The Lotus and The Rose

*To Derek
With best wishes*

THE LOTUS AND THE ROSE

Sharad Keskar

AuthorHouse™
1663 Liberty Drive
Bloomington, IN 47403
www.authorhouse.com
Phone: 1-800-839-8640

© 2011 by Sharad Keskar. All rights reserved.

No part of this book may be reproduced, stored in a retrieval system, or transmitted by any means without the written permission of the author.

First published by AuthorHouse   08/03/2011

ISBN: 978-1-4567-7933-7 (sc)
ISBN: 978-1-4567-7934-4 (hc)
ISBN: 978-1-4567-7935-1 (ebk)

Printed in the United States of America

Any people depicted in stock imagery provided by Thinkstock are models, and such images are being used for illustrative purposes only.
Certain stock imagery © Thinkstock.

This book is printed on acid-free paper.

Because of the dynamic nature of the Internet, any web addresses or links contained in this book may have changed since publication and may no longer be valid. The views expressed in this work are solely those of the author and do not necessarily reflect the views of the publisher, and the publisher hereby disclaims any responsibility for them.

To England for Jane

AUTHOR'S NOTE

The Lotus and the Rose is a novel inspired by my intimacy with Indian Anglophiles, who saw in the Raj the prospect of a united India, democracy and an end to caste discrimination. Many were upper/middle-class Indians, who had an English education, worked with the Raj, served in the army, the civil service and the judiciary. They aimed to emulate the fairness and efficiency of their Rulers, and for their co-operation the Raj rewarded them with status and friendship. But after Indian Independence, that past was an embarrassment and something to be reticent about. Yet, a love of things English remained; and because they faced no threat from anti-Raj nationals, they kept their posts. Transition was smooth, promotion fast—one even became Prime Minister, and is reputed to have told the American Ambassador that he was the last "Englishman" to govern India.

After 1947 some Indian Anglophiles failed to shed their admiration for what they saw as a time of good government. They were at home in English society, where the "brown" Englishman's civil charm often won the heart of an Englishwoman.

The "lotus" and "rose" are symbols of India and England and the novel, set in both countries, fills a literary lacuna, where Anglophilia and intermarriage foster a sense of unease, displacement, delusion, even solitude, but an accommodation despite of it all.

Sharad Keskar
March 2011

PART 1

The Anglophile

PROLOGUE

The bougainvillaea was dying. The once beautiful garden looked wild. But, as Dinesh shut the gate behind him and joined his wife, more pressing worries occupied his mind. The future and the freedom he longed for was his, yet he could not overcome feeling a sense of loss and apprehension. And now, what most troubled his conscience was the thought he had not been quite open with Sandy. He needed to be alone, to sort things out . . . but she was talking, talking about the poor state of the garden. 'Shanti, for God's sake, let it rest! And, for God's sake, speak in English!'

Shanti stamped her foot and raised her voice. 'So you poke fun! I've had enough of you correcting my English.' She brushed aside his pacifying hand. 'And don't tell me to keep voice down. Look at garden! Huh! English. You, of all people! England returned. Big deal. So vot! You're still an Indian.'

'I ask you to speak in English only because these people here understand Hindustani; and you're drawing attention.'

'Then do something. You're boss now. Stop them. Hundreds have turned up.'

'Can't be more than sixty or seventy . . . The garden's not that big.'

'Last year, this time, the garden vas so luv-ver-ly. No?'

Dinesh took a deep breath. 'Lovely,' he said inaudibly. He had no interest in gardens but remembered the recent incident she had provoked. Unhappy with their own garden she threatened to sack the *mali*, their old gardener, who had been with her family long enough to be part of it. Seth Agarwal, her father, tactfully persuaded the old man into believing he was only being asked to employ a helper. It was a lie and old Gopal knew it. He played along till, softened by a cash hand-out, he considered his *izzat*, that is his honour, satisfied; and any humiliation suffered, fully compensated.

'Actually,' Dinesh said, placing a cautionary forefinger against his lips, 'they've been without a gardener for some time. Emma Aunty took a personal interest. But she's been ill. These people . . . No, I can't drive them away. They loved her. And are behaving with dignity . . . stop making faces, Shanti. I won't.'

'Then, just don't involve me.' She waved a hand and entered the cottage. He stayed by the porch and inspected the twisted, wilting branches of the bougainvillaea. Above the roots, cuts made by a sickle or machete were smeared with turmeric paste, and on the flower-bed lay a heap of marigold heads. Dinesh knew enough about mountain folk to realise this was no act of vandalism but some peculiar ritual. He moved to the side of the porch where wisteria once climbed. The trellis had come loose. He pressed it into place, but it sprang back with the twang of a bow string. He grunted, dusted his hands, entered the cottage and went up the stairs into the bedroom. There he studied Sandy's limp body as it lay on the four-poster bed. How he hated that bedroom and everything "English" about the cottage! And he had made certain Sandy knew it was the cause of the rift between them. Now, all hope of reconciliation was gone. But, in his last letter to Sandy he had made a well-argued case for the way he felt. Every convoluted sentence was meticulously crafted. Besides, after that terrible humiliation Sandy had suffered in England, Sandy had good cause to hate the English; and having settled in India, it was insensitive of him not to see that an English life-style was an affront to India and to Dinesh, who he knew was a member of the local Indian National Party. But Sandy had ignored the letter, so surely his, Dinesh's, resentment was justified. "Gandhi uniquely and non-violently freed India from Britain's yoke, and Indian spirituality offers you tranquillity and freedom from all vanity." Dinesh prized that sentence, in his letter to Sandy, and he quoted it whenever he could, mistaking for admiration the silence with which it was received. But there was no mistaking Sandy's silence. That was a snub and Dinesh resented every unspoken moment of it. He sighed with deep relief and, having salved his conscience, an urge to be sententious gripped him. 'Shanti!' he called.

Shanti ceased rummaging the chest-of-drawers in the next room and came out to join him; sullen for having been interrupted. Her Indian dancer's hour-glass figure—narrow waist, full breasts, rounded hips, taut as a Khajuraho temple sculpture—froze in a pose of artful indignation. He pointed to the bed. She approached saucily, her bangles jangled with every jerk of her arms. 'See, Shanti, that peaceful expression on his face? That's the serenity of despair and defeat.' She wondered why despair and defeat should take on an aspect of serenity, but said nothing. She seldom did when he was in declamatory mood. Besides her mind was on other things. There was much to explore in the cottage, and now she had time and opportunity to satisfy her curiosity.

'Such folly!' her husband went on, 'sheer madness. Look at this room?'

Shanti nodded reluctantly. '*Arrey*, but Emma vos English, vos she not?'

Dinesh shook his head. 'Yes, but more Indian than him and became more so with the passage of time. Took to wearing saris. Even in public. Aunty's not to blame. Anyway, what place does all this have on the secluded slopes of Mcleodganj? I ask you? None!'

She nodded, remembering the long talk they had some months ago, when she agreed to play the good Indian wife and accept him, unquestioningly as her "Lord". It was the measure of that loyalty to him, to remain unmoved by his bombast. It wasn't easy and it did not suit her temperament. She wondered how long she could keep it up. Hadn't she strayed a little, moments ago, when she snapped at him in front of the local peasantry? But hill folk, she told herself, were simple. They came as mourners and wouldn't have noticed. Still, she must guard against future lapses and criticisms. These sacrifices were worth making if they helped to persuade him to let her continue her dancing lessons . . .

And Dinesh was mistaken. If he had understood his own vision of India, he would have seen that incongruity was India's charm. No one, apart from him, seemed to mind Sandy's cottage and life-style; nor was it alien to the history of Mcleodganj. For though it is now less like the Pennine village it was, peeping through the crumbling bungalows and colonnaded verandas is its palimpsest, in the run-down church, where a Viceroy lies buried. A sad, not wholly inglorious, memory to the Raj.

With every passing decade, Mcleodganj gets its boost of new life. In the 1950s, rich Punjabi residents, in search of more salubrious locations, moved into its upper reaches, there soon to be nudged by the stream of Tibetan refugees pouring down from the high mountain passes. Today, twenty-five years on, timber huts and *chortens*—snug among tree ferns, pines and rhododendrons—still retain a makeshift look, while the beauty of the Himalayan foothills succeeds in hiding a growing squalor.

And Dinesh need not have been troubled by Sandy's "English" cottage and garden. It was being reclaimed. The fading hollyhocks round the perimeter were being engulfed by the a creeping wilderness and the carefully nurtured rose garden had disappeared with recent neglect. Untended lilies, pansies, sweet-peas and geraniums, were being replaced by the hardy Indian marigold and every trace of an English garden was fading. Now as he stood looking out from the bedroom window, the scene below was unlike anything he had known. The reverent and silent invasion of the garden by Kangra and Tibetan men and women continued. As they enter, men and women separate. The men, vacant-eyed, squat on the dry lawn. The women, with faces hidden by shawls and stoles, move to the patio at the back of the house, where one, with a high-pitched wail, leads the rest in a plangent chant. Above that sound, Dinesh can hear Chandu Lal, the estate manager, calling out to someone to shut the gate, beyond which, the bridle path winds down to the farms and orchards of the valleys below. He should have locked that gate earlier and not left it to Chandu. After all, Sandy was dying and it was up to him, as Shanti earlier had pointed out, the new *malik*, the "boss", to take charge.

He saw Chandu greet, with folded hands, the men and women gathering outside the gate, and with a commiserating shake of the head, asking them to leave. They roll their heads in response but stay on by the gate. Some sink on to their haunches with a rooted obstinacy; others climb the rocky mound behind the paddock, where a tethered chestnut pony, with bulging brown eyes, studies their presence with equine disdain.

Most of the men are farmers, who cultivate the rice terraces on the slopes above the valleys. Some are *coolies* who carry goods for those who will hire them. Two *gaddis* or shepherds, who, every year, in late summer, on their way up into the hills, halted to rest at the paddock, approached the gate and leant sadly on their staffs. Chandu opened the gate and let them in. There is no protest from those shut out.

A group of Tibetan men and women, among the first to arrive, sit cross-legged on the terrace below the bedroom window. Heads bowed, they rock their bodies and drone monotonously as they rotate hand-held prayer-wheels. At their head is Sona, a middle-aged woman. Her face—its olive skin stretched taut over high cheek bones—is serene. She is wearing a multi-coloured embroidered apron over a long black dress or *chuba*, silver earrings, and a turquoise necklace. Her uncovered head reveals raven black hair, neatly combed and tightly pressed down. She holds a crucifix in one hand and a prayer-wheel in the other. Her lips move soundlessly and her eyes are shut; but she knows who is at the window looking down on her.

Dinesh is annoyed with her. She should have arranged the preparation of a simple meal of puris and spiced potatoes for the people assembling outside. Instead, she had left the kitchen in the morning to lead the silent funeral procession across a stream into the Old Cemetery. On her return, she insisted on being left alone. Her concern, she had told him, was only for Sandy . . .

He, unable to join the procession, had watched from that very window. Leaning on his walking-stick, he stared desolately, as Emma's coffin was carried past the wooden gate, into the slender pines and deodars, A soft grey mist hid the pall-bearers, and for a brief moment the coffin floated in the air, till like a falling leaf; it sank below the crest and out of sight . . . Turning from the window to face the room, he saw her on the bed. There she was! Smiling that same sweet smile with which she greeted him every morning. Always she stayed in bed till he was up and till Sona brought them a tray of tea. The vision went. The bed was empty and made. 'Emma!' he whispered, moving towards it, till in a dreadful fit of shaking, the stick fell from his hand. He snatched wildly, fists uselessly flailing the air. The bed receded. Again, she was there, beckoning to him with raised arms. He reached out and falling forwards grasped at the bedclothes. They slid down with him as he desperately clung and pulled ... then darkness ...

Dinesh turned to look for a chair and realised Shanti was no longer with him. She had slipped away and had gone back to rummaging in the adjoining room. He tiptoed to the open doorway. 'There's nothing there for you,' he said, making her jump. 'And leave things the way you find them or I'll have, Sona,' he jerked his head in the direction of the window, 'at my throat.'

Shanti groaned and slammed the drawer shut. 'Okay, then in that case I'll go to kitchen, only. *Arrey*, vot vit that *tamasha* going on outside ... if I don't go now, you'll get nothing to eat.'

'Dinesh slapped his forehead, 'Oh, I forgot to mention! Don't worry about the food. Mohan Singh's wife ... I always forget her name ... it's like yours.'

'It's not. Bunty. He calls her Bunty. Everyone calls her Bunty.'

'Anyway, she's arranging for ... she's providing a meal for everyone. Soon. I hope. But you could help.'

'Oh, Gawd no! Believe me, she needs no help. Best not to interfere. She's not going to do anything herself. Mohan is rich man. She'll send her *khansamah* to town.'

'Khansamah?'

'Cook! You know?'

'Yes, of course, I know. But I wish you wouldn't use words I associate it with the Raj ... Oh, never mind!'

'Anyway, she needs no help. Mohanbhai also runs a canteen. They can arrange to get a lot of help and fast. I bet, all she'll do: make a lot of *puris* and serve them with pickle, mango pickle. She's got jars of it. You'll see. Also she's a great one for ordering people about. Madam bountiful, Bunty bountiful, von't lift a finger. So why should I?'

He chuckled. 'You got the "why" right. But really, Bunty's quite friendly, though I know you don't like her.'

'But you do. It's those flimsy blouses she wears ... I've seen you, many times, staring down at her big big titties'

'They are no match to yours ...'

'But vot I say is true. Happened before. Last month only. Remember, ven her son Balbir passed High School. Big, big party they gave. I helped. All she did . . . gave cook instructions . . . even gave him her keys, so lazy she is. You know, she trusts that fellow completely. I bet he lies and cheats her. Mother taught me to keep everything under lock and key. Servants are not to be trusted. Such crooks, I tell you.'

'Keep your voice down. Walls have ears.'

'Anyway,' she spoke above a whisper. 'You know how time vas spent? In her room. Sitting on bed, drinking ice-cold *lassi*, and she, showing off her jewellery.'

'Those poor people outside will have to wait a long time.'

'Don't worry about them. They are patient like donkeys. They expect nothing. Just live in hope. That's vot life on the land teaches them. Father wouldn't have bothered.'

He nodded. 'But that's not the point. It's what Emma would've done and did, which matters. Every Christmas Day and the Easter day . . .'

'Emma and Sandy fed these people? Yes, yes, I remember now. Heard all about that. Letting these folk to trample all over garden.'

'You exaggerate. No one trampled. These people may be uneducated but they're not uncultured. They treated Emma aunty like she was some kind of goddess or saint . . . You didn't know her. Your father wouldn't let you come here.'

'Today even. He didn't vant me to come . . . this time I told him the house belonged to us. Just mention property and father's ears go prick, prick.'

Dinesh secretly disliked his father-in-law, but ever watchful to hide it, pursed his lips. 'I still think we ought to make some gesture. At least send our cook's wife to help.'

'Khushvanti? Vy not the cook himself?'

'She'll be the right sort of person to organise some of those women outside to go with her. Besides, I've sent . . . why am I so bad with names . . . I mean the cook . . . ? I've sent him to fetch the doctor. Can't think why he's not back. Sona is to blame for this whole mess up. You keep away from her as much as possible.'

'I took an instant dislike to her. This Sona woman. Gives me the creeps.'

'I'll tell the cook to help, when he's back.' Dinesh peeped past her into the adjoining room. Beside the chest-of-drawers and large wardrobe, were two steel trunks. 'It's the linen room! What were you looking for?'

'Did she not have jewellery?'

'You little *Puggli*! What a waste of time and effort. Why didn't you ask me? Do you see that rosewood chest on top of the cupboard . . . one moment, I'll get it down.'

'Open it! Open it!' Shanti cried excitedly.

'Read the label. It says: "For Kitty".'

'This Kitty, some relative?'

'Never mind,' he said placing the chest back.

'Can't see 'y this Kitty should get everything.'

'Most of it is Victorian antique jewellery. Not anything you'd like. But I'm surprised at you. You've got more jewellery of your own than any one woman ought to have, for her own good. Now off you go.'

'Okay! But don't call me *Puggli*. You joke, but to servants *puggli* means mad.'

'In front of servants, I won't. Behave like the rich woman you are and good wife and I shall forget to say it . . . except when we . . .'

She stretched a hand to keep him at arms length as he approached her. '*Bus, bus!* Gawd, I've had it tonight. But listen,' she flirtatiously banged his chest with her fists. 'Listen. I've got something to tell you about this Sona. This supposedly saintly Sona. And don't think I'm scandal mongering, huh.'

'Later, later!' He gestured as if to shoo her away. 'Now, what's the matter?'

She was pointing to Sandy. 'Seen that? *Arrey*, his hands. Sandy's hands.'

They tiptoed to the bed. She pointed. Clasped in Sandy's hands were two plaits of chestnut brown and grey hair and a small leather bound book. 'Is that some holy book?'

He nodded. 'Book of Common Prayer.'

'Vate till I tell. Things I saw happening here,' she said.

'So you were here before I got back. I said after eleven; and to meet me at the gate?'

'I met you at the gate.'

'But, you got here earlier?'
'I vas early. And there was no one. All at the funeral. So I . . .'
'But Sona returned early. I happen to know that.'
'She didn't see me.' She tossed her head. 'And if she did, so vot. She is no more than a servant.'
'Don't ever say that, Shanti. Don't ever call her a servant. I'll explain later.'
'You know, you're a *darpoke*. A big, big coward.' With a provocative swing of her hips, she went down the stairs.

Dinesh drew a chair and sat by the window. He stared down at Sona and resting his elbows on the sill, cupped his face in his hands. Shanti was right. He was afraid of her. Sandy and Emma had never made Sona's position in the house clear to him, but he had his suspicions. She was allowed to treat him like an errant little brother, and they were more fond of her. Sandy's papers confirmed that, and made clear Sona's entitlements. A trustee had been appointed because she was illiterate. He needed to find out how much Sona knew. First he had to wrestle with the events of the morning. Their confrontation after the funeral service had left him angry and intrigued. Without consulting him she had arranged for Emma's coffin to be left in the chapel and instructed Ran Singh, their chowkidar, to keep watch over it till sunset. Far from raising any objection, Ran Singh spent his own money, buying candles, joss-sticks and *chameli* blossoms. But her strangest behaviour that morning was ordering the grave to be dug wide enough for two coffins. It was absurd. He told her so and asked, first in English and then in Hindi, what it all meant. Trembling with anger she replied: 'I being true daughter, I do right things.' Then she went into a tirade of accusations, and pointed out how she had cared for Emma and Sandy, while he was at to boarding school and then in England. That he was son only in name. He had tried to allay her feelings. Speaking a mix of English and Punjabi, which she found easier to follow, he agreed he had been away, in England, for some time, but that had nothing to do with now. Now he wanted an explanation of her present conduct. She told him to shut up and insisted on being left alone. He gave in. There was no point countermanding her instructions. She was determined to have her way and he did not want anyone to see his authority openly defied. Pretending he had left her in charge, he took the longer route back to the cottage. This was the forest road that went past Mohan Singh's timber and turpentine distillation plant. It was deserted. He walked round to the back and saw Mohan Singh locking the gates of his timber yard. Mohan turned to greet Dinesh with folded palms. '*Nameste*! Dinesh *babu*. Do, please to accept my heartfelt condolences! God is great! This tragedy will be a most terrible shock to your father . . . will it not?'

'He is not my father,' Dinesh protested.

Mohan Singh regarded him with genuine astonishment. '*Arrey Bhai*! What talk is this? He's your father; in truth, is he not, to all sense and purposes? Consider now his feelings. What must he be going through? *Achcha*, okay, no time for . . . come, *challo*, I'll walk with you. In any case, I was coming over to pay my respects. I've shut up shop for the day. As mark of respect.'

Dinesh told him that Sandy had left strict instructions not to be disturbed. 'Not even by me. He lies in bed, eyes shut. Hasn't spoken a word.'

Mohan scratched his beard thoughtfully. Then with a solemn roll of his head said: 'Sandy can't live without her. *Mia aur bibi*. Husband and wife. The two were one and inseparable. Now the great man's nothing to live for.' He sighed. 'I must do something. Some gesture of respect, because, as I say, he was a great man.'

'Great?'

'Oh, yes! Great and good man.' They started to walk. 'Please, I understand. I'll not disturb your father. May God give him peace and grant his wish. But somehow I must pay my respects, if only to do a *darshan* of their dwelling place. And *hahn*, to offer my condolences to that fine daughter of the house, Sona.' He took out what looked like a Chinese chop-stick from the top pocket of his tweed jacket and used it to tuck the loose hairs of his grey beard under the black hair-net he wore over his chin. Then he adjusted his blue turban. Even for a Sikh he was a man of unusually pale complexion and blushed as he caught Dinesh watching him. Abruptly he stopped his tidying and turned to gaze into the distance. The closely set grey eyes, large hooked nose, and full bearded cheeks, made him look owlish. '*Challo*,' he said, 'let's go.' And the stumpy legs of this stocky man set off at the brisk pace of one used to the hills.

The Lotus And The Rose

'I've just come from the Church, we . . .' Dinesh began trying to keep pace with him.

'Yes, I was there. My good lady wife too. She was most insistent. But there was no need. We all, the whole family, had the greatest respect for Emmaji. Of course, we did not enter the chapel. Though son Balbir didn't hesitate. Did you not see him? He took his turn to carry the-the box . . . The boy was in tears. You know, I'm thinking he had a crush on Emmaji. Old as she was, she kept her figure.' He looked down at his rotund figure and smiled wanly. 'White women do. Not like our women. Once wed, they relax and spread.' He began to laugh, remembered the occasion, and checked himself. 'She was a good woman. The perfect wife. A veritable Sita.'

'Sita? Emma was an Englishwoman! A Christian!'

'So what?' Mohan forced a smile to hide his irritation. 'Sita is Sita. Emma is Emma. A good woman's a good woman. Saintliness is not only an Hindu virtue. Religion, my brother, is second to people. When I say Sita, I'm mean the epi-tummy of womanhood . . . across all barriers, creeds, nationality . . . What is the matter? Are you unwell?'

Dinesh shook his head and waved a hand. 'I'm all mixed up. Yes, they were good to me, but I can't forgive his crass, foolish, so very . . . idiosyncratic, attitude. He may have been good, but he was also foolish.'

'To be good is to be foolish. *Baap re baap!* In today's world is it not foolish to be good? Goodness is a kind of foolishness. That's why this bloody world finds saints so boring. My friend, foolishness doesn't matter. Goodness is a monument to itself.'

Dinesh often found Mohan Singh verbose and tiresome to follow. 'I didn't mean that foolishness. It was easy for Sandy to be . . . be good. He came from a rich princely family . . . and, as you know, his home life was happy too. He had no cause to be bad.'

'Look Dinesh. Now I'm speaking like elder brother. I knew him better than even you did. Let me say, you do him great wrong. I know about the anti feelings you harbour. If I may say so, you take things to extremes. You're so anti-British . . . and that's because in London you mixed with commies and stupid Indians who want to rewrite history, just to suit their *izzat* . . . their pride. One day they'll even prove the Brits were never in India. Okay, so Sandy was pro-British.

But he wasn't anti-Indian. My father also admired the Brits. Only in the last ten years of his life he joined the Congress Party. Before, like Sandy, he was Anglophile also! Many Indians, in father's time and before, were. Even Nehru and Gandhi admired the Brits. Maybe Sandy idolised the Brits . . . no, English—he insisted on that distinction. But that aside, he was a kindly man. So be forgiving . . . show some sort of gratitude. He did a lot for you.'

Dinesh nodded, compressing his lips to stem mixed feelings of frustration, anger and contrition: 'This is unfair,' he said, looking away. 'It is emotional blackmail.'

Mohan gripped his arm. 'I don't know what you mean. But listen, as elder brother it is my duty. *Hosh mein ao!* Get a hold of yourself.'

Dinesh shrugged himself free and walked ahead.

They reached a point where the road looped on a spur overlooking the valley and the bridle path leading to the cottage. Mohan nudged Dinesh and pointed. 'Look, is that not Sona? Something's wrong. She's running towards the gate!' Dinesh stared but made no response. 'She's an angel of mercy,' Mohan Singh added and when he failed again to get a response, asked: 'Surely, she's allowed to be near him?'

'More demon than angel,' Dinesh grumbled, 'she's a law unto herself. Everybody, including Emma and Sandy, let Sona have her way. And she takes full advantage of it.'

'But where she is,' Mohan rolled his head solemnly, 'there's *shanti*. By that I mean peace—not your wife Shanti.' He grinned. But Dinesh was not amused. 'Well, I guess Sandy's made Sona the exception. I wouldn't be surprised . . . She may rule the roost but also she's been doting daughter of house, totally devoted to their welfare.'

Dinesh shrugged his shoulders. Neither spoke till they reached the gate. Mohan was genuinely astonished by the crowd of people in the garden. 'It's wonderful! I told you . . . greatness and goodness! The reward of goodness is homage. Look! Such a gathering. Pilgrims at the shrine! Take pride, my friend. Your mother and father are honoured.'

Dinesh winced. 'I don't like it. Something uneasy in the air. It's to do with these people. It's as if they're willing something to happen.' Mohan seemed not to hear.

'This is no way to talk.' Mohan said. 'They are mourners and deserve consideration.'

'Yes, and expecting to be fed.' Dinesh looked at his watch.

'Dinesh *bhai*, you can't drive them away. The meal, simple, howsoever small . . . it's an obligation. Every society, the world over, has its love meal. Is it not what the Greeks call "agape"? Hindu puja, Christians communion . . . also what Emma would have done?'

'She was the wife of a rich man. Her generosity bought their affection. It's pure and simple *mutlab* . . . cupboard love.'

'Please! This is not time or place for sarcasm or hurtful words. Let me contribute as my mark of respect. Allow me, no, in fact I insist! Leave it all to me and my good wife. The meal. We'll provide the meal. It will be a simple one. These folk understand. They don't expect a banquet. Just something to help them stay here as long as they want to.'

'All right,' said Dinesh. 'Since you insist. But I'll pay for . . .'

'*Arrey bhai*, don't insult me. Am I a beggar? We have cooks and staff. Also I run a canteen for my workers. The factory is shut, not the canteen. At such times my Bunty is in her element. She'll even organise some of the women here to help make the puris. No "buts", "whys" or "wherefores" . . . You know the saying: *takaloof mai hai takaleef*. Yes, formalities are a pain in the neck. Now go in. Go, go. See you later.'

Dinesh looked about him. Shanti was to meet him at the garden gate. He looked at his watch and simultaneously felt a tap on his shoulder. 'Shanti, you gave me a start! Where have you been hiding?'

'Here, in crowd only. And don't ask. I didn't want to be seen by that Sona person . . . or for that matter Mohan Singh. You took long. I've been waiting, and waiting.'

Dinesh clicked his tongue. He knew she was lying. Instinctively he felt she had been in the cottage and had come out while he was in conversation with Mohan Singh . . .

Turning from the window, Dinesh pushed the chair back and tiptoed to the bed. He searched Sandy's pale, handsome face for signs of life; the breathing was imperceptible. Dinesh bent forward and sniffed. The distinct scent of rose-water, which he associated with

Sona, also had a faint aroma of fermented wheat and almonds. Was it *chang*, that Tibetan brew? He straighten himself and remembered the scene of Sona hurrying down the bridle path. Now his suspicions were aroused. He had to know what Sona had been up to . . . and there were other things he wanted to talk to her about . . .

Sona's breathless race up the stairs into the bedroom had startled Shanti, who found herself trapped in the adjoining linen room. Trapped because, from the landing, the linen room was exposed. Shanti held her breath and remained very still. The communicating door was ajar and it gave her a clear view of the bed. She pressed herself against the wall only to be startled once more by a loud cry of dismay. She peeped cautiously.

Sona had found Sandy on the floor, by the bed. He had fallen awkwardly, in a heap, under the bedclothes. Shanti watched Sona lift him effortlessly on to the bed. Drawing back she marvelled at the woman's strength. Sounds of sobbing now reached her, then stopped as suddenly as they had started. She peeped again. Sona was bent right over Sandy. A low mumble from her was answered by a moan from the bed. A moment later Sona sat up and pressed a hand against her mouth, as one does to stifle making a sound. Then she bent over Sandy once more and whispered for some time into his ear, her face pressed against his. Suddenly she jerk upright, cocked her head and listened. She sprang from the bed and went to the window and saw Dinesh and Mohan Singh coming down the hill. Shanti, who momentarily lost sight of her, now heard hurried footsteps coming towards the linen room. Telling herself she had no need to be afraid of Sona—after all, was she not now mistress of the house?—she steeled herself for a confrontation. But Sona turned off at the landing, sped along the gallery above the trellis-enclosed veranda, entered her own bedroom, combed her hair, put on her earrings and necklace, removed the crucifix from the wall and, after some hesitation, picked up the prayer wheel from its quilted casket. Then she went down the fire escape that spiralled down from her little balcony into the garden . . .

Dinesh returned to the window. The scene was much the same except that Sona had disappeared. He spun on his heel, but before he could get to the door, she was facing him. He recovered himself. With a nod in her direction he tried to walk past her but felt himself wrenched back by a hand which caught his arm in a vice-like grip. He winced.

'You here?' There was a wild look in her eyes.

He made no attempt to free himself. Memory served. This peasant woman was as strong as an ox. 'I have a right to be here,' he said evenly. 'This is my house.'

'No.' She pointed to the bed. 'His!' She took a deep breath and released his arm. 'Go now. Take wife.' She indicated the adjoining linen room. 'I know, she there.'

'My wife's in the kitchen,' he said smugly. His arm was still smarting but he resisted the impulse to rub it. He tapped the pocket of his raw-silk jodhpur jacket, took out a buff envelope and shook it under her nose. 'This Sandy's. In here, all this, mine.' She stared at him unmoved. Then, with a pretence at magnanimity, he added: 'you too. You okay. You keep your part of cottage for as long as . . .' He stopped. She waited. 'And—and you are free. Free to do what you want. Not have to work. Not be servant . . . I mean free to do what you like . . . There's also monthly allowance. Money for you.' He gave a discreet cough. Then switching to Punjabi he said: 'The lawyer, Vakil sahib will tell you all, everything. You are now,' he coughed again, 'Sandy's daughter.'

'I know,' she said, and smiled as she walked to the door. There she stood and with a slight toss of her head, indicated that he should leave the room.

Dinesh went across the patio—where the now quiet peasant women sidled on their haunches to make way for him—into the kitchen. Shanti was talking to Khushvanti. He raised a hand before she could speak. 'So, Khushvanti is still here?'

'I'm going,' Khushvanti said sullenly, and Dinesh realised he had interrupted a spell of gossip. He stared as she waddled out of sight, recalling the trimmer, buxom woman of ten years ago, who let him satisfy his curiosity by guiding his hand inside her blouse. He was fourteen then, and though he tried on many later occasions to find her alone, it was an intimacy she never permitted him to experience again.

'Shanti,' he said, 'you should go too. It'll be a nice gesture. Besides,' his libido now aroused, 'a little exercise will help you lose those spare tyres!' He made a feint to grab her waist. She giggled, ran out of the kitchen, stopped to give him a coquettish glance, then hitched up her *salwar* under her *kamez*. Dinesh lost interest.'

In the bedroom, upstairs, Sandy stirred. To his half opened eyes the room appeared to swim with moving shadows and flashing lights. Muffled voices, coming from a distance, punctured his waking dreams, while the pain and loud thumping in his chest sank into paralysis. He shut his eyes. A phantom weighed down on him, whispering, in Punjabi: "all will soon be over and all will be well." His tried to nod, to move his lips, but only a moan escaped as his body began to float. Then a drowning wave swept over him and he struggled, gasping for air. He felt a pressure on his mouth, and a memory of staring out of a window, of reaching out towards the essence of his life, turned into a vertiginous fall, a cold, suffocating hurtle into blackness. Intercepting arms cradled him and set him adrift into consciousness. He shut his eyes, clinging fast to a clear need never to open them again for some reason deep within his psyche—that of a child's burrowing under blankets to recapture a lost dream and from which refusing to wake.

Ghostly shadows now ceased to move, till they were dispersed by a vision so very dear to his heart . . . a vision of England . . . a seaside, and of him running towards a familiar cottage . . . towards Edith and Ted. 'Emma's on the beach', Ted pointed. 'Go, Sandy, talk to her.' 'Make Emma see sense!' Edith was saying, her face hard with the polite reserve of middle-class England. He was amused, even charmed. 'No, not this time! Not ever. Never!' he heard himself say, as he raced across the sands towards the gently lapping waves of a sheltered cove. 'Sandy! Sandy!' Emma's face rose, like a corona breaking through dull skies . . . Her smile banishing the pensive sadness of her drooping mouth . . . the grey of brooding England pierced by a high bright sun . . . 'Sandy! Sandy!' Her voice so distant yet unmistakably hers. He answered: 'Yes' . . . Reaching out . . . reaching . . .

Sandy died that afternoon. Dr Sharma told Dinesh there was nothing he could have done. 'In my opinion, nothing wrong with Thakur sahib, I mean medically speaking. He wanted this. This is what he wished. Therefore, it could not be prevented.'

CHAPTER ONE

In 1934, a Bailey bridge, long since gone, spanned a creek in south Bombay where, for a mile on either side of it, a railway ran on a high embankment. Below, on the banks of the creek, silently and secretly, a slum had arisen. This sprawl of huts rested perilously on bamboo stilts and discarded railway sleepers, above the black, oily ooze of sea marsh and effluent—human sties, at the mercy of the tides that ebbed and flowed, threatening, with sluggish disregard, flood and disease.

Under roofs of salvaged materials—sacking, boards, flattened tin canisters, rotting struts and reeds, weighted down by rope and stones—the slum dwellers fought a losing battle against Bombay's pitiless monsoon, and what the rain spared the wind did not. Rising waters burst makeshift gutters and the flooded, filthy drains swept through their shelters, leaving them drenched, derelict, and clinging to the little they had: earthen jars of grain and oil and cooking utensils. All else is left to be retrieved or scavenged, when they returned to rebuild. For the Bombay dream, that in this city of promise, one day, the poor, hard working *coolie* will be king, lives on.

Municipal officials posed an added threat to these illegal tenants. Bespectacled clerks in black pill-box hats, brown waistcoats, white *dhotis*, and umbrellas tucked under their arms, come accompanied by policeman armed with *lathis*, to conduct rare but punishing raids. The squatters flee, only to return and resettle, like shooed off flies. But strangely one hut remains unmolested by man and nature. Its brick walls and corrugated iron roof provide a haven for labourers ready to blow the day's wages and drown their sorrows in drink. To this canteen a well-trodden path runs obliquely from the bridge, down the steep embankment into the wide courtyard where, above the entrance a reed thatched lean-to offers shelter from the sun. Here the proprietor places tables and benches, not for the slum-dwellers, but for clients from the suburbs. His fame for producing the best palm-toddy and a rum-like spirit, had spread. A few regular customers are privileged to sit inside the hut, where two noisy electric fans stir the fetid air. Clearly he is allowed to ply his trade, for policemen are seen entering the hut—after battles with the squatters.

There are no policemen today and a spirit of wild bonhomie prevails. A well-dressed man, drunk and disorderly, stumbles out of the hut, refuses the help of two companions, and ignoring the path, staggers up the steep embankment. He slips and falls, but with amazing alacrity stands up again. Soon his knees give and he folds like a deck chair, on to his heels. By now he had drawn everyone's attention and their laughter. Turning on his detractors, he snarls. They cower, because he is a man of importance. Tackling the slope again, he stretches his arms like a tight-rope walker and tip-toes, one step at a time. But the gradient forces his head back; his body arches over while his arms rotate like the sails of a windmill. He falls and rolls down to whoops, jeers and hand-clapping.

'What a guy, mun! Helluva chap!' Frank D'Silva's laughed, an odd laugh, that was very like the kick-starting of a reluctant motorbike, and in keeping with that impression, stamps a foot, as if operating a foot pedal. 'Can't hold his licker, mun. Bloody hell, eh, Dally? Say something, mun! What do you think about your Headmaster sahib, now? Hey?' Leaning forward, he stamped his foot again and stuttered a guffaw.

Dayal Singh, the man addressed as Dally, looked down at the frightened little boy, holding his hand. 'This is no place for a five-year boy. What a *tamasha*!' He shook his head gravely. 'Why bring the boy along? But, no, I forget. This is all your doing.' He wagged an accusing finger, rolled his head in what was neither a shake nor a nod, but some philosophical position in-between.

'Gorn mun. Every evening he goes for daily walk. You know. Met by chance on the bridge. Decided to have a quickie. Simple. You were here, as usual, in the grog-shop.' Frank started to laugh but stopped when he felt a sharp kick against his shin and the boy's tiny fists drumming against his thighs. 'Hey! Watch it little fellow.' He pushed the boy away from him. 'Your dad's having fun!' Then going down on his heels he gripped the boy's shoulders. 'Just fun. Okay?' He studied the child's face. 'Okay. Now, you wont tell Mummy?' The boy's large eyes stared angrily at him; then he began to cry. 'Hey, come on, mun.' Frank, wiped the tears off the child's face with a bare hand and the boy shied away from the stench of Frank's nicotine stained fingers. 'There's a good chap. Don't tell Mummy and I'll buy you a nice drink. Pic-Me-Up? Yes, you'll like that. Nice, nice golden soda? Hey? What say you?'

The boy stopped crying. He weighed the offer, then nodded. 'And a *jelaby*.'

'Okay, dokay, you *charlak* fellow. Eh, Dally! Cunning fellow, isn't he. No?'

'Don't try to involve me in your *badmashi*.' Dayal snapped. 'Bloody mischief-maker then laughing like a donkey. I was here. My usual,' he raised two fingers horizontally to indicate the amount . 'One *chatak*. No more. I drinking for pleasure and relaxation. But you, like most East Indians . . . come here to get drunk.'

'Goan, not East Indian.'

'Goans, East Indians, the same. You fellows don't know when to stop. And then you look for mischief and fun. Is no good.' He shook a slender finger like a metronome and rolled his head solemnly.

Frank stared at Dayal with a sheepish grin.

'I don't like this one bit.' Dayal went on. 'You better make sure the boy says nothing to his mother. How you call yourself a friend of Headmaster sahib? I won't say more in front of boy. But as his father's chief clerk, I ought to protect my boss from the likes of you. You maybe a guard on the railways, but you're still a stupid donkey. No match to him. Yes, my Thakur sahib's a scholar . . . with, with Oxforword accent.'

Frank frowned at this irrelevance. 'The boy. He's only a *buccha*. Five-year old. He'll forget before he gets home. You'll see!' He thumped Dayal's back and placed an arm round his shoulder. 'Hey! come on, we're old friends!'

Dayal wobbled his head as Frank nudged him with a conniving grin.

The boy, who had been listening intently, understood more than they imagined. He knew, intuitively, they were a bad influence on his father—he even suspected Dayal to be no less guilty than Frank. He was angry. But he liked Frank and, the muscular Dayal, even more. He shivered. Instinctively Dayal squeezed his hand. 'What, Sandy baba? What?' (Years later Sandy will wonder how his father could face a subordinate who had seen him so disgracefully drunk; and he would then come to realise that Dayal had been loyal and discreet.) 'Mummy will know,' he blurted out, involuntarily.

'He's right, Frank,' Dayal's eyes widened. 'We'll face music, and as usual I will get all the blame. How can I look Mrs Thakur, that so noble lady, in the eye!'

A cry from the embankment made them look up. Sandy's father had scrambled up the slope. 'My Gawd! He'll kill himself!' Frank shouted and ran up the embankment. Dayal tugged the boy, who stood rooted by the sound of an approaching train and the sight of his father waving his hands, shouting and charging towards it like a mad bull. 'Come on, Sandy, baba!' The engine blew a long piercing whistle.

'Daddy! Daddy!'

'Stop him Frank, you bloody fool!' shouted Dayal. 'Get hold of Thakur sahib!'

Frank pounced on Sandy's father, pulled him back and with his full weight pressed him to the ground. The train clanged past at a great speed with a whoosh of steam and grinding iron. 'That's the Madras Express!' Frank slapped his forehead. 'Phew! Gawd! Skin of the teeth, man.' He forced a laugh. 'Why does he get like this? Boister-bloody-rus. You should see my boss. Great toper! But, bloody-hell, when he gets drunk . . . the fellow goes off to sleep.'

'Hixon? That bloody Anglo-half-Indian? Tommy rot! Don't talk to me about him. I have seen the fellow bawling and shouting at top of his voice, calling all Indians "bloody natives" and . . .' Dayal looked at Sandy and checked himself.

'Yeah! But he's a big guy. People shit in their pants when . . .' At a signal from Dayal, Frank checked himself. 'But his wife's like a small mouse. Always appears gobrified,'

'Gobrified?'

'Yes, man. Frightened, you know. Can't say more with the boy around.' Frank stood up and dusted his knees. 'Hey, hey, watch him!' Frank tapped out another guffaw.

Sandy's father had rolled on his side and was now up on his feet. He began to rock and drunkenly raising and lowering his voice, started to sing: '"O show me the way to go home, I'm tired and I wanna go to bed. I 'ad a drink about an hour ago . . . its gone right to my 'ed" Come on Laddie! Sing!'

Sandy giggled. He had heard the song a few times before and tried to join in, but the singing stopped as abruptly as it began. His father had fallen forward on to his knees. Sandy thought his father looked strangely small as Dayal propped him up against Frank. 'He's hurt. See, blood on forehead.' Dayal bent down and wiped his hand on the grass.

Sandy began to cry. He found a stone and threw it at Dayal. 'I'll tell mummy!'

Dayal lifted him up like a feather and swung him on to his broad shoulders. 'Sit there! Hold my head tight.'

The four of them made a strange picture. A small man in a well-tailored dark suit being frog-marched between two big men and a little boy perched on the shoulder of one of them. Sandy's tiny hands clasped Dayal's chin. He had stopped crying.

Sandy's mother said nothing. She inspected her husband's forehead, declared it was just a nasty graze and told the men to put him to bed. 'I'll attend to it.' But when they left, she put her arms round Sandy and holding him to her breast, rocked gently. Her dark, luxuriant hair, which should have had more grey at her age, fell over her shoulders. She usually wore it tied back in a bun, but before retiring to bed she would untie it for Sandy's ayah to comb and brush and weave into four thick plaits. Sandy liked it most when her hair was down, as it was now, free and flowing. He ran his little fingers gently through her hair and drank in the carbolic aroma of her soft skin. He was secure now, and he smiled as he lay his head on her shoulder and burrowed deep into her breasts. She was humming and he thought she whispered: '*Bechara*! My poor, little boy!' He did not give it much further thought for soon he was fast asleep.

The next morning he opened his eyes to see his mother bending over him. From her conspiratorial expression he knew she was about to share a secret. He sat up. 'We're going to uncle Jagdish, in Rajnagar.' She smiled with glee. 'To be with grandfather.'

'Raj-na-gar,' he chanted thoughtfully.

'Yes, Rajnagar.'

Sandy raised his hands to be carried. 'What's gran like? Will we sleep on the train?'

His mother regarded him with pride. 'Wait and see, my beautiful *Uckalji.*' She took him in her arms and hugged him. Then she put him down.

'My name is Sandy.'

'And Uckalji. That's what your big sister Mona called you yesterday, when she kissed you bye-bye. I think it's a nice way of saying "little genius". She picked him up and rolling him like a rattle from side to side, kept repeating: 'Ickle Uckal! Ickle Uckal! Little Genius.' She put him down. 'We will spend two nights on the train.'

Sandy danced about the floor excitedly, but froze when his father entered the room. His mother turned to the open wardrobe and pretended to search for something.

Mr Thakur waited, glanced at his pocket watch, and began to wind it. 'I've got to leave in half an hour,' he said.

'Breakfast is ready', she said without looking at him. In the mornings she always wore a long house coat and round her waist a heavy silver chatelaine. Everyone in the house knew her approach by the sound of those keys. 'I'll get the sugar out from the food cupboard,' she said sullenly as she walked past him. The sugar was always kept locked away from the servants, as were other items like flour, rice, ghee and spices. Perishable foods were kept in what was referred to as the meat-safe. The meat-safe had meshed doors and rested on four large unglazed pottery bowls that were filled with water to discourage marauding ants and cockroaches.

An English breakfast was a meal Sandy's father introduced into the family after the years he spent in England—that was before Sandy was born. And so the smell of fried bacon and eggs invaded the dining-room as Nathoo, the bearer, entered carrying a tray. Sandy's mother placed an EPNS sugar bowl on the table, and they sat down in silence. Mr Thakur cleared his throat. 'During the school hols, it's good to breakfast together.' He got no reply. 'Where's Dolly?' Dolly was the youngest of Sandy's three sisters.

'Nathoo!' Sandy's mother called out. *'Jera chhoti babee ko bulao.'* The bearer gave a nod and left the room.

Like Sandy, his elder brother and sisters also had anglicised pet names, a common practice among middle-class Indians. Sandy's given name was Sandeep. That, and the fact he was born with light brown hair, earned him his sobriquet, which stayed, even though his hair grew darker soon after his first birthday.

The servants, respectfully referred to the boys as "babas" and the girls as "baybees", while prefixes singled out a particular sister: "chhoti" for the youngest and "barra", for the eldest. And for the one in the middle, the prefix was descriptive. She was "mothi" baybee, because as a child she was fat. In time, that changed to "moti" which, minus the aspirant, means "pearl". Sandy never knew his eldest brother, and any reference to him was said in hushed tones. Being a late child, the gap between him and that brother was seventeen years, and seven years between him and his nearest sibling, Dolly. There was no rivalry for parental affection between Dolly and Sandy. She was glad to have that attention transferred to Sandy. In fact, she adored him, and as they were close friends, she was surprised he ignored her when she came to the table.

Sandy was looking at his father intently. He wanted to chat about the forthcoming trip. A long journey by train was an exciting prospect and many questions about it buzzed in his brain. 'Will there be more bridges or more tunnels?' he longed to ask, but wondered if his mother wanted him to keep the trip a secret.

'So,' said Dolly. 'You're going on a long trip with Mum?'

Sandy started, then nodded vigorously. He looked from his mother to the plaster on his father's forehead. He couldn't understand why she had not chided Frank and Dayal. Suddenly he remembered Frank had not kept his promise of the drink and jelaby. The memory of that hurt. He pouted and sniffed. 'Now what?' said his father impatiently.

'A nice start to the holidays you've made'. His mother mumbled, pushing her plate away from her.

'That will do! Not in front of the children.' His father warned gruffly.

She sighed and kept silent. Nathoo reached for the teapot and poured her a fresh cup of tea. He waited after adding some milk. She nodded and took a grateful sip.

'Dolly coming too?' Sandy asked his mother.

'Can't,' said Dolly. 'Got to mug for my exams.'

'Why?' Sandy quizzed.

'She's must study hard and do well,' said his father, 'if she wants to join her sisters at their school. It's a school for bright children.'

'St Columba's, Malabar hill'. Dolly anticipated her brother's questioning glance.

'Far from Daddy's school?' Sandy asked not knowing why.

'Quite', said Dolly. 'Finish your egg.'

Sandy looked at his father with alarm and then up at his ayah, standing behind him. He knew his father disliked food to be wasted and he solemnly watched the ayah mash the boiled egg for him. Then he began to gobble it up with affected gusto. The ayah, who also doubled as the cook, was Nathoo's wife; a slight woman with a refined but pock-marked face and of a complexion much lighter than her husband's. His serene face had the smoothness and glow of polished teak.

'You're not going to keep this up,' said Sandy's father. Dolly and Sandy knew he was talking to their mother. Their parents never referred to each other by name.

'Well, I suppose life must go on!' She said, trying hard to disguise the bitter tone in her voice. 'This time I *will* travel first class. It was a mistake travelling by Inter when I brought the servants from Rajnagar.'

'Five years ago, Inter for ladies was comfortable.' Sandy's father spoke gently.

'Did I tell you, Sandy, you were born in Rajnagar?' She did not wait for an answer. Instead she addressed her plate firmly: 'We'll travel by First. Jagdish will pay for the tickets if you think I'm being extravagant.'

'No need for that. I've denied you nothing.'

'Jaggers!' cried Sandy, wide-eyed. 'Handsome uncle Jag...Jaggers?'

'Yes,' said his mother. 'Jaggers, uncle Jagdish. He used to carry you. Remember.'

'Puch! Puch!' teased his sister, making a face. 'You used to kiss him non-stop.'

Sandy pouted.

'Dolly!' warned her mother. 'Leave the boy alone.'

'What about me?' asked Sandy's father, with the first smile of the morning. 'Am I not handsome too?'

Sandy stared. 'Yes,' he said, 'but your eyes are red.'

'Handsome is, as handsome does,' mumbled his mother.

Sandy's father stood up. He threw his napkin on the table, and walked to the door. His wife followed him. 'We'd better stop buying bacon and sausages from Fernandez,' he said. 'Frank said something nasty about the way those pigs are reared.'

'You had to wait till Frank told you. I've been saying this for sometime.' She gazed at him. 'You needn't worry. I've been ordering from the farm in Thana.'

'See,' he said affectionately, 'you always get your way.'

She touched his arm. 'That was no place to take the boy. And if you're going to drink yourself to death, you don't have to tell tall stories: "Taking the boy for a walk". What a lame excuse! Have I ever stopped you?'

'I wasn't thinking,' he said. 'Anyway, you're ensuring it won't happen again. About the boy, I mean. About the other matter, I'll try hard. I promise!'

'At this rate, drink will make you lose your job and your pension.'

He looked at her earnestly. 'Help me!'

'I've tried. You don't need my help. Give up the low company you keep. Take that temporary transfer to Poona. I know you hate your job. But it's not for long. You can hold out for a year. Till you get your pension, surely?'

'How long will you be away?'

'I don't know. Mix with men of your own standing. Jagdish says they're looking for retired officers, around sixty, willing to serve in the army as recruiting officers.'

'I know. I was there. I don't know why he thinks soon there'll be war in Europe. He's unhappy that his English friends think more of the King's Silver Jubilee than of the possibility of war.' He paused a moment. 'If I go to Poona, next year, and take on the job of an Assistant—it'll be assisting—Recruiting Officer, will you join me?'

'Yes.'

He took his solar topi and walking stick, and strode jauntily out of the house.

'Sandy! I've been looking for you. What are you doing in the kitchen?'

'Playing "mango man" with Panchu.'

Panchu jumped to his feet. 'Salaam memsahib! Cooking the dinner now?'

Sandy's mother shook her head. Panchu could see she had been crying. 'Memsahib, what is doctorsahib saying?'

She took a deep breath, then, speaking in Urdu, told Panchu not to worry about dinner. She would warn him if something had to be prepared. 'Sandy, come with me.'

'Why?'

'Because Grandfather is dying,' she said. 'You must say goodbye to Grandad.'

Pancho mumbled something which Sandy vaguely understood. He looked up at his mother. 'Tell the doctor to make him better.'

She picked him up and rested him on one hip, then quickly put him down again. 'Oof, you're heavy!'

He took her hand. 'I'll walk,' he said with adult dignity, 'I'm six, you know.'

She led him into her father's bedroom, the second largest room in a house that the builders had not quite finished. [One day, because of its sprawling nature, it would be sold and refurbished into a primary school.] The heavy curtains were drawn, and in the darkness, amid the clutter of ornate furnishing, brooding silhouettes of men and women moved noiselessly. Sandy was awed. Most were strangers to him, but on either side of the massive high bed, on which his grandfather lay on a sea of pillows, were familiar faces of his uncle Jagdish, and Dr Mark Peterson. They talked in hushed tones, while a nurse in a neat blue and white uniform, propped up the dying man. As she did so, Sandy saw the back of his grandfather's body, emaciated, naked to the waist. He was wearing a night cap. Sandy looked away and at the grey terrier curled up at the foot of the bed.

'Nancy!' he called, but the bitch merely twitched her ears and ignored him. He looked for Tinker—the dogs were never apart—and spotted the golden retriever stretched flat on his side, asleep under the bed. (Years later Sandy described the scene to Emma as being so like that depicted in the painting of the Earl of Chatham on his death-bed.) A sharp and unexpected cry of pain from the bed found its echo in the muted wails from the moving shadows. Sandy looked up, terrified. Women had appeared from nowhere. They were in front of him, heating and applying glass beakers to the dying man's bare back, where some remained stuck to the body. Ugly alternating pop and thump sounds made him tremble. 'They're hurting Nah-nah!' he cried. 'Tell them not to hurt him!'

His mother covered his eyes and pressed him against her side. 'Father's in great pain. This is supposed to help.' A moment later she screamed. 'Stop it! Stop it! Let him die in peace!' And, pushing the boy away, rushed to the bed to help her father to lie back into the pillows. Sandy saw her terror-stricken face and began to howl and stamp his feet. Then he ran to her and buried his face into her pelvis. She pressed him; and the sensations evoked were deeply consoling to both mother and son. They remained very still, till Tinker, the dog, rose from under the bed, cowering with his tail between his legs. He went to the middle of the room, raised his head and howled.

'Ajmeri!' Sandy's uncle Jagdish called.

'*Huzoor!*' A lumbering muslim chowkidar came up from behind him out of the dark shadows. Jagdish told him to take the dog out. Instinctively Tinker made a dash for the door, turned, and barked at the bed. The bark turned into a long mournful bay. Ajmeri caught up with him and the dog left the room whimpering.

'Come,' Sandy's mother sighed. 'Say bye-bye to Nah-nah. Don't be afraid.'

'No! No!' pleaded Sandy backing away.

'There now. I'm with you!' They moved to the bed. 'Oh, look! Jagdish, look!'

The dying man was pointing to the ceiling.

'Light the chandelier!' cried Jagdish. '*Jaldi! Jaldi!*'

The house stirred. Moments later the candles in the chandelier were lit. A warm glow from the rose-coloured Venetian glass filled the room.

CHAPTER TWO

'Whenever you want to criticise the British Raj, you come up with the "divide and rule" slogan. It's meaningless. Yes, it is. India was a divided country before the British came. There was no India. India was the creation of the British. The idea of Indian nationality was their gift to us.' Sandy looked at each of them in turn.

'Utter nonsense!' Hari snarled. 'What do you mean?'

'What I mean couldn't be more obvious. And here's another case in point. Look at us! My mother tongue is Marwari. I don't speak it because father never spoke it—at least not to us—because my mum spoke Urdu, as Hindu families from Lucknow, do . . .'

'You speak Urdu?' Satish interrupted.

'No, because father couldn't, and mother used it only to address the servants.'

'Get to the point,' Hari said irritably.

'My point: English unites us. Helps us to reach out and communicate with each . . .'

'No bloody excuse. We could have had another common language. Hindustani . . . Admit it, *yar*. Your family spoke English so they could suck up to the Britishers. All bloody power tactics and nest feathering.'

'And your family? Speak for yourself. Let's not start insulting each other's family. There'll be no end to it. English brought us together. You're Punjabi, Ramesh Gujarati, Satish Bengali, and here we're communicating in the only way we can.'

'Because of bloody Macaulay.' Hari grumbled. 'When was that Satish, *bhai*? Satish knows. He's our Bengali speaking History lecturer, from Government College. Sandy, Satish is an authority. Go on, Satish. Tell this fellow. Put him right. Thinks he's bloody clever because he went to Oxford. Another one of those "England-returned" empties.'

Satish looked at Hari with the pained expression of one reluctant to be involved. 'I suppose that would be the, er 1830s . . . 34 or 35, I think. Macaulay decreed that English was to be the medium of Indian education.'

'But that makes my point. He saw the need for a common . . .'

'No, Sandy,' said Ramesh. 'Left to us, we would've made Hindi our lingua franca . . . or, maybe, Hindustani, that mix of Hindi-Urdu which is the language of the cinema. We understand each other in Hindustani as well, if not better, than in English. In my own case, I produced a Gujarati film, *Circus Clown*. It has Hindustani version, not an English one. You're thinking about middle-class educated Indians, like yourself.'

'This fellow won't know Hindustani.' Hari derided. 'This so bloody *angrez* fellow only goes to the English cinema.'

'Come on, Hari. We all see English flicks.' Satish said. 'Hindi ones are stupid. All that singing and dancing, and lovers chasing round trees.'

'*Arrey*, Satish, don't give this fellow ammo. We're not talking about that.'

Sandy grinned. 'Satish, can we be a modern society without English? Can we teach Science or Medicine—or for that matter liberal democracy—without English?'

Satish clicked his tongue, reluctant to take sides.

'Never mind. English words,' Sandy went on, "have found their way into all Indian languages. Words like "time" and "line" and "station" . . ."cricket". So many others. We use a lot of them without realising. Take the title of Ramesh's film. It's English. Even a *coolie* knows what *Circus Clown* means. It's paranoia to assume everything the British did was a conspiracy. Many Englishmen were opposed to making English the medium of education. They had more to lose than gain, because the English language educated us into democracy and so on to freedom and independence.'

'But what business had the bloody Brits to be here in the first place?' Hari jerked his thumbs, raised his eyebrows and looked at each of them in turn.

'Just that. Their business. Trade. They came as traders, not conquerors. A small but often forgotten fact.' Sandy paused for effect. 'And, in fairness, you must admit, left to ourselves, there would not have been one nation for a lingua franca. Even Hindustani was the result of the Hindustan the British made possible.'

'Divide and rule!' Hari burst in. 'Don't bloody laugh. Say what you like. They used cunning tactics . . .'

'As did all foreigners who ruled India. Equally, one could say, that Indian rulers used the English for their own ends. And, by the way, I do know a good deal of Hindustani. My cousin in the army spoke it.'

'*Arrey*, don't talk about Roman Urdu and Army Hindustani to me. I know all about that stuff. "*Jaldi, jaldi,*" and "*Thik hai*", and when stuck, turning to your JCO, saying: "*Shabash!* Carry on, Sahib".'

'What's a JCO?' asked Ramesh.

'Junior Commissioned Officer,' Sandy explained. 'They used to be called VCOs. Viceroy Commissioned Officers, as distinct from King's Commissioned Officers.'

'And,' pounced Hari with a triumphant air, 'tell me why it's a rank you only find in the Indian Army. Britishers couldn't talk to the men directly. They spoke in English to the JCOs, and the JCOs spoke to the men. Interpreters. *Arrey*, I also got cousin-brother in the army. He's telling me, these bloody army types, officers like our Sandy's cousin, copy the Britishers. Yes, even now. "Pass me that *dahl-ka-maffick*" . . . and, in officers mess, they still don't serve Indian food—sorry, I should say "native" food . . . and listen, listen, this is really taking cake . . . calling each other English names—George, and Harry, and what else . . . yes, Krishnamurti, becomes Murphy. Someone else became Momby because he came from Mombasa .'

'That's a red-herring,' Sandy said. 'All close-knit groups use jargon and nicknames . . . for the sake of camaraderie and affection . . . to be distinct.'

'What is this red-herring?' asked Ramesh.

'By that this *sala* means I'm talking rubbish,' interjected Hari. 'Just limey talk.'

'Can we be gentlemanly? There's no need for abuse. We're supposed to be friends.'

'Satish, he won't know what *sala* means.'

'I've never understood why "brother-in-law" is a term of abuse,' Sandy said.

Satish grinned. 'What brothers-in-law do to sisters is an even more common abuse.'

Hari glared.

'Come on Hari. *Bahainchode*, sisterfucker? And then there's mother . . .'

'*Bus, bus,* Satish, enough. But why do Indian Officers still copy the Britishers by still having these J.C.Os. And don't talk about bloody tradition.'

'You're wrong to think British Officers did not speak directly to their troops. Many painstakingly learned Hindustani. But the troops themselves did not speak the language. They came from areas and villages with their own language and dialect. It's a problem for Indian Officers too, still is. And as JCOs were promoted from the troops they had to be used. And they were useful towards the gradual handing over of power to Indians . . .'

'Or to placate Indians,' Satish said, 'while holding on to real power.'

Sandy ignored Satish's intervention. 'The rank is also an incentive. Any uneducated peasant soldier can rise to be a JCO . . . And when I said red-herring, I simply meant we were straying from the point. Seriously, Hari you have to agree, Hindi isn't enough for the unification of India. South Indians question why the lingua franca has to be Hindi and not Tamil or any one of the languages that millions of them speak. Besides we needed English to talk to the British on equal terms. Wouldn't you have wanted that?'

'Look, they should've learnt Hindi. Bloody hell! What business had they to be here, if not going to speak our language. You've got it wrong. English Education was to their benefit. Meant to create a tier of brown Englishmen types, like you and your titled grandfather, to help run the country for them. An Indian official class of boot-lickers! A second tier of half-educated babus. Lackeys of imperialism, they kept the Raj going.'

'This is typical of you, Hari. Whenever you find yourself in a corner, you attack my grandfather. Now for the last time get this into your head and keep it there. He and his father had an Indian title, in their own right. One of them turned down a knighthood.'

'Yes, Hari *bhai*', Ramesh said. 'Keep parents out of this. No insulting of elders.'

'Thanks Ramesh.' Sandy gave him a brief grateful smile, then turn to Hari. 'Lies and abuse don't alter facts. But to answer your question about the English not learning Hin-Hindustani—clearly some did—but many saw no need to. They were the rulers. When the Mughals ruled India they brought Persian and Urdu. They gave us their language. We took it on. What's Hindustani if not bastardised Persian. They gave us their culture too. What the world recognises as high Indian culture, art, architecture, poetry, music, is Mughal. The Taj, the symbol of India, is Mughal.'

'Correct! True!' said Satish. 'Think about our Lucknowvi Hindus—like Sandy's mother's family. Hari, all the Hindu landed gentry of Delhi and UP area speak a highly literary and cultured Urdu. Talking about lackeys, what about the Hindus in the court of King Akbar. They served the Mughal Empire. Politics is a human survival strategy. And where there's power and wealth, there you'll always find *chumchas*.'

'Red-bloody-herring!' Hari blurted, 'except about *chumchas*!'

Sandy laughed, though he wasn't quite sure what Satish meant and dare not ask in case Hari pounced on him. But, intuitively, he correctly guessed it had something to do with servile flatterers.

'You're not going to like this, Hari,' Satish went on. 'I see no great virtue in being Indian. What's wrong with being what we are: Bengalis, Punjabis, so on and so forth? Better off, I say. Some states were better governed by Rajahs than the provinces were under British rule.'

'No, no. I totally agree. Put your hand there, Satish *bhai*! But this Sandy is bloody lover of the English! He would have been happy if Brits were still here. Eh, Sandy?'

'Not true. Chains are chains even if they are golden. And that, Hari, was said to me by an Englishman.'

'I think,' Ramesh said, 'it's unfair to confuse Sandy's admiration for the Brits.'

'English,' Sandy quietly interposed.

'. . . with a slavish mentality. And Satish, with respect, I have to disagree about Rajahs and Nawabs being good rulers. Most of those bloody chaps were despots living in the Dark Ages. Wait. Let me finish. That case in Punjab . . . somewhere in Punjab! The Rajah bloke who arrested Nehru. Put him in chains . . . dumped him in a filthy prison teeming with rats. The Brits deposed the fellow and released Panditji. Remember?'

'Okay! One or two bad cases but, but . . .' Hari turned on him angrily. 'Why this! Why mention once in blue moon cases. Exceptions bloody prove rule. This Sandy wouldn't know these things—living as he does in foolish paradise—now you've given the fellow more ammo—ammunition.'

'Hari,' said Sandy. 'Since you think I'm an apologist for the British, why should you imagine I wouldn't know about such a superb case of British justice, just as I am aware of the reluctance with which some British judges sent Gandhi to prison.'

'Enough, Sandy,' Satish said. 'Don't make a big thing of it. Applies both ways. One or two cases don't make them saints.'

Hari stared at him blankly. 'Okay, okay, Sandy, how would we have lost out without what you call English education?'

'I've already said how! English broadened our horizons, opened to us science and modernity—technology, western philosophy and the politics of rights and freedoms. At least admit, Hari, the British have a sense of fairness; that they're democrats?'

'Fairness! In the name of bloody fairness they kept clever talented people down and promoted incompetent sycophants.' Satish said, and they all stared at Sandy.'

'I find that hard to believe,' said Sandy. 'The British do not like flatterers.'

'I don't know about that,' Satish enjoined. 'They most certainly hated clever people. They saw them as potential troublemakers.'

'Well, not just Indians. Their own people have been on that receiving end. It's in the British character to suspect talent and genius.'

'You see!' Hari clicked his tongue and gave a wry smile. 'This fellow defends them, say what you like.'

'It's a characteristic that's hard to understand when, more than any other nation, the British are among the talented people in the world. No point shaking your heads. Face facts. Off the top on my head I'd say Britain has produced more Nobel prize winners in every sphere than any other nation.'

'One day,' Sandy, 'the Americans will break that record.'

'But, Satish, for the size of the country . . . its something to wonder at. It's odd why they distrust genius and often pursue it to destruction. Satire and self-deprecation is one of the main stays of British humour—which is essentially anti-intellectual.'

'Huh! You mean their school-boy humour.'

'One could write a book on English humour. I'm talking about its anti-intellectual aspect . . . one cannot be devoted to puns and word play without undermining concepts.'

'True, they don't take life seriously.' Ramesh rolled his head.

'Ramesh is a great fan of Oscar Wilde,' Satish said. 'But I don't accept this idea of the English being the most talented nation on earth. Sandy, where . . .'

'Did I say England? I meant Britain. The Scots . . .'

'Shut up, *yaar*,' Hari interrupted. 'Satish meant Britain.'

'All right,' Sandy raised a placating hand. 'Think of all the great inventions—"firsts" from Britain. And is it not commonly agreed Newton was the greatest scientist ever . . .'

'True.' Ramesh gave another solemn roll of his head. 'Britain has the most "firsts" in every sphere, including, sports. I'm helping Pitoo, my youngest brother, to mug up for the General Knowledge paper . . . this year, 1952, for the UPSC exams! You know, Union Public Service . . .'

'And paradoxically,' interrupted Sandy, 'ignoring genius, talent and the hounding of great men is also peculiarly British. Think of the many times pioneers and inventors have been ignored. Great men, such as Hastings and Clive, impeached or driven to . . .'

'Shut up! Enough. Those two were corrupt bastards. As for "firsts". Who knows. Imperialists make claims and exploit their power, right, left and centre. Exploiting talent, skills, resources. Like the Yanks are doing now. Using all German scientists to, to . . . Prizes mean nothing. All that politiking behind those Nobel prizes. Prizes, never for the deserving. Exploitation is greatest talent of

West—robbing ideas, standing on other shoulders. Napoleon said Brits were a nation of shopkeepers. I say, they're a bloody nation of bloody robbers.'

Sandy chuckled. 'The Empire is fairly recent British history. Think of the discoveries and inventions in Tudor and Stuart times. Newton aside, in the field of Medicine. Men like Harvey, Jenner . . . What's the point. You question everything I say. Even the fact that the Industrial Revolution started in Britain.'

'If you knew the Ancient Hindu scriptures, you'll know all those great scientific ideas occurred to our ancestors. Here in India.'

'That's nonsense! Where's the proof. You can't place myths against facts. If our ancestors were so wonderful, why are we . . . well, industrially, still developing?'

'What about Da Vinci?'

'What about him?'

'Did he not .'

'Yes, but the evidence of his genius is in black and white . . . and on canvas.'

'He had wonderful ideas, maybe,' Ramesh intervened, 'but none of them would have worked. Imagination is not the same thing as invention.'

'Ha, yes,' said Satish. 'I speak as historian. Every invention has a long technological history behind it. Each must await developments. You can't have steel tools before the discovery of iron and the development of steel. How could our ancestors have flown in aircraft before the-the discovery of aircraft materials, and-and the invention of engines?'

Hari was scowling. Suddenly his face lit up. 'Sandy, you want evidence? Okay. The Ashoka Pillar. There, in front of the Kutab Minar, in Dehli. Solid iron and no rust. BC! Before Christ! Long, long ages before that Brit what's his name . . . ?'

'Bessemer,' prompted Satish.

'*Hahn*. How do you explain that, Sandy? There's evidence.'

'I can't explain that. And there are other things of India's great past, I can't explain. But it does not answer my question. Why haven't we benefited from past knowledge? Much of India's greatness is in art and philosophy, not in science or in any technological progress. What is lacking in the Indian . . .'

'Hey, now you listen to me!' Ramesh interrupted angrily. 'Not taking sides but this is where politeness must end. How can you, an Indian, deny your culture and heritage. Shame, *yaar*, you should be ashamed?'

Sandy stared at Ramesh. When he spoke he was barely audible. 'Not everyone wants to be identified by their culture, or, for that matter, be imprisoned by it. There's such a thing as individual freedom, Ramesh, and if you are a democrat, you . . .' He stopped. All eyes were looking past him. He turned. Hari's sister, Veena, had entered the room.

'*Bus, bus!*' she said. 'Enough of all this talk. Such a waste of time. All talk, talk, and nothing is going to change the world one bit.' She looked at Sandy and smiled. 'Come on all of you. *khana's* ready. Lunch is on the table.' She wriggled her chin and wrinkled her nose with petulant coquetry. None of this escaped her brother's notice.

'Challay, chaloo!' he said. 'Let's eat. Come on, Veena! Lead the way.'

'Go, go! I'm not stopping you. You know the way. I'm going to wash my hands first. As he passed her Hari growled, almost inaudibly, in Punjabi: 'I know what you're up to. Behave yourself. I'll tell Ma. I don't approve of this shameless behaviour.'

'Tell your great grandfather if you like. You're not my chowkidar.'

Sandy tried to circle them, but she caught his sleeve and detained him. 'Let me see your hands? *Chee chee*, filthy! Come. Wash them.' She pushed Sandy as he tried to remonstrate that his hands were clean.

She giggled. 'In any case, you need to wash them before *khanna*. No forks, knives and spoons in our house.' In the bathroom, she thrust the soap in his hands. 'Take, I will pour the water.' She filled a small brass ewer from a bucket.

'Hey!' warned Sandy, 'you'll get it all over me. Join the others. I'll do it myself.'

'I won't splash it. Promise.' She drew nearer. 'There, stretch your hands over the basin.' She was behind him, and as she poured the water he could feel the softness of her young breasts against his arm. It aroused in him both a thrill and a trepidation; and the cake of soap flew out of his hands. With a nervous laugh he retrieved it.

'What's wrong, Sandy?' she asked and leaned even more heavily against him.

'Nothing.' He was determined not to encourage her. Hari burst in.

'Veena! What's this. Have you no shame? There are other guests to attend to. And Ma's alone in the kitchen.'

'Nonsense! What about the servants?'

Hari caught her arm and led her out. Sandy could hear her raised voice. 'Hari, you're such a bore. Interfering all the time. Why don't you mind your own business.'

'I'm minding my business! My business as your elder brother.'

At the table Sandy realised that in fact Veena had an ally in her mother. Both were paying him undue attention and, for their own reasons, both he and Hari were alarmed. Soon his worst fears were confirmed when Veena's mother cornered him after the meal. 'Becoming Christian, you know, means nothing. You're still a good Hindu boy from a good Hindu family. I know your mother wery vell. I should speak to her. It's time she thought of your marriage. You should be married, soon.'

'But Ma!' intervened Hari, who made sure he was within earshot. 'That's none of our business. You know, fellows!' he raised his voice. 'Veena is soon to be engaged to Vinod Sharma. His father and I've come to some understanding.'

'As if I don't know,' said his mother. 'But, nowadays a girl should have some choice in these matters. In any case, stupid boy, I was just curious to know Sandy's plans for the future. You've made big big *tamasha* for nothing.'

'I've no immediate plans, said Sandy. But I'm happy for Veena. Congratulations.'

Hari's mother pushed her son away from her. 'Donkey!' she said, and drawing her sari over her head shuffled into the kitchen and was soon heard shouting at the servants: 'Oh, God! *Toba, toba*! these servants will be the death of me. When will you donkeys ever learn?'

Sandy smiled, relieved to see that Veena had forgotten him, and brother and sister seemed reconciled. Now she was all blushes; giggling and sticking out her tongue at Hari. Relived, he realised that her brief flirtation was mere coquetry. He turned and looked out of the window. Through the palm trees, that marked the perimeter of the Oval Maidan, the imposing Victorian Gothic buildings of Bombay University and the Law Courts shone in the late afternoon sun. Then something out of the ordinary struck him. The flags over the grey-slated roofs were flying at half-mast. He wasn't sure but thought he knew why; and wondered why no one had remarked upon it.

Soon after lunch Ramesh suggested a game of Bridge, but Sandy made his excuses and took his leave. As he walked down Queen's Road, he knew he was stepping into a new chapter of his life and the certainty of never again visiting Hari's family. He caught a taxi outside the Eros Cinema. They passed the news-stand on the steps of Churchgate Station. A banner headline read "King George VI is dead".

'Want paper, sahib?' asked the Sikh taxi-driver.

Sandy looked away. The news brought a lump to his throat and a boyhood memory returned. He was fourteen and had just finished reading Ernest Raymond's novel of Gallipoli, *Tell England*. 'Is it a sad book, Sandy?' his mother had asked. 'No.' he lied, unable to hide his tears, 'I mean yes.' He took the open book across to her and pointed. She read aloud. "'Tell England, ye who pass this monument,/ We died for her, and here we rest content.'" She looked at her husband, who looked up from his book but said nothing. 'You're a romantic, Sandy,' she said smiling. Sandy wiped his face and went to his father and asked what that meant. His father thought a while, then said: 'A romantic, laddie, is someone who believes in myths in spite of being aware of realities. Can young lives, cut short, rest content?' 'Never mind, Sandy,' said his mother, prompted by his puzzled expression, 'the world is meaningless without romance.' 'Indeed,' added his father, with a gentle cough, 'reality is prose, romance is poetry. But one must never loose one's grip on reality . . .' Sandy feared he had and would do so, only too often . . .

'Stop at the next news-stand and buy me a paper,' he asked the taxi driver.

The Sikh wobbled his head. When he did stop, he was to return shortly. 'No paper. All gone. Sold out, sahib.' But before starting the engine he turned to Sandy and added: 'You know Sahib, I was driver many years with English boss. He give me photo of King Emperor.' The turbaned head rolled thoughtfully as the car moved on.

CHAPTER THREE

The Georgian House
St Andrew's Road
Winchester
28 August 1958

Dear Sandeep Thakur,

    I have seen your letter to Colonel Franks and have to tell you that my husband died two years ago. Your kind letter would have stirred old memories of his time in Poona. I am sure he would have enjoyed reading your letter and meeting you.

    Yes, we met once, but my memory of that meeting is rather vague. You were just a boy then, so I suppose we will have changed beyond recognition.

    Ted is a doctor and has just folded up his practice here and moved to London. I will tell him about you when he next writes and gives me his new address.

With best wishes
Edith

5 Rutland Mansions
Riverside Gardens
Hammersmith
30th August 1958

Dear Mrs Franks,

I was sad to receive your letter, and reproach myself for not getting in touch earlier, especially as I have been in England since March 1956. But, until now, I have found all my energies and attention taken up by matters, the details of which I shall spare you.

I will always remember with fondness the friendship and kindness Colonel Franks showed towards my father and me. For that reason alone I would like to meet you and visit his grave.

Winchester is not far, and if you can find any free end of a week between now and the end of September, I will try to make my visit as brief as possible.

Yours sincerely
Sandy

Winchester
15 September 1958

Dear Sandy,

I am sorry for the delay in replying to your letter. But I did give Ted your address and since then I gather that the two of you have met and recalled boyhood memories of the Christmas vacation he spent in India.

You could, if you like, spend a Saturday and Sunday with us here in Winchester. Ted will try to manage a time that will suit both of you, and bring you down in his car.

Best wishes
Edith

> PS I must warn you, Ted likes making an early start to avoid traffic. E

※

'Gosh! That's a Rover 75.'

'Yes, but suffering from chronic rheumatism. Keep you fingers crossed and pray she doesn't die on us today.' Ted grinned. 'It's dad's car. I've my eye on a second-hand Austin A105. You know, the sporty, two-toned affair.' He picked up Sandy's suitcase and put it on the back-seat. 'Get in.' As the engine sprang to life he patted the steering wheel affectionately. 'I haven't yet found a garage I could trust in London, but my chap in Winchester knows her insides like the back of his hand.' He boxed Sandy's arm. 'Sorry, I'll shut up now. I'm a bore when it comes to cars. There's a Penguin Guide to Hampshire in that glove-what's-it.'

'Thanks.' A moment later Sandy shut the book and stared out of the window. It had been a dull morning, but now, against a brightening sky the silhouette of Hammersmith Bridge loomed large, while below, the mist had lifted to reveal the silver glide of a placid Thames. 'The greys of England sustain me,' he remarked, 'as it did Whistler.'

'Still in love with England!' Ted sniffed.

Sandy gave a monosyllabic affirmation. He studied Ted's clean-cut profile but failed to link it with the gangly youth he first met in Poona in 1941; and though Ted could not be more than thirty-two, he looked older. The thick, wiry brown hair was white at the temples and the rakish thin moustache at odds with the solemnity of his deep-set grey eyes. 'So, Winchester's the family home town . . . city?'

Ted nodded. 'Father's family. Mother's a proud daughter of Bedfordshire. Even boasts an ancestor who knew Bunyan. I tease her about it—when she lets me—about how it explains the puritanical streak in her. Father was spiky, you know what I mean, High Church. One always felt he'd end up a Roman Catholic. He did.' Ted stifled a yawn. 'Of course, you're High too. I have to remind myself you're Christian.'

'And you?'

'Don't really know, old boy. Never give it much thought.' He shifted in his seat. 'Someday I will . . . that is, think upon it. When death stares me in the face.'

'And the name Franks. It suggests Norman ancestry?'

'Father was tall and long-faced? I see. You may be right.'

'And you were a Wykehamist—manners maketh and all that?' Sandy laughed. 'I'm just showing off.'

'You could've been one too. Father had plans to . . . You were nearly thirteen when we last met. He wanted you to join me and I was to take care of you. He was fond of you.'

Sandy smiled wanly, but said nothing.

'I remember looking forward to it, at the time. It's the paternal in me, you know, and you have the "I'm-lost-look-after-me" sort of look. What did happened? Or rather, why didn't it happen.'

'Sorry, belatedly sorry, my father should've written to explain. He and I were keen, but we knew it would break mother's heart. I'm a late child and the youngest.'

'Well, it probably was the right decision for you.'

'I'm not so sure, as you can see, here I am.'

'But the school you went to wasn't so unlike our public schools.'

'Quite a few of those in India.'

'But yours was, or is, a famous one. I forget the name.'

'The Princes School. Founded by Lord Mayo.'

'Had an old Etonian Headmaster. Timson. Was he still there in your time?'

'Yes. Bachelor. Suave. Always immaculately dressed. Drove an MG.'

'How did you manage that? To get into that school, I mean.'

'What was I doing in a school for princes? Family links. Jaggers, my uncle Jagdish—being a nawab, was an old boy.'

'That grey building, we just passed, was, I'm reliably told, the convent school Vivien Leigh went to . . . and Maureen . . . the one who played Jane in the Tarzan films. Know this part of England?'

'Driven through. Once on my way to Guildford. Also, last summer. There was a wedding. Chris Thompson's. Chap, on the same training course as me.'

'The chap who bought your car?'

'Yes.'

'Do you miss it? The car. I would. You should've held on to it.'

'Bought it on a whim. I didn't really need it. And now my school's within walking distance. But, yes, I miss it.'

'So, you did a post-graduate course? Somehow, I don't see you as a teacher. Much too debonair and bookish . . . I suppose the last bit fits. What's the school's name?'

'Browns, a private school. Someone I met at the wedding, who's now my colleague, she arranged an interview with the headmaster. And I got the job.'

'Did you charm her into pressing your case?'

Sandy laughed. 'Steady on. She's spoken for; and Clarke—he's the Head—is the sort who makes up his own mind. Merit, dear boy, sheer merit, I assure you.'

'Sorry that was below the belt. But you're a likeable chap. Your face, dear boy, is your fortune. And you were in Balliol. One of the sons of Belial.' Ted sniggered.

'Oxford doesn't count. I left after two terms.'

'And why didn't you get in touch when you were in Oxford?'

'1950 was a horrible year. Father died and then, when I thought I'd return to Oxford, there were family problems to settle. Yes, a year of . . .' Sandy checked himself as a twinge of guilt overcame him. It was also the year he met Bill Clayton and the start of a dear friendship. He would find another, more suitable, time to share that with Ted, who appeared not to have been listening and was now humming a familiar tune.

'That's from *Gigi*. The film won nine Oscars.'

'More than it deserved.' Ted fell silent, then asked suddenly: 'Are you married?'

'No.'

'Why not?'

'Never stayed in one place long enough to . . . and the years just rolled by.'

'Didn't mean to pry. You see, not all Englishmen have that reserve you so admire. But if we're to pick up from where we left off, the long gap has to be filled. Besides I wondered . . . You don't mind my asking?'

'Ask away, I've nothing to hide.'

'I was going to ask, if you encountered any racial prejudice here; though clearly none from your colleague and this Clarke chappie.'

'I've been lucky. But I suppose it'll come when least expected. By the way, Clarke told me, after the interview, that he served in India. In Bangalore. Army Supply Corps.'

'Some luck then.' Ted hummed a tune. 'Mabel trained as a teacher, too.'

'And where does she teach?'

'She doesn't. After all that, she didn't take it up. She's a dress designer. Runs a boutique in Carnaby Street. I did ask her to join us, but she can't.' Ted compressed his lips and shook his head. 'She's going to Paris . . .'

Sandy waited, then asked: 'And Kitty?'

Ted drew a breath, puffed his cheeks and blew. 'Kitty's with Ruth, Mabel's sister. She, that is Ruth, has a flat over the shop.'

'I suppose the business is doing well.'

'Yes. It didn't at first, but in the last year or so there's been a buzz in the market. Mabel found it hard to operate from Winchester. So we decided to come to London, not, I hasten to add, to better my prospects. I had a good practice in Winchester.'

'Was it hard to find a place in London?'

'That never was a worry. Father bought the Holland Park house, when he returned from India. We haven't been there long. We had to wait till the tenants left. Repairs, and now decorating, which Mabel enjoys doing when she gives herself some time off. Come over and see us when its ready.' Ted stared solemnly ahead. Then his face lit up. 'You'll like Kitty. She's a caution. Delightful.'

For sometime neither spoke. Ted hummed. Sandy smiled, idly turning the pages of the Penguin Guide. 'The first time.' Ted said suddenly. 'Your first trip to Guildford? What was that about?'

'Oh, just an outing. By myself. Exercising the car, as it were. I went to Stag Hill, and watched them working on the new Cathedral.'

After another long pause Ted said: 'I should warn you about mother. Comes across as rather aloof and unfriendly. Don't let it worry you.'

'I won't. I got that impression from her letters.'

Ted returned to his humming. 'Take in the landscape. It gets better at Wisley and the Hog's Back.'

'I will. It's the most beautiful country in the world . . . England is.'

Ted coughed discreetly. 'I won't argue. We could do with more sun. Shall we stop at Ripley, for coffee?'

'I'd love that. Actually, I'm dying for a cup of coffee.'

'And the car could do with a break.' Ted looked at his watch,' we're making good time. Yes, bang on schedule. We should be in Winchester ten thirty, elevenish . . . sorry to drag you out of bed, but it'll give you time to freshen up before lunch. Cigarette?'

'No, thank you. I didn't know you smoked.'

'Only minor vices, as my father used to say. Father managed to give it up soon after retirement. I don't smoke much. But on long drives it keeps me awake. Filthy habit.'

On the top beam of the heavy oak gate, ash grey with age, were chiselled the words "The Georgian House". A gravel drive, box-hedged on either side, led up to the house. Ted got out off the car and stretched his arms. 'If mother's in the garden, she won't know we've arrived. I'll see.' He returned. 'Yes, she's not in the kitchen. Follow me."

'Gosh!' said Sandy. 'The house is just as I imagined from your father's description. Now those green rosettes on the roof. I've seen them once before. Houseleeks?'

'Spot on. Hope they last, because I've no intention of climbing up there again. I'll take you to your room. Bring your case. Through here. This is the pantry, kitchen and there's the dining room. Over there, the library, or rather study, leading into the living-room.' Ted led the way up the stairs. 'These boards creak, but don't let that worry you. We have thick walls. This is my bedroom . . . ours when Mabel's here. And this is yours, next to mine, separated by the bathroom, which we share. We knock on each other's doors when the bathroom's free. Or leave the door ajar when done with it. Mother and Emma have their own. You'll find towels in that chest and there should be a packet of blades and a razor in the small cupboard next to the mirror. There's also a lavatory downstairs next to the study.' He pulled open the door and crossed the room to open a window. 'The other three bedrooms overlook the garden. We're not so lucky.'

Sandy wondered about Emma. A maiden aunt? Perhaps an old nanny? 'So, there are five bedrooms,' he asked for lack of something to say.

'If you count the box room. It's been father's for sometime. No one goes there, well, except Emma. Call if you need anything. When you're ready we'll meet downstairs in the living-room and I'll introduce you to the mater.'

When Sandy entered the living-room, Ted was on the narrow terrace outside the French windows. Sandy drew in a deep breath. 'It's beautiful! Who's the gardener?'

'Mother. And we dare not interfere. But a little man comes twice in the week.'

They walked up a path, between herbaceous borders, towards a neat square lawn in the centre of which was a small circular pond with a simple fountain. On the right edge of the lawn, a narrow flag-stoned path led to a garden shed and leaning against its door was a red Raleigh bicycle. Along the far end of the lawn were beds of over-blown roses, and behind them, a line of poplars screened the house from a quiet lane. At the opposite corner of the garden shed was a greenhouse and on a deck-chair, in front of it, wearing a large straw hat, was, Sandy presumed, Ted's mother.

'Hello, mother! This is Sandy.'

Sandy hid a mild astonishment as he took the hand she limply offered him, because the woman who stood by Ted looked nothing like her son. He knew he was about an inch shorter than Ted, which would make Ted just under six feet, but the wiry, slim, erect woman before him barely reached his shoulder, in spite of the tall straw hat she wore. It cast a shadow over a thin pale face with greying hair and dark non-committal eyes. 'So you're Sandy?' Her voice was clear and strong. 'How do you do!'

'How do you do, Mrs Franks!'

She removed her hat and stared. 'You've grown into a fine looking young man.' She looked younger than he had expected and handsome in an understated and sombre way. 'You can't possibly remember me!' She added with a fleeting smile.

Sandy hesitated. 'We met once, briefly, but I have a clear memory of that meeting.' Then with a rather sheepish smile he added: 'Because I wanted too.'

'I have the advantage of seeing photographs my husband took of you and Ted. You had a soft and delicate face. That hasn't changed.' She looked away. 'We're lunching at one, Sandy. I may call you Sandy and do call me Edith?' She faced him. 'Would you like coffee and biscuits in the meantime. Or indeed, a drink?'

'Nothing right now, thank you. But I'd love to be shown the garden.'

'Well,' she looked at her watch. He noted her movements were brisk. 'It'll have to be a quick tour. I'm expecting Mary, our neighbour, in fifteen minutes.'

'Why Mary?' queried Ted.

'Why not. She's lending a hand and is lunching with us. And Ted,' her face clouded, 'about Emma, we better not rely . . . excuse me, Sandy.' She led Ted aside and spoke as one not wishing to be overheard and yet not too concerned if anyone did. 'Emma's been her usual enigmatic self. Up early. I don't know if she's had breakfast, but when I came out into the garden, she was by the pond, painting. And now she's disappeared.'

'Didn't you remind her about lunch?'

'Yes. It didn't seem to register. You know, I never press when she's melancholic and peculiarly sullen. I'd rather she stayed away than drew attention to herself. Lets not mention her, shall we? It does annoy me. Why can't she say where's she's going?'

'Because you don't ask, mother. Are George and Trevor coming too?'

'No. Out for the day. Fishing.'

'Sorry, I must phone the garage.' Ted turned and walked briskly towards the house.

Edith sniffed and joined Sandy. 'Now, where shall we begin? It's not a big garden. And at its best in June.'

Sandy sensed a slight impatience in the tone of her voice. 'Why don't you let me potter? It's a good size, and I do think you've achieved a lot, single-handed!'

'Did Ted say that? He exaggerates. A little man comes twice in the week.'

'Mother!' Ted called out from the terrace. I'm taking the car to the garage and I may have to leave it there. I won't be more than an hour. Back in time.'

'Take Sandy with you, because in a few minutes I have to be in the kitchen. He can seen the garden later. After lunch.'

'Of course.' Ted came out to join them.

'Actually,' said Sandy, 'I'll visit the cemetery. Is it within walking distance?'

There was an uncomfortable pause.

'I'm sorry, but I would like to visit your husband's grave, Mrs Franks.'

Edith sighed. 'But of course! Why you're here. It's not hard to find. Go down St James's Lane. Hilltop cemetery is past the bridge over the railway. Can't miss it.'

'I'll drop you there,' said Ted, 'and collect you on the way back. I'll try not to be more than forty minutes, with or without the car.'

In the car, after a while, Sandy asked, 'was I out of line? I mean, did I blunder? You know, mentioning your father's . . .'

'Don't give it another thought. It's not what you think. She just forgot.'

'And you? Have you got . . .'

'It's been two years. As a doctor I was prepared for the end long before it came.'

They stopped outside the cemetery gates. 'This is it,' Ted said. 'As I said, not far.'

'And it really is on a hill, or should I say the slope of a hill. Peaceful, isn't it.'

'Yes. And the sound of the occasional train emphasises that peace.'

'How apt. Trains and the idea of a journey.' Sandy said almost inaudibly.

Ted got out of the car. 'You don't mind if I don't . . .'

'Just point me in the right direction.'

'You see the paths? Take the one that goes uphill, then before you get to what looks like a war memorial, the path turns left to a grassy patch under a chestnut tree. You can see the top of it from here. Father's one of four graves. You can't miss it. Sorry, have you lost something.'

'I was looking for a flower stall.'

'Not today. Sundays, and then only in summer. Meg Robinson, who tends a vicarage garden, opens a stall. I'll leave now. If you don't want to wait, go back down this lane, take the first turning right and carry on till you see the house.'

The grave, when Sandy found it, was a simple white marble slab on a granite base, and bore a plain black marble cross. Below that the legend read:

Colonel Ian Basil Franks
Hampshire Regiment
1891-1956
I am the resurrection and the life

Sandy had hoped to place a single rose on the grave. He bent down, touched the stone, and as he stared at the inscription, he saw himself, a boy of twelve, on a high stool next to his father, behind the long, polished teakwood counter of the Poona Station Canteen, serving, tea, biscuits and cigarettes to grinning black soldiers of the Afrika Corps. They came amid a clatter of mess-tins. "Attention!" someone shouted, and hobnailed boots struck the platform, raggedly; then a shuffle as a sea of khaki parted to allow a tall, slim figure, in bushshirt and Sam Browne belt, to come through the divide. "Sar'Major!" the figure barked. "Get those packs off their backs! Give the boys a rest. There's a whole hour before they board the troop train." The soldier addressed stiffened and saluted. "Sah!" The tall officer calmly acknowledged the salute with a brisk tap of his swagger stick against his peaked cap. "Jolly good, carry on, Sar'Major." He turned and walked towards the counter. Sandy's father whispered: "That's Colonel Franks, my boss," as the Colonel's face broke into a wide grin. His thin clipped, white moustache stretched across his lean face, and his blue eyes, set deep under grey eyebrows, had a mischievous twinkle. "So, you're Sandy, eh?" Sandy recalled giggling as the Colonel prodded his father's midriff with the cane. "Thakur, you ruddy scoundrel, you've a good-looking lad, you have, blast you!" He laughed and prodded again. "Tell me, young 'un, have you seen a Bren Gun Carrier? No? Then come with me. Thakur! the boy can come with me in the jeep. I'll take him back to the office. See you there in an hour.' He looked at Sandy quizzically, and tousled his hair. "Ah, one other thing Thakur, old horse. Did I tell you my son, Ted's down here for Christmas? Meant to. Anyway, have tea with us. It would be good for the boys to get together. Can you? Good. Come on then, Sandy." Sandy, proud to be with someone as important as the Colonel, was thrilled as they cut a swath through the troops to his jeep . . .

A long siren-like whistle jerked Sandy back to the present. He turned towards the sound and looking down the slope of the hill, saw a train speed under the bridge below the bank; and as the shrill of the whistle faded in the distance, he suddenly felt he was no longer alone. He turned back. Looking down at him was the most angelic face he had ever seen.

'Hello', said the apparition; and he imagined its translucent blue eyes widened.

'Gosh! I mean, hello!' Sandy waited, but the young woman did not speak. Her eyes rested on him with that frank regard he found so attractive in English women. 'You are real? I mean, I didn't hear you . . . you aren't going to suddenly vanish?' Strange stirrings within him made him stammer. He quickly recovered and though he couldn't see why he felt the need to explain, said: 'Somebody I knew. Colonel Franks.'

'Then you must be Sandy.'

He gaped. 'You have, as they say, the advantage of me.'

'Mother told me you were coming.'

'Mother?'

'Colonel Franks was my father.'

He noted her lips tremble as she said "Father". 'I didn't know he had a daughter?'

She didn't answer, but came down the slope to his level. He raised a hand to steady her. She took it without hesitation. It suddenly dawned on him. 'You must be Emma?'

She nodded.

'And you've been here? How is it I missed you?'

She pointed to the cedar tree. 'I was sitting there. Painting.'

The Lotus And The Rose

'You paint? Wonderful. Can I . . . may I?'

She shook her head. A gust of wind blew her brown shoulder length hair against her slender neck. 'I'm not happy with it.' She sighed. 'Were they talking about me?'

The question took him by surprise. 'Yes. But I didn't know, then, you were Ted's sister.' He smiled encouragingly. But all he got was a pout and a thoughtful tilt of the head. She turned to go. 'I'm sorry,' he said, 'sorry I came empty-handed, but I didn't get the chance to bring flowers.' He waited. 'Your father must have meant a lot to you? Silly question.'

'Nothing and no one means more to me.' She said with childlike vehemence.

'Of course. We, your father and I, couldn't have met more than a few times, but I grew fond of him.' A gentle thought struck him. 'I'm sure he'd want you to let go . . .'

'But I don't wish to let go!' She frowned darkly.

Someone called out. It was Ted, and he was waving frantically from the gates.

'You can help me pack,' she said. 'Then we'll join Ted. Promise you won't peek.' She smiled, and as he followed her, he knew, with instant yet absolute certainty, he was in love.

Ted met them half-way down the path. 'Hello there! I see you've met Emma.'

'I say Ted, you didn't tell me you had a sister?'

'Didn't I! Terribly sorry. Must've slipped my mind. Odd, though . . .' He shook his head. 'We must hurry. Mustn't keep mother waiting.' Emma put her things on the back seat and sat down. Sandy sat in front. Ted leaned over to Emma: 'Are you all right, about lunch? Good.'

She hadn't spoken but before her brother could start the car, she tapped him on the shoulder. 'What's odd?'

'He turned round. 'Odd? Did I say anything was odd?'

'Yes. Something to do with Sandy not knowing about me!'

'Oh, that! Nothing, really, Sandy. I thought it odd, because Emma was born in India. In the hills. Murray, which I gather is now in Pakistan.'

'And where was Emma when we met in India.' Sandy glanced over his shoulder. He noted, for the first time, she was wearing a plain white blouse and a blue skirt; and that her figure, though full, was not obviously so.

'She was not quite two and with her aunt in Wales.' Ted started the car. 'Mother, I have to say, hated India. The stay in Murray was her happiest. She left for England to serve as an ambulance driver.'

'But I saw your mother in 1944.'

'Yes, at the farewell party your father gave us, or rather gave my father. Mother felt—noblesse oblige and all that—that we should be together as a family on father's retirement. So we came to India, except Emma, of course.' The car turned right into the drive of The Georgian House.

'Mother only went to supervise the packing and to make sure daddy didn't leave the rose-wood chest behind.' Emma said almost mechanically.

Ted laughed. They stopped outside the door. Emma sprang out. 'I'll change. Tell mum I'll be down soon. If you're making drinks, I'll have a martini, sweet . . . with ice.'

'What about your stuff?'

'Later.'

Sandy's head was buzzing. If Emma was two in 1942, she would be nineteen now. Ten years younger than him! Even more intriguing was the twelve-year gap between Ted and Emma! Was she an accident? Did she know it? Ted appeared to have read his thoughts. 'Are you wondering about the age gap between us? Well, the gap was even greater between mother and father. At least fifteen years. Mother couldn't have been more than twenty-one when I was born. It was a caesarean birth and she decided never to go through that again. But in 1938, father was posted to India, a special assignment; and mother was quite thrilled about it. Dad decided to spend his furlough or long leave in India to pick up the local language . . . Marathi I think, but . . . anyway, they holidayed in Murray . . . Emma's the result. By the way what did you think about her painting?'

'I wasn't allowed to see. But I'd like to. There must be others.'

'Yes, do. They're quite something. Uncanny talent for someone so young.'

They entered the dining room. 'You back?' Edith called from the kitchen. She came out wiping her hands on her apron. 'I thought I heard the car. Has he fixed it?'

'Yes. Something small I'm ashamed to admit, but all the better for expert attention. We're making ourselves a drink?'

'It will have to be a quick one. Lunch in ten minutes. We've got our drinks, Mary and I, in the kitchen.'

'And mother, Emma's here. Down in a moment.'

'And where did you find . . . never mind. As you can see, I've laid a place for her.'

A tall, matronly woman with large high hips entered the room. She walked with the forward stoop and tottering gait of one used to talking to children or patients in bed.

'Ah, Mary, this is Sandy . . . oh, dear I've forgotten . . . and I've been talking about you!'

'Sandy Thakur,' prompted Ted, from the sideboard.

'Yes. Sandy, this is Mary Williams.'

'How do you do,' said Mary, in a high-pitched voice. She shook his hand firmly and her lips moved soundlessly as she studied his face with rheumy dark eyes that darted.

'How do you do,' said Sandy.

'You'll do well,' she said, 'as a teacher, I mean. I can see children liking you.'

'I hope you're right. The thought of facing a classroom of children terrifies me.'

'You'll be . . . Ah!' Her mouth opened and her eyes widened. She was looking past him. 'Now, there's a sight for sore eyes! My dear, you look radiant!' She tottered past Sandy and warmly hugged Emma, who smiled reluctantly.

'Anything I can do, mother?' Emma asked.

'No, it's all done. Keep the men company.'

'For little Emmy,' smiled Ted, handing her a martini. 'And Sandy, your sherry.'

'Goodness!' exclaimed Edith. 'My manners! Sandy, this is my daughter, Emma.'

'We've met,' Sandy bowed.

Edith and Mary exchanged glances. Edith said. 'And where, may I ask?'

'At the cemetery.' Sandy said taking in Emma's blue and white polka dot dress.

There was an awkward pause, another exchange of glances then Edith said: 'Bring your drinks to the table. Ted, are we having wine? Yes. Emma, the wine glasses. It's meat pie. Not those, Emma, the usual. Sandy, I hope you like pies?'

'I can't wait.' Sandy said politely.

'Good. Visitors to this country imagine we live on boiled beef and carrots.'

'Or roast beef and Yorkshire pudding,' chimed in Mary.

'Sandy's no visitor,' said Ted. 'He's more English than I am.' But seeing his mother a little vexed, he changed tack. 'If it's one of your short-crust affairs, mother, we're all in for a treat.'

'Do sit down. Ted opposite me. Sandy on my right. Mary on my left, then Emma.'

Lunch was served, the wine poured, and the conversation flitted from Sandy's new career in teaching to Ted's move to the house in Holland Park; finally to India. It turned out, Mary's grandfather had been a Circuit Judge in the Chota Nagpur district, and that on retiring, he and an uncle, who served in the Army Education Corps, helped to found a school in Hazaribagh. Throughout all this Emma was silent, and though Sandy tried to include her, she showed no interest. But he sensed her occasional frank gaze on him and was tempted to meet it. Her regard was artless and Sandy was fascinated, even thrilled, till he realised they were being watched—not by Ted or Edith, but Mary. He turned to face her. She forced a smile. 'D'you know Hazaribagh, Sandy?' she asked defensively. Something in the tone of her voice caught everyone's attention.

'Hazaribagh? No, not really.'

'And don't you miss India?'

'Not in the least! I do have links with India, of course, but home is where my heart is. My heart's here.'

'I see. But it's odd, don't you think, or should I say unusual. I know many who lived in India, who'd give anything to be back there again. And George, my husband, told me of an Indian, who after his first dismal winter in a poky London flat—packed his bags and flew back to sunny India.' She chortled unconvincingly. 'I mean, this country has a miserable climate. Cold wet winters?'

Sandy sensed hostility and was a little puzzled by it. 'I know.'

Ted laughed. 'Mary, I was serious when I said Sandy's more English than I am.'

'Can he be? Is that possible?' Mary stared at Edith, who shrugged her shoulders.

'And,' Ted continued, with a slight sweep of his hand, 'not just Sandy, but several members in his family had long links with England. Also, I'm sure Sandy's flat in Hammersmith is anything but poky.'

Sandy spread his hands in a gesture of modesty.

Mary inhaled sharply. 'A large flat?'

'Comfortable,' Sandy said.'

'On a teacher's salary?'

'I don't think Sandy relies solely on a salary.' Ted said calmly.

'Dear me! Sorry! If I've caused any offence. Sor-or-ry.'

'It's all right, Mary,' Edith broke in. 'I sure Sandy's not offended.'

Sandy smiled. 'I'm not. But I disagree about the climate. Like much in England it's unique. I love those dull, sultry days you find nowhere else in the world. And, because of the climate, you have beautiful trees and meadows.'

Mary grimaced. 'I can't imagine our climate being envied. It's all right for the young and healthy. Not for the bronchial and rheumatic!'

Edith got up. 'That reminds me, Mary, I've got something to show you. It's a snap of Sandy and . . .' She went to a side table and picked up a cabinet sized pewter frame, which had been turned face downwards. 'Sorry Emma, you won't mind. I took it from your room. But it used to be in the study. I don't know much about the picture. Sandy can tell us. You see, Mary, I wasn't in India much of the time Colonel sahib was there.'

Sandy got up and stood behind them. It was a black and white photograph of a tall man grinning happily into the camera. He was wearing an open collar bush-shirt and his trousers were tucked into high-laced jungle boots. A hand rested on his hip, the other on the shoulder of a boy, who was also grinning but whose face was turned up towards the man. 'That you?' Mary Williams pointed to the boy. Sandy nodded.

'Let me see,' said Ted joining the group. 'Yes. There's no mistaking that face. You see,' he giggled, 'the budding Rupert Brooke profile. That sweep of hair . . . and the way it falls over the forehead . . .'

Sandy boxed Ted's arm. 'My uncle in Rajnagar has a copy of this.'

'And my husband had an enlargement made from it. Of himself.'

'It's a good one of Ian,' said Mary.

'Frightfully good,' agreed Edith. 'You can't have missed the enlargement in the living room.'

'Thought it looked familiar. Amazing what one can do with photographs these days.'

'When was this taken, Sandy?' asked Ted.

'I can tell you exactly. New Year's Day, nineteen forty-four.'

'The year he retired,' Edith said. 'But where. It's clear you are standing by a jeep. I recognise the bonnet . . . I expect your father took the photograph?'

'No, Major Rankin did. He drove the jeep.'

Edith sniffed impatiently. 'I can see a hill in the background, with a summit's like a ship's funnel?'

'That's its name, Funnel Hill. Not far from Poona. On the road to Goa. Ian, I mean the colonel, your husband, wanted very much to get to the top. He nearly gave up.'

'What do you mean?' Edith frowned.

'Rankin accompanied us half way up the hill, then decided to sit it out and wait till we got back to him—he had a bad leg. We, the Colonel and I, set off till we got to the base of the funnel. It was, what we feared, a cliff of solid, sheer rock, and a steep climb. We had to cling to every finger and toe-hold we could find. Then he lost his nerve. "I'm afraid Funnel Hill will remain unconquered by me," he said.'

'But he did get to the top,' Emma burst in, with feeling.

'Yes.' She was now close behind him. He turned to face her. "I wouldn't let him give up. There were only another thirty feet left.'

'That then, is father's victory smile.' She gave a little clap. Then reached across the table and took the framed photograph from her mother. 'I'll put it back,' she said, and left the room. Edith shook her head.

'Did you see,' interjected Mary. 'She ate like a bird.'

'As always," Edith sounded a little irritated.

'But she was quite good today,' said Ted. 'Two glasses of wine, I counted, and a second helping of Mary's lovely lemon tart! And, she looks less pale than usual.'

'A little pancake for the occasion, I expect,' Edith patted her cheeks. 'Anyway, I'm glad about the wine. It'll be good for her . . .'

'Mother, you know she doesn't use make-up. Sorry Sandy. Just family talk.'

'Anyway she's been far from well. You're the doctor, I needn't tell you.'

Mary looked from one to the other and nodded a little dubiously.

Emma re-entered the room. 'Coffee? Shall I, mother?'

'That'd be lovely, dear. Not for me. Just the four of you. Have it in the garden. But first, all hands to help clear the table.'

Sandy picked up the nearest thing he could find. The large pie dish. 'Where does this go?' He asked, thoughtfully regarding the remnants of the pie.

'I'll take that!' said Edith. 'I should've said except Sandy.'

'And,' said Ted, as he brushed past Sandy, 'don't volunteer to do the washing up, either. Come along, I'm dying for a cigarette.'

Sandy laughed.

'You and Sandy can put the chairs out by the pond.' Edith said.

'Edith, Trevor and George should be back after six,' said Mary, annoying Edith by her irrelevance. 'You're welcome to have supper with us.'

'Awfully kind, Mary, 'but I've planned supper.'

'Tomorrow night, then. We're away at Andover for lunch, but we'll be back for tea. You know, Trevor would like to . . .' Mary nodded towards the kitchen.

Edith gave an understanding nod. 'Yes, thank you. Just Emma and me. Ted's driving back to London, with Sandy, soon after lunch, tomorrow.'

'Ted!' Emma called out, 'Sandy can help me with the tray.'

'There you are,' said Ted, 'at last a genuine plea for your services. I don't need help with the chairs.'

'I'm glad you're coming for supper tomorrow, Emma,' Mary said, peeping into the kitchen. 'You haven't seen Trevor since he went on his course. Not since Easter!'

'Has it been that long?' asked Emma absently. 'When did he get back?'

'Almost two weeks, now.' Mary said dryly. They entered the kitchen, and Edith ran the Ascot water heater. Then with a nervous laugh Mary added, to no one in particular: 'He's a good lad, Trevor is. Serious, conscientious, a bit bashful, which is no bad thing. I've been at him to call on friends, but he won't budge. Loves the outdoors. Forever planning expeditions, and, oh, Edith, I forgot to mention, early next year he is going to South Africa, for two years. To help on my brother's Farm.'

Edith turned the Ascot off. 'I'll rinse, you wipe. Sorry, Mary, I missed that.'

'I was saying, Trevor's going to South Africa, for two years. He'll work on the farm. Derek's farm.'

'Good. So he'll put to use what he's learnt in theory. It was an agricultural course he went on, was it not?'

'Yes. It's really Trevor's farm. I mean, his eventually. You've met Derek?'

'No. What made you think I've met Derek?'

'You haven't? No, of course. Silly me. He was in England five years ago, when we were in Newbury. Oops! I better concentrate, that nearly went the way of all . . .'

'Leave the dishes, Mary. Just do the glasses. I suppose Trevor likes South Africa. A beautiful country, I gather.'

'Yes, indeed. I've such happy childhood memories.'

They looked at each other. Neither spoke, while Sandy leaned against the door that led into the kitchen. But he noted an exchange of glances and the flicker of conspiracy that, intuitively, he knew went beyond anything they were saying. They were an oddity. One small and alert, the other large, lumbering, hesitant. Yet, clearly they were friends and over them hovered, he felt, an air of tacit understanding.

'I think it's time Trevor took the next big step.' Mary was holding a tea towel as she leaned forward and whispered in a voice that crackled like an ill-tuned radio. 'He'll be twenty-six when he gets back. Marriage will do them both a power of good. As will living in South Africa. Large bungalows, gardens, servants and a climate that's just the ticket for you know who. This moping about, it isn't healthy you know.'

'Couldn't agree more.' Edith tossed her head in Sandy's direction. 'Hush!'

They continued to talk in subdued tones but not inaudibly. Sandy thought to move away but he also realised that that would draw attention to himself and to the fact that they could be overheard. So he stayed, midway between Emma and the women.

'Two years could make all the difference!' Edith added. 'Time heals . . . But I wish he'd show more interest. You know, a little more gumption, and charm. Sometimes I wonder if he is interested in girls, you know what I mean?'

Mary drew herself up with a sound of escaping steam. 'He *is* interested. Just doesn't show it. A mother knows about these things. You know, sounds and things . . . bathroom, marks on the sheets!'

'Mary, please! Anyway. Those things prove nothing . . . but let it go.'

'Trevor's easily put off. Or, dare I say, he gets no encouragement.'

'There's a general lack of interest. On both sides, I mean.'

'What about a holiday there? You and Emma. Next winter?'

'That won't be right, not yet. Ted wants her to take up an art course in London, or even a job in the British Museum. But she refuses to leave. As I said, give it time.'

'But this business of daily visits to the cemetery. Really! It's unhealthy. Fathers and daughters should never be that close?'

'As I said, Mary, at the risk of being repetitious, give it time. It can't go on like this. She'll stop when she . . . We'll talk later.'

'Yes. We've got other times to talk . . . And we must involve George.'

All this time, Sandy, whose eyes were scarcely off Emma, was intrigued to note her increasing annoyance. She slammed a tray on the kitchen table, kept glancing at the two women as she looked for cups and saucers. These she put on the tray, noisily, and a jug of milk which spilled as she banged it down. Then with a sigh she turned and pointed to the tray. As Sandy took it, she whispered, 'go ahead, I'll bring the coffee pot.'

'We're a chair short,' said Ted as Sandy reached him. 'Never mind, Emma likes to sit on the wall of the pond. Ah, Emmy, I see you've forgotten the sugar. For Mary.'

'I'll get it,' Sandy said. 'I've seen the sugar basin.' On the way, he passed Edith and Mary and heard Edith saying: 'She knows she doesn't have to work, but really, I don't mind what captures her interest as long as it gets her away from Winchester.' Then on seeing Sandy, she called after him: 'You don't have to go upstairs, there's one next to the study, downstairs.'

Sandy waved a hand, entered the kitchen, found the silver sugar basin, and turned to realise that Emma had followed him. 'You enjoy giving people a start.' He said.

'I suppose you know they are talking about me?' she said.

'You mean here, in the kitchen, during the washing up?'

'Don't pretend.'

He loved her directness. 'Well, it's none of my business.'

'It's none of theirs either. Mary's a persistent gossip . . . I mean busybody.'

'It really doesn't matter. I'm not sure I understood any of it.'

'Good, because it's all so horrid!' She swung round and walked ahead. He followed with a bemused smile. Damn the cliché, he thought, but she really does look even more beautiful when she's angry.

The coffee cups were large, for which Sandy was grateful. Mary changed her mind about coffee and joined Edith near the greenhouse. He watched Emma study them with knitted brows and the thrust of a petulant chin. The expression on her face so amused him that he burst out laughing.

'It's not funny.'

'I'm sorry, I tried hard not to laugh. But it is funny, you know.'

The corners of her mouth trembled, then broke in a smile. 'You're being horrid.'

'What's going on? Don't leave me out.' Ted said.

Emma shook her head. 'Later Ted.' She got up.

'Now, where are you going?' Ted inquired.

'To my room.'

'Finish your coffee.'

'Thank you, I forgot.' She sat down again and held her cup in both hands.

'Emmy. I'm taking Sandy on a tour of the town and a walk up St Giles's Hill? You could join us, if you want to.'

'I want to read. Will you be back for tea?'

'We'll find a tea-place in town. But we'll be back by six.'

'Ted, are you going to include the Cathedral?'

'Sandy's doing that on his own, tomorrow morning. But we'll check Sunday's service timings. So he'll get a peek.'

'You don't have to. It's eight and ten.' She put her cup down. 'I'm going in.'

'Tell mother we'll be back by six,' Ted called, but she did not hear him.

❧

An hour later, in the city, Sandy and Ted were caught in a sudden rain storm and decided to take tea earlier than planned. Ted had been unusually thoughtful, saying little except to point to places of interest. But in the restaurant, after tea, he leaned forward: 'Sandy, I should tell you, though you probably know it, in some strange way, you were closer to father than I was! He was sad at the thought he would not see you again.'

'Nonsense! Ted, how could you say that? He didn't write to me or to my father.'

'He saw no point writing. But I'm serious. He talked about you many times.' Ted stared at his empty cup. 'That was a moving story you told . . . about the climb up Funnel Hill. I can't look back on any such intimate moment together, with father.'

'But, you were fond of each other. That's the impression I got, those years ago.'

'Yes, affection—kindly . . . distant. What boarding school does. When he returned to England, I was nineteen and about to move to London, to study medicine. We bridged the years as best we could and remained friends. Dad did his bit. Bought a house and lived in London.'

'What about Emma?'

'They were very close, as you will have gathered.'

Sandy nodded and wondered about Ted alternate usage of "father" and "dad". It was intriguing and sadly touching. 'Emma was barely seven,' Ted went on, 'and while he was in India, she idolised the man she had only seen in photographs and told was her father.' He toyed with the knife on his plate, pushing the crumbs of a fruit cake to one side; then he gave a brief chuckle. 'I remember meeting the boat in Southampton and how through-out the drive back to Winchester, I was aware of father staring at me. We were expected after tea, about this time, and as we turned into the gates I saw little Emma leaning out of the bedroom window, waving frantically. Later I learned she had been waiting at that window for hours, yet she didn't come down to greet us. She stood on the landing, surveying father with a solemn face. He held out his arms. "Aren't you going to kiss father?" he asked. "Daddy! Daddy!" she screamed and threw herself at him—literally. He had to catch her! They clung to each other—as if nothing else and no one else mattered. And that's how it remained.'

'So his death would have come as a great shock to her?'

'I have never been more anxious for her then and since. For a long time she spoke to no one. Even now, it's obvious to most people, she hasn't got over it. She won't accept the fact of his death. Hence these visits to the cemetery. She was sixteen when he died, and after that school was impossible. I tell myself that she's young, that time will heal, that time's on her side . . . but we worry. Mother and I. Mary and other friends also.'

'What can I say? A new life. Love, marriage. A new job, a new home?'

'I don't know. She's shown no interest in men, or anything except painting. She can be very intense . . . Everything she takes up becomes a cause. Father became a cause, too. There was a time she wanted to be a nun. That and religion became a cause! She paints with fervour, like one who sees nature and its preservation, a cause also. By the way . . .'

'Does she still want to be a nun?'

Ted studied Sandy's face for a moment before answering. 'Can't say. She's not one for giving up easily. The phase may have passed. I hope so. She was very young then. Twelve or thirteen. But something happened to take her mind off it. A tubercular patch on her lung. Father took her to a mountain village in Spain. In the Pyrenees, a rest-cure. A year later she was back, cured, but while there, in the Sanatorium of the Immaculate Conception, the cult of the Madonna impressed her. It was all, how shall I put it, "very immaculate".' Ted smiled. 'Why am I telling you all this? I'm being a bore. Sorry.'

'No, you're not. You're talking because you're remembering your father.'

Ted shook his head. 'No, because you made her laugh. I can't remember when that last happened. Since father died, I've been afraid, especially after those early long days and nights . . . we tried but nothing we could . . . she was inconsolable. We, mother and I, grew anxious, afraid she'd do something terrible to herself and because of that we let her be—she seemed better for those hours spent by the graveside . . . Then you turn up and do something we couldn't.'

'I suppose, because I'm a stranger, ignorant of a past she's conscious of.'

'There has to be a cue for laughter. Tell me about it? I've just said that you've done a good deed, and I'm grateful. Truly grateful. You'd understand if you only knew how concerned I am about Emma. Mother too, in her way.'

'Well, in the kitchen, your mother and Mary were washing up . . . They kept their voices low, but I could hear, and guessed they were talking about Emma. Her reactions amused me. As simple as that. Laughter was infectious, I suppose.'

'Is that all? Mary's a bore. She's fond of Emma and keen to get her hitched with her son Trevor.'

After a pause, Sandy said. 'I can't say I understood what all that talk was about.'

'Well, I thought there'd be more to it. I would have sworn it was a happy laugh.'

Sandy wanted to ask about Trevor and how Emma felt about him. But he checked himself. It was hardly the right thing to do. Besides, his curiosity would betray his own feelings and jeopardise any chance of seeing her again.

The rain had stopped. The late afternoon light, piercing through the dark, washed sky, lit the wet buildings of the High Street and lent the pale biscuit medieval stone, a golden glow. The vision was compelling. Ted said Winchester had never looked more beautiful. They passed Hamo Thornycroft's statue of Alfred the Great, turned right off Bridge Street, continued along the river, and crossed it near the Mill. Then uphill to the foot of the steps of St Giles's Hill.

'Race you to the top?' said Ted. They stood, looked at each other and laughed, then climbed the steps, stopping at intervals to view of the city. At the top Ted pointed to the College, the Cathedral, the Cloisters and Chantry. 'When it started to rain,' he said, 'I was afraid you'd miss all this, but now, look. Isn't that stunning?'

Sandy nodded. 'Absolutely. If I haven't said anything, it's because in spirit I've been here before. For long my soul's been one with this Blessed Country—capital B and C.'

Ted looked at Sandy quizzically. 'You're a sentimental Old Chump.'

'You know,' Sandy said, 'people don't associate art with England, yet everything about England is man made.'

'But we have great landscape artists. Constable, Gainsborough... Turner?'

'And Wilson. I know. And in the true spirit of this nation of garden lovers, English artists worked with nature. The Pre-Raphaelites... still, it's France, Italy and Spain that we think of...'

'Absolutely! They had the Old Masters.'

'Yes, and why this is the birthplace of democracy.'

'With a monarchy and an aristocracy? I don't see...'

'From King Alfred onwards, concern has always centred on land and the people. I'm a monarchist, here, but I couldn't have been one in France, or anywhere else... Tyranny and extreme government produce grand art. Remember Orson Welles, *The Third Man*, that bit about democracy and brotherly love producing only the cuckoo clock?'

'You argue your corner well. But it's still a corner. As an Englishman I ought to be flattered by your obvious love for England. But... oh, never mind. Shall we get back to the car.' Ted glanced at his watch. 'We'll be back earlier than expected.'

At the Mill crossing they paused to look at the ducks. 'About England,' Ted said abruptly, 'after having met mother and me, and

Mary, yes particularly Mary, you must have a revised opinion about the English reserve you admire.'

'I'm not so sure about you. Even less about your mother. There are reservoirs of reserve in both of you, all the better concealed by frankness. Frankness, you know, is also an English virtue. You may not open up easily, but when you do, it's open straight dealing. But, I have to admit, Mary did surprise me.'

'Mary's Irish. Or rather has Irish antecedents. What about that other famous English trait: hypocrisy?' He laughed. 'That got you stymied. And I'm not convinced about the frankness. Deal with hypocrisy, first. Where does that fit in?'

'I try not to fit that in.' Sandy chuckled. 'Hypocrisy is a kind of reserve too.'

'You're being kind. You may have wriggled out of that, but not very cleanly.'

'Your father, was a paragon of "Englishness", to coin a phrase? I'm sure he was.'

'Possibly. Remember, he was in India and playing a role—he and Englishmen like him, in their various professions, doing what was expected of them. That aside, there always was, or had to be, a strong element of hypocrisy. Nothing to do with reserve.'

'Being aware of the role one plays in life is not hypocrisy; and surely not, if inspired by a sense of duty.'

'Granted. But I can't, wholeheartedly go along with that . . . not without reservations.' They started to walk again. Ted gazed at Sandy for a while, then asked: 'And Emma? Does she fit your bill?'

'I think Emma is the most English of all. From the little I know of her. I do believe she's being herself.'

'Not herself, not with the present trauma of loss weighing on her. Such a happy child she was. But you may be right. Her school teachers remarked on her reserve. They used that very word and what they termed "innate dignity". We thought they were being kind to a dreamy, religious and rather pious-minded girl.'

'They ought to know,' Sandy mumbled. Already he saw in Emma, a strange young woman who looked at life with indifference and registered emotions without perceptible enthusiasm. In the car, Ted startled him by asking: 'You want to know about Trevor? Yes, you do. You want to know if he made her laugh.'

Sandy smiled. He suspected a trap was being laid for him.

'I don't mind telling you. Your charming disinterest, my dear chap, has prised it out of me. The last thing I'd expect Trevor to do is to make anyone laugh . . . and Emma's a tall order. A nice enough bloke is Trev, nearer her age, but deadly earnest and, I have to say, a single-minded bore. The sort who'll do well at work but socially lacking finesse. I mean, polite without the spark that makes all the difference in winning a gel's heart. In short, a chap rather like me.'

'I don't believe it. About you, I mean. I've seen your wedding snap in the living-room. You've done well. Mabel's a handsome woman.'

Ted laughed. 'Like your choice of words. Handsome as only a strong-willed woman can be. But, to be fair to Trevor, Emma hasn't given him a chance to be confident. Far too mature for him. But, given time, some kind of understanding will be reached.' Ted threw an inquiring glance at Sandy.

Sandy was on his guard. He met Ted's gaze unflinchingly, feigned indifference, gave a nod, and said nothing. He knew his chances of seeing Emma rested on this. He must hide his interest in Emma till fate dealt him a better hand. It was one thing to be in love, quite another to win love. He would need time and opportunity to woo Emma.

There was an awkward pause. Then Ted said suddenly: 'I'm being a lousy host.'

'*Au contraire*! I'm having a wonderful time. I know doctors are pressed for time and you've been generous with . . . sorry that sounds terribly patronising. But . . .'

'I mean, you're my guest and I've already involved you in family matters. Also, I feel I've been unfair to Emma. Bad form, or as father would say "a bloody poor show".'

'Not if you look upon me as a friend?'

'I do. Of course, I do.' Ted stopped the car outside the gates of his house. 'I'll drop you here. Go in. I'll be back soon. We'll have a drink. Mother likes a whisky and soda before supper and we've run out of soda. It's about the only thing she's picked up from India. From Ooty, "snooty Ooty", so she told me.'

'Yes. Very *pukka*. Very "Army in India". Actually, I'd love a whisky and soda, too.'

'Good. But back to your love for England and the English, I must warn you, now that you are here, in time, that will change. You've led a privileged and sheltered life, and you've been lucky till now. Romantics block out the realities of life. I wonder what sort of chap you would be now, if dad had his way and we were in college together?'

'Are you suggesting life in a Public School would've been too tough for me?'

Ted spread his hands and smiled. 'Yes.'

'I'm no softie, Ted. As I said, we have schools in India, which mimic Winchester and Eton; run by prefects, who let privilege get to their heads. Certainly my school . . .'

'Indians are soft, philosophical. I can't imagine an Indian school prefect, who's ready to insult and abuse or swish a cane. Sandy, your England is from books. It's one thing to read about fagging, quite another to actually fag.'

'But I gathered Winchester was among the first to be the most liberal . . .'

'Yes. And Oakshott, a most likeable Head . . . but I'm not sure you'd have been happy in Winchester. God! Now who's being patronising. Sorry. I'm talking rubbish. Forget it. Bright chaps can handle any situation. I soon learned life was easier for a prefect, and you're brainier than me. Father wanted me to watch over you.' He laughed. 'It would have been a tough job. Good-looking chap like you, getting the wrong sort of attention, if you know what I mean?'

'There's no need to explain. One meets that sort of thing everywhere. I've come out of it all safe and unscathed.'

Ted shook his head. 'Sorry. I've lost all the good manners and discretion Winchester taught me. Well, see you anon,' he said, and drove away.

Sandy walked up the drive towards the house with a sense of relief. Clearly he had succeeded in dismissing any suspicion Ted may have had. He stopped. Someone was playing the piano. The music was faintly familiar—something his sister Dolly used to play. He entered the hall. The living-room door was ajar. He could see the back of an upright piano but not the player. He coughed discreetly and went in. Emma looked up and quickly looked down again. She had been crying. He pretended not to notice, but walked round and stood behind her. She stopped playing. 'Please don't stop,' he said gently. 'I'm sorry. Would you like me to leave?'

She reached for the small handkerchief on top of the piano and stood up.

'Was that. "Fur Elise"? I'm no judge of . . . but that was good.'

She gave a short nervous laugh. 'If you heard mother, you'll know I'm third rate.'

'At any rate, I think you're good.'

She sniffed and looked at him sideways. Then sat on the piano stool and waited with hands poised above the keys. 'Since you're obviously no musician,' she said, 'I'll play.' After a few bars she stopped again. 'I can't play if you stand over me!'

'Sorry. I'll stand in the corner, till I'm forgiven?'

She sniffed like someone trying hard not to laugh and shut the piano. 'Where's Ted?'

'Buying soda. He'll be back, soon.'

'And, have you had tea?'

'Yes, thank you. Ted dropped me at the gate.'

'Mother's still in her room. She couldn't have heard the car.' She sighed. 'Make yourself at home. I'll see you later.'

She was about to leave when he said. 'So, I'm not to see your paintings?'

'Do you really want to?'

'Yes. I wouldn't say it if . . . I'll never lie to you.'

Her deep blue eyes searched his face. 'Come with me,' she said simply, and led the way through the hall into the study. She started to shut the door, then left it open.

The room was long and narrow with large sash windows opposite the fireplace and walls lined with books. A heavy oak desk faced the door and on its faded baize top was a glass inkstand and a carved walnut wood letter rack which could only have come from Kashmir. Behind the desk was a high leather-backed chair under a tall standard lamp. She went to the desk and from the large central top drawer, took out a blue portfolio. 'You'll have to sit down. Some drawings are quite small.'

Sandy was not prepared for what he saw. He was looking at work which had been executed with the precise detail and skill of a botanical artist. 'Gosh!' he exclaimed, 'but this is fantastic! Beautiful!

The Lotus And The Rose

I really . . . you must know . . . I don't have to tell you. It speaks for itself. Such delicate draughtsmanship. Quite honestly, anything I say sounds like flattery. But its the truth.'

She had been standing close to him, at times leaning over him to turn the drawings. Now she moved back with a slight shrug of her shoulders and shut the portfolio. A small drawing flew out of the pile. Both made a sudden move to retrieve it, and her cheeks almost brushed his lips. He could so easily have touched her, as he longed to do, and plead accident as an excuse. But her indifference suggested nothing more than that her proximity was a necessity, and in her calm assured manner there was an indefinable something. It warned him that any liberty would be severely reprimanded and seriously inhibit any growth of friendship or trust.

'Thank you,' he said. 'I'm absolutely bowled over.'

She leaned against the desk looking down at him with an expression of deep pathos. Then a wisp of a smile played bewitchingly at the corners of her mouth. He tried hard to detect anything more than innocent friendliness; and failed. The sound of Ted's car on the drive broke the spell. She looked up. 'Teddy's back! I'll put these away.'

Ted peeped into the study. 'Ah, there you are. I thought you would be in the living-room.' He search their faces as if to discover an explanation. 'Where's mother?'

'In her room. I've been showing Sandy my drawings.'

'Oh, good. Were you surprised, Sandy?'

'Yes. Astounded.'

'You've been painting, Emmy?' Ted pointed to her neck below the chin.

'Sometime ago.' Emma said, as she put the portfolio into the desk drawer.

'Here, let me.' Ted went up to her. She let him wipe the spot with his handkerchief. 'It's oil paint!' He said, as Sandy wondered what he would have said and done had he seen the spot, and rued an opportunity lost.

'You paint in oils as well?' Sandy asked.

'Doesn't she half.' Ted said. 'Quite large and brilliant ones.'

'I'd love to see those!'

Emma wrinkled her nose. 'They're not as good as Teddy says.'

'Oh come, Emmy. Let Sandy judge for himself.'

They went upstairs to the room next to Emma's bedroom. Sandy remembered Ted pointing it out as his father's bedroom and which now he realised Emma used as her studio. A smell of linseed and turps greeted them as they entered. Emma crossed the room and raised the large window that overlooked the terrace. 'When did you do this?' Sandy pointed to a canvas leaning against the wall.

'Almost a year ago. It's not finished.'

'It has such power. Dark sky, clouds, the gloom . . . typically England. Yorkshire?'

'I've never been there. Dartmoor.'

'But, of course, silly me. The tors. So, you sketch outdoors and paint later.'

'There's excellent stuff in that pile, there,' Ted interjected. 'I want her to exhibit them in a gallery of a friend I know, but . . . right, I'm off. Got to call Mabel.' He looked at Emma, and Sandy saw her return a pained but sympathetic look. 'I think mother's in the kitchen. We could all do with a drink. Emma? Ten minutes?' Ted put an arm round her. She leaned affectionately against him. 'I've got to, phone. I won't be long.'

She freed herself. Then went to the window overlooking the garden. 'Please don't ask to see those paintings,' she said without turning from the window. 'How are you going to the Cathedral tomorrow?'

'I'll walk.' He drew nearer. She was looking out into the distance. Her raised chin stretched her slender neck and made her eyelids droop. Only Botticelli could have done justice to that profile, he thought. Her proximity made him tremble and saddened by the thought that after tomorrow he may never see her again, he took a deep breath. He was in love, but it was absurd. Away from her, he would have to fight it, immerse himself in his new job and forget. But the desired object of his present love, whatever its future, was here beside him. Suddenly he saw a purpose, a responsibility for the happiness of this beautiful girl. He must light up those contemplative blue eyes, and drive away the sadness that made them tearful and indifferent to the joys of being alive. He would give in to this need and bear any pain. He had known lust before and knew how easily he responded to physical beauty. So, why was this different? What about it made the past cheap and irrelevant? Now, as he drank in the contours of her loveliness, his feelings were not libido, but an altruism inspired by something new and special stirring within him: a longing to be with her always.

She turned to face him; and the probity of her gaze struck him like a bullet. 'What is it?' she asked with a slight frown.

He laughed nervously like one caught red-handed. 'Sorry. I didn't mean to stare.'

'Do you think I'm beautiful?'

He stared with astonishment and increased discomfiture at her directness. 'Very', he said. 'Absolutely stunning!' And as he said it he was struck by the thought that although her father had been strikingly handsome, and both Edith and Ted were pleasant to look at, she resembled none of them. 'Surely you must know that. Need you ask.'

She had turned away. 'It's of no use to me. I feel empty.'

'Good Lord! Why! Who doesn't want beauty! Beauty is also for others . . . I mean, for the beholder as well . . . even if it is of no use to you.'

'I hate attention. I hate being physically desired . . . I should've done what I wanted . . . when father became a Roman Catholic . . . I wanted to be a nun.'

'A bride of Christ? But you are His, eternally. In the meanwhile, someone else may need you, for this lifetime. Have you thought of that?'

She frowned. 'You're clever with words. But it's clever nonsense.'

'Not if it's sincere.'

Her frown deepened.

'Emma, are you telling me you don't love yourself?' The question leapt out of him without warning.

'Sandy, it is more important to love others.'

'Then love me', he whispered, taking a deep breath to calm himself. 'A good friend of mine once said, loving your neighbour as yourself, does not mean you mustn't love yourself. How can you properly understand love if you don't begin with yourself? That must be the meaning of "charity begins at home".'

'Loving yourself can become a habit. Charity which begins at home stays there.'

'So young and so cynical!'
'What?'
He shook his head. 'That was harsh.'
'What was harsh?' Ted took them by surprise.
'Sorry', Sandy said, 'have we kept you waiting?'
'I wouldn't argue with Emma. She's a thinker and has an answer for every question.' Ted looked at his sister with a tender smile. 'Isn't that so, my little philosopher?'

"Not this time," Emma murmured as she turned from the window and walked out of the room. Halfway down the stair she stopped and looked at Sandy. 'You could borrow Ted's bicycle. I'll come with you. I always bicycle to church.'

'Yes, if that's all right by you.' Sandy was struck again by her unpredictability.

'I usually go to Christ's Church.'
'I'll come with you if you prefer to go there?'
'No. You should see the Cathedral.'
'Well, then if it's okay by Ted. I mean, if he's not using his bike.'

'Teddy's a heathen,' Emma's beautiful smile went as fast as it came.

Sandy was intrigued by those occasions when Ted became Teddy to both Edith and Emma and what it meant in a family that was both near and distant to each other.

'It's in the garage,' Ted said. 'I'd checked the tyres for air, first.'
'We'll do that now,' said Emma. 'Come, Sandy.'
'Emma! Mother. She may not . . . about tomorrow.' Ted made a face. 'Forget it. Just make sure you're back in time for lunch. I need to leave for London at three.'

In the garage they found the bicycle. 'It's a B S A,' Sandy said. 'The tyres are fine. Is yours the red one against the shed? I thought so. Shall I fetch it.' He took a few steps, then stopped. 'You've got a visitor.'

Emma came out of the garage. 'It's Trevor. Mary's son,' she mumbled. 'Hello! Are you looking for Ted?'

'Eh? Ah, yes! Well, not really. Thought I'd come over and say hello.' Trevor came nearer. 'I say, you must be Sandy?' The evening light behind him put him in silhouette, and made his rather nasal voice sound disembodied.

'And you must be Trevor.' Sandy advanced with an outstretched hand. Trevor's face was fresh, fair and freckled, but his most striking feature was his red hair, which though thin, sharply outlined his high forehead. As they shook hands, a slight shift of Trevor's head revealed a pair of friendly brown eyes.

'Well,' Trevor said, bashfully to Emma, 'I'll see you tomorrow evening. Bye!'

'Goodbye!' Emma and Sandy said, almost in unison.

Trevor stared, digging his hands deep in his pockets, turned as if to go, then froze. 'Since I'm here, I'll say hello to Ted.' After a pause of indecision, he turned round and dragging his feet on the gravel, walked down the path towards the kitchen.

Sandy and Emma looked at each other. She sensed he was about to tease. 'Don't say anything if you're going to be horrid?'

'No,' he said, taking in a deep breath.

'What is it?'

'Is he "the boy next door"?'

'Yes.' She frowned. 'But you mean something else.' She turned and walked into the garage. He followed her. She stopped. 'The answer is yes and no.'

He smiled smugly. She's no child. She knew what he meant. But what did *she* mean?

The kitchen door opened and Edith came out. 'Emma!' She called. 'Give me a hand with the supper.' She waited till they passed her into the kitchen. 'By the way, I'll leave it to you or Ted to lay breakfast tomorrow.'

'I will, mother. As I always do.'

'I breakfast late, Sandy,' Edith explained. 'So I won't see you till you get back.' She was looking at Emma as she spoke. 'Emma, did you know Trevor's here?'

'Yes. He came to the garage.'

'Oh, Emma. I despair. Your manners child. Why didn't you come in?'

'Is he still here?'

'We shall see.' They entered the dining room. 'Has Trevor left, Ted?'

Ted nodded.

'That boy's painfully shy. Hard to believe, he'll be twenty-six.'

'When will that be, mother?' asked Ted.

'When will that be, Emma?'

'Why should Emma know, mother?'

'She doesn't,' said Emma. 'She's laying the table and wants to know if she needs to put out the soup spoons.'

'Yes, Emma, we're having soup.'

'Drink, Sandy?' Ted indicated the sideboard. 'Help yourself.'

'I will, thank you.'

'Take it into the living room,' Edith said. 'There's a bowl of nuts there. I'll check what's on the box. We could watch a bit of television after supper.'

❦

When Sandy came down for breakfast only Ted was seated at the table. 'Ah, good morning, Sandy. Help yourself.' He indicated the side-board.

'Thank you. I see you've had breakfast, Ted. Sorry I'm late. Overslept.' Sandy said, recalling how he did not get to sleep till after midnight.

'Well, it won't matter if you're a bit late. I'll pour you a cup of coffee . . . or tea?'

'Tea, please. Milk no sugar. Thanks.' Sandy wondered where Emma was, but dare not to ask. Ted put the cup of tea next to him. 'There's some cold toast.'

'I won't, thank you. I don't want to be too late.'

Ted stared at him quizzically. 'Emma's gone ahead. I've made a rough sketch of the route. You can't miss the Cathedral. And since you're late, you may not find her during the service. But Emma said she'd meet you after the service in the cloisters. Here, I've marked it . . . where it says bicycle stand. Get there promptly because she'll go to earth if anyone else approaches her.'

'I'll try to find her before then. But thanks for telling me.'

Sandy cycled to the Cathedral with a heavy heart. It was painfully clear he did not occupy Emma's thoughts as she occupied his. Last night, at supper, she seemed not to notice him, and was locked in

The Lotus And The Rose

her own world. Then after the BBC news, she left the room and did not return.

He found the bicycle stand in the Deanery, south of the Cathedral, near the cloisters, pressed the spring lock, removed the key and inspected the other bicycles. Two were red, and though he was by no means certain, one looked very like Emma's. He walked round to the great west door and entered. Looking down the longest nave in England he gave up any hope of finding Emma. The silence puzzled him. 'Am I very late?' he whispered to the sidesman as he took the books offered him. The sidesman, an image of Rudyard Kipling, arched his heavy brows. 'The service starts in five minutes.'

Emma had got it wrong. The service was Matins at 10.30. "Kipling" gestured and Sandy followed him 'There's plenty of room in the front pews.' Sandy expressed a wish to be in a quiet corner. He bowed and turned into the north aisle. It was deserted. He looked across the crowded nave and scanned the pillars of the opposite aisle. She was nowhere to be seen. He chose a pew behind a pillar and below the board with hymn numbers. The organ boomed. The congregation rose. The choir processed from the north transept and disappeared behind the Rood Screen. Someone, with a limp and a walking stick came up his aisle and sat down a few pews behind him. 'Thank you, dear,' the voice of an old man wheezed. Then there was an almost noiseless movement next to him. He did not turn to look. "*Rend your heart and not your garments, and turn* . . . He craned his neck to see round the pillar. The speaker stayed hidden from view. "*Dearly beloved brethren, the Scripture moveth us in sundry* . . .". He leaned over his pew and, in his present disappointment, sought solace in the beauty of the Prayer Book language.

'Sorry,' came a whisper and he felt a light pressure on his sleeve. 'Forgive me!' He trembled. The voice was one he had by now committed to memory. She was wearing a beret pulled down at a slant across her forehead. It was dark brown and made her hair look many shades lighter. 'I'm sorry, I've been unforgivably rude . . .' Her eyes reflected the prussian blue of the patterned scarf she wore over a khaki trench-coat. Buttoned at the waist, it parted to reveal a knee length beige gabardine skirt.

He covered his lips with his forefinger. 'I'll think about it,' he whispered, 'but you'll have to be very good from now on.' He tossed his head towards the altar as the priest solemnly intoned: "*accompany me with a pure heart and humble voice, unto the throne of the heavenly grace, saying after me.*"

Amid a great buzz of shuffling feet and dragging furniture the congregation knelt and joined in the prayer of the General Confession. The drone of many voices rose up to the rafters, then settled into a confiding buzz. During the Service, she neither joined in the responses nor sang the hymns. It suited Sandy, who was never very fond of hymns.

'You are horrid, you know,' Emma said, as they moved out into the aisle. 'Horrid to make me giggle in church. I've never done that before.'

'Well, think what the Lord has missed. He gave you a beautiful smile for the world to see. A lighted candle, not to be hidden under a bushel.'

'You're impossible,' she frowned.

'Sorry. Are you cross?'

'No. Eucharist will follow Matins so, we won't be able to look round.' They moved towards the crowded West door. 'And we can't wait, if we are to get back in time for lunch.' She twisted his wrist and looked at his watch. 'We've got ten minutes. If we go up this aisle and back down the other . . . Oh, no! It's been roped off. Sorry, I've ruined your plans.'

'Sundays are invariably difficult because of the services. I'll take a peek on our way back to London, if Ted can spare fifteen minutes. But you can help me do what I really came to do and wasn't able. To put flowers on your father's grave.'

Her eyes melted into the clearest expression of gratitude. 'I'll do it for you. Promise. You won't find a florist open today.'

'I know. I did think of stealing flowers from your garden. It didn't seem right. But I have a plan. You'll see. First, join me for coffee. Please! Say yes you will!'

'Where?' she asked simply.

'On my way here I saw a restaurant, could've been a pub—serving coffee till noon.'

She made a pained expression. 'I don't care for pubs or restaurants.'

'Please come! If only to make amends for deserting me this morning!'

She turned and walked ahead. He followed as she slipped past people making her way to the Cloisters. He was right about her bicycle. 'You haven't answered me,' he pleaded. 'I promise, we won't spend more than twenty minutes?'

They were shown a table on a terrace under an awning. He helped her with her coat and draped it over the back of her chair. She sat down, removed the grips which held her beret, shook her head, ran her fingers through her hair, held the locks above each ear in turn and opening the grips with her teeth, slid them into place. He ordered coffee. Two tables away three young men were engaged in lively banter. Two were seated, and the third, referred to as Alastair, stood over them. He wore a blazer and flannels, and every time he emphasised a point, he struck his palm with the edge of a squash racket. One of the two seated saw Sandy and gradually became aware of Emma.

'I say, Alastair,' he beckoned confidentially. Alastair bent over to listen. There were whispers and giggles. Alastair sat down. 'Smashing!' he said.

Sandy chuckled.

'What is it?' Emma asked. 'Why are you laughing?'

'You've caught the admiration of three young men. None, of course, a patch on me, so I'm not worried.' He grinned.

She made a face. 'They could just as easily be fascinated by you!'

A tall, thin young woman placed a tray of coffee before them, smiled briefly, and on making sure they did not required anything else, left them.

'You're terribly good-looking.' Emma said in a matter-of-fact tone. She watched as Sandy poured the coffee. 'Just milk, thank you. And, of course, you're different.'

Sandy was intrigued. 'If I were alone. But they're trying to get your attention.'

'Well, they won't.'

'You're beautiful; and for your own good you must see that. You must be prepared for the attention you're always going to get.'

She made a face. He sat back and looked at her. 'The fact that you are unaware of your beauty adds to your charm.' She stopped him with an abrupt gesture. He felt the blood rush to his face and his mouth went dry. He took a sip of coffee and looked up to meet a sweet smile. It encouraged him. 'Emma,' he said, 'Is it too early for me to say, what I'm dying to say?'

'No, I mean, yes. Please, you mustn't.' She looked away. He had misread the smile. The young men had resumed their banter. 'There, you see, they've lost interest.' She gazed at him with a pained expression. 'Sandy, you must have met so many beautiful women. All far more sophisticated and charming. Looks don't last. Charm does. I lack charm. And I'm all mixed up. You'll be hurt. I'll only hurt you.'

'You have natural charm. For me, that's better than sophistication. And I'll refuse to be hurt.'

She shook her head. 'I'm a misfit.'

'Because you're matchless.'

She spread her hands, palms upwards, in a gesture that reminded him of the painting of the Madonna in the Duomo at Perugia. 'Please stop this,' she said, and lifting her cup in both hands, finished her coffee. 'You're different from what I expected. I knew you'd be good looking—from that snap, with daddy. But I expected someone older, like Ted.'

'I'm only two years younger than Ted. Good grief! Am I too old for you?'

'No! I'm twenty next month and . . . I've forgotten what I was going to say.'

'You were saying you imagined I'd be older . . .'

'Yes, but I didn't mean too old for me.' Suddenly she appeared older, in command of the situation. 'And a moment ago you looked quite the sullen little boy lost!'

He sighed. 'Before we met, I was cool, calm, and in full control. Not now. Can't you see why?' He pointedly stared at her lips. She frowned. He despaired. She really did not know what he was talking about. At least he could not tell if she did. God, he thought, am I being unfair? She's a child. He watched as she let a finger play wistfully on the rim of her empty cup and noted, with some surprise, that her hands, though slender, were large. 'Would you like another cup?' He asked.

She shook her head. 'I know how hard and selfish sophisticated people can be.'

He wondered if she was thinking of Ted's wife, Mabel. 'I've no use for, nor am I looking for sophistication.'

She closed her eyes and sighed deeply.

'You expected someone older and strong?' Sandy continued. 'I'm no weakling.'

'I don't know why I said that. In fact I hoped you'd be as dreamy and romantic as you looked then. I was talking nonsense. I wanted to stop you . . . protect you from me.'

The three youths had left, but two other tables were now occupied. One by a young couple with a child in a push chair. The other, nearer to them, by two elderly women. Sandy stood up and whispered as he left the table, 'I'll be back, soon.'

He returned a short while later with a wide grin. 'Mission accomplished.' He stayed standing. A moment later the tall lady came up to them. 'Lucy's bringing the flowers. They were picked this morning . . . ah, here she comes.'

'Thank you. You are kind. And you must let me pay for them?' said Sandy.

'No sir. Just what's on the bill.' The tall woman replied with a finality and left.

Lucy came up to the table and presented Sandy a bunch of flowers. She was a pretty girl, about twelve years old, with happy brown eyes and waist-length auburn hair tied by a wide pink ribbon, into a large bow, above her fringed forehead.

'Thank you, Lucy. Have you gone through a lot of trouble putting these together?'

'No, not really.'

'And what flowers are they? You must tell me. I know nothing about flowers.'

'Chrysanthemums mostly, lilies, and those I think are . . . I've forgotten what . . .'

'Michaelmas daisies,' said Emma

Lucy grimaced. 'I should've known that.'

'That's Emma, Lucy,' said Sandy. 'She knows all about flowers and shrubs and trees, and she paints them beautifully, on paper and canvas.'

'That's clever, I wish I could. I can't draw.'

'Come on, Lucy!' Her mother joined them. 'She'll talk all day given the chance.'

'Well, once again, thank you.' Sandy stood up and watched Lucy and her tall mother disappear indoors. Then he turned and helped Emma with her trench coat.

※

At the cemetery gates she said: 'I won't go in. It's different when I'm alone.'

'I understand. These things take time. I thought I'd never get over my mother's . . . But I was lucky to have Bill.'

'Who's Bill?'

'A very dear friend of mine. He works in India. We first met at Oxford. I wish you could meet him. Bill's a *Sadhu*—that's a kind of sage who leads an ascetic life, a hermit, a Christian *sadhu*, but to people in India he is a holy man. Bill said, we live in sad times, and the world will never quite recover from the bereavement of war. He said we ought to mourn but not be angry, or worse alienated.'

'You had better hurry. We have to get back for lunch.'

When he returned, she was sitting on the grass mound outside the gates, hugging her knees. The lower part of her skirt had fallen back, exposing her knees and part of her thighs. He offered his hand. She felt light as he pulled her on to her feet. She avoided meeting his eye and he knew why. She had been crying.

They bicycled silently till they got to the house and turned into the drive. 'Emma! Emma, wait!' He held her handle bar. 'Before we go in, may I say . . . I know, it's silly, and none of my business, but I'll feel awful if I didn't.'

'What is it, Sandy?'

'This may be a safe country. But you shouldn't go about by yourself.'

'If I do, I don't stay out late; and I don't go to places I don't know. The cemetery shuts in the evenings. Besides, it's on a slope, so no part is hidden from Jimmy's place.'

'Jimmy?'

'The caretaker. From his cottage the whole cemetery is visible.' She pushed with her foot, briefly stood on the pedals and rode towards the garage. When he got there she was nowhere to be seen, so he went into the house by himself.

Edith greeted him as she came into the hall from the kitchen. 'Where's Emma?'

'Hasn't she come in?'

'She didn't answer, so that must have been her. There's cold cider in a jug, there on the table. Help yourself.' She went in then peeped. 'Did you get to see the Cathedral?'

'No, not really!' And he was reminded of Lucy.

'I didn't think you would. Not on a Sunday morning. So, where have you two been? I assume Emma was with you?'

'Yes. We had coffee; and I was able to find flowers for the grave.'

'Hmm' She grimaced. 'Ted will be back any moment.'

Sandy saw the cider tray, poured himself a glass, and stood in front of the French windows. He stared with the nervous tension of one determined to cherish a scene he reluctantly must leave behind. Then he walked to the upright piano, raised the lid and passed his hands lightly over the keys. Within his peripheral vision a shadow moved; and he knew she was in the room.

'Are you thinking of playing?'

'No, I was remembering you. I can't play.'

'Would you like a cheesy cracker?'

She was wearing a blue and white striped apron over a high collared plain red dress with three-quarter length sleeves. 'Sorry I left you suddenly. I felt like a quick wash and change.' She held out a bowl. 'I'm helping mother in the kitchen.'

He moved close up to her. She did not retreat. He checked himself.

After Ted arrived they had lunch almost immediately. The conversation veered from Winchester Cathedral, the drive back to

London and to some building project at Ted's house in Holland Park. Coffee, this time prepared by Edith, was had on the terrace, but a passing shower forced them to return to the living-room. Edith pointedly asked why Sandy was strangely quiet. Sandy apologised and said he was thinking about his new job and the school. He excused himself and went upstairs to pack. Shortly afterwards he was down with his suitcase. They were waiting in the hall.

Ted greeted him. 'We could spend some time in the Cathedral, if you'd like, Sandy.'

'Thank you. But I mustn't delay you, Ted.'

'Would you like one of my drawings?' Emma said.

Sandy gaped. 'Of course! Thank you. Yes indeed!'

'Come with me and choose one.'

They went into the study. She took out her portfolio and Sandy chose the small drawing on the top.

'Don't you want to see the others?'

He shook his head. 'I could spend hours looking at them, But this will do.'

'Why that one?'

'Because it brought us close together.'

Her face was a picture of bewilderment. 'Haven't we been close all morning?'

'Yes. But if you remember, this picture fell out and . . . I'm being silly. Sorry.'

'I'll put it in this.' She took a cardboard tube and opened one side. 'You see, I'd planned to give you a drawing.' She rolled the picture and put it into the tube. 'But you don't know what this watercolour is about?'

'I do. It's of the tree next to the garage.'

She looked at him. Her lips parted and closed. 'There.'

He took it and held out his hand. She put her hand in his and said. 'Goodbye.'

'Goodbye! I suppose we won't see each other again?'

'I suppose so,' she echoed mechanically.

Ted stuck his head round the door jamb. 'All set?'

They came out into the hall. Sandy shook hands with Edith. 'Thank you, for inviting me. I've had a wonderful time.'

'Goodbye, Mr Thakur,' she said. 'It's been a pleasure to meet you. I wish you well.' She was smiling, but something behind her eyes told him that it was very unlikely she would invite him again. He watched her turn to Ted and give him a formal hug and kiss. 'Drive carefully.'

Emma kissed her brother. She turned to Sandy. He held out his hand once again. But this time she drew near, held him with both hands, raised herself on her toes, and kissed his cheek. In his astonishment he failed to kiss her back.

'Really, Emma!' cried Edith. 'You're so unpredictable!'

After a short awkward pause Sandy said, 'There's no virtue in being predictable.'

'Bah! Absolute piffle,' Edith gave a dismissive wave of her hand. 'Why?'

Sandy wished he hadn't spoken. 'The truly creative person is unpredictable.'

'To be predictable is to be reliable. That is better than being creative . . . or foolish.'

'It's a question of choice. Some of us prefer the calms . . . or do I mean doldrums . . . of reliability; others the excitement of creativity.' Sandy studied Edith as he spoke and felt like a golfer who sees his hurried loft making straight for a bunker. He smiled with all the charm he could muster. 'I'm not saying one is better than the other.'

'Thank you for that gracious concession!' She glared stonily.

'I see what Sandy's getting at,' beamed Ted. 'Who said: "Variety is the spice of life"? Eh, mother? Emma?'

'What's that got to do with it?' Edith smirked.

'It's "the very spice of life,"' said Emma. 'Cowper. But I would hope I'm reliable too.' She turned and started to climb the stairs.

'I know the poem,' Sandy said. Emma stopped to face him. 'It's "The Timepiece" and includes the lines, "England, with all thy faults, I love thee still—My country!"'

'Why would you remember those lines?' Edith demanded.

Ted chuckled. 'Sandy's an Anglophile, mother.'

'That's very commendable, I'm sure.' Edith sighed.

'Well, thank you again.' Sandy bowed. 'And may I extend you an open invitation to dine with me? Anytime you're in London?'

'Thank you, Sandy. As a bachelor I don't expect you to return my invitation. Ted, I'll walk with you to the car. Then I'll shut the gate after . . . ?'

Sandy tucked the rolled drawing under his arm, picked up his suitcase, and glanced up at the stairs. Emma had gone.

The car was parked in the drive quite near the gate. 'I'll reverse out on to the road,' said Ted, when they were in the car. 'Keep a lookout on your side, Sandy.'

They reached the gates. 'Clear on my side!' Sandy looked back. She was at the upper window, facing the drive. She waved. He waved as the car turned; and the face and the house were left behind. For a time Ted did not speak and Sandy was grateful to be left to think. The wrench of being separated from Emma occupied his mind and his heart sank as every passing minute increased the distance between them. Nothing in the way they parted or in the way Edith looked at him, held any hope of seeing her again; and the memory of the happy hours spent with Emma conspired only to wound him. He relived the sensation of that kiss, realising at the same time that it would be foolish to make of it anything more than what it was, a farewell. Once again he saw the absurdity of his romantic dream. He was thirty, not an adolescent. Yet such pain as he now felt had the infatuation and rapture of a first love with an intensity that was the worse for coming late and catching him unprepared. And she had made it beautiful in those hours spent together, and herself a prize worth winning.

They had left the High Street, driven up Magdalen Hill, and were now cruising on the open road. He looked at Ted and for the first time wondered at his long silence. 'How's she running?' He asked. 'The car?'

'She's running well.' Ted kept his eyes on the road and spoke in a tone of voice that Sandy thought was meant to discourage conversation. But a moment later Ted asked: 'Were you waving to Emma? It couldn't have been mother?' He chuckled.

'Yes, she was at the window. I waved back.' Ted said nothing. 'I'm sorry,' Sandy continued. 'I've blotted my copy book with your mother. I'd no business to butt in.'

'With mother, sooner or later, people blot their copy books. I think Mary's the only close friend she has left, though they've little

The Lotus And The Rose

in common and often get in each other's way. Surprised they're still friends. She's genuinely fond of Trevor. And that's typical. Mother likes gauche young men, so she could patronise without being maternal. She has a deep dislike of being maternal and delights in domineering and being in control. So Trev gets her vote. She takes a sadistic delight in seeing a mismatch. If she were in the army she would want to train the awkward squad.' He clicked his tongue. 'As a boy, I remember how she sided with friends I disliked and would insist on inviting them to any do she organised for me.' Ted laughed and gave Sandy a sidewise glance. 'On the plus side, like all busybodies, mother's an excellent social worker. The Dean was sorry to lose her when she stopped attending the Cathedral.' He paused and hummed a tune. 'You're the sort of chap to rouse women's maternal instincts.'

'Oh come, come. I mean, you can't know that for certain.'

'So you were being gallant by rushing to Emma's aid? There was no need for that.'

'I thought Edith was a bit hard on her.'

'Emma's superbly unruffled by anything mother says. And mother never goes too far. She's steeped in all the new permissive trends—Spock, Dewey, Montessori—but they get on. Mum in the role of a big sister. Sarcasm is the limit of her nastiness. I may be wrong, of course. But clearly, Emma feels no constraint.'

'And your mother would find that frustrating.'

'Meaning?'

'Emma being unpredictable.'

'We'll turn in here for a break and a pot of tea. I always stop here on my way back to London. They serve excellent teas. You know Sandy, to be fair to Mum, Emma can do rather strange things. And since father died, I'm sorry to say, quite mad at times.'

They entered the low-ceilinged parlour of a Victorian cottage and sat at a table that was genteelly laid for afternoon tea. Ted moved a slender glass vase of delicate pinks to one side. 'I recommend the scones . . . You're spot on about the mater.'

'I'm sorry I didn't mean to . . .'

'Mother's manipulated as long as I can remember. And it used to infuriate me, till I learned to ignore it. Emma was always better at dealing with it. But poor dad bore the brunt. He had a hard time keeping up with mother's moods, and always gave in.' Ted turned as a young man approached them. 'Ah, Paul! Where's Betty?'

The fair-haired boy smiled. 'I'm Eric. Mother won't be back for sometime.'

'I see. Terribly sorry, calling you Paul. I've done this before, haven't I? Mistaking you for Paul. You look more like your brother than he does, what!' Ted looked up and grinned. 'Ah, yes. Tea and scones, please. Thank you.' He waited till Eric left the room. 'Paul and Eric,' he explained, 'are twins. Soon they'll be doing national service, which means Betty'll close down this place if she can't find someone to help her out. Husband was killed in Cyprus. Gunned down in a bar while off duty. He was a sergeant-major in the army. Father knew him well. They were in India about the same time.'

'When was this? I mean when was he killed.'

'About three years ago.' He stared quizzically at Sandy. 'Something's on your mind, old chap. You seem a bit preoccupied?'

'What makes you say that?'

'I thought you were a bit . . . unhappy about something? Oh, by the way, sorry about the Cathedral. But there's not point just having a peep. There's a lot to see. Chapels and paintings, a black marble font, oh, and the Great Winchester Bible . . . I've been a rather neglectful host. I should have taken you there first.'

'There wasn't enough time, and it was good to get a general sweep of Winchester. I am glad you invited me. Grateful. You've been an excellent host . . . But, odd you should ask. I mean what you said earlier. I thought you were somewhat distant yourself.'

'Well, I've been steeped in my own . . .' Ted puckered his lips, then whistled through his teeth. 'You may as well know . . . bound to find out sooner or later. It's Mabel. I had expected her to join us yesterday. But said she couldn't because of stocktaking. That done, she decides she'd like to . . . well, have a break. That's was the upshot of the call this afternoon.'

Sandy waited.

'It's Kitty I'm thinking off. I don't care what Mabel does . . . if only she wouldn't insist on dragging the child along.' He gave Sandy a quick glance. 'Sorry, to involve you in this, but apart from you and Emma . . .'

'Emma knows . . . ?'

The Lotus And The Rose

'Oh, yes. I couldn't turn to mother . . . Yes, you've guessed it. Mother likes Mabel.'

'There's nothing I can sensibly say. I don't know Mabel or the situation.'

'It doesn't matter. Feels good to talk to someone who has nothing to say.'

'Can't you put your foot down.'

'Mabel's excuse is that Kitty can't be left unattended, and that she never knows what time I'll be home. She's right, you know. Women with careers and ambitions shouldn't marry doctors or policemen.' He laughed involuntarily. 'I was about to say, a doctor's wife ought to be patient . . . mother thinks I'm making things worse by a lack of trust.' He stared at Sandy. 'I don't have suspicions. I know. I know she's having an affair. I've even seen the chap.' Ted stopped as Eric came in with the tea.

'It's Ceylon tea,' said Eric. 'I remembered.'

'Yes, thank you. Good. Ah, clotted cream! You're in for a treat, Sandy. Don't wait, tuck in.' He helped himself to a scone. Thanks, Eric.'

'But your concern for Kitty has to do with Mabel . . . As a mother?'

'There's the rub. Mabel's a good mother. Kitty's well cared for. But I want Kitty's company. She's my one consolation. Kitty's a rare and wonderful child . . . I was hoping to show her off to you.'

Sandy smiled as he recalled the schoolboy chant: "If the sister you must win,/ With the brother first begin." 'I would love to meet Kitty. When do you expect them back?' He asked, trying to hide the excitement in his voice.

'Wednesday.'

'You can't go back to an empty house! Have dinner with me. I dine out in any case. We could go to the flicks first and,' he added carelessly, 'forget our troubles.'

'You can't have troubles! Ah, the tranquillity of bachelor-hood! But, yes, I'd like that. Are you sure? Thanks. An evening in the cinema. Yes, and I won't mind what we see, as long as it's not *Peyton Place* . . . not because it's about family problems, but the music, the background music . . . I'm tired of hearing it. Every juke-box in

London plays it. What about *Pather Panchali?* If it's showing . Did I pronounced it correctly.'

'Perfectly.'

'One of my patients told me about it. And you're the right person to go with. You know enough Hindi to fill in what's lost in the subtitles?'

'It's in Bengali,' Sandy said, and they laughed. 'Incidentally, I met Ray, the Director, when he worked for an advertising agency in Bombay. I don't mind seeing it again. I'm a great one for the cinema. There's also *The Wind Cannot Read*, some of it was shot in India, or *Indiscreet?* Ingrid Bergman?' He grinned at Ted's raised eyebrows.

'I'll leave it to you. First, I must go to the surgery. Tell Willoughby I'm back. Clive and I share the practice. We were in college together. Drop you first if you like.'

'No, I'll be happy to see your surgery. Then we can go on to my place.'

Ted lit a cigarette, took two deep puffs and stubbed it. 'I'm trying to give up. You do smoke, occasionally?'

'Yes. Is it that hard, trying to give up?'

Ted giggled. 'It's easy. I'm doing it all the time, as Oscar Wilde is supposed to have said. Shall we powder our . . . ? You go ahead, I'll follow later.' He made a sign to Eric, took out a note-book, wrote in it, tore the page out, and handed it to him. 'Give my regards to your mum and tell her that's my new telephone number.'

In the car, Ted boxed Sandy's shoulder. 'I'm looking forward to this p.m.'

Sandy smiled and stared ahead. As the car sped towards London his thoughts once again returned to Emma; and with it returned a sense of despair.

'Sandy, as soon as things are settled in Holland Park, you must come over. I'll call you. You've got to meet Kitty.' Ted dug into his tweed jacket to hand him a postcard-sized buff envelope. In it was a black and white photograph of an enchantingly beautiful but solemn little girl. The thick fair hair was parted in the middle and two plaits rested on her shoulders.

'Kitty?'

'No. Emma, when she was nine. I brought it for Mabel to see. There, someone in the family who looks like Emma. That could be

Kitty! She's six but the likeness is uncanny. Except the hair. Kitty's dark.'

Sandy returned the photograph. The haunting beauty of the face sharpened his pain. 'I hope you won't mind my saying this,' he coughed discreetly, 'but I'm intrigued that neither you nor your mother seem aware or proud of Emma's stunningly beauty.'

'Emma hates compliments, and I know enough to feel sorry for any man smitten by her, bar Trevor. He has no great expectations.' He gave Sandy a sidelong glance.

Sandy caught his breath. He had no reason to doubt Ted's judgement till now; and what Ted said next confirmed his doubt. 'I said Emma hates being complimented about her looks. Clive did, about three years ago. She avoided him like he were the plague!' He laughed. 'Clive's happily married now, but hasn't forgotten the incident.'

'You think she'll never marry?' Sandy looked at Ted. The smile of open friendship which met his glance cheered him. With Ted around there could be a chance of meeting Emma. Even if he never returned to Winchester, she might visit Ted in London. Though she had revealed an aversion to Mabel, she might be close to Kitty and she certainly was to Ted. And surely Edith occasionally came to London, with Emma! He dare not ask. Even a casual inquiry risked the chance of betraying his feelings.

'Probably.' Ted hummed a tune. 'We are a family of free and detached members . . . I don't know how else to describe us. We give each other space. Comes equally from my father and mother . . . Besides, there's the great age difference, between Emma and me.'

The car slowed down. Ted uttered an inaudible curse. 'Hope the road-works won't delay us. No, he's letting us through.' He waved. 'Thank you! Could have been worse.'

'The road-works?'

'No, I was thinking about Emma. Which is worse, to heartlessly exploit one's beauty or keep it hermetically sealed from the world? What do you think?'

'Hard to say. The former? Exploitation is always bad. It involves other people.'

'What's virtuous about the latter?'

'By not being the former. The virtue of beauty unsullied . . . Venus preserved is better than Venus vandalised.'

'Romantic humbug!'

'No, think of the rose. Think of flowers. They please without . . . without blackmail.'

'Twaddle. But I'll concede. Few would put it so romantically. It's the poet in you; and I don't mean to mock. Anyway, if Emma marries, it'll be to please mother.' Ted whistled 'Mind you, she surprised us by the peck she gave you. Extraordinary! There you are. Didn't I say, it's the maternal instinct you arouse. And she gave you a drawing! Count yourself privileged.'

'I have,' Sandy said. He had to know if at any time she would come to London. 'Do you as a family get together for Christmas and or Easter?'

'We used to, when father was around. Just family. By the way, have you plans for Christmas? You'll be welcome to join us.'

'Thank you. I'm free.' Then Sandy remembered he had accepted Sally Watson's invitation. 'Oh, except Christmas Day, itself.'

'You sly dog. It's a woman? Tell me I'm right?'

'Wrong.' Sandy jeered. Ted was suddenly the boy he met in India years ago.

'I don't believe you!'

'Sally, the colleague I told you about. I accepted her invitation weeks before we got in touch. Christmas with her family in Windsor. Don't give me that look! I've told you she's engaged and he's certain to be there.'

'You don't have to explain.'

'Stop ragging. I truly regret not contacting you before. We should've kept in touch. If you knew the lengths I went to, to get your father's home address!'

'I'm more to blame. I left Bombay without warning or exchanging addresses.'

Sandy steeled himself to ask the one question uppermost on his mind. 'Does the family always spend Christmas in Winchester? What about London?'

'Mother hates London. Now, she invariably spends Christmas with Mary.'

'I suppose, Emma as well?' Sandy tried to sound unconcerned.

'No. Just mother.'

Sandy looked away. Ted seem in no mood to expand and it was hardly politic to pursue the matter. For a while neither spoke. Then Ted said: 'Emma looks forward to Christmas . . . but not in the way the rest of us do.'

'With friends?'

'Emma had few close friends. Two, as I remember. Ex-classmates. And now it's just Clare. Wendy married last year and lives in Scotland. Emma spends two weeks over Christmas in Wantage . . . in a convent. She actually looks forward to it. This will be her third Christmas there. Clare's a nun. Once, both planned to be nuns. Look, why not bring in the New Year with us. Yes? Good. The house'll be in good shape by then. And by then, you will have met Kitty . . . and Mabel.

CHAPTER FOUR

It would be two years before Sandy saw Emma again; and their second meeting was to be as unexpected as the first. Till then, mercifully, the interval saw him hard at work in school and fairly active during the holidays—though he did view the approach of each vacation, except Easter, with dread. Easter was a respite. Since 1956, he spent every Easter at Stoke Poges with Una, Bill Clayton's mother, and there, in 1959, he decided to return to writing the novel he began four years ago; hoping it would help him forget Emma. Then in the summer of 1960 he heard that his uncle Jagdish—"Jaggers"—was gravely ill and, that August, flew to New Delhi. At the airport he was met by his uncle's chauffeur, Arjun. Taking turns at the wheel, they drove the old black Wolseley all the way over dusty roads to Charbagh. "Junior", as Sandy affectionately called Arjun, told Sandy that after a bungled prostrate operation, his uncle had to be rushed to hospital with septicaemia. When he regained consciousness he asked to see Sandy.

'*Baba*, Jaggersahib, he weery ill. Weery thin. Like rake.'

'Is he still in hospital?'

'No, *baba* sahib. At home. He tell doctor he no die in hosbidal bed. He wanting to die at home. But he not die.'

'Junior, I heard you, but now, tell me truthfully. Is my uncle dying?'

'*Baba*, no, no! He *phalwan*. Strong man. I taking good care of him. Egg, hot milk, whisky. Two times daily.'

'What about a nurse? He must need someone?'

'Dat taken care of. Night time. Good Anglo-Indian. Miss Antic Hay.'

The Lotus And The Rose

'Annette Hay?'

'Dats vart am saying. Antic Hay.'

(Sandy had learnt not to laugh at this wry old man, behind whose hollow eyes and comic expression lurked a shrewd intellect. Once he had—for the first and last time—fifteen years ago, when Arjun got his present job. Sandy was at the interview. "I'm failed B.A.," Arjun had informed Jagdish and Sandy giggled. His uncle frowned. 'No Sandy, don't. How else can he tell me that though he has failed the exams, he's done the course? It makes a lot of sense.")

'Yes,' said Sandy. 'I remember Annette Hay. She was from the corner house in Alwar estate. Thin, quite pretty.'

'Now fat. Not so pretty.'

The village of Charbagh, fifty-one miles west of Ajmer, was little more than a large oasis in the desert state of Rajasthan. But it had the reputation of being a health resort famed for the medicinal property of the waters from four clearly marked and protected wells. Temples were built over them, and gardens or baghs—hence the name Charbagh, which means four gardens—within the premises had assembly halls for the distribution of water by caste-marked priests who sat on raised platforms. Utensils of any kind were not permitted, and the waters had to be drunk from cupped hands reverently held under chins. There was no charge for the waters, but priests had a canny ability of singling out non-Brahmins, who were served water out of long spouted zinc containers in distinction from the shining brass ones reserved for Brahmins and the ostensibly rich. Temple bells rang throughout the day and during festivals, late into the night. Luckily for Sandy, his uncle's mansion was outside the village, and the sound of the bells, muffled by distance, had a soporific effect. So any discomfort Sandy suffered was due more to the fact that he no longer was acclimatised to the Charbagh summers: dry hot days, sandstorms after sunset, and sudden showers that made the nights damp and heavy. As for the waters, no amount of filtering could rid it of its peculiar brackish taste. But pleased with his uncle's progress, Sandy felt able to leave after a short stay. He was also able to see his sister in Poona before flying back from Bombay to London, where on arrival he telephoned Ted.

'Good, Sandy, glad to hear all's well.' Ted coughed. 'Sorry dear chap, had a mild touch of the flu. Mabel and Kitty are in the Lake District. I'm stuck here. But we've got a new girl for Kitty.'

'What happened to Millie?'

'Nothing. She couldn't stay the extra hour Mabel wanted her to, and now that Kitty is day-schooling we need almost full time help. Oh, by the way, before you left, did you promise to take Kitty to the park? She hasn't forgotten. Yes, when you're here next. What? She shamed you, did you say? Well, Emma taught her the names of flowers. I wouldn't have fared better . . . What? The line's awful. I didn't hear? Yes, they'll be back on Sunday. Saturday next will be fine. I make a note of it.'

Sandy entered the garden and walked towards the deck chair on which Mabel's elegant figure reclined. 'Hello, Sandy,' she said, shading her eyes to look at him. Then with a languid feline movement, she stretched her shapely legs and raised her angular, bony frame to its full height. Having never stood in such proximity before, Sandy realised she was almost as tall as him. Many men, Sandy thought, would find this sophisticated woman attractive. He was not among them; and he knew she knew that from the first time they met. Now, something about her face coincided with a recent memory. On the chest of drawers in his uncle's bedroom, in a silver frame was a black and white signed photograph of Gertrude Lawrence. Mabel's steely grey eyes studied his. 'Why, Sandy,' she said. 'I believe you're staring.'

'Terribly sorry, Mabel, I thought, for a moment, you reminded me of someone.'

'And who would that be?'

It suddenly occurred to Sandy that Mabel would hate to see herself as anything but original. 'No one,' he said. 'I realise I was mistaken.'

Her nostrils flared, he imagined, in disdain.

'Hello there, Sandy!' Ted called from the far end of the garden and came towards them followed by a lumbering and unusually large Irish Setter. 'Good afternoon! And meet Tinker. Are you fond of dogs?'

'Afternoon, Ted. I adore dogs.'

'I wanted a Basset hound. You know, the goofy kind. We tossed for it. Mabel won.' He sniggered. 'If you'd like to give a Basset a home, tell me.'

'I couldn't. Not in a flat. It's not fair. To a dog, I mean.' Tinker rubbed against him and sniffed his hand. Sandy held the hand over his head. The dog drew its ears back, wagged his tail and whimpered. He bent down to stroke its sleek head. A movement behind him and an electric thrill, set his heart racing.

'Guess who's here?' said Ted.

Sandy knew before he looked up and turned to face her.

'Emma arrived this morning. We didn't know she was coming till yesterday.'

'You're looking well,' said Sandy, finding his voice.

She gave a slight toss of her head. 'Thank you. You look well, too. I gather your uncle's much better.'

'Yes, thank you. And how's . . .' he stopped.

A groan from Mabel made the three of them look at her sharply. 'I think we can all do with tea,' she said sardonically. 'Where's Kitty? Speak of the devil.'

A girl ran out of the house and across the terrace towards them. The dog sprang forward to meet her. 'Tinker!' commanded Mabel. Both dog and girl froze. The dog retreated making the sound of a deflating balloon.

Kitty quickly recovered herself. 'Sandy!' she cried, skipping towards him excitedly. She grasped his hands and swung them from side to side. 'You've forgotten me!'

'Oh, no. I haven't!'

Kitty giggled. 'Oh, yes you have! You went right through the dining room and into the garden. I was at the table, with Angela. Didn't you see us?'

'I did. But I thought you were doing homework.'

'Anyways.' She blocked his path, her arms akimbo. 'I'm ready for our walk and our talk . . . oh, and . . .' Turning on her heel she did a pirouette. 'the Jane thingy book.'

'Kitty! You'll go nowhere! Not in that dress. That's for Wednesday.'

Kitty stamped a foot.

'I thought I told Angela.'

As if waiting for her cue, Angela came out on to the terrace. 'Sorry, Mrs Franks, but Kitty insisted.'

'Kitty must do as you say. But we'll let it pass. I'm not so sure about that dress now. She looks twelve instead of eight.'

All this while Kitty stood poised with hands clasped and held away from her; a tilted head, downcast eyes, and a foot stretched to rest lightly on a toe. Sandy choked. It was clear the child was taking ballet lessons.

'You look silly, Kitty.' Mabel growled. 'Stop that.'

'Come on, Mabs. Have a heart!' Ted mumbled. 'Avoid scenes, please.'

'Then don't interfere.'

'If you don't want her to look twelve at Wednesday's party, let her wear it on now. She may want to look twelve this evening. It wouldn't matter if she did?'

'Ted, I wish you wouldn't,' Mabel said through clenched teeth, 'contradict me.'

'Dad, shall I wear the white dress with the blue sash?'

'Yes. Or the green blouse with the tartan skirt. You know, I like that.'

Kitty ran in, and Angela, after a hesitant look at Mabel, followed her, leaving behind a vague memory of a small and neat young woman. She was the sort of person one sees but fails to notice.

'We'll have tea in the sitting-room,' said Mabel. 'It'll save Angela having to carry things on to the terrace.'

'Can't trust her with your fine china?' Ted chuckled.

Mabel ignored the gibe. 'She'll be with Kitty. So Ted, you could lend me a hand in the kitchen.' She did not wait for an answer. 'Kitty's been rather silly, today.'

Ted laughed. 'She's got a crush on Sandy.'

'That's a silly remark, even if it's true.'

'I remarked upon it precisely because it's silly.'

Mabel shut her eyes with a pained expression. 'I didn't mean silly innocent.' She turned to Sandy. 'What is it all about? I don't understand. When I said to Kitty that Angela should accompany you, Kitty insisted she wanted only to be with you. It's not the sort of thing I want to encourage. And if Ted hadn't . . ..'

'Mabel!' said Emma, 'I think you're being crude!'

'Indeed!' agreed Ted. 'And downright rude.'

'Sorry, Sandy. I didn't mean it the way it came out.'

'But Mabel,' said Sandy, 'you must remember? When I was here last, just before I went to India? Kitty's school had a showing of *Jane Eyre* and we, Kitty and I, talked about it, and she wanted to see the book. It's beyond her age range, I know, but it's a childlike curiosity . . ."Is there really a book of the film? Or is he pulling my leg?" That kind of thing. She's genuinely intrigued by the idea of seeing the story in words, which is no bad thing.'

'But, of course,' said Ted. 'Don't give it another thought, Sandy. A child's curiosity ought to be met with frankness, you believe that Mabel, don't you? Sandy's here on my invitation, and Kitty asked me to remind him of his promise.'

'For heaven's sake! Who's disputing that!' Mabel snarled.

'I promised her a walk in Holland park and to read passages from the book,' Sandy said. It so happens I forgot to bring the book, so if we can get her mind off the whole . . .'

'We have a copy,' Ted said. 'I'll get it. Come on, Tinker.'

'Let her handle the book, Sandy,' Mabel said confidingly. 'Kitty's a precocious and avid reader. Don't underestimate her.'

In no mood to let her have the last word, Sandy said: 'I don't.'

The large coffee table in the sitting-room displayed cups, plates and napkins. 'That is nice. Angela's showing some initiative,' said Mabel. 'She has also made the sandwiches. That was a great help. I'll do the rest. Do we have to wait for Ted?'

'Yes.' said Emma, firmly. Just then Ted entered the room.

'Did you find it?' asked Mabel.

'Find what? Blast! The book. I'll get it. Let's get tea going first.'

'Yes, Ted. I can do with help in the kitchen.'

'But we can't all be in the kitchen, Mabs. Emma can keep Sandy company.'

Sandy sat down with a grateful sigh, while Emma sank into the winged-back chair facing him. At last they were alone! Any moment now she would look up and, uneasy at the thought of meeting her gaze, Sandy studied his hands to hide his apprehension. He had longed for such an opportunity and rehearsed a declaration of love that would win her heart, but the interval between their meetings presented him a gap too awkward to bridge. Having despaired of ever seeing her again, worse, of seeing her and being made desolate by the fact her life was irrevocably separated from his and pledged to another, unnerved him. Anything could have happened. Two years was a long time. He had to find out! But first he must steel himself. Time had not dimmed his love, but that was a love for a remembered face. Could the years have wrought a change that would break the spell she had cast on him? He looked up. She met his eyes with the same steady, absentminded, artless, soft blue gaze. Changed! If anything, she was lovelier! The sage-green upholstery of the chair heightened the chestnut tones of her hair and the smooth whiteness of her face. Perhaps he detected a subtle maturity; a disinterested, almost spiritual aloofness? All so very elusive. The hair! Now was that different? Less full? She turned away and he saw her profile. No. It was as luxuriant as he remembered it, but drawn over the ears, tied high at the back in a thick plaited pony tail. Its effect on those finely chiselled features was a vision of Ancient Greece. 'Aphrodite!' He murmured.

'What?' she asked huskily.

'You've changed the way you do your hair?'

'I do this sometimes. After I've washed it. I suppose I look terrible.'

'You can't, even if you tried.'

She looked away, not embarrassed, but like one who has dismissed a statement as empty. Mabel came in with a tray. 'Do help yourself with plates and napkins.'

She left the room. Emma stood up.

'Please don't go! I'm not usually at a loss for words. I just don't know where to begin. Try and understand why! Surely you already do!'

She shook her head, handed him a plate, napkin, and sat on the sofa next to him.

'Your mother's well?' he asked irrelevantly.

She nodded.

'And, er, the Williamses? Your neighbours?'

'Do you really want to know about them?'

'Gosh, no! I really want to know about you!'

'I can't think what to say. I really have no news, Sandy.'

'Then is no news good news.'

'What do you mean?' She smiled. 'It depends, what you mean by good.'

After a pause he asked: 'Did you go to Wantage this Christmas?'

'Yes.' Then she said abruptly. 'Trevor is back. He's been away in South Africa.'

After another pause he asked: 'How long are you here?'

'I go back tomorrow.'

'So, it's goodbye again!'

She studied his face, 'I'm back on Wednesday. I start work at the British Museum.'

'Will I see you again? I must, unless . . . unless,' he whispered, 'unless you want to break my heart.'

He could feel her eyes on him. Softly she said: 'Yes. If you want to.' Then almost inaudibly. 'You didn't write.'

He stared. 'How can you be so cruel! If only you knew! I was dying to write.'

'But you didn't.' She said simply.

'You gave me no opening. No hint. You said, we may not meet again.'

'I did. Is that all I did?'

Sandy shut his eyes tightly. 'O God! What a fool I've . . . I could've written sonnets to you! Poor, but heart felt ones.' He looked at her and saw he had gone too far.

'You mustn't embarrass me. I want your friendship. To keep in touch with you. And to keep your letters. I know they will be beautiful.'

'Just pen-friends?'

'But able to see each other.'

'Do you understand how I feel? There can be no one else, in my life, Emma!'

'In so short a time? You hardly know me. I don't wish to hurt you. Sandy . . .'

They started. A little face popped up behind and between them. It was Kitty. She had crept in and now she rested her chin on the top of the sofa

'Have you been here long?' Emma asked.

Kitty made a humming noise, raised her brows, turned her eyes towards the ceiling and gave a wicked grin. 'You like Emmy, don't you, Sandy?'

Emma placed a finger on Kitty's lips. 'Hush!' she said.

Kitty stood on her toes, reached out over the sofa, put her arms round Emma's neck, and pressed her face against hers. 'But I want you to like Sandy!'

Emma did not answer. They made a pretty picture; and Ted was right. They were so alike. But as he watched he noted differences more significant than the obvious physical ones. Kitty's merry brown eyes retained their twinkle even when she was not smiling. While in Emma's solemn blue depths, there was, not only an absence of coquetry and guile, but also a good measure of wariness. Kitty showed every sign of growing into one of those vivacious women that men find irresistibly attractive; and Sandy, though not immune to their charm and bubbling spirits, found the company of such confident women a little inhibiting, whereas Emma's rare tranquillity, emboldened him. With her he could relax, be himself, and find her inner strength sustaining. Kitty was Martha to Emma's Mary . . .

In the kitchen Mabel said to Ted: 'Edith won't thank you, you know.'

'What on earth are you talking about?'

'About bringing them together.'

'By them you mean?'

'Yes, keep your voice down.'

'What of it? Good for Emma, I say. When father died, she lost the only company that made her happy. Now she can be with Sandy without running away and locking herself in solitude. Anyway, I know Emma. Nothing serious will come off it. They'll just be good friends. Mind you, I wouldn't want him to be hurt or get the wrong idea. But Sandy's a sensible chap. Can't see him . . .'

'Oh, do shut up, Ted. None are so blind as those who will not see. Men are such fools. It sticks out a mile. There's a lot brewing out there, even right now. Being other worldly doesn't make her immune. She's innocent enough to be . . . to be seduced. Don't underestimate Sandy. Women go for his type, and he's good-looking.'

'Very good looking. I suppose you're hurt he hasn't . . . Sorry, that was below the . . .'

'You poor man! To think you could wound me! Well, it's none of my business, as long as you make that clear to Edith. That clear, I'll admit, any one who can shake off her isolation is doing some good. You know what I mean. Such a waste! She would have made a superb model . . . that distant non-committal look my sister has in mind. But she won't even try out our new line of dresses!'

'I don't blame her. All your stuff is indecently short.'

'Oh, come on. That frock, yes frock, she wore yesterday. Awful.'

'Awful? Emma looking awful? She couldn't, what ever she wears.'

'I'm speaking about her clothes. It's the forties and not in fashion.'

'One can look awful in the latest fashion. Emma's no fool. She knows what suits her. Remember she's an artist, with excellent taste.'

'I'll admit very light or very dark colours suit her, but I assure you, however good you look, people still talk if you're out of fashion.'

'Shall we drop this. Emma doesn't care a fig what people think. She is not a child. She's an independent woman, in every sense.'

'And what is she going to do with her money? (I assume you also meant financial independence.) And why is she coming to live here?'

'I'm not prepared to go into any of this, except to say she'll be paying her share. I've asked her to stay here because we have room and because I don't want her to be on her own in London. Nor does mother. Is that the milk? Right, put it on the tray. I'll take it in.' He started to move, then stopped. 'Remember, if one is to go by father's intentions, legally this place is hers. You ought to know we can't sell it without her consent.'

'She can have the place as far as I'm concerned. I'm no beggar. My business is doing very well, thank you. I'd love the opportunity to have a place of my own.'

'You would. That's not the point. By the way, Sandy is a decent chap. So let's not have any more of what ensued in the garden.'

Ted entered the sitting-room. 'There, the very best Darjeeling . . . And what plot is my little Kitty hatching. I see those beady scheming eyes . . . Hey! Kitty don't! You'll knock the tray. Now!' he lifted Kitty fondly in his arms, kissed her and put her down.

'I see fairy cakes! Oh, daddy you remembered.'

'And Chelsea buns,' added Mabel. 'Now, plate and napkin first, and sit by me.'

'Right,' said Ted, 'before I forget I'll get the book. Won't be long.'

'What's daddy looking for?'

'*Jane Eyre.* The book you wanted to see.' Mabel replied.

'I've got it. I asked Angela to find it. It's on my table, daddy!'

Ted was back with the book a moment later. 'Good beginning,' he said reading the opening sentence aloud.

'I think it's silly,' Kitty said. 'Why can't she go for a walk?'

'Kitty,' said Mabel. 'Don't speak with your mouth full.'

'People can always go for walks, if they want to.'

'You couldn't have gone yesterday. It rained all day.'

'I could? With my mac and umberella, I could.'

'Umbrella, darling. But would you want to.'

'If it's important . . . and I want to . . .'

'Now you're being tiresome. There are times when we can't do what we'd like to.'

'Kitty knows,' said Ted. 'Don't you, Kitty? Tell me, what or who could stop you going out? When it's got nothing to do with weather?'

'People?'

'And when it's not other people, we stop ourselves because we think we should.'

'Sandy's going to read the last bit to me. I love his voice, daddy. He reads better than Angela. Don't you like his voice, Emmy?' Kitty's eyes twinkled wickedly.

Emma smiled briefly. Ted said: 'Sandy speaks a damn sight better than I do!' There was something in his manner which reminded Sandy of Colonel Franks. 'Here, Sandy.'

'Can I have it!' Kitty squeaked. 'Let me hold the book, daddy?'

'After you've finished your tea and washed your hands,' said her mother evenly.

The Lotus And The Rose

'Let's all seriously get on with tea. I'm famished,' said Ted. 'And Kitty, the sooner you finish your tea, and er washed your hands, the sooner you can look at the book.'

Kitty put her plate down and wiped her mouth and hands with her napkin. Then she showed them to her mother. 'I suppose so.' said Mabel languidly.

'Now,' said Sandy, 'where do I start?'

Kitty did not answer. She had put the book on his lap and climbing up next to him, leaned forwards and peered at the last page. She read aloud: "Reader, I married him." Then she frowned. 'That's funny. Why not just say, I married him?'

'It sounds better.'

'Why, Sandy? Why does it sound better?'

'Some things which are beautiful can't be explained. They just are.'

Kitty caught Sandy's sly glance at Emma. She turned to face her mother. 'Mum, can Emmy come with us to the park.'

'Your aunt Emma,' Mabel spoke with deliberate emphasis, 'may have better things to do. Anyway I thought you wanted only Sandy.'

'That's 'cos he knows books and things . . . and stories. And Emmy . . . er, aunt Emma won't stop me asking questions. Would you Em . . . aunty?'

'Of course, I won't Kitty and it's a nice afternoon for a walk in the park.'

Mabel threw a triumphant glance at Ted, then she forced a smile. 'Better still, Kitty, why don't we all have a walk in the park? I'm sure daddy would like to come too!' She picked up a tray, and thrust it in Ted's hands. 'Help me take things into the kitchen.'

'Oh, daddy!' pleaded Kitty. 'It's going to take so long! And I want to go now.'

'You three go ahead. We'll catch up. Now run along.'

In the kitchen Mabel hissed: 'Ted, you can be so naive! You know what our Little Madam's up to? She's playing Cupid.'

'I'm not going to treat Emma like a child, Mabel.'

'Emma's not my worry. It's Kitty. She far too precocious.'

Ted placed the tray on the sink and threw his hands up in despair. 'Now, what's all this about. You've got what you wanted. Kitty's not alone with Sandy . . . besides, you have got no right involving me in all this . . . this chicanery. I've got things to do, and the last thing I want is kill time in the park.' He sighed. 'For God's sake, Mabs! Sandy's a gentleman. I don't think Kitty's crush is anything like what you had for older men at her age! I'm sorry, but you asked for that.'

Mabel glared angrily. 'That's pathetic. You can't hurt me! Don't even try. I was going to say, I think *Jane Eyre's* been forgotten. I know she was tickled by the story's romantic ideas, but now all that has been transferred to Sandy and Emma, and for all the excitement she'll get out of it.'

'I see, you've moved to . . .'

'Yes, and I rather it didn't happen here. I don't give a hoot about the outcome, but your mother must know I did everything to discourage it.'

'Emma's not interested in men, not in the way you think, or in marriage. She's a sweet sad girl. If, and that's a big if, she's making any new decisions for herself, then it's her business, and I shall, as I always have, stand by her. But I don't believe there's anything to be concerned about. When push comes to shove, her happiness comes first. Personally, I'd rather it was Sandy, than that poor boring boy, Trevor.'

'Then there's nothing more to be said.'

'You've got nothing against Sandy have you?

'No. But I know the type. Old fashioned, intense, romantic, single-minded . . . from my point of view, a bore.'

Ted sighed. 'Good for them. And I assure you, he's far too intelligent to be a bore.'

The door opened and Kitty peeped in. 'Daddy,' she said, 'we're waiting!'

'But I told you to go ahead?'

'Sandy said we should wait.' She looked from one to the other. 'What's wrong?'

'Nothing, darling,' said Mabel. 'Go ahead. Tell Sandy we've changed our minds. Daddy's got work to do. Now treat that book with care.'

Kitty held out the book. 'You keep this for now, dad. I think we'll just walk . . . ;

The Lotus And The Rose

When they returned from the park Emma took Ted by the arm: 'About tomorrow. Ring Clive and tell him you're coming. Have your game of golf. You haven't spent a Sunday together for ages. And you don't have to see me off.'

'You're going at eleven. I'll still have the afternoon. Can't have you hanging about alone at the station.'

'I won't be alone. Sandy'll be there.'

'I see.' He studied her face. 'If that's what you want. But he hasn't got a car?'

'He's coming in a cab.'

'That's settled then,' said Ted. Later, he told Mabel that he hadn't seen Emma look more radiant. "If Emma is genuinely happy, then for the sake of her health it's best not to interfere." Mabel shrugged her shoulders. It suited Ted. Sharing his thoughts with Mabel increasingly seemed to give her opportunities to attack him. But he had his own fears about Emma's growing attachment to Sandy. He knew Emma could suddenly and inexplicably retreat within herself and even act against her own interests; but if Sandy's charm proved to be a force to be reckoned with, could Emma extricate herself if she wanted to? But, if male charm was not something Emma was susceptible to, there had to be something else she saw in him, and if that something made her happy, he would, come what may, not be an obstacle.

Wednesday began with all the promise of a bright autumn day. But late afternoon saw an overcast sky followed by wind and rain. Before that, Ted had been called out on an emergency, which involved a sixteen year-old school girl taken from the playground, by ambulance to the nearest hospital. He waited in his surgery till she had been operated upon for appendicitis, then drove through driving rain to find Mabel in the sitting-room watching television. She ignored his apology, glanced at her watch, stood up and butted her cigarette. 'You care more for Clive's family than your own. He ought to do his bit.'

'Mabs, I've had a hard day. I'm tired . . . and how can you be so heartless. Clive's son is just ten months old?'

'And why should that pose a problem? Fiona doesn't work. She's home all day.'

'He does cover for me, when I take a day off.'

She waved a hand.

'I need a drink!' He sighed. 'Would you like . . . I see you've had . . . Where's Emma?'

'Hasn't left her room since she arrived. Didn't want tea, Angela asked, just wants to be left alone. As usual. You know how she can freeze people out. But I'll see her while you change. I haven't been here long. I've had a lousy day too! Got drenched to the bone! What does that look mean?'

'Nothing. Yes, the rain's been hell these past few hours. Leave Emma to me.'

'Gladly. I hate it when she's moody.'

'I had hoped you two would get along. She's well read and mature for her years.'

'Maybe, but we've got nothing in common. Besides, I've little spare time.'

'And where's Kitty?'

'With Angela, having supper. Don't be too long.'

The two-storied Victorian house had twice been extended at ground level. First, to include a central annexe, which was now the dining room and later, a new wing of two rooms and a bathroom, for guests. This wing could be reached from the conservatory beyond the dining room.

'Hello Angela. Has Kitty had a good day?'

'Daddy! Daddy! sit by me. You're so late?'

'I have to see Emma. Give daddy a big kiss. There. Why the long face?'

'Emmy won't come out of her room. I knocked. Angela did too.'

'She must be tired. I'll find out. Finish your supper.'

He tapped softly on Emma's door. 'It's me, Ted.' The door opened. 'Are you all right? What are you doing in the dark?' He put his arm round her. She put her head on his shoulder. 'Hey! Chin up. We can't have this. You've been crying? Whatever for?'

She did not answer.

'Why didn't you tell Sandy to meet you? Have you phoned him?' She nodded. 'And is he coming?'

'She shook her head.

'He can't make it?'

'I told him not to come. But I've agreed to meet him on Saturday. Ted! I feel terrible. I feel as if I'm . . . I'm being unfaithful. Unfaithful to father.'

'Because of Sandy?'

'No. Coming to London. Leaving daddy . . . behind . . . alone out there!'

'Emmy, we've been through all that. Remember what you said last week? How you felt father was always with you? And remember what Clare said . . . You've got daddy's great coat—to wrap around you when you read, so you can feel him close to you? Dad loved you and he wouldn't want you to be like this? Now, I'm going to turn the lights on, and you're going to have a drink and a good dinner.'

'I'm so tired!'

'So you will be, if you haven't eaten all day. I've told you, again and again, you need to eat well to keep strong. What are you doing on Saturday? You and Sandy?'

'I don't know, yet.'

'Are you going to invite him, earlier . . . before Saturday?'

'I don't know.'

'Do you intend to keep seeing him? You realise I'm conniving. Mother'll find out. As a friend, I can't stop him calling, but if she should think I'm encouraging . . .'

'It's none of her business.'

'But she and Mary have made it their business.'

'Oh, Teddy! You know I feel nothing for Trevor.'

'And for Sandy?' He waited a moment. 'You seem to like his company.'

'I want to be alone . . . he lets me feel I'm alone . . . he makes being alone feel nice, yes, even a little exciting . . . I mean, I like to listen to him. He teases . . . and makes me laugh.'

Clever Sandy, Ted thought. Or maybe Sandy was, as he always knew, just a nice chap. 'You used not to care much for teasing . . .'

'He's gentle too . . . and sensitive. But I'm afraid to hurt him. Sometimes, I feel, we've always known each other. I've thought about him, you know, even before we met!'

'From that snap of him with father? So, you were ready to like him?'

She nodded. There was a pause. Then he said: 'I understand about Trevor. About any man for that matter. I didn't think there'd ever be a man in your life. You know what I mean. Emmy, Sandy's much older than you, so I hope you know what your doing and can keep things in check? You know what I mean?'

She started and stared wild-eyed at him. 'He's not too old for me!'

'And, you know, he's in love with you.'

'Yes. I think he's in love with me because he's in love with England.'

'I don't follow.'

'I think he's determined to love an English girl as part of his love for England.'

Ted laughed. 'You could be right, but believe me, he loves you because you're you. As any man would if you'd let him.'

'But I must also be a symbol of his love of England.'

'Emma, he's in love with you. I had my suspicions from the time the two of you first met, and now I'm certain of it. And Mabel knows. She saw it the moment she saw you two together. You have to be sensible and careful. He's my friend. And I too wouldn't want him to be hurt.'

'I'll do nothing to hurt him.'

'Why aren't you discouraging him, as you did others.'

'I've not encouraged him. But that doesn't answer your question.' She sat down on the edge of her bed with a deep sigh. 'I can't seem to get angry with Sandy!'

'Then you do care.' He sat down next to her. 'Ask yourself why? Why you haven't shown interest in men before, and why is it different with Sandy?'

'I'm afraid of love,' she said sadly.

'Being afraid is not going to help. Do some serious thinking and make up your mind. In the meantime, don't let things get out of hand . . . get too physical. Don't look at me like that. You're playing with explosive stuff. I'd imagine he can be jolly seductive. And what if he pops the question?'

'Oh, Teddy! I want his friendship. I don't want to think about marriage or . . .'

'Sex?'

'Can't men and women just be friends. Can't he love me as he loves England?'

'You think love of country is platonic? It can be passionate. Full of expectations and illusions. But you may be lucky. Sandy's too much of a gentleman to press you.'

'Yes. He always apologises if he thinks he's gone too far.'

'Give it time. If you like him, as I think you do, and he's patient, love will come naturally. But don't be deceived. He may not be able to possess England but he'll want to possess you . . . his English rose. And you. You can't want to be with him and remain unaffected. You'll change too, because you can't take without wanting to give.'

She gave a little shiver. 'Then I shouldn't see him? Is that what you want, Ted?'

'It has to be your decision. Use your head,' he tapped her forehead affectionately, 'not your heart—which is more than I did. There're a lot of cobwebs here. You've got a lot of clearing out to do.'

'Poor Teddy! There was no one to advise you.'

'Well, as far as mother was concerned, Mabel could do no wrong. And father was no judge of women. But I can't blame others. I was old enough. Now, back to the present. I don't want to see you like this. Sandy's no Mabel. See him by all means and be happy. And if there's any advice you need . . . I'm a doctor, remember.'

'Oh, Teddy, I'm so lucky to have you as a brother! You won't forget to collect my painting things when you go home next week?'

'I won't forget. By the way, how did you know he was an Anglophile?'

'I've known for a long time. Daddy talked about him. He told me that he hadn't met anyone, let alone a boy, who loved England so. Why he wanted Sandy to study here.'

'In Poona, when we were boys, Sandy showed me his scrapbook. He had cut out and pasted all the "This England" pictures from *The Children's Newspaper*. The one edited by Arthur Mee.'

CHAPTER FIVE

That night Emma sat up in bed and started a letter to Sandy, begging him to bear with her, give her more time, and postpone their meeting till . . . She couldn't finish the letter. She scrapped it and having decided that she wanted to see him, fell asleep.

It was pouring with rain when she woke up. The house was still and apart from the muffled drumming of heavy rain on the terrace, no other sound reached her. It was late but refreshed and hungry and all the better for having made up her mind, she went into the kitchen and made herself scrambled eggs, toast, and a pot of tea. These she put on a tray and sat by the window. The rain trickled down the panes in a network of darting streams. Outside, in the light diffused by washed grey skies, the pastel pink and yellow of the water lilies glowed luminously in the garden pond. A longing to draw and paint overcame her. But she knew she would have to wait till Ted brought her paints. A low bark and a whining sound caught her attention. Tinker was sitting plaintively by the door. She smiled. 'You're not allowed in the kitchen! No use looking at me like that. I can't let you out either. It's horribly wet. Later, when it stops. Off you go! Go on!' The dog seemed to understand, and obediently slinked away.

After breakfast she went into Ted's study. There was a book on his desk she had not seen before. It lay open. The chapter was about Peggy Guggenheim. She read all five pages of it. It would be wonderful if she could use her money to lead an independent life? A sense of loneliness saddened her till the thoughts of Sandy brought comfort. The telephone rang. It was Ted.

'You up? And you've slept well. Good. I rang earlier. What? Yes.'

'Ted, I've decided to see Sandy.'

'Then you don't have to do anything. You were going to meet him on Saturday.'

'Yes, but I'd like to change it to Sunday afternoon.'

'Why?'

'I like being home in the evenings. Saturday evening, means restaurants or shows.'

'Then you had better telephone.'

'I can't. Not till after five this evening. And Ted, you know I hate telephoning. Ask him over. This evening.'

'Hang on! Yes, I have his number. He can come over for a drink. You know we are going out this evening. Dinner. Not to worry. I'll square it with Mabel.'

She did not answer.

'Come over and we'll lunch together. If the weather improves. Give me a call. Hello! Emma, you there?'

'Thank you. Some other time. I'd like to read. I've seen a book on your desk.'

'Ah, the Sieveking. *Eye of the Beholder.* It's good. About tonight. Will he stay on after we've left?'

'I don't see him doing that.'

Sandy arrived at twenty past six, not long after Ted, who greeted him and helped him with his coat. 'Ever the immaculately dressed man about town. Can't believe this is off the peg. Do go in. Glad you could make it. Ah, here's Emma.'

Sandy bowed as he lightly held Emma's hand.

'Well,' said Ted, pursing his lips, 'anyone who can make Emma blush deserves a drink! Sherry?' Emma nodded and went into the kitchen. 'Still wondering how a chap like me could have such a beautiful sister?'

'Yes, I mean, no! Don't do yourself down. You've got that distinguished Ronald Colman look'

'You mean a tired look.' Ted grinned. 'By the way, I hope you're hungry.'

'Not really.'

'Find room. Emma's taken a lot of trouble with the snacks. Let me get the drinks. You can take hers to the kitchen.'

'You're sure? I mean, if that's okay by you?'

'Yes. Emma's got something to say. Why you're here. Don't look so anxious. I'd advise you if I didn't know you're far more adept at handling women.'

Sandy laughed. Then took the drinks and turned to find Emma coming towards him holding a tray. He put the drinks down. 'I say, "Angels on horseback"? Takes me back to guest nights at the Mess. Officers' Mess, in New Delhi.'

'I hope these will be as good. Mother's recipe.'

They sat down with their drinks and were silent for sometime. 'Emma,' he said, 'you'll be by yourself tonight. Have dinner with me?'

She shook her head. 'Please don't ask . . . Hush, now! We're not alone. Kitty, you should be eating your supper.'

'Yes,' said Kitty. 'Can I have one of those?'

'Tell Angela. There're some in the kitchen. You won't like it.'

'Hello, Kitty. Sorry, I didn't see you!' Sandy said, putting his glass down.

She ran up to him and raised her hands. 'Pick me up?' He did. She kissed him. He put her down. 'Goodnight, Sandy,' she said as she ran out of the room. He waited till she had gone, then he turned to Emma. 'You have something to tell me?'

Emma patted the sofa. 'Sit here by me,' she said and took his hand. 'Don't ask for reasons! But can we meet on Sunday instead of Saturday?'

'Anything you say.'

'Sunday afternoon. After Church. After lunch? She studied his face solemnly. 'I want you to be a friend. To go for walks. Visit museums, galleries . . . that sort of thing.'

Ted entered the room. 'Sorry, but I need to nibble some of these.' Then he lowered his voice. 'I know, I'm not going to enjoy dinner. I've never cared much for Italian. Tomatoes with everything. Sandy, any good at tying bows?'

Sandy stood up. 'Here, let me.'

'Excellent. Should have remembered. An officer and a gentleman always ties his own bow. Thanks. I see cucumber sandwiches! Don't miss those. No one makes them like Emma.' He kissed her on the forehead and left the room.

'I'll pack some of these for you, before you go, Sandy. Then you needn't go out for dinner.' Emma said.

Half an hour later Sandy decided he should leave. She saw him to the front door and handed him a biscuit barrel. 'You can bring it back on Sunday. The box I mean.'

They moved together into the hall. In the dim light from the sitting-room her eyes gleamed strangely, catlike, and it quite unnerved him. She offered her hand. 'Goodbye. Sorry to bring you all the way here just to tell you about Saturday.'

'Don't apologise. Being with you makes everything else unimportant.' He raised her hand to his lips. She quickly withdrew it. Then smiled.

'You off!' Ted called out from within. 'Can we drop you somewhere?'

'No, thank you Ted. I'll be all right. Give my regards to Mabel.'

'Bye!' Mabel called from within. 'Sorry I didn't say hello. Make up for it next time.'

※

Sunday afternoon outings became a regular pattern with Emma and Sandy and in time Sandy noted how increasingly more relaxed she became. He knew it was unwise to press or cajole her into doing anything that might upset or make her tense. So he took things at her pace. Only patience and consideration on his part would allay the fears or concerns she seemed to have. Fortunately, patience was one of his virtues, but he also felt amply rewarded to be in the company of a woman of such rare beauty; and his aim to woo and win Emma provided all the incentive patience needed. Sandy's mother had once told him that charming people not only liked to be charming but they also enjoyed seeing its effect on others. Now he understood what she meant. She had taught him to observe social niceties and from an early age elegant manners and etiquette not only left their stamp on him but also appealed to him, making him appear, at times, old-fashioned and quaint. All that both intrigued and amused his colleague, Sally Watson. 'You know, Sandy,' she said, cornering him one day in the staff-room, 'your need to emulate, to be more than yourself, explains why you're an Anglophile. Your style of romance is of a bygone age. But it suits you.'

'What on earth do you mean?' he had asked, knowing exactly what she meant.

'You're lapping it up. I'd call you pompous if you weren't so damn good-looking.'

'You've planned this ambush, Sally?' The wicked gleam in her eye warned him to escape. But he stayed. He liked Sally.

After a pause she said: 'I saw you with her, last Sunday.'

'And?' He bit his lower lip and nodded encouragingly.

She shook her head with affected gravity. 'Where on earth did you find her?'

'Isn't she the most beautiful of God's creatures?'

'I was some distance away. A painting. Lifeless. A damsel from the Court of King Arthur.' Sally giggled. 'Don't tell me she's also in distress.'

'Careful, you risk my ever trusting your judgement,' he said, amazed at how intuitive she was, even in jest.

'A Tennyson heroine. But why you are blind to other kinds of feminine beauty.'

'Not true. And why were you tempted to call me pompous?'

'You can't be an Anglophile and not be pompous. It goes with the role.'

'But I ain't acting.'

'Don't change the subject. You can't have known her long?'

'Wrong. I met her three years ago.'

'And you turned me down for her!'

'And we've been seeing each other for a year . . . over a year. Emma I mean.'

'I don't believe it. Seeing? You mean courting, serenading. Playing the mediaeval knight to the demure maiden. How old is she?'

'Twenty-three . . . twenty-four.'

'Just off the cradle and ripe for seduction. But clearly you haven't.'

'Haven't what?'

'Made love.' She caught his arm. 'You haven't even kissed her.'

'I'm not going to be tempted by your baiting.'

'But I'm right. Come on! Admit it.'

The Lotus And The Rose

'You can't know! Not by looking! That's ridiculous!'

'I can. Just by looking. Couples who have—not to hurt your tender feelings—more than kissed, look relaxed. Those on kissing terms, are dreamy, eager. And those who've just about held hands, look like the two of you did, straining on the leash.'

'You're being puerile.'

'I rest my case. Sandy, this is 1962 and spring.' Sally laughed. 'She reminds me of my eldest sister on her first date. Hetty was in her mid-twenties before my father let her go out on a date. I was the rebel in the family; "the bolter". Hetty confided in me. But that was the fifties! Sandy, the world has changed since—since . . .'

'Four years ago? I suppose Emma and I are stragglers. Refusing to come out of the fifties. And what's this about my turning you down. You were engaged. Still are.'

'Not seriously. I'm a free spirit. A hungry young woman.' Sally giggled. 'Anyway, you're not even of the fifties. I'll grant you, Medieval is a bit unfair, but you two are positively Edwardian.'

'Hungry for angry. That's clever. But Sally, freedom has a price.'

'Now, that's what I call pompous. Take it from me, Sandy, you'll never kiss her if you're going to wait till she asks.'

That was three months ago. Now, as he and Emma walked down the steps of The National Gallery, and stopped to gazed across Trafalgar Square, he wondered what triggered the memory of that encounter with Sally? Quite spontaneously Emma took his arm. 'Am I pompous?' he asked abruptly.

She looked at him perplexed and at once he realised she was the soul of acceptance—that rare non-judgemental, intuitive breed of humanity who see through externals to reach the inner person. He gave her hand a grateful squeeze. 'Forget what I said. But is there anything about me you don't like?'

'I'm fond of you,' she said simply. 'Let's take the tube from here.'

'Wouldn't you like tea first? That nice place in the Strand?'

'I want to get back.'

The train was crowded. Facing each other by the sliding doors he asked: 'Emma, are you all right? Is something the matter?' She shook her head but avoided his eyes.

At the next stop a man pushed past them, and as he did so, dug Sandy sharply in the ribs with his elbow. Sandy turned to face a gaunt elderly man about his own height. The man glared with hostility. 'Yeah!' he said. 'Wha'er staring at?' Then with a curl of his upper lip he growled: 'Leave our bloody women alone! Stick to your kind.'

Sandy turned away, taken aback. 'Good grief! Is he talking to me!'

'Take no notice,' she whispered.

But the man lurch forward and thrust his face at Sandy. 'Oh, so la-de-bloody-da!' Then he turned to Emma. 'Excuse me, love! Didn't quite hear you?' He waited. 'He's not pestering you, is he?'

Emma moved closer to Sandy.

'Huh!' The man snarled. 'It's a bloody shame. Lovely girl like you with the likes of him. A bloody native! Upstart darkie.'

Emma suddenly rounded on him. 'Shut up! Go away!'

The man rocked back and gazed wide-eyed. 'I meant well, love!' His jaw dropped visibly. Sandy stared, too, fascinated by the wild look on her face. An expectant hush filled the compartment. The man, aware he had caught the stony attention and disapproval of the other passengers, he addressed them, speaking to no one in particular: 'I was protecting her! For her own good. This is the thanks I get!'

Emma took in a sharp breath. 'You stupid, ignorant man!' She burst out. 'He's a hundred times . . . a thousand times more of a gentleman than you!'

The man curled his lips again and muttering inaudibly moved away.

A couple next to Sandy stood up. The woman touched Emma's arm. 'That was terrible. Here, you two, take our seats.'

'That's awfully kind of you.' said Sandy. 'I'll stand.'

'No, young man.' insisted the woman. 'Sit next to her. She's quite shaken.' Then she glanced up at her tall companion. 'You agree, George, don't you?' The tall man nodded solemnly. Sandy decided George was her son.

'Thank you,' said Sandy. 'I'm terribly ashamed for not facing up the man.'

'Goodness. no! It would have made things worse. There, you'd better . . . she's a bit weepy now.'

The train stopped. Some passengers got off. A seat next to Emma, on the other side, became vacant. The woman sat down and put her arm round Emma.

'I'm all right,' Emma whispered. 'Thank you.'

The woman looked at the unpleasant man who was among the passengers getting off the train. 'You ought to be ashamed!'

'Don't you start!' the man barked.

'Oh, go on!' snapped George. 'Off you go!'

The doors shut. The train moved. Sandy stood up. 'We get off at the next stop,' he said to George. 'That was quite a shock.' He forced a laugh. 'First time for me. I really wasn't prepared for it. I thought the English were the politest people in the world . . . er at least, no open betrayal of prejudice.'

The tall man chuckled. 'Stiff upper lip and all that. Well, now you know. But I'll grant you his conduct was quite exceptional. He's probably had a hard day, and will hate himself when he gets home. Unless, in his own uncouth way, he thought he was being chivalrous. She's extraordinarily beautiful. You're a lucky man.'

'Sorry, I didn't hear the last bit?'

'Never mind. Here's your stop. Goodbye, and watch how you go.'

Emma stood up, thanked the woman and took Sandy's arm. They left the station and crossed Holland Park Avenue in silence. He watched her, wondering what adverse effect the incident may have on their relationship. 'Say something, anything.' He said.

'I've never felt so angry and frustrated.'

'You were magnificent.'

'Let's walk through the park,' she said, and to his delight she squeezed his arm.

'Yes. Of course!' He pressed her hand gratefully against his side. Gently, she freed her hand, lifted the strap of her handbag higher up her shoulder, then folded her arms and walked with a thoughtful swing in her gait.

'You must think me a coward. But I was absolutely unprepared . . .'

'I don't blame you for looking surprised and confused. I had to say something. I know how you love England. I was angry for you . . . for England too.'

'I'm not really a coward, you must believe me.'

'There was nothing to do. You heard what that lady said. You could have made matters worse. I did the wrong thing.'

'Well, that's the last time we go by public transport. I wish I hadn't got rid of my car. I'll soon remedy that.'

'Don't let a chance incident put you off. We've had good times.'

'But think of it. With a car we can go farther afield.'

She stopped by the gatepost. 'They're home early. Ted's left the gate open.' She closed the gates between them and standing on the lowest bar leaned over him. It was something he remembered her doing before. 'Sorry, I've made you miss tea,' she said.

He shrugged his shoulders. 'Are you all right now?'

'Yes.'

'Happy? So I don't see you next Sunday?'

'And the Sunday after that.'

'A fortnight! That would kill me!'

'I want to paint. Ted's taking me to Kew that Sunday. Or rather he'll drop me off and pick me up later. He doesn't like the idea of my being there all day by myself. He did wonder, but it's not fair to you. You'd be bored.'

'Me bored? Never!' Then mimicking Humphry Bogart, Sandy added: 'Not while I'm looking at you, kid.'

She gave a short shy laugh. 'I make faces when I paint.'

'Good, then I'll know you're real and not a goddess to be worshipped from afar. Oh, please let me come. Please?'

'Promise you won't distract me?'

'Absolutely. And let's not trouble Ted. Forget Kew. I know a lovely spot not far from Denham. You'll love it. A canal lock and a river that runs almost parallel to the canal—and wild flowers on the banks!'

She looked doubtful.

'I'll hire a car for the day. We'll have a picnic and I'll bring a hamper from Fortnum and Masons.'

'No, you won't.' She got off the gate. 'Leave that side to me.' She smiled. 'I'll ring you nearer the time. It'll have to be after church.'

'I'll pick you up here.' For the first time since he met her she seemed unconditionally happy.

The Lotus And The Rose

'I'm going in now,' she said, turned, started to leave, stopped, and returned. 'Shut your eyes.'

Instinctively he knew not to ask why. He closed his eyes and a moment later felt a light kiss on his lips. Then he heard her run away. The front door closed behind her.

It was the second time she had kissed him, but if he was intrigued by the first, he was pleased by the second. Patience had been rewarded. Could he be bolder in the future? A nagging thought . . . was it an intrinsic part of his character to hold back? Was he failing to recognise the signals she was giving? But how was he know what were the right moves and responses? It was too big a risk to lose all by a careless move. He faced a hard task, made harder by the fact that she was undoubtedly a complex, even mysterious, person, with an obvious and disarming innocence. Was she innocent? No woman, his mother once told him, ever is. By now, there had been ample evidence that beneath her sad facade lay an inner strength and maturity.

Next day she telephoned him. 'Hello. Sandy!' Then the line went quiet.

'Emma? Hello, I'm listening! Shy after yesterday? Why? Oh, that. Perfectly natural. Do it more often, and the shyness will go.'

'You're being horrid.'

'Honestly. Make it a habit, till it no longer matters; and let me return it. Better still, let me do it first, then you can return it in self-defence.'

'Now you're teasing. You must promise—if you want me to come with you—you won't talk about it. Promise you won't mention it? Behave as if it never happened?'

'Anything you say, my sweet dilemma.'

'What do you mean?'

'A lot: "*dil*" in Hindustani means "heart". So Emma's my *dil*; so dil-emma.'

A pause. 'I don't know what to say when you ramble on like that.'

'I've booked the car. It's going to be a Beetle. Probably, a horribly orange one.'

'Sandy, you're sure you won't be bored. I'm quiet when I paint and it takes time. I've not had anyone with me before . . . except father . . . and he'd go off to sleep. No, this would have been the first for Ted.'

'It'll be just fine. I'll catch up with my reading. You'll need sensible walking shoes.'

'Meet me here after church, after ten. Wait in the car. I'll come out to you.'

Sandy arrived promptly at ten. The morning was dull with a misty drizzle. She came out with Ted, both sheltering under a large umbrella. Ted carried what looked like a small hamper, and she, a canvas bag containing, he assumed, her painting stuff. They stopped half-way down the path and faced each other in earnest conversation. Sandy got out.

'Hello, old horse!' Ted beamed. 'It'll be a shame if the rain keeps up, what?'

'The forecast promises a fine spring afternoon.' Sandy looked at Emma, who having avoided meeting his eye was now standing silently in front of the passenger door. He took her bag and shut the door after she got in. 'The boot's no use Ted. Put the stuff on the back seat.'

Ted tapped on Emma's window. She wound the window down. He kissed her. 'Enjoy yourself,' he whispered. Then aloud to Sandy: 'Drive carefully, old chap.'

'Wilco.' Sandy stood to attention, gave a mock salute, then laughed as he got in the car. 'I was right about the car. It's horribly orange.' She nodded and he passed her an Ordinance Survey map. 'I've marked the route. Be my navigator.'

'Oh, I'd love to do that! I love maps.' She exclaimed, suddenly coming alive.

'You look so very young in that outfit.'

She was wearing a beige linen shirt and a navy blue pinafore dress. 'It's new. I went shopping with Mabel yesterday. I'm afraid all my clothes are out of fashion. She chose a dress for me and I chose this.'

'What did she choose?'

'A long sleeved dress with a high waistline. There was one with a dropped waistline, I chose that, to please her. Mabel despairs. But I don't like dresses that are too short, or too long.'

'Yes, your dresses are knee-length and slim. Where do you find them?'

'I've got patterns and mother makes them. She makes her own too. She's good.' She glanced down at the map. 'If we're going to Denham, this can't be the direct route?'

'Parts of Iver Heath are worth seeing. I wasn't serious about navigating. I know the area. This is a longer way but it'll give time for the rain to stop.'

'What if the rain doesn't stop?'

'Then we'll find a quiet spot. You can paint from the car. I knew an artist who drove around the Peak District doing just that.'

She looked away. 'I should get cross when you tease me,' she said suddenly. 'I don't know why I don't... Oh, look, the sun! It's coming out! We mustn't miss it.'

'Straight to Denham, then.'

An hour later he crossed the bridge over the Colne river and drove off the road into the car park of a pub. 'It's eleven forty. Let's go in and have a cup of coffee. Then I can arrange to leave the car here. You may like to freshen up. And we'll come back here for afternoon tea.' He got out and opened the door for her.

'Where's the river?'

'About two hundred yards behind you. You see that lock in front? We head for it. That's where the canal and river meet. The embankment is rather steep, but after that we follow the towpath. I'll carry your bag. Can you manage the hamper?'

'Actually, I'll carry my bag. I'm used to it. And the hamper is heavier. Ted's put in glasses and a bottle of wine.'

Later, as they walked towards the cottage by the lock, she whispered her surprise at seeing quite a few people about. 'We'll be moving away from the canal,' he assured her, 'to a quiet corner—still undiscovered, I hope.'

They stood over the lock gates and watched a canal barge rise as the lock filled up. Nearby, two boys were offering bits of bread to a white goose with startlingly pink eyes while an excited man, evidently their father, was trying to record the event on his twin lens Rolliflex camera. Sandy waited till they moved on, then he led the way behind the cottage, where a narrow path wound past bramble and elder, into a clearing. Here the river flowed sluggishly under a frail iron footbridge, designed in miniature to resemble a suspension bridge.

'It is beautiful, Sandy, but are you sure we're not on private land?'

'It's private on the other side of the bridge. We're keeping on this side. Now, if you stand on this stump, you'll see the weir beyond the bridge, and where the river takes a sharp bend. Do you see that grassy knoll? Past the willows? The patch of grass below a large tree? That's the spot.'

'I see some large rocks behind the tree.'

'Yes. One upright like a pillar, and an even larger one lying flat like an altar stone of ancient ritual. Why the smile?'

'Ted warned me you're a romantic. Can we get to those rocks?'

'Yes. Keep close behind me, I'll protect you from the nettles.'

She laughed. 'Those are not nettles. Anyway, I'll use my canvas bag to protect me.'

'What's in it?' He asked.

'A sketch book, a camp stool, a few paints and brushes.'

'I hadn't noticed you had thick long socks.'

'I'd only just pulled them up.'

'God, she's beautiful,' he mumbled to himself as he lifted the hamper above his head and brushed past the bushes. They reached the high bank and began searching around.

'These boulders are granite!' She patted one of them. 'Strange. There are no other rocks in the area.'

'Are you hinting they were brought here by some ancient, iron age tribe?'

She did not answer. 'Oh, look at that fern in the cleft of the rock. Shall I start or do we lunch first?'

'It's your day. Do as you wish. A bit early for lunch. Give it an hour. Where are you going to work?'

'On that flat rock. And you? Where will you be?'

'Somewhere there, within call, if you need anything.'

'I won't need any . . . but you could spread the ground sheet which is at the bottom of the hamper.' When she was settled he asked if she'd like a drink. 'No, thanks. May I see the book you are reading. The poems of John Donne . . . we did Keats in school.'

Less than an hour later she was back, standing over him. 'How are you getting on?' He asked.

'I've made a few sketches. After lunch I'll do a little more work on them,' She knelt on the ground sheet facing him and opened the hamper. 'We've got two scotch eggs, a pork pie cut in quarters, cucumber and salmon sandwiches. Please help yourself.' She handed him a plate. 'You know, the Donne poem, which begins "Go and catch a falling star". Do you agree, nowhere, lives a woman true and fair?'

'I don't think any man does. Not unless . . . We haven't got glasses.'

'Oh dear! Sorry. Drink from the bottle. It's stout. Ted packed that for you. There's coffee in the thermos flask. Enough for both of us.' She burst out laughing. 'I don't know why I'm laughing, but it's the way you looked at me.'

For a long while they ate in silence. 'A penny for your thoughts,' he said at last.

She gave a little shrug. 'I've been thinking about you. Thinking and wondering why you waste your time on me. Why you want to be with me.'

'A million molecular reasons which together form your beautiful shape.'

'Sandy, be serious. Tell me why.'

He dusted his hands, leaned back on them and stared at the branches overhead. Then he took a deep breath. 'Because,' he gazed at her intently, 'because I love you.'

She drew near. 'You must know, have known, livelier women than me?'

'But not anyone as beautiful as you are. More than that, you're fascinating, talented, well read, sweet, innocent . . . everything I want, everything most men would prize in a woman. I'll be the luckiest man on earth if you'll be mine, mine only. Don't say beauty isn't everything. It is for me. That's how it began . . . where it began for me . . . there in the cemetery, at first sight . . . and you haven't done anything to make me stop loving you.'

She sat back, side-saddling her knees together and resting on one arm—reminding him of the little mermaid in Copenhagen.'

He waited as she wistfully traced the hem of her pinafore with her fingers. 'I'm not innocent.' He sensed a note of sadness in her voice. 'It's easy to love beauty, but what about virtue and goodness?'

He laughed. 'You're not suggesting you have neither. You haven't had time to be wicked. As for innocence. That's what I meant, when I said I prize beauty. Beauty is more than looks. It is alive. The soul of beauty is virtue. Every artist knows that.'

'But virtue, goodness, even innocence . . . in the end, are they not boring?'

'Only to the shallow fun-loving world of today. I'd be a fool not to recognise virtue as . . . well, a good thing. The world may ridicule virtue but it can't do without it. People rely on goodness and good people. But, why all this talk? The simple fact is I love you. Analysis murders love. Like taking a rose, pulling out its petals to see how it is formed.'

'You're too clever for me. You mustn't be. And you mustn't love me.'

'You say that because you don't love me? What can I do to make you love me?'

'Nothing.'

'Do you love someone else?'

She shook her head. 'If I did I wouldn't be here.'

'Then what? Do you find me dull? Someone said, sincere people are boring.'

She raised herself on her knees. 'Was she pretty?'

He sat up with a start. 'How do you know it's a woman?'

'I guessed. I'm beginning to know you. It matters to you what women think of you. With men you'll fight your ground, but you want women to understand and like you.' Father was like that too.' She turned away to peer into the hamper. 'Pudding? I've got a chocolate mousse pudding for you.' She handed him a ramekin and a teaspoon.

'Thank you. But you, Emma? Do you like what you understand?'

She shook her head. 'Oh Sandy, Mother thinks we're an odd couple.'

'Mother!'

'She's here.'

The Lotus And The Rose

'What! In London?'

'She arrived last night.'

'So, she knows you're out with me?'

'She's known about us for sometime. That's why she's here'

'And she thinks we're odd?'

'"Flotsam and Jetsam". That's us.'

Sandy laughed. 'I suppose you're Flo and I'm Jet.'

'Don't laugh,' she said with a frown, which on a less attractive person would have been a scowl. 'Mother was perfectly horrid last night. But it doesn't matter.' She sipped her coffee thoughtfully. He wanted to ask why but decided not to. 'Don't forget your coffee,' she said, taking hers to the camp stool on the flat rock.

He tried to read, but couldn't concentrate. So he put down his book and watched her till she stopped and held out a jam jar. 'Sandy, I need water for my brushes.'

He sprang up, took the jar to the stream, filled it and gave it back to her. She smiled. 'Sandy, when I said you don't have to do anything, I meant there is no one else. You and Clare are dear to me.'

Her knees were level with his lips. He leaned forward and kissed them.

'Now let me work,' she said, as if nothing had happened.

He read fitfully till a heaviness overcame him. He lay on his back, put the book over his eyes, and drifted into sleep.

He awoke with a start. The afternoon seemed brighter. He sat up and as he got used to the glare, saw her with growing clarity. She was sitting next to him, her back resting against the tree trunk. 'Have you been here long?' He asked.

'Did I wake you?'

'Have you finished?'

'For now.' She reached behind her and rested her sketch book on her knees.

He crouched beside her. 'I don't suppose you'll let me see what you've done.'

She put the sketch book away and drawing her legs up rested her chin on her knees. His face was within inches of her perfect profile. He gazed mesmerised. Daring, he let his index finger touch her hair and gently trace its sweep over her ear. She froze. 'You were blond?'

His voice trembled. 'Ted showed me the photograph of you aged nine.'

She gave a slight shiver. He lightly kissed her cheek. She shrank like a timid creature cornered by its predator. 'You shouldn't have done that,' she said faintly.

'Are you angry?' he asked.

She shook her head. He stood up. She offered her hand. 'Help me up!' she said.

He pulled her up but did not let go of her hand. Instead he wrapped their clasped hands behind her waist and pressed her hard against him . . . and as he kissed her long and full on the mouth, his free hand rested on her breasts. The soft yielding warmth filled his whole being with a deep comforting sensation, meeting, for the first time, a need which began at his mother's bosom. And as he drank in the carnal pleasure of their embrace, another vision from his subconscious gripped him—one that had lain dormant since the age of fourteen when, on first seeing Botticelli's Venus at the Uffizi, he felt a deep urge, sexual, but at the time inexplicable, to penetrate the fleshy reality of that ideal woman . . .

And Emma, taken by surprise, stayed still long enough to test for herself a new and peculiar thrill that flowed like an electrifying current through her body. Then she raised the hand which hung limply by her side and pushed and wriggled till she was able to free herself. 'Sandy!' she cried. 'Why? Why spoil everything?'

'I don't care!' he said. 'I'm glad. All I've done is show my love in the only way I possibly can.' He turned his back on her and slowly sank on his knees. 'God, I've been a cad! Forgive me.'

'I don't know what to say. Maybe I'm to blame, Sandy.' She stood in front of him and lightly brushed his hair from his forehead. 'I forgive you. There now, stand up.'

'I can't! If I did, you'll really see how I feel. And that will shock you!' He laughed. 'God, this is humiliating.'

'I don't understand, what's so . . . ?' Wide-eyed, she stared at his hands crossed over his crotch. Intuitively she understood and decided not to press the question. 'It's all right, you needn't say.' She sank down next to him. 'I feel funny too. Funny peculiar.'

'Oh, my sweet darling. I'm sorry. I've behaved shamefully. Come, rest your head on my shoulder and give me your hand. I'll be good . . . trust me.' After a while he asked. 'Is that better?'

'Yes, thank you. Do you think that couple there, near the bridge, saw us?'

'They're far too absorbed in each other. Anyway, what if they did. We didn't go as far or even half as long at what they've been up to.'

'I should have known this would happen. We'll have to stop seeing each other.'

'Why? For heaven's sake, Emma! That will crush me. It'll destroy me!'

'I don't want to stop seeing you, but you must promise not to . . . again. I love you, Sandy. I want to be with you . . . and I'm not afraid to be with you, but I fear that kind of love. Say you understand! The pain of that fear. That kind of love. It's messy . . . and it'll kill all the loves I know. That may sound like rubbish but it isn't. I can't explain. I'm so mixed up, Sandy.'

'You are thinking about your father.'

'And the Church . . . and Clare, and painting, and Ted.'

'You'll never lose them, even if you let them go, and those loves need to be set free. Every kind of loving wounds, but wounds have to be healed. They may leave scars, but, well, scars are battle honours, to bare with pride. The love I offer is a possessing one, to be shared . . . an umbrella to shelter under . . . a love to enjoy, to make you and us happy . . . I know, all this sounds silly and as sticky as treacle, but I'm desperate. I so need you. I can't lose you!'

'Don't Sandy! Please no more. I'm so numb. I can't think!'

'Promise, at least, when you're in a mood to give, you'll think of me! Remember, it's not only me; others are not going to leave you alone. Edith, Mary, they have their plans. You'll end up with Trevor. You can't want that?'

'Oh, Sandy! You're going to make me cry.'

'Please you mustn't do that. I'll stop. Come, let's do the English thing. Restore our spirits with a cuppa. Tea and sympathy?'

She whispered: 'There's Clare. I've known her for years.'

'Do you love Clare more than me?'

'It's a different love and it's clean. She loves God.'

'Loving God has to involve being passionate.'

'But God makes no demands.'

'Touché. So, am I just going to be like a brother to you?'

'I have a brother,' she said, folding the ground sheet and starting to pack up.

'Then your love for me, whatever it is, can't be platonic. Admit it or pay a forfeit.'

'I'll admit nothing. But I'll pay a forfeit.' She stood on her toes and gave a quick peck on his cheek. 'Hurry,' she said, 'it's getting late.'

'Good, Lord!' he exclaimed, looking at his watch, 'we are late for tea. It'll have to be a drink. And we won't be back much before seven.'

'I don't care,' she said firmly. 'I'd rather not spend a long evening with mother.'

Neither spoke much during the drive back to Holland Park. 'Stop there,' she pointed as the car went up Campden Hill and drew to a halt in a leafy corner. The late evening lent the sky a warm salmon glow. 'Stay here, Sandy, stay a while.' He switched the engine off and they remained seated in the car. 'Sandy, you look so handsome in this light,' she sighed and lay her head on his shoulder. 'Thank you for a lovely day.'

'Thank you for lunch . . . for everything . . . for being you. I will never forget today.'

They stared ahead in silence. 'Emma,' he said, after a pause he was afraid to break. '*Lawrence of Arabia* is on again in Mayfair. We could see it together. A matinee?'

She shook her head. 'I don't know, Sandy. Walk me to the gate.' She slipped her hand into his, then stopped and look at him. There were tears in her eyes.

'Hey! Now, what's the matter? Why? He felt for his handkerchief. 'It's clean.'

'I know. Everything about you is clean. May I keep it. Thank you. I'll always keep it pressed to my heart.' She smiled briefly and put his handkerchief into her blouse.

'Don't talk as if we won't be seeing each other again!'

'I'm glad you were the first,' she whispered, 'to kiss me.'

'Like Rapunzel you've shut yourself in a tower . . .'

'A tower of my own making. Is that what you were going to say next?'

He stopped. 'Yes, and let down your hair.' He grinned and tried to draw her to himself, but she freed her hand and moved away. 'Emma, please!'

'Sandy, for you own good, you must try to forget me.'

'Never!' He said with a vehemence that startled her. 'Sorry. But I won't let you go. I can't! The thought of another man having you will kill me.'

'I may never marry? I won't let mother bully me.'

She walked towards the gate. He caught up with her and held her back. 'You're far too beautiful. Now that you are out in the open world, men will fall at your feet. You must know that already in the few weeks you have started working.'

'I've told you, Sandy, I won't encourage that kind of attention. Now, I must go in.' She opened the gate and moved into the long shadows of the failing light. There half way up the drive she turned, and waited as if undecided. He walked up to her. 'Sandy, I can't invite you in. It's a bit awkward. I don't think mother wants to see you.'

His pride was hurt. 'Much as I love you, I will not grovel. But don't leave without telling me when we meet next.'

'We can't for sometime. It has nothing to do with this afternoon. I'm going back to Winchester on Tuesday with Mother . . .'

'But your work?'

'That was temporary. I could've told you earlier but I didn't want to spoil our day. I'll write. I'll write often. I'll write always . . . till you stop writing.'

'And where shall I write to?'

She thought for a moment. 'Write to me, here. I'll ask Ted to keep the letters.'

'Yes. But you've got more to tell?'

'Yes. About a fortnight from now, we will be on holiday in France.'

'We means your mother and the Williamses? Trevor will be there?'

'They have a cottage in France. I shan't stay longer than a week. If they plan to stay longer, I'll return on my own. I've told mother.'

'And you'll . . .'

'Yes. I'll tell you. Sandy, when I'm back.' She drew near, leaned forward awkwardly and rested her head on his chest. He kissed her forehead. 'Goodbye Sandy!'

'Not goodbye! Never that.' She move away and looked at him sadly. He suddenly remembered. 'Gosh! Emma! Your stuff?'

'Keep my things. Give the hamper to Ted when you next see him.' She turned and saw her mother walking down the path towards her. Sandy braced himself.

'Good evening, Edith,' he said.

Edith glared at Emma. 'I thought you were never coming in?'

'That's patently not true,' Emma answered brusquely.

'You know what I mean,' Edith said icily. 'Go in. I'd like a word with Sandy.'

'Mother, there's nothing to say to Sandy which you can't say in front of me.'

'Don't be tiresome, I shan't keep him long.' She waited till Emma went indoors. 'So, young man. You two have been going out without so much as a "by your leave"?'

'I don't understand. I have had Emma's consent. She's not a minor.'

'And for someone of your upbringing is that enough? Never mind. I don't mean to be unfriendly nor do I dislike you Sandy . . .' She took a deep breath. 'And I suppose, I must thank you for being honourable. I assume, as her escort your behaviour has been impeccable—what one may expect from an officer and gentleman?' She looked at him steadily. 'Now, I'm asking you, as a gentleman, to bow out of her life.'

'Bow out? Why? I shall bow out when Emma tells me to.'

'Hear me out. I want you—as I said, I'm not being unfriendly—I want you to think about someone else's feelings besides mine and Emma's.'

'You mean Trevor's.'

'Yes. How did you know? Never mind. Yes, Trevor. Mary—you remember Mary—and I, we more or less assume Emma and Trevor will finally get together.'

'An arranged marriage, in a liberal society?'

'Nonsense! Nothing is being arranged—are you being ironic, using the word liberal to me? They've known each other for a long time. Emma's no prisoner. It'll be as she wishes . . . decides. Of course, we hope she sees our plans for her future as a sensible way to settle down. Women have to be practical, Sandy. When one is not, as it seems in Emma's case, then the good common-sense of women who know better, is called for.'

'You do Emma an injustice. She's more than sensible. She's also a good . . .'

'Goodness and good sense don't go together. And, young man, you might pay me the compliment of my knowing my own daughter.'

'And what if you force her into joining a convent . . .'

'That's different . . . anyway, I happen to know, it's no longer something she . . . really, none of this is any business of yours.'

'I have made it my business and I don't see why Trevor should have any greater consideration . . . I mean, I deserve as much. Let Emma decide.'

'You astonish me, Sandy. I am asking you to stop seeing her. Do you realise what you're doing to her reputation. You have been seen together. In these matters the world always assumes the worst.'

'Edith, I love Emma. I have since I first saw her and I have no intention of . . .'

'I feared this. I wish you hadn't told me. And I'll ask you not to spread it about. Has Emma accepted? Has she said she loves you?'

'Not precisely. But she still wants to go out with me.'

'I'm sorry. In that case I am free to press what I'd prefer her to do. For the sake of friendship, I sincerely hope you'll get over this-this infatuation. This is schoolboy stuff, Sandy. You disappoint me. A bachelor, eligible in every way, you're a prize for any gal. I gather you get an allowance from a rich uncle—the sort of thing one reads in novels—and that your clothes are tailored in Saville Row?'

'What has that got to . . . what are you trying to say?'

'I'm reminding you that you're highly attractive and eligible.'

'But not good enough for Emma.'

'I neither said nor implied . . . *Au contraire*, the implication is clearer in its suggestion that you're too good for her. Think. I'm doing you a favour.'

'I'm not too good for Emma. No one is. I hope she doesn't find that out. But I am certainly more worthy of her than Trevor. He shows little interest.'

'You can't know that for certain. And why do you think you're more worthy? He's at least nearer her age. But, whatever your intentions, you won't get anywhere with her.' She waited. 'She won't be touched, you know. She hates physical contact.'

He saw the trap and checked himself in time. Compressing his lips, he shrugged.

'And, if ever, if ever she did, it would only be in a moment of madness. It will mean nothing to her. She's quite mad, you know. I thought you'd see that.'

'Good grief! Edith, how could you! How could you speak of her like that? She's a little unworldly, awkward maybe. But I rather like that. And if she's mad, she is less and less each time we meet.'

'Goodnight, Sandy, and goodbye.'

He watched her retreating figure, and waited till the light in the hall went out and the house shrouded in darkness. Then he walked to the car and drove with the attention of one bent on putting aside the happenings of the immediate past.

Writing came easily to Sandy, but after his fourth unanswered letter to Emma, he dried up and found it impossible to continue. It was increasingly hard to pretend he mattered to her and he grew angry with himself for being so hopelessly in love. Three weeks had passed since his confrontation with Edith and, with no calls from Ted, he despaired. But in the fourth week Ted called. 'Sorry, old chap. Didn't forget . . . but you must see how bloody awkward my position is. I've had it out with the mater and decided it is best to leave it to her and Emma to sort things out . . . What? No, I haven't heard from Emma. Abso-bally-lutely no idea where she is. Back from France? Oh, yes; weeks ago. I've put your letters in her desk. Had to hide them from prying old Mabs. Well, nil, as they say desperandum, old boy. Emma's never been a great one for letters. But, if she promised, she'll get back to you . . . The mater and Mary Williams may well have driven her into the arms of Clare at the Convent.'

Ted's call did little to alleviate Sandy's sense of desolation. He poured himself a large whisky and searched for a cigarette, but gave up when he couldn't find one. He needed help. Someone he could open his heart to. Then he remembered Bill's mother, Una. She knew, because he had told her about Emma last Easter. And she was happy for him. He rang. Could he see her as soon as possible? She invited him to come over on Saturday night to spend Sunday with her. Tomorrow was Saturday. He looked at his watch. Dinner and cinema? Why not! He patted a low pile of exercise books and smiled. Not many left to mark. He would do the rest when he got back from Stoke Poges. He showered and dressed, as he always did, for the evening. Ignoring the lift, he took the stairs and going through the foyer glanced at the table where the caretaker left the post. Nothing but a picture card! He looked at it and his heart raced. It was from her. "Dear Sandy", it read. "Forgive me. I can't think what to write. I think of you every hour of the day. The week has passed. Tomorrow I leave for London, love, E. PS. I can't stop thinking of you.' He studied the date on the frank. It had taken a fortnight to reach him! He ran up the stairs, two at a time, to his flat, put a fresh sheet in the typewriter and sat staring at it. He looked out of the window. It was raining. He studied the card again. It was a picture of the Basilica to Joan of Arc at Doremy. The door bell rang, and rang again. He started with a cold sense of foreboding. The bell rang for the third time. He went to the door and opened it. It was Emma. She looked wild, wet and beautiful.

Emma had said she would ring after lunch but Sandy stayed by the telephone all morning. There was no reason why she should ring earlier than she said she would but Sandy hoped she might. He even tried calling but got Edith—a curtly polite Edith—on the line. She told him Emma had had a bad night, was not to be disturbed, and would call him if she wanted to. At eleven he telephoned Una. The trip to Stoke Poges had to be cancelled. Lord! what a mess he had made of things last evening!

'Una? Dear, dear Una, I'm miserable! Utterly, hopelessly. Forgive me, but as things are I can't come over . . . Sorry! I know you'll understand . . . Hello! Hello! Are you there?'

A slight pause preceded the deep tones of a familiar voice—soft, warm, and a little shaky. 'Now, Sandy, calm down. Tell me all, and don't worry if you can't come over. I don't mind in the least. Now, what's the matter? Tell mother.'

'Oh. mother, I'm so desolate!'

'I've got that bit. Wringing your hands won't help. Now go on.'

'I've been such an idiot. Emma came to see me . . . Yes, at my flat. It was brave of her and-and, I made a mess of everything. When? Yesterday, evening, not more than a few hours after I rang you. I said and did all the wrong things, and there's nothing I can do to make it right. Yes, we quarrelled, or as good as . . . she took me by surprise. I was hurt, because she hadn't written, so foolishly, instead of saying the right things . . . I failed her.'

'Stop this breast beating. As good as, means you didn't actually quarrel.'

'She asked for advice, asked what she should do. Stupidly I kept mum.'

'Asked for advice, about what?'

'A decision that affected her whole life . . . and mine. She turned to me for help, and I failed to reach out to her. I should've been level-headed. I should've been thinking of her . . . instead of being touchy and sensitive. I can't understand what came over me. I've been a fool . . . The thought of losing her forever is unthinkable. And now I can't reach her. What can I do to make things right?'

'There you go again! Rambling, not making sense. You still haven't told me.'

'Haven't I? Sorry.' He paused to think. 'Well, I told you about Edith and Mary, her neighbour. They're close friends. They've planned this for a long time, they want Emma to marry Trevor . . .'

'Trevor? Who's Trevor?'

'Trevor's Mary's son. The chap she's going to marry . . .'

'I thought there wasn't any chap in her life . . . till there was you.'

'Yes and no. It's a long story.'

'Never mind, carry on.'

'I'm certain they pressed Emma after they returned from France. She was there on holiday. Trevor was too. Now he's here. They're lunching together, today, when he's going to ask her to marry him!'

'But if she doesn't care for him, she won't accept.'

'She will, if she thinks it's the right thing to do. And why she asked for advice. She's not the sort of girl to think about her own feelings . . .'

'But, she must know marriage is big step . . . the biggest. However sweetly docile she is, I can't see her willing, not with you around, to marry—just to please her mother.'

'What shall I do?'

'Sandy, there's more to all this. Yes, you've been blind, and for quite some time, and you've missed the broadest possible hint or do I mean compliment any woman can offer a man. Tell me exactly what she said? Did she actually say she going to accept?'

'Thinking of accepting. I couldn't believe my ears. I stared at her lost for words. The Indian in me wanted to cry out: "You can't! You don't love Trevor! What about me!'

'But you played the tight-lipped Englishman and said nothing. Sandy, you silly boy. She was trying to get you to say something, not anything. The right words. Words she wanted you to say. Clearly you did not. What, in the end, did you say?'

'I said it was a decision she had to make for herself.'

'Good heaven's, Sandy! I'm surprised. Not like you to be so insensitive. Surely you wanted to shake her, plead with her, beg her not to be influenced by others. That she couldn't marry Trevor because *you* wanted to marry her. It was a cue for a proposal. Why didn't you? Why didn't you say you wanted to marry her? That's what she wanted to hear from you.'

'Because I wasn't sure she loved me enough . . . and I was afraid she might say that.'

'If she didn't love you, she would not have come to you. A modest girl like Emma would not have come to your flat, or see any reason to visit you if she didn't care.'

'I've been a fool! I see her now, standing by the door, about to leave saying: "I may as well get this marriage business over and done with!"'

'And you stood on your pride and turned ironical?'

'I said, convenience was the worst reason for marrying.'

'And she said she didn't see why, in time, she couldn't grow to love Trevor?'

'Yes! Those very words!'

'And you, heavens above! Sandy, don't tell me you asked if this was the end.'

'Oh, yes!. She stamped her foot. Said I was being impossible. Was I?'

'I would have slapped your face. But then I'm not Emma.'

'But why?'

'Have you at anytime said you wanted to marry her?'

'Did I need to say it! She must know how much I love her. My letters are full of . . .'

'Not enough. You had to pledge yourself—not just your love. A woman must have the exact words. To be certain; and to hold it against you if you renege, or at any time when she feels you ought to renew your pledge. Women are eminently practical. Your silence must have hurt her deeply.'

Sandy groaned. 'What can I do now? It's too late!'

'It's never too late to tell a woman you want to marry her. If she accepts what's-his-name's proposal—she might now out of sheer pique—it's not the end of the matter. Give her the chance to choose even at this eleventh hour. It may be hard on him, but if he's waited for Mary and Edith to push him, he's not worthy of her and deserves no quarter. All's fair, as the saying goes, in love and war. He'll survive. Men like that do.'

Sandy sprang to his feet, excited. 'I know where they're lunching. I'll go there. Now, before he's had the chance to say anything . . .'

'Whoa, m'lad! Hold your horse. Is she's the sort of girl who'd like scenes? No. Well, then, don't make matters worse. Wait. be patient. And we better keep this line free, just in case. But I think you could safely wait for this evening, or tomorrow.'

'And if I don't get a chance. If her mother . . .'

'Find one. Make certain of that. Also put it in writing and make it the best letter you've ever written. You'll be all right. I'll remember you in my prayers. Bill will be happy for you. He's always said you'll make a good husband. Have you eaten? Make yourself something, now. And come over for Whitsun. Bring Emma along.'

The Lotus And The Rose

Sandy broke an egg into a bowl, whisked it, adding milk, sugar, and a sprinkle of nutmeg. Then he dipped in two slices of bread, waited till they soaked up the liquid, poured the mixture into a buttered shallow dish and placed it under the grill. Then he opened the kitchen window and gazed over the roof tops at the river. Hammersmith Bridge gleamed green in skies washed by overnight rain. He took a deep breath and tried emptying his mind, but the sight of the bridge brought back the memory of that misty morning drive to Winchester three years ago . . . and with it the haunting beauty of the face in the cemetery . . . The letter! He raced to the desk, stared motionlessly at the sheet of paper on his typewriter. How shall I begin, he wondered. "Darling Emma! Can you forgive a foolish man?" No. I'll write "Emma will you marry me?" He looked at the telephone, threw his head back and sighed. "Sweet Jesu!"

The telephone gave one ring and stopped. He sat up with a start and stared at it dumbfounded. He got up, walked to the cooker and turned off the grill. Then he went back to the telephone. It rang. He snatched the receiver. 'Hello!'

'Sandy!' It was Emma.

'Yes! Darling it's Sandy, I love you.' A pause. 'Emma? Hello! Are you there?'

'Yes.' Another pause. 'Sandy, will you . . .'

'Emma, I can't hear you!'

'Sandy, will you marry me?'

'Of course! But that's what I was going to ask you. What about Trevor?'

'We talked. In the cab. We both knew it was hopeless. I got off at Swan and Edgar. That's where I am now.'

'So you haven't had lunch? Of course, you haven't.'

'Have you?' Her voice was clearer and more confident.

'No. It's under the grill.'

'We could share it.'

'No, it's dreadful. A kind of bread pudding. Mother's recipe. Tastes like nothing I remember. Give me time to get to you. I'll take a cab. Meet me at The Royal Academy. In the restaurant. You know, we've been there.'

'You haven't answered my question.'

'I have! Yes, yes, a countless times yes! I'll say it with flowers if I find any. I love you and I want you to be with me forever. I've been a pompous idiot, not to say it to you when you were here. Darling, Emma, be my wife.'

'I'll be in the forecourt, Sandy. Not the restaurant.'

'What's that sound? Are you in a telephone thingy?'

'Quick! Go on, there's time. I knew you cared.'

'Loved, as I've told you, from the day we first met!' The telephone went dead.

Sandy arrived at The Royal Academy carrying a pot of African violets. The forecourt was crowded but he saw her almost immediately. She was sitting on a step in the far left hand corner, crouching like one trying to be inconspicuous and looking, Sandy thought, so like The Virgin in Rossetti's *Annunciation*. Curiously, Emma's own thoughts were back in those convent years when at fourteen she wanted to be a nun; but ill-health—a mysterious, persistent fever, and a long convalescence at a Spanish mountain village—ended that aspiration. He put the flower-pot down and stood at the bottom of the steps. She looked frail, vulnerable. He feared to startle her. She saw him, stood up and smiled. She held her handbag in the crook of her arm, and brushed down the front of her ivory white dress; then nervously played with a double stranded necklace of amethyst beads.

'Forgive me!' he spread his hands apologetically.

She stretched out a hand like a child offering it in trust and for protection.

'My God! I'm the luckiest man in the world. Tell me I'm not dreaming? That you meant every word you said on the telephone.'

'I don't joke,' she answered simply.

'Then say you love me! Say you'll be my wife. Say it again. I must see you say it.'

'Hush, Sandy, not here!'

His hands trembled. 'Let's find a place to eat. Oh, I got these.' He picked up the flowerpot. 'Couldn't find anything better. I'll make up for it, later.'

'It's too late in the day to find flowers. We'll be lucky to find lunch. I adore African violets. Thank you.'

'I'm sure the restaurant across the road will give us lunch.'

'At a price.' She stepped down and pressed against him. 'I'm not very hungry.'

'We'll celebrate with the best champagne they have? Yes? That settles it. Something light with it . . . an omelette? No, I remember. They serve excellent *hors-d'oeuvre, tapas*. Or whatever. I confess I've been there before, many years ago, with my uncle. It was a nice place then. I hope it hasn't changed.'

They crossed the court and into Piccadilly. 'Why didn't you contact father then?'

'I was entirely in my uncle's hands—a young man, accompanying a rich uncle on a holiday tour of Europe. Anyway, it was probably a good thing. You'd have been so little that I couldn't have looked upon you again with all the lustful desire I do now.'

'Was it the uncle you . . .'

'Yes. Jaggers? He's been like a father to me. But don't change the subject. All I've had is one stolen kiss, eons ago, and here we are about to marry, behaving like an old couple, as if we're out on some anniversary celebration. Emma, yesterday, if only you rushed into my arms . . . there wouldn't have been any misunderstanding. I'm wholly to blame, and I dread to think how nearly I could have lost you.'

She took his arm as they entered the restaurant. 'I was cross with you, Sandy,' she whispered calmly. 'But I'm here now, which proves I love you.' They were shown a table. The waiter, promptly took their order, sensed the occasion and assured them to leave everything to his judgement. When he left she reached across the table and held Sandy's hand. 'Don't look at me like that. You'll have all the time in the world to do whatever you like.'

'God, does it show!' He studied her face. It was alight with absolute sincerity. 'Just you wait . . . you're going to be treated like no woman's been treated before. Last night, I was mad, stupidly proud. Nothing and no one now is going to take you away from me. Though l dread the day you realise you're the most beautiful woman in the world.'

'When I do, I will remember, if it wasn't for you, Sandy, I would never have known what it is to be in love.'

He looked down at their clasped hands. 'Gosh!' he whispered. 'How brown my hand looks against yours.'

'You have lovely hands. You move them beautifully. It was the first thing I noticed about you. Your hands.'

'I suppose it's the result of the time spent in Tuscany.' He grinned.

'Why were you in Tuscany?'

'I was on my way to England when I got the mad idea of staying in Florence, long enough to write about the Medici. I soon realised it was a waste of time. I had nothing original to say. Besides my sister spoiled me.'

'Sister! In Italy?'

'Yes. Quite a bit older than me. Married an Italian POW. She was a WAC in Delhi. Italian POWs were sent there. Those known to be anti-fascist were debriefed and asked to contribute towards the war effort. After the War she went with him to Italy.'

'And your father let her?'

'She made sure he had to.' He grinned as he studied the frown on her face. 'She was pregnant . . . Her only daughter was born during the voyage.'

'You said she spoilt you?'

'I mean, she gave me money to spend. More importantly, her husband Nino—his name's Giovanni—has a friend who let me spend a month in his flat in Venice. That was a turning point. I've led the life of a traveller, never long at any place. But Venice is a dream . . . but dreams are fleeting. It's not a place for staying on. And England has always beckoned . . .' The waiter brought a tray of neatly arranged *hors-d'oeuvre*, and a bottle of champagne, which he poured with great finesse, and left them. Sandy raised his glass. 'To us,' he said.

She took a sip, her eyes widened. 'And England.'

'England's special. It's always been my deepest regret I cannot call England my own, because it's not my birthright. That's an Anglophile's tragedy. Still, it's home.'

'Tell me more about your sister?'

'I mustn't bore you. I don't even know how we got there. Hey, listen! Why don't we honeymoon in Italy?'

'Oh. Sandy! That would be wonderful!'

'How soon can we marry? Emma, I can't wait.'

She blushed. 'As soon as we can. I'll get a job.'

'You don't have too. We'll be okay, financially. And there's my flat.'

'Tom Ashworth—a publisher and old friend of my father—likes my work. He said, just what you said, that my work was like Marianne North's.'

'Have you seen her stuff at Kew? Kew Gardens.'

'Yes. But not since father took me. That was years ago. I wanted to be like her, and dreamed of travelling the world with a paint box . . . I even imagined meeting you on my travels.' She sighed. 'It would never have happened. I was a girl then and not brave or adventurous enough.'

'Marianne North liked the hill-stations of India. Maybe she was brave but, I gather, she was never alone. Not in Simla . . . she had a large escort and a posse of servants who accompanied her into the hills. But then the Viceroy may have insisted.'

'She hugged herself. 'Say you love me.'

'Actions speak louder than words,' he said, failing to keep a straight face. 'Lean forward and I'll kiss you.'

'You're being horrid. You know we can't reach. Ted tells me you're a poet.'

'Good Lord! Did he mention my slim volume of verse?'

The waiter came and deferentially inquired if everything was to their satisfaction. Sandy thanked him. 'We better tuck in, Emma. Can't disappoint the chap. Here let me choose for you. Look! I don't believe it. Didn't you make something like this.'

She shook her head. 'No. These are delicious!'

He laughed. 'You said that so seriously. You're a good cook. Believe me.'

They ate silently for sometime, then she said: 'Mother thinks I'm idle.'

He raised his brows. 'You are. My idol. I'm joking. Try the rolled ham. The fillings are out of this world. She can't be serious.'

'She thinks dad spoilt me. But daddy understood me. He said he'd make sure I was financially independent.'

'Ted doesn't mind? About the will I mean.'

'The will was as much Ted's idea. They drew it out together. Dad knew Ted has a well-established practice . . . it's also something to do with Mabel. And mother has the house in Winchester. Ted's like a father to me.'

'I know. And I'm only two years younger!'

'Ted looks his age. You don't.' She peered at the tray. 'There's a lot there I'm not too keen to try. Are those quail's eggs?'

'Yes. Have what you like. I'll send for the menu.'

'No, Sandy, don't. There's more than enough here.'

'Were you suggesting, earlier, that your father didn't care much for Mabel?'

'Yes. Poor Ted. He comes . . . we all come, very low in her priorities. She cares only for her boutique. And to be fair, Kitty.'

'I was very fond of your father.'

'I know. But you were a boy then. He would be proud to see you now, looking so handsome . . . and he would have seen how much I loved you.' Suddenly the expression on her face changed to one of anguish. 'You hurt me yesterday, Sandy!'

'But, my sweet. I thought you'd forgiven me?'

'When did you first come to England?' He detected a catch in her voice.

'When I was four. This was before I met your father in India. I only know I did. My parents were here on a long holiday. Then I came twice with my uncle, in my teens.'

'And this time, this last time on your own?'

'April 1956.'

'Sandy, daddy died on the 30th of October, that year.'

'Emma, I'm truly sorry. I should've kept in touch.'

'He was my whole world. I miss him terribly!'

'I'll make up for all the pain you suffered and I'll give you all the love you deserve. Your father will know. I believe that. I'm not just saying it.'

'But why didn't you come in fifty-six?'

'Darling, you know how it is. Life is full of regrets. Time flies, good intentions fall by the wayside. I was in teacher training college, and the next year mother died. I took time off and stayed with Bill; for comfort. I was so devastated by the news of her death. I know what it is to lose someone you love. Why I understand how you feel. Not to be with her, at the end, is a constant regret.'

'So, why did you come to England?'

Sandy grinned, 'I was running away from marriage or rather pressure to marry. For two years my family had been pressing me to marry. A girl was found for me. I'd have been married in '55, if they had had their way.'

'Was she pretty?'

'Yes. At least from her photograph. I never actually met her.' He smiled. 'No, not pettier than you, no one can be or has been, or ever will be.'

'An arranged marriage? But don't Christians in India follow Western customs. My father said they did.'

'He was probably thinking about Anglo-Indians—I mean Eurasians. And yes, some Indian Christians. But, in many ancient families, conversion to Christianity meant little or no change in life-style and values. So an arranged marriage isn't that unusual. And apart from my immediate family, all my other relations are Hindus.'

'How did you escape it, the marriage, I mean.'

'My two allies were my mother and Jaggers. Mother told them to leave me alone and Jaggers really quashed the whole affair. He understands me best. We've been close. I've lived with him for years and studied at his old college. We are alike in many ways, but I can't say I know him. He's a man of infinite reserve, westernised and widely travelled.'

'Is he, like you, an Anglophile?

'I'm not sure. If anyone else in the family was, it was dad. But changed, after Indian Independence and turned mildly anti-British, and so, at times, hostile to me.'

But your uncle doesn't mind you being an Anglophile?'

'No. And it was in his library I found books by Anglophiles. Dixon and an American named Drew. There were others. In the thirties and forties the world thought well about the Englishman. My family has been closely associated with the British for generations, so it won't surprise me if he was. He's different now, living very much in the style and manner of a nawab or landowner, He is a Hindu, bur steeped in Mogul culture . . . Emma, what's the matter?'

She was shivering. 'Sandy, suppose your family is against our marriage.'

'It's up to me. I'm a free man. And your family is known to mine. They'll be happy to know I am getting married—having more or less given up on me.'

'You could, at any time, catch a plane and disappear, and leave me broken . . .'

He laughed. 'Emma, my little dilemma! Can you see me doing that?'

'Your uncle could stop your allowance.'

'Then I shall marry you for your money.' He grinned.

'Yes!' Her face brightened.

'I'm joking. I didn't marry the girl my family wanted me to and Jaggers stood by me. He knows an Indian wife was not for me. He won't stop my allowance. And he knows about you. I've told him. How we met and how beautiful you are. Years ago, when he was a young man in Europe, he loved a French woman. He let his family talk him out of marrying her. He warned me not to make the same mistake. "Marry the woman who'll make you happy", he said, "Don't let her go." Well, I won't.'

'I love you, Sandy. Will that be enough to make you happy?'

'That's all I ask.' He held her hands. 'Believe me, Jaggers would be delighted when I cable the news. He'd love to see you if he could travel. But he's a sick man.'

'He sounds loveable. Does he mind being called Jaggers?'

'No. But when we wanted to get round him it was *mah mah*. That means uncle—mother's brother. Father's brother is *cha cha*.'

'Is he's married?'

'Yes. But in all my years with him, he's been alone. Alone, that is, in a big house run by servants. After an adventurous past, he now lives like a recluse. I don't pry. He likes that. But, yes, he did marry, and soon after, installed his wife in a house in Jodhpur and was off on his travels. She didn't mind. On his return they agreed to live apart, and have ever since.'

'And children?'

'None. Why I'm like a son to him. On the day I got my exam results, I was sixteen, he was happy I'd done well and said he was going out to order a new suit for me. But he returned, late for dinner, drunk. The cook and the watchman put him to bed. I dined alone, then picked up a book to read . . .'

The Lotus And The Rose

The waiter came up to the table. 'Would you like a dessert, sir?'

'No, thank you,' said Sandy. 'Could I have the bill?'

'You were reading?' She prompted.

'Yes, I remember the book . . . one of the best books on India . . . *Indian Mosaic* by Mark Channing . . . about an hour later, I felt a hand on my shoulder. I knew it was him. He was sober, tearful and standing by my chair, splendidly robed in a deep red *kaftan*. He told me I reminded him of his father—my grandfather. That night he gave me this signet ring.'

'It's beautiful and it has your initials'

'That's grandfather's, we have the same . . . S-T.' The waiter came with the bill. Sandy paid it and they walked towards the door. 'It's raining!'

'Excuse me, sir, but the lady's left her handbag.'

Emma started. 'I've never done that before! Thank you.'

The waiter bowed. 'You and madam may wait in the coffee lounge till the rain stops. It'll be all right.' He led them to a room with sofas, chairs, two large coffee tables, and a clear view of the street.

'Thank you,' said Sandy. 'We'll be off as soon as it stops.' The room appeared to be empty but Sandy chose a corner far from the entrance to the restaurant. They sat close together. She took his hands. 'Sandy, I've done an awful thing. Sorry. I've left the pot of African violets behind! On the steps of the Royal Academy.'

He laughed. 'Never mind, someone will have given it a home by now.' He put his arm round her waist, then at a sudden thought withdrew it.

'What is it,' she asked.

'How will your mother and Ted take the news? Trevor would've told them?'

'I telephoned Ted before I spoke to you. It was Ted who suggested I call you. He had no doubts about your feelings towards me. As for mother, we'll soon see. I know she would rather I married Trevor—but that has nothing to do with your being Indian. If that's what you're thinking.'

For a moment he was taken aback by her intuition. 'And . . . well, I'm jealous. Emma. You must have loved Trevor enough to be prepared to marry him?'

'No. I was being silly.'

'What about those years without me, the years with Trevor.'

'He seemed more keen on Ted's company. They spent hours tinkering in the garage. His other keen interest is dancing, which I hate. We went once. I was awful. Trevor is easily put off. Which is good. We don't have to worry about his feelings.' She put her handbag on her lap, passed her hands through her necklace, till it rested on her thumbs. 'What would you have done if, to please mother, I'd accepted Trevor's proposal?'

'I'll tell you all about that later, but before you rang, I had made up my mind. I was determined to confront you and stop you. Begging you to marry me . . . insisting that you choose between us.'

Her lips trembled. 'You must understand how close I was to losing you. I want to know, that whatever happened I was never going to lose you, because I do so love you. Oh Sandy!' She covered her face and sobbed gently.

'Please! Emma! Believe me, it was a moment's aberration. If only you knew what I went through. I tried ringing you after you left and despaired when I got Edith and not you. Then I rang Bill's mother—I'll tell you about Una later. She strengthened my determination. I would have gone through hell and high water to get you back. If you hadn't phoned, I would have found a way to tell you. Yes, today!'

She sniffed and searched her handbag. He offered his handkerchief. She took it. 'Thank you.'

'If it wasn't for my stupid gentlemanly scruples, I'd be kissing you now, and to hell with what the world thinks.'

'But I love you for being a gentleman!' She looked up at him. Her smile grew till it tucked the corners of her mouth into prominent dimples.

'Now you look like Vivien Leigh,' he said.

Two women entered the room and sank into the chairs nearest the doors. They were talking excitedly and almost incessantly. One was unmistakably American. But the voice of her English friend caught Sandy's attention. He knew it only too well. The American was facing him. Little more than a girl, she beamed with the health and vigour American tourists seem almost invariably to have. She had caught Sandy's glance and whispered to her companion. A pretty blonde head leaned forward and peered round her winged-back chair. 'Why, Sandy! You rogue!' With a jump and a bound she was almost across the room. 'What are you doing here? Were you at the Summer Exhibition?'

'No,' he said limply, aware that while she spoke her eyes were on Emma.

'Aren't you going to introduce me . . . us?' The American girl had joined them.

'Yes. Of course!' He quickly recovered. 'This is Emma Franks. Emma, this is Sally Watson, a teacher and, for my sins, a colleague.' He laughed.

'And this is Tracy Feldman from Boston,' Sally said, still grinning.

'Hi there!' said Tracy.

'Now, Tracy,' Sally went on, 'here, indeed, is someone who's studied England with a love which passes my understanding. He knows more about England than I or any of my friends do . . . or care to know.'

'Now, is that a fact!' Tracy transferred a bemused look from Sally to Sandy.

'Sally exaggerates,' said Sandy.

'It's true,' said Emma quietly. Her chin went up, the upper lip drooped, the eyes grew large and solemn. Sandy drank in the vision. It was the "blessed-damozel-leaned—out-from-the-golden-bar-of-heaven" look; and he yearned to embrace her.

'We dropped in for an early cup of tea. Join us!' Sally said. 'We'll get a table sooner if we are four. Sandy?'

'I thought the restaurant wasn't full.'

'It is now.'

'Thank you but we've just had lunch. Yes, a late lunch. We've been waiting for the rain to stop.'

'The rain stopped ten minutes ago!' Sally's eyes had a distinct twinkle.

'So it has! So it has. Well, we better be going then, before it starts again.' He shook hands with Tracy. 'Nice meeting you. Enjoy your stay in London. Bye, Sally.'

They stepped out on to the wet pavement. The air was heavy, the skies uniformly a deep grey, while all around the buildings were spot-lighted with a revealing white light, a phenomenon Sandy associated with England. 'Left? Right? Where to?' he asked.

'We could stroll a bit in Green Park, then the tube to Hammersmith.'

'Hammersmith? My place?'

'Yes. There's plenty of time. I don't want to get home to mother before Ted. Ted said he'd try to leave early but couldn't promise to be home before six.' She took his arm and for a while they walked in silence.

'She's pretty,' Emma said suddenly.

'Sally?'

'And wearing one of Mabel's inventions . . . an A-line sleeveless dress.'

'I like what you wear. Honestly!' He turned to look at her, his lips almost brushing her temples, and from his height guessed she was five feet six inches tall.

'What is it,' she inquired, turning to meet his gaze.

Sandy started. Her face had never been so close for study and he was struck by the clarity of her features. The afternoon light picked out specks of gold on her thick, soft, chestnut hair, which framed her face and slender neck in sharp contrast to her pale skin. But it was the rare melancholy gaze of her blue eyes that he found unsettling. It would take a hard man to hurt her, he thought.

'You know,' he stopped by a shop window, 'I've never bought you a present. We could choose something together? A dress of your choice?'

'Yes, but not now. Let it be a surprise.'

'A wrong choice would be a waste.'

'Choose dark or very light colours. Plain not print. Knee length.'

'Size?'

'Ten.'

'There's something else I have for you. You'll see.'

She was twisting her necklace thoughtfully and appeared not to have heard him. 'Sally,' she said, 'isn't the sort of person one would expect a teacher to be . . . like.'

The Lotus And The Rose

He chuckled. 'Sally's a chameleon. You saw her as you would in the staff room and outside school. You won't see that side of her in the classroom. Quite a disciplinarian.'

'I envy women who are vivacious and socially at ease. Women like her.'

'I'm glad you're not like Sally. I couldn't relax with someone like Sally. It's tiring to be on one's toes, constantly. Don't change. Remember the Fred Astaire song: "Oh, but you're lovely, never, never change . . ." something like that.' He grinned down at her.

'I can see, Sally is very fond of you.'

'She's a tease. I wasn't going to be another notch on her six-shooter. You're miles more attractive . . . no, wrong word, she's attractive, you're beautiful.'

At the park gates he stood aside, and as she went past, bent down and lightly kissed her lips. She responded, awkwardly. He tried to kiss her again, but she slipped by, then waited and took his arm. 'Not in public,' she whispered.

'This is a civilised country. People don't stare.' He said.

She started to walk. 'Do you find me cold and distant?'

He thought for a moment. 'I don't know. There has to be passion lurking behind all that calm beauty. One can't be artistic or religious without passion. You've been such a challenge, you know. But I liked challenges. Like a mountaineer facing Everest, I had to conquer you, because you're there and can listen to all this rubbish and not giggle.'

She pinched his arm and gave a reluctant smile. 'You can't be serious for long. It's one of the things I love about you. Anyway this mountain came to Mohammed. It had to be you. No one else.' She pressed against him.

'The words of another song: "It had to be you".

'You're so widely informed. The children in your class must love you.'

'I don't know what to say. But now. How long must I wait before I can crush you up and smother you with kisses?'

'Later,' she said with the solemn composure of one who gave the proposal serious consideration. 'Yes. I like you kissing me. Why do you laugh?'

'Not for anything you said, but because of the way you said it.'

'You're being horrid. You get away with a lot because of your charm. Everyone you meet must find you charming.'

'I've failed dismally with your mother?'

'No. She may resist it, but I know she finds you charming.'

'Not enough to want me as a son-in-law.'

'If she wasn't so set on my marrying Trevor, and wasn't such a great friend of Mary, I don't know what . . .'

'Ah, Mary! Now there's someone who distinctly dislikes me.'

Her face clouded. 'We're going to have to face mother this evening, and she's going to have to accept you. Ted will be there to support us.'

'Poor chap. He must wish we hadn't placed him in this position. How soon?'

'What's the time?'

'Four-thirty-five . . . thirty-six.'

'There's time. We'll go to your place, for tea.' She stopped and pointed. 'Let's go though the trees and sit there on that grassy slope for a while. Then we can make our way back to the tube.'

'Yes. Remind me to telephone Una, Bill's mother. This morning I woke up fearing my world had come to an end. That I'd lost you, especially after your mother wouldn't let me speak to you. I phoned Una and she gave me hope and all the courage I needed. She's like a mother to . . .' he stopped. She was not listening. The wild look in her eyes shocked him. She began to tremble. Suddenly she freed herself and ran away from him. He caught up with her and with a firm grip on her arms, turned her round to face him. She struggled to free herself. 'Emma! What is the matter?' Then as he held her pressed against the trunk of a plane tree, she calmed down. 'Please! Emma, I'm going to let go. People will think I'm assaulting you. There. Please. Stay calm.'

'Is everything all right?' Asked a small man leading a Springer-spaniel.

Emma nodded and put her arms round Sandy, who raised a reassuring hand. 'Help me, Sandy! I'm afraid! Afraid of the future.'

'You have nothing to fear, Emma!

'Promise me, you'll always love me!'

'Always. I promise. There now, take deep breaths. Why this sudden anxiety?'

'I'm all mixed up. I wanted be like Clare . . . at peace in a Convent. But now I want to be with you. Promise, you'll stand up to mother . . . that you won't take no for an answer? You can be proud, sensitive. She'll use that to-to have her way.'

'Nothing will stop me. We'll elope if we have to. I could take you to places in India where you'll find all the peace you want. I'll always be there. I don't need to work, you know that.' He looked about him. 'Oh, to hell with decorum!' He gathered her in his arms and kissed her repeatedly, and in the intervals between kisses she whispered in his ear: 'Say you'll never leave me and after I'm gone you won't hold another woman like this!' She tried to push him away. 'You must promise me that!'

He stopped. 'What on earth are you talking about? You're not going anywhere!' Then he understood. 'Tommy rot! You'll outlive me. Women outlive men. We're stuck with each other—forever, like limpets on the rock of eternity.' He started to laugh.

'There. Life's a joke to you.'

'Men to whom life is a joke find comfort in women to whom life is a prayer. Kipling wrote that or something like it.' He felt her fingernails dig deep into his wrists and tried not to wince. Then the pressure released and the frown on her face cleared. She was her sleek beautiful self again.

In the train, as they sat side by side, and unaware of the other passengers, she took his hand and rested it on her lap. He smiled gratefully, recalling Ted assurance, that Emma was so indifferent about her looks, that his only rivals would be books. 'I could live with that', he had replied, but now, it was what Ted said later which troubled him. "Emma can be suicidal. If it wasn't for my father's library, she wouldn't be here today." 'Emma', he whispered, did I tell you my uncle has one of the finest collection of books I have seen in any home; and he's willed the whole lot to me?'

She raised his hand and kissed it. 'Ted's told you a lot about me.'

Her clairvoyance startled him, 'Yes,' he said.

'Ted's on our side.' Then she asked: 'You love England, and you're a British citizen. Why didn't you live here.'

'Because of my mother, I couldn't while she was alive. She would have been heart-broken. Me too. We were very close.'

'And will your love for England ever fade?'

'I see no reason why it should. My England's an ideal, not a reality. It doesn't exist . . . rather it exists because I want it to. Sometimes, in some places, and with some people, I get a glimpse of the myth, and a frisson that makes my England real. It's strange.'

'What is strange?'

'That I came to Winchester. The most English spot, to meet an English family, and fall in love with a most English rose. So now, tell me about your father. I gather he was active to the last.'

'Yes! That makes it so painful. He died in his sleep. No warning. No last words. Just a memory of a serene look on his face. I was there. I had been reading to him. There's nothing more to say.'

'What were you reading?'

'*A Glastonbury Romance*. Powys was one of dad's favourite writers.'

'John Cowper Powys? He's mine too.'

'Three more stops,' she said absently.

Sandy looked up to meet the steady gaze of a thickset, elderly man wearing a bowler hat. He looked away. Not again, he prayed, not again! What's happening to my beloved England! Must they only see my colour and not my love for England—deeper, so much deeper than theirs? Resolved to save Emma from another assault, he faced the man, and struck by a familiar look about him, smiled disarmingly.

'Forgive me for staring, but at the risk of appearing awfully rude, young man, aren't you Sandy?' Turning to Emma he tipped his hat with a slight nod of the head.

'Yes. I'm Sandy.'

'Friend of Clayton, Bill Clayton? Thought so. Never forget a face. Remember me? Bill's neighbour, or as near as one can be to his large estate. We played a set of tennis together. You partnered Bill . . . two years ago, or was it three.'

'I remember now. One of the quickest sets I've played. You and . . .'

'Jenny, my wife.'

'You gave us a trouncing.'

'I don't know. You and Bill were out of practice. Surely.'

'Yes. I'm sorry I should've recognised . . .'

'Don't give it another thought. Your attention was absorbed by a charming young lady.' He bowed to Emma and tipped his hat again. 'Travis, George Travis.'

'Emma Franks,' Sandy said, 'we . . .'

'This is my stop. My card. Call me, when you're next in Stoke Poges.'

'Thank you. We certainly will. Quite soon in fact.'

'Good!' George jerked forward. The train ground to a halt, the doors opened and closed, and he was gone. Sandy looked over his shoulder with a hand poised to wave, but George Travis's head was firmly fixed in the direction he was going.

'Gosh, Emma, I should have recognised him, but when you've last seen someone in a T-shirt and shorts, it's a job recognising him in a pin-striped suit and a bowler hat.'

'He could have ignored us. But, I rather liked him.'

'Sometimes even the most reserved among us are curious. I can see him telling his wife: "I say, Joan, do you . . ."'

'Jenny.'

'I say Jenny, remember that Indian chap Bill brought with him for tea? Two years ago. Later we played tennis and thrashed them hollow? Well. I saw the whippersnapper earlier this p.m., sitting next a lovely young gel. Can't see what she sees in him . . .'

'Hush, Sandy, you're drawing attention.'

'We'll see him again because I'm going to introduce you to mother. I mean Una, Bill's mum . . . the most beautiful mother in the world.'

'You're so full of passion,' she said without smiling.

Sandy's flat was on the first floor of a Mansion block. Its red-brick, Victorian facade had been maintained but the interior was refurbished and modernised. A small entrance hall separated the kitchen from the large dining-cum-living-room, with sliding doors opening into a spacious bedroom and en suite bathroom. In front of these doors, a long sofa, with a square coffee table in front of it, faced two high, north-facing bay windows. One window opened on to a small balcony. The room was bright and airy.

Emma sank on the sofa. 'I long for a cup of tea.'

'It won't be long now. Biscuits, I'm afraid. If I knew you were coming I'd have baked a cake . . . No, stay put, you won't know where things are.'

'Then I'd like to . . .'

'Of course! But give me a minute.'

Sandy dashed into the bedroom and reappeared some moments later. 'I've put out a fresh towel on the bed. Make yourself at home.'

'Thank you.' She entered the bedroom and pulled the doors a fraction behind her.

Sandy went into the kitchen, opened the refrigerator and at once realised he had run out of milk. He remembered the Bengali family on the ground floor. He dashed down the stair-well and knocked on the door marked "A K Ghosh". Old Mr Ghosh's hand pushed the post flap. 'Hallo, 'allo! Yes, please. Which number wanting, please?' Sandy explained. 'Oh, yes, yes. I'm telling the good wife.' A latch moved. The door opened. 'Come in, come in, young sir.' Sandy slowly followed the shuffling gait of Mr Ghosh. The old man was wearing a *dhoti* and *kurta*, which surprised Sandy, who had till now always seen this wiry and dapper man in a three-piece tweed suit. 'This is kind of you *babuji*. And I am really sorry to trouble you and your wife.'

'*Arrey*!' said the old man. 'No need thanking and all that rot. If we Indians can't help our own . . .' He did not finish the sentence. 'Just wait here.' Old Ghosh had moved down the passage and now stood in front of a cane and bamboo screen, behind which, Sandy rightly guessed, was the kitchen.

Sandy knew old Ghosh through his son Ajit, who owned a Bata Shoe shop on Chiswick High Street. In the past, he had even dined with the family and on his way down to the flat, to borrow milk, he was embarrassingly conscious of having turned down several invitations recently. The "good wife" was a quiet mystery. He had never seen her, as the meals were laid out on the table and the men dined alone. Only sounds of her movements in the kitchen pointed to her existence. Now he stared at the screen with a measure of curiosity, and a moment later was rewarded by the appearance of a plump, heavily bangled, hand holding a bottle of milk. This was quickly followed by a round face and large black eyes—eyes that contrasted sharply with the circle of vivid red powder on a forehead fringed with curly white hair. 'Long time no see, Sandy?' The apparition spoke in a high octave, and without waiting for an answer disappeared.

Old Ghosh was looking oddly at Sandy's china jug. 'Will that be sufficient?'

'It's just for tea,' said Sandy. 'Thank you. I hope you both and Ajit are well?'

Old Ghosh wobbled his head, shut his eyes and smiled enigmatically. 'And how fares it with your honourable self?'

'I'm well, thank you. See you soon. Must rush now.' Sandy backed towards the door. Old Ghosh followed him.

'You know, a good Indian woman makes a dutiful wife. Faithful and virtuous.'

'Of course,' said Sandy, a hand on the door knob.

'I'm only wanting this to say,' old Ghosh went on, 'I've great experience of the world. I've travelled and seen everything. I saw you with this white . . . this English woman. Hobnobbing with their likes is dangerous. Must not mind my speaking.'

'Thank you,' said Sandy. 'But I'm not hobnobbing. She is going to be my wife.'

'Wife!' Old Ghosh raised his hands in horror, shook his head woefully and clicked his tongue several times, disapprovingly. 'Oh, my God! Hope you know what you're doing! You will regret this greatly. Don't mind my saying so. These western women are too free and flirtatious.'

Sandy regretted not saying from the start that Emma *was* his wife. He opened the door and faced the old man. 'You can be right, but not in this case.'

'But see. Would a virtuous woman come to a man's flat?'

Sandy thought quickly. He leaned forward and whispered: 'She is, indeed, the most virtuous woman, I assure you. She is here only because we're eloping. Running away. Her family is against the marriage; most against.'

This time not only were the hands raised in horror but the old man's jaw dropped, and inside the red *paan*-stained mouth the tongue wagged. 'This is prejudice! Colour prejudice! Who do these fellows think they're? I know from your name, you're from most worthy family. Good-looking fellow like you! And not so *kala*, dark-skinned. Were you white, they'd be touching your feet and pressing you most hard to marry . . .'

'Precisely,' said Sandy and shut the door behind him. Back in his kitchen, he put the jug on the tea tray, crossed the hall and peered into the living-room. The sliding doors seemed not to have moved since she went in but he could hear soft, cat-like movements in the bedroom. He returned to the kitchen and turned the electric kettle on. While it sang he reviewed the day's happenings. Events had moved so fast he needed time to digest their full impact. In a matter of hours he had been transported from a state of desolation to one of utter bliss; more, the once unattainable vision was here, real, in the flesh, tangibly and soon to be a vital part of his life! He thought of what old Ghosh had said and smiled complacently. 'Oh, Emma,' he whispered to himself, 'can I ever prove how much I love you! Will I ever be able to erase the memory of the hurt I gave you yesterday, when you came to me in a storm of quiet desperation? God forgive me!' He made the tea and carried the tray into the living-room. She was standing, framed in the open doorway, undressed and wearing his black, cotton, dressing gown. It fell loosely about her.

'Ah!' he said, 'now I know what *décolleté* means. You do look incredibly beautiful! But, you mustn't do this to a chap without warning. I could have dropped the tray.'

She came up and put her arms round his neck. 'You don't have to be a gentleman any more.' He tried to kiss her but she moved back a little and stared at him hard and long. 'My sweet Sandy, I've always loved you, before we met, from that photograph of you with daddy.'

'But you were going to join a convent!'

'Because I didn't think we'd ever meet, and because no other man seemed to interest me. But remember how I shocked mother by kissing you, that first day . . .'

'And I thanked my lucky stars. But why won't you let me kiss you now?'

'I will. First we'll have tea.' She sat down. He poured and handed her a cup, which she drank in silence, while he noted her lips betray a slight tremble. He waited till she put her cup down. Then she stood up and solemnly held out a hand. He took it, telling himself that even a hint of a smile would ruin the magic. She led him into the bedroom and sat on the edge of the bed. 'Now kiss me.' He felt like a boy invited to play doctors and nurses. He kissed her, gently. She lay on her back. 'Love me. Now. Here.'

He pulled her up into his arms and caressed her. 'My sweet, my darling Emma, are you sure you want this? There's no . . .'

'I do! I do! I want to face mother knowing there's no turning back . . . that nothing she can say will alter my commitment . . . our commitment.' She shivered. 'I'm afraid.'

'There's nothing to be afraid about.' He kissed and undressed her tenderly. Then he lifted her, surprised at her lightness, and laid her on the bed so that her head rested on the pillows. 'I'll be back in a moment,' he whispered. He undressed in the bathroom and on returning smiled to see her, as he left her, lying very still, her eyes tightly shut. She had made no attempt to cover herself. He looked at her, then kissed and lightly touched her all over. 'Sandy, I'm all tingly!' She opened her eyes to find his face inches from her and shut them again and felt the full weight of his naked body on her. He whispered but all the electric tremors in her body prevented her from hearing. A sharp pain made her cry out but soon it didn't seem to matter, and she yielded, not coldly or passionately, but in generous surrender—a surrender that heightened his libido. He had only to look at her to want to make love again and, after his lips explored every undulation of her body, yet again. A soft moan, a tender pained expression on her face warned him he was hurting her. He paused with sudden concern, but she tightened her arms round him and drew him to her, whispering: 'Yes, yes!'

He lay back with a sigh. She stayed very still. Then he turned to her and traced the contours of her breasts, kissing and squeezing them. She pushed him away. 'Haven't you had enough?'

He smiled. 'You'll have to tell me because I'll never know.'

She sat up and looked at him. Her eyes travelled up and down his body.

'You can look at me now,' she said, lying down again on her back.

'If I do, I will want to make love again.'

'No, don't. It hurts. And we must think of getting to Ted's place.'

They lay alongside and neither spoke for a while. Then she said: 'That snap of you with my father. I must have been three when it was taken. I pressed daddy to give it to me on my fifteenth birthday. "I suppose you can have it," dad said. Then he added, "its no good. I don't think I'll ever see him again." Oh, Sandy, that was so sad.'

'Yes, my little one, it was. Why did you want that particular photograph?'

'I don't know. It was a good one of father.'

'Fifteen, you said. Was it then you turned to religion?'

'Yes. My last years in school. Two other girls in my year were also keen to be nuns. The other girls called us the "The Dames Templar" just to be horrid. We didn't care.'

'Why, how did that name come about?'

'During a school debate, Clare, my best friend, one of us three, said that our bodies were temples of the Holy Spirit.'

He turned towards her 'And I have violated the temple!' Her frown made him regret his frivolity. 'Sorry. Forgive me!' He kissed her on the mouth. 'Stupid of me.'

'Yes.' She felt between her legs and looked at her hand and jumped up. 'Sandy! It's bleeding! And I've stained your . . .'

'It's all right, darling. Don't give it another thought. Is it still bleeding?'

She felt herself again. 'No. not really. I'll wash the sheet for you.'

'Forget it. There, you rest a little while I have a shower and dress.' He got out of bed and put on his dressing-gown.

She propped up the pillows and sat up in bed. 'You look pale and romantic in that gown,' she said. 'Black suits you.'

'And you look ravished but beautiful. Innocent too. I feel a cad.'

'I'm not innocent or ignorant. I've read what I ought to know. Read about love and marriage.' She watched as he searched a box on top of the chest of draws and lit a cigarette. He inhaled deeply, blew three perfect smoke rings and grinned. He inhaled again but broke into a spasm of coughing. 'Served me right for showing off.' He said.

'I didn't know you smoked? I don't like the smell of cigarettes.'

'Then, here goes.' He turned round, butted his cigarette, crossed the room, bent over her and kissed her. 'Isn't it wonderful. I don't have to fret or long to touch you. I can kiss you as much as I want.' He waited for her to nod, then kissed her forehead, her eyes, her nose, her chin, and her mouth. 'Now, have I left anything out?'

She nodded. 'Yes. These.' She pointed to her breasts.

He took each of them in his hands and squeezed gently. There were tears in her eyes. 'Why?' He asked. 'Why the tears?'

She shook her head. 'I've seen what marriage does . . . and how soon love dies.'

'Are you thinking about Ted and Mabel?'

'I was also thinking about mother and father.' She repressed a sob and he felt her teeth bite hard on his shoulder through the dressing-gown. 'I loved Daddy. When he was alone, I wanted to be with him.' She sighed. 'We won't let that happen to us.' She covered his mouth with a hand. 'Hush, don't speak. I can't see that happening.'

'You truly have the most beautiful eyes in the world. You mustn't worry. I've got nothing else to do but love you.'

Abruptly, she pushed him away. 'Can I shower first?' She pulled the sheets with her and went into the bathroom. 'I won't mind if you smoke. Almost everyone does.'.

She came out of the bathroom with the bath towel wrapped like a sarong and her hair spread wide over her shoulders. 'I'll wash the sheets after you've . . . why are you looking like that?'

'If you're going to keep looking differently beautiful from time to time, I don't see how I'm ever going to do anything else but keep making love to you.?

'You'll soon get tired.' She said matter-of-factly.

He laughed. 'You're a rum one. We'll honeymoon twice as long as anyone else.'

'If that's what you want.'

He laughed again. 'I must take you to the Musée D'Orsay. In Paris.'

'Why?'

'First, let me see you. Please!'

She opened her towel and held it by the corners outspread behind her.

'You remind me of a painting there. Except she is holding a pitcher of water.'

She covered herself. 'Sandy, it's a terrible sin? What we've just done? Yes, it is.'

'But we're getting married. That's a mitigating factor. Or penance enough.'

'I wasn't joking.' She picked up her petticoat from the back of a chair. 'Now hurry, with your shower. Sandy, what if you've made me pregnant?

'The same answer. We are husband and wife, as good as.' We are getting married. Immediately? Are we not?'

'Yes. Hurry now. Oh wait!' She stood on her toes and kissed him. 'Thank you, for setting me free.'

When he came out she was dressed and looking immaculate. She let him kiss her but the palms of her hands pressed against his chest. He raised his brows.

'We mustn't do that again,' she said, 'not till after we're married.'

'What? Kiss?'

'No. That thing. You know.'

'Suppose I can't wait?'

'You'll have to. To make our wedding night special.' She shut her eyes. 'Sandy, it feels sore!'

'Oh, my love!' He cupped her face in his hands. 'I am sorry! Forget the sheets. I'll take care of that. Now, you sit on the sofa. Here, look at this book on Italy. My sister gave it me. It's by a German photographer. The pictures are stunning.'

'Wear your charcoal grey suit. I want you to look your best. Impress mother.'

He rubbed his chin. 'I'll have a quick shave. The charcoal suit it is.'

When he entered the room dressed, she stood up and starting from the back of her neck, ran her fingers through her hair, lifting and spreading it above her ears, exposing the nape of her slender neck. She shook her head and let the hair fall. It was something he had seen her do often and though it accentuated her feminine charm, the gesture was artless. 'Sandy, why are you smiling? Tell me. But not if you're going to tease.'

'My teasing is a kind of serenading. I couldn't ever make fun of you. You are up there . . .' He gestured with his hand. 'Come. Let's take a cab.' As they crossed the road, he said: 'I've decided to get a car. I've seen one. A good second-hand one.'

'Someone you know?'

'Getting to know. There's a house I pass everyday on my way to and from school. I saw a car parked on the drive, as good as new; a Ford Zephyr. It has a "for sale" notice and a reasonable price tag. Last Friday I stopped to look at it when a dapper old man came down the drive. Something about his walk and his trim white moustache held my attention. He asked if I was interested and I said I was but that I hadn't quite made up my mind. He wanted to know if I was from India, and told me he had spent many years there, in the Punjab. I said the Punjab was my stamping ground too and asked what he was doing in India. Anyway, the astonishing thing is that not only had he been in the Indian Army, he was in the same corps as I was—Education. In Pachmarhi, a hillstation in Central India—before my time. Strange, don't you think?'

'Yes,' she said thoughtfully. 'But some things are meant to be. Like us.'

'He's given me till Wednesday to make up my mind, invited me to tea, and in the spirit of comradeship said he'll knock a few pounds off the price!'

'And you're sure it's a good buy?'

'It's just clocked twelve thousand miles! Harry Collins, that's his name, retired last month. He worked for one of those department stores on Oxford Street—I forget the name. Said he'll introduce me to the memsahib.' Sandy laughed. 'Ah, a cab! Taxi!'

They sat quietly for some time. Sandy sensed an air of anxiety. He held her hand. 'You've been wonderful, darling. Nothing to be anxious about. Your mother's had her way. Now it's time you had yours.'

'And there's nothing she can say which will change your mind, Sandy?'

'Nothing.'

'It's not her style to make a scene or argue, but she can be cutting, cold, distant. It made father unhappy. "For goodness sake, Edith, say something," he'd plead. It always ended with everyone giving in to her. She's used to that.'

'Where does my beautiful, dreamy, artistic, sweet Emma fit into this family? I knew something of your dad. All of you are so different.'

'Yes, I suppose so. I've never thought about it. Father was army to the core—Ted tells me—I only got to know the sad old man who turned to the Catholic Church and to solitude. Ted's the ideal doctor. Mother's a good committee woman. Sandy, be strong.'

'Look at it this way. We're not asking, we're telling her. We know how it ends. We are going to be together come what may.'

Sandy paid the cab. 'Don't go in yet, Emma.' He held out a small purple velvet box and opened the lid. 'My mother's engagement ring. Wear it as a token of our pledge.'

She took the ring and held it in her palm. 'It's beautiful. What is it?'

'An opal with two rubies. Opal was her birthstone. Opal for October. Yours is topaz. November. You shall have that too. Gosh! it fits perfectly. That's uncanny.'

'Another one of those strange things!'

'Yes. There. Now, you have my mother's approval.'

'I feel strong now. Kiss me.'

Ted answered the door. 'Have you been here long?' Emma asked.

'Twenty minutes. Hello Sandy.' They shook hands. He turned to Emma. 'You look radiant! That's good. So, Sandy's what the doctor ordered?'

Emma kissed her brother. 'Look!' She raised her hand.

Ted held her hand to the light in the porch. 'So the die is cast. Well, steel yourselves, she's on the warpath—not noticeably, but most assuredly.'

'Have you told her?'

'Yes, Emma. I rang her to say you'd turned Trevor down and that you two would be here later this evening.'

'Teddy!' Sandy thought Edith's voice sounded different, unrecognisably strident.

'Yes. mother.' Ted replied, then whispered: 'by the way, we're all invited to dinner. This is typically mother, Sandy. And she'll use it to effect.'

'By that, you mean she'll attend to you and ignore us?'

'You bet, Sandy, and it can be rudeness personified.'

'I see. And, since it's not the fatted calf, what's for dinner?'

'Roast lamb,' replied Ted with a light chuckle.

'Poor Trevor,' sighed Emma'

'Oh, don't worry about Trevor, he's gone.'

'You mean back to Winchester.'

'No. He has a friend in Watford. They're going fishing tomorrow.'

'What's keeping all of you?' Edith blared from within.

'Coming mother!' Ted called back. Then he whispered: 'Let me be the first to congratulate you two.'

'Thank you,' said Sandy, 'now lead us to the slaughter.'

'Isn't he a bit of a wag,' Ted said to Emma. She nodded stifling a giggle.

'Hello! Edith,' said Sandy.

Edith ignored him. She was standing with her hands in the pockets of her gingham apron. Her mouth twitched and puckered as she glared at Emma. 'This is a nice turn up for the books, young lady!'

'What do you mean mother?'

'You know very well what I mean. But, I shan't say anything now. Dinner's ready. I know it's early for Ted, but things can't be the way we'd like them to be.' She pursed her lips at Ted, raised her eyebrows like double question marks and drew her chin in. 'Will you see to the drinks. I'd better save the lamb from disaster.'

'I'll give you a hand,' said Emma.

'I can manage, thank you.'

Emma followed her into the kitchen. 'It'll be all right, Sandy,' said Ted. 'Let's have a drink. Mother's as good as her word. She'll say nothing. A cold shoulder is about the worse thing Emma will have to face. Whisky? I'm afraid there's no soda.'

'Water will do.'

'We'll forgo the ice? It means going to the kitchen.' They sat with their drinks and faced each other. Something in the way Ted stretched his legs triggered a memory. But Sandy couldn't place it. 'Mother's unfair to Emma. She believes Emma only cared for father. Indeed, Emma was very fond of him. Adored his company—which may explain why she likes older men—but mother's wrong. Emma cares for her too. Since father's death their need for each other's company grew. Emma even gave up the idea of going to university, to spend more time with her. It was mother who distanced herself when she discovered he'd left all the money to Emma. Well, all that's academic now. Just thought I'd mention it. Emma's made her decision, I can see that, and I'm happy for both of you. But I won't pretend it would have been a lot more convenient if she'd decided to marry an Englishman.' He sipped his drink. 'Ugh! we need ice.' He started to get up, when Emma entered the room wearing a blue-striped apron.

'I found some nuts,' she said. 'Did you want something, Ted?'
'Ice.'
'I'll get some.'

Ted waited till Emma left the room. 'Don't get me wrong. You're a damn sight more English than the lot of us, but the world outside won't always see that. I know Emma'll be happy, what is more important she'll be unhappy without you. I mean that. I'm sorry if a moment ago I sounded a bit negative.'

Sandy made a deprecating gesture. 'Ted, there's something I want to know?'

'Go ahead. Ask. You're family now.'

'Tell me . . .' Sandy stopped. Emma came in with the ice.

'It'll be another ten minutes,' she said.

Ted's eyes followed Emma as she left the room, and Sandy noted they were not as blue as his sister's. Her blue had a frankness that was unsettling, while his grey had a friendly twinkle, and once again triggered that earlier sense of *deja vu*. This time Sandy recognised it's past echo. He was being reminded of the colonel, Ted's father.

'You know, Sandy, I've been concerned about Emma. She had all the makings of a spinster. A deeply religious phase followed by a desire to be left alone. Then, frightfully withdrawn after father's death. I reminded mother. We were both intrigued by the way she took to you. It wasn't what either of us expected. While you positively do not oil your way around the floor, you do ooze charm from every pore.' He chortled. 'Mother is less cold than you think. but for reasons of her own, can't see you as her son-in-law. You see, once her mind's set on anything, she has to see it through; and she hates losing face . . . remember she'll now have to face Mary.'

Sandy leaned forward. 'This is no game. We're in deadly earnest. I mean, while I shall ever, for the rest of my life, wonder what your beautiful sister sees in me, I can assure you, and speaking for her too, it's not mere infatuation.'

Ted stared at him. 'You don't have to tell me.'

'And are you really on my side?'

'Of course, because I'm on Emma's side. Only patience could have won her, and you've been patient. She may appear cold, but I know there's passion. But I worry about her and frankly I want your assurance, because, if you don't mind my saying it, you have all the qualifications of a philanderer.'

'Good grief, Ted. India's no training ground for a philanderer. The opportunities are almost nil. And it wasn't just patience. I persevered. Also, I have to say, some of what appeared to be patience on my part had something to do with my fear of being rejected. I loved Emma the first moment I saw her. Yes, when you picked us up that day at the cemetery. Besides, Emma is matchless. There can be no rivals. Who can replace her?'

'I had to make sure. I know, there's more to you than just good looks. Emma is a sensitive and unique sort of gal . . .' He clicked his tongue. 'I remember us, Mabel and I, taking her out one birthday, her birthday, for a dance. Mabel invited a young chap to join . . . Emma's not one for dancing but, he coaxed her on to the floor. All went well, reasonably well, till I gather he tried to get closer than she wanted him to . . . she pushed him and walked away. I'm afraid, I know she's not one for the physical side of love—if you gather my drift. That's something you'll have too . . .' Ted stared aghast. 'What does that look mean? Sandy! You haven't! I'll be damned!'

'Damned?' Edith was in the room. 'What on earth are you two talking about?'

'Society, mother, and politics. Do we come in now?'

'No. We'll have to give it a few more minutes. You don't like it rare. But you could see to the wine.'

'I should have guessed,' continued Ted as his mother's retreating figure passed through the dining-room into the kitchen.

'You are not going to get a full confession . . .' Sandy chortled. 'Religious people aren't innocents. They have an innate wisdom. Bill Clayton, have I told you about Bill?'

'Yes, you've mentioned him. The missionary monk who works in India?'

'Yes, a celibate who, for long periods, retreats from the world; and yet, he has a profound understanding of human social psychology.'

'I must say, Emma was, unusually for a girl of her age, always very much together . . . till father's death. Kitty's like that too. Profoundly intuitive.'

'By the way, where's Kitty?'

'I thought it best she went with Mabel and they spent the night with Mabel's sister. I thought Mabel's presence tonight might have proved unhelpful.'

Ted stood up, went into the dining-room, and produced a bottle of wine just as Edith and Emma entered the room with the lamb. 'I'm afraid it's red wine. Run out of white.'

Edith pursed her lips and looked unblinkingly at the leg of lamb. 'Teddy, you carve. So, you sit here. Emma next to me.'

'Mother!' said Emma lowering her voice. 'I won't talk if you ignore Sandy. And as there is nothing to discuss, your attitude towards Sandy is all that interests me.'

'Are those your last words?' Edith fumed. 'Well, I'll have mine, if I need to.'

'Mother,' Ted intervened. 'I hope we'll all be civilised about this. There really is nothing to discuss. You've made a lovely dinner. Let's make it a happy one. Yes?'

'*Et tu brute!* So it's three to one . . . I see you cleverly packed Mabel off. But, Teddy, I'll have you know I'm not just anybody. As Emma's mother, I deserve respect and courtesy. You can't condone Emma's conduct. She goes out with one man and comes home with another. And, has the audacity . . .'

'Come, come, mother. It's not as if it's a complete surprise. They've been seeing each other for years. It would have been a far greater surprise, and a cruel one at that, if after all that time Emma ended her friendship with Sandy, and no explanation.'

The Lotus And The Rose

'Get on with the carving.'

At a nod from Ted, Sandy went round with the wine. Edith waited till everyone had been serve with meat and vegetables. Then she took the sauce-boat and, rather heavily, splashed gravy over her plate. 'Emma needn't have stopped being friends with Sandy.' She said, rather emphatically dabbing the table with her napkin.

'Mother, I have to say this,' Ted said. 'Your own conduct in this matter you need to think about. You had no right to push Trevor on to Emma, when it was clear she never had any interest in the boy, whatever.'

'Emma didn't have to marry. Equally she didn't have to jump from the frying pan into the fire!' She looked at Sandy. 'I suppose you find that funny.'

'Edith, I assure you I take that remark seriously. I don't mind being described as the fire. I am not without passion.'

Edith repressed a smile.

'I suppose,' Edith gave Emma a stern look, 'Ted's got a point there . . . the unhelpful situation created by Sandy and Emma seeing each other—Ted has to take the blame for that—but I trusted Sandy to be a gentleman, and I wasn't to know Emma needed help.'

'Help!' Emma burst in. 'Whatever do you mean?'

'Advice, my dear. You had shown no interest in men before—I can't put it better—let alone turning up suddenly, as good as married.' She inhaled sharply through her teeth. 'I do hope you haven't . . . You two haven't, by any chance, done anything foolish?'

Sandy laughed. 'Foolish? It really depends what you mean, as Professor Joad would say.' He looked at Emma. A faint smile played on her lips.

Edith pushed the cream potatoes towards Sandy with a thump. 'I shan't waste time trying to fathom that. I'm sure you're being very clever, if not a little cheeky. There was a time when it was "Mrs Franks this" and "Mrs Franks that". She looked at Ted. 'That smirk makes me think you know something I don't know?'

'Mother, you and I can play guessing games. They don't have to enlighten us.'

'And, mother,' Emma piped in, 'you insisted on Sandy calling you Edith.'

'Yes, darling! I don't need reminding. I'd also prefer Ted to call me Edith.'

'And there really is no reason for you to worry about anything. We're not going to embarrass you or involve you at all. Sandy and I plan to marry without any show or fuss, as soon as we can. Next week if possible.'

'I'm your mother! And you're telling me. I'm not involved?'

'I mean, you have a choice not to be involved. And if it's easier, tell Mary we've been foolish and gone too far.'

'That's most considerate,' Edith said. 'I mean it. I shan't talk about this again. I'll gladly wash my hands off the whole affair. I suppose Mary will be consoled, her son is not going to marry a . . . a whore.'

'Mother!' Ted exclaimed. 'Now, where are you going.'

'The kitchen. To check the pudding. Life goes on.' She paused behind Sandy's chair and lightly touched his shoulder. 'Well, young man, count yourself lucky. Emma's paid you a great compliment. Or do I have to compliment you on your powers of seduction!'

'Mother,' Emma said emphatically, '*I* asked Sandy to marry me.'

'Wonders never cease!'

The rest of the meal was eaten in silence but, as the earlier tension of the evening eased, ample justice was done to the *Creme Caramel*. The table was cleared. Ted made coffee and brought it into the sitting-room. 'Scrabble? Anyone?' He asked. 'It's early.'

'What about songs at twilight, by the piano?' teased Sandy.

Edith laughed. 'One game, then I'm off to my room.'

Later Emma walked with Sandy to the gate. 'I should have telephoned for a cab.'

'I'll enjoy the walk to the tube,' he said. 'It's been quite a day.'

She shut the gate after him and leant against it. 'How I wish I was going home with you! When do I see . . . oh, don't forget to phone Una.'

'I won't. Thanks for reminding me. Tomorrow? Will I be seeing you?'

She thought for a while then shook her head. 'No. I couldn't trust myself.'

'Wednesday then. On Tuesday there's a staff-meeting. I'll have the car that evening. An inaugural drive into the West End. We'll dine out?'

'Yes, but before dinner you must take me somewhere. Not for long. A few minutes?'

'Where?'

'I'll tell you when we meet. In the meantime, as I'm free, Ted's will help me with arrangements at the registry office. A church wedding would embarrass mother.'

'I know. Four weeks for the Banns, then the ceremony itself. Sorry. I suppose this is denying you something you dreamed about.'

'No. I never dreamed of getting married. We want to be married soon, don't we.'

'Yes. But I should be the one helping with the arrangements?'

'No, Sandy, please! Let me do everything . . . till you have to. Say yes!'

'Yes. I'll cable my uncle . . . and Bill.'

She leaned over the gate and raise her face to be kissed. She was less clumsy and he kissed her hard and long, till she was breathless.

'I'll come to your flat,' she murmured. 'Tomorrow, if you wish.' In the dim light of the street lamp her eyes shone with aroused desire. How soon she had changed from the girl he first met. For a fleeting moment a mild nervousness overcame him.

'Wednesday,' he said. Her body trembled. Her eyelids closed, the upper lip drooped. She was his Emma again. 'Now,' he said. 'I want you right now!'

She kissed her forefinger and touched his lips softly. 'I reserve my place,' she smiled. 'I saw that in a film . . . but I think the man said it.'

CHAPTER SIX

The next day, during the lunch break, Sandy telephoned Harry Collins, who confirmed he could collect the car on Wednesday. He put the receiver down to find Sally Watson waiting to pounce on him. There was no escape.

'You've been dodging me!' She said'

'Have I? Anyway, I'm off to get a sandwich.'

'I'll come with you. Is it the transport cafe or Jimmy's Kitchen?'

'I thought you had school lunches?'

'Either you come with me or I go with you. Choose. You're not escaping me.'

'I've brought a sandwich, so I'll make myself a coffee and sit here.'

'You swine! You lied! You'll pay for that. I'll make do with the apple in my locker. Get your sandwich, I'll make the coffee, then you can tell me all about her.'

'I don't see why I should. I've seen you with Peter, I don't grill you about . . .'

'I'll tell you anything. I can't help it if you're not curious. Emma? Tell me all.'

Sandy ignored her. He opened his lunch box and sat by the window overlooking the playground and began to eat. Sally joined him and handed him a cup of coffee. So,' she said, 'suddenly it's spring and the quiet man's found him a mate.'

He signalled his lips were sealed, then burst out laughing. 'Sally, you're incorrigible. You're in the wrong line of work. You would've made a good journalist, prising all the tittle tattle you want by the exercise of your charm.'

'Thanks for the compliment, but clearly I'm not your type!'
'Stop it. All pretty girls are my type, or once were.'
'Tell me about Emma?'
'The Greek goddess! Can't believe my luck.'
'You're obviously in love, since you see more than there is. She's beautiful in a demure, unfashionable way. I bet she reads Tennyson.'

He looked away.

'And she's quite busty, which too is unfashionable.'
'I've no complaints. How can busts be out of fashion?'
'She's like Black Forest Gateau. You know, Sandy, there's a whiff of domesticity about you. I see "Home Sweet Home" embroidered on cushions. What a waste. You have looks, a sharp mind, but blind to the world. Look around you today! London's coming alive and free. You're still in the age and literature of Empire. I should've have guessed you'd fall for a woman with an Art Nouveau, or do I mean Victorian, look?'

'You're wrong. Her looks are classical and the classical is never out of date.'

'In a 1940's dress?'

'Whatever she wears, she looks smashing. The whole point about clothes is to look good in them. Why follow fashion if it's not your style? Envy doesn't suit my gal Sal.'

'Not envy, resentment. Why should anyone look good without trying? She's the type that makes women like me look soiled and frivolous.'

'No Sally. Don't be harsh on yourself. All right, I'll say it. You're terribly attractive and accomplished. Emma wished she could be like you. At home in any society.'

'But you quickly disabused her of that. You want her the way she is. A domestic pet, tremulous, trained, obedient, so you can live like a sultan in a harem of one.'

'You're being unfair. I'm not responsible for the way she is. I found her as she is, and I like as she is.'

'And thanking your lucky stars for having struck gold. Yes? Then I'm not being unfair. Women like her, spoil men. They're bad for men.'

'If she wasn't around, you couldn't guess who I might have chosen?'

'Me?'

'Possibly . . . after some taming of the shrew.'

'I'd make a good wife, I would,' she said fluttering her eyelids demurely.

He laughed. 'You'll find a better man and a better husband.'

'Damn you. I just wish you weren't so good-looking.'

'A slap and a compliment. But you've got Emma wrong. Women like her always have their own way. Because they're loved and they know it and subtly use it.'

'I believe you're capable of great love and she'll be happy because of it, but you'll never know what she really wants. She won't tell you. You'll put her in a cage, maybe a gilded one, but still a cage. Don't turn on that little-boy-lost look. You know I'm right.'

'You see too many films. Dash it! A chap has a right to choose wife and home to suit his needs. Like colours one lives with. If I like yellows, you can't criticise me for not going for reds? And what . . .' He stopped as Bailey, the Geography Master, came in with Alan Bryce the caretaker.

'There!' Bailey pointed to the wardrobe in the far corner. 'You'll find a large map of the world on the top. No, not . . . hello! where did that come from? Yes, it'll do fine. And tell Mrs Wilson I'll need it back here at the end of the day.' He then became aware of Sally and Sandy. 'Am I interrupting any . . . that reminds me, the kitchen staff wondered where you were, Sally. They've kept your lunch. I said you might be held up.'

'Thank you, Richard. I'll go now. It was sweet of you,' said Sally.

'Don't mention it. That's what we oldies are for . . . to look after you young 'uns. Oh, don't miss the pudding. It's Black Forest Gateau. Have I said something funny?'

❧

On Wednesday Sandy met the irrepressible Babs, wife of Major Harry Collins. Babs was confined to a wheelchair, but Sandy couldn't remember meeting a more endearing and cheerful person before. Her clear, musical voice was, at times, almost operatic, so that, often, she seemed to chant rather than speak. 'Come in, come in, Mr Thakur. I may call you Sandy? Of course, I can! You're just a boy. Now, Harry tells me you're a schoolmaster. A brave man to take on such a task. Children these days lack discipline . . . no, not there, Harry! Sandy will sit here, next to me, at the table.'

She sat erect, with chin tucked in, as her eyes twinkled over half-moon spectacles. On the table before her, on a tray was a silver teapot, jug and sugar basin. On another tray were bone china cups and saucers. There was also a seed cake on a crystal glass cake-stand, plates of sugared buns and cucumber sandwiches. 'No, darling, not that side. That's my deaf side. Sit here. Now you can call me Babs and we can talk about India. Harry served in India for twenty years, you know! Happy days.'

'Now, Babs,' beamed Harry, 'Sandy can't stay long, he's meeting a young lady.'

'Is he now, indeed! Well, well. Do I hear wedding bells? Wonderful, wonderful! Bring her with you next time and plan to spend a long Sunday afternoon. We have a lovely garden at the back. All Harry's handiwork. He's good, so very good with his hands. Harry, why don't you show Sandy the garden?'

'I will, Babs. Later. Let's have tea first. He'll want to look at the car.'

'It's all there. Vicky's done us proud. Our brisk little helper, Sandy, is a gem. The seed cake's my recipe. You must be ravenous after a hard day at school?' She passed him a cup and Sandy noticed she had beautiful hands, which he spontaneously reached out to hold. She gave a little start and laughed. Her eyes, which scarcely rested on any object for long, were dark amber, and contrasted sharply with her soft, snow-white hair. The face was a delicate pink and wrinkled, but they were the wrinkles of one who saw life serenely and with good humour.

'We left India in 1948. After Independence and that awful partition business, and Mr Gandhi's death. Harry was in Poona then, but I was still in Quetta, and travelled back to Delhi in those overcrowded, blood splattered trains. But, I love my India. Did Harry tell you we're going back?'

'Back to India?'

'Yes. I've longed to go back all these years, and now, at last, we can. I see, he didn't tell you. He does forget things. I can't spend another winter here. I know what you're thinking. But there's little the doctors can do for me here. Besides, India is home. My family has been there for generations, and my brother's settled there. Do you know the South. Bangalore, Ooty, the Hills. The Nilgiris, I mean?'

'No. I haven't been further south than Mhow. I wasn't long in the army.'

'We know Mhow . . . and Ahmednagar. Harry was an instructor in both those places. But I'm neglecting you. I talk far too much. Sixteen to the dozen, as mother used to say. Do help yourself, then I won't feel guilty.'

'I am. I'm making quite a pig of myself. I loved the cucumber sandwiches; and the seed cake's wonderful. You must give Emma the recipe.'

'I will, when you bring her. In the meantime you must take a piece for her. Harry will find an empty tin. By the way,' she whispered, as Harry left the table, 'you must bring her over soon. Next month my son will be here helping us to pack.'

'Would Sunday after next be all right?'

'Yes, that will be fine. Come for lunch. I'll warn Vicky.'

After tea Harry said he would take Sandy to inspect the car. 'Cheerio!' Babs trilled. 'It was lovely meeting you.' She started to wheel the chair.

'Allow me.' said Sandy. 'At least part of the way?'

'Awfully kind of you. Just to the door. Thank you, dear boy.'

For an inexplicable moment Sandy was reminded of his mother, and Bill's . . . and of all mothers. He bent forward and kissed her forehead.

'Bless you, dear boy. And happy driving. It'll be in excellent condition. Harry's so good at looking after things. Goodbye.'

For the first ten minutes of the drive he said nothing. Then turning to her, he asked. 'What do you think of the car?'.

'I know nothing about cars, Sandy. But I'm glad it's not a Mini. Is it as good as the one you had?'

'My old Riley? This is easier to handle . . . But I mustn't bore you.'

After a pause she asked: 'Have you known a lot of women?'

He started, then laughed. 'In the biblical sense? Do you really want to know? Sordid details and all?' She was looking out of her window, playing with her necklace. 'Yes.'

'What makes you think I've known, inverted commas, many?'

'When we made love, I was afraid. Nervous. Not you.'

'I was, you know. I thought it stuck out a mile!'

'I won't mind. Tell me.'

'As long as you know there never can be another woman. That you're unique.'

'Tell me.'

'Just two. Neither should count as serious affairs. The first time was in Lucknow—later referred to by my friend, who arranged it, as the "relief of Lucknow".

'Why?'

'Because it was the first time for me. I was nineteen, at this friend's house or rather palace. He, a Rajkumar, that is a prince, saw it as part of a host's duty to arrange for nautch girls—singing and dancing courtesans—to entertain us after dinner. We were four young men, ex-school mates. Quite drunk. I don't remember much about it except that it was Good Friday. That meant nothing to the others, but I did feel awful about it for a long time, and now, telling you about it. Sheer bravado. This may sound a lame excuse, but she was a prostitute.'

'It still counts, Sandy. And the second?'

'Must I? This one was an embarrassing experience. Let me off the hook?'

He kept his eyes on the road. 'I won't talk about it again,' she said.

'She was married with children. But no man around. As I said, it was embarrassing. Please don't ask me to explain. Sufficient to say, I realised how inept I was. It started me on all the manuals I could get hold of . . . *Married Love* by Stopes or Ellis . . . others. Sorry, one moment.' He swerved suddenly. 'Sorry, again. But he ought to know better than . . . Good grief! The poor chap's hit a bollard.'

'And what about here? Ted said, men drive a Riley to impress the girls.'

'Ted thinks I've the makings of a philanderer. I plead "not guilty". A few innocent dates to be left in their wrappings. I'm no saint but I'm fairly old-fashioned, morally, I mean.' He stopped at the lights. 'I wish I hadn't . . . Makes me feel unworthy of you.'

'Don't feel bad. You're older than me. I can't expect you not to have . . . I'm not the jealous type . . . No, I am, but I won't be if you'll look after me?'

'I don't deserve you. So young, so fresh, so beautiful. It's you I'll have to watch. I, an old Menelaus afraid of some young Paris, stealing you away from me?'

'You're not old.' She lay her head lightly on his shoulder.

'You know Emma, for three years, you made me suffer.'

'I know. I've been horrid to you. I was so mixed up. You should have been bolder.'

'I was afraid of being rejected. And you didn't acknowledge my greeting cards.'

She sat up. 'I have no excuse. I could've got your address from Ted. But I tried not to think of you and give in to feelings I was afraid to have. I'm so glad, Sandy, you did not give up on me.

'With Ted around there was every hope we would meet again, as well as the fear it might be too late.' He whistled. 'But after two years, I too tried to forget. I started to write . . . to help me forget.'

'I never meant to hurt you. I was confused, unhappy. How was I to know what I felt was love! I needed time to understand what it meant to love you . . . to be in love . . . to be loved by you. That's why I wanted to be with you . . . why I came to London, why I was grateful you still wanted to be with me. She reached out and traced the contours of his lips. He kissed her fingers without taking his eyes off the road. 'All's well now.'

'Yes, let's not dwell on the worse that could have been.'

'I like the title: *Marmalade for Breakfast*,' she said. 'I saw the chapters you gave Ted. You can be so funny. You observe the English with such humour, and yet I know your love for England is a serious affair. But you should publish it.'

'I couldn't finish it. I've set it aside. There are lots of books about the English . . . and better ones than I can ever hope to write. I've little new to say.'

'Write about the long history of your family links with the British. That'll be new.'

'I'll think about it. Encourage me. Here we are, Marble Arch. If I went up Oxford Street, I could turn left for Marylebone High Street?'

'Yes. I'll tell you where to stop. It's the Church at Spanish Place. If you can get to Manchester Square, we can leave the car there. Where are we going for dinner?'

'The Rangoon. Following orders. Got a cable from Jaggers in reply to mine. Soon my account will be the better for five hundred guineas. His wedding gift. Happy?'

She pressed her face against his shoulder.'

'He's asked for a photograph of you.'

'I don't have any. Nothing recent.'

'I have. The one I took last summer—at Polesden Lacy, with Ted and Kitty. You were looking out of a window and as you turned towards me, I clicked.'

'I remember now. Do you like it?'

'Yes. You can't make a bad photograph, even if you tried. It must be wonderful not to fear the camera and not to have to adopt a this-is-my-best-side pose.'

She looked away. 'One day my looks will go, then there'll be nothing left.'

'Nonsense. A pretty face may lose it's looks, not a beautiful one. And don't forget, your art? You have great talent. And all those hours of reading will enter your soul.'

She did not speak and for a time only the purr of the car could be heard. He turned into Manchester Square and parked the car. 'Why are we here? You said you'll tell me. What is the matter? I don't ever want to see tears again!'

'I'm all right. They're happy tears. Four years before daddy died he became a Roman Catholic. You see the church? Father brought me here twice. It's why I wanted to come so I could tell him about us. I'll say a prayer for both of us.'

He smiled, and put down her pale and fragile look to her navy blue dress. He leaned over to kiss her. She raised a hand to ward him. 'Sandy, I shall die before you do. And you're going to feel cheated.'

'Why, Emma, why bring this up, now?'

'Ted told me it would be fair to tell you. I have a weak heart, Sandy. I've known it since I was fourteen. And I don't know if I can have children.'

'I don't care. I have you. That's all that matters. Anyway, nothing is certain in life, and medical science is always discovering new cures. Tomorrow is not yesterday. Have you seen a specialist?'

'After father died, Ted was concerned about me. Mother too. They did insist I saw a heart specialist. I refused.'

'You're young. Your heart will strengthen with love and care and contentment. I'll give you all that.' He cupped her chin. 'Where's the tranquil Emma I used to know?'

'It didn't matter before. It does now. You mustn't feel bound to marry me.'

'But I am. I love you. Anytime together is better than no time?' He raised her chin. 'I'll take good care of you. From today I banish all sadness.' He kissed her, gently, then looked at his watch. 'The Church, will it be open?'

'It's a Roman Catholic church. Come, Sandy. We won't be long.'

As they entered, she opened her handbag and unrolled a black veil and put it over her head. 'If I didn't know better,' he whispered, 'it would seem that everything you do is designed to tantalise me.'

'Hush, we're in church!' She dipped her hand in holy water, crossed herself, entered a side chapel and knelt before a statue of the Madonna and Child. The flickering glow from the candles lit her face. Her eyes were shut and as the face under the veil took on the stillness of sculptured marble, an air of sanctity created a hiatus between them. Her lips moved soundlessly. He studied the downward curve of the upper lip and the orchid pout of the lower one. She kissed the cross on a rosary wound round her folded hands, then rose to light two candles. He went up and put his arm round her waist. 'This is for us,' she whispered, 'and this candle for father. In my prayer, Sandy, I've said sorry for having slept together before marriage. Don't giggle. Horrid boy! There now, put some coins in the offertory box.'

In the porch he took her hand. 'I'm sorry for giggling. Society may frown, but God understands. We haven't done anything terribly wrong! What we did was beautiful.'

'And all beautiful things need God's blessings.' They crossed the road to the car. 'It makes sense to respect our bodies.'

'Of course. When do I next pay my respects?'

She dug her elbow into his side.

'I like to see you smile and glad you don't get cross with me. Ted said you can be quite short-tempered. I find that hard to believe.'

'Ted's right. That's how I know I truly love you. I've changed. I want to give in to you, indulge you . . . as if you were my dearest and only child!'

He stared at her amazed. She was earnest.

A lanky, morose looking young man loped past them. 'Oh, man that's beautiful! It's really beautiful, man. Do your own thing. That's what it's all about.'

They gaped. 'Was he speaking to us or talking to himself, Sandy?'

'I don't suppose we'll ever know. Sounded American.'

※

When they were shown to their table in the restaurant she whispered: 'Don't order too much, Sandy. I'm not a big eater.'

The tall Indian waiter bowed. 'I'll come back when sahib's ready.'

'Don't you love this place?' Sandy asked. 'It's a pocket of colonial England and I'm told modelled on Raffles, in Singapore. It also reminds me of the Pachmarhi Officers' Mess. I suppose, because of the waiters. The white uniform, turbans, gloves. "Bearers", we called them.'

The waiter returned and was about to turn away when Sandy said: 'Yes it's all right. We're ready.' The waiter bowed and gestured and immediately two other waiters came carrying trays. 'Emma, they are following my uncle's instructions to the letter. I hope you won't mind, but the meal's been ordered in advance. It's Northwest Frontier food. You'll like it. *Kebabs*, and a special Mughal Emperor's *biryani*, with raisins and nuts. Not too spicy—the Emperor Shah Jehan's favourite dish—and, of course, Champagne.'

She stared as they laid the dishes on the table. 'Sandy! This is far too much.'

'When you've had enough leave something on the plate. Otherwise they will keep on serving you. I have to carry out Uncle Jagdish's instructions.' He took out his notebook and unfolded a piece of paper. 'And for pudding we're having a rich *Kheer*, ground rice cooked in full cream milk, with almonds.'

The meal eaten, the table cleared and coffee was served. 'That was wonderful, you will tell Jaggers, Sandy, I thought every dish was neat and delicious. The pudding too. Give me his address. I'll write to him.'

'He'd like that. And you can enclose my photograph of you.'

'Tell me about this afternoon. I forgot to ask.'

'Oh, yes, the Collinses? They're a sweet couple. But you'll see for yourself. We've been invited to lunch on Sunday after next. I said I'd confirm it this week. It's the only time. They leave for India in five weeks.'

'Sunday after next is fine. They'll be meeting Mrs Thakur.'

'Gosh! Yes, but of course.'

'But, I've got nothing to wear.'

'Nothing suits you best,' he mumbled.

'What did you say?'

'Nothing. Just teasing.' He stirred his coffee. 'Strip-teasing.' He laughed.

'I don't know what you're on about. But your eyes have a wicked look.'

He pushed his coffee aside and leaned forward. 'Please come back with me.'

'Be good. A few days, then you can do what you like. To your heart's content. I do mean that. Don't expect too much from me in that sort of thing. But I'll give myself to you completely. I'll not deny you.'

'God, I don't deserve you, and I was cad to press you. Sorry.'

'But, promise you won't marry again. You won't let another woman take my . . .'

'Darling, you must stop this, you really must!'

'Just this one last time. I want to hear you say it. It will make me happy.'

'I give you my solemn vow . . . it will be an easy one to keep. I wouldn't want to live without you.'

The Lotus And The Rose

'I'm being possessive and horribly selfish.'

'No. I would feel the same. If you were to survive me I couldn't bear the thought of another man touching you . . .'

'I couldn't bear the thought of another man touching me!' She interrupted.

'No more of this. It's ghoulish, sentimental and I dare say non-intellectual.'

She stopped and looked hard at him. 'Let's stroll along the Embankment,' she said. We can leave the car where it is.'

'Yes, it's a pleasant evening.'

'Sandy, I've never understood why is it better to be cynical rather than sentimental?'

'I suppose, to parody T S Eliot, cynics cannot bear too much reality. Human beings shy away from commitment. To be sentimental is to be committed.'

It was a dark night and the Thames Embankment was almost deserted. A man in a trilby, bent over a walking stick, felt his way up the steps of Hungerford Bridge. He shuffled and the tapping of his stick against the iron railings, broke the stillness of the night. The river lapped and splashed against the solid stone blocks below Cleopatra's Needle. Emma was smiling and he thought the shape of her head and the whites of her eyes and teeth reflected a sphinx-like quality. 'There's no one around,' she said with a slight shiver and drew closer to him. Is it very late?'

'Eleven-thirty,' he said glancing at his watch.

'Help me up!' she said.

He lifted her on to the parapet. 'Your so light!' She stood up and rested against the rump of the bronze lion. He buried his face in her pelvis.

'Sandy!'

'Marking my place,' he grinned and sprang up to her. She lifted her hair off the nape of her neck and shook her head. A dimly lighted boat chugged past, and from the radio in its cabin came sounds of garbled singing. 'Have you heard that song before?'

She listened. 'Sounds like screaming.'

'It's popular. There. Did you get that. I've heard it before. "I want to hold you hand . . . Please let me hold . . ." It's sung by a group of long-haired youngsters.'

'I've never been interested in songs, Sandy.' Her face was in deep shadow, but he could feel her eyes on him. 'Mother is right. We're an odd couple, limping in a world that's rushing into new freedoms that challenge all that's old and beautiful. We are on the threshold of a silly decade. Don't you think so?'

'Who cares! We're well out of it. We've found our rest and built our nest.'

'I'd like to read your slim volume of verse. Ted thinks there's a lot of poetry in you.' He hugged her, and she turned within his grasp, put her arms round his neck, pressed hard against him, and whispered: 'Love me, Sandy! Love me. Take me to your place.'

He kissed her. 'It's late, Emma. I must take you home. See. I can be noble.'

She did not speak during the drive back and he wondered why. He glanced at her. She had her head resting against the seat, her face turned towards him; and though her eyes were shut he was certain she was not asleep. When he stopped at the gate of Ted's house he felt her hand in his. 'Forgive me, for being unreasonably jealous. I know, you say I shouldn't be, but even beautiful couples break up.'

'You funny little thing. Cheer up.'

'How did you manage not to fall in love before you met me?'

'Because I've always been on the move. Ted asked the same question. After college I joined the Army Educational Corps and I've travelled a lot with my uncle whenever we could. But, I have had a long love affair, which is still going strong, though nothing you need be jealous about.'

She frowned, then her face cleared. 'You mean England?'

'Yes. There is no history or literature like England's. Do you know I've travelled and seen much of Britain. Holidays, long weekends. Yes, alone, I needed to be alone, in castles, churches, cemeteries. Thrills not to be shared.'

'But now, you will . . . with me? I've seen almost nothing of England!'

'But, of course, my love. You're my tangible piece of England. My compass.'

'Sandy, do you want to make love to me. You can. Here in my room. In my bed. No one's awake. I've got my keys. You can slip away later.'

He gazed down at her. The erotic desire in her eyes shone clearly in the dim light and belied what she earlier had said about simply surrendering to his sexual needs. He smiled and squeezed her arm. Then they walked softly round to the back of the house.

CHAPTER SEVEN

'There are no absolutes, Sandy.' Nigel Carr laughed derisively.

'Ideals are absolutes. Children ought to be educated as if there were. Their idealism will be destroyed soon enough. Why the rush to take away innocence and trust. They'll discover relativism and the subjective world of half-truths all too soon, and when they do, they'll need a template of absolute principles to compare or condemn values. How else can they exercise judgement and restraint? The search for the worthwhile is what education is about.'

'You seem to have given this some thought but that doesn't mean you've found the right answer. I see no benefit in delaying the inevitable. Delay can create traumas.'

'What about checks and balances? And common sense and consideration for others? Respect for authority? All these demand constraints. The subjective outlook is a self-justifying one. Selfishness can be rationalised.'

'And self-discipline?'

'It has to be taught. You know that. Moral development: *pace* Piaget and Freud.'

'So you'd advocate hypocrisy. You do have strange views about hypocrisy. I know. Sally told me. Hypocrisy is a kind of politeness, you say.'

'I don't encourage hypocrisy. I simply accept it as an unavoidable aspect of human nature. One hopes it'll be used less and less but it remains part of the civilising process. We're all hypocrites. You can't be a parent without at sometime being one. Think. We journey through tunnels, rites of passage, before finding the light.'

'Ouch! But say what you like. Education is for increasing freedoms not to impose restrictions. Cliches are excuses, excuses for justifying pain and hardships.'

'Can one banish hardships? Even tyranny has its uses.'

'Here we go again. The British Empire was a good thing?'

'Indians learnt . . .'

'Through slavery . . .'

'We were never slaves.'

'You look at British History as if it was a Boy's Own book of Adventures.'

'Brits were never tyrants. Their actions were tempered by justice, democracy and a code of good conduct. Hastings, Clive, and Dyer were questioned, even hounded.'

'It was humbug . . .'

' . . . and they admired opponents who stood up to them . . .'

'That, Gunga Din, especially that, was all hypocrisy!'

'I see, this is going to be a circular argument.'

'Oh, for God's sake!' snarled Nigel. 'Can we be serious?'

'You want to ridicule my stance, yet you're as much a moralist and pedant as I am, You are Rousseau to my Voltaire. Much of the philosophy in progressive education is romantic, naïve, short-sighted and even hypocritical; and the worst kind of hypocrisy is pretending that self-interest and manipulation don't exist.'

'And Nigel,' Sally chimed in, 'don't forget your own guru, John Dewey. He said: educationists must furnish the environment.'

'Precisely, my dear Watson,' agreed Sandy. They looked up to see Sally Watson grinning down at them.

'I thought you were on my side, Sally?' Nigel said petulantly.

'I am, Nigel. But I was following Sandy's logic. And I . . .'

The door opened, and the Headmaster poked his head in. 'Anyone seen David?'

'Try the gym, Mr Clarke.' Sally said.

'Oh, Tom! Can I have a word?' asked Nigel.

'Can't wait. You'll have to come with me,' and the door slammed shut.

Nigel sprang to his feet. He tapped Sandy's shoulder. 'Wait for me after school. We'll take the tube together. It's important.'

'Can I join you two?' Sally raised a brow, 'or is it a boy's outing?'

'It's a free country.' Nigel grimace and rushed out to catch up with Tom.

'Now, what is he up to?' Sandy said.

'Watch out,' warned Sally, 'Nigel's a scheming bastard—don't worry we're alone. He wants to find out if you're applying for the post of Deputy. Are you?'

'Hadn't even crossed my mind. I note, he's on first name terms with Clarke?'

'Showing off. I know Clarke resents it. But they were together in Repton. Sandy, you've got as good a chance of getting it as any of us. Clarke is rather fond of you.'

'Getting what? Oh, the Deputy Headship.' Sandy shook his head, 'No. I'm not really interested in promotion. Not even sure I want to make teaching a career.'

'But you're so good. The children love you. You must know there are children who wish they were in your class. You'll make a good deputy.'

'What about you? Applying, I mean.'

'Yes. I will apply. But I won't if you are . . .'

'Please do. I shan't change my mind. And Nigel?'

'Hasn't an earthly. Mind you, Clarke could surprise us all by getting an outsider. I won't mind. Rather that than Nigel.' She stared at him mischievously.

Sandy looked away and passed his fingers through his hair. 'I see you're about to change the subject. I know that look. Wasted on me. But, a word from an older and wiser mind. You could do with Peter's steadying influence and sobriety. Stick to your plans and invite me to the wedding.'

'I'd drop him like a shot at the slightest hint from you. Lord! Was that the bell?'

'Yes. Send not to know for whom the bell tolls.'

She laughed. 'More a case of saved by the bell.' As they went down the stairs she asked: 'Tell me, how's the demure Emma?'

'You're wrong about Emma. You've only seen the tip of the iceberg.'

'Is she an iceberg?'

'You don't miss a thing! No, she ain't. Sally, you pretend to be worse than you are.'

'And does she pretend to be better than she is? No, don't answer that. So you two are committed.'

'Couldn't be more committed.' He grinned.

She took out her key to opened her classroom door. 'Wait for me in the playground after we've seen the children off. You need protecting from Nigel.'

They waited in the corridor for the children. Tom Clarke's voice could be heard calling out each class in turn. The doors from the playground into the corridor opened, and the children entered like consecutive waves rolling on to a beach. A low murmur began to take on the volume of a roar, but its promise of reaching full expression was quelled by a single bellow from Tom Clarke: 'Quiet!' This was followed by: 'And keep in line!' It was at such moments that Clarke's military past achieved its distinct echo.

'Isn't he wonderful!' gasped Sally. I mean it's jolly nice of Clarke to give us these extra few minutes. In my last school we had to bring the children in from the playground ourselves.'

'So you do approve of his stern discipline?'

'Foolish not to. It makes our job easier and . . .'

Her voice was drowned in a sudden crescendo of adult admonitions: "Stop running!" "Settle down!" "Don't bang the desks!" "Coats neatly on the pegs!" "Not on the back of your chair, Eliot!" "Get rid of that, Stuart . . . into the bin!" Suddenly all was quiet. The sound of Tom Clarke's brisk footsteps down the main corridor, seemed to emphasise the silence.

Colonel Brown's Preparatory School for Boys, famed for discipline and excellent academic results, had Londoners—those wary of "progressive" education—scrambling to get their sons on its roll. As for the dapper Headmaster, Thomas Horace Clarke, no praise was fulsome enough. In his late fifties, he still had the springy stride of the boxer who thirty years earlier had been his Regimental Bantam-weight champion. Now, this always immaculately dressed and bushy-whiskered, brusque-mannered man, struck awe in hearts of children and parents alike. But the facade belied his innate gentleness. If at times he was stern, he never was harsh, and always quick to endorse good behaviour.

After school Sandy waited for Nigel in the playground, having earlier sent a message with one of the boys to tell Sally where he would be. 'Hello!' she called, with a wave of her hand. She came up to him and with a conspiratorial hiss said: 'Do you know what Nigel was overheard saying to Clarke? I have this from a reliable source.'

'The school secretary?'

She compressed her lips. 'About you. Nigel told Clarke you were a scholar and that he couldn't see what scholarship has to do with teaching in a prep school.'

Sandy looked at her with a quizzical arch of an eyebrow. 'And Clarke agreed?'

'No. He said something to the effect that knowledge informed theory and from that came authority. That's the gist . . . There's Nigel.' She waved. Nigel walked towards them but was immediately waylaid by the caretaker. Turning back to Sandy she added: 'why didn't you tell me you were leaving?'

'Was that also from the same reliable source?'

'It wasn't going to be a secret for long. Clarke will announce it at the staff-meeting tomorrow. No one knows why you're leaving, but we'll soon . . .'

'A sudden decision. Had to be, and I didn't want a big fuss to be made.'

'But you can't stop me giving you a present. I'm buying you a jacket.'

'You don't know my size. Don't waste money on something I can't wear.'

'I know your size. I've inspected your jacket on its hanger. Many a time I've planted a secret kiss on the lapels.'

'You're impossible. Why do you want to give me a present?'

'It'll give me an excuse to kiss you,' she teased. 'A custom when presents are given.'

'Get me a book. One of those arty things for the coffee table. And I'll kiss you back in self-defence.'

'Give me a name or two. Artists?'

'Botticelli or Burne-Jones.'

'How predictable. It'll be Matisse or Picasso. With the message: "Yours in spite, Sally".'

'Does Nigel know? About my leaving.'

'Know what?' Nigel had joined them unobserved. 'Never mind. I'm afraid I've got to sort something out. The caretaker's got two of my boys outside Tom's office.'

'Not the terrible twins.' Sally giggled.

'Can I have a quick word with Sandy? You don't mind Sally, but . . .'

'That's all right Nigel. I'm no longer curious.' She swung round on her heel and made for the school gate.'

'Look Sandy, have you applied for the post of deputy?'

'No.'

'Why not? Look, I know it's none of my business, but you've a damn good . . .'

'Not interested.'

'You shouldn't just think about yourself. Do it for others. For minority interests? For Indians . . . for immigrants.'

'Now you're being pompous.'

'Speak for yourself! You believe we're tolerant and fair but you won't test that belief because you wish to preserve a myth. And myth it is. That is a lot worse than being pompous. It's self-delusion. I bet you wouldn't have got this job if you didn't speak like an Englishman.'

'I think testing and putting pressure to get the result you want is unfair. All of us weigh our chances before applying for jobs. Why do it, just to make a point. I hate the idea of taking up a cause with an ulterior motive. There's a lot of this going on these days. People ostensibly having axes to grind.'

'What's wrong with showing solidarity on behalf of the weak . . . oppressed?'

'Nothing. As long as they're not used as pawns to further one's political aims.'

'Rubbish. Anyway, I can't wait. I'll just say this. It's a pity you didn't apply, for the sake of your own enlightenment and education.'

'I wish I could. Only to prove you wrong.'

Nigel scowled, shrugged his shoulders and dashed into the school building.'

The next morning Clarke was late to the staff-meeting. This unusual lapse, and Sandy's absence caused a stir among the waiting members of the school teaching staff. They arrived together. Clarke apologised for the delay and without further explanation got down to routine business. 'Finally,' he said, 'and sadly, I have to tell you that Mr Sandeep Thakur will be leaving us at the end of this month.' He paused to let the news sink in then added: 'Mr Thakur, very considerately—because of the school tests next week—has asked for no public announcement to be made just yet. So I must ask you to keep this to yourselves. I will, in the last week, about a fortnight from now, inform the school at a special assembly. Mr Thakur has to return to India to sort out property and financial matters at home, due sadly to the death of his uncle. On behalf of us all, I wish to extend our sympathies and best wishes. We will miss you, Sandy. I am particularly grateful for the useful contributions you have made here at Browns. I hope you and your wife have a safe trip to India. Now that all of you know why Sandy cannot apply for the post of Deputy, I suggest we end all speculation on the matter and inform you that two candidates, a Miss Boulting and a Mr Davis are visiting the school this week. A good day to you all.'

Colleagues gathered round Sandy, made suitable noises and dispersed. Sally stayed till the end. 'Wife! You sly dog! Why didn't you tell me? Is it Emma?

'Who else. It was all very hush-hush. Just four at a Registry.'

'And a shot-gun?'

Sandy laughed. 'Her brother Ted and his friend Clive.'

'I see. Trouble with mother. When was this?'

'Two years, this Saturday.'

'Absolutely astonishing! Where have you two been hiding yourselves.'

'Sally, you must come over before we go. I'll fix a date.'

'I'd like that. Two years! Will I also hear the patter of little feet?'

'No. Emma can't have children.'

'I'm sorry.'

'It's all right. I knew before. Actually I never gave the idea of having children much thought. My happiness didn't include or depend . . . I'm not putting this well. Whatever I say, will sound heartless.'

'You needn't explain. Your type thrive on unrivalled attention. Mind you, I'm not all that keen on having babies either, but I suppose they'll come in due course. I bet, I'm as fertile as compost.'

It was Wednesday 26 May 1964. Later in the day, Tom Clarke sent a note round announcing the death of Jawaharlal Nehru, Prime Minister of India.

CHAPTER EIGHT

'Why is he talking about bananas?' Emma asked.
'He isn't.'
'I distinctly heard him say . . .'
Sandy laughed. '*Banana*, singular, is Hindustani for "to make". *Banana, banao, banaya, bannega* are all to do with making.'

She wasn't listening. She was watching the cobbler fascinated. 'He is so good and so fast.' She said. 'He needs shoes for himself. His feet are so terribly cracked.'

'No shoe. No want shoe.' The cobbler grinned up at her showing a red tongue and widely space, bitumin-stained teeth. He was working by the roadside, squatting on his left thigh, which lay flat and tucked under him, while the right leg was upright. As he bent over his work, his cheek rested against the right knee. 'See, see!' He slapped the sole of his left foot. 'Strong *chumara*. Like leather. More, more strong than this.' He held up the sandal he was repairing, flexed it, gave his head a brisk wobble. 'Stronger than this,' he muttered to himself. When he had finished, he studied her sandal and with a thoughtful nod declared his satisfaction. 'There, I mend it. Okay!'

Emma tried the sandal. 'Yes, thank you.' She pushed the other sandal towards him. 'Now, this one too. You can speak English.'

'Dis nothing,' he addressed Sandy. 'Speaking better, long time gone. English now forgotting. Twenty years with British Army. Twenty!' He looked at Sandy and grinned widely. 'Army *mochee*. Yes. I army *mochee*.'

'*Mochee* means a cobbler.' Sandy said. The man gave his head another wobble.

Emma shuddered. 'I can't bear to watch. That needle looks lethal.'

The man took a length of cotton twine and doubled it, Then stretching his right leg before him, he looped the twine round his big toe, twirled the four-ply thread with his palms into a single strand, and sealed and stiffened it with a ball of beeswax. Emma watched the gnarled, wrinkled, but skilled hands as the fingers looped and knotted the twine over the hooked needle which pierced in and out of the leather sole. The deft invisible strength in his hands denied their weak appearance. When he had done, Sandy threw a few coins near his feet and led Emma away.

'Sahibji! Sahibji!' the man called after them.

'I don't think you've given enough.' Emma said.

'Tactics. Nothing is enough the first time round. I should've settled the price before.' Sandy held up another coin. The *mochee* jumped up, took the coin, bowed and touched his forehead. Emma was shocked to see the small, shrivelled and undernourished man.

'You're tall for an Indian, Sandy,' she said. 'Most Indians I see are rather puny.'

'Northern Indians are bigger than those from the South. Height also has to do with caste and wealth. Sweepers, tanners, mochees are low-caste. Also the "pariah", a word of Indian origin, who are without caste, the lowest of the low. I put my being tall to the Raj and a diet of "bangers and mash"; meat pies, cauliflower in white sauce, chocolate blanc-mange and custard.'

'Why was that? I mean how . . . ?'

'I was six when I was first introduced to English food. Our cook would occasionally produced roasts and stews. But I was properly introduced to a full English diet in an English home. It's a long story. I should have kept in touch with that family. I was nine when they left India. There you are, now you know I'm a self-centred prig.'

'You were far too young. You can't blame yourself.'

'No excuse. I'm lazy, when it comes to writing letters. Two years later I met your father and Ted. I didn't keep in touch with them either and I was old enough then!'

'Still, you would've been about twelve. I was sixteen when I wrote my first letter.'

They walked out of Kelly's Lane towards the Railway Station and the Madar Gate bazaar. The November morning was warm. Sandy removed his jacket, slung it over his shoulder and studied the sky. The night's freak sandstorm left a dust-filled sky, and as the bright sun shone through, it cast a golden haze over Rajnagar. In the diffused light, the town's prominent landmark, the yellow sandstone, Gothic, Victoria Jubilee Tower, shimmered. The uneven flagstones of a pavement too narrow for a teeming humanity, forced them to spill on to Station Road, which was crowded with rickshaws, bullock-carts, honking lorries and shouting taxi-drivers. In mute contrast, above the chaotic, noisy traffic, electrocuted flying-foxes hung from slack electric cables like a string of ragged, hirsute buntings. Terrified by this strange sight overhead, Emma drew closed to Sandy. He took her arm. 'Don't worry, they won't fall on us.'

'How did you meet this family?' She asked, determined to shut out present scenes.

'The Ashworths? Quite by chance and not far from here. Less than a mile behind that clock tower is an artificial lake, edged by marble pavilions, built by Emperor Shah Jehan of Taj Mahal fame. It was an unforgettable evening of fireworks and public celebration to honour the Silver Jubilee of King George V. Military bands were beating the Retreat on the wide lawn behind the pavilions—I'll show you the spot, remind me. My uncle, as a prominent citizen, had seats in one of the pavilions, and in that same pavilion was this young English family. Well, Paul was considerably older than this wife Molly. I couldn't keep my eyes off John, their son. We were the same age, though he looked younger. I was fascinated by his head of golden hair, which was straight and cut in a fringe right round his head—as if someone had used a pudding bowl to align the scissors. He was friendly and chatty. We talked toys and books. He had a lot more books than I had, and a train set I longed to play with. After the celebrations, his father, that's Paul, asked my mother if I could spend Sundays with John. She agreed. Those were happy days.'

'So it was Sunday dinners. But didn't they cook Indian meals?'

'Well,' he shrugged his shoulders. 'In the thirties and during the war, the British thought it important to stress their distinct "English" life style. An attitude which trickled down to their servants. Cooks proudly boasted they "only cooking English".'

'And don't you think that was wrong? On part of the British, I mean.'

'Let's say, I understood why. Ruling the Empire was like a game of poker. Compare the size of England and the extent of an Empire ruled by a supposedly invincible power. The whole thing was a gigantic bluff waiting to be tested. So they really had to establish a "race apart" myth. To project superiority was an important tactic. So in an India of four distinct castes they became the fifth, separate and above all. They were more lax in the eighteenth century. The Indian Mutiny changed that.'

'What was Paul doing in India?'

'I don't know what he was doing here in Rajnagar, but very soon after meeting John, Paul was appointed Headmaster of a Primary school in Pachmari, a hill-station in India. When the family left I thought that was the end of our friendship. Then mother received a letter from Paul saying there was a place for me at the school and that although it was a school for English children, I wouldn't be made to feel out of place. I wasn't.'

'And your mother didn't mind.'

'No. because Jaggers told her it would help his plans to get me into Princes College.'

'Here in Rajnagar. Why would being in an English school help?'

'The English mixed more freely with Indian aristocracy. The more so as both began to attend the same schools. Years later I was again at Pachmari, but the school was no longer there. I heard that the Ashworths were somewhere in Somerset, but I was then in training to be an officer in the Indian Army.'

'Did you make inquires when you settled in Britain?'

'Too late. I did find the village in Somerset and the graves of John's parents.'

She put her arm round his waist and hugged him. 'And John?'

'On his mother's grave there was this inscription: "And in memory of their beloved son John who was killed in a mountaineering accident in Austria." He was nineteen.' He stopped abruptly. 'Would you be disappointed if we did the market tomorrow since it's getting impossibly crowded. Instead let me show you where the Ashworths lived when I was a boy. If I can find the place. Shall we? You've got me all nostalgic.'

'Don't forget we're lunching at the Princes College.'

'Professor Shyam doesn't expect us before one.' He looked at his watch. That gives us two hours. If we make an early start tomorrow we'll beat the crowds.'

'Is that Madder Gate? The arch through that wall which looks like a fort?'

'Madar. Yes. Beyond the Gate is a narrow street which leads to a beautiful mosque and a shrine—the tomb of a *pir* or muslim saint. The patron of beggars. Every year, on his feast day, *pilau* rice is cooked in two huge cauldrons, that are ten feet wide, five feet deep. Then at a given signal the contents are looted in record time. Two men, specially equipped and dressed, jump inside these huge pots and help clear the contents, so I'm told. It's said that Akbar, the Great Mughal King, visited the shrine to pray for a son. His prayers were answered. Beyond that shrine, a path goes to that fort you see on the summit of the hill.'

'Oh, let's walk up to see that!'

'Tomorrow. But now we'll take a rickshaw. A bicycle rickshaw to save us time.'

'Must we? The thought of sitting behind someone puffing and sweating. It's awful.'

'Would you prefer a taxi? There're some at the station . . . across the road. But you'll be denying the poor rickshawallah a wage. Better for him to sweat than starve.'

'Yes. I forget. All right then.'

'I'll chat to take your mind off the poor fellow; *and* the stray buffaloes, which seem to fascinate you endlessly.'

She threw her head back and laughed. Her laughter always intrigued him. The mouth would open, slightly wider than her smile, and soundlessly.

There was no difficulty in finding a rickshaw. Three were circling them like vultures. Sandy chose the sturdiest rickshawwalla, for Emma's peace of mind. 'I think our man's a muslim,' he said.

'How do you know?'

'Subtle things. That black vest, white pyjamas, the orange, henna-dyed beard and no moustache. But,' he went on as the rickshaw came up to them, 'the clearest proof of his religion is that locket-like thing he's wearing. The tiny silver box round his neck, that is a *tabiz* . . .' He broke off and addressed the rickshawalla in Urdu. 'Fraser Road? *Kithna?* How much to Fraser Road.'

The man took in Emma perceptibly. 'Fraser Road? Phive. Only phive rupees.'

Sandy gave Emma a warning look. 'Leave this to me,' he mumbled. Then he said to the man. 'We not tourists. I used to live here. Went college here. Princes College.'

The man puckered his lips, unconvinced. 'Okay,' he shrugged. 'Phor rupees.'

'Tharee rupees, eight annas!' called out another rickshawalla within earshot.

'Shut your mouth, you sister fucker!' Sandy's man swore in Hindustani, and Sandy, avoided Emma's inquiring glance. He had no intention of translating this fulsome abuse.

'Listen!' Sandy said in Urdu. 'I'll give you five, if you will wait for fifteen minutes on Fraser Road and then take us on to Princes College?'

The man studied Sandy with wry admiration. 'So you knowing some Hindustani?' He laughed, not unkindly: 'But you no speakin' okay. Sahib making too many missing takes.' He dismounted, wobbled his head and proudly slapped the oil-cloth upholstery with a resounding thump. '*Chalo, sahib aur memsahib!.* Vee go.'

As they climbed into the rickshaw, Emma whispered: 'That's only six shillings!'

'Still twice the amount he would've got. Believe me he's made a killing. We're probably spoiling the fares for others.'

The road was lined with ogling men, who scratched their crotches as they gaped. She looked away. 'It will be a relief to get away from here. I know you keep telling me there's no hostility, but I can't get used to it.'

'Indians are great balls scratchers!' Sandy mumbled.

Emma banged a fist sharply against his thigh. 'You don't have say the obvious.'

The rickshaw sped down the road to meet the steep incline of Mayo Bridge. The rickshawalla stood on his pedals but when he began to struggle Sandy told him to stop at the foot of the bridge. 'We'll walk and meet you at the top.'

'The man dismounted with a grateful shake of his head. 'Ahmed', he said. 'My name Ahmed.' He pushed the rickshaw up the slope. On their way up Emma stopped and leaned over the parapet. 'A lot of the buildings here use this grey-green stone, like this bridge, which is grand.'

'Large and Raj. Rajnagar was an important Railway Junction, and probably still has one of the largest railway carriage workshops in the country. Careful where you lean. That space is used as a spittoon . . . and sometimes they miss.'

She sprang back, then seeing his pained expression added with concern. 'You poor thing! I don't mean to be squeamish. I'll get used to it, if I took in less. There's much in India to be proud about, Sandy. Even from the little I've seen.'

'We are an ancient people, but there's so much ugliness about. It doesn't take long to make me unhappy here. Thank God I can live in Britain.'

They walked on in silence. Then she said: 'You were talking about Rajnagar.'

'About it being a railway centre. Yes. There was a large British community here and an even larger Anglo-Indian one—Anglo-Indians, as Eurasians came to be called, more especially those of Irish descent. They ran the Indian railways for the British, and talked openly about one day "going back home", that's England. For that and much else they were despised by both the Indians and the Brits. After Indian Independence, 1947, some did go, but many were shunted off to Canada, Australia, and Rhodesia. It was an awful business. They had to prove some percentage of British blood. A sort of Plimsoll line below which some sank. Now that,' they crossed to the other side, 'that Nursing Home, run by Roman Catholic nuns, is where my Italian niece was born.'

'Dorothea?'

He nodded. They reached the top of the bridge overlooking the rather dilapidated Sahara Hotel. 'Cross over to the other side and you'll see St Mary's Church, where I went to Sunday School and fell madly in love with Patricia Kinsella—forever my image of Alice in Wonderland. Don't look at me like that! I was only here during the hols and I was eleven when she went out of my life forever. Good Lord! This is dreadful!' They were standing at a gap in the parapet where an iron stairway led down to a little bridge of railway sleepers over an open drain of stagnant, black, oily sludge. The stench was overwhelming.

'Oh dear,' she said, looking decidedly uncomfortable. 'I'd want to forget that.'

'That wasn't there.' He searched beyond the filthy culvert for the field, where he played cricket on Sunday afternoons and where it banked up to a low hill on which the church stood. The steeple was just about visible but the field was hidden by what could only be described as a gigantic chicken coop; which it was, and explained the constant din of countless cackling hens. He turned enquiringly at the rickshawalla, who had come up behind them.

'Many years now', said Ahmed, rolling his head.

They climbed on to the rickshaw. 'Behind the church there was a small lake. Is that still there?' Sandy asked Ahmed.

'No, phinished. No lake. *Khatam*, phinished. Now growing vegetables. No *pani*, no water.' Ahmed shook his head, then violently cleared his throat and spat. 'I coming here Sunday morning time. Bringing memsahibs to church. No Padre, no English memsahibs. Anglos, two maybe three, left. Indian priest now. I bring old Hamilton memsahib from Jaipur Gate. You know Jaipur Gate. Near college, only.'

'Gosh!' said Sandy. 'She'll be nearly ninety.'

'Who?' asked Emma.

'Mrs Hamilton. She was quite old when I knew her.' Sandy then spoke to Ahmed in Urdu, and the two had a long conversation. 'I've just been telling him,' he explained to Emma, 'that Mrs Hamilton was our neighbour and that we lived in a house behind hers. "Ah, the *bhoot bangla*," he says, meaning, the haunted house. Why it was called that no one really knows. But it had a certain atmosphere. It's going to be a school.'

'School? A big house then.'

'Ramblingly big. There were rooms I dreaded going into without a servant or adult member of the family. A *Turn of the Screw* sort of place. It was my grandfathers house. You'll see. Tomorrow we'll be moving into the small cottage in the grounds, which will become the headmaster's residence . . . fortunately, it's near Madar Gate. The cottage needs a lot doing to. A bit rough, lacking facilities. I'm sorry, but it just for two days. I need to sort things out with Panchu and Arjun. Then we'll go on to Charbagh.

'Sahibji, you not *ghussa* . . . angry . . . I calling *bhoot bangla*?'

Sandy waved his hand. '*Aur*, Bartlett memsahib?'

'*Uski mauth*. Phinish. Dead. All dead. All family dead. Now many years gone.'

'Good Lord! That's sad news, Emma. I knew Pamela Bartlett, Mrs Hamilton's only daughter. Married a police Inspector. Three children. Penny, the eldest, was my age.'

Ahmed stopped the rickshaw and got off the saddle. He spoke at length in Urdu, too fast for Sandy to follow, but he got the gist. 'Dreadful. He says that Bartlett was posted to Delhi as a Superintendent. But not long after, a murderous gang broke into their bungalow and murdered the whole family. No, the youngest survived. The boy's *ayah*, who was sleeping next to his bed, picked him up and ran out of the house.'

'*Badla*,' said Ahmed

'Revenge? A revenge killing?' Sandy translated as Ahmed went on. 'It seems that the boss of a ruthless gang was killed during a police siege, and as it was known that Bartlett was the officer in charge, they . . . well you can guess the rest.'

'You go. See church. I wait here.' Ahmed said. He pointed to the gravel path that ran alongside the high fenced perimeter of the poultry farm. 'This short-cut. I wait here for eight annas. Maybe one rupee more?'

Sandy smiled. 'Okay, one rupee. Not one paisa more.' They climbed the path up to the church. The sandstone gate pillars were there, but not the beautiful cast-iron gates, as were the raised green lawns and flower beds, much the worse for neglect. He spotted the remnants of the summer house, but the oak bench which was in front of it was gone. That was the bench on which pretty Patricia Kinsella sat, her frilly skirt neatly spread under a white pinafore. With her carefully brushed auburn hair she was the picture of a wondering, but aloof "Alice". He recalled being stricken by the large hazel eyes and the sullen poise of her carmine lips. He turned to look for the bed of tall sweet-peas behind which, one happy Sunday, she allowed him a chaste kiss, indicating the exact spot with a finger. The plot was there but not the sweet-peas, while within a border of pansies, lay an unkempt display of ball chrysanthemums.

'Amazing,' Emma said. 'Did they try to recreate a little bit of England?'

'Yes. Along the perimeter were hollyhocks and behind the church, a rose garden and orangery. Here, on either side of the West door were two sago-palms.'

'And the church, Sandy. That could be anywhere in the Home Counties.'

He tried the door. It opened. They entered the cool darkness of the nave. Out of the dazzling light it was sometime before they could see anything. She found a pew and sat down.

'Are you all right?' he asked. She nodded. 'Tired?'

'Sandy,' she whispered. 'I need to go.'

'Oh, heck! I don't know if there's a lavatory, or one clean enough!'

'Don't fuss! Keep your voice down. And before you ask, I did go before we set out.'

'We can try the Sahara hotel. Can you last? Ten to fifteen minutes?'

She nodded. The vestry door opened and a little man in a black cassock came out and walked along the side aisle. 'I'll ask,' Sandy said and strode across to intercept the man, who saw him coming and stopped.

'Oh, hello,' greeted the little man. 'I'm Father Joshua.' He was small, fat, with curly black hair and soft brown eyes. His cassock was dusty. 'Please to forgive me, but I've been up there.' He pointed to the belfrey. 'Removing sparrow's nests.'

Sandy took the extended hand and explained about Emma.

'Not to worry. Wait one moment, I'll bring key.' Father Joshua re-entered the vestry and returned almost immediately carrying a plastic bucket.

'Oh, Sandy! I could die.' Emma sighed when he joined her.

Father Joshua led them, through a side door, out to the back of the church. The rose garden was gone. Where it should have been was a large concrete floor, on the one end of which was an easel and blackboard, while at the other end was a Nissen-like hut with its roof of corrugated iron. The priest filled the bucket with water from an oil drum next to the door of the hut, which he opened and shut behind him, A sound of a great splash of water was heard before he emerged with a pleasant grin and gestured to Emma. 'Yes please, good lady.' He said and pointed to the door.

Emma, who was experiencing emotions worse than stage-fright, smiled bravely and gingerly shut the door behind her. The bowl was clean but wet. She sat on her hands and realised there was no paper. An empty, cracked china container, on the wall next to her, bore the legend "Bromo" in indigo, and below at knee level a tap dripped into a blue, chipped, enamel mug. She used a tissue from her handbag, which she kept to get rid of later, rinsed her hands in the rusty brown water in the mug, and dried them on the back of her cotton khaki slacks, under her navy blue bush-shirt. She felt uncomfortable but welcomed the hot dry air outside. Sandy and the priest had moved down the crazy flag-paved pathway. They turned towards her as she came out.

'I'd take advantage of the facilities,' she said to Sandy, directing a charming smile to Father Joshua.

'My very thought,' mumbled Sandy and made for the hut.

Father Joshua smiled widely and rolled his head. 'Not meaning to be inquisitive, but he's your husband, no?'

Emma nodded. 'He lived here from the age of five or six and attended this church. That was before the war . . . and then again when he was in college.'

'I see! I see! But he's Indian, and this was the Englishmen's church? How . . .'

'I believe, a branch of the Thakur family . . .'

'Sorry. Did you say Thakur? But they are a most renown family. People here well remember them. Rai Bahadur Thakur was Zamindar. Big landowner. But a Hindu!'

'He was Sandy's grandfather. I'm still learning about the family.'

'Father Joshua,' said Sandy, joining them, 'do give me your address. I'd like to make a donation towards the church, once I've settled my affairs here.'

'This is most kind of you, Thakur sahib. Please may I offer you a cup of tea.'

'Thank you, but we have a luncheon date.' He looked at his watch. 'We are running late. Emma, we'll have to give up on Fraser Road . . . You see, Father Joshua, I knew an English family who lived there, and I wanted to see the house . . .'

'Nothing to see now. Fraser Road is closed. Grand bungalows all gone. Re-building. Making into flats . . .' He rolled his head. 'One moment. I giving you picture post card of St Mary's Church, with my address.'

'Sahib! Sahibji! Salaam, salaam sahib!' The familiar voice was none other than that of their erstwhile rickshawalla, Ahmed. '*Hut! Huttoh!*' He shouted to the mob that were closing in on Sandy and Emma. '*Bazoo! Bazoo! Huttoh! Yeh mera malik.* He my sahib! *Mera shareef malik.*' My good sahib.' All this he accompanied with a constant ringing of his bicycle bell. The crowd gaped and then began slowly to give way. Ahmed's head could be seen bobbing above the crowd as he pedalled his rickshaw towards them. 'Sit! Sit! Come memsahib, come sahib.' They climbed into the rickshaw as he dismounted to turn the vehicle round. The crowd started to close in again. Ahmed stood on the pedals and addressed them in Urdu, with a mix of abuse and appeasement. 'Go, go! Go home! Have you no shame! Haven't you got sisters, wives, mothers. *Arrey,* what? Harassing this noble couple. They are husband and wife. Look at their faces. They are big people!' Once again the crowd retreated and started to disperse as he rode through them. 'This,' he added. 'is not that kind white woman you see in cinema. You donkeys think all white woman want only one thing.' He made a rude gesture by clenching his fist and gripping his elbow. Someone laughed. A contagion of laughter rippled through the crowd easing the tension.

They passed under Madar Gate, meandered through market stalls, and not till they were on Station Road did Ahmed stop. Then he let the rickshaw freewheel slowly and turning to Sandy slapped his forehead, tut-tutting at the same time. 'What sahib you thinking. Most foolish thinking. Taking white woman to that place? There, *arrey* with no guide, nothing? Dargah is now bad place. Not for toorist now.'

There followed a conversation in Hindustani between them. Sandy sucked in his lips shamefacedly. 'I wanted to show memsahib the famous Dargah!'

'No, no. No good place. Next time go anywhere, first checking with me. Okay?'

Sandy sat back, angry with himself. His enthusiasm had caught him off guard, and realising how unwise he had been, tried to shut out the vision of Emma stripped and brutally violated. He had been a fool to expose her to such danger. But now, the more he thought about Ahmed's intervention the more unclear recent events became. Was the situation really as sinister as Ahmed was making it? Was the crowd simply curious and no harm intended. He waved Ahmed on. 'Princes College,' he said. Ahmed moved on, but there was no way of stopping his commentary on Sandy's ill-judged actions. 'Most danger for Memsahib, but sahib, in more danger! In Mussalman place always someone there to protect woman. But you Sahib, Hindu. They no like Hindu . . .' At the foot of the bridge he dismounted. 'Sahib and memsahib is married?'

'Of course!' Sandy said sternly, his face so visibly angry that Ahmed quickly changed tack. 'But memsahib is good . . . also most bee-ooti-full.'

Sandy ignored him. He looked at Emma. She was her usual calm self. 'Forgive me. I am sorry I put you through all this.'

'I'm all right,' she murmured. 'Let the man go. Please do as I say.'

'*Kitna?*' asked Sandy. 'How much?'

'Like yesterday. Phive, only.'

Sandy gave a fiver, then produced another. 'This *baksheesh* for help.'

Ahmed shook his head. 'No, no. That I do in name of Gawd. Gawd is Great.'

'I want you to have it.' Sandy turned to Emma. 'You offer it to him.'

She took the note. 'Come on Ahmed. Take it or memsahib will be offended.'

'Okay,' said Ahmed. 'But where you go? I take you.'

Emma shook her head, took Sandy's arm firmly, and led him away.

'That was a bit abrupt,' he said. 'After all he did prevent an ugly incident. Darling, weren't you afraid? I was.'

'Terrified; for a while.' She glanced over her shoulder to see Ahmed ride away. 'He was overdoing it. There were women and children in the crowd. And, no different from the other crowds we've come across.'

'So you think I've been hoodwinked?'

'Yes, by ten rupees.' They laughed.

In a room darkened by shut windows and blinds drawn to keep out the afternoon heat, they lay naked on the bed, studying with increasing apprehension the eccentric rattling of the ceiling-fan. 'If I switch it off the heat will be stifling.' Sandy said.

She sat up, shook her head and raised her hair from off the nape of her neck. 'Make it go faster, Sandy. I've never been so hot in all my life.'

'That's the North Indian summer for you.' He dabbed his chest with a towel. 'Any faster and it will come crashing down on us.'

'Sandy, are you absolutely certain it'll be worse if we open the windows?'

'It's a furnace outside. Panchu kept the room shut to keep the heat out. This is the worse time of the hot season. We couldn't wait till November. Arjun's wire was urgent. He had a buyer for uncle's sprawling estate. People change their minds if you give them time to think things over.'

'Yes. I'm sorry to fuss. The evenings are pleasant. I'm having a wonderful time.'

Sandy got up and toyed with the fan switch. 'It's on full. I'll tell Panchu to get an extra fan. A table fan. He should be back soon. I asked him to expect us for tea.' Sandy came round and sat on the edge of the bed. 'Just one more night. We'll be comfortable tomorrow. The rooms in my uncle's house are air-conditioned.'

She kissed him.

'Emma, I'm thinking of selling everything, even though I have a special affection for the house. It's far too big, and there are gardens and orchards to maintain. And we live in London. The place needs a big family, like the Kapoors. They will be the new owners and have a string of servants to keep it in good trim.'

'Your uncle would want you to keep something; and it would be nice to have a place in India to come to occasionally. What about that cottage you told me about?'

'The cottage in the hills? Fern Cottage? You like the idea of it? You can have it.'

'Our home away from home!' She gave a little excited clap. 'I imagine it's pretty?'

'Yes. But I wonder what state it is in. I was a teenager when I last saw it. There's a garden, a field, a paddock and ponies. You'll be taking on a big job.'

'Sandy, you've got me all excited. We'll work on it together to make it ours . . . Don't look at me like that? I feel so vulnerable lying like this. No, Sandy! Stop. Why ponies?'

'Transport. We're miles away from the nearest town.' He bent down and kissed her. 'This is to help you to forget the heat.' He lay on top of her.

'Didn't work the first time. You're insatiable.' She pushed him away. 'It's been less than two hours since . . .' A noise in another part of the house made them jump up. They listened. Shuffling feet approached the door of their bedroom. 'Sandy?' She whispered.

'Quick', he said. 'Make yourself decent. Here.' He threw her bathrobe, walked to the door and called out. 'Panchu?'

'*Hahnji*. Salaam *baba* sahib!' There was a pause. '*Chai?* After-the-noona tea?'

Sandy raised a finger to his lips to discourage Emma from getting the giggles—a gesture she failed to see in the darkness. He shouted at the door. '*bahut achcha, dus minut ke bad.*' He returned to the bed. 'I've told him to bring tea after ten minutes.'

'Then I'll have a shower,' she said and was about to put her feet into her shoes.

'Stop! Phew! don't forget what I told you. Bang the shoes to make sure nothing has crawled into them. Absolutely vital! There may be scorpions about.'

On entering the bathroom her face fell. The room was bare. In the far corner of the flag-stoned floor, a low wall surround enclosed a small tiled floor which sloped towards a drain-hole. In the middle of the floor was a two-foot square slatted board, and above, a loose, rusty shower-head was attached to a pipe, which came in through the outside wall. She inspected the shower-head, then tried the tap. It juddered, hissed, rattled and spat loudly. 'Sandy! There's no water.'

'I should have remembered. Panchu warned me the taps don't run in the afternoons. Do you see a bucket of water and a large aluminium mug next to it?'

'There's an oil drum or barrel full of water . . . yes, and a mug.'

'Keep dipping and filling the mug and pouring the water over you. That's the Indian way. I'll give you a towel.'

'And the dressing-gown.'

'Right. Come out after he's brought the tea. I'll tell you when.'

When she came out, Panchu was standing by the bed staring at the ceiling fan. Then he went to the regulator and gave it a sharp bang with his fist. The fan groaned, picked up speed and steadied itself.'

'Wonderful!' Emma cried delightedly.

Panchu gave her the widest grin she thought a human face could possibly make. He pointed to the chair next to the low table. 'See, missy baba. For you. Hot, hot *jelabies*.'

'Thank you, Panchu, that was sweet of you.'

Panchu rolled his head.

She smiled as she watched his tubby figure waddle out of the room and shut the door behind him. 'How does he know I like jelly babies?'

'*Jelabies*, schwweetheart,' Sandy said, mimicking Humphry Bogart, 'bechossh I told him, "of all the sweets in town she had to choose these."'

The door opened and Panchu peeped in. 'Dinner, baba?'

'No, Panchu,' Sandy said. 'Going out.' The door closed.

'He calls you baba. And he's not like other servants. Much less obsequious.'

'Panchu is family. Known me since the year dot. Now, he's caretaker of this house. The poor man feared he'd lose his family quarters when the school takes over. I'd told Arjun, I'll only sell this house on condition they employ Panchu and house his family. They've agreed. Panchu's got a two-roomed hut in the local *bustee*. A kind of slum.'

'Two rooms! What about a bathroom and lavatory.'

'A *bustee* usually has a communal stand pipe or two.'

'You mean they bathe in the open?'

'Next to the stand pipe. Of course, they wear something. As for the other, well, it's the wide open spaces or the side of the road. That's why these settlements are outside towns and not places one cares to visit. I pressed him to bid for something better, but Panchu wants to be near his son and grandchildren. They live in the same *bustee*.'

'Poor chap. I like him. Can't you persuade the Kapoors to take him on?'

'The Kapoors have their own servants. Servants in many Indian families are members of the household and for generations. For instance, Panchu's father, and for all I know, his grandfather were with my family. But all that's changing . . . has since the War. Many of my generation had joined the army. The railways too, offer better paid jobs. If you're worried we could take him with us to the hills. But the man's nearly seventy. Foolish to uproot him. In any case he wont come.'

'What about a pension?'

'Darling stop worrying! I won't let him starve.'

There was a gentle knock on the door and Panchu entered and stared at the tea tray with a look of disappointment. 'Missy baba not eat?'

'If I eat anymore, I shall become fat.' Emma enunciated slowly.

He shook his head. 'No. Not now. When baby coming, then missy baba go fat.' He picked up the tray and Sandy opened the door for him.

'Panchu,' said Sandy, 'take the *jelabies*, don't leave them.' He turned to Emma. There were tears in her eyes. 'Darling, that's the sort of thing servants say.'

'Oh, Sandy! I'm sorry. Sorry I can't give you . . .'

'Now don't get broody. I count myself lucky. I'd make a terrible father. What you said earlier: "just us", that will do nicely.'

'Why do you laugh?'

'I was reminded of a Marx Brothers film. During an argument, Chico, the one who speaks with an Italian accent, is asked: "Don't you believe in justice?" "Of course", says Chico. "I believe in justice. I'm just as good as you."'

'You have a facile sense of humour.'

'Come now. This will cheer you. I've an Army Ordnance map that shows you where Fern Cottage is.' He opened his brief case, took out a map and spread it out on the bed. 'That's north. There's Delhi, Simla . . . follow this range of mountains westward. There's Dharamsala. Ten miles further into the hills, towards Dalhousie—above this small lake, near the village of Rajkot, is the cottage.'

'Is anyone at the cottage, at this moment? A caretaker?'

'Nathoo. Panchu's younger brother. If you like Panchu, you'll like him. I've known him even longer. His wife was our cook in Bombay. They are both there, taking care of the place. Arjun goes there, every few months, to check all is well It is a risk to leave a house empty these days, especially with the influx of refugees.'

'Tibetans?'

Sandy nodded

'Oh, Sandy! I can't wait.'

'We'll go as soon as we can. Here's an old snap Arjun took. That's me with Jaggers in front of his house. And here's one of Junior, I mean Arjun, wearing a *sola topi*.'

'Jaggers and you look like father and son. Both so very good-looking.' She returned the snaps. 'The family, who are buying the house, will we see them?'

'The Kapoors, no. They take over from December.'

'So what's going to happen to Arr-joon?'

'He'll return to his village near Jodhpur, with a good pension. Jaggers has seen to that. Though Junior never has been short of a bob or two.'

'Sandy, if we are flying back to London from Delhi, we could see your sister.'

'After we've been to the hills? Yes, we will be doing that. At Charbagh I could do with your help supervising the packing and crating of my uncle's books, and an item or two of furniture. Junior's booked two lorries to take it to Delhi. It's sweet of my sister to offer to store them. I hate imposing on people. Hey! just occurred to me. I should've thought of this before. No need to trouble Dolly. Panchu can travel with the lorries, not to Delhi, but straight to Pathankot. Look, that's Pathankot, near to Dharamsala.' Sandy jabbed the map with his forefinger. 'Jaggers kept a garage there. Ideal for storage.

He had two cars. One is now in Charbagh. So there'll be ample space. But I can't postpone seeing my sister next week. She lost her husband recently and wants to talk to me about little Dinesh's future. She would like him to go to a school in Somerset.'

'How old is he?'

'Five or six. A bit premature. I'll get Arjun to go with Panchu. He'll drive the Austin Healey back to Delhi, then we can drive it to Dharamsala. More fun. Actually, with the car we can go up to Macleodganj. The last bit is a pony trek. Can you ride a pony?'

'I've never ridden a pony.'

'Not to worry. Terribly docile. They walk a steady pace however much you prod them and know their way to the cottage. I've found someone to replace Nathoo, who'll be happy to return to Rajnagar. It'll please Panchu. The brothers can travel back on the lorries. Ransingh, the chap who met us at the Airport, takes over as chowkidar—watchman. He will keep an eye on the place. He was a soldier in the Army. Batman to Dolly's husband. He'll make a good *chowkidar*. I'm fond of him. An honest man.'

How old is Dolly?' Emma asked, as they got into a taxi.

'Queensway!' Sandy told the driver. 'About Ted's age.'

'I don't think she likes me.'

'She said you're beautiful.'

'I'm tired of being just a face.'

'Dolly wouldn't compliment you if she didn't like you. Don't read too much into her sullen moods. They have nothing to do with her husband's death. She's had a hard time. Something went badly wrong in their marriage. But I thought she seemed more relaxed after our chat.'

'She has no time for her son.'

'Dinesh? You've noticed that?'

'The only attention he gets is from the maid.'

'His *ayah*. He hardly knew his parents, and from early childhood he's lived with relatives and friends. So he'll take to boarding. Dolly asked me not to tell you her story till we're back in England, but I may as well. She had been in the Army Nursing Corps and when she got demobbed the family suddenly woke up to the fact she was well into her thirties, and pressed her into an arranged Hindu marriage.

Mahesh seemed a decent, pleasant chap, liked by all, even by Dolly, but quite soon after marriage he lost interest in her. Each posting became an excuse to stay away, and he lived like a bachelor in the Officers' Mess. Dolly stayed with her in-laws, till she could bear it no longer, and ran away to mother. Before mother died, she begged Dolly to contact Mahesh, and retrieve their marriage. Then, according to Dolly, I knew nothing of this till now, without any explanation, Mahesh applied for early retirement. Instead, he was posted to Army HQ here. Soon he saw the advantage of being socially seen with his wife—as you can see, Dolly's a handsome woman. But when Dinesh was born, Mahesh returned to his old ways of avoiding Dolly and any further sexual contact . . .'

'Did you find out why?'

'He preferred the company of men.'

'You mean he is a . . .'

'Yes. That's the conclusion Dolly came to. There's no absolute proof of it.' Sandy looked at his watch. 'We're early.'

'Then let's walk along Queensway. I've seen such pretty things on the pavements.'

Sandy stopped the taxi outside The Imperial Hotel and they walked back towards Connaught Place in silence for a while. 'The world's a sad place.' Emma said wistfully.

'My prescription, for what it's worth. We can't cure all the ills of the world, but we can make it a good place if each one of us resolve to make at least one person happy.'

'One may want to, with that one person but sometimes even that is impossible. What does that look mean? You would say we must make it a duty, an obligation. Oh, Sandy you'd make a good father!'

'Hush, Emma.'

'Who's the man Dolly wants us to meet?'

'No one I know, but I've a strong feeling he's been around for sometime.' Then he added, after a thoughtful pause, 'young Dinesh does look terribly like his father. So, it's understandable why Dolly finds it hard to like the boy. It would also be hard for both of them. Dolly and the new man, I mean.'

'After dinner let's give them time to be with each other. We could see a film. Or is it too late to get tickets?'

'We'll do that. I had a chance to discuss Dinesh's education. She was reasonable. I got her to agree he should be educated in India and then do a post graduate course in England. I said I'd help. I hope you don't mind.'

'Not at all. We have the money. I've been wondering what I could do with mine.'

'Do what you want with your money.'

'Oh, look at that!' she said.'

'Handloom House?'

'No. The jewellery on pavement. Who are those women?'

'Tibetan refugees. You'll see a lot more when we ride through Macleodganj.'

'Some are so young. That's pretty. That necklace and earrings set.' Emma knelt down to take a closer look. 'I think these are turquoise.'

'Nice for you.' A hand brushed Emma's cheek as it held a earring against her hair. She looked up and her gaze was held by eyes of the deepest black she ever saw. But there was something else about those eyes. 'Thank you,' she said breathlessly. They moved on. 'She's beautiful . . . serenely beautiful.' Emma looked back. 'She's still looking at me! I'll never forget that face. Her skin's like gold against her jet black hair. She's no more than a child.'

'About nineteen or twenty, I'd say. Don't keep stopping and looking back. You'll only raise her hopes.'

A few yards ahead Emma turned, she told herself, for the last time, and saw a gang of young men gather round the Tibetan girl, who was looking very distressed.

'Go, please! Go. *Jao!*' Emma heard her say. 'Sandy, those boys are being horrid to her! What are they saying?'

'Keep moving. We can't get involved. She'll know how to handle such situations.'

'Supposing she can't. And whatever they're saying, its got the poor girl all agitated.'

'They're not interested in jewellery. They want to know if she's selling her body and offering to take her in a taxi. We should move on. It probably happens everyday.'

'She's far too young. She could be new. It could be her first day in Delhi.'

'No. She has to be with someone. Someone who's keeping an eye . . .'

'Stop them! Quick! Sandy stop them. Please she's looking so unhappy. There, she's seen us. I'm going to her.'

'Emma wait! I'll do it. Stay close to me, in case the boys get cheeky.'

'I will. Thank you, sweet Sandy.'

'Hello there!' Sandy called out. 'My wife,' he said, addressing the young woman in Hindi, 'has changed her mind. We'll buy those earrings.' Then back in English: 'Excuse me, gentlemen. Please, do you mind? Or if you're buying something, we'll wait?'

The young men, indistinguishable one from another, drew back. 'No, no!' said one of them, with a rapid roll of his head. 'You first.'

'Thank you, you're so kind. But I insist you finish your business first.'

One of the group started laughing. 'Fellow's putting a lot of *kunny*. You know? He is showing off. Putting on style. Speaking like a limey to impress the whitey.'

'Bilu, you're a donkey. He said wife. Idiot.' The speaker sharply tapped the head of the young man, presumably Bilu.

'*Chalo*, let's forget it and go to the coffee house,' said a new voice.

'No, *yaar*, try the Alps. They've got a dance band now.'

'Hang on!' said Bilu. 'Don't give up so easy. They won't take long.' The young men stopped and, from across the road stood around watching and waiting.

Sandy turned to Emma, who was kneeling on the pavement, apparently talking to the Tibetan girl. 'Take your time,' he whispered. 'They'll eventually give up.'

'I've no intention of leaving till they've gone. Sandy, she understands and speaks a little English and she's terribly grateful we are here. What's your name?'

'Sonam,' said the Tibetan girl.

'That means "gold"' Sandy said, 'Sona is gold.'

'Sona?' repeated the Tibetan girl. 'Yes, yes! I be Sona.'

'Take the set. Necklace, bracelet, ring . . . the lot . . .' He knelt beside Emma. 'They are still waiting. Listen,' he said to Sona, 'trust me. Pack up, come with us.'

She stared at him. 'Where?'

'There,' he pointed. 'Imperial Hotel. Emma, we are going back to the Hotel.'

Emma reached out and held Sona's hand. Sona nodded and gathered the corners of the black mat and bundled the jewellery into a canvas satchel. 'Okay,' she said striding ahead. Emma and Sandy followed. The young men gaped. Then putting their arms over each others shoulders, moved on. 'I could phone the police from the Reception Desk and ask them to keep an eye on those young men. How much do we owe her, Emma?'

'One hundred and forty five rupees. That, could you believe it is for the lot.'

At the hotel gates Sandy paid Sona. 'That's okay. Keep the change.' He looked at his watch. 'Emma, it's almost time.'

'I can't move Sandy, she's holding my hand!'

'Preese, I work for you. Preese take me. Any job, I do. Good servant I be.'

'But Sona,' Sandy said, 'we don't live here!'

'Anywhere I come. No fammery. No mother, no chirren, I arone.' Then she started speaking desperately and rapidly in a mixture of English and Hindustani.

Sandy translated. 'She's all alone in the world. Says that she worked for a rich old Hindu woman in Jawalamukhi—which by coincidence isn't far from Dharamsala—and with whom she came to Delhi. But the woman died some weeks ago . . . She says she's a Christian, an orphan, who worked in a Catholic mission in Kalimpong. Right, Emma, we . . .' But Sona had gone on her knees and clung to Emma's feet. 'God, I feared this.'

'Preese! I be good servant!' Sona cried. Her beseeching eyes stirred Emma to tears. She cupped the girl's face in her hands. 'Sandy,' she said hoarsely, 'it's a strange and lovely coincidence. I have to help. I'll give her a home. She can live in our cottage. We have to do this. If you love me, you can't refuse to make room for her.'

'There's no shortage of room. But we're not going to be there much ourselves. I mean for holidays only . . . some holidays, not all.'

'But she can stay there. It would be good not to leave the cottage empty.'

'Emma, we've got a watchman to take care of the place.'

'She can take care of the cottage itself. Don't keep looking at your watch, you're frightening the poor girl. We'll only miss having a drink in this chap's room.'

'Wait, that man is a waiter, I'll get him to take a message to Raj's room. Strange, I remembered his name.' Sandy hailed the waiter and went up to him. When he returned he said: 'That's settled. I sent a message to say we'll be with them in fifteen minutes, and will meet them in the restaurant. Now, darling we have to be sensible. We can't jump into . . .'

'Why not, Sandy?' Emma stared at him with trembling determination.

'We don't know who she is! We only have her story. We can't take on anyone . . .'

'Why not? People employ servants on flimsiest references—you told me so. She's not just anyone. She's special, I know, in my heart, she is.'

'I suppose, if she agrees to a salary, it will protect us from any charge of abduction. And she is an adult. Lord, here comes trouble. Judging from Sona's reaction, she must know this woman. Where has she been all this time!'

A spectral old woman, in a long black robe, came up to them. Her deep lined face seemed carved in granite. She spoke rapidly. Her lips scarcely moving, produced a flow of unintelligible words. But Sona was paying close attention. 'Mother?' Sandy asked. Sona, shook her head and taking the satchel from off her shoulder, thrust it into the old woman's hands. The old woman stared implacably, till Sona waved money under her nose. The woman beamed, took the money and turned to leave. Sona tugged her back. Reluctantly the woman handed Sona thirty rupees.

'She Legjin. Her make jewellery. I sell for she.'

'Sandy?' Emma squeezed his arm. 'I've never asked for anything, till now.'

'Do you have a piece of paper? Wait, it's all right. I'll use this shop receipt. We won't need it.' He raised a leg and wrote on his knee. 'Sona, this my address. Come tomorrow morning . . . ten.' He gave her the paper and gestured the number ten with his hands and again on his watch. 'Ten o'clock. Morning.'

'I not forget.' Sona bent down and touched his feet. 'Tank you! Tank you! I be good. With you, aurways.' Then she turned to Emma and kissed her hands.

'Sona, listen carefully. This my name. Sandy. Now, this Legjin, Will she stop you?'

'No, no. She nothing. I alone Sona. I coming.'

CHAPTER EIGHT

'Emma, I'm sorry. I agreed, some time ago. I can't withdraw now. I'll be breaking my word. Please understand! I promised James. I can't let him down. Not now. Besides, I was quite keen at the time. Still am. And for heaven's sake, where's the harm?'

Emma sighed. 'Then there is nothing more to say.' She studied his reflection in the long mirror, He was tying his bow. 'I wouldn't want you to break your word. But you were unwise to accept the invitation.'

'Damn this bow!' cursed Sandy. 'Sorry, finish what you were saying.'

'You should have told me at the time. Consulted me, even.'

'Believe me I would have. Am I not the consulting type? One reason why I never can surprise you with my presents. Actually, James and I had discussed this very early on; you weren't around then. It was before,' he added with a teasing grin, 'you pledged to honour and obey.' He blew his cheeks. 'You knew last Friday and said nothing when he was on the phone this morning.'

'Because I hadn't read your lecture. I have, now, while you were in the bath.'

'Well, what do you think of it?' He turned round because she said nothing. 'You know how it is? When one feels strongly about something one longs to share it with others. Please say it's not awful. My lecture, I mean, not my face.'

She smiled. 'Of course, not. You write well. It's informative, well argued and you'll say it beautifully. But if you take questions you'll be attacked. Not everyone will agree with you. Less and less these days. It is unfashionable to be an Anglophile.'

'I don't care. There, how do I look? Don't say "as always", I want to look better than that. Gives a chap confidence to know . . . seriously.'

'Your face is your fortune, Sir, she said.'

'So you married me my pretty maid.' He turned to face her. 'Hey! why the petulant face? I wanna pet you, when you look pet-u-lant.'

She went to him and resting her face on his back put her arms round his waist. 'Do I really deserve you, Sandy!'

'Don't steal my lines.' He pulled her round in front of him and pointed in the mirror. 'Look! Men must envy me your looks. Vivien Leigh, but altogether more, yes, more mysterious . . . and bigger breasts.'

'Thirty-six is not big . . . Ah, that hurt! You're so crude at times. And did I promise to obey? I can't remember. Was it a Prayer Book wedding?'

'God. I don't remember.'

After a pause she said suddenly. 'If life's a joke, Sandy, Anglomania is a joke too.'

'It's absurd, I know. I can't help myself. England's History is so grand and real, and English Literature so vast and splendid. I'm amazed at people who remain indifferent.'

She moved away and sat on the bed. 'Sandy, be good. Listen. I know you've got a sharp mind and you'll stand up to your critics. But even if you win the verbal battles, the war is lost. To be an Anglophile is an eccentricity. I know how you feel. I know and understand your sentiments . . . My bath's ready.'

He followed her into the bathroom. 'Why don't you come? To support me?'

'You haven't had the chance to tell Sir James about me. Can't spring a wife on him, at the eleventh hour. How did you meet him?'

'I knew his son, Roger, in Bombay. He was in the British Council—Roger was. And then I spent a few weekends with the family at their country home, in Burwash, Sussex. Near Bateman's, Kipling's house . . . ?'

'And were there any young women in the family?'

Her expression was artless, almost innocent. He laughed. 'Alas, no!'

She turned the taps off. 'Straighten your bow.'

The Lotus And The Rose

He brushed the steam off the bathroom mirror and peered. Then he looked at his watch. 'The car will be here in ten minutes.' She had dropped her dressing gown and slipped into the bath. He kissed her forehead. 'Do me a favour? Emma, please. Please say you'll come.'

'Yes,' she said simply.

'Good I'll feel better knowing you're there?'

'Have I got enough time?'

'An hour. Forty minutes to dress, twenty to get there. Take a cab. It's The British Society. I'll leave the Programme and address on your dressing table.'

'You're sure I won't be too late.'

'It's a bit of a dash, but you have some leeway. The minutes and Chairman's report come first. It's their AGM. My talk's the last item and the highlight of the evening.' He chortled. 'I'll tell James you're coming. Later I'll introduce you to him.

'What shall I wear?'

'What about that beige dress and the amethyst earrings and necklace.'

She smiled. 'You never forget that. It's almost threadbare. No, it's evening. I'll wear something dark to go with the garnet necklace you gave me in Charbagh.'

Sir James Pollock, founder and Chairman of The British Society, was stout, florid, and completely bald. He surveyed the gathering before him and beamed benignly over his half-moon, gold-rimmed spectacles. 'Any other business? Then Fellow Members,' he said rising, 'may I introduce our guest speaker, Mr Sandeep Thakur. It has been my good fortune, nay privilege to know Sandy, as he won't mind me calling him, for many years now. He's an engaging and illuminating chap to be with. Sandy was in the Indian Army Education Corps for a short time and later did a spell of teaching here. Although he is widely read in English History and Literature, and Philosophy, he insists he is not an intellectual, in the Orwellian sense of the term, which for my money makes him a very wise person to meet. The title of Sandy's talk is "Britain's Legacy to the World", and as I know we are in for a fascinating and entertaining evening, so without further ado . . . but before he starts may I crave a moment of his time, on a matter he has till this evening hid from me. I understand Mr and Mrs Thakur have just returned from India, and that his wife is seated among you. May I, on your behalf, invite her to join us here on the podium. There! Will someone kindly show Mrs . . . thank you, Peter.'

There was applause and turning of heads as Emma was led up to the dais. Sandy's heart went out to her as he watched her downcast eyes and flushed face. He could not save her from the embarrassment she was suffering, so he stood up, hoping it would help and what he saw and heard made his heart swell with pride. A distinct gasp and buzz rose from the audience in clear response to her radiant beauty. She was wearing a deep maroon dress, which emphasised the fullness of her figure and gave her height. She looked up. The lights playing on the deep red of her garnet necklace, set her skin aglow. Their eyes met. Her blush disappeared and was replaced with a dimpled smile.

Sir James bowed and waited till she sat down in the chair next to Sandy. 'So, this is Sandy's charming secret, but', he raised his hand, 'we shall be meeting Emma socially after Mr Thakur's talk. And now it remains only to say that Mr Thakur will be happy to answer questions at the end of the lecture and we'll allow a little more than the usual fifteen minutes. Mr Sandeep Thakur!'

Sandy collected his papers and went up to the lectern. He thanked Sir James for his welcome and his audience for the privilege of speaking to them. 'The story goes,' he began, 'that during a visit to Britain, Mahatma Gandhi, when asked what he thought about British civilisation, replied: "I think it would be a good idea." There was a stir in the hall and some loud laughter. 'I tell the story to remind us of two great legacies the English gave the world: a comprehensive Language and a dry but delightful sense of humour. There are other gifts. The list is an impressive and unique package, which I would like to present to you, and to which Gandhi, unintentionally, drew attention. In other words, I'll answer the question Gandhi was asked, and in doing so, make, I hope, a plausible distinction between civilisation and culture. Would you also allow me the occasional lapse of not making too fine a distinction between Britain and England. For while British is the civilisation, English is the culture I'm thinking about.

'Civilisation to me is a process and the loom that weaves the threads of cultures into its tapestry. Culture is plural and every civilisation the result of interacting historical influences. A culture which shuts itself from other influences, remains a cult and never flowers into a civilisation. British civilisation started with a debt to Rome, while English culture owed much to Celtic, Saxon and Norman influences, and with the founding of a kingdom by Alfred the Great. Then, as this island kingdom by the sea discovered not just Europe, but new lands, world trade, maritime greatness and Empire, a civilisation typically civil and typically British, began to spread. Culture is subjective and fluid; civilization is objective and needs to be fair, firm and dependable. In other words, while culture is flexible, civilisation is less so. You may understand what I'm getting at if I were to say that the Raj was the meeting of the most cultured country, India, and the most civilised one, Britain. So, what do I mean by civilised. Europe is more cultured in the arts than Britain, but not eating frogs and snails is more civilised.' [He paused for laughter to die down]

'But the civilisation of Imperial Britain bore seeds of it own destruction: Freedom, civil justice, self-government, and having had to surrender supremacy to peacekeeping, turned into an experiment of policies with politics. The dissolution of the Empire itself was brought about by the English language, and the present situation, sad to say, is now ripe for breakdown. Hopefully, this breakdown may neither be too swift nor disastrous. The strengths in the conservative nature of English Society may yet save and maintain its unique quality. The thread of Englishness need never snap or ever run out. I believe it will remain an unbroken weft in the weave of the World's tapestry. Unless there is a loss of morale and moral fibre. That risk is always there.

'In the past wherever Britain went, it's civil machine went with it. And as the Empire spread, other nations became British, for "Britishness" is a protean state. Britain also changed—not immediately or gradually, but imperceptibly. From 1815 to 1914 she was the dominant world power in a position to bask leisurely in what came to be called *Pax Britainnica*; and able to exercise, in spite of 1857, a gigantic bluff of being invincible. The strength which made the bluff possible came from British morale. In her encounters with European powers, one may say, from 1066, it thrived in an atmosphere of growing confidence, pomp and circumstance, and Britain settled down, to an increasing sense of privacy, exploration, invention and discovery to, as it were, cultivate their own gardens, and build a democratic institution that was the envy of the world. People, property, and rights were protected; but ironically, as I said before, the seeds of democracy sown abroad, grew to shake the foundations of an Empire on which the sun had never set.

'I do not subscribe to the view that all civilisations have travelled the same distance, or that all cultures are equal. Civilisation as distinct from culture has more to do with the climate of government and civil matters—laws, rights, duties, responsibilities and the freedom of the individual; and once established becomes a template that is a goal itself. The subjectivities of a community, shaped by geography, tradition, customs, and their expression in religion and art, creates a culture that informs a civilisation, without destroying that template. In civil morale, tolerance and justice are firm objectives of civilisation, while in cultures, a hierarchy exists. A culture which offers greater freedoms and equal opportunities to men and women has to be superior to those that do not. It is also possible to have a high culture but a low civilisation. As an Indian this apparently strange conclusion is clear to me by linking Science with civilisation, Art with culture. A high culture can be so steeped in dogma and ancient superstition, it becomes blind and nonsensical to Science. But where civilisation has struck a balance between science and culture, that civilisation is on the road to utopia.

'It was science that made Western Civilisation more inventive and practical than that of the East, because the mathematical genius of the East, in reaching the West, achieved its apotheosis in men like Newton. Britain, in giving birth to the Industrial Revolution, became, if not the most cultured, the most civilised nation, and from her laboratory of studied pragmatism, the most concerned for good governance. We laugh at the British, who when faced with a problem form a committee, or on seeing a queue, join it, but we are also witnessing civilisation in progress and right action.'

Sandy then briefly expanded on the British character, its traits and inventive genius, by listing their outstanding contributions to world Literature, Science and Medicine. 'As you're a self-deprecating

The Lotus And The Rose

lot, I know this will not swell your heads, but it's time you got a pat on your backs.'

The audience, who listened to Sandy's talk with all the encouraging signs a speaker could ask for, now grew restless. Chairs creaked and heads turned round to catch, what seemed like the rumble of a gathering storm of dissent. Rising from the back of the hall it rolled towards the front. Hushing and hissing protests met somewhere in the middle. Sandy stopped. He looked at Sir James and raised his eyebrows. Then smiled. 'Forgive me ladies and gentlemen, but, with apologies to P.G.Wodehouse, I suspect a giant raspberry is about to arrive, as I hear the distinct beating of its wings.' He waited as a tall, thin man stood up. He was trying to speak, his face red with the effort.

'Mr Chairman! Mr Chairman, sir!' He spluttered. 'There's an obnoxious little man behind me. His constant mutterings interfere with my enjoyment of what I think is a damn good talk. Sir, I ask that he-he be thrown out . . .' He nodded violently. 'Sir!'

Sir James stood up and raised a placating hand. He was not smiling. 'Thank you, Major Newton-Dunn. Whatever the provocation, it would be helpful, all round, if we kept our tempers. This is a free country. Ladies and Gentlemen! Please! Need I remind you, it's customary to hear out our guest speakers, without interruption, till they have finished! If you disagree about anything, kindly frame them into questions and you'll be given the opportunity to ask them. I see the evening promises to be a stimulating one, let it also be polite one . . .' He smiled. 'My apologies, Mr Thakur for this . . .'

'You're a fascist!' A shocked hall caught its breath and the hush was emphasised by the sound of slow handclapping and murmurs of support.

'I cannot see you, sir. Kindly stand up!' Sir James shielded his eyes and peered.

A chair at the back of the central aisle fell back with a mighty crash as a large West Indian drew himself up. 'Sorry man. But ah mean . . . you may like what this fellow . . . this, what's his name, Mr . . . ?' He looked about him to meet a sea of stony faces. A single prompt from the back failed to reach him. The prompter leant forward to whisper and Sandy got a glimpse of his face. There was no mistaking it. It was Nigel Carr, his past colleague at Colonel

Brown's Prep School. The face of the Indian next to him was also familiar, though he couldn't immediately put a name to it.

'Ah mean to say, Chairman,' continued the West Indian, 'You may like . . .'

'It's customary to give your name and . . .'

'Ah ain't givin' no names, man. What d'yer want my name for . . . eh!' Clearly the man was losing his temper. 'I ain't no licker of white man's boots like your . . . Thakker chap.' (The prompt had reached but the mishearing caused the hall to burst into laughter.) 'Oi, what's the bloody joke? . . . Makes me sick listnin' to him goin' arn and arn. Me, ah can't take no more of this. Dat's awl ah've got to say.'

'And all I've got to say,' rejoined Sir James, 'is that I'm no fascist. You are free to speak your mind. Those who prevent others from speaking freely are the true fascists.'

'Ah'm not free to speak my mind. You know that, man. You may say ah'm free, but I ain't . . .' The big man waved his hand dismissively. 'Ah'm not stayin' to argue with the likes of you . . . Don't worry about shuttin' me up. Ah'm a goin' . . .' He moved towards the exit, and on reaching the door, turned, hesitated, threw up his hands, and was gone.

'Mr Chairman,' Sandy said after a pause. 'I wonder if it would be all right to take questions now and keep my closing remarks till later, if there's time?'

'Very well, Mr Thakur. That might ease the tension.' Sir James rose again. 'Yes, Ladies and Gent . . . I beg your pardon, the chair recognises the presence of its eminent patron. My Lord, Ladies and Gentlemen. We'll take questions now. Please raise your hand, and on being invited to speak, give your name, and if you wish, occupation, then ask your question.'

'Correct me if I'm wrong . . . sorry, Nigel Carr, and I'm a teacher. Correct me if I'm wrong, but I assume Mr Thakur that you're an Indian?'

'Please ask your question,' the Chairman intervened.

'Mr Thakur, can you explain why as an Indian you're an Anglophile?'

'I'm British. You know that Mr Carr, since we worked together. 'But I understand the point you are making. There's nothing to explain. I suppose an Anglophile has to disclose his loyalty, unlike an Englishman. An Englishman who loves his country is a patriot which, for England's sake, I hope you are.'

'Hear! Hear!' Someone shouted from a side aisle.

'But,' insisted Nigel, 'as an Englishman, I don't see your England. I recognise some ingredients, but you've made a myth and a mirage. I ought to be flattered, but what you say is not the reality. The things you say of England exist largely in fiction and fantasy, and in any case of no value today. You . . .'

'Oh, shut up Nigel!' Said a familiar voice, which Sandy instantly knew was Sally's.

Nigel sat down as the Indian next to him stood up. It was Hari. The intervening years had wrought changes. Hari had grown fat and bald, yet there was no mistaking him. 'You're talking about most ordinary people and making extraordinary claims on their behalf,' he said. 'You've not changed, so I won't waste my time, thank you.' He sat down to murmurs of 'Name! Name!' and 'What's the question!' Hari jumped up. '*Arrey!* He knows my name. Hari Chander, in case he's forgotten.'

'Hello, Hari. It's been a long time.'

'Not long enough for me, Sandy.' Hari popped up and sat down again.

'*Touché*. But Hari, a nation which produced Newton and Shakespeare, and more winners of Nobel prizes than any other single country . . . who ruled an Empire, possibly the largest the world has ever known, has to be extraordinary. But may I enlarge upon some of Mr Carr's implications, with Sally's permission . . .' He grinned into the middle distance. 'It is the sad lot of Anglophiles to be surprised, to be disappointed. They are invariably advised to spend time in England to rid them of their illusions. I am taking the cure, but till the cure is affected, allow me my small illusions. We should, all of us, be allowed to keep romance alive. When romance dies, love dies . . . decency dies too. We need sentiment—even mirages—to make life bearable. Facts aren't enough. Men and women don't die for facts. And if the present England is as you see it, the England of History and Literature is, as I see it. And I'm sorry your vision of it has been obscured. Yes? The gentleman in the tweed suit.'

'Walter Legge. I had intended to be critical . . . but you shame me, sir . . .'

'He doesn't shame me!' cried Hari doing his Jack-in-the-box act. 'I'm ashamed an Indian talks like that. He's a lackey of imperialism.'

'Instead of abuse, I'd prefer a sensible question.' Sandy said.

'Mr Chander,' Sir James intervened, if you interrupt again, without invitation from the chair or the speaker, I shall have to ask you to leave.'

'I'm respectable businessman,' Hari mumbled audibly.

'Then you should know better. I'm merely asking you to observe niceties. I find the evening is turning out to be entertaining. I'd like to extend "Questions" time, if you have no objection, Sandy?'

'Indeed, no. My answers may cover all I had left to say.'

'Joan Mason. To be an Anglophile or even a patriot, is neither intellectual nor a fashionable thing to be. I can't think of any great person who was or is one.'

Sandy cast a sidelong glance at Emma, expecting to meet a "didn't I warn you" look. Instead she was staring calmly at the questioner with an air of soft melancholy. 'Let me see,' he said. 'We have just had the state funeral of a very great Englishman and patriot, ergo an Anglophile too—but I'll take your question to be directed solely to Anglophiles not born in this country—I give you Handel and Henry James. Pevsner? Mendelssohn? Possibly . . . a sixth of Americans, and many of India's leading citizens . . . I see that ridicule is not for the great and famous Anglophiles, but for simpletons like me. Be that as it may, but I'm still young, give me time.' He laughed and the audience joined in. 'That great hymn to England by Shakespeare in *Richard II* stirs Anglophiles, surely patriots too. Now, the other half of your question. Is it an intellectual pursuit? Simple answer, "No", followed by "so what?" I'm content not to be an "intellectual". The intellectual outlook is narrow and intolerant of greatness. Its sin is conceit, worse, self-conceit.'

'The Revd Bob White,' announced Sir James, 'has a question. Yes.'

'We don't make much of our heroes, or victories or achievements... and some of us would like to be spared the embarrassment of praise. Do we lack the equivalent of the "American Dream"?'

'Indeed! But if the English did have it they'd be less attractive. Understatement and the stiff upper lip are part of their charm. They prefer to celebrate defeats and disasters. A moment ago I wondered at the extent of the British Empire, and yet the British are not a nation of conquerors, tyrants or of goose-stepping armies. The Empire was, to use a school-boy phrase, "accidentally done on purpose.". it was carved in an amateur spirit of adventure and enterprise by a people said to be the most nomadic of races—having set foot in every corner of the globe. They are also the most democratic. They build an Empire, then take themselves to account. Hastings was impeached; and Clive hounded to suicide. You're a nation of poets. I suppose poets make good soldiers—the sort with strong morale and moral tenacity. But those other qualities: eccentricity and humour . . . they are not the stuff of slaves or tyrants.'

'Robert Danvers. I see laurels in preparation. Before they crown you with it, may I strike a note of criticism. It is impossible to defend Anglomania, or any mania for that matter, without resorting to gobbledegook. I'll grant your answers to questions have been adequate, but what went before was a splash of balderdash. Not boring, far from it. You've won the approval of a large section of your audience. But what you've said made little sense, or made sense to others for wrong reasons. Pandering to nostalgia; to patriotism, that refuge of a scoundrel—to earn yourself applause, even a rousing cheer.'

'Thank you,' said Sandy. 'In all that I cannot discern a question. Beware, gobble-degook is contagious . . . Oh, and Hari, I just remembered. You and I as boys have seen the terrible results of that disfiguring disease and killer, small-pox, and I am ashamed I omitted to mention the contribution of that modest and very great Englishman, Edward Jenner. The World owes him a debt of eternal gratitude.'

Sir James stood up. 'We must leave time for Mr Thakur's closing remarks. He is due a rousing and deserving cheer. Mr Danvers is right about the laurels but not for reasons he stated. One last question. Sorry, Joan, you've had your turn. The lady behind you has had her hand up for sometime. Yes.'

Sally rose, and Sandy became conscious of Emma looking at him. 'Sally Watson. Teacher. I'm curious to know what George Orwell said about intellectuals, and why our guest speaker is happy not to be counted among them?'

'I hope I don't do Orwell an injustice. But if I remember rightly, he thought they had divorced themselves from the common culture of the country. I could quote chunks of what he said . . .' Sandy rustled through his papers. 'I came prepared, knowing someone might ask. Here it is . . . I'll pick the best bits: "They take their cooking from France and their opinions from Moscow . . . form an island of dissident thought. England is perhaps the only great country whose intellectuals are ashamed of their own nationality . . ." He goes on: "The Bloomsbury highbrow with his mechanical snigger, is as out of date as the cavalry colonel." Orwell hoped that patriotism and intelligence will combine again. There you are . . . But when I said I was happy not to be counted an intellectual, I wasn't suggesting I was not intelligent.'

The hall laughed. Sally thank him and sat down. Sir James nodded and Sandy began his closing remarks. 'Mr Chairman, it was not my intention to flatter or offend. More than anything else this talk has enabled me to consider my own position. So far my life has been a search for the England I read about as a child and fascinated me as a young man . . . The England of my father's time, of books, of history . . . All searching is introvert, personal and subjective. I was not being didactic, merely sharing with you the dreams and enthusiasms of a fan of England, trying for a moment, to set aside the gloom of change and decay I see on the horizon. Briefly I looked back with regret. Yes, nostalgia and images of old still grip me . . . making much I've said, perhaps foolish. But, Britain's incalculable legacy to the world wins my admiration. My England walked like the ghost of Hamlet and pressed me to speak for her. I've done that and my own perturbed spirit can rest. And to those I've annoyed, I ask for gentlemanly allowance—incidentally, the concept of "The Gentleman", is an English one, and a word, not to be found in other languages. In turn I'll concede to them this assessment of the English made by Cardinal Newman. I quote: "I consider Englishmen the most suspicious and touchy of mankind; I think them unreasonable and unjust in their seasons of excitement, but I had rather be an Englishman than belong to any other race under heaven. They are as generous as they are hasty and burly; and their repentance for their injustices greater than their sin." Thank you, for listening.'

Sandy sat down and Emma took his hand. She was smiling. Sir James Pollock waited till the applause died down. 'Thank you, Sandy. There's little I need say. The eloquent applause speaks for itself. Your tributes to this land and its people are generous. To our faults you attribute humour and where others see snobbery and hostility, you see polite dignity and diffident charm. We may be, as you say, Athens to America's Rome. But to the smug among us, those who boast of an unsinkable England, may I remind them of the Titanic, which is remembered not for the tragedy it was, but as another one of our fairy tales, told by idiots and signifying nothing. Indeed, we need truth and romance and you walked that tightrope with skill. But, we must not repeat the mistake we have so often made throughout our history: remembering the poetry and heroism but forgetting the loss. I suppose, if this is inevitable, history will, as you say, still keep on record the memorable innings we staged on its playing fields. Thank you. Now, friends it's time I released Mr and Mrs Thakur in your midst. Drinks are being served in the foyer. Soon the chairs in the hall will be moved and stacked against the wall to give you more room to move about.'

Before taking Sir James's proffered arm, Emma managed to whisper to Sandy: 'I'm so proud of you. You were wonderful.' Then he began to lose sight of her as the freely moving audience surged forward in all directions. Many waylaid him and held him back. Nigel Carr pushed his way through and gripped his hand. 'Great speech. Truly, sorry to be contrary. I didn't mean to be. But I knew that would get the best out of you.'

'Where is Hari?' Sandy asked.

'I believe he left, no! He's behind me.' Nigel side-stepped, then moved away.

'Congrats!' Hari grinned, 'I see, you've won the hearts of the stinko pinkos.' Sandy frowned, but Hari's face expressed genuine friendliness.

'I'm not sure how to respond to that.' Sandy said.

'When you come to your senses,' Hari replied, 'we'll be there waiting to welcome the return of the prodigal. Till then goodbye. Historically, India is a patient country. Oh, yes! Regards from the family and friends in Bombay. So you've married a great beauty.

Hope it works out . . . you know how flighty English girls can be. No offence meant.'

'None taken.'

'You remember my sister Veena. Husband's now MP.'

'Who did she marry?'

'Oh, of course, you never met Dilip Tandon! They've got two children. Both boys.'

Sandy felt a tug on his sleeve and he turned, as Hari folded his hands in a farewell *nameste*, to face Sally. For a moment neither spoke.

'So, "you'd rather have a paper doll to call your own than a fickle minded girl like me?"' She sang, then gave a sly wink

'Yes.' Sandy chuckled. 'And when I come home at night she will be waiting.'

'You know the song? Are there no limits to your . . . I must stop teasing, really. I have been unfair. Emma's lovely, and you're a lucky man.'

'Quite a coincidence you and Nigel being here.'

'Most people here are in education. I won't keep you. Emma will be wondering where you are. Sandy, I'm leaving teaching. I'm getting married . . .'

'Peter.'

'No, not to Peter.'

'That petered out?'

'Ouch! You were always one for puns. The children in school remember you for that particularly. Now, promise you won't drop dead. It's Nigel. I'm marrying Nigel.'

'Nigel!'

'You promised.'

'I don't believe it! Nigel! You do like living in the eye of the storm. The two of you are always at each other's throats?'

'I know. Never for long. Had a tiff earlier this p.m. I refused to sit with him because he insisted on being with that fat Indian. But Nigel's talent for rooting out gossip makes him interesting and he's devoid of jealousy. He's leaving too, much to Clarke's relief.'

'How is Clarke?'

'The Clarkes of this world go on for ever and stay the same.' She laughed.

The Lotus And The Rose

'Lucky Nigel. Does he deserve that fetching laugh?'

'He's a poppet. Come to our wedding. Must go, I'm holding up the queue.'

'I'll join Emma, they can follow me. By the way, who was the big West Indian?'

'There's nothing to stop anyone coming. He's in education too. Well sort of. Nigel says he's the caretaker for some big school in Pimlico. I really must go. Your chairman is bearing down on us with Emma. She looks cross.'

'No. That's her "what do I say, I haven't been listening" look.'

'Bye, Sandy.' She kissed him.

'Goodbye, and give Nigel my congratulations. Sir James!'

'Sandy I was hoping to introduce you to Lord Fenton. He had to rush. But he has invited the three of us to lunch at his club. I'll call you and tell you more about it, but we, Emma and me, accepted on your behalf. I have a surprise for you. I knew Emma's father. We were in Sandhurst, together!'

'I must love you because I hate you', she said.

Sandy stared at her. She was in one of her melancholic moods again. 'Emma, what do you mean. Why do you hate me?'

'A little and not all the time. I hate you for making me love you, for disturbing my, my inner peace. That's what I had before I met you.'

'Peace? Your silent world without people? No one, not your father, not God, would have approved of a world that shut out so much goodness.' He took her in his arms and she yielded with a sound that was almost like the purr of a cat. 'If hate keeps you in my arms, then hate me.' She turned her head away and he kissed the back of her neck. 'In spite of all that, you love me! I know you do.'

She nodded. 'Love changes us, Sandy. It's upsetting. And it hurts.'

'You like it when it hurts?'

She pushed him away. 'You reduce all I say to base desire.' He lifted her and lay her propped against the pillows. 'You wicked man. You've planned this right down to the pillows.' He kissed her, slowly unbuttoning her night dress. 'What are you doing?'

'Undoing what you've done up.'

'Stop. First talk to me, then you can have your evil way with me. I've been thinking about the cottage and little Sona.'

'Little? She's a big woman by any standards. You've seen her moving things around. She's got wrists like forearms.'

'It'll be a lovely summer. Can we stay till autumn?'

'If you like. I'd like to buy a house in Sussex. I've dreamed of a place in Sussex, as far back as I can remember. Now I can afford it.'

'Where in Sussex?

'Alfriston . . . Rye . . . You know what Charles II said of Sussex? When he fled to a boat waiting to take him to France? He turned on his horse, looked across the Sussex Downs and said: "It's a country worth fighting for." That was when he was King in waiting.'

'Sussex is beautiful. It can wait, till after we're back?' She knelt on the bed, resting on her heels: 'Sandy, how will the furniture from Charbagh get to the cottage?'

'At snail's pace. Lorries, then by bullock cart, and from Mcleodganj by coolies. They unpack the stuff, take it to bits, carry it on their backs and plod patiently uphill. That's how it is at hill stations. I've left it in Arjun's capable hands. He'll ensure the dining table and four-poster bed get there first. The wardrobe and bookshelves can be left in Pathankot, for the time being.'

She nodded absently as she smoothened the bed sheets. 'This flat is far too small for us,' he said. 'You need room for your work and to store your paintings.'

She nodded again. 'It's sad. We made love for the first time on this bed.'

'I won't leave the bed for anyone else to sleep on. I promise.' She put her hand out and he pulled her beside him. 'Are you happy darling? Sometimes I wonder.'

'Oh, yes Sandy. Happy ever since I met you. Why do you ask?'

'Because of what you said earlier.'

'Oh, don't pay any attention to that.'

'And often you look so sad.'

'But I'm not. I'm not one for laughing. Laughter, happiness isn't what life is about. Life's serious. One has only to think to stop laughing. It's unthinking to laugh all the time. Sadness is more in keeping. I feel that, don't you?'

'The eternal note of sadness.'

'Do you know . . .' They both began simultaneously. 'You first,' he coaxed.

'Were you going to ask if I knew Arnold's "Dover Beach"? Yes?'

'Maybe smiles are there to give sadness a rest.'

'I feel silly smiling all the time. You know, when I'm really unhappy. You're so good at that. Sandy, don't you like me the way I am?'

'I have always loved your sad face. But you have a beautiful smile. Your face is like England. Cloudy till the sun breaks through. Then it's glorious. I've said this before . . .'

'It's England you love, not me.' She put her hand inside his dressing gown and snuggled up to him. 'I'm being silly. I'm the saddest happiest woman in the world.'

'So now, when your mother calls us "flotsam and jetsam", tell her we've landed on Dover Beach.'

'Sandy, don't give any more talks like the one you gave tonight.'

'I thought you liked my talk. You said you were proud of me?'

'I was, am. You're clever with words. You fight your corner well . . .'

'But I'm still in a corner. Someone else told me that. Never mind, go on.'

'Most of those who cheered were only pleased about the good things you said about England . . . not because they recognised themselves. Sandy, the English may have been enlightened rulers but did they really appreciate Indians? They used Indians like you to make their administration work, but did they treat you as equals? To think that noble families like yours could be pushed around by common, less cultured Englishmen . . .'

'You've been listening to Dolly? No, you needn't feel bad about it. My sister and the rest of my family are right. My father changed from admiring to actually disliking the English. But I can't help myself. It's like falling in love. The heart has it's reasons, and all that guff . . . I could no more stop loving you just because someone tells me that as an Indian I should marry my own kind. Logic and love don't mix.'

'I said you're good at arguing your corner. You shut me up, even though deep down I feel there's has to be a flaw somewhere.'

'Yes, the flaw is that people fall out of love, or use good sense to fall out of love.'

'Or because they've been hurt. I won't hurt you, but, I'm afraid England will.'

'I was afraid of that. Not now. Not ever. Because there'll always be you!'

'Oh, Sandy! You're either the greatest lover in the world or the greatest fool.'

'That's a tautology . . . and it's taught me nothing. There, what a beautiful laugh.'

'I hope you won't become famous, even a little, and we don't have to go to parties and lectures and . . . I don't care much about meeting people and chatting. I hardly said anything this evening. Fortunately, Sir James talked so much, he didn't seem to notice.'

'I thought you were wonderful this evening. And I liked it when you said you were proud of me. Only you matter, Emma. I won't put you through anything you hate. I'm not ambitious. Just this once. I couldn't turn down Terry's invitation. I taught his son and I feel we must.'

'Yes,' she said sleepily. 'Leave me tonight . . . Have you read *Honest to God?*'

'No, but I know about it.'

'Don't. It's awful.' With a sudden movement she sat up. 'It's a book which is going to destroy the Church.'

'I'm already disillusioned by the Church. Rome beckons me.'

'Oh, Sandy, is that true?' She fell back against the pillows. 'Father became Roman Catholic towards the end. Sandy, when you decide, let's do it together.'

'How can I. Not while Bill is around.' he said and looked at her. She was asleep. He pulled the covers over her, turned the bedside lamp off, lay on his back and staring into the darkness prayed. 'Jesus, make her strong!' The darkness and silence deepened. He could not sleep. He drew closer and gently put an arm around her. She slid back and pressed against the hollow of his body. 'Rest!' she murmured. 'Rest!'

CHAPTER NINE

The King's Arms had no designated car park; cars used the waste land behind it. 'When things are settled in court,' Terry said, 'I'll get my car park. Not long now.' He winked.

'What about the path running through that land? It must be Council property!'

'Na, Sandy. That's no path. Children crossing to the swimming pool from the School have beaten that track.'

'Then what's that barrack like thing running alongside?'

'Dad says he can't remember why or who build it. No one knows, 'cept it was built during the war. The pool's behind the barrack. Got a direct hit. Yer know wha' I mean. One of those doodlebug things. For years they've bin diggin', more off than on, lookin' for unexploded bombs and all that lark. It's boarded up, same as the school. As for that barrack thing . . . some dark goings on . . . don't ask. But it'll go when dad gets his car park. Council will take over the rest. I've seen plans. Goin' to build blocks, twenty storeys high, named after famous writers. The barrack one will be Dickens. Sue! We've bin neglecting our guests.'

'We have had a lovely time, Susan,' Emma said. 'We really ought to be going.'

'Yes, Terry,' Sandy said. 'We ought . . .'

'Hey, come on. It's early. Twenty minutes to closing. One last for the road?'

Sandy smiled and shook his head. 'Thanks, it's quite a drive back. We've had a wonderful time. I'll bring the car round to the front. Emma can wait here.'

'You should wear a mini, a pretty thing like you,' Sue said suddenly. 'It's the fashion dearie! Go on. Show off those lovely legs. Look at me!' She straightened her tight skirt, which had creased and travelled up her thighs. 'And I've got fat, I mean fat, legs. Look at 'em. Eh? Thighs, I mean.'

'My thighs are fat too,' a red-faced Emma said diffidently.

'Never! She ain't got fat thighs . . . eh, Sandy?' Sue giggled irrepressibly.

Sandy grinned. 'I won't be long.'

'Come, luv. We'll wait in the parlour,' Susan said. 'Give us a honk, Sandy, when yer round. Na, yer don't have to go through the saloon bar! Terry'll show you out.'

Terry led Sandy through the kitchen to the back door. They shook hands. 'I'm glad all's well,' said Sandy. 'Do give my regard to your father and tell Dave I wish him all the best. I knew he'd do well in school. He was one of the brightest pupils, if not the brightest pupil, in my class.'

'Yeah, but I still worry about the kid, Sandy. Still misses his "best teacher". Sure you can't spare some time?'

'He doesn't need tuition.'

'Great in maths, I know. But English . . . and History?'

'I'll see what I can do. Maybe late Friday afternoons?'

'Thanks!' Terry smiled gratefully. 'I'll bring him to you, so you won't have to come to this lousy area. I don't want the kid to fall behind. Mind you, he talks real posh like, these days. Some of the locals take the micky . . . who cares. I want 'im to 'ave the best. I mean, wha' is a dad for? 'E's not going to be like me. I missed on eddication.'

'But Terry, you've done well for yourself.'

'Money? Yeah. But Dave's a genius. I want him to get to university and out of this dump.' He glanced over his shoulder. Yer 'no' I think Sue's taken to your wife. A quiet one, ain't she? Bit shy, won't you say? But there's Sue for yer. She'll get one talking . . . even those . . . wha' yer call those priests chaps?'

'Trappist monks?'

'Yeah, them. Dad says she can talk the 'ind legs off a donkey. Right, won't keep yer. Thanks for coming. Fridays then.'

The Lotus And The Rose

'Yes. I'll give you a call and confirm the time. Goodbye and thank you. It was an excellent dinner. Remind Sue. It really was.'

Sandy's car was parked against the wall of the boarded-up school, next to the brick doorway which bore on its lintel the legend "1886" and below that "GIRLS". It was not far from the pub but it was a heavy, dark night and the dim light from the single lamp on a gate post emphasised the shadows. As he passed the gate, Sandy side-stepped to give way to two young women.

'Hello, handsome!' said one as she nudged the other. They giggled. Sandy crossed the road and glancing back, saw the girls join a noisy group of young men outside the pub. They were seated on motorbikes and he wondered why he missed seeing them as a foreboding sense of fear seized him. He shouldn't have come, still less brought Emma with him! All at once the motorbikes burst into life, growling and roaring intermittently. Above the din he heard raised voices. One reached him with ominous clarity. 'Tony, no! Tony, it's none of your business . . . Ow! for God's sake! Please!' The girl's voice ended in a scream. 'I wish I 'adn't said anything. We were just larkin' about. For the last time, Tony! Tony! I'll never go out with you again. Tony! You hear me! Never!'

'Ow! Shut yer fuckin' gob. Stupid bitch!' Immediately the roar of engines became deafening as headlights pierced the area with blinding beams of white light. 'Oi, off my bloody way!' Sandy quickened his pace. He could now see his car less than fifty yards away, but found two motorcyclists already blocking his way, heading him off towards the long barrack-like building. A large car was parked in front of it. Sandy prayed it would be occupied. A headlamp spotlighted him.

'We'll teach 'im not to muck around with our girls, won't we Chris?' The voice of the speaker had an odd quality—a sort of studied mimicry of a familiar film star. Sandy shaded his eyes. He couldn't see the speaker. Turning to avoid the dazzling beam he said: 'Sorry, but if you're talking to me, let me assure you, you are mistaken. I'm not from this area. I don't know any of your girls.'

'Oh yeah!' said the one called Chris. 'And 'oose that floosie with yer in the pub?'

'That's my wife.'

A duet of derisive laughter greeted Sandy's reply. 'Oi! Pull the other one, matey. It's got bells on.'

'Honestly, that's the truth. That's no floosie, that's my wife.' Sandy forced a laugh, hoping it would help to ease the tension. But it received a sullen silence.

A light shone from the casement window of the disused barrack behind him, only to go off again. Sandy looked about him. It was closing time. There ought to be a general exodus from the pub anytime now. He toyed with the idea of making a dash back to it, but found to his dismay he was cut off by two other motor-cyclists. They turned their headlights on and off when he moved towards them. One of them, dimly visible by the light on the gatepost, wore a jacket of a shiny, black leather-like material, an American policeman's peaked cap and dark glasses. 'It's my girl you made a pass at,' he growled and, dismounting from his bike, stood with his feet spread apart, arms were folded and head nodding menacingly.

'Tony! Tony!' A girl's voice came from behind him. 'I was larkin'. He did nothing!'

The man looked back. 'I said, shut up. 'E'll do nothing, no more. In't, Billy?'

The man addressed as Billy left his bike too and stood next to the young man Sandy assumed was Tony. Billy was short, bull-necked, with a clean shaven head that caught the light. 'Yeah, we'll teach the bastard a lesson 'e won't forget.'

They were not to be placated. Sandy backed up against the barrack wall behind him. He would defend himself as best he could, fight back. He could not stand up to four of them but he would gain time and time may bring help. Surely they would leave him when the owner of the big car came out of the pub to collect it! The thought of injury made his hands tremble. 'Anyone there! Hello!' His voice sounded hoarse, hollow and strangulated. 'Hello! Help!' The only response was the girl's repeated appeal to Tony. Then her voice faded as she moved away. Sandy called out again. Someone very near to him sniggered and he realised there was a figure alongside him.

'Grab him Danny,' Billy hissed and immediately Sandy's arms were pinned back by hands travelling up to the back of his neck. He remembered the close combat training he had in the army and attempted to kick and grazed the shins of his assailant, only to find the man was wearing full leather boots. A tightening of the half-nelson grip pressed his head down. Once more the light from the barrack window came on, staying on long enough for him to see the others. Tony with the dark glasses was in the middle. On his right, Billy now had the dim gate lamp behind him. He was waving a baseball bat in a threatening and sinister manner. The third figure on Tony's left was in shadow. He appeared to be tall and lanky.

The window from the disused barrack behind him suddenly opened. 'Oi! What's going on there!' The shout from the lighted window, caused the three to freeze, and Danny, who was pressing Sandy's neck against his chest, loosened his hold, allowing Sandy to raise his head a little. Now the other three could be seen clearly. The tall thin man seemed disinterested. Hands on hips, he appeared to be looking at the other two. 'Danny,' he said, 'it's Glen White.'

'Bloody hell, Tony!' hissed Danny. 'I left his gang. I'm not staying.'

'Hang on, Dan!'

But Danny's grip weakened and with a determined effort Sandy managed a loud and desperate plea for help. 'Help! For God's sake, someone help me!.

'Who've you got there?' The window spoke again.

'A wog. Just muckin' around. Showin' 'im he's not wanted here.' Tony said.

While he spoke Sandy manage to strike hard on Danny's knee and was able to free himself. He faced the window. 'I'm a friend of Terry. His father owns the pub. My wife is in there.'

'Doesn't sound like a wog to me,' said the window.

'Then he's a wop,' said Billy with a mechanical laugh.'

'Take it easy,' the window went on. 'I don't want the police here.'

'Let's go, chaps.' The tall nameless onlooker said. .

'Bugger off Chris,' said Tony. 'Quick Billy, wind the bastard! Break his legs!'

'Hey! Look!' said Chris, taking the tone of one able at last to make a valuable contribution. 'Look, your sis is here?'

Tony spun round. 'Pam, what the hell are you . . . ?'

'Tony, for God's sake, scram! Lorna's gone to the pub to phone the police!'

'Fuck!' said Danny. 'Stop the bitch!'

'I'm off!' said Tony. 'Billy do something. Then get the fuck out off here!'

'Come on, Dan!' Billy shouted. 'Grab hold of the bastard.'

Sandy saw Billy rush towards him with a raised bat. He acted quickly. Putting all his strength in a desperate effort to free himself, he lounged forward, sank his teeth into the wrist that pressed against his chest and kicked back hard against Danny's knee. Then he swung round sharply, pushing Danny in front to meet Billy head on. 'Jesus, Billy! You stupid bastard! You've landed me a solid crack.' Danny sank to the ground, with hands nursing his forehead. 'Tony! Get back here!'

Sandy was free. He backed against the wall, raising his hands in a placating gesture. Billy and Tony started to advance towards him. 'Stop! Listen! Listen! You're making a big mistake!' They seemed not to hear. Sandy decided to make a dash for it. If only he could do something to divert their attention! He looked around and spotted a big red car on his right. It was a Jaguar. He dashed to the car and took out his keys as if to open it. 'Come on Dan, don't let the bugger get away. Danny wiped his hands, joined the other two and, together, the three moved towards the red car.

'This yer car?' Tony asked, changing his voice to sound distinctly American. 'Hold it, guys!' He lifted his peaked cap, ran his fingers through his thick black hair, put the cap on again, then pushed it forward so that the peak fell over his brows. He looked at Sandy askance and repeated: 'This yer car!' Not waiting for an answer he turned to the other two, who were watching him intently with wide grinning faces. 'He must be some guy, Billy. 'E deserves our respect.' From the front pocket of his jacket he took out a packet of *Camel* cigarettes. "Ere, have a fag.'

Sandy, a little confused, hesitated a moment, then advanced nervously and helped himself. 'Thanks,' he said hoarsely. The others giggled and Sandy realised that Tony was mimicking Marlon Brando. This was confirmed a moment later.

'Give him a light, Danny!'

'Sure Marlon,' Danny laughed and struck a match to light Sandy's cigarette. Then he immediately positioned himself between Sandy and the wall.

Chris coming out of the shadows joined the group. 'She won't talk,' he said to no one in particular. 'Not for some days she won't. But she got to the police. What's up?'

Tony chuckled and kicked a pebble with the toe of his right boot. 'Yer know, this is some guy. Seen 'is car?' He caressed the slope of the car boot lovingly.

'You don't say!' Chris said.

'Stop mucking around, Tony,' said Billy, looking at his watch. 'If the police come . . .'

'My girl's got a bashing because of 'im.'

'I'm off,' said Chris. 'Come on. We've scared the livin' daylights out of 'im. Leave him. 'E won't come here again. Dan, yer comin'?'

''Arf a minute, boys. We'll go toge'er,' Tony growled. 'We've got bikes, remember? We'll be off in time. Gimme the bat, Billy.'

'Don't bash my car!' Sandy cried.

Tony raised the bat high and hit the rear screen. It bounced back to his surprise, but on the second strike the screen caved in with a hollow thud. He laughed fiendishly and quickly smashed in the tail lamps.

'Oi! You!' Shouted the window and a head leaned out. 'Wha' the 'ell are you doing to my brand new car. You little cunts. I teach you . . . Boys, get the bastards!'

'My God!' Tony stared in absolute terror. 'Quick, the bikes!'

There was a stampede. Cursing, swearing and panic stricken cries came from every confusing direction. Torches flashed in the darkness. Soon a new but triumphant voice called out. 'Got his bike, Ken! Gave me the slip, but I've got 'is bike.'

'Good, Pete. But I wan'yer and Jimmy to get the stupid fuckers. Can you believe it? There's one actually going back to the car! He's mine.'

'Billy!' Tony warned desperately. 'What the fuck are you doing? They've got 'old of Chris's bike. He needs a lift. Come on! Danny's skidaddled.' A motorbike burst into life and tyres screeched in a skid. Then the sound of its engine faded into the night.

In the confusion Sandy stayed by the car and waited for a chance to escape unseen. He ducked as a flashlight almost spotted him. He backed and buckled as a blow struck him behind his knees. He fell forward on his hands, tried getting up, but felt one of his ankles held in a vice like grip.

'I've got the bastard, the cunning bastard!' Billy hissed. 'Can't let 'im go arfer wot 'e's done to us. 'Is car 'e said! Yer get out of 'ere, Tony. They 'aven't seen me.'

'Na, Billy. First I'll smash the living daylights of the sly piece of shit!'

Sandy twisted on to his back to see Billy lying flat on his chest. He brought his free foot crashing down on Billy's face. Billy howled, releasing Sandy's ankle. But as Sandy tried to stand up, he saw Tony advancing on him with the baseball bat, too late to ward off the blow, which struck him in the pit of his stomach. Breathless, he crumpled to the ground and stared up to see the bat coming down on him again. There was no escape. In an attempt to protect his face, Sandy tucked his head between his elbows, raised his knees and curled up into a foetal position. The blows rained down on him. In the dark some went awry. When they struck, the pain was excruciating and numbing at the same time. Billy, now recovered, joined in the attack, kicking him in the small of his back and below his knee. Sandy heard a sharp crack and a different kind of pain brought with it a strange sensation of drifting into space . . .

'Ow, bleeding hell, let me go Glen. Do us a favour!' pleaded Tony. 'Swear we didn't know 'oose car . . . Billy! Billy do something! Billy! Don't leave me!'

'Grab that bald-'eaded turd, Pete! Don't let'im get away. As for you, you piece of shit, yore comin' with me.' Glen's large head of curly red hair shone like a saint's halo round his silhouetted face. 'See how many rounds you last when the gloves are on.'

Sandy heard none of this. Sounds and voices had faded. All was black and silent . . .

'Glen! Cops will be 'ere any minute,' Tony cried. 'You don't wanna be here . . . Ow! Ken that hurt! I swear! True! I 'eard some bloke from the pub say the Bill's coming.'

'Cheeky bastard. What makes you think I'm worried about the Bill.'

'Glen, we got two of them,' said Ken. 'One got away.'

'It's that twit. Danny. I know his voice. He won't escape. Put those two in the back seat. He's coming too.' Glen dragged Tony by the collar towards the car. He tripped over Sandy's huddled body and pushed it with his foot. 'Why did yer? Bloody clowns. Looks a decent chap an' awl. And take off those stupid glasses. Look a prick in 'em.' Glen snatched the dark glasses off Tony's face and stamped them underfoot. Then he opened the car door and shoved Tony in.

'Those were special,' moaned Tony. 'Cost me a tidy.'

'Shut yer mouth. Yer goin' to be sorry you ever heard my name. Pete! sit with the boys. Ken, you drive. First, help me move this Johnny. Don't want to run over 'im. O bloody hell! Look what you done to my car. Bloody twerp. Yer'll pay for this and no mistake. Right, now nice 'n' easy Pete. Don't wanna get attention. Just the side lights. Jesus Christ! They've smashed the lights and all.'

Sandy woke to a weightless sensation. Floating in giddy space he thought he heard a clear whisper, soft, near, so very dear and familiar to him. He opened his eyes. Emma? A bright light behind a circle of peering, shadowy faces, confused him. 'Emma?'

'Hush,' she whispered in his ear. 'I'm here, my love. Holding you.'

'Emma, I've failed.'

'What did he say?' Someone asked.

'No, Sandy. It's all right. Not here . . . not now. Don't talk.' His head lay cradled in her lap. She sighed, bent down and murmured: 'No, darling. You have not failed, my sweet. England failed you. But we have each other! Live for me! Please, live for me!' He tried moving his head. 'Hush, don't move. Stay very still!'

He shut his eyes. 'I've made an Indian out of you.'

She smiled and rocked gently. He slumped and for the first time she felt his weight.

'Gangway! Please, move back.' It was Terry. Emma didn't look up.

'Sorry, luv. How was I to know? They're scum, who did this.'

An arm was gently laid on Emma's shoulder. 'The ambulance are 'ere, luv.' Susan sounded very different. 'They want to . . . let them, luv.'

Emma shivered. A deeper, firmer, masculine voice said: 'Now you must leave it to us. We'll take it from here.' She shook her head. They came alongside. Passively, she watched as they started lifting him on to a stretcher. Suddenly she threw herself across Sandy. 'Mind the bottle!' said the same voice.

'No, no!' Her eyes were wild. 'I'm not leaving him. I'm staying with him. You can't stop me. He's alive, I know! Is he? Tell me he is . . .'

'She's 'is wife,' Susan said.

'I guessed that, ma'am. Don't worry, we'll handle it.'

It was that same warm and soothing voice and Emma wanted it near her. 'He's shut his eyes!' She cried. 'Sandy, darling open your eyes. Look me! He has to live!'

'He'll live. You don't have to worry. But now he needs our help. He can hear you.'

'Sandy! Sandy, don't let them win. Speak, my darling! Say something!' He opened his eyes slowly. Her shadow fell over him and he saw only the golden lining of her hair.

'He'll be all right.' Strong arms took hold of her and lifted her on her feet. 'You can come. But you must be good and quiet. That will help.'

'Thank you.' she said.

He helped her up; and she saw him for the first time. 'You look like a cricketer,' she said absently. 'From the West Indies.'

He grinned. 'Here, put this on. It's just a white overall. My name's Garfield.'

The doors shut. The siren wailed. The ambulance moved. Inside, Emma looked at the overall Garfield had given her. Her dress underneath was blood-stained. 'Sandy,' she sighed gazing at the plasma bottle. 'Dear God, don't let him die. Fight, my love. For my sake! Fight!' She wanted to scream, wondered if she had, and stared at Garfield with alarm. But no sound had left her lips. Sandy turned his head towards her. '*Bibi*', he murmured. She tried desperately to remember. Shouldn't she know the word. "Wife?" 'Yes, oh yes! Sandy,' she said, 'I am your wife. Your *bibi*. Your *bibi's* here.'

'Everything will turn out fine,' Garfield said. 'Relax, lady.'

She nodded and as she sat back, a renewed strength and determination filled her. In her thoughts she was saying: 'Now, I know for certain, I love him. I'll take him away from this horrid place, to India; to our home in the hills. Yes, Sandy it will be the way you dreamed; surrounded by things you love. Your own

England, in India.' She closed her eyes and as she prayed for his life, the cottage came to mind. The tiled roof cottage; their little secret, tucked away, snug in the Himalayan foothills . . . refurbished the way she had planned. She saw him happy, walking with her in the garden; on a pony; on winding bridle paths and hilly lanes . . . the evening chill . . . the red sunsets . . . the crumbling Victorian Church, silhouetted against a lavender sky. And Ransingh mending the perimeter fences . . . the *mali* planting hollyhocks, raking the beds for sweetpeas. And dear, dear Sona, by her side, always, when she needed a woman. Her heart filled with renewed hope . . . and what of England? England didn't matter anymore. Nothing and no one else, mattered. They would live with hill folk: honest, caring, simple in life . . . in death. And the hills! The calm, snow-capped hills! "I will lift up mine eyes unto the hills" she intoned. A low cry woke her from her reverie. She bent her ear to his lips.

'What have they done to me?' He asked softly.

She kissed him lightly, letting her lips linger awhile, trying to recall the passion with which he crushed hers. 'Never mind, dearest. We're together. All is well.'

The ambulance came to a halt, reversed some distance and a moment later the doors opened. Garfield stood alongside as the stretcher was removed, steadying the bottle. He helped Emma down, gently restraining her as the stretcher was rushed to the emergency ward. Then he led her to a waiting room. 'You have nothing to worry about. No danger at all. Physical injuries just need time to heal. Stay here. Is there anything you need? Do you wish to telephone anybody?'

'Thank you. Yes! My brother. He's a doctor. Doctor Franks. Could you telephone him. Ask him to come . . . I'm sorry. I can't think of his number.'

'You leave it to me. If he's a registered doctor, I'll find him.'

'This is how all dreams end. Not with a whimper but a bang.'
'Several bangs, Sandy, by the look of it.' Ted smiled.
'You mustn't make me laugh, it hurts,' warned Sandy. 'Where's Emma?'
'Behind you.'

Sandy raised his chin and turned his eyes upwards. 'What have I done to deserve that beautiful face.'

'You didn't have to do anything. I was yours from the start.' She said simply.

He lowered his chin. 'I must look terrible. Black and blue, I suppose, all over.'

'Your arms and legs, mostly.' Ted said.

'I covered my face, I'm so vain. It was my first concern.' He looked down. 'But why can't I move? Am I strapped down? And is that my leg up in the air?'

Ted nodded. 'Yes. Got to go now. Take care. I'll drop in sometime tomorrow.'

Sandy waited. 'Why are you hiding from me?'

She came round, sat by the bed and taking his hand she pressed it to her lips. 'Don't look at me like that?'

'Are we alone?'

'As good as. Darling, it's good to see you looking well. It's been so long.'

'Is everything all right? Can you guess what I'm thinking about?'

'I can tell from that wicked look. They've told Ted . . . not about that . . . generally. That in time and with care and exercise, you'll be almost as good . . .'

'Almost? What does that mean?'

'A limp. The left shin's broken . . . your ankle too. They've put it together. I mean, set and put in plaster . . .' She began to cry. 'They've done their best.'

'Then don't cry. It could have been worse. I'll walk again. Won't I?'

'Oh, yes. Just that limp, because your left leg will be a bit shorter. Ted says, with specially built shoes, it will be hard to tell . . . But, you're not listening.'

'I am. How long, before I can . . . you know?' He squeezed her hand. 'When you look at me like that I get goose pimples; always did.'

'It won't be long, knowing you.'

'So everything's all right in that quarter.'

'I'm afraid so.' She looked away to hide a smile.

'But I won't be able to move, for sometime?'

'Speak for yourself . . . There, you make me say things.'

'This evidence,' he thought, 'of lessening inhibition, is a new found joy.'

Anyway,' she stood up. 'You can fly, even if it's sometime before you can walk. I'm taking you home.'

'But, there's the matter of the court case and hearings . . .'

'No!' she scowled. 'You must promise to put it all behind you. Sandy, please! There are enough witnesses for the police to make . . . someone named Glen White, is their key witness. He knows all the four . . . louts. There's Terry also. And Sir James will pursue the case as far as he can take it. They won't go unpunished. Please! Leave it to Ted.'

'You're wise and beautiful.'

'And I love you. More than I ever did.'

'Is it beauty and the beast syndrome. I must look monstrous. Does that turn you on. I'm teasing. Tell me, has Ted been here before today?'

'Yes, several times since . . . And mother too. She was here yesterday.'

'Why do I keep forgetting.'

'It's the drugs,' she said, remembering her relief when Ted told her. 'You will keep drifting in and out. It will go when you stop taking them.'

'You're so far away. Come closer.'

She sat on the bed, took his hand and placed it between her breasts. 'Now rest.'

'Thank God. I know now, I'm not impotent.' He studied her questioningly.

'But it wouldn't have mattered. I hate it when you worry about that. Sex is not the most important thing in life. Henry James has said it is overrated.'

'But you like it when we make love.'

'Because I love you.' She lay her head against the edge of his pillow. 'I love best sleeping next to you, with your arms around me. I feel secure.' She sat up.

'Ah, the dimples.'

'Dr Phillips said he hadn't met anyone quite so determined to live.'

'Because of you. You can tell him that. But can one choose to live?'

'Do you believe in the power of prayer?'

'Yes, Emma. At least, I want to. And I certainly think I do.'

'Oh, Sandy! I prayed. How I prayed!' She hid her face in her hands and sobbed.

'You al'right? A passing nurse came up to them and asked. 'Are you al'right?'

'Will you come to see them off, mother?'

'No, Ted. And don't press me,' said Edith. 'I did my bit, visiting him in hospital.'

'But you may never see them again?'

'Some day, when it matters, or when I pluck up courage, I'll come with you to India. I don't matter to them, now. I hate feeling spare, unwanted.' She sighed deeply. 'It's no use. I'll never understand Emma. She's so complex. Impulsive when she gave no sign of her being passionate. I took her to be asexual, despite her very obvious charm. It's why I thought Trevor would be right for her. Here she's now, positively blooming.'

'We owe that to Sandy.'

'Of course, Ted. I'm not an idiot.'

'Then you'll understand when I say that she has never been without passion. No one who paints like her can be anything but full of passion. She loved father with a passion, and Clare. She loved the Church with a passion; now, this Tibetan girl. And the cottage. India will be next, if it isn't already. I fear she will never return to England.'

'Are you suggesting her passions come turn by turn?'

'No. She'll collect passions till there's no room in her heart.'

'Her great aunt Thirza was like that.'

'Damn Thirza! Don't you see I'll miss her! Emma's not like her. For one thing she's Christian. She'll never kill herself in despair as agnostic aunt Thirza did. Someone said: the alternative to Christianity is pessimism.'

CHAPTER TEN

              Fern Tree Cottage
              24 October 1983

Dear Dinesh,

 Your letter has made me regret telling you why I left England. I waited, all this time because I hoped you were now old and mature enough to be philosophical about it. I'm also sorry if I've been a general disappointment to you, but nothing about the way I live gives you reason for anger and downright rudeness. I don't remember, since you were sixteen, telling you what to do. You have been free to plan your life and career with my full support. And on your 21st birthday, I appointed you manager of my estate.

 You don't mention Shanti in your letter. I assume you are happy with your wedding arrangements. We did not get involved, knowing it is how you wanted it. I think July is a bit of a rush to marry, but you have chosen well to get Mohan Singh to represent you. He's a good organiser. I'm uneasy about your future father-in-law. I hear he is bit of a ruthless "godfather". It may be gossip. But you and Mohan know the local scene better than I do, and I don't wish to offend. Still, caution and wise moves always pay. Mohan tells me that Seth Agarwal insists you and Shanti live in the "Big House" as it is locally called. I know she's an only child and he is a very rich man, but it breaks

Hindu custom. I suppose he is protecting Shanti from Christian contamination!

So you will be home for Diwali and Christmas. Incidentally, I have no idea what you have to show for your time spent in England. Clearly, diplomas are of no importance to you—count yourself lucky to have a financially assured future—but I have to say I was sad you gave up at the Polytechnic and got yourself mixed up in the political activities of a rather dubious society. From what I hear I can only hope you exercised caution and kept away from anything which was not your quarrel. Don't be used. You've got every right to make up your mind about this, as I have to ask you not to involve me or my personal details for propaganda purposes. "The Republican" is not just left wing, it is a militant, anti-establishment tract—fascist in fact. The Establishment, however much you despise it, gave you more freedom than your group is prepared to give others. It's true I'm for integration rather than multiculturalism, whatever that means—how does one create a common curriculum from several cultures? A little learning is a dangerous thing and while some knowledge of a variety of cultures help promote understanding, can it give unity or identity. Surely, you don't believe in separate development. In any case, to be truly multicultural, you have to be as much one as the other—that is, as much British as Indian. Tolerance is seeing another person's view and accepting it as equally valid to your own. If you think you know it all, you'll be tempted to prescribe, that is arrogance. To be involved in society is to take part in it and make in it a useful contribution. One can't do that without understanding its culture. There is no self-respect, pride or dignity in despising a society in which you seek education. That is ingratitude. Integration and integrity—are "good" words.

You say, I'm more English than the English, and that that makes me a traitor. I'll try to explain, though I see no need to defend myself. I admire the English, still do in spite of everything. They were in India, long enough to establish a democracy. I liked what I saw, as did many members in our family. Mine is a personal choice, without a mission. I do not ask others to follow me. You accuse me of being disloyal. What am I betraying apart from what you want me to be? In what way does a private choice adversely affect India. Whatever you think, I'm not playing a role, or being a ridiculous Malvolio as you put it, making an ass of himself. Don't belabour your points. I'm simply being loyal to myself—no more playacting than anyone who pursues a hobby or career is playacting. I fell in love with the idea of England—the culture, land and it's people; even it's climate. Love defies analysis. Lovers meet rejection. I met it violently in one sad instance. It was just bad luck, but no cause to reject what is good about England. Crime has no national boundaries. I wouldn't expect you to reject India if you were a victim of a crime here or to take an actual incident, because you were held up at Palam airport, and your cassette recorder confiscated. Do you recall the abuse you so richly hurled at your country then? My unhappy incident produced heart-warming responses from friends; even an apology from someone in the Home Office. The police behaved impeccably. My assailants were caught and punished. Not enough you say. For that show of regard I thank you. But far more hurtful than the memory of that unfortunate experience in England is your attitude towards me.

You will find Mohan Singh more understanding of my position. But then, like me, he is a philosopher. This letter is not to chide or insult you. On the contrary, I envy the scientific mind. It is of more use to society. Scientists drive the world forward, but philosophers provide the brakes for reckless drivers—here I go, waffling again, another one of my failings—but I can't deal with hypothetical cases or claim dissatisfaction where none exists. If injustices are rife, you and your friends should have no difficulty finding real and present cases to redress. Use the world's best judicial system. Later, if you must, shake the dust from off your feet when you return to permanently settle here.

Become the true son of India you want to be. (It's still an advantage to have "England returned" on a CV). By all means, persevere with vigour, political and social reforms in India. India could do with your enthusiasm and anger. Corruption & poverty, anywhere, deserve the attention of crusaders. But don't press me for an article of a past incident I know the "Republican" will use to fan hatred.

I have written at length, not to bore you, but in the hope you'll take it seriously. In times ahead it'll help us to know, we gave each other room for understanding.

I'm happy. Emma remains all that my love of England is. I have surrounded myself with the things I love. Mohan Singh has done me a great favour. He has transported the books I left in Pathankot by handcarts and ponies to the cottage. As for the cottage, I've documented two stipulations. First, it is not to be sold. Second, should you find no further use for it, or if you settle elsewhere, the cottage goes to Bill Clayton or Miss Das—both for whom you have shown respect, I am happy to say—to dispose of. They could use the money or the property. As things promise to be, the cottage and land will eventually become part of a growing Tibetan landscape. One can't predict the future.

I've provided Sona with a regular allowance. Do remember she is not a servant. She is a member of the family and she took good care of you in our absence, when you were a boy and your ayah suddenly took ill and died. Now you are to be responsible for her welfare. Nothing can be proceeded on the cottage until she leaves of her own accord.

Keep this letter. One day it will be useful. We brought you up in the way my sister, your mother, wished, a Hindu; and why you were pupil of Pundit Bhaba. Ironically, like Gandhi, he is more "Christian" than the best of us. He told Emma, Gandhi's favourite hymn was "Abide With Me". I told her, I thought it was "Lead Kindly Light". She said it didn't matter as that was not the point of the story. Anyway, what you know about Christianity comes from him and not from us. I'm trying, in a lumbering way, to get you to see that ideals and beliefs don't have to exclude people.

I'll close now. It's been physically tiring. My fingers find typing difficult and writing impossible: so this is a labour of love.

As ever, Sandy.

PS Ted has been a great help to me and to you in England. Moneys banked there are at his discretion. I know Edith likes you. When she was here last year, she told me how much she enjoyed your walks together. Indeed, for her age she's very fit and active. S

CHAPTER ELEVEN

'The truth is destructive,' said Pundit Bhaba. 'It destroys gradually.'

Dinesh frowned. 'But why, Punditji? And why gradually?'

'Because, *beta* Dinesh, life is the gradual discovery of truth, *hahn*. And with every new truth discovered, something in us, and in the world, dies. You see, basically, life is expediency. And what is expediency, but falsehood!'

'Why is expediency falsehood?'

'Because there is no need for urgency in this world. Urgency is man-made. So, truth is never expedient. And we can never know the whole truth, because we are not gods. Therefore, truth is what we believe to be true. So, belief itself is false and, therefore, not truth. That's why I say that we're bound to be unhappy if, one, we search for truth and, two, persist in believing our truth is Truth; truth with big T.'

'Then, punditji, are you saying, we mustn't have beliefs?' Dinesh stared past Pundit Bhaba at the black stone figure of Ganesh, freshly garlanded with marigold and jasmine.

'No, no, no. One may cherish and foster one's beliefs as long as one knows they are false, *hahn*. And if at the end we do not care whether they are true or false, then only will we find contentment.'

'So truth is destructive because life's an illusion.'

'Now you are learning. And this is why one shouldn't have ideals, because, finally in the face of truth, ideals are delusions. In a perfect state, there are no ideals.'

'Like we say in Hinduism: *maya*. All life is an illusion.'

'Not just Hinduism. All religions hold life to be an illusion. In the sense that religions point towards something beyond earthly turmoil. Ultimate reality is far beyond human experience and so making human experience ultimately false.'

'So we may lie and live a lie. Can that be a formula for happiness?'

'Happiness is itself a falsehood. We are really seeking contentment, and merely, the satisfaction of our base cravings.'

'But,' said Dinesh, driven to distraction, and making a mental note not to visit Pundit Bhaba again, 'if there is no such thing as happiness, can we know when our cravings are satisfied?'

'We lie to delude ourselves till we're content. The goal of contentment is neither a highway nor is it a pilgrimage. It's an inner journey. Some, those who can't tell lies or who can't face the truth, never attempt it . . . the journey I mean. Sensibly, perhaps.'

'So contentment is in learning to live with lies. But it's wrong . . . to tell lies.'

'But I'm not thinking about lies which conflict with law. Just philosophical lies. Lies which placate, not implicate.'

'How can one tell lies and not be aware of it.'

'By force of habit. Attaching value to your lie, making a philosophy out of a lie.'

'I see. So if one is aware that one is lying, one is unhappy. But if the lie is the result of what one is striving to achieve, then one has found contentment.'

'Now you are following me. As long as one's strivings do not infringe the law or hinder others. That about sums it up.'

'But that is advocating hypocrisy!'

'I have nothing against hypocrisy. Do not confuse hypocrisy with dishonesty. It is the modus operandi of all civilised societies. It's a kind of politeness.'

'There has to be a flaw. There can be no defence for lying or hypocrisy. Or are you saying that saints and martyrs are fools for not protecting themselves by lying? I mean, how does a truthful coward survive?'

'By getting rid of all cravings, desires, ambitions . . . yes, and especially spiritual pride. You see, son Dinesh, one does not have to choose contentment. You may choose the path of truth and forever wrestle with life—forever lead a restless life. Think upon this. A contented life is one without excitement. Without meaning. The truth, if I may quote what Christ said, will set you free. Such freedom is a fulfilment; and such fulfilment is exciting without excitement.'

'But, Punditji, how can anything be exciting without excitement?'

'By having a clear conscience.'

'But Shakespeare said, that conscience makes cowards of us all?' Dinesh did not know why he said it, or where it would lead. But he longed for Pundit Bhaba to reach an end. Maybe that end was imminent, for the Pundit had paused and was looking at him with an enigmatic smile.

'Son, Dinesh. Shakespeare, great man as he was; great psychologist, but he was all over the . . . this and that and the other. He was no theologian. I say, people who can't lie shouldn't. Would you not rather live with a conscience than without one, and thereby avoid striving to gain happiness? There is solace even in a tragic destiny. What you have forgotten is the human spirit. Human spirit overcomes misery, if that spirit, sustained by *karma*, good works, seeks salvation. But let me say this, finally. Hypocrisy is a romance and heaven is a dream, and that is what most of us need in life.'

Dinesh rose to his feet, folded his palms, bowed, touched the punditji's feet, and retreated in utter confusion.

'Uncle Sandy,' Dinesh said, looking out of the window, 'can I ask you something? Is it possible to fall in love with anyone and anything, if you make up you mind to.'

'It depends on the sort of person you are.' Sandy smiled, aware that Dinesh's use of the prefix "uncle" meant he was genuinely seeking help or advice.

'I was thinking of you and Emmaji. And Shanti and me.'

'Is it not obvious? I see, you want to press the case for arranged marriages? Well, it doesn't matter if love comes early or late, as long as, in the end, it lasts.'

'I just wanted to say that when I'm anti-English, I've no personal animosity towards Auntyji. I think Aunty is—is wonderful and-and, a good person.'

Sandy softened visibly. 'Lunch is being laid out on the lawn. Are you staying?'

'No, uncle. Thanks. I did tell Aunty on my way up to see you. Shanti is at Mohan Singh's house. I'll be joining them. There, as you can see, the table is laid for three. And Sona's back from the Post Office.'

'Well, give our regards to Shanti, Mohan and Bunty.' Sandy limped towards the stairs and reached out for the banisters.

'You're not wearing your special shoes?' Dinesh asked with genuine concern.

'It's far too hot in them. These Italian moccasins are cool and comfortable.'

After lunch Sona led Emma to a low deck chair and placed cushions behind her back. 'Now, I get stool for feet.'

'I'm all right, darling. Stay with me.'

'Not ar'right. Keep feet up, doctor say.' Sona looked down, arms akimbo, at Emma. Then she went into the verandah. Sandy smiled and drew a cane chair next to Emma. Sona came back with a stool and more cushions.

'Thank you, Sona.' Emma watched Sona clear the table and waited till she carried the trays to the kitchen. 'Sandy, has Dinesh been horrid to you?'

Sandy sighed. 'No, not today. Seemed a bit subdued. He's so mixed up. At least we talked. Not much. He's fond of you.'

'That's not enough. It doesn't make up for his hostility. And not a word of thanks?'

'Thanks? Ah, for the wedding expenses. No. I never expected any. I kept them down to the minimum. Luckily, the girl's side bore the brunt. I wasn't going to compete with her father's lavish spending. I hope you don't mind not seeing Shanti?'

She shook her head. 'Dinesh didn't answer your letter? I didn't think he would. Do you think he'll manage the estate for long?'

'No, I think Shanti's father will make him an offer he can't refuse. But, as you know I've made Bill a trustee, and made sure Sona's taken good care of. I've also left a large account for Ted to manage.'

She turned her head away from him. 'My sweet! I've given you nothing . . . nothing of us . . . no child to . . .'

'Please, my love. You promised not make yourself unhappy. And me.'

'But I don't like the idea of you giving up everything because of me. You can still have children after I'm gone. You're only fifty-four.'

'Are you suggesting I should limp around looking for a womb to let?'

'I'm serious.' She paused and stared at him. 'There's Sona. I know she loves of you. Women know these things. She's strong and young. I won't mind, she's a good girl.'

'Girl! She's not much younger than you . . .'

'She'll do it if I ask . . . I don't think she'll need much persuading.'

They hadn't heard Sona approach. There she stood looking down at them benignly, her hands spread out affectionately. Then she let them fall helplessly against her sides.

'What is it?' Emma said gently. 'Come Sona, please come to me!'

'You both rike children!' She knelt and buried her face in Emma's lap.

'There now.' Sandy patted Sona's head. She wiped her face on her sleeve. Sandy offered his handkerchief. She looked at it, then at Emma. Both laughed.

'What's so funny?' Sandy asked.

'How he saying, long ago. "Use hanky, Sona, not sleeve!" So nice gentleman.' Sona said, her smile displayed a beautiful set of even teeth. She grabbed the handkerchief and giggled. 'I no give back. Now I go kitchen for tea. I tell cook, make hot sponge cake.'

'Not for me, darling,' Emma said.

Sona sucked air through clenched teeth as she cupped Emma's face lovingly. 'For Sandy and doctorsahib. Doctor coming soon.' Then she went indoors.

'Yes, of course . . . The doctor.' Sandy said absently. 'Did Ransingh arrange a *dooli* or *jampan* to fetch him?'

'No,' said Emma. 'Don't you remember? We lent him one of our ponies. Pleased he was, too, because he has to come up often. Come, sit next to me. And darling please look at me. Sandy, why won't you look at me? Do I look old and terrible?'

'Good Lord, no! That's what's so cruel. You look young, beautiful as ever. Forty-four. I don't, no one does believe it. Look at you, so sylph-like, in spite of the Indian sweets you love. No tyres round the tum-tums.' He laughed as he pinched her.

'There never was danger of gaining weight. Please don't look sad. I'm sorry. You wanted to spend May in Italy and I've been so involved with Sona and "The Women's Welfare" group.'

'I forgot all about Italy. I love to see you happy. And I'm happy to be with you and my books. And I love watching you gardening and painting; and I love . . . making love.'

'But you've stopped saying nice things to me.'

'Emma, that's unfair. So not like you. What is it? Something's the matter, my love. Something's worrying you. Talk to me? Not about children . . . or about dying.'

She looked away. 'The garden's not what it used to be. You haven't noticed. Our cook has.'

He sighed. 'I gather Mohan Singh's building an extension. But, thankfully, whatever he does won't block our view of the lake. We're quite sheltered from neighbours. That clump of poplars, on the slope below us, screens us . . . It's ours . . . I must remind Dinesh.'

'We've seen such changes! Mcleodganj has changed . . . I like her'

'Her? Who or what are you thinking about?'

'Bunty. Mohan's wife. She calls me *Neelum*.'

'You must know why? It means sapphire. Your eyes.'

She looked down and touched her ringed finger. 'It doesn't seem so long ago!' She sighed again. 'This sapphire ring Bunty gave me. Mohan was unhappy about it. He said a sapphire can be unlucky. She told me to test it by putting it under my pillow. If I had a bad dream, I wasn't to wear it. I did have a bad dream. But I don't believe in that sort of thing. You don't either. Do you?'

He shook his head.

She gazed at him. 'I dreamt you were back in England. That you were alone, and without me. I dreamt of Sona too. She was here, but sitting in a bus. I was calling out to her, frantically! But she did not hear . . . Or rather she, ignored me.'

'It's only a stone. An inanimate thing. It can't harm you.'

'India is full of . . . remember the fuss over horoscopes for Dinesh and Shanti? There had to be an auspicious date for the wedding.'

'The whole thing is a con. What about Bunty's son, Balbir? I couldn't help noticing that he couldn't seem to take his eyes off you.'

'Calf-love. He's a shy and awkward nineteen-year-old. Dashes about wanting to do things for me or just stands at a distance gaping, blushing. Bunty's quite tickled by his infatuation. That's all it is. You've have no reason to be jealous. I can never understand why Indians are so keen on fair skins?'

'Their idea of fair. Not the pink and blotchy reds and mauves of British men in India. More the pale alabaster of the *topied* mems. But all men love the fair and the fragile.'

'What about Tennyson's "dusky" maidens?'

'The other day he, not Tennyson, Balbir told me he had seen an actress who looked just like you. He had just been to a matinee showing of *The Third Man*. "Uncle, uncle he said, Emmaji looks like her, ditto." I suppose he was thinking of Alida Valli.'

'He calls me *Bhabi*. That means sister, doesn't it? I'm too old for that.'

'All these compliments can turn a girl's head.'

'Stop it. I don't like it. Don't tease, Sandy.' She frowned and pulled her hand away. Then relented and gave it back to him. With a tired smile she squeezed his hand. 'You turned my head. It's stayed turned towards you. But you've stopped writing those little poems, as you did for my birthdays. It's been two years now.'

'As it happens, I've a small present for you. A pocket edition of Donne's poems. Leather bound. No bigger than the palm of your hand. Here, it belonged to Jaggers. He had it specially printed and bound.'

She took it gleefully. 'Have you written something in it?'

'Not a poem. I dare not. That would be an affront to Donne. But I've penned a line.'

She read: '"Never forget that first time I kissed you." Thank you. I've never, Sandy. Kiss me now.' He did. She quietly turned the pages of the little book. 'It must be quite old. The first page is missing.'

'I suppose there may have been something very private written on it. Something he could no longer keep, or which no longer applied.

'Sandy, I am sorry about Italy. We could next April. What about this September?'

'Moti will be away with her son, six months from August. In Mauritius.'

'You mean, Perla. I know Moti means pearl. But she prefers to be called Perla. Will she be hurt, about our not coming to Italy this . . . ?'

'Not in the least.'

'She's sweet, generous, but of your three sisters I like the one in Bombay best.'

'Ranee. I too, though I don't know much about her. Except that she didn't marry and cared for my father to the end. She went into politics and was an MP for ten years. She would have been the right guardian for Dinesh, but Ranee couldn't stand him.'

'She has great dignity. The name, Ranee, suits her. And your brother? It's curious that none of you talk about him.'

'Ashok? The eldest. Poor chap. I never knew him. Did I not tell you about him?'

'You did. But remind me.'

'He and father never got on. Ashok was sent to a boarding school in Simla. Then one day he disappeared. Just vanished. I'll always regret not pressing my parents to tell me more. I sensed a conspiracy to keep hush-hush what was clearly a scandal.'

'Your sisters were old enough to know more?'

'Only about the pre-school years. There's an amusing story. When little, he looked at a portrait of George V, and asked: "Mummy, why do they sing God shave the King".'

Emma smiled. 'He might be still alive. Somewhere.'

Sandy shook his head. 'Father found out he enlisted in 1940. Was sent to Burma, and not heard of till—he must have named mother as next of kin—she got a telegram on VE Day, of all days . . . Ranee was the only one she told. But father knew, I don't know how. Ranee swears she never told him, There were rumours. Desertion, liaison with a Burmese woman. But . . .'

'What is it? What is the matter?'

He was staring down the path and beyond the gate.

'Has Dr Saxena arrived?'

He nodded. And started to limp down the path.

'Stay with me, Sandy!'

He turned. She beckoned. 'Now, promise you will be brave. I'm so much better.'

He bent over and whispered. 'Let me take you inside.'

'Wait for Sona. If he's gone to the paddock she will have seen him. No, Sandy wait! Oh my love, you must look after yourself. You look weak and exhausted!'

Dr Sudhir Saxena came out of the bedroom looking grim. Sandy's mouth went dry. He swallowed. His throat hurt and under his vest the sweat was icy. He shivered as he accompanied the doctor downstairs into the garden. They were silent till they reached the gate. 'Thakurji,' the doctor said, 'Mrs Thakur has been taking capsules? And all the medicines? I'm hoping so.'

'Oh, yes. Sona sees to that. The half aspirins too. Just as you said.'

'Fine, fine. Then all has been done. Now what can I say.' He raised his brows and took a deep breath. 'I'm most sorry. Indeed, I am baffled—totally—baffled, as to what else to do.'

Sandy swayed. The doctor held out a hand to steady him. Sandy nodded gratefully. Grim faced, he said. 'Do your best. Spare no effort . . . money, as you know is no . . .'

'I know. Such talk is needless. I have also consulted colleagues. Better than the best. No stone unturned. You see, she is getting weaker daily. I can barely hear her pulse!'

'But she looks well! I can't understand.'

'Thakur sahib. Have you not noted her movements are slow? That she tires easily. Note under her eyelids. She's anaemic. Severely so.'

'Is there nothing you can give her. Liver tea?'

'Thakurji, your wife's getting all right treatment, but she's a delicate lady, and a long history of congenital heart . . .'

"For God's sake, Doctor! What is wrong! Sorry, I didn't mean to raise my voice.'

'No matter. I understand. Auricular fibrillation among . . . other things too. Systolic murmurs in the apex—it's hard to explain the case. Best to be frank. Nobody has been negligent. She will go like a leaf in the wind. One thing I know, she will not suffer and for that, God be praised.'

'It's unfair! So unfair!' Sandy raised a hand as the doctor was about to speak. 'No, don't tell me life's unfair.' There were tears in Dr Saxena's eyes. 'Forgive me. I know you have done all you can.'

Dr Saxena spread his hands. 'Destiny is with the gods. We Hindus have saying: when mortals achieve perfection, the gods want their company.' He shut his eyes, forefinger pressed against his lips. 'She will have dignity. I see so much indignity, Thakurji, that I can assure you, dignity is a blessing. The gods will grant her that, because your worthy wife is herself a goddess.' He rested his hands on the wooden gate and stared into the distance. '*Hari Om!*' *Hari Om*! He murmured.

In the paddock beyond the gate, Harnam Singh was brushing the pony lovingly, while the animal stood noisily absorbed in the contents of his nose-bag. 'I cannot live without her!' Sandy whispered. The pony shook the bag off his head and looked up.

'Why not take her back to England? I don't think there's anything they can do there for her, but maybe, it's the right thing to do.'

'She won't hear of it. She will never go back.'

'Why for this? England is most beautiful country! I spent two most happy years there. Actually,' the doctor grinned sheepishly and gave his head a slight wobble, 'I was in Scotland. Still, but why won't she?'

'It's because of me. It's a long story.'

'Oh, yes. I know. Dinesh told me. However, at present she's too weak to travel. Had you been in Delhi it might have been more practical. By air, I mean.'

'I could arrange a helicopter flight to Delhi but, as I said, she won't return to . . .'

'That's true, doctor sahib. I'll never return to England.' Emma joined them. She was wearing fur-lined Tibetan moccasins that Sona had given her and her gold-embroidered, maroon, cashmere house coat, having caught the evening light, lent her pale cheeks a deceptively healthy glow.

'But sister, please, I merely suggesting temporary visit only. No need to worry about Sandy sahib. We'll take care of him.'

'I wouldn't dream of going without my husband.'

'Indeed! Please forgive.' Dr Saxena smiled. '*Miah bibi*, Husband wife, always being together. This is talk of the Ganj.'

'And I cannot do without Sona. I want to be here.'

'But your brother. He is doctor . . .'

Sandy had raised a hand. The doctor desisted. An awkward silence was broken by Sona calling out from the porch. She said something in Tibetan and to the amazement of the Doctor, Emma answered her.

'Sister! Wonderful! Hearing you speak Tibetan.'

'Emma's always been good at languages,' Sandy said wanly.

'You should seek an audience with the Dalai Lama, sisterji.'

Emma was watching Sandy with an expression of deep concern. 'I have seen him, doctor sahib, some years ago. I believe in a good man's power of prayer.

Dr Saxena raised his palms. 'What can I say!'

'You don't have to say anything, Saxena sahib.' Emma said, her eyes still on Sandy.

Dr Saxena folded his hands in salutation. '*Achcha*. I should be taking my leave. But I also hear Padre Sahib will be with you some time soon. A most saintly man. I saw him the other day. He was wearing saffron robes like sadhu.'

'Bill Clayton,' said Sandy, 'likes to be called a Christian Sadhu.'

Emma took Sandy's arm. 'Doctor sahib, I want you to know, I couldn't have had a better doctor. I know the walls of my heart are too thin to face an operation. So, I am not being foolishly obstinate about treatment in England.'

'Thakurji is unhappy. I am trying best to tell, but failing to explain.'

'I don't believe nothing can be done!' Sandy burst in. 'I will take her back!'

'Hush Sandy, I don't want to die alone in a hospital, however grand or wonderful it is.' Sona came out to them carrying a tray. 'Please doctor, do have a drink. Whisky and soda? It's the way my husband likes it. No, don't refuse. Drink to my health?'

'That I'll surely do, sister.' He poured the soda. 'Have some too. Churchill, he lived long life because he sipped weak whisky all day. Here, Sandy sahib, join me.'

Sona led Emma inside. The men watched them go through the porch. 'Soda's cold. You have ice-box?' Dr Saxena asked, but Sandy was not listening. He leaned forward. The whisky glass fell from his shaking hand and smashed to pieces.

※

'Darling don't be afraid to make love to me.' Emma looked up tearfully. He took her in his arms and held her tightly. 'Kill me, Sandy! Crush me to death.'

He kissed her fondly. 'I couldn't.'

'I'm dying, Sandy. Let me die happy, like this in your arms.'

'Emma, if you die, I'll kill myself.'

'Oh, darling? Will you do that for me? Keep me company.'

'Yes, I couldn't live alone. I'll find a way. I promise. It's as it should be for us.'

'But it's a sin.'

'It wont be the first time we've sinned. Remember?'

'And mother knew. Ted knew.'

'Yes, they knew.'

'Sandy! I'm so afraid.'

'Yesterday, you were happy. You were smiling?'

'I feel I'm being sucked in . . . into . . . something horrid, empty. I shouldn't be afraid, I know.' She paused. He waited. He wanted to cry out. 'Lie down next to me.' He did. 'Sandy I dreamt about our holiday in Arran, when we followed a stream, up a valley and climbed Goat Fell? On our wedding anniversary . . . then the dream changed. I was a child again, with father. He pointed to the picture in my bedroom . . . Bellini's Madonna . . . then the child's hands . . . hands from a cloud . . . a big white cloud pulling me in.'

※

They lay awake. The curtains were open and the window framed a starlit sky. Only their breathing broke the silence. She giggled. He turned on his side and pressed against her. 'What is it?'

'Nothing.' She was remembering their honeymoon in Venice, and the moment, when she woke with a start to find him stark naked in the morning light, standing on the bed, looking down at her. "Awake! Beloved! Behold the sight, your sultan's penis, caught in a noose of light!"

'Tell me?' He drew her hard against him.

'Nothing. You were so wicked. I'll tell you in the morning. Sleep now.'

'You'll forget. You always do.'

'It won't matter,' she sighed, then whispered. 'I'm so tired, so drowsy . . .' A dull constricting pain ran through her like an electric current. She sank into his body. The warmth of his pressure eased the pain. 'You've always made me laugh,' she said. 'The silly things you say . . . and do. Sandy, I love you! I've never said it often enough.'

He kissed her neck. It was time to affirm his love, to express gratitude for a life that had answered his, that had filled and comforted his every longing. A strong desire to make love overcame him.

'Sandy,' she murmured intuitively. 'Be gentle. Don't put all your weight on me.'

He turned her towards him, till she lay on her back and, in trying to take his weight on his elbows, came down heavily and ineptly between her legs. He apologised. She made no protest. It was too dark to see her face. He spread her thighs. She felt cold. 'My demon lover!' He heard her whisper from a darkness deep beyond him. He made love, awkwardly, breathlessly. Exhausted, he rolled off her and lay on his back. Slowly he raised himself and sought her lips, kissing her, twice. She made a faint sound, a deep unsettling pathos gripped him. He fell back and lay very still.

'Have you made love to Sona,' she asked, scarcely above a whisper. He started. A dim light from somewhere turned the smooth skin of her face to marble. Her eyes were shut. He studied the fine straight nose, the full sullen lips and was reminded of Millais's *Ophelia*. That painting always depressed him.

'You didn't answer me?' she said.

'The answer is no, never, not ever. Why would I?'

She sighed deeply. 'I won't mind.'

'You ought to! We been through all this before. Don't punish yourself. How many times must I say, I've loved you every moment of our lives?'

'I want to keep hearing it . . . even after I'm gone.'

He felt his heart breaking. 'I'll die loving you! I've told . . .' his voice began to trail.

'Did you know, Sona's clairvoyant?' She murmured, but he had fallen asleep. His breathing grew deep and regular. She became anxious and afraid of sleep, and wanted so much to hear his voice. 'Sandy?' She listened and waited. Then slipped out of bed, landing on her hands and knees. The night was pleasantly warm but she shivered as she groped for her shawl that lay at the foot of the bed and wrapped it round herself. 'What! What!' he called. Rolled on his stomach and drifted back to sleep.

She felt her way towards the window. Through its mosquito-wire-mesh, the starlit garden appeared like a scene painted on canvas. A light breeze rustled the leaves and gusts of wind swayed the branches of the ilex trees, casting ghostly shadows. Turning away, she moved to her favourite emperor cane chair and sank into its cushions. Then she drew her feet up, hugged her knees and in this foetal position sobbed quietly. 'Oh, Sandy! Will this be the last time? Will we never make love again? Lord Jesus! I don't want to die! Spare me! I can't leave him . . . Mother! O mother . . . Will you understand . . . when I'm gone . . . forgive the years of absence? You're strong, very strong. It's unfair! Why Mother? Why didn't you give me strength. Strength to live! Why do you hate me? You were horrid when you came here. I hate you for ignoring me . . . leaving me, sick and helpless . . .' She covered her face in her hands. It felt cold and wet. She must rest and think of nothing else but sleep. Imagine that black square. As a child it had helped her to sleep. "Emma, Emma!" 'Father? Is that you?' She sensed his presence till from the shadows a strong hand held hers. She felt a peculiar thrill. The years swept back. She was a child again. He was pointing to the rose bushes above their Anderson shelter. "Emma, Emma!" The voice, now louder, more real, came with a warm breath against her ear. She looked down. Sandy was holding her hands and kneeling beside her.

'I didn't want to startle you. What are you doing here? Please come back to bed.'

'Sandy, did I wake you? I'm sorry.'

'No. Sona woke me. She heard you crying. There, put your arms round me.'

'Sona? Is Sona here?'

'She sleeps in the box-room next to us. For sometime now. Remember?'

'She must know all about us. All our loving? Does that matter?'

'It doesn't matter. Of course it doesn't. She would know, wherever she is.'

'Stay with me.' He leaned forward, put his head against her heart and whispered, sadly: 'Don't stop, dear heart, don't stop.' Then aloud to her: 'Emma, you have always been brave. You are the strong one. Without you . . .' He stopped. Sona was humming "Rock of Ages" to a familiar tune. She must have learned it at the Christian Mission in Ladakh. He glanced over his shoulder. In the adjacent room, a lighted candle flickered.

'Sandy! I'm afraid of dying . . . afraid of the darkness . . . the journey alone.'

'There'll be no darkness. I know. You've been magnificent . . . comforted and given hope to others . . . you won't be alone. I'll be with you. I've made that promise. We will journey together . . . You have my promise. Now come to bed.'

They lay together in a silence lulled by Sona's humming. Emma chuckled. 'Poor girl. I wonder if she knows the words.' Suddenly she asked: How is your injured leg?'

'Right now. Pins and needles. It'll go,' he added forcing a laugh.

'Sandy? Us being together, how can you be sure . . . ?'

'By the power of prayer. Not just mine; Bill's, Sona's, yours . . . All ours together. Sona knows what we want. She'll see to it. There is nothing to keep me here.'

'But Bill? He would think it wrong?'

'He'll pray for forgiveness . . . Anyway it's not as if I'm in the best of health. Hush now that's all settled.' He took a deep breath and drew her hard against him. 'We have been talking nonsense. You'll be well. Fight. "Do not go gentle . . . rage, rage against the dying of the light".' She took the hand that held her and gave it a feeble squeeze.

Sona had stopped humming. Sandy looked up to find her standing over him. 'She okay, now.' Sona pronounced. 'Sleeping till morning time.'

He clutched her broad wrist and whispered urgently. 'Now, Sona. Now?'

'No. Wait. Now too soon.'

CHAPTER TWELVE

Dinesh, having planned not to visit Fern cottage while Bill was there, arrived the day after Bill left for Dharamsala. He thanked Sandy for sending a pony with Harnam Singh. 'Have you acquired a new one?' He asked.

Sandy frowned. 'Pony? No. Didn't you recognise Chameli?'

'The mare? No. I know Dr Saxena's riding Hira. I saw Harnam on Ravi so I thought the pony he was leading couldn't possibly be Chameli. I also thought you may have lent her to Bill.'

Sandy laughed. 'Bill! Can you imagine Moses, I mean Bill, on one of my ponies? His feet would scrape the ground. He may as well walk, which he prefers. Walking is a part of his philosophy. Christ did. A pity you missed Bill. We expected you two days ago?'

'I wasn't sure if there'd be room.'

'The guest room was free. You know Bill prefers the loft above the stables.'

'Also part of his theology? Away in a manger.' Dinesh giggled defensively.

'But I understand why you stayed away. Harnam told . . .'

'God, am I being spied upon?'

'Nonsense. Look, sorry I mentioned it. I hope you won't take it out on him. Harnam is a good man. Now, you must promise me that. I insist.'

Dinesh shrugged. 'I don't expect loyalty from anyone while you're around. Sorry, I had to say that. It's the typical mentality of Indian minions. Anyway he's leaving at the end of this month, so he told me.'

'Is he? You see, I'm not told everything. Contradicts what you just said. Don't underestimate the Sikhs. Pity. He'll be hard to replace.'

'I've got someone lined up.'

'Hmm. I hope you won't make drastic changes to the staff. When you do, make sure no one gets less than six months severance pay. I'll add a codicil in my will to ensure Ransingh gets a pension for life.'

'I met Dr Saxena. He saw Bill in his sadhu outfit? It's phoney.'

'Phoney! How would you know? Leave it. I'm not in a mood to argue with you. We have a lot to do.'

'You can insult me, and I mustn't protest?'

'I won't insult you if you don't insult my friends. You may be a militant Hindu, but you must know that the rest of the Hindu community regard Bill as a saint,'

'I don't deny that, Sandy. Just this Sadhu business. A wolf-in-sheep clothing.'

Sandy waved a hand. 'Now, have you had breakfast? Good. Then we'll get down to legal matters. I don't have to be around, but Nanavati—you haven't met him, but he's one of our lawyers—he'll fill you in. Hand me my stick. Thank you. He's a good man, Nanavati. I trust him absolutely.'

'Nanavati. Is he Sindhi or Parsee?'

'Parsee, but not *passe*. Never mind. Just a silly joke. He's in the garden. It a fine day, so we can work there. Not much paper work now but there's a file for you.'

Late in the evening Dinesh received a message by runner from Shanti. It didn't make sense, so he decided to leave for Pathankot in the morning. He rode to Dharamsala with Harnam Singh, but before handing back the pony he asked Harnam to accompany him to a *halwai* shop, where he bought a half *seer* of *burfi*—Emma's favourite sweetmeat. 'The best and freshest,' he said to the *halwai* in Hindi. The man adjusted his *dhoti* and made a great show of washing his hands over the side of the shop, creating a small pool on to the pavement below. He then drew a large *thali* of the fudge-like confection and cut it into diamond shapes. '*Dhekko* sahibji. Made last night only.' He offered a piece to Dinesh to taste. 'Good', said Dinesh. 'Put lots of *varak*.' The man applied the flimsy silver leaf on top of the sweets with a flourish. 'Good for blood and . . .' he flexed his arm and struck the elbow with the palm of his other hand, in a vulgar gesture suggesting male sexual potency. Dinesh handed the packet to the syce and instructed him to make certain 'memsahib' received it in person. Then he tipped the syce handsomely, to make sure, although he did not doubt Harnam's honesty.

The bus station was crowded and the queues long and noisy. Dinesh waved to draw the attention of the booking clerk behind the grille. The man nodded and sent a minion out to him. 'I want one seat on the Pathankot bus.' Dinesh said imperiously. The minion bowed with folded palms, rolled his head in a figure of eight and led the way to the bus. 'And.' Dinesh added. 'see that I get my usual place. The single seat up front, next to the driver!' The man stopped and cringed obsequiously. The front seat he deeply regretted was not available. If only the sahib arrived ten minutes earlier! He pointed and Dinesh saw a refrigerator roped to the seat. A seat by the door was the next best thing. Dinesh examined the hard cushion with a critical eye as the minion dusted it with noisy flicks of the cloth duster he carried over this left shoulder. Forcing an ingratiating and toothless grin, the man waited. Dinesh made a face, slapped a five rupee note into the man's open palm and dismissed him with a wave. The man protested the tip was not necessary—he was only doing a job—but pocketed it with practised dexterity and left before Dinesh could change his mind.

Dinesh placed his small suitcase on the vacant seat next to his own and sat down with an air meant to discourage boarding peasantry from daring even to think of sitting next to him. He relaxed after the bus left with the seat not taken, but he knew his luck would soon run out. There always were important passengers and buses made detours to collect them. One such obligatory stop was at the well by the tamarind tree, where Seth Sonlal, a rich merchant, built himself a house and a temple in honour of Hanuman, the monkey god. So Dinesh was pleasantly surprised when the bus took the direct route out of town and saw, for the first time, the rear wall of the temple and its huge tempera painting of Hanuman leaping into the sky with one hand lifting a mountain and the other holding his tail. A chorus of *'Jai Mahadev! Jai Hanumanji!* (victory to the great god! victory to Hanuman!) came from the bus passengers. These hill folk had welcomed the addition of a Hanuman festival to their other

The Lotus And The Rose

religious celebrations and their reactions to icons were spontaneous, almost Pavlovian. Now they sat glumly, feet cocked up, heads resting on their knees, allowing the movement of the bus to rock them to sleep.

The bus jolted to a stop. Inquiries were ignored by the Sikh driver, who went past the passengers to the back of the bus where, after some discussion with his assistant, he returned to his seat, reversed the bus some distance, turned into a dirt road and after a mile or so, left it and drove up a gravel hardened jeep track towards what looked like a derelict cherry orchard. He turned off the engine, dismounted and stood outside with his back to the passengers. Once again he ignored a barrage of inquiries, yawned and stretched himself. A big man behind Dinesh stood up, scratched his crotch impudently and got off the bus to urinate behind a bush. Then he cleared his throat and spat. 'What is the matter?' he asked the Sikh driver in Punjabi. 'Why the hold up?' The men sized each other for a while and spat almost simultaneously and with emphasis.

'*Doh minoot*,' answered the driver sullenly. He unrolled his turban and retied it.

'Is it twelve o'clock?' chirped a voice from inside the bus, loud enough for the Sikh driver to hear. The question was immediately greeted with a roar of laughter. The Sikh swung round and glared at the passengers angrily. The big man shrugged and returned to the bus. The Sikh relaxed, flashed a good humoured smile and with a glance at his bright metal watch said: 'Still one hour to go, brothers.' All laughed.

Dinesh did not join in the laughter. Someone tapped his shoulder and explained. '*Arrey*, at twelve noon, these Sardarjis go crazy. He saying only eleven now.'

Dinesh nodded, pushed the glass of the window down and leaned out to take in the scene behind him. On closer inspection the orchard turned out to be a dilapidated and unkempt Christian cemetery. Through the trees he could make out a marble cross and gravestones askew among the tall grass and weeds. An angel with a broken wing stood under a slate canopy while on its right, under what was once a lych-gate, was the effigy of an old man. The effigy came to life and moved toward the bus and Dinesh recognised the Reverend Father Bill Clayton.

Bill Clayton was wearing a plain brown shirt and khaki shorts. Holding a stout staff he walked with the long strides of a giant and the dignity of a Biblical Patriarch. Behind him came four men carrying a large wooden crate. As they neared the bus the Sikh gave Bill a military salute and to Dinesh's astonishment the whole bus stirred to life. 'Beel! Padre Beel sahib! Baba Beel sahib!' The bus emptied and soon Bill was surrounded by smiling faces, greeting him with folded palms. The crate was taken up to the roof of the bus with a great deal of advice and fuss.

'What have you got there? Dinesh asked, inviting Bill to sit next to him.

Bill Clayton was very tall, thin, and ascetic, with twinkling blue eyes, a white beard, and a deep tan which emphasised the wrinkles at the corners of his eyes. He had a full head of long white hair, swept back and tied in a pony tail behind a sturdy neck. He sat down with a grateful sigh and looked steadily at Dinesh. 'So, how's my Danny Boy,' he asked. 'And what's the latest news of your uncle?'

Dinesh turned away, awed by the bent figure looming over him. He saw at once why Sandy nicknamed him Moses. 'Sandy's well. As far as I know.'

Bill raised his brows and shook his head. Taking a sharp breath he slapped his knees. 'You'd like to know what's up there?' He smiled. 'Yes, you do. Did I tell you about my maternal grandfather? Well, he was a missionary in these parts years ago, and died in a minor epidemic of small-pox in 1910. He's buried there.' Bill indicated the cemetery, as the bus began to move. 'It was the year my father arrived in India to join him. I had no difficulty finding the grave. There aren't many graves and India's climate is kind to inscriptions. I was told, over his grave, there was a beautiful Victorian cast-iron cross. That.' he pointed to the roof, 'took some finding. It lay buried, far from the headstone. I mean to restore it.'

'That cemetery has lain neglected for years.'

'But not vandalised or defiled. Indians respect the dead. But, why replace the cross? Respect. Respect for someone I heard so much about but never met.'

'We cremate our dead.'

'True. Though you bury saints. Some at least.'

They were silent for a while. The bus descended into the plains and Dinesh felt the pressure on his eardrums. It was also considerably hotter and as they slowed down past a cluster of sun baked mud huts, the driver shouted 'Bhojpur!'.

'This will be a forty-minutes stop,' said Bill.

'Let me buy you lunch?' said Dinesh.

'That's kind. Yes, thank you. Bhojpur is famous for its puri and potato *bhaji*.'

They got off the bus. Bill stretched and looked about him. 'It's been three years since I was here. It hasn't changed. That tin hut is new. What does that notice say?'

'"Lavatory for tourists guests only",' Dinesh read.

I suppose we could be tourists for the day . . . oh, and that cafe! That's new. But I'm glad to see the food hut is still there—underneath the spreading banyan tree.'

'I'll order lunch,' said Dinesh. 'Shall we find a less crowded spot?'

'Yes, if you wish.'

'There, under the mango tree by the ruins. The stone steps are in the shade. But I see they are bringing out chairs and a folding table for us. We'll have to stay here, Bill.'

'Just as well. The ruins, as you call it, is a shrine, still in use.'

Dinesh returned, followed by a little man carrying two steaming *thalis*. 'Hmm, this smells good,' said Bill, 'and they've included a pickle. *Bangan,* is it?'

'Yes, aubergine or brinjal.'

'Did you know brinjal is a corruption of brown jolly?'

Dinesh seemed not to hear. 'One moment,' he said, 'he's gone without asking for the money.' After a brief conversation with the man he said. 'They won't let me pay for the lunch, because of you. They see you as a holy man. But you're not wearing . . .'

'Dear, me! That's naughty of Madan—he's the proprietor.' He waved and Madan folded his hands in greeting. 'We know each other. I've helped his son in a small way. But that was some years ago. This is a beautiful and hospitable country.'

'So, you've been away three years? In England?'

'Yes, almost three. Stoke Poges. My mother died the year before last. I didn't tell Sandy till I got back. It broke his heart and saddened Emma too. My mother was fond of them.'

'I'm sorry. May I offer my belated condolences.'

'Thank you. Ninety-two was a good age. I was glad to be there... she had fallen asleep in the chapel and died peacefully.'

After lunch Bill suggested a walk. At the shrine they took off their shoes and sat in the shade on the stone steps. 'Danny, you do realise both Emma and Sandy are far from well, and you haven't been seeing them as often as you should.'

'I'm increasingly involved in my father-in-law's business.'

'Yes, I know. That sounded almost Biblical.' Bill smiled encouragingly.

'What do you mean?'

'The story of Jacob who worked for his father-in-law.'

'Are you still in the Ganj? I thought you were working in the Gharwal Hills.'

'I'm here to carry out mother's wishes. That plot of land, in the cemetery, belongs to what was once the Pilgrim Missionary Trust—since 1855, a good fifty years before that terrible earthquake. The last surviving member of the Trust was my mother. She had all the necessary papers and the ledger of burials since 1886.'

'And has the Government of India accepted your claim?'

'Indeed, they have accepted it and, after letters to and fro, agreed to let us carry out repairs and restoration. Sandy wields a lot of influence. Work's started on the chapel.'

'Chapel?'

'Yes, there was a small one there. Mother wanted it rebuilt in memory of her father.'

'Was your mother in India too?'

'That's how she met my father. Mcleodganj was different then. Family's links with India go back generations. The chapel walls still stand. Not visible from the road—as is the old bridle path from it to Sandy's cottage. I bet you didn't know about the path. For three miles it winds through pines and deodars. One can see Sandy's bedroom window from the chapel. The path is in surprisingly good condition.'

'Then the cottage must be old too. I know, Sandy's uncle bought it in 1946 from a retired English civil servant.'

'Geoffrey Bell. I met him in 1941. I had come over from Dalhousie, and it was the first time I was invited to preach in Mcleodganj—at St John's. There is a lot of waste land within the compound walls. I plan to build a school.'

'A school? Near a cemetery?'

'It's a small graveyard, and as the graves are near the chapel, it can be walled off.'

'So the cem . . . graveyard, is part of the land.'

Bill nodded. 'The lych-gate is on the end of the chapel compound. The chapel is in a hollow because most of the land slopes uphill. The school will be at the far top end with an orchard between the school and chapel graveyard. The school will be the first thing you'll see coming up the valley.'

'But not if you are coming from the bridle path you just mentioned.'

'No. But it's a private path, as you'll find out when you study Sandy's estate.'

'Well, I know, Sandy told me, your family is one of the landed gentry, so presumably you have funds for the project. A rich man in Sadhu's clothing.'

Bill grinned. 'Not all the landed gentry in England are rich. But, let me put it this way, money is the least of my worries.'

'What about Stoke Manor?' (Dinesh knew Bill was the last of his family). 'You'll be going back? Eventually?'

Bill sniffed. 'No,' he said sharply. 'I intend to live, work and die in this country. The house is to be put to good charitable use.' He looked up. 'It's not a mango tree but the good old *neem*. An unusually large specimen.' He puffed his cheeks and blew. 'Did you know, Sandy had planned to buy the Manor, and Mother was happy about it, but there was that terrible incident!' He paused. 'Great shame! To think how well India treats me, and how badly England treated him. Well, not England, but you know what I mean.'

'Sandy learnt nothing. He still loves England.' Dinesh waited for a reaction. 'He has an infinite capacity for self-deception. In spite of what happened, he'll find some way to affirm his myths of England. He's done the rounds of Henley, Lords, Last Night of the Proms . . .

He's still a member of the Kipling Society.' He should've stayed on. And he didn't need to work or expose himself to the low element of English society.'

'Had he stayed, you wouldn't be here. He planned to sell his properties in India. It's what his uncle expected. Sandy was not a selfish man. His decisions bore other people in mind. You, Sona . . . of course, he would have kept the cottage, for Emma's sake, as a holiday home.'

'I would've found my way back to India, to be a more worthy son of India.'

Bill tapped his forehead. 'He could've stayed on, as you say, in spite of all, if Emma let him. After that incident, the very love he had for England made her hate it. But like the wise woman she is, she knew he needed the myth and that it would never do to hate what he loved. Solution? Exile. And in exile longing.'

'What a rigmarole! All for nothing. Forgive me but talk about myths, absurd loyalties and self-inflicted wounds, is a waste of time. It's talk about nothing.'

'Nothing! Young man! History is not bunk and myths are not without foundation in reality. Ideals take root, become meaningful. If nothing else, the long winding queues of impatient cricket crowds outside Bombay's Stadium is proof of that.'

'All right, so the Brits left their mark, but there are more reasons for Indians to hate than to love them. They took our freedom and exploited our wealth.'

'All this is debatable and proves we're all susceptible, dear boy, to self-deception. All of us have our myths to which we cling. I don't take sides. Either one's an anglophile or one is not. There's nothing ridiculous about either stance.'

'To love a country that's not your own? Is ridiculous! "Breathes there a man with soul so dead, that never to himself hath said, this is my own my native land . . ." that was said by an Englishman.'

'A Scot. Sir Walter Scott. But I take your point. To love one's adopted country is less foolish than saying: "My country right or wrong". More rational to choose where love is, than to love blindly? There is no right or wrong in matters of the heart.'

'I won't argue. I know you're a good friend of Sandy.'

'And of India.'

'Then try to understand what I'm driving at.'

'That India needs all the loyalty she can find? But India can afford to be generous as she has been, a refuge, a haven, a spiritual home for all. I love India. No Englishman is angered by that. No one in England thinks I'm a traitor to my country. He might think I'm eccentric—at worst he'll strike me off his list of friends. Dinesh, do you think less of me for loving India more than England? To put it another way. Would you condemn a person for reading an author you dislike?'

'I think,' said Dinesh, 'we should get back. Our bus driver is signalling frantically. Let me just say this. It is a matter of *izzat*—a matter of honour. In England, I found it hard to explain why Indians find it hard to mix in western society. It is not because they feel inferior, but because they feel superior.'

Bill laughed. 'The British/Indian love/hate relationship is maintained by hypocrisy on both sides. One moment. I must thank Madan and Hazari Lal for lunch. You go ahead and tell the driver to give me a minute.'

Minutes after the bus got going again, Bill nodded off. Not for long. He woke with a start. 'Don't let me sleep, Danny. Keep talking. Anything to keep me awake.'

Dinesh stared thoughtfully. 'Tell me more about Sandy. You met him in Oxford?'

'Briefly, though it feels we've known each other for ages. I'm many years his senior. Hard to believe. He'll be fifty six or seven. Slim and still has his boyish looks.'

'But you are fit and active.'

'So was Friar Tuck. What made you ask about Oxford.'

'Sandy said you were the cleverest man he knew.' Bill looked away, a little abashed. Dinesh added. 'Why I wanted to meet you when I first came to England.'

Bill sighed. 'Sandy is the noblest man I know. Clever? I'd rather be noble.'

'Why is it better to be noble than clever?'

'To be noble is to be whole. Easy, open. Both eclectic and esoteric. Cleverness, even when not confused with slyness, is narrow, single-minded, bent on success, ruthless and lacking of understanding. You disagree? You would rather be clever?'

'Nobility is medieval. The stuff of romance and legend. Noble people are portraits. Portraits do nothing. They simply decorate the walls of history and are of no practical value. Just reminders of time wasted.' Dinesh glanced at Bill smugly.

'Nobility is of no practical value? You may be right, but that's unIndian. Cleverness is bereft of spirituality. And how would you define genius?'

'Genius, is infinite capacity for taking pains.'

'That's a *cliche*. As is: genius is ninety-nine per cent perspiration and one per cent inspiration. No one who is not noble or sensitive ought to be called a genius. There's more art than science in genius. It has, like all virtues, creativity.'

'Bill, I know sermons are your trade, so you're good with words, but spirituality has been India's downfall. We welcomed migrants and invited invasions . . . often surrendered and swallowed pride. We must build a new India. You use words to dodge questions.'

'That puts me in my place. So I'm an artful dodger. But all of us twist language to justify our attitudes. A very human failing and, sadly, the bane to philosophy.'

'A philosopher has been described as a man in a dark room looking for a black cat that isn't there.' Dinesh grinned.

Bill laughed. 'And a theologian, as one who finds it, I know.'

Dinesh frowned. The conversation, he thought, had taken a peculiar turn. 'You and Sandy are very alike. You both don't seem to care what people think of you.'

'Dinesh, that's because neither of us are politicians. Sandy loves England for what it gave the world. Language, literature, democracy, and . . . Go on, say what you want to.'

'I was going to say, and Pox Britannica. Add hypocrisy to the list.'

'They may have bluffed their way into building an Empire. But the British did try to create a just society. They may have failed, but give them marks for trying.'

'May I speak frankly?'

'Be as insulting as you like! I'm old enough to realise insults don't change facts.'

Dinesh winced. Bill waited. Dinesh clicked his tongue impatiently. 'I forget what I was going to say.'

'You say Sandy and I are close. But in a way I'm closer to Emma. We love India and Indians. I may be open to the charge of hypocrisy, but not Emma.'

Dinesh's face lit up. 'If you love India for what it is, why are you here?'

'I don't understand. Why wouldn't I want to be with the most hospitable people in the world? With people I love?'

'Then, why do you want to change them? That's your purpose as a missionary.'

'That's the narrow view. I like Indians, but that does not mean I think they are perfect. The life of any relationship is communication. That includes giving and sharing. Even taking. As in marriage, partners subtly change each other, often without realising.'

'You're being clever again. Christian Missionaries undermine culture. Religion and culture go together. Conversion is subversion.'

'Slogans are for people who think in black and white. Realities in life turn black and white into grey, without making a grey world. A black and white world is an ignorant one. I've found a pearl of great price and I want to share its beauty with people I love. I speak of truth with a capital T. The giver of that truth tells me his Truth is not just for me or for keeping under wraps. It's good news for all. Conversion and subversion are what all teaching is about. The moment you express an opinion you do it to subvert. It is not for nothing that conversation and conversion are a close construct.'

'But here in India, your "good news" has created people disloyal to their country.'

'That's sweepingly unfair. There are outstanding examples of Christians who have worked and fought for India's freedom—to say nothing of the fact they founded the Congress party . . . Hume, Andrews, Besant. Many Indians, I know, became Christian for the wrong reasons. You can't say that of Sandy! Christianity is not responsible for bad Christians. Nothing in Christianity stops Christians being good Indians. Oh, by the way, Christianity came here before it went to Britain.'

Dinesh sneered. 'I don't go along with the St Thomas legend.'

'Christians were in Cochin and Madras long before Europe traded with India, and before much of Europe was Christian. But to return to your earlier target, me. I'm more interested in sharing a message than making converts, which in India, is not easy. I find little objection to anything I say—how do you convert people who agree with you—but if as a result there is a change of heart, I leave it to them to join or not join the Christian community. I've baptised no one in all the years I've been here.'

'But then, you're not a good missionary. Shouldn't you be an earnest Christian? And why do you want to be called a *sadhu*?'

'A Christian *sadhu*.'

'It's a contradiction in terms. A *sadhu's* a Hindu.'

'A leap, not a contradiction.'

'And what about not being a good missionary, by not spreading your gospel.'

'A missionary does best to point away from himself to a greater truth. Whether I'm good or bad is relevant only to that extent. I don't set out to be either.'

'My point is, you can't be any kind of real sadhu. You're a rich man.'

'There are Maharishis, Hindu gurus, far richer, and go about in Rolls-Royces.'

'But you agree, Indians who mimic Western habits and life-styles look ridiculous.'

'I see where this is leading. There's nothing wrong with Western values. They spell democracy. Sandy is no mimic. He is being himself. In those formative years, between seven and ten, he lived with an English family and their English nanny. His westernised uncle Jagdish, your great uncle, gave him free rein. Trips to Europe, a year at Oxford.'

'I blame uncle Jagdish and the school he sent Sandy to. A school for Indian Princes. Those lackeys of Imperialism. A school run like a British Public school with an Etonian Headmaster. But now he should choose! He is not unacquainted with Indian Culture.'

'Sandy's a British citizen. Let it rest. You know the saying. Live and let live? You are more of a missionary than I am, and an ideologue at that.'

'It's a mystery to me why he had to live with an English family? As a boy.'

'I'm sure your grand parents had good reason.'

'And that business of the family involved in the war effort, and with Colonel Franks, Emma's father.'

'Sandy's father served under Colonel Franks. Circumstances do affect people's lives. Think about your own boyhood. Now, my turn to ask questions. What is a true Indian life-style? Where in the urban homes of educated Indians will you find it? And is not what passes as high Indian culture, in fact, Mughal?'

Dinesh compressed his lips.

'Incidentally,' Bill did not wait for an reply, 'compared to the British, the Mughals were ruthless—at times using the sword to forcefully convert Hindus to Islam. Strange you don't condemn those Hindu sycophants who were members of the Mughal Court, and who married their daughters to Muslim princes? They were far, more loyal to their Muslim rulers than the anglophiles you condemn, were loyal to Britain.'

Dinesh scowled and avoided Bill eyes.

'I know how you feel,' Bill continued, 'I understand. I'm sympathetic. I'm happy the British left India. I want all peoples to govern themselves in whatever way they choose, But you're extreme in your criticisms and if I may say so, that's unIndian.'

'You don't understand.' said Dinesh sullenly. 'My concern is now. The Mughals had their critics. You don't understand my concern. The harm of a foreign religion.'

'Christianity is not foreign. I've explained that. What makes you think you can shut the door against influences? Science and Technology? That has brought changes.'

Dinesh looked at his watch and shook his head. 'Anglophilia is stupidity.'

'Stupidity is human. Romance is human. All of us are foolish about something. We suffer for love just as much as we suffer for truth. Sandy and Emma take each other for granted and live without getting in each other's way. Relationships like theirs don't bear analysis. They are to be celebrated.'

'This kind of love talk is not what one expects from a priest!' Dinesh growled.

'Why? Why shouldn't priests talk about love. They should do it more often.'

Dinesh changed tack. 'If there are no heated debates or expressed convictions in a relationship, that relationship is dead . . . without heat or fire. Dead.'

'You can't believe that! Having known them?'

'It's easy for them. They only have each other. Yes, Sona and I may be part of the family but they remain apart. Being together is easy without children.'

'You think not having children makes it easier?'

'In their case, yes. You're making them out to be saints!'

'They're not, nor are they trying to be. Few saints are as blessed as they.'

'Cushioned by wealth and without children, the relationship of Sandy and Emma has neither been tried nor tested. They lived in a sort of dream.'

'Below that dream is absolute trust . . .' Bill's voice faded. He was looking through the mud-splattered window at the landscape. It was a pensive look, a seeing beyond the here and now. His next move took Dinesh by surprise. He put an arm round Dinesh and gave him a tight hug. 'I am sorry. Forgive me!'

Dinesh stared in astonishment. 'Forgive what? You mean all that was banter?'

Bill nodded. 'C S Lewis was right when he said pride is the worst sin. And I include intellectual pride. But what I said was not unreasonable. Belief is not truth.'

'So the Gospel you preach is not true.' Dinesh grinned with satisfaction.

'I didn't say that. In the Gospel, I see "the truth". I don't believe in my truth but in someone else's. The truth of Jesus. He is the Truth. But I have apologised.' Bill smiled. He released Dinesh. 'Not long now,' he mumbled, stifled a yawn and rested his head against the window. Then he shut his eyes and fell asleep. The evening sun silhouetted the patriarchal profile as it froze into effigy once more.

Dinesh got up quietly and stood behind the driver. They were on the outskirts of Pathankot. In the distance the *terai* spread before them. The driver looked at his watch and said with a roll of his head: 'Sa-topping bery soon now at Pathankot bus sa-tand.' Dinesh went back to his seat. Bill was awake. Dinesh said: 'We'll be there any minute now. It will get dark rapidly. Are you all right for the night?'

The Lotus And The Rose

'I'm being met. In fact,' Bill put his glasses on and pulled the window glass down, 'there they are.' He waved. Standing by a white jeep was a tall, sad looking man, the obvious deputy of the large matronly woman in a sari and cardigan. She was standing in front of him, arms akimbo, staring through horn-rimmed glasses at the bus, as it entered the busy square.

'You know,' said Bill, 'Indian Christians make the finest goat *pilau*.'

'You mean *biryani*?'

'I mean *pilau*. But I won't dwell on it. Dinner could turn out to be rice, *dahl* and *subjee*. Are you vegetarian now. I assume Shanti's is? You loved a good steak.'

'I still do. Shanti's family describe themselves as "chickenarians".'

Bill chuckled. 'How very Punjabi. Eggs, chicken, but no other meats.'

'One soon forgets about missing meat if one's given a really good vegetarian meal.'

'I believe that. Danny, I won't embarrass you by introducing you to my friends.'

The bus honked its way through the crowded bus station. Bill stood up and bumped his head on the roof of the bus. 'Always forget. Still, no serious harm done,' he said, as he rubbed his head. 'I'll say goodbye. But could we meet again? It has to be tomorrow. Tomorrow morning? I leave for Delhi, late afternoon. Ten? I'll buy you breakfast at the Madras Hotel. It's important, we meet? Save me having to sit up tonight to write what I want to say to you.'

'Of course! I'll be there. At ten. I know the place.'

A puzzled Dinesh watched the big man disappear into the milling crowd. Then he crossed the square into the courtyard of a two-storied mansion. Looking up he saw Shanti leaning over a small balcony. Looking back he saw Bill and his escort by the bus. Bill's hands were raised towards a silhouetted figure on the roof of the bus. No doubt, Dinesh thought, he was collecting his Victorian cast-iron cross.

The convenience of living over the bus station had its disadvantages. Always a light sleeper, Dinesh found the noises of a bus station kept him awake. So, when the *dhaba*, the street café, at the entrance to the square, chose to entertain its diners with amplified music, he would often go down there for a glass of piping hot sweet tea to chat with the proprietor. Tonight the *dhaba* had wound down early and by midnight the only sounds were those of metal pots and pans being scrubbed clean, rinsed and put away. His eyes grew heavy. The clanging mingled into a familiar evocation of his childhood . . . the jangle of bright lacquer bangles and the happy vision of his pretty *ayah*, Radha, throwing him up in the air to fall into her musical arms and against her ample bosom. The only loving, comforting physical warmth he knew as a child was the softness of her arms about him. He opened his eyes and turned to find Shanti's face next to his. Dinesh groaned and fell fast asleep.

When Bill arrived at the ground floor restaurant of the Madras Hotel, the stone floor was being washed by a man who splashed water from a shiny brass bucket and followed it with great sweeps of a stiff broom. Bill, in a white cassock, waited well out of range of the brown spray sent up by the broom. The man stopped, threw the broom down and invited Bill to enter. Inside, he was greeted by the proprietor, a man with large bulging eyes and oily black hair. He wore a clean. white cotton vest and a *dhoti* no bigger than a loin cloth. Bill asked if the restaurant would serve him breakfast and in reply the man wiped his hands on the tea-towel over his shoulder and disappeared. Bill waited. The man reappeared with a dishcloth, wiped a green formica-topped table and placed a chair under it. Bill sat down. For a moment they eyed each other.

'*Ek?* One only?' asked the man raising his brows.

'No,' said Bill. 'Two. *Doh*,' and pointed to Dinesh who could be heard telling the man to let him pass.

'Good morning!' greeted Bill, 'Well timed.'

The man with the bulging eyes left them and soon returned with two glasses of water, placing them with a bang on the table. He drew up another chair, shut his eyes and without a single hesitation recited the names of several South Indian dishes.

'I know what I want,' said Bill. 'A *masala dosa* and some strong sweet coffee.'

'I'll have a plain *dosa*,' said Dinesh.

'I wonder if we'll get that delicious coconut chutney,' Bill said in passing.

'*Sambhar* vit *masala dosa*. Chutney vit plain *dosa*,' recited the man.'

'I've never seen you in a cassock before,' said Dinesh.

'I said Mass this morning at the Mission.'

'Thursday?'

'Now, as to the purpose of our meeting, shall we wait till after we've eaten?'

Dinesh nodded and took in the empty restaurant. 'I see you've chosen the gap between the crowd which comes before ten and the one which comes after eleven.'

'Yes. I'm sorry. It's rather a late breakfast. I suppose Shanti made you eat?'

'Tea and a light *paratha*, sometime ago. There's room for a *dosa*.' Dinesh put a hand over his mouth and stifled a yawn. 'Sorry, can't think why. I slept well. I suppose you want to talk about Sandy and Emma.'

'And about you. This isn't going to be easy, but I have to try, Danny boy! I want to help. You may rightly think it's none of my business, but I am making it my business. I love all of you, the whole family, and that includes Sona.'

Dinesh looked away. 'Did you have a good night?'

'Yes. The Mission House is a well-furnished establishment.'

'Where is it?'

'Just beyond Chakkar Bazaar, on the road to Nurpur.'

'That's two miles from here! At least! You-you walked, of course!'

Bill nodded and Dinesh stared at him. He knew Bill was well into his seventies.

The food came, steaming hot, on silver *thalis*. They ate in silence. The man who had been sweeping the floor was now arranging tables and chairs, and almost at once customers began to file in. The coffee came in small glass tumblers. Bill tested his for hotness. 'Emma,' he began, stopped, and smiled. 'You know, she adapted herself to many things in India, bar this. She couldn't take to drinking tea or coffee from a glass.'

'It burnt her lips. The hot glass.'

Bill toyed with his glass. 'Emma hasn't long to live. She can go anytime.'

Dinesh recalled the strange impulse he had to send that gift of sweets. His mouth felt dry. He took a sip of coffee. 'Why are you telling me this?'

'Because you ought to show concern. It'll be good for you and for them. Soon, it will be too late. Besides, I don't think Sandy will live long without Emma, and I'm sure he wouldn't want to. And once they have gone, I think, in time you'll regret not having made your peace with them. Particularly Sandy.'

Dinesh shifted uneasily in his chair. 'Bill, I don't want to hurt your feelings. They maybe kind, caring and generous, but, nothing and no one is more important to them than each other—well, maybe Sona. Look, for years I've lived my own life. They treat me like a guest. They're not concerned. I've been free to chose since I was eighteen.'

'Danny, my boy. There's such a thing as gratitude.'

Dinesh passed his hands through his hair desperately. 'What do you want of me?'

'First, accept what I'm asking is reasonable. Be forgiving. Accept Sandy for what he is. Show him you value all he has done for you.'

Dinesh avoided Bill's eyes.

'It's important for Sona too.' Bill added.'

'What has Sona got to do with it? We're hardly on speaking terms.'

'She senses your hostility to Sandy. Remember she's fiercely loyal.'

Dinesh went sullen and silent. Bill reached out a large craggy hand and gripped him firmly by the wrist. 'All right, forget all I've just said. Do it for your own sake. We have been talking about happiness and contentment. An accepting and forgiving attitude is the surest way I know of achieving contentment. You don't have a lot of time.'

'I can't leave here before Sunday.'

'Be there by Saturday.' Bill got up, paid the man with the bulging eyes and thanked him. He rested a hand on Dinesh's shoulder as they left the restaurant. 'Another favour I ask of you.' He felt deep in the pockets of his cassock and from a notebook removed a piece of paper. 'This is my address in Delhi, Old Delhi. I'm at St Stephen's House for a week. Now, you must promise to tell me at once if there's any emergency? That's the phone number. Add the code for Delhi. Tell me, whatever happens, even if you think it's too late. I'll come as soon as I can. Don't lose this slip.'

'There won't be any emergency, but I'll do what you ask.'

'Thank you. This is where we part,' said Bill. 'I take the highroad!'

They shook hands warmly. 'Bill, I don't know if I've thanked you enough for all you did, in the past, for me. You know I didn't venture much in England, but I did take full advantage of your, and your mother's generous hospitality. And, of course, Ted's.'

'I've written to Ted and I'll phone him if that becomes necessary. Strange. When I left England to work in India, I thought I'd never see Sandy again!' Bill's huge frame shivered. 'We have to brace ourselves . . .' He suddenly looked very old and tired.

'I'll return on Saturday. Bill, you can rely on me. I'll do what you asked.'

Later that day, on his way to the railway station, Bill left a letter at the *Dhaba* to be delivered to Dinesh. He wrote: "I've had to write this, having thought again about all our discussions. Let me try to set down with a directness your intelligence deserves, the nub of my appeal. I defend Sandy because (and Forster wasn't the first to note it) there are many Indias. It is wonderful how those Indias survive side by side. It is exciting to live in a country where one is always wrong-footed. No one can ever be wholly right about India, not even Indians, because always there's someone with some peculiar knowledge we are not privy to. This Indian kaleidoscope isn't just a myriad of patterns. Each India has to be seen against it's own backdrop of community, geography and religious observances. As your ancient scripture, the *Puranas*, have it, we tread on a razor's edge. One India can be viewed with intolerance, censure, and even hatred, by other Indias. I love India as a home of spiritual values, for its long and continual search for truth and of non-violence; and yet, even as I say it, I am filled by a great sense of guilt, as if I am ignoring reality and living a lie. The spirituality that embraces India can do with an injection of Christian charity. Hinduism has renunciation, resigned piety and salvation through good works but omits love, affirmation of life and community service. Foster an appetite for life, which is not the same as taking up a cause. Being focussed is not the same as having an appetite for life. Reformers refuse to accept life as it is. But failure makes them intolerant. There's a time for anger, a time to question; and a time not to question God. Question society. We are accountable to God, but God, who gave us stewardship of the world is not responsible for our actions. As someone said, God gave us the gift of life and the way we live it is our gift back to him. Life is both reality and illusion. It is either a satisfactory state of affairs or it isn't; and the society we create for the good of all. Concentrate on that achievement but don't omit the poetry. Why be extreme when there are always happy mediums. Living alongside Nature means Nature has its part to play. Where we don't find redress against Man and Nature, against those slings and arrows of fortune, should we leave it to heaven or find strength in ourselves? "Sandy's life has meaning. He does not claim it to be exemplary or wise, but without such people the world is a mean place; without sentiment or sensitivity, it will have only expediency, politics and propaganda. If you still think he is absurd, therefore dangerous, then I am sorry for you. I defend him as I defend a good book. I don't believe you wish to be a burner of books?

"Without individuality we're slaves living in a world that is neither new nor brave but on the edge of doom. Nationalism takes patriotism to extremes and you know what has been said of those who take refuge in the latter. A kind world is a free state of tolerance and brotherly love. Even at a distance love is better than hate in proximity.

"This is a poor letter. It lays bare inadequacies. But it will have to do. I'm sleepy. Remember your promise. With love, Bill."

Dinesh made no immediate sense of the letter and put it down as ramblings of an old man. But he resolved to study it again and being a man of method, opened his filing cabinet, removed a file marked "Bill" and placed the letter in it. He caught sight of the file cover. Below "Bill" he had written something in parenthesis. After a moment's thought he took his pen and neatly crossed the phrase "a dangerous man" and carefully replaced the file. He fished out another folder. Under "The Anglophile" was the phrase "a foolish man". After some thought he replaced it and locked the filing cabinet.

✼

'Sandeep', she whispered.

'Yes, Emma?' With Sona's help, he adjusted himself against the pillows so that she could rest more comfortably in his arms. 'What is it?'

'Is this it? This the end?

He shut his eyes. 'No. You must not leave me! If you want me to live.'

Her breathing was short and irregular and at intervals she caught her breath.

'Are you in pain? Emma, are you in pain?'

She tried to move. 'I can't see you!'

With an effort he bent his face towards her and held her chin. Her eyes opened. They were tired and hollow but bluer than he remembered. Her lips moved soundlessly. Then suddenly her voice was clearer. 'You'll kiss me goodbye, when I go . . .'

His head fell back and burying his face in the pillows, he tried to stifle a sob. 'Sona,' he whispered. 'Sona!'

Sona came out of the shadows and placed a firm hand on his shoulder. He nodded and looked at Emma. Her eyes were half shut. 'Emma!' he cried in panic and shook her. Slowly her eyes opened. 'Emma! I'm coming too! We'll be together!'

She shut her eyes again. He detected a slight smile and her breathing was perceptibly calmer. 'Read to me, Sandy. Read to me. I want to hear your voice.'

'*Leave it to P-Smith*?' he murmured with a chuckle.

She smiled feebly. 'Our Psalm.'

Sona thrust *The Book of Common Prayer*, opened on Psalm 121. He set it aside. 'I know the words.' Sona closed the book and backed into the shadows.

'"I will lift up mine eyes . . ."' He stopped and started again. "I will lift up mine eyes unto the hills: from whence cometh my help. My help cometh . . ."' He looked through the gap in the curtains of the open window. The afternoon was bright and mellow in the

April sun. The Virginia creepers, which decked the deodars, were in full leaf. A gentle breeze whistled softly through the branches. He pointed to the window. Sona pulled the curtains well back. Together they raised Emma to face the window. Beyond the trees the snow-capped Himalayan foothills stood purple against a golden sky. Sona propped up more cushions to keep Emma from slipping back. Then she sat on the other side of the bed and stroked Emma's forehead tenderly . . .

Sandy whispered the Psalm. "'I will lift up mine eyes unto the hills: from whence cometh my help. My help cometh even from the Lord: who hath made heaven and earth . . .'" He paused to see Emma looking out with a happy smile. She closed her eyes. He continued. "'He will not suffer thy foot to be moved and he that keepth thee will not sleep . . .'" She grew heavy, her lips moved . . . she sank, and died in his arms.

A shadow pass over him. Sona drew Sandy away. Then she raised Emma, removed the pillows and gently laid her flat on the bed. She tidied the sheets, cradled Emma's head in her strong arms, hollowed two pillows and gently let the head back to keep it from rolling. She stroked Emma's hair, which in the early morning she had combed and tied in two plaits. The plaits now rested over each shoulder: rich, warm chestnut skeins, upon a soft blue night dress.

Sandy had slipped off the bed to the floor. Sona lifted him on to the chair by the bed and covered him with Emma's shawl. He clung to it for comfort, then grew faint, shut his eyes as a choking darkness engulfed him . . .

When he opened his eyes, Sona was standing over him holding a tall china tankard. 'Chang,' she whispered and bent over him. 'Drink, Sandy, now you drink.'

He looked up. 'Have you been crying?'

She nodded.

'Why?' He frowned.

'Drink.' She held the tankard with both hands and lowered it to his lips.

With a sudden realisation, he clutched her hands desperately. 'Yes, yes.'

CHAPTER THIRTEEN

'Doctor Saxena, this whole affair is bloody strange,' Dinesh said sullenly.

'You're talking about the garden? "The Garden of Emma", as Thakurji called it. *Arrey, bhai*, it had to go. She was dying. Naturally the garden must die too. And now you see why Thakur sahib did not replace the *mali*.'

Dinesh frowned. 'What's all this about the *mali*? What happened to the *mali*?'

'When the *mali* ran away, Thakurji let the garden go. He did not employ another.'

'Rammu? Why, what happened?'

'Three four months now. You were not here. Frightful scandal. This fellow Rammu left in a hurry. Indecent hurry. Thakurji was angry but he lost interest. He managed to placate the local *kissan*, farmer by compensating him. That chap was hopping mad.'

'Which farmer? Why compensate a farmer? And for what? Mohan Singh, do you know about this.

Mohan Singh gave a start. 'Sorry, I wasn't listening.'

'Mohan is worrying about the woman, Sona.' Dr Sudhir Saxena grinned.

'She seems to have disappeared, Dinesh babu.' Mohan Singh said.

'*Arrey*, she'll be back.' The doctor waved a dismissive hand. 'I was talking about Rammu and the *kissan* affair.'

'The tale of the farmer's wife?' Mohan Singh sniggered.

'Except,' giggled the doctor, 'it was the farmer who wanted to cut of Rammu's tail with a carving knife.'

'I hope, when you two stop behaving like schoolboys, I'll find out about Rammu.' Dinesh said. 'I'm in charge now. I must to know these things.'

'You know this farmer chappie,' said Mohan Singh, wiping the tears from his eyes and visibly trying hard to contain himself. 'He was a long time devotee of our respected Emmaji, bringing her gifts of fruit and maize, at harvest time.'

'Why was he compensated?' Dinesh began to lose patience. 'Seriously.'

'Your Rammu was seducing this wife.' Mohan suppressed a giggle. 'It seems the affair had been going on for sometime. Rammu visited the farm on the excuse he was advising the farmer about fertilisers . . .

'But rogue was fertilising his wife.' Dr Sudhir chimed in and laughed.

'Eventually,' Mohan continued, 'as happens in these cases, they were found out. Red-bloody-handed, if you see what I mean. The farmer actually caught them together and gave them a thrashing. Oh, yes, both. Later he chased after Rammu but somehow the fellow gave him the slip . . .'

'He's younger and faster. Rammu is.' The doctor interjected and giggled.

'Then he went into hiding. That is Rammu. Nothing was heard of him for days. But he returned, or rather secretly stole in, here, took his belongings and disappeared.'

'What about the farmer?' asked Dinesh. 'Did he go to the police?'

'*Arrey bhai*, you should know, simple folk don't go to police.' Mohan said. He was sober now. 'The farmer, what's his name . . . Dhanraj? Yes, Dhanraj.'

'Go on,' said Dinesh, 'the name is not . . .'

'He came here to Sandy. Made a big scene. But for two thousand rupees the chappie agreed to let the matter drop.'

'And now,' said the doctor, 'that his wife is pregnant, he quietly accepts peoples congratulations, to the extent, he believes he is the father.'

'A thousand in the first month,' Mohan Singh continued, 'and the other thousand three months later, only on condition the woman, his wife, was not harmed. This was Emmaji's idea. I know because I was present. Sandy asked me to be present.'

Dinesh sniffed. 'So the matter is settled, finally.'

'Yes. Except you'll have to pay him that thousand, in a week or two. These people may be plain and simple, but they are also practical. Pride has a price.'

'Only a bachelor like doctor sahib will say a thing like that,' Mohan Singh rolled his head. 'A peasant values his *izzat* as much as any of us. The immediate problem now is finding a new gardener.'

'I must take my leave now,' said the doctor. 'I've tied the pony, over there by the gate. I won't be needing it now.' He dusted his hands. 'Thanks for the loan of it.'

'Wait, doctor sahib,' Mohan Singh called. 'We'll walk back together.'

'Before you go, Dr Saxena,' said Dinesh. 'May I have a word in private?'

'I'll wait by the gate.' Mohan Singh said as he walked away.

'I won't keep you long,' Dinesh led Dr Sudhir Saxena to the porch and pointed to the bougainvillea. The doctor shrugged. 'What are you trying to find out, Mr Dinesh?'

'I want to know if the root of this plant is poisonous. The sap?'

'Forget this bee in your bonnet. Let me tell you finally. Once and for all. Thakurji was dying. He needed the slightest shock to die. He died naturally. If you have any suspicions about Sona, I can't go along with that accusation. Besides I am no expert upon herbal drugs and plant poisons.'

'Should I involve the police?'

'No. Absolutely not. In any case they'll have to consult me. And I'm quite positive there has been no hanky panky. No *dahl mein kala*.' Dr Saxena gripped Dinesh firmly by the arm. 'Leave it. There's been a tragedy, but everything that has happened is as it should be. They would not have wanted it in any other way. Sandy would think himself fortunate. Now, I go, asking you not to do anything which will break our friendship.'

At the gate Mohan Singh said: 'Why did you return the pony? I do believe Sandy wanted you to keep it.'

Dr Saxena sighed. 'Dinesh must know that too. Never mind. You see Mohan, it will always remind me of them, and I . . . I don't want to live with sad memories.'

❈

Fern Tree Cottage
30th April 1985

Dear Ted

Thank you for understanding why I wrote instead of sending a cable. As you correctly guessed the peculiar circumstances demanded privacy. I know from past experience that the man in the post office is a bit of a gossip. Also, by writing, I was able to give myself time and thought, through prayer, to find words more adequate than just a cablegram. I am happy you too felt that by knowing they were together, even in death, the pain of bereavement is less. I also hoped this letter gives you time and space to wonder about there being more to life and death than its bare biological fact. Please come when you can. I understand, as they would too, why you couldn't come at once. I hope things will sort themselves out for Kitty.

I often say a prayer by their grave—work on the school building breaks for lunch—so I find time to be with them. You ask if "resurgamus" is grammatically correct, but what you went on to say is more important. Pedantry has no place here. The point is, Sandy chose the word. It's a fitting epitaph for one who created his own certainties. Buried with him is the only certainty he had the privilege of experiencing—the reality of Emma's love. Sandy had seen the grave of William Morris which had the Latin singular "resurgam", "I will arise". It's quite logical for Sandy to assume "resurgamus" is "we will arise". Yes. Sona and I knew Sandy was determined not to survive Emma death.

What a rare soul Emma was! I said something of this to Dinesh. He has mellowed, I think, and is showing genuine interest in the school project, and has drummed up local interest and some support for it. He leaves for Bombay seven months from now.

I can't write more. For someone to whom words come easily—far too easily—I am astonished I can't console myself. But there will be words and time for us together. So I await your arrival. I understand why you want to make the trip alone and would rather not be met. To know you will never again be able to see a loved one in this life is harsh, and a great burden.

Dinesh is letting me stay in the cottage for as long as I need. Having been here twice before, you'll have no difficulty finding the place, even though Mcleodganj has changed physically and is alive with refugees, pilgrims and tourists. Just bear in mind the cottage is four miles up the road to Dalhousie. The hamlet is Rajkot. Turn off by the lone Tulip tree before you get to the lake. It will all come back to you from then on.

Love, Bill.

PS I should have said, turn right by the Tulip tree. Left will take you to Mohan Singh's place. That reminds me. About Sona. We must protect her by dismissing the rumours about her having anything to do with Sandy's death. She may have played the angel of mercy but Dinesh must not get any inkling of that even if its true. Mohan thinks Sona may have gone back to Tibet. I don't think so. I think she is lying low for a short time and someone knows and is protecting her. Though I must admit it's not like her. Bill

The ample and ebullient Miss Monica Das, the woman Dinesh had seen by the jeep at the Pathankot bus station, drove Bill and

Ted to the cemetery. 'Maami,' said Ted—no one who had spent any length of time with Monica Das could escape her insistence on being addressed as Maami or Auntie—'did you know Emma?'

'No, no!' She spoke with the unintended emphasis of one who is always out of breath. 'But I heard of her. Oh, most certainly, yes! Now and then, people would talk about this strange couple, living far far away, in some lonely cottage, you know, above the lake, away from it all. That sort of talk. And they being sort of good kindly people, that sort of thing. But I don't go very far from mission, unless part of job, when one has to. Okay, now I must *chalo*, must go, otherwise those people will go away. People are so impatient these days, you know. What to say. No rest for the wicked!' She laughed; and her whole body rippled. 'Oh my! Just look at Bill. Father Bill?'

'Yes, Maamiji?' Bill was going through the satchel that was slung across his chest. He found an envelope. 'Give this to your friends. Tell them to post it in Delhi. It will reach quicker that way. It's stamped.'

'Now you're sure?' she wheezed, staring at Bill over heavy black rimmed spectacles. 'Sure you don't want me to come back for you? I can. No problem.'

'We'll walk back to the cottage. Ted will go on to Mohan Singh's, where he and Dinesh will spend the night. They have organised an expedition for tomorrow.'

'This being to look for that woman, Sona?

Bill nodded. 'I'll take the last bus back to Pathankot. I don't need to be met. The walk will do me good. And for supper, a glass of milk and a few plain biscuits.'

'What is this *khama-khai* formality? *Khansama's* there till ten. He'll heat curry and make fresh *chapatis* just like that, *phata phat*. She patted her palms alternately in a mime of *chapati* making. Again her entire body rippled. 'Milk, "Thumbs Up", always there.' The jeep shrank as she got into it. 'Just take things easy.' She started the engine; and with a roar and a skid of tyres on rubble, the jeep sped away. They watched the trailing cloud of red dust till it passed behind a rocky outcrop, turned and walked up the grassy slope. Half-way up, Ted looked across the valley. 'It's beautiful! But not quite the Scottish Highlands mother compares it with.'

'It is what it is.' Bill said. 'The conifers, oaks and fruit trees are quite unique to these foothills. The oak is not the English oak we know. It is evergreen. Ilex or Holm oak as Emma correctly identified. That tree, for instance is a horse-chestnut, quite unlike those in England. Lower and wider. The nuts are inside brown pear-like fruit. However, those graceful deodars and that magnificent rhododendron tree is a vision of Eden. Soon it'll be a ravaged and exploited Eden. By the way, Emma has captured much of it.'

'Yes.' Ted cleared his throat. 'I must thank Dinesh. He has arranged for me to have them, watercolours and oils. I'll fill the walls of her room in Holland Park.'

They reached the rusted iron gates of the graveyard and together had to lift one gate. It swung back, snapping a hinge. Bill examined the solid oak gate posts. 'A lych-gate was here. I plan to restore it and build a gate house . . . two rooms, verandah, kitchen and bathroom. That'll be for Ransingh, *chowkidar,* our watchman. It has a clear view of the area. You'll remember Ransingh when you see him.' Bill dug his hands into the leather belt round his waist, threw his head back and stared wistfully into the distance.

Ted marvelled. Yesterday, in a loose saffron robe, Bill was the *sadhu.* Today, in a worn out white cassock, army boots and hair tied at the nape of his neck by a shoelace, he was the eccentric clergyman. Ted coughed. 'And the town is behind that ridge.'

The huge frame, frozen in contemplation, suddenly came to life. 'We're on a spur looking away from the town towards the plains.'

'And you were right about Mcleodganj. It's a Tibetan town now.'

Bill gazed at him benignly. 'You want to ask where it is?'

Ted nodded.

'At the far end. There, where the ridge falls steeply, by the lone larch. You could go ahead? I'll wait here for them.'

Ted shook his head. 'I can't face it without you. Not being a believer, I don't have your spiritual strength. Sorry!'

Bill raised a hand. 'I assure you, believing is hard work.' He smiled. 'Were you and Emma . . . close? I know about the age gap.'

'I can't say. But Sandy certainly brought us closer than we were. Odd, meeting an Indian more English than oneself. I've always felt we had no right to rule India, much less foist on them an alien culture and language. I've met quite a few of these dislocated Indians we created. Brown Englishmen. Sandy was different. Nothing false or studied about his Englishness. He made me see the Raj wasn't a total disaster, not even from an Indian point of view. But I don't have to tell you this.'

'No, please go on. It's good to talk.'

'His rather naive charm made one overlooked the fact he had a brilliant mind.'

'Indeed, he was one of the most charming and intelligent of men.'

'Fortunately, he was also a good man.'

'That was part of his charm.'

'A quality mother deeply suspects. Something to do with her puritanical upbringing. She got on well with Dinesh' Ted looked at his watch. 'Are we early?'

'Punctuality is not an Indian virtue... was it not Kafka who said, impatience drove us out of Eden and impatience prevents us from returning. Mohan Singh is bringing Dinesh in his Land Rover.'

They came to a point where the path crossed another at right angles. This one, paved with flagstones, showed signs of recent repair. Looking down it, through an avenue of birch, cypress and yew, they got a glimpse of the chapel and the fading blossoms in the orchard beyond. They crossed it till their grassy path disappeared gradually into broken ground and a patchwork of weeds and bracken. 'We have to go through this.' Bill said. 'This trench was the result of a landslide soon after the great 1905 earthquake.'

Ted stared awe-struck by the scene before him. Above the broken ground, a densely wooded slope climbed in a steep curve towards a sheer rock face, while on the right a glade descended gently below the ridge, ending in a circle of spruce and juniper. 'Like a stairway to heaven,' he said. Then he noted the larch set apart from the trees and behind it a grassy mound.

'There's a story about that larch,' Bill said quickly. 'Planted by my grandfather after a trip to Nepal. He carried the sapling in a flowerpot on the back of his mule, though he didn't expect it to survive. It did. A Nepalese larch planted by an Englishman where no other larch grows!'

They started to walk again, losing and regaining sight of the glade as they entered the trench and climbed up its incline. 'I'm told that Emma did a lot of good work in the community and was regarded as a saint. Bill, is that typically a Hindu . . . ?'

'Indeed.' Bill brushed his forehead. 'In the last years when she wasn't strong enough to go by pony, she went to the Ganj by *jampan* or *palki*—sort of sedan chair carried by four men. The local folk greeted her with folded hands and followed it. She would wear a sari on those occasions and because she looked like an Indian goddess, it looked more like a Hindu religious procession.'

As they approached the grassy mound by the foot of the larch, it was less green; and the significance of the freshly turned earth struck Ted with an excruciating impact. Bill gripped his arm. 'There you are, Ted. Here they come.' Ted turned to see Mohan Singh jogging ahead, frantically waving his hands. 'Hullo there! Mr Franks, Bill!' Behind him slouched a sullen Dinesh. They waited for Dinesh. Then Bill led them to the grave.

They stood, heads bowed as a gentle breeze stirred the branches above them. In the wooded hollow beyond a strong wind swept downhill whistling through the leaves of a *jamun* tree, while a loping chipmunk stopped to raise itself, paws folded, alert, watching a lone *hoopoe* bird pecking among the fallen purple fruit. Then as suddenly as it started the wind died to a stillness made intense by the careful tapping of chisel on marble. Bill left his satchel against the larch after he took out a mauve stole. He kissed the stole, put it round his neck and knelt. A moment later Ted knelt by him, while Mohan and Dinesh shifted uneasily.

Ted broke down. 'No! Not like this! I won't leave them here. It's possible. Yes Bill, even now. After all, they are British! I can charter a flight. The money's there. Sandy's money.'

Bill said nothing.

'Emma did not want to be in England? That is what I believe,' said Mohan Singh. He waited, but no one spoke. 'She was one of us and a holy woman. Leave them. It may not be England, but neither is it India. They made this *zamin*, this earth, their own. Let it be a monument to their love . . . like how Taj Mahal is.'

Bill rose, removed his stole, picked up his satchel and took Ted aside. 'Mohan has a point.' He opened his prayer book and took out a folded piece of paper. 'Sandy wrote to me. His last letter.' Bill gave the letter to Ted. The letter read:

"My dear Bill, I hope this letter gets to you. I was told you are at Ranikhet and that Fordham House would be the best address to find you. Bill, I am desperately unhappy. My guardian angel is leaving me. I can't live without her. There's only you and Sona to turn to. It's a pity Sona can't write. I've tried to show her how to use the telephone at the post office but she'll have none of it. Talk to Dinesh, get him to contact you at once should anything happen to either of us. You must be there, however late. You always were a great comfort to us. Your mother too. How I miss her. She was as welcoming as the Gospel of St John . . . I am beginning to wander . . .

"I couldn't finish the letter last night. Could we be like the Koestlers? Would you absolve me? I know it isn't the Christian thing to do. But Sona knows how I feel. She understands. She'll help. It's solace to know Emma and I are together, as we were in life: a consolation not to be missed! Sandeep.

PS The dream we dreamed was not denied us. PPS. Indeed, cheap music is potent! S."

Ted returned the letter. 'Typical of Sandy, that postscript. Even in the darkest hour, something light to underline the tragic.'

Bill carefully folded the piece of paper, placed it in his Bible and put the book into his satchel. 'My Mother believed he was the soul of the son she lost in childbirth. By some strange coincidence, they had the same birthday, although my brother Ambrose would've been Sandy's senior by five years.'

'And did Dinesh contact you?'

'He did. I came as soon as I could. There's an inscription I'm having prepared. It's meant to give both intimacy and anonymity. That tapping you heard. As Dinesh is next of kin I asked for his approval. He said, "do whatever you think is right for them."' They joined the others and all walked silently through the trees, along the edge of the orchard, to the chapel.

'That chapel,' Ted said, 'could be a chapel in Sussex.'

'It was an attempt to echo the small church in Alfriston. I've been lucky to find most of the dressed stone and roof tiles. The beams will have to be replaced, eventually.'

'They seem to be doing a good job.'

'Indian masons are the best in the world and make do with fewer and simpler tools.'

Inside, the chapel was plain and bare, and on entering it, the nostrils were assailed by the strong smell of distemper, lime and damp earth. There were no pews and the dark cemented floor stretched unevenly from the west door to the step of the chancel railing. Beyond this was a low teak dais, where a simple rose-wood table served as an altar. On this, a plain wooden cross was flanked and dwarfed by two large cast-iron candlesticks. The only other furniture were three oak benches placed in the middle of the nave. The chapel was wedge-shaped, being narrowest at the altar and widest at the west door. On the floor, in a far corner by this door, squatted a feeble looking old man with chisel and mallet in hand. When Bill entered, he lay down his tools and stood up—just tall enough to reach up to Bill's waist. He wore a brown waistcoat over his shirt and short pyjamas that reached just below the knee. Without looking up he raised a hand to his forehead in salutation, while a faint smile cracked his parchment-like skin. He adjusted a pair of tiny brass-rimmed spectacles, held together by copper wire, and tied behind his clean shaven head. Behind these he constantly screwed up his bleary eyes.

Bill studied the marble slab the man had been working on and patting the man's back said: '*Shabash! Bahut achcha!* This is Bholaram, my old friend from Agra.' Bholaram wobbled his head, then crouched down once again over his work. 'He's working from that.' Bill pointed to a sheet of paper and a sketch of a rectangle in which was written "SANDY & EMMA," under it "WERE HERE", and below that, "RESURGAMUS".

'Should it not be "are here",' suggested Mohan Singh.

'They are no longer "here",' said Bill, 'if you get my meaning.'

'Oh, that is most beautiful thought,' Mohan beamed. 'And the latin word?'

'"We will rise again".'

Mohan Singh nodded thoughtfully.

'But,' Ted frowned, 'what about antecedents? This sets them adrift. In time people may wonder "Sandy who" and "Emma who"? It's too like graffito carved on a tree.'

'Anonymity is what they always wanted.' Bill returned the drawing to Bholaram.

'You must excuse me now,' Dinesh said. He looked at Mohan Singh. 'Coming?'

'*Arrey bhai*, go ahead. Wait by the Land Rover. I'll join you in a minute.'

From the open frameless window the path was clearly visible. They watched Dinesh hurry down it. He did not look back. Mohan Singh clicked his tongue. 'Forgive him. He is all mixed up. Okay, *bhai sahibs*, see you later. And Padre sahib, when it's finished, the memorial I mean, tell me, because my family would like to pay their respects.' He extended both his hands and gripped theirs in turn. Then he left.

'I'm afraid we've lost Dinesh forever!' sighed Bill.

'I find it very hard to like him,' said Ted.

Bill sighed. 'It's a blessing Sandy and Emma didn't have children. They were far too absorbed in each other to be good parents. Dinesh got everything except parenthood. A pity. He was rather fond of Emma. I think she found it hard to overcome her instinctive dislike . . . that or she was fiercely loyal to Sandy. But I agree he's hard to like.'

Ted turned away. 'Is that Indian marble?'

'Yes, from Rajasthan. I forget the name of the place. They have a beautiful word for marble: *Sang marmar*. I left it to Bholaram to order and get it here. His chaps brought it in the day before yesterday.'

'Are they from Agra too?'

'No. The poor man freelances and recruits local help. Masons to do the brick and cement platform, and *coolies*, the hard tasks of fetching, carrying, and cement mixing. They're around somewhere. It's the lunch break. Lunch is taken anytime after eleven.'

'I like the idea of the raised brick platform.'

'Yes, a Mogul concept. The platform will cover the width of both graves, and the single marble slab will be embedded in the centre.'

'I gather Dinesh did attend the funeral?'

'And the chapel service too. He stood alone and apart from the rest.'

'What is he going to do in Bombay?'

'Manage one of his father-in-law's hotels. That PS in Sandy's letter rang a bell.'

'It's from a song. "Long ago and Far Away".

'We should be going. I'll be here again tomorrow.'

'*Arrey, ho! Bhai, roko!*' Bholaram called out from the window. He left the chapel. They saw him walk up, bow-legged towards the ridge.

'They're going back to work,' Bill explained. 'He's asking his men to wait. You see the two men in front. They're Muslims. The white skull caps are a give away . . . I expect you know I was close to them; Sandy and Emma. Sona too. I want to tell you about an occasion when we happened to be walking in St John's churchyard. Sandy and I agreed that graveyards were sad places but, that as gardens of the resurrection they ought not to be so. He felt this was because the inscriptions on the headstones contained messages which cling to mortality; by the finger nails. His very words. After some thought, we all felt it wasn't necessary for gravestones to be like identity tags, and Emma—this Ted, is for you to remember—Emma, quite in her own train of thought said, she always was intrigued by poems signed "Anon". They gave her a peculiar thrill, because unclaimed poetry was selflessly reaching out to all humanity. As if the messenger did not want to come in the way of the message.'

Ted leaned heavily on the window sill. 'What a pity. I wish I knew her better. But that wasn't to be. And my Kitty will constantly remind me of her.'

Bill put his arm round him.

Before they left the chapel Bill lit a candle, said a short prayer and went into a tiny vestry. Following him Ted entered. Bill removed his cassock to reveal a pair of khaki shorts, boots and thick socks, which he pulled up to his knees. Ted repressed a giggle. 'Sorry, I couldn't help it. You look the old colonial shikari.'

'There's an old army surplus shop in Old Delhi.' Bill looked at Ted's feet. 'Good. Glad you remembered to wear heavy shoes.' Then he took the long sturdy staff which rested in a corner of the room and led the way down the tree-lined path. Some way along it Ted stopped to look back at the chapel and the grave, then he caught up with Bill. 'When the marble slab is laid I'll bring my camera. Did you have much difficulty getting permission to . . . ?'

'In India, with patience, you get what you want. Indian bureaucracy maybe slow but it's not heartless. More often than not they are helpful and always sympathetic. And, as you know, the Thakurs were held in high regard. One of Sandy's elder sisters, Ranee, is a prominent citizen of Bombay, with influence in high places.'

'Has she been here?'

'She's an invalid. Incidentally, only Sandy and his parents were Christian.'

They were silent for some time. Then Ted asked abruptly. 'Did Sona have a hand in Sandy's death? Dinesh is angry about the rumours flying around and upset the doctor hadn't been called to attend to Sandy after Emma died.'

'Dr Sudhir's visits were frequent. I trust Sona's innate good sense. She knew them best. At the end, Emma and Sandy wanted all the privacy they could get. This is how I see it. Sandy died because he wanted to and through the power of prayers. The prayers of three loves. His and Emma's and Sona's. A doctor had no role in any of these.'

They walked, once again, in silence. Then Bill added. 'I suppose you think all that talk of prayers is unscientific mumbo jumbo?'

'No, not at all. As a doctor I've known of strange happenings. One is always aware of the paranormal. You must know that famous one about Sir James Frazer's wife . . .

'He of *The Golden Bough* fame? I think I . . . but, go on.'

'On seeing her dead husband, she bade him farewell, went back to her bed, turned her face to the wall and died. Ah,' he stopped and nodded in the direction of the lych gate. Bill shaded his eyes. Coming down the slope towards them was a lean and very erect man, carrying on his back an olive-green kit bag. Bill waved. The man came to attention and gave a smart military salute.

'This is Ransingh,' Bill said, 'a *jat* from Rothak and ex-soldier. He was wounded during India's war with China and had to retire on medical grounds.'

Ted was immediately struck by Ransingh's handsome face and military bearing; and though he was smaller than Bill, his slim, powerful built in no way dwarfed by him. He wore the olive-green uniform of a soldier in the Indian Army and his close cropped hair, though noticeably grey, oddly complimented a face that was brown and as smooth as polished bronze. But it was the eyes which held Ted's attention. Deep-set and alive, they gave the impression of looking at and through to a tranquil vision beyond.

'*Ki hal hai?*' asked Bill grinning widely.

The man smiled, flashing a set of immaculate teeth. 'Memsahib's brother, no?'

'Yes,' said Ted, 'but I don't look a bit like her.' He held out his hand. 'You were Sandy's watchman. We met once before.'

Ransingh saluted. 'I bringing food and drink . . . for you.' He opened his bag and took out a large orange plastic box and two glass bottles. The larger contained a milky tea and the smaller one lime juice. 'I also, two galasses, inside.' He put the things back and handed the bag to Bill.

'Our lunch!' laughed Bill. '*Bahut meherbani!* Thank you.'

'No problem.' Ransingh answered.

'Take the bag Ted, I'll have a word with Ransingh. He is to supervise the building of his own gate house. I'll explain the layout to him.'

'I'll sit there, on the rock under that tree and I might try some of that cold tea.'

'It's cold but it's not tea. It's *chang*. You may not like it. It's an acquired taste.'

Ted decided to forgo the drink and sat down to watch the two men. He could hear them though he could not follow their conversation. After sometime Bill returned and sat next to him. 'Ransingh would like an extra room. I should have remembered. But a good thing in the longer term. He'll train his son to take over when he retires.'

'I'm sorry, but I don't know what you're talking about?'

'Ransingh has a son. I haven't met the lad. They've recently got together. Till now, the boy was at the Convent school in Kalimpong. Miss Das helped to get him there.'

'What about the boy's mother?'

'Sadly, she killed herself not long after Vijay—that's the boys name—was born. It was during the war of 1962, I mentioned earlier. Vijay means victory.'

'How dreadful. Why did she do that?'

'A terrible misunderstanding. She was told that Ransingh had been killed. Whoever told her got the wrong message. The thought of widowhood among Rajput women is still anathema. You must have heard about *suttee*. It's against the law, but still happens on the quiet. And, of course, poor Ransingh didn't know he had a son.'

'When did he find out?'

'When he returned to his village after a long stay at the Military Hospital in Dehra Dun. The villagers and relations got a nasty shock when he turned up.'

'And how does the ubiquitous Miss Das come into it?'

'Vijay, a sickly, premature baby, was taken to the Ranikhet General Nursing Home. Miss Das was a nurse there. A slip of a girl then.' Bill smiled. 'D'you find that hard to imagine. She's younger than she looks, you know.'

Ted laughed. 'But didn't Ransingh claim the boy?'

'Normally a woman in the family would have fostered the boy, and Ransingh did have a sister. But there's so much poverty in villages. The woman had children of her own. And there was Monica Das, even at twenty, exuding every maternal quality, and promising to see the boy was given education and career opportunities . . . So, Ransingh and his sister consented. I shouldn't say boy. He'll be twenty-three, at least. I gather he speaks fluent Tibetan, so he'll be useful in my school.'

'School?'

'Yes. Shall we make a move? I know a nice spot by a stream where we'll lunch. Yes, a school. That pleased the authorities and helped a lot towards getting all the necessary sanctions needed. A school here will protect this area from being exploited or occupied. The cemetery, rather graveyard, is a small part of the land; and private. There have been no burials since my grandfather's, till now. Mine will certainly be the last. Just fourteen graves. The Forsyths were distant forebears. Haven't a clue about the Duckworths. Tea planters, I presume. So as the graveyard is just the bit of ground between the chapel and the conifers, it can be walled off, leaving all that wide grassy incline between the hill and the orchard, for the school building.'

'And the orchard?'

'The school will maintain the orchard, which would provide a wonderful diversion for the children.' Bill stopped. 'Am I walking too fast?'

'I could never match your strides.'

'We're almost there. You see that ledge? Up there under that birch?'

'I give up. That's far too steep!'

Bill laughed. 'From here, yes. But we're not taking it head on. Behind that line of rhododendrons, a gentle track leads off this path to the ledge.'

It was as Bill said an easy climb. Ted cautiously tested the ledge. 'Man made?'

'It was used as a *machan*. A huntsman's platform. It certainly commands a wide area of the path and valley below.' Bill sat down heavily. 'So to lunch.'

Ted gave up on the *chang* and had to be content with the lime juice to cool down the hot curried aubergine. 'And what's this?' he asked.

'Ah, that's *churma*. It's a sweet and perfect antidote to a hot curry. I adore the stuff, which means it's bad for me. Quite simple to make. It's just a very thick, slow baked *chappati*, crumbled in *ghee* and sugar. Have a taste. Use that plastic spoon.'

Ted put a tentative spoonful in his mouth. 'Um! Yes! Quite farmhouse cakey.'

After lunch Bill stretched, put his hands behind his head and leaned against the rock. Slowly his eyes closed and remained shut for sometime. Ted studied his face. He knew Sandy's nickname for Bill, and indeed something about the sculptured head resembled Michelangelo's Moses. Bill opened his eyes and gazed wistfully across the deep valley. A spasm shook his great frame. His eyes filled with tears. He turned away.

'It is all right, Bill. I know you were very fond of Sandy.'

Bill gave a wry smile. 'The sorrows and tragedies of other people remind us of our own. When we weep, we weep also for ourselves. That is from one of Sandy's poems. We regret what we rue. Did you know he published what he laughingly called his slim volume of verse?'

'Yes. *Terror Incognita*. It wasn't well received. He meant to follow it with *Terror Infirma*, but gave up the idea. He was too much of a wag and punster to be a serious poet. And he knew it.'

'I've seen worse poems. I'm no judge. But he had a way with words.'

'Bill, did you know his affectionate nickname for you?'

'Moses? Yes. He had another, which he believed I did not get to hear of. A young Spanish priest, a Benedictine Brother, Sandy met in Delhi told me. He remarked upon my height, and Sandy replied: "Yes, Sierra Padre". Much to the young man's delight.'

'How very apt. You must be almost seven feet?'

'Not really. Six nine and shrinking.' Bill reached for his staff and raised himself up with visible effort. 'I'll show you something. It's just a short climb.' They got on to a grassy knoll behind the ledge. Bill put on his glasses. 'There!' he pointed.

'Why, indeed!' cried Ted. 'It's the cottage! It looks no more than a mile away!'

'As the crow flies. But, regrettably we have to stick to the path. Two winding miles of it. We'll get there, after another short break, in a leisurely hour or so.'

'I suppose this path's no longer used. I hope, unarmed as we are, it is safe. And what about wildlife?'

'In theory we're between the tiger and the snow leopard. Both have vanished. There is wild life—civets, hog-badgers, wild goat, barking deer and, with some luck, you may get a glimpse of the beautiful Himalayan, yellow pine marten.'

A mile further up they rested. Ted was about to sit on a fallen tree but Bill warned him off. 'You would have been devoured by ants. Look!'

Ted stepped back. 'Ants? They're the size of beetles!'

Bill pointed to a flat stone slab laid over two rocks. He sat down, leaning heavily on his staff. 'I wouldn't walk here after dark. After today, I won't need to do this again. I'm tired. You'll be all right tomorrow. They'll use ponies. They're not great walkers.'

'Did you see that bird? Smaller than a magpie. Black, with a swallow-tail. There.'

'Drongo, or king crow. Plucky. Always ready for a fight. Emma was a close student of nature. I learned a lot from her, particularly about plants and flowers. In the early years we enjoyed what we called our nature walks. Poor Sandy. He was often house bound because of those old injuries. She always carried the book of Indian flora and fauna, which Sandy gave her—written by a Jesuit priest who lived in Goa.'

Ted remembered how she loved such walks from a very early age, and regretted the number of times he had to turn down her begging invitations to accompany her. 'What about dates!' Ted cried suddenly. 'Just struck me. Dates on the gravestone, birth, age . . . that sort of thing. Never mind, I don't see why anyone need know.' Ted looked at Bill quizzically. 'I expect the truly religious are truly romantic. Were you ever in love? I say I'm terribly sorry! Didn't mean to pry.'

'Did I always want to be celibate? A monk, wedded to the Church?' Bill raised his chin and brushed his scanty white beard thoughtfully against his neck. 'As a young man I was rather keen on marriage and family life. There was Amy. I met her in Oxford. My last year there. A tender-hearted girl . . . Some years older than me . . . She sang beautifully. There was no reason to wait. So we decided to marry. Mother liked her too and Amy stayed with us in Stoke Poges while the banns were published. Then some days before the wedding, Amy suddenly decided to drive down to Kent—she had an aunt in Deal.' Bill paused. 'There was an accident . . . With Amy I buried all desires for love and for marriage. I left Oxford. Went to Jerusalem and entered an Anglican seminary.'

Ted shook his head penitently. 'This is terrible. I've been unthinking and clumsy. But didn't this tragedy in your life shake your faith?'

'There was none to lose. Like all arrogant students, I started an agnostic and a man of the world. I had money. We knew passion, Amy and I . . . I found faith in Jerusalem.'

'I made you relive those moments. I'm sorry.'

'You needn't be. Recent events have made me think about it. It's distant and past. I can now talk about it. Sandy and Emma knew.'

Ted got up and looked vaguely about him. He crossed the path and gazed across the valley. Bill waited a moment before he joined him. He knew without having to see. Ted raised a hand. 'I'll be all right.' He took a deep breath. 'It is hard. I've so little faith in which to seek refuge. Kitty's christening was the last time I went to church. Gosh, they are so alike! To look at Kitty is to see Emma!'

'That will be a great help. You will love Kitty even more.'

'Poor little Emma! Miles away from home!'

They stood together in silence for sometime. Then Bill said: 'It's getting dark.'

Ted nodded. 'How far now?'

'Not long now.'

They surprised Baldev, Mohan Singh's servant, who was patiently expecting them to arrive at the cottage gate. He folded his hands in salutation and gave Bill a note from Mohan Singh. In it Mohan insisted that Bill spend the night at his place, and not go on to the bus station. He would arrange to inform the Mission.

'This is typically generous of Mohan. Actually, Maamiji will know if I don't turn up soon after ten. Ted, you go with Baldev. Tell Mohan not to worry about me. I'll spend the night here in the Cottage, But don't tell him that. I don't feel like company tonight. Lie you must.' He smiled. 'We're all sinners.'

'But this place is deserted. Sona's disappeared. And it doesn't seem as if, what's his name, Ransingh, will be back . . . I also believe the generator is switched off. There'll be neither electricity or water! And what about a meal tonight?"

'I'm not hungry. My room's there, above the stable. I've a tin of biscuits and an oil lamp and a bottle of water. I need nothing more. Go. Don't keep Mohan waiting.'

'Sure you'll be all right?'

'Yes. I always carry a torch and a box of matches.'

'Goodbye then. I'll see you day after tomorrow, at the chapel'

'That fellow,' said Mohan Singh, 'says, that Sona was seen on this road, setting out for Tibet and somewhere there she lost her footing, slipped and fell down a ravine.'

'That's awful!' Dinesh shivered. 'What a way to die! What do we do now?'

'Make further inquiries.' Mohan Singh said. 'We must make sure.'

Ted sat down on the wall over a culvert and waited. He looked up the valley and at the steep rocky path. 'I can't walk much more.'

'We're near the end of our search,' Mohan said. 'Not far. You see that *chorten*? The white stupa like temple just below the skyline?'

'Yes, the one with flags and a large painted eye. I suppose I can make it there.'

'Good. I was going to add we don't even have to go that far. You see where the path takes a dip. That's where Laddie lives. We can't see his hut. But, he has a full view of the valley. And as this is the road to Ladakh and ultimately Tibet, he keeps watch on all the traffic going to and fro.'

'Is he some Government official?' Asked Ted.

'No, no. The fellow is a recluse. Hermit. Built himself a hut in front of a cave. Sits by the wayside and blesses travellers.'

'That's the cave where they say St John, the Evangelist lived,' Dinesh said. 'People believe he is still alive. John. The old man of the mountains.'

'*Arrey*! No. Your mixing up. That cave is somewhere in Kashmir.'

'No, Mohan. You're thinking about Jesus, whose tomb is in Kashmir.'

'Why is he called Laddie?' Ted asked quietly.

'Why Laddie? Oh, because he's a Ladakhi. Some Englishman mispronounced it and the name stuck.' Mohan grinned. 'Now everyone calls him so. But I don't believe he's from Ladakh. He's from Tibet. And, one thing more, Dinesh *babu*. If Sona was with a group of Tibetans and fell to her death, he would know.'

'Why?' asked Dinesh.

'Haven't you heard how Tibetans disdain death and respect nature. Well, they hack the dead body to pieces with an axe, exposing it to the elements. That is what I'm told. I mean, it's not all that shocking. Parsees also expose the dead to the elements. In their Well of silence. There's one in Bombay's Malabar Hill.'

Ted stood up. 'Why don't we find out if he's seen her?'

"Laddie" hadn't seen her. He recognised Sona from the photograph Dinesh showed him. He was sure he would have remembered seeing her. He was also certain there had been no accident. Ted told this to Bill, when they met the next day at the chapel.

'I'm afraid,' said Bill, 'all of you have had, what my mother called "a wild goose chase". Sona's alive and somewhere near by, in hiding. I also believe I know who is protecting her. Come with me to the grave. I'll show you something.'

Someone had planted a red flag by the grave and next to it was a neat mound of stemless marigolds. Bill pointed to this and the white scarf tied to a low overhanging branch of the larch tree. 'If we've had a mysterious visitor, only one person can know who it is.' He turned to Ransingh, who stood behind him at a respectful distance and asked in Hindustani. 'Was it's a woman?'

They studied each other impassively. Ransingh nodded with visible reluctance.

'You know this woman?'

Ransingh displayed the discomfiture of someone unused to lying. 'My sight isn't what it used to be,' he said. 'I could see she was harmless, so I didn't pay too much attention . . . Padre sahib, no great wrong been done.'

'No wrong,' Bill said in Punjabi, 'on the contrary, she has shown great love.'

'Then forgive me. I am respecting her wishes. Please do not press me further.'

'All right,' said Bill, 'we'll say no more.'

'Do I have your permission to leave?'

Bill nodded. Ransingh turned to leave, then stopped and faced them. 'In one hour I bringing lunch.' He said in English. His eyes rested on Ted. 'This time cold beer. Ice?' They smiled. 'Thank you, Ransingh,' said Ted. 'No need for ice.'

Ransingh gave one of his rare smiles; an apologetic smile, as if to say: "No ice, with beer, I should have remembered!"

Bill waited till he was gone. 'Now I know, Sona is alive and well and Ransingh is looking after her. They've been discreet. Kept, whatever relationship they had and have, a secret. I wonder if Sandy and Emma had any inkling. I'd be astonished if they did.'

CHAPTER FOURTEEN

The photographs and letters Ted Franks brought with him from India, lay spread on his mother's dining table. He watched her as she impassively glanced through them, but the occasional sniff and monosyllabic grunt held his curiosity. After a while she got up and left the table. A little peeved he began to gather the items. She stopped him. 'Ted, leave them. I'll look at them later. Give me a sherry. We'll lunch in the kitchen, so the table can stay as it is.'

Ted studied her face as she sipped the sherry. 'You've given me far too much. Never mind.' She was a picture of good health and as she sat against the light, her face seemed devoid of wrinkles. Nothing about her reminded him of Emma or, for that matter, of himself. She made an impatient gesture. 'Oh, do stop staring and sit down! If you must know, I did shed a tear or two. But I'm not going to do it now for your benefit. I can't see what useful purpose it'll serve.' Her mouth twitched as she shrugged and massaged her forearms briskly, 'I'm eighty. I've had my share of sorrows. The last thing I want to hear from anyone is comforting, consoling noises.' He waited. 'Poor souls! A foolish pair if ever there was one.' She sniffed. 'If he wasn't a rich man, they wouldn't have survived as long as they did.'

Ted lit his pipe and pulled on it sharply. 'That's what Dinesh keeps saying. About the money side. But that can't be the full answer, as you well know.'

'I suppose they suited each other,' she continued. 'A misguided and impractical pair. I know he was charming, good-looking; an imprudent man married to a religious, or do I mean pious, simpleton . . . both full of impossible ideals.'

'Simpleton? Mother, you do Emma an injustice. Or are you suggesting Sandy took advantage of her? No one could. She saw through people. She was no simpleton. You never seemed to care what she did. Explains why you missed her subtleties.'

'She knew how I felt, but she had to do things her own way. Never consulted me. Certainly not since your father died. She was like him, obstinate.'

'Obstinate!' Ted tapped his pipe against his heel.

'I wish you wouldn't do that! Yes, she was obstinate. Well, strong-minded. I'm not saying she was rude. She had a way of ignoring you; doing her own thing.'

'Independent, strong? That's no description of a simpleton.'

Edith Franks compressed and pursed her lips in rapid succession. 'I really wish you wouldn't talk to me as if I'm a moron. As a doctor you should know better. People are many things. She was physically weak, delicate, but mentally strong, though she could be terribly apathetic. And in all that there was an element of foolishness. I suppose he had the right kind of charm or used the right kind to make her feel she was having her own way. He was clever, but with romantic notions too foolish to contemplate.'

'He was sensitive. She had talent and yearnings. Did you try to understand Emma?'

'Tried? Of course I did! I was against her marrying him and she knew it without my having to spell it out. But once her mind was made up there was nothing anyone could do to discourage her. With your father away in Poona and you in college, I thought we, Emma and I, would be close. I was mistaken. Clearly she had made her own little world from which I was excluded or in which I was the wicked witch and your father was the prince. From the day he returned, after all those years, she clung to him like a limpet. I know what I'm talking about. I didn't shut her in any tower. She did it herself and very effectively. Huh! Little bound us to each other. I am bitter. Why shouldn't I be? All the years we could have had together she denied me.'

'Emma was a sweet child and father gave her the sort of attention she needed.'

'She knew nothing about men. Apart from father fixation she avoided them. Locked herself in her dreams of heavens knows what. Remote and spells of brooding silence.'

'And we did nothing to break into that locked-in world. Father did. Sandy did.'

'Stuff and nonsense! I was much too indulgent. An occasional smack would've done her a power of good. She needed to be shaken out of her stupor.'

Ted re-lit his pipe and puffed thoughtfully. 'Sandy did. He tried and he succeeded . . . I feel terrible we didn't. There's no getting away from the fact she missed the fun, all the fun of childhood. He gave it back to her, called her his fairy's child. In their early days.'

'That makes me sick. That's the sort of romantic nonsense, which lust inspires men to wallow in. Yes, lust. Your hearts are in your trousers. You want girls, not women.'

'At least he was good to and for her.'

'I wish you'd face up to it. Emma was odd . . . oh all right, unique if you want. She had religion up to here. And it's nonsense for me to have a sense of guilt or imagine she was sadly neglected. She liked being the way she was and why no one, apart from the nuns in the convent, liked her. They would. Religious people are masochists. She could have been seduced from all that if any of your namby pamby college friends, and I'll include Trevor too, made the effort or persevered. Sandy did. I'll give him that.'

'Mother, you forget, Emma was beautiful. No man would have given up easily if he thought he had a chance. If my friends were not persistent, remember, they were much older and knew other women. Sandy was luckier. Because of father she had a romantic idea of him. Remember the photograph of father with Sandy, which she kept? Also, he loved her too much and with open sincerity, any woman would have been overwhelmed by it. She hated mere flirtation and walked away at the slightest hint of it. Once he won her, Sandy could tease her with impunity, which secretly she enjoyed.'

'Because he was a boy. He posed no threat to her . . .'

'Boy! Sandy was at least ten years older . . .'

'He looked and behaved a boy. Fairy child, my eye! She was the dominant partner, even if he did seduced her. I regret letting her come to London . . . But all this talk is such a waste of time. Why we . . .' A faint smiled turned the corners of her thin lips. 'I mustn't be harsh. He did make her smile. It was heartening to see her smile. She had a beautiful smile. She could have achieved so much with her looks. Pity.'

'She made a home, a happy one too. Not many can say that. And she won the hearts of simple people. They treated her like a goddess, there, in India, hill folk and Tibetans. You saw that for yourself.'

'Babes in the wood,' Edith mumbled and blew her nose violently. 'I don't know who the doctor was who attended them. Couldn't have been any good. She might have lived longer, here. In London, I mean. And you would have attended her.'

'There was nothing anyone could have done, anywhere.'

'If she had married Trevor. We could at least have been together, a family.'

'I don't know. I didn't care for him. He showed little interest. Well, now we know why. You don't accept it but I always suspected he was gay.'

'Rubbish. He married Maud and they have two children.'

'But it didn't last. And, mother, Sandy was not a complete stranger. We knew him as a boy. Father knew quite a bit of his family. I hope it wasn't because he was Indian, that . . . you know what I'm driving at. Can't see what else one could have against him?'

'I shall ignore that.'

'You didn't speak to her for years after she married, or write. And when you were there you pointedly ignored them, giving undue attention to that awful prig Dinesh.'

'There you are! So, I'm not racist. They had to know how I felt about marrying against my wishes. Do I not count for something? Still there's no use crying over spilt milk.' She emptied her glass and went back to the photographs. Ted tapped his pipe. 'You don't seem to get much out of that pipe, Ted.'

'I'm trying to give up, by making difficult the pleasure of smoking.' He laughed.

'This one! This one of Emma. I don't remember seeing this. She looks radiant.'

'I spotted that too. It was on Sandy's desk.'

'There's a strange inscription. "My dilemma!" Why has he split dilemma? And what does it mean. She was no dilemma. Quite transparent. Whatever her moods, you knew where you were. Poor child!' She put the photograph to one side, covered her face and sobbed. 'She was my baby.'

He put his arm round her. 'I'm all right,' she whispered, and moved his hand.

'It's three words, mother. Sandy's little joke. "My Dil Emma". Three words. "My Heart Emma". "Dil" is Hindustani for heart.'

'Sentimental rubbish. Oh, look!' she exclaimed. 'The photograph you were talking about. Father with Sandy, which was always in her room. Maybe you were right about always being in love with him.'

'Not seriously. She kept Sandy waiting for three years.'

'She was still very young, timid, afraid of sex.'

Ted shook his head. 'We'll never know.' He turned to leave the room.

'Don't go, Teddy. Come here. Put your arm round me.'

He did, a little wonderingly. A soft squeeze on his hand made him look down at the carefully combed grey head and the trembling lips of her tight mouth. Lips that never spoke his father name. He bent down and kissed her.

After a while she asked: 'Do you really intend to go ahead with your divorce?'

He nodded. 'If it wasn't for Kitty's problems and my trip to India, I would have filed for divorce by now . . . We've been separated for two years. Why do you ask?'

'You don't have to listen to Kitty.'

'Kitty's got nothing to do with it. Twenty-eight years of hell told me I should have done it long ago.'

'Mabel is a proud woman. I feel for her.'

He removed his arm and faced her with hands on his hips. 'And my feelings? Oh, mother you can be impossible at times!'

He spun on his heel and left the room.

Kitty was thirty-four when she arrived at Nurpur Mission House. Miss Monica Das had planned to meet her at New Delhi's Palam Airport, but as Kitty insisted on taking the train, Maamiji met her at Pathankot.

A flurry of chattering and excited servants ran out to meet the jeep. They trotted alongside it, as it entered the Mission Compound.

Kitty gasped. The large stone manse with its wide verandahs on either side of a portico decked with lush wisteria, took her completely by surprise. 'Maami! It's lovely!'

Miss Das rippled with delight. 'So, you like your new home? Good. It will take another year before your own little bungalow is ready. Maybe little longer. It will be at the back. Work has started already.' The large woman cupped Kitty's face and gave her a matronly hug. Kitty felt like a chick under its mother's wing, and liked it.

'You don't have to build me a bungalow. A room will do. Bill is leaving the cottage, Sandy's cottage to me. Dinesh . . . do you know Dinesh?'

'Yes, yes. I knowing. He stopped here for two days before going to Bombay.'

'Well, he gave the cottage to Bill, soon after Bill got the school going.'

'But you can't live in cottage and work in the School . . .'

'I'm looking forward to the pony rides.'

'Okay, okay! We shall see. First you settle here. Getting to know people and all that. Then we shall see.'

On the steps of the portico stood the patient, neatly turned out staff of the Mission House. They greeted Kitty with broad smiles, wagging heads and folded palms. One of them handed Miss Das a garland of marigolds, which Miss Das put round Kitty's neck. 'Welcome! Welcome, my dear! Just look at her? All excited. Thirty-what? She looks twenty. My! Oh, my! I expected to see grown lady, but she's no more than a girl. *Heh, na?*' She surveyed her staff and their heads wobbled in united agreement. 'See? You're most welcome. A breath of fresh air!'

Kitty hoped to be introduced to each member of the staff, but Miss Das hurried her indoors. 'Come, come. I'll take you to your room. Then we will have *khana*—lunch. You're hungry, no? Must be, poor thing! So long journey. Tired? Then rest a little.'

The servants followed them, insisting on carrying every item of Kitty's luggage, even her handbag. Ted had warned her she would be pampered and fussed over. The room was large and everything in it was large: the bed, the windows, which overlooked the portico, as was the desk by the bed. She touched the wood. So this is teak, she told herself as she slipped off her moccasins. The stone floor felt refreshingly cool.

'*Achcha*, rest now. Shortly someone will come to take you to the dining-room, and after that I'll introduce you to all and sundry.'

'Thank you, maamiji.'

'Oh, so pretty. Now I know what your aunt looked like. Everyone saying you're spitting image of her.'

Kitty blushed. 'No, maamiji. My aunt Emma was more beautiful.'

EPILOGUE

Three years before Kitty's arrival at Nurpur, her decision to leave England and join the Mission as teacher and social worker, was made on a day she would never forget. Early that morning a package had arrived, addressed to "Edward Franks Esq". It was a cold, clear January morning. Something, Kitty couldn't think what, had woken her. Having slept fitfully through the night and unable to get back to sleep, she climbed out of bed, put on the blue Kashmiri dressing-gown her father had brought from India, and opened the curtains. Shading her eyes she peered through the window-panes. The pale, golden glow of dawn silhouetted the leafless twigs of birch and hawthorn; and the brier thicket, along the brow of the hill behind the church, cast weird shadows on the gravestones. She glanced down and saw, below the window, clear footprints on the snow-covered path between the front gate and the door. But her curiosity was not aroused. If the post had come, she knew there would be nothing for her. There hadn't been for the past five months. John obviously had decided to ignore her letter. She was now past caring.

The long case clock outside her father's room chimed the quarters. Kitty listened and waited till there was stillness once more, then tiptoed downstairs to the kitchen, poured a glass of milk, drank it and returned to her room. She lay awake in bed, restless till the clock chimed again, got up, untied the bundle of letters next to her bed and with a sigh of relief found the letter she wanted. She read it, not once but twice; folded it lovingly, put it in her dressing-gown pocket and went down to the living-room. There she sat on the window-seat by the latticed bay windows.

It was later than she thought. The central heating was on, while outside, the snow-covered lawn sparkled in the clear brightening light. Kitty hugged her knees, shut her eyes and fell asleep, unaware that her father, was sitting in the shadows by the fireplace, having read the contents of the package he had received by recorded delivery. Kitty had first been awakened, though she did not know it, by the sound of the doorbell.

Ted stood by her. He waited sometime before he shook her gently. Kitty opened her eyes, yawned and stretched her arms. 'Are you all right?' he asked.

'Good morning,' she cooed, 'is mum up too?'

'I wouldn't expect her to be. Remember, we were up till the small hours, or should I say, were kept up . . . I'm not complaining.' He tousled her hair.

'Sorry! I've been such trouble!' She sprang up, put her arms round him and swayed. 'Sorry for all the heartache I've caused. Dad, I've always loved you. Oh, how I wish I'd found someone like you.' She moved back and held him at arms length. 'But that's all behind me now. I've made my mind up.' With a pert gesture of a hand and a pirouette, reminiscent of the child he knew, she chanted. 'The past is past. I'm going to be good. Very good. I'm going to do something new and exciting.'

Ted laughed and shook his head. 'Tell me.'

'I've decided to go to India. And I'll teach in Bill's school.'

'You said nothing of this last night!'

'I've decided, this morning, an hour ago. Dad you must help me!'

'And what about your divorce?'

'That's just it. John will give up. India's the last place he'll follow me to. You know what he thinks of India. And he doesn't have to know where I am.'

'Don't you want to marry again, have a family. You're young? At thirty-one you still have all the time in the world to start a new life.'

'Promise me you'll help!'

'Are you absolutely certain you want to join the Mission at Nurpur? Well, if that's what you want, I'll help. It'll be a very different life. A lonely life and not an easy one.'

She gripped his shoulders. 'Don't look sad, daddy! Can't you see I'm happy. I see a useful life ahead. I've been . . . oh, I can't say it! I've been a disappointment. But I've had enough men in my life. I won't ever make a good wife or mother. I'd rather be alone.'

'And little old me? I'll be alone, now more than ever.'

'No, daddy! Don't make it hard for me. We'll see each other more often! You must come for long holidays and stay with Bill at Fern Cottage, or at the Mission. You said the Mission House are planing to board tourists in the holiday season?'

'That fell through. Nurpur is much too isolated. I mean transport wise.'

'Never mind, there's the Cottage. I could settle there and look after it; and you when you come.' Kitty hugged her father. 'Oh, daddy, please!'

Ted nodded resignedly. 'It's all so sudden.'

'I had to be sure. This letter helped. It's Sandy's letter. Uncle Sandy. Read it.'

Ted took the letter. 'This is two years old, more.'

'I should've given it more thought then. It came when I didn't want to know. I've been a fool.'

The letter read: "Dearest Kitty, Thank you for the snaps. You look so like Emma and yet different. I suppose that's because you and Emma are on the opposite sides of the bra-burning divide—a joke, to tell you I'm not a 'fuddy old duddy'. So read this letter to the end and promise you'll listen and not mind listening.

"As family we care for you, terribly. You're no longer a child with endless time on your hands. So, you can't go on living the way you have, without hurting others and burning yourself out. The 60s slogan of doing your own thing, leads only to behaving unwisely. Wisdom comes from knowledge and understanding and not from freedom to act on impulse. You admit marrying John was a mistake. In so short a time he has made you unhappy. My heart goes out to you. But I have to say, it's a lesson from which to learn. Grown-ups are as often right as they are wrong.

"It was sweet of you to pay me compliments I'm sure I don't deserve. You have a generous nature and I'll try to be worthy of your trust . . . Some adults see children about to run into a wall and believe by keeping mum, children will learn what it means to 'bang one's head' against it. I know walls and let me assure you, if you haven't already found out, it hurts like hell. My most important advice is to suggest you spend more time with your father. As a doctor he has been in touch with people and the world and now that he has retired, let him be the good father he wants to be. Love hurts. Lovers hurt each other. When love is creative and a dynamic flame, it's worth keeping that fire going. But when the fire has gone out, don't stir or trouble with the embers, unless there's fuel to bring it to life again. But then there's "Time's Winged Chariot". It is getting to that time when you must settle down and take life for the gift it is and give up playing with fire.

"Dear girl, be single-minded. Concentrate on what is rewarding and on that alone. If you do, serenity lies ahead. I wish I could return to forty and be forty forever. For most people it is a time when much of the stresses of passion and adjustments are over; the mountains climbed and a calm plateau reached. Life's journey begins here and the views are beautiful. Before that, all was preparation. If you're constantly packing, unpacking, the journey can't begin. Finish your packing, get rid of those items which are too heavy to carry and weighing you down: and set off. Don't miss out on the views and all the wonderful dawns and sunsets of a tranquil life. Much love. Mr Sandman—you called me that when you were little—well, Mr Sandman brings you a dream!

"PS The single life is not without its blessings. Think of my friend Bill. He quoted someone saying that we should live as if each day is our last, and added that that is only half of it. Also, live as if each tomorrow is a new adventure. S."

'Dad, why are you smiling?'

Ted handed back the letter. 'In Camelot Sandy would've been a Knight of the Round Table. That's the serious Sandy. I was amused at the thought of the schoolboy in him. Emma wrote to me about this very letter. She asked Sandy to write to you. He agreed, adding, he was going to ask you to be promising and not promiscuous.' Ted saw Kitty frown. 'It amused me then. I've ruined the punch-line by forgetting something.'

'I'm teasing, dad. Of course, it's funny. Funny, ha ha, I mean. And clever.' She gave her father a quick hug. 'I'm sorry about last night. But Mum did get at me.'

'After last night's row, she'll suffer an apoplectic fit when she learns you're planning to live and work in India,'

'I don't care. Oh, but dad, you do approve, and you're going to help!'

'Yes, through Miss Das and Dinesh too.'

'Thanks dad. I know it's none of my business, but why is Mabel here? I thought . . .'

'She's here for your sake. Not mine. She came to offer you a job in her Company.'

'Why after all this time. She didn't seem to care.'

'I see my mother, your grandmother's hand in her sudden interest.'

After a thoughtful pause she said: 'You didn't mention Bill? He'd help.' Something in the way he looked alarmed her. 'What's the matter?'

'It's a pity you never met Bill.'

'But I did! On holiday in India. That giant of a man. Uncle Sandy's friend.'

'So you did. Gosh! You'd have been fourteen or fifteen then!'

She looked past him and went to the sofa by the fireside. 'You had collected the post early this morning? What's in that packet?'

'Papers from Bill's lawyers.' He picked up the brown paper packet. 'A strange, rare coincidence, your decision. I can now show you the plan of the school buildings.' They moved to the dining area of the L-shaped room. Ted turned on the light and spread the papers on the dining table. 'The school will be run by, the Mission—an incentive to get them to see the project through. I'm a trustee.'

'Daddy! Something's happened. It's Bill. What's happened to Bill?'

'He told the Mission he was going to Tibet. I knew that. He wrote to tell me about his trip. Well, he hasn't been seen or heard of, since. Five or six months have past.'

'What do you think has happened?'

Ted shrugged. 'They haven't said more than that he's simply disappeared. Miss Das, that's Maami, wrote to me about Bill's disappearance, but I didn't think it important at the time. He was always appearing and disappearing. Now his lawyers have sent these papers. So they must know. There could have been an accident. I've seen, with my own eyes, the path the locals call the road to Tibet. It's stony and steep. Doubly dangerous after a snowfall. Some parts, beyond the bit I reached, are precipitous. He probably lost his footing.'

Kitty had covered her mouth and looked at her father with terrified eyes.

'He told me he often looked at those great mountains and thought of Mallory. "What a wonderful and heroic way to die", he said. "Symbolic of man dying as he reaches out beyond himself." Bill was a dear and special person.' Ted gazed sadly at her. 'Kitty,' he began, then he slumped forward with his hands on the table; and wept.

Kitty put her arms round him. 'My sweet father!' She whispered. Kissed him and rested her head on his bent shoulders.

'I'm ashamed to cry.'

'No, dad! There's no shame.'

'Bill said that in facing the death of others we weep for ourselves. He's right. I am thinking about my own sorrows. I tried to hide things from you. After all, you had your own difficulties. I wondered sometimes if you guessed about your mother and me?'

She nodded. 'I knew.'

'When you say you knew, do you really mean you know? For how long?'

'Dad, you're such an innocent. I probably knew from the beginning.'

'You mean when you were eleven—twelve?'

'Yes. Don't worry about it. And I knew for certain when we were in India, and mum didn't come with us.'

Ted dug his hands deep into the pockets of his cardigan and stared at the table.

'Besides,' she continued, those frequent letters from Nairobi, and mums trips to Rye, and the long weekends away from us.' She sat heavily on a chair. 'You poor thing. You should have ended it long ago. Not worried about me. And begun again with someone who would have cared for you . . . the way you deserve!' She shook her head. 'You're straight out of a John Buchan novel. Bill too. You know what I mean. Stiff upper lip and all that. Just the types to confirm uncle Sandy's mad ideas of the English. Oh, why daddy? Why didn't you do something.'

'Because it would have been irresponsible and because of the pain and the anguish it would've caused . . . most of all, because I would've lost you.' He sighed. 'We won't talk about it anymore. Now, if you're serious about India, you need to do some courses, and learn an Indian language. Punjabi, I'd say. In the meantime, we'll plan a couple of trips to India and see how the school is getting on and what you're taking on. By the way, this is Bill's letter to his solicitor and this is his note addressed to me.'

Kitty read: "Dear Ted, I'm sorry to burden you with this, but I have no one else—and in case anything should happen, you know something about my project. Please see it through. I forgot to mention—it was sometime ago—the idea of a school was first suggested by Emma. When the time comes, you might help Miss Das in interviewing teachers and staff. She thinks very highly of you and may press you to send her some books on education. There's a good chap. Bill. PS Look after Sona and Ransingh."

Suddenly they were aware of Mabel's presence in the room. 'Good morning, Mabel,' said Ted. 'I didn't hear you?'

'Good morning. Was that the postman? Earlier on?'

Ted nodded.

Mabel stared. Her habit of keeping her lips tightly shut had, in time, drawn hard lines at the corners of her mouth, otherwise she was still a handsome woman with cold grey eyes. Her blue rinsed hair was neat; for any impact sleep had on a head so frequently coiffured, was repaired by a few flicks of the brush. 'I know the village post is erratic, but why turn up at such an unearthly hour? Why do you allow people to take advantage of your soft nature!'

'You can say that again!' trilled Kitty.

Mabel glared at her daughter.

'It seemed earlier than it was, Mabel.' Ted sounded very tired. 'I did ask Tom, as a special favour, to bring anything from India as soon it came. I've been a bit anxiously awaiting news about Bill. And it happens to be the first Monday, when Tom drives to Chesham. He likes an early start. So the choice was morning or late evening.'

'And you had to choose to live in the middle of nowhere.'

'I love this cottage. I find it suitable and convenient. You came without warning.'

'Kitty happens to be my daughter, and I don't need your leave to see her.'

'Mother,' Kitty said acidly, 'Kitty is a woman and not a child!'

'Congratulations. And when you make some sensible, mature decisions, I shan't forget. If I think of you as a child it is because you behave like one.'

'That,' said Ted raising his voice, 'is uncalled for.'

'Shut up Ted! Have you forgotten last night. What has madam to say for that?'

'Madam is sorry about last night. But,' Kitty folded her arms, 'madam has a lot to say. To begin with I'm not a bit interested in working in anything as frivolous as the fashion industry. I haven't finished, mother. Wouldn't you like to know my plans for the future. My mature and sensible decision?'

Mabel flashed a brilliant sneer. 'No, Kitty. I've heard enough. I'm going to have a bath. And I shall leave for London before lunch. I suppose without your company.' She turned with regal dignity and left the room.

'That was harsh,' said Ted. 'Tell her. Over breakfast. I'm afraid she'll decide to have nothing to do with you. She's your mother and probably will outlast me.'

'It doesn't matter. And it's too late, anyway. When your divorce came through, I had to choose. It was the easiest decision anyone has had to make.'

Ted folded the papers on the table and put them back into the large envelope. 'We'll look at these again, sometime later, shall we?' he said sadly.

Kitty took his arm and led him to the window-seat. They sat down and stared at the sky which had begun to cloud over. 'She never really cared for me.'

Ted gave a moment's thought before speaking. 'She was constantly told you were so like Emma; and she disliked Emma.'

'You never thought of having more children?'

'It was going on long before you guessed. Since you were three. He was an Italian. A dress designer or tailor, I don't know. I didn't suspect . . . I mean, he looked and . . . well from the way he walked and talked, I thought he was one . . . well, I was the wrong.'

'You believed he was gay?' She laughed. 'Don't punish yourself. Mother would've been the same whoever she married. Sexual fidelity is not her style.'

'If nothing else, Kitty, I kept my pride. I didn't go around, my horns on display.'

'Horns? I see,' Kitty laughed. 'Cuckold. And you hung on because of me? God! I've been such a burden to you.' Suddenly she burst into tears. 'Nothing I do will ever make up for those lost years.'

'There now, please stop!' He hugged her. 'You've had a hard time, too. I'll try to make up for that. I feel responsible. I adored and probably indulged you. Now, I'm happy you've chosen to do something . . . something you'll find fulfilling.'

They looked through the panes. 'It's getting dismal,' Ted said.

Kitty wiped the panes with the palm of her hand. 'It's started snowing again.'

'I really shouldn't let Mabel drive in this weather.'

After a pause Kitty said. 'Yes. I'll tell her she should wait till tomorrow.'

He hadn't heard. It will be snowing on those mountains, he thought, and in his mind came the vision of a clearing in a pine forest and a grave beneath a larch . . . He saw a gentle snowdrift moving down from the ridge into the wooded glen, softly obliterating two names. 'Oh Emma!' he mouthed softly. Kitty heard him, stroked his wide forehead, and ran her fingers through the curls of his white hair.

Higher in the mountains of Tibet a heavier snowfall covered the rocks and a human body made one with them . . . one within a bleak landscape, stark in its promise for those yearning to believe in love, life, hope and eternity . . . For we as ripening seed are sown to germinate and shape other lives. Had he? Ted wondered if as a father and physician he had reaped a good harvest of blessings. 'Come with me to the pub,' he said.

'Yes. But why?'

'I've a sudden longing to be with people. They serve breakfast, you know. Geoff will be there. He knew Jim Corbett in India. Corbett, the great hunter, who protected Indian villagers from man-eating tigers and wrote about it.'

'I don't know him. Corbett I mean. But tell me about him when we get there. I'll get dressed and warn mother we'll be back for lunch.'

'Turn on the wireless as you go.'

'And dad, change into boots, you can't wear those outside.'

⁂

Kitty lay on a bed in a room at the Nurpur Mission House, remembering her father's enigmatic smile, as he waved goodbye . . . till it merged into the many brown faces pressed against the glass at Palam Airport, where a turbaned Sikh first asked if she had electrical goods to declare, then flashed a perfect set of white teeth and let her through. And as she relived the long, long train journey to Pathankot in the "First Class Women Only" compartment, her eyes grew heavy . . . the train's rolling sensation crept back on her, and with it there drifted in a subconscious memory of a rocking cradle . . . She fell asleep.

⁂

PART II

THE HINDU

"But there is neither East nor West, Border, nor Breed, nor Birth . . ."

Rudyard Kipling

CHAPTER FIFTEEN

Ted Franks examined the window and lightly touched the framework. 'The rain is getting through.' He took out his handkerchief and wiped his hands. 'The putty needs replacing. I'll get Jim to do it.' He wiped the misted glass and peered into the garden. 'It's awful now but should be fine in time for your walk after tea. The weather chaps get it right, sometimes. Now, remember, while it's light. You don't want another fall?' He turned to face his mother and smiled, conscious of their rather formal relationship. 'As for Sandy, I have to disagree. One of the most intelligent chaps I've known. You may not think he was an intellectual. But believe me, he was that too.'

'I didn't expect you to agree. Just wanted you to know what I think.'

'That playful, boyish charm gave people the wrong impression. Made it hard to pin down what he stood for. His love for England, poetry and Emma, was rather obvious.' He paused. She waited. 'For Emma? Surely you believe that. It's better to be constant about some things than never to be constant at all.' He grinned.

'Don't be pompous, Ted!'

'Pompous? You mean trite or . . .'

'I meant what I said. Sandy wasn't intellectual enough for me. He was a romantic, not an intellectual. One can't be both. By defending him, you attack me.'

'Mother . . .' Ted began, then checked himself. The last thing he wanted to do was hurt her feelings; and though he knew her to be immune to criticism, she was looking unusually frail. 'Even when he was being—what you call—silly, nothing he said, even in jest, was simple. Always a sense of something profound would peep through.' He laughed. 'I remember some years into their marriage—asking him if he believed in angels. "Of course," was his immediate answer, "I'm married to one". I was amused, even pleased—he was talking about my sister—but I was also intrigued. I thought he was joking. He wasn't. He was deadly earnest!'

'I suppose that might disarm most people. But it's old-fashioned, sentimental. All right for my generation, not his. Do you believe in angels?'

'I don't know, mother. I don't give these things much thought.' He took a deep breath. 'Maybe I ought.'

'Rubbish!'

Ted studied his mother with undisguised admiration. She's magnificent for her age, he thought. 'Talk about believing, Emma believed in everything and everyone. Well, it explains why she never lost her temper, for one thing.'

'That's poppycock! She could be quite brusque. I should know. You wouldn't... nor Sandy. She doted on him, as she did your father before. And you were the ideal image of a big brother, precisely because you were away for long periods. Also because of the age gap. There was method in that madness. She could twist you round her little finger. As she did your father too.'

'But she never was demanding or difficult, and shut herself in a world of her own.'

'Only after Ian died.'

He started, surprised at her using her husband's first name. He could not recall when she last did that. She was staring at the carpet with compressed lips. Then with a sharp intake of breath she met his gaze implacably. He had only seen her cry once. That was when he was a boy and she had news of her mother's death. Was she going cry now! 'I should know Emma better than anyone else.' Her voice shook. 'Before Ian died she'd talk sixteen to the dozen... she could be sullen at times, till she had her way.'

'It didn't matter. She was a good girl. Never did anything unseemly?'

'Dinesh knew that side of her! I mean about those cold moods which simply cut you off. Like being sent to Coventry.'

'Dinesh is a self-centred prig and no judge of anything. Emma was never critical of anyone. Not even of him. She was so accepting.'

'Never critical of anyone? Well, even if that were true, you couldn't say never. How can you be certain? Besides one can be both critical and accepting.'

'That is even better.'

She shrugged. 'I suppose she was accepting. She would have accepted Trevor if Sandy wasn't around and been an equally good wife to him.'

Ted puffed his cheeks and shook his head ruefully. 'She'd have only married Trevor to please you. Then there'd have been another unhappy marriage in the family. Did you know that Emma had a rare quality and one that awed people. A serenity, people said, that was rare for a westerner. Many in the local Indian community, called her *Devi*, which is Hindi for goddess.'

'Yes, yes, I know what *Devi* means. But many women in India are called that. It's often used as a term of respect.'

'Yes mother, but in her case, it was more than just that. She, and Sona too, were held in special regard. But, to go back to you and Emma, I thought you two got on fine. That you spent happy hours together and that you were the dominant one—I mean this as a compliment. You even chose the clothes she wore?'

'Mabel thought so too. Emma didn't care about fashions—about what was "in" or what was "out". And she wouldn't let me get rid of my old frocks. Mind you, they were tailor-made by the Cantonment *durzi* in Poona.' She chuckled. 'The man was a rascal but an excellent tailor.'

'What made you keep them?'

'Sentiment. Why does one keep anything which has outlived its use? Emma loved trying on my frocks, dresses—should remember to say dresses—long before they fitted her. Sometimes I wondered if there was more to it than just dressing up . . . if you get my drift—you know, psychological? Her infatuation with your father? Taking my place.

'You needn't elaborate, mother.'

'It didn't always strike me as healthy. Fortunately, he was an upright man. At least I think so . . .'

'I know so. He was as straight as a . . . they don't come any straighter. Dismiss any suspicions in the area of . . .'

'I have. Can't think why I said it.'

'You've often said she was a great help in the kitchen. That's where many a mother and daughter relationships are forged.'

'Spoken like a man. Yes, she liked housework, but on her terms and when the mood took her. But more hours were spent locked away in her room—reading or painting, or at the piano. And God knows what she did for whole afternoons at the cemetery!'

'Why didn't you go with her? I'm sorry, I know it's not for me to say this. I know your feelings about . . . but you could have . . . once or twice . . . for her sake?'

She looked away. The rain had stopped. The late afternoon light from the window bathed the room with an orange glow. She rose with the help of her stick and walked stiffly to join him at the window. He knew she would not answer. His father's death was a subject upon which she maintained a resolute silence and he was never to learn why. 'I said the evening would turn out fine.' He rubbed the glass with his elbow and pointed to the garden, aware, for the first time since he arrived from London, that the water-lilies had not come out this year . . . Emma's lilies. 'The sensible thing now, for us', he added, 'is to forget.' Ted wanted to say more but knew she hated sentimentality and giving her the last word should clear the air. He waited, trying not to smile. It came.

'Don't be soppy, Ted.' She went back to her chair and with her stick indicated his favourite armchair by the coffee table. 'I want to talk to you about something else.'

'Are we back on the subject of Mabel's letter?'

She nodded. 'Why it had to be Poland? Of all places!'

Ted grimaced and made a helpless gesture with his hands. 'Ancestral voices? It's where here family came from.'

'Do take this seriously. And you needn't remind me she's a Pole by descent. But I thought that that connection was broken. Past and forgotten? Who's left there?'

'A great uncle, with an unpronounceable name, somewhere near Danzig. He may have left her money . . . which she doesn't need. As you know, she's got bags of it.'

'She didn't have to shut the business. She was doing so well. Wasn't she?'

'I think she'd exhausted her talent. Mabel, mother, was very much a woman of the sixties. The grunge—or whatever you call today's trend—is not her scene.'

'Nonsense. Anything goes these days. We're straying from the point. I don't like the idea of you living alone, now that Kitty's gone. Ted don't you think you should . . .'

'Mother, this is futile!' Ted stood up. He lit a cigarette, walked to the window, then turned to look her. 'Can't we spend time together without you mentioning Mabel?' He clamped his jaw, then opened it. 'Anyway, why won't you let me see her letter?'

'Because she expressly asked me not to give you her address.'

He chuckled. 'What makes her think I'm interested? The nerve, to imagine I'd want to contact her after all this time?' He waited with raised eyebrows, then quickly added as his mother was about to speak: 'And don't tell me that I should've been firm, or that I didn't know how to handle the woman.'

'I wasn't going to say anything of the kind!' Her mouth twitched petulantly.

'How do you handle a woman, who earns twice as much as you do and is no longer in love with you?' He asked sardonically.

'By putting your foot down. If you had been firm with her there would have been no scandal and no divorce. I'm old fashioned enough to be embarrassed by those sort of things happening in the family. Not for religious or moral reasons. And not just one but two divorces in the family.'

'You promised to leave Kitty out of this? And, I distinctly remember your whole-hearted approval of Kitty's divorce.'

She growled and looked away.

'What were you going to say? Earlier on? When I interrupted?'

'Never mind!' After a pause she added, 'and I don't recall talking about Mabel the last time you came.' She sniffed sullenly and rubbed the back of her hands. 'I shan't talk. You persist on misunderstanding me. It is most unfair. You should apologise.'

'I'm sorry mother. I just want you to accept Mabel is out of my life and I want you to realise I'm jolly glad I don't have to think about her.'

'You're just like your father.'

'Now what's that supposed to mean?'

'Nothing.' She pursed her lips and the hands on her lap quivered with emotion. 'I see you've taken up smoking again?'

He went back to his chair and sat down, took a deep breath and leaning forward to stub his cigarette, searched for an ashtray.

'I've got rid of them . . . rather, Betty has. Get a saucer in the kitchen.' When he returned she asked. 'When, indeed, did you start smoking again?'

'I don't know. Six months? You must know. I've smoked in front of you before.'

'You should know better. I'm sure you advise your patients to give up smoking and don't smoke in front of them?'

'Mother! It's three years since I gave up my practice.'

'You could have been a consultant. Can't understand why you turned that down. You could have made a name for yourself, and money.'

'That's all behind me now. I'm enjoying my retirement and . . . and my writing.'

'Such a waste of time. Who will want to read the story of . . . never mind.'

'If you cared to listen, there is a lot about Emma and Sandy that is fascinating. Particularly the sort of person Emma became in India.'

She waved a hand. 'I was trying to help. I mean, about you and Mabel. With Kitty away, I thought you . . .'

'Mother, this is repetitious! And for Pete's sake mother! I hope you haven't been interfering. You don't seem to realise this—Mabel won't thank you for trying to bring us together. You should've seen her face light up when I told her my decision to . . . The sigh of relief from her was such, I bet it could be heard for miles. I'm not complaining. It was a great weight off my shoulders too.'

'Why did you take the blame?'

'You know. We've been through this before?'

'Remind me.'

'Well, keen as she was about the divorce she wasn't going to expose her guilt or her affairs. It didn't matter to me. It was the quickest, least sordid way of getting what I wanted.' He grinned.

'She may have ridden out into the sunset untarnished, but it also saved me leaving a public court wearing horns as large as antlers.'

She laughed.

'I do so love it when you laugh.' He got up and kissed her forehead.

'How is the book getting on?' She murmured softly. 'Don't take notice of what I say.' She patted the hand on her shoulder. 'I suppose I come out rather badly in it.'

'A little insensitive perhaps.'

'Yes, I suppose I'm insensitive. I've been thinking of Emma, a lot recently. She was so dreamy and unprepared for the world. That's what being religious did for her.'

'Emma was unworldly. Is that the same as being religious? Possibly. But I'm not so sure. She had a strange indifference to life and to people about her. We know why. She was so completely infatuated by father and, of course, was never going to meet anyone like him in her generation.'

'Rubbish. You don't mean some kind of sexual hang up made her a frigid? But now we sense a contradiction; or have I got you wrong? Whatever, she was an innocent.'

'She was too bright to be innocent. Too talented and interested in literature and art to be ignorant. A little self-absorbed, apart from father's, she liked her own company. His death left a lacuna. A cavity, into which she dug herself.'

'I don't know what you mean.'

'To be unworldly is a kind of wisdom, with its own measure of satisfaction.' He smiled. 'I'm quoting. You never met Bill Clayton? A giant of a man physically. And mentally too, and seemed bigger than his six feet six. Sandy called him "Sierra Padre". He had many names for Bill. "Moses" was another. Bill was a monk, or rather, because he did not belong to any monastic order, a priest who was celibate.'

'I saw him once, briefly. Very impressive. Do you think he took advantage of her? Sandy, I mean . . . advantage of Emma.'

'If he did, she wanted him too. Emma was no moral weakling. I've seen her freeze men in their tracks with a look. Sandy was right for her. She couldn't have found a better husband. Certainly not a more patient and adoring one. And Emma knew it.'

'If you've told me this once, you've told it to me a hundred times. You loved him too. You encouraged them. I mean, you did nothing to stop them.'

'I couldn't, not after seeing how happy Emma was to be with him. I did think about it, because of the pressures on such marriages. I'm glad I didn't.'

'She gave herself to him all right! Yes, even before they were married. Oh, I knew! They couldn't hide it from me. They were far too relaxed in each other's company, that night, when she sprang the news. She took the one step that would make it impossible for me to object. She knew I would know . . . so maybe after all you're right. She wasn't innocent. I wasn't going to let a bastard ruin the family name, let alone a striped one.'

'Striped one? What a terrible thing to say!'

'Don't look at me like that. I'm no racist. I'm merely being factual.'

'Even so, it's not always the case. The child could've taken after Emma. Still, didn't we all envy Sandy's olive complexion? I did.'

'Anyway, it wasn't to be. I hoped there'd be a grandson, striped or unstriped.' She sighed deeply. 'It's a mystery why some women turn out to be barren.'

'In her case a blessing. Child-birth would've killed her. I'm astonished she lived as long as she did with that heart condition. There again, we have Sandy to thank.'

She mumbled and her face clouded with a suddenness that surprised him. When she spoke her voice was low but distinct. 'I suppose you're proud of the part you played in all this?'

He stared at her with an expression of sheer exhaustion. It was the same accusation she made on the day he returned from Heathrow after seeing Sandy and Emma off on their honeymoon in Italy. He said nothing then but now he was determined not to let it pass. She was looking away. He waited.

'You brought India into the house and India took Emma from me.'

'What do you mean? India was here long before me! You and father brought India. Britain brought India!'

'Don't be obtuse, Ted. You saw what was coming. Mabel did and wanted to stop it. You could've stopped inviting him to your London home.'

'We're going round in circles. I needed him too. What with Mabel's attitude. He was good company. He never spoke about Emma, until I brought her into the conversation. We've been through this and we're agreed he was the best thing that happened for her. Without his patience, gentleness, she would've remained a spinster or worse, in some institution . . . depressed, suicidal.'

'Poppycock! She had reserves . . . there was her art . . .' Her voice grew shaky and she began to tremble. 'Ted, he took her away . . .' She reached a hand out to him. He leapt up and took it in both his hands. 'And now you've let India take Kitty as well.'

'I will always miss Kitty,' he said. 'But she's not a child. And now she's happy in her work. You've seen her letters. Here she was irresponsible, with far too many temptations to keep her that way. You hated the sort of life she led.'

She took a deep breath. 'Poor Sandy!' she murmured. Ted was taken aback. She shook her head. 'I was hard on him, I know. I shall regret that as long as I live. And as I believe the mind lives on after death, I suppose it will be my eternal regret.'

For some minutes neither spoke. Then she said: 'Why wasn't she arrested?'

'Arrested? Who are you talking about?'

'That Goldie woman. The one whose name meant gold. The young girl—though I suppose she's no longer young—the woman they adopted . . . the Tibetan.'

'I know who you mean. What about her? Why should she have been arrested?'

'Charged or prosecuted? Whatever.'

'I still don't understand . . . ?'

'Didn't she murder Sandy? Or helped him die—which in my book is still murder. Didn't she? She knew a lot about herbal medicine. Don't you remember? She gave me some minty green concoction when I had a tummy upset . . . Delhi belly the doctor called it. A useless man . . . Emma would have been better cared for here.'

'No, mother. He was a good man. He knew his stuff. I should know. Indian doctors almost without exception are good. Emma didn't need specialist attention. Love and aspirins. She got both.' Ted leaned forward, 'where did you get this idea of Sona . . . yes that's her name . . . where did you get this idea about her doing anything to Sandy? You mustn't say things like that. There's no evidence. None that would link her . . . except the fact she was there when Sandy died.'

'We'll never know. The doctor prevented Dinesh . . . I know the boy wanted some kind of *post mortem* or police inquiry.'

'There, I said the doctor had more sense than you credit him. He would've known if Sandy had been poisoned. Sandy wanted to die and willed himself to die. These things happen, rarely, but they do. Besides Sandy wasn't overly robust . . .'

'Overly?' she sniffed

'He never quite recovered from that awful incident. If Sona gave him anything . . . and remember she was devoted to Sandy, it would've been something to help him with the trauma of Emma's death. And she wouldn't have done that without Sandy's insistence. But this is all conjecture. I don't believe any of it. Sandy used all the power of his will, and willed himself to die. As I said, these things do happen.'

'Dinesh said there was a sickly sweet organic smell in the room. At first he thought that was the Tibetan beer she gave him.'

'Chang.'

'Whatever it's name. Perhaps she put something in it. Though we will never know.'

'The desirable result was achieved. Personally, I think Sandy was dying. He could have gone first. In one of her letters Emma expressed her concern about his health. He himself wrote that he couldn't bear the thought of living without Emma.'

'I go along with Dinesh. I believe it was a conspiracy that involved not only Sona and Sandy but the doctor as well.'

'I repeat. It was a fortuitous death. Sandy was spared all the suffering of a desolate and inconsolable bereavement. But how on earth . . . I see. Dinesh has written to you?'

'I got his letter last week.'

'After all these years?'

'Yes. It was a long letter. He was opening his heart out. The poor boy . . .'

'He's nearly thirty.'

'He has such feelings of guilt. Feels he behaved abominably to Sandy . . . Emma . . . That apart, the boy's unhappy. In trouble. I wish I could help, but I don't see how I can!'

'Take care. One never knows with Dinesh. You said trouble? What trouble?'

'I'm tired now, Ted. I'll tell you next time.' She struggled to get up. He helped her. 'Thank you,' she said. 'Before you go, leave a note in the kitchen for Betty. Say, I'll only have a poached egg on toast for supper.'

'By the way, where is Betty?'

'On an errand. I haven't forgotten. Pity she's not back, you'll get your present when you come next. Enjoy this evening. Sorry I can't be there but I haven't the strength to be sociable and Spalding's wife can be so erudite. There, I've even forgotten her name, and she wouldn't have forgiven me for that.'

'Thank you, but you needn't have troubled. I'm too old for birthday presents.'

'It's just a shirt and a tie to go with it. You haven't been dressing with the care you used to.' She gave a tired smile. 'You were a beautiful baby. My only baby for years. I wasn't to know, eleven . . . thirteen years later, I'd have Emma. She was Ian's daughter . . . You must believe that. There must be no doubt. Emma was your father's daughter. Whatever our disappointments, we never broke the rules. We had, if nothing else, the moral discipline so sadly lacking these days. There, now, kindly open the window. It's turning out to be one of those sultry evenings I love.'

'Goodbye, mother,' he whispered, and as he bent down to kiss her, she held his face in her hands and peered deeply into his bewildered grey eyes. A strange feeling gripped him. She sank back into her chair. 'You haven't seen me cry and you're not going to now. Off you go . . . and don't forget the note for Betty.'

When he left the room, she was sitting very still, gazing through the window at the dying light. That's how Betty found her the next day—not slumped, her patrician head in silhouette—dead. Later, Ted found the letter addressed to him. It was in the top drawer of her writing desk and read: "Dear Ted, Don't feel sad about Emma. You were a good brother to her and she loved you for it. As for me,

I hope I shall meet her and make amends. Sandy too. I don't know whether these things can be. But it's good to believe. I do, really. I have lived too long. Long enough to see you old and alone. Try not to be alone. Get Kitty to come back. India can't be good for her, not now, and things are unlikely to improve. The house in Winchester is hers now. Sell the house in Chalfont St Giles and get together again. Love Edith."

CHAPTER SIXTEEN

Dinesh looked out from the balcony of his luxurious flat on Malabar Hill. He was in his blue, hand woven, cotton dressing-gown and having just had a shower, a towel of deep indigo rested on his shoulders. He had come out to take in the panoramic view of the haunts of Bombay's moneyed classes, for the last time. Sacked from his post as Chief Executive of Agarwal Hotels Limited, the company flat had to be surrendered. He had no idea who was replacing him and though he could have stayed on till the end of the month, he had no intention of waiting to find out or, as it was already mid-June, of being stranded by the monsoon rains. Seth Agarwal, had moved with a suddenness that was both clandestine and ruthless. But Dinesh, by now, familiar with his father-in-law's methods, was not caught unprepared. A hired furniture van had already collected his desk, a table, four chairs and two book shelves, with instructions to deliver these to a named depot in Dharamsala.

He dabbed his face with the towel, then took out the watch in his dressing-gown pocket and studied it. The large Rolex watch gleamed opulently in the morning light. He smiled as he remembered that the Company had not included it on the list of items to be returned; and though money was the least of his worries, he would keep it.

It was eight o'clock on the morning of June fifteenth. The heat and humidity of the monsoon season of wind and rain was making its ominous presence felt. On the horizon, beyond the grand sweep of Marine Drive, he saw dark, foreboding clouds gather. A low rumble of thunder, like the roll of distant drums, reached him. He turned. Below him the uniformed girls of Sacred Heart Convent High School were lining up for their morning assembly. He clicked his tongue and gave his mouth a wry twist, as his mind went back ten years almost to the day of that holiday in Mussoorie, when he rode his pony past the tall gates of another school for girls; and picked out the girl who was to be his wife. She was by the half opened gate, ushering the other girls in. He recalled her, as she was then, full and firm breasted, a slimmer, more cheeky, Shanti. 'Stop staring at my boobs! Everyone's keeps staring at my boobs.' She giggled. 'All you men have a filthy minds. Go, go, you're not supposed to be hanging around here.'

'I wasn't staring at you. I happened to be passing.'

'They all say that,' she retorted coquettishly. 'Passing and making passes. Anyway, you von't see anything again. Today, last day, tomorrow the holidays begin.'

'And you live here?'

'No, no. I live near Dharamsala, I mean Pathankot.'

'God, what a coincidence! I'm from there. Well, not quite, higher up the valley.'

'I know,' she retorted, with a nautch dancer's movement of her neck. 'I've seen you in the market. Once with some Tibetan woman bossing you around! Hurry! hurry! [this to the girls] stop being so inquisitive. Learn to mind your own business. Late for school you know . . . [then back to Dinesh] . . . I know about you. I got daddy to find out. You're doing higher studies in England. No? And so talking like a bloody *angrezi* fellow.' She giggled. '*Arrey*, struck dumb? Don't remember seeing me? Why? Am I not pretty?'

To that he had replied, simply. 'I think you are pretty.'

'Sexy too!' Again she wriggled, making her large eyes dart from side to side like a Kathakali dancer. 'I'm Seth Agarwal's daughter.'

'Incredible! But I know your father! I mean I know about him.'

She pushed in the last comer with "get in you starey cat" and shut the gate behind her. 'His only daughter,' she said through the bars of the gate, 'so, you see, there'll be big, big dowry. Make a good Indian wife. Not like flirty English girl-friends.' He had bridled at that taunt and shouted back. 'I'm a Nationalist. I don't like anything English. Just then a voice below him called out "Shanti" above the school bell. Another Shanti!

Dinesh turned from the balcony. 'If I was thirty then, instead of twenty!' He shut his eyes and cursed the day he set eyes on her.

'A good Indian wife!' he growled under his breath as he entered the adjoining air conditioned bedroom. For the last two months, he had confined himself to this room, with its attached bathroom and balcony, avoiding to see any other part of the flat associated with her. He threw himself on the bed and rested on its cool sheets. There was a gentle knock on the door. 'Anthony?'

'Good morning, sahib! *Chhota hazari.*' His man servant entered carrying a tray and looked nervously at his employer. 'Sorry sahib, morning tea.'

'That's all right Anthony. You can say *chota hazari*, if you like.'

Anthony put the tray on the bedside table, knelt and began massaging Dinesh's legs.

'Listen, Anthony. Very important. Pack the two suitcases and leave everything else as it is. Then put them in a taxi. And, as I said yesterday, we must not leave together or be seen together. Take the suitcases to Bombay Central Station. I gave you money?'

Anthony patted his shirt pocket and rolled his head in affirmation. 'Yes, sahib, safe with me. I put safety pin on top pocket.'

'Leave the suitcases in the Luggage Office. Don't lose the ticket. Then back to my office. Hand over the keys of this flat. Then back to wait outside the station. I'll meet you there. One hour from now, to take train to Poona.'

'Poona! Then sahib, V.T. Station. Not Bombay Central.'

Dinesh smacked his forehead. 'Victoria Terminus! Yes, yes.'

'No worry, I wait outside V.T. for sahib. And I . . .' Anthony stopped massaging. He sniffed and wiped his tears with the back of his hand.

Dinesh sat up. 'Anthony, it is safest for me to be in a hotel. If you work for me, your life is in danger. They will catch you in the market and beat you till you tell them where I am. They may even kill you.' Dinesh stared at his crestfallen servant, who was sitting frog-like on his haunches with head bowed between hands resting on his knees. 'God knows, Anthony, how much I'll miss you. You're best cook and honest man.'

'Sahib, tea going cold! I make you fresh?'

'No, Anthony. Leave it. I'll get breakfast at Natraj cafè. You tidy up while I dress.' Dinesh stood up and watched his faithful servant and relented. Three months severance pay seemed inadequate.

'Anthony! Put that tray down. Listen to me. Your brother has a Grog-shop in Goa, yes? Why not work with him?'

Anthony shook his head. 'It small shop. After paying rent, family *kharcha* . . .'

'You mean family's expenses? He's got a family?'

'Two boys going school.'

'Then what about finding another job here? You have good supporting letters.'

'Job hard to getting these days. Also being Roman Catholic, more hard.'

'If I give you double money, you will have six months to find a job.'

'Thank you good sahib, God bless you, master!' Anthony bent down and touched Dinesh's feet. 'Maybe I find work in Goa. Sahib come there sometime. Nice place.'

'Listen. I'll take you there. Give myself a holiday in Goa. I'll see your brother. I will help him with money if he takes you on as a partner.' Anthony grovelled again. 'No, no Anthony. Stand up. For four months you have been good friend. I told you more than any sahib tell a servant. I have lot money but my life so very bad. I made a *kharab shaadi*—bad marriage. Also, I was not being good to kind uncle and aunt. Showed them no respect. Maybe, this God's punishment.'

'Young people, sahib, always making mistakes.'

'I'm a Hindu. You know what bad *karma* is? Bad action. Bad work is punished.'

'Christian not think that. We asket God to forgiving. He makes okay.'

'But what about the people we hurt? It's never okay for them.'

'They also know. They forgive. They also okay. That's how God makes okay. But sahib, I'm thinking. Sahib, take car. Why leave car? Your car. We go by car to Goa. I know way. I worked many years for Brown Car Company.'

'Then wait on steps outside VT Station. I come in car. We get luggage.'

When Dinesh Thakur arrived outside the Victoria Terminus station, Anthony was nowhere to be seen. The day was hot and humid. Had he moved to a shady part of the station forecourt? Dinesh parked his car in a bay under a *neem* tree and scanned the forecourt. Then he noticed a small, but rather noisy and abusive crowd in the far left hand corner, where the set of steps disappeared into a blind alcove. A blue uniformed policeman with a pill-box hat and a long *lathi*, was making a leisurely but threatening progress towards them. The crowd began to disperse. Some were teenagers, who on seeing the policemen pointed to a body on the ground and giggled. '*Nasha, daru pia*'. 'He's drunk; fully loaded', a lanky youth addressed Dinesh. The policeman began to prod the body that lay on the ground. It was Anthony. He was bent double, with his arms pressed against his stomach. A low moan indicated he was still alive. '*Thairo!*' Dinesh called out with the natural authority of a man of his status. 'he's not drunk. I'll take care of him. Tell the constable.' He addressed the lanky youth who translated the message to the policeman in Gujarati. The police constable walked towards Dinesh. He pointed with the *lathi* and spoke angrily. 'I know English!' Dinesh raised a placatory hand: 'He is my *naukar*, my servant. My car is there. Help me to put him in the car.' At the sight of a foreign car, the policeman smiled ingratiatingly. 'Bring car this place', he said. When Dinesh did that, he helped to carry the groaning Anthony and laid him flat on the back seat of his vintage Alfa Romeo, which Dinesh had bought in Gwalior, from a member of the Maharaja's family. 'Little blood coming from tooth,' the policeman said, 'otherwise he okay.' Dinesh thanked the policeman, who hesitated. Dinesh took out a ten rupee note from his wallet and gave it to him. 'This is for a cup of tea.' The policeman deftly pocketed the note and, mumbling that there was no need for it, as he was simply doing his duty.

Dinesh opened the back door of the car and bent over Anthony. 'Can you talk?' he whispered. Anthony opened his eyes painfully and nodded. 'Sahib, they came, but I not tell.' He spoke pausing for breath between words. 'They asked for you, but I not tell.'

'Good man, Anthony. What did they do to you?'

'They *maro* me a lot. Beat me, knock me down . . . kicking stomach.'

Dinesh realised it was pointless to ask about the suitcases. He also noted Anthony's shirt pocket had been ripped off. 'They stole the money?'

'They throw money at people and run away.' He tried to sit up.
'No, no. Lie flat Anthony. Don't move.'

But Anthony insisted. He sat up with painful difficulty, clutched his stomach again and bent forward. 'It better this way.' Then he felt the trickle of blood down the right side of his mouth, and wiped it with the back of his hand. He rolled his tongue around his teeth and sucked in. 'They break tooth. Why memsahib's father so angry with you? He using *goondas*. Bad men, who beat people up. What you done sahib?'

'Seth Aggarwal, knows many bad people, all over India.'

'But why so angry?'

'Because I am leaving job and memsahib. That is an insult to his honour. Now, let me take you to hospital. There's a cut on your head that needs bandaging.'

'No hosspittal here! Think sahib. They expect you go there.' He moaned and rolled in pain. 'Take me Goa . . . Hosspittal there.'

'That will take many hours. You need to see a doctor.'

'Sahib is good driver. Get there soon. I okay for long time.'

'We'll stop at Ratnagiri. In the meanwhile you must have Anadin.' Dinesh opened the boot and returned with a silver hip flask of brandy. Drink this and take these white pills. They are for pain.'

'Not with brandy, sahib.'

'Then I'll stop somewhere soon and get you a bottle of soda water.'

They arrived in Goa the next day before noon. Earlier Anthony had received medical attention at Ratnagiri Hospital, where, later in the car park they rested for a few hours. Now Anthony lay bandaged and heavily sedated. Dinesh spoke to him but when he got no reply he panicked, stopped the car, jumped out and accosted the first person he saw. 'Hello, what is this place?'

The stranger was tall, with curly black hair and thick lips. 'This is Mapsa.'

'And where's the nearest hotel?'

'You're looking at it, mun. Across the road. Cost you, mun. Rich tourist only. You one of them? Can you spare a fiver?'

With a hurried thank you and a wave, Dinesh got back into the car and drove into the Hotel Braganza. He booked a room and was told he could park the car at the rear. 'Are you the manager?' The thickset man at the counter wore a smart suit. 'No. I'm owner, proprietor, but we have a manager. Can I help you, mun?'

'I want someone to ring for an ambulance. I have a very sick man in my car.' The man stared at him. 'He needs urgent attention. I don't care what it costs.'

'Then, sir,' said the proprietor in a tone of deep respect, 'leave it to me. My wife is doctor also. That your car. Good car, mun. If you think of selling, mun, then . . .'

'No, not now. Don't waste time, please!'

'I'm going now. You, there. Bell boy! Take . . . no luggage sir? Show sahib room number nine.'

'You said your wife is a doctor. Could she arrange to get my man to a Hospital?'

'Don't worry, mun. She calls, ambulance comes pronto. But it will cost yer.'

'As I said, money is no object. Could she see he gets urgent attention and a bed. Not left to lie on the floor. Thank you, and oh, I'll need a toothbrush and a night suit.'

'Certainly, sir. The hotel has shops; everything you want, mun. Lunch now. Dinner from seven to ten. Please sign, here. My name is John Fernandez. Nice to do business with you sir. Not to worry. Leave it awl to me.'

'Good. I'll rest now, but I'd like to visit my man in the hospital this evening.'

'Hotel chauffeur will take you there, sir. Not far.'

'Then I'd rather walk. I could do with a stretch.'

'Hundred, two hundred yards from Church. You can see Church from here.'

'Could I have a wake up call. 4 p.m. I'll have tea before I set out.'

'At precisely 4 p.m. Dinesh's room telephone rang. It was not the receptionist but John Fernandez on the line. 'Ah, Mr Thakur. Do me the honour by joining me for tea. Take your time. I'll be in the Restaurant.'

Half an hour later Fernandez welcomed him with open arms, and led him to a table, Almost immediately a waiter laid a tray, poured two cups of tea, placed plates of cakes sandwiches and scones and left. 'This is kind of you, but I'll just have a cup of tea and be on my way,' Dinesh said. 'I would like to get back before dark.'

'Your wish sir, is my command. My card. I've drawn a rough map of the way. As I said, not far. Also a slightly longer scenic route. I'd hoped to discuss some business, it taking just a few minutes. It can wait.'

'We have a few minutes. Tell me, do you by any chance, besides this hotel, own a grog shop . . . or bar, here in Goa?'

'Why, Mr Thakur, I own many grog shops?'

'I thought you might. I've heard of one somewhere on Colva beach.'

'Yes. Lucinda's Bar. My wife's name. Managed by a fellow called Denzil Lobo.'

'Good grief! He's my man's brother!'

'Your man! The fellow in hospital? What surprise, mun.'

'Then *I have* a business proposition to make for you and Denzil Lobo.'

'Mr Thakur, I can guess, so let me save you time. I have no intention of selling the property. It's far away from other bars I own, but it's my only toe-hold in Colva.'

'All right, don't sell. He pays you rent? Well, from now on. I'll pay the rent. I want my man to work for him. Bill me each month. I can arrange a standing order. Trust me'

'Okay. Look, if you're so keen, I sell the shop. Market price, but on one condition. You throw in the car, gratis?'

'My car?' Dinesh smiled as he stared at Fernandez. It already had occurred to him that his car would provide the necessary bait, and while he was sorry to lose it, it was proving to be a millstone round his neck. A distinctive car like his was easy to trace. 'All right, Mr Fernandez. But first I need it to get to Poona.'

'Take my driver. He'll drive it back. First we'll complete the paperwork before you go.' They shook hands. Fernandez coughed discreetly. 'One more thing, Mr Thakur, may I suggest you don't stay here longer than three days.'

'I had planned a week's holiday.' Dinesh said a little irately.

Mr Fernandez shook his curly grey head. 'For your own good.'

Dinesh froze, as the full import of the remark struck him. 'You know something?'

Mr Fernandez nodded. 'Seth Agarwal is a smuggler. He has contacts in Goa.'

Dinesh took a deep breath. 'You know him?'

Putting on a poker face was not in Fernandez's repertoire and he had long since given up trying. He dodged the question. 'What people do is none of my business, mun. I make suggestions and people can take it or leave it. But, let's say I don't like this Seth fellow. But I'm ready to do business with any chap who has good money.'

'My money is good and it's my own. Do me a favour. Please keep this transaction secret? For my man's sake.'

'I have many secrets, mun. My head is bursting with secrets.'

'Anthony, is no longer my servant. When I leave Goa he will have no information to give anyone about me. He's a fellow Goan, like you. Help him.'

'There are Goans and Goans,' Fernandez said cryptically. 'Not to say I won't help. Denzil said he had a brother. I know Denzil. His family. A good chap, mun, is Denzil. Well, once this deal is complete, I'll have no more interests in Colva Bay. But I cannot keep your presence here a secret for long. I look upon you as a friend. So a drink to our deal and your health. You must try my *feni*. The best in Goa. My speciality. Made from *caju* fruit. You know *caju*? Cashew?'

Dinesh regretted that glass of *feni*. He felt weak in the knees and queasy. Outside the hotel it was hot and steamy and his sweat-drenched shirt clung to him like poultice. He opened his shirt and blew down it, wondering if the oppressive heat had heightened the potency of the *feni*. He would take the scenic route in the hope that time and fresh air would wear away its effects. Supporting himself by leaning against the iron railings of a low bridge, he stared at the channel of water which flowed towards the silver sands of a beach fringed with coconut palms. In the distance a fishing boat, tied to its moorings, rolled gently, and on the shore, men, naked to their waists, dragged a long net as they sang a ballad. Dinesh looked without seeing. He wondered for how long he would have to be on the run. His decision to divorce Shanti had, naturally, angered her father and it was reasonable to expect the Seth to sack him. But it never occurred to him that his life would be at stake. And now, after the savage attack on Anthony, this threat took on a nightmarish quality. He could contact the police when he got to Poona but, without any concrete evidence, there was no reason for them to take him seriously, let alone offer to protect him. He had tried to get Shanti to answer his letters and get the Seth's threat in writing. But Seth Agarwal was no fool. Instead, he had sent his trusted chief accountant Munshi Popatlal to convey the threat verbally. 'Thakurji, you making big mistake. With respect, I say, don't go for divorcement. I am here to tell you, if you do, he will send *goondas* of the worst kind. Should you persist, he will see to it that you are killed.' 'Then I shall go to the police', he had replied. 'That,' the Munshi tutted, will not help. They will not believe you. I shall deny this conversation and you can prove nothing. The *goondas* will strike and disappear into thin air.' 'Munshiji, tell me why the Seth seeks revenge. Shanti, in all our years of marriage, has lived with her father more than she has lived with me. He indulges her every whim. He interfered. Ruined our marriage and in the two years I worked at the Bombay office, she has been with me less than three months. We have no children. Most of my Bombay friends think I'm a bachelor.' 'In that case,' rejoined the Munshi, 'let matters continue same way. Live in Bombay. Have good time on your own. In that sin city there is scope for all sorts of fun roguery. That is my advice.' 'I can't Munshji. And why should I keep up appearances.' 'Why this strong *nuffrat*, this deep hatred of Shantiji? Is there *dahl mein kala*? Some dirty business?' Dinesh smiled as he recalled the eager expression on the Munshi's face. Clearly he did not know the whole story. How Dinesh ached to open his heart! Then as if he had read his thoughts, the Munshi said: 'In court, you'll have a jolly hard time to prove anything, and do you know how many judges are in the Sethji's pocket?'

The St Francis Xavier hospital was clean, efficient and the Goan nuns who ran it, polite and extremely helpful. They assured him that Anthony was as well as he could be under the circumstances. No bones were broken, even the suspected rib-cage was intact. The pain was no longer acute and he was able to walk about. If Mr Thakur could make himself comfortable in the Waiting Room, a nurse would bring Anthony to him.

'Why can't I see him where he is?'

'Sorry, but the doctor is doing his rounds,' said the Chief Matron, who was a nun.

'Doctor is not going into general ward,' blurted the young girl who stood next to her, and then shrank under the matron's steely gaze.

'General Ward? Why is he in a general ward? I know what general wards are like. I specifically asked for him to be in a casualty ward, or any ward . . .'

'But sir, he is after all a servant.' The girl said, seeking a nod of approval from her superior, but failed to get even a glance.

'Mr Thakur,' the older woman said. 'This is not like other hospitals in India. All our patients have beds. No one sleeps on the floor. When you see him, you'll be satisfied. Of course, there are black patches round his eyes and the right side of the face, but you must have noted that already.'

Dinesh shrugged. 'If it's only a matter of recovering, I'll come in the morning and take him back with me. But I'd like to see him now.'

He was shown into a waiting room and offered a cup of coffee. He refused. It was dark. The Matron turned on the lights. 'Ring that bell if you change your mind about coffee,' she said. 'He will be some time. I'll personally see that he has fresh dressings and bandages.'

Dinesh waited uneasily. He had to face an innocent man who had suffered injuries because of him. But the good news he had for Anthony would be some recompense.

Anthony came in wearing a head bandage and a surgical collar. It hurt to see his bruised face, but his typically wide grin confirmed the matron's diagnosis. Dinesh rose to prevent Anthony touching his feet. 'You're a good man, Anthony. I'm sorry, because of me you have suffered. But, I've good news. Mr Fernandez, who owns the Catherine Braganza Hotel, happens to be your brother's landlord. But I have bought the shop at Colva Bay, and it is yours.'

'God will bless you. My brother Denzil, he honest man. He pay you rent on the dot. And I come and work for you always. Here or Punè.'

'No. As I said before, you must stay here. I can't keep you. I plan to stay in hotels. It is the safest thing for me. I may even leave the country. You will be Denzil's landlord. I'll make that legal, you know, *pukka*.'

'May St Francis protect you and give you long life. But my good Sahibji, you spend lot money. Money staying hotels. And now no job having. How you live?'

'Don't worry about me. You must also promise not to talk about me to anyone. And you must not tell anyone that I've gone to Poona.'

'I was fool. Big fool, telling you about Shanti memsahib. Forget sahib. Go back, live like before and keep old job.'

'No, Anthony, you did right. No man wants to be a cuckold.' Anthony gaped. And Dinesh, realising there should be a healthy gulf between a master and servant, decided not to explain. 'You see, Anthony, these things get found out. And I would have been unhappy to learn, that knowing, you kept it from me.'

'Yes, sahib. It is bad what memsahib did. Why her father not see this? He is bad man to want to kill you.'

'It's matter of *izzat*. Family pride. Divorce is shame. You said what you suspected. But I saw for myself.' Dinesh checked himself. He walked to the window and gazing out recalled the shocking scene. How he had tiptoed barefoot up the stairs of Shanti's dance master's room and peeped through a chink in the wooden door. There she was, naked below the waist, dancing, posing before the man, who sat cross-legged, beating a lewd rhythm on the *tublas* in front of him. Dinesh, sickened with disgust, watched, and though, all he could see was the back of an oily long-haired head shaking excitedly, he imagined the libidinous desire in the man's pan-chewing red lips. She had shaved her pubic hair and as her swaying hips drew nearer, the man's hand stretched out to touch. She sank on her knees, her hands reaching behind her back to undo the bright coloured bodice. Completely naked she lay back. The dance master rose, tugging at his dhoti . . . Dinesh, jerked involuntarily as he recalled the fury with which he kicked the door open, and the force with which his foot struck the naked bottom of the dance master. It sent the man sprawling over Shanti, smothering her screams . . .

Dinesh turned from the window and laughed as the farcical nature of the incident struck him now.

'Sahibji? Is sahibji okay?'

Dinesh took a deep breath. 'Yes. Anthony, I'm okay. Now, tomorrow I'll take you back to the hotel. Fernandez will give you a room in the servant quarters till you can join your brother. I have to leave the next day.'

'See that young lady in a plain sari.' Fernandez tried not to point. 'There.' The Hotel restaurant was rather full. 'Can't miss her. By that potted sago palm. You can see she's European, English, maybe Swedish. They are wrong shape for saris. No hips, mun.'

Dinesh shrugged. He had had enough of large hips.

Fernandez grinned. 'She's not a bad looker, mun'

Dinesh was getting tired of Fernandez's increasingly familiar manner and glad their acquaintance would soon end. He concluded this familiarity was to demonstrate that in their short business relationship, he, Fernandez, had the upper hand. 'I must be getting on,' Dinesh said gruffly. 'May I have the bill, please?'

'Don't forget to take my driver along?'

'Ajit Singh? Couldn't even if I tried. He's been watching over that car like a hawk.'

'Now, suppose I was to say. No bill. On the house. No charge.'

Dinesh laughed. 'I'd still say you haven't done too badly. The Café Lucinda, I am told is little more than a hut with a thatched roof.'

'But it has, as they say, potential. The Lobos will thank their lucky stars, mun. Also, I made big concession for the car.'

Dinesh nodded. He was pleased that all the formalities of their business transaction had been satisfactorily completed in Anthony's presence, though he started to regard Fernandez with a measure of suspicion. He couldn't think why.

'Okay then, when you get to your hotel in Poona, you hand over car to Ajit Singh.'

The vulnerable position Dinesh had placed himself into, now struck him. Was it safe to let Fernandez know his whereabouts in Poona? 'Look', he said, 'I blame myself for complicating this deal. Damn the car. Keep it. Save Ajit an unnecessary trip.'

'Then how are you going to get to Punè? By taxi cab?'

'Maybe I'll hire a car.' Dinesh answered cagily. 'I'll risk the delay . . . You won't give me away for a few hours?'

'If I can . . . I make no promises, mun.'

'In fairness I must warn you. It's going to be hard finding spare parts for the car.'

'*Arrey*, Mr Thakur, you're talking to Fernandez. If it is the last spare anything, I'll manage to get it. Never you worry, mun.'

'Excuse me! Are you the manager?' It was the sari-clad young woman by the potted palm. Her sari was of unbleached muslin with a blue border of pale pink lotuses. Her cotton, saffron blouse was worn high, accenting the breasts and revealing the waist.

'No, madam. He's in the Reception Hall. Can I be of service?'

'I've paid my bill. But he promised to find me a bus and railway timetable.'

'One moment. I'll check with Reception.' Fernandez picked up the telephone by his elbow, dialled a number and waited. Dinesh studied the young woman closely. He put her down to about his own age. She was quietly pretty without actually being beautiful, and owed much of her attraction to her splendid firm figure, which the shabbily draped sari failed to conceal. For him, her charm lay in her open and easy manner of speaking. He could not quite place her English accent. It seemed more northern than southern, but disguised by a university education. Fernandez put the phone down. 'Sorry, but I don't know why he made that promise. No trains leave from here. Buses leave from the bus stand when the driver has enough passengers. You'll have to make enquires there. Go straight down the main street. About half a mile or so.'

'I'll take you there,' Dinesh said quietly. 'I mean, I'll be your escort. You shouldn't go there by yourself.' She faced him squarely. Her deep set hazel-brown eyes unnerved him. 'It's all right. I—I—I'm a married man, you can trust me.' His expression of abject discomfiture made the young woman, who was trying not to giggle, burst out laughing.

'Sorry,' she said, 'you're very kind. Yes, thank you.'

Relieved, Dinesh gained confidence. 'Mr Fernandez, there's only my old shirt and vest in the car. Chuck it. Turning to the young

The Lotus And The Rose

woman he said: 'As I'm leaving Goa, I too could do with some information about coaches or taxis.'

'I've got to collect my bags. They let me leave it in the cloak room.'

'I'll wait in the lounge,' he said, surprised at the slight excitement in his voice.

A moment later she was back, holding a small leather suitcase and a backpack. He grinned. 'Neither go with the sari.'

'I know, but I had to see the Cathedral, and nothing else was decent enough.'

He took the suitcase from her. It was surprisingly light. Outside he asked if she had been staying at the Hotel. 'The Braganza? You're joking. Far too expensive, and even if I could, I wouldn't want to. I came in for an English breakfast. I do that sort of thing occasionally. One has to watch what one eats and drinks in India.'

'Indeed, even those who think they are immune are often laid low.' Dinesh smiled. It had been a long time since he was able to talk English freely to anyone without having to consider his listener. 'Have you been long in Goa?'

'Two weeks.'

'Alone?'

'No. I came with Jonathan. We quarrelled. He left two days ago. I think he found me a bit of an embarrassment.'

'I can't believe that. Any man would be proud to be in your company.'

'But I can quite sympathise with him. He works for an oil company and apart from jeans and shirts this is all I have to wear.' She spread her hands in a childlike gesture.

'Admittedly, it's rather "Hari Krishna". You know what I mean.'

'Yes, but I drew the line at shaving my head.'

He glanced at her thick, light brown hair, drawn loosely into a bun behind her neck, and at the fringe over her broad forehead. He had to be strong. This was no time to fall in love. 'But, he shouldn't have left you alone in a strange country.'

'Oh, I'm no stranger to India. And I rather let him down. Well, surprised him. I was not the person he expected. I've been through a sea change. Do you know the play?'

'*The Tempest*? Yes. Sandy and Emma were great lovers of English literature.'

'Sandy and Emma?'

'They brought me up.'

'So you had English parents? Foster parents. I did wonder. Your English is good.'

'Emma was English but Sandy was Indian. Sandy, nickname for Sandeep. I studied in England too, for part of my education.'

'Was? Are they?'

He nodded. 'There, that must the bus stand.' He pointed across the road. 'Or rather the booking office. I don't see any buses. Where . . .'

'Poona, I mean Punè.' She stopped, making him step back on to the pavement. 'We can't go on like this. I'm Alice Turnbull.' She held out her hand.

'Sorry, yes,' he said, taking the proffered hand in his. 'I'm Dinesh Thakur.'

'So, you're married?' She giggled. 'Sorry. It was the way you said: "You can trust me, I'm married". It's the married ones, one has to watch out for.'

'Yes, that was silly. It's just that you made me nervous, and I wanted . . .'

She looked at him and her eyes seemed to soften.

'Alice,' he said. 'I want to make you a proposition.'

'As a married man?' she giggled again and he noted she laughed easily.

'No, no. Regarding Poona. I'm going there. We could travel together?'

She shook her head. 'I'll be travelling third class, after I get a bus to the nearest train station. And I can see that you've never travelled third in your whole life.' She laughed. 'I see "Air-conditioned First Class" written all over you.'

'Just this once. Can't you make an exception? If you agree, I can book . . .'

'It would be against my principles.'

'If *I* paid for it, *you* wouldn't be breaking . . .'

'Technically.' She paused. 'Clearly, your wife isn't with you?'

'No. We're div—separated. Recently separated. I'm not telling stories. Please, Alice, I'm longing to find someone, to whom I can talk about it.'

'To whom? How very correct.'

'It's the pedant in me. I was pompous, bombastic . . . now, I too am undergoing a sea change . . . Gosh! You've got beautiful sherry brown eyes . . . Alice, think it over. Don't answer now. Think it over a cup of coffee. There must be a restaurant near here.'

'You'll find me boring company. Or do you want just a shoulder to cry on? For that, you want someone you know . . . I don't know you.'

'Mine is the one situation where a stranger is the ideal person. You'll find out why.'

'All right. But if we don't make arrangements soon, it might be too late. And I must be in Poona, tomorrow morning at the latest. I could do without coffee?'

'Alice, transport, public transport is slow and unreliable getting anywhere. So if you need to be in Poona by tomorrow, we'll go by car. First I need to return to the Hotel'

'Oh, Denis, sorry Dinesh, I couldn't go back there!'

'Wait for me in the hotel lounge. Promise you won't run away?'

'Maybe I should, but I won't. There, an Englishwoman's word is her bond.' She laughed, and he so wanted to kiss her. 'Who's Anthony? I heard his name mentioned.'

'Anthony is, or rather was my servant. He got badly beaten up.'

'Why, what did he do?'

'Nothing. It was because of me. Part of my story. I'll tell you later. Do you really have to be in Poona tomorrow?'

'It's not a matter of life and death. But if I can't, I'll have to telephone my friend.'

'Jonathan?'

'No. A girl friend. Much more important.'

'May I ask something. This quarrel with-with Jonathan, was it just a lovers tiff? Sorry I'm being presumptuous, forgive me.'

'Lovers quarrel? He's a relation . . . my mother's cousin, and years older than me. Not that, given the chance, he wouldn't . . . It's all very prosaic. Separate rooms and all that. Mother asked Jonathan to keep an eye on me. Reluctantly he agreed. I could see he was longing to be back in Bombay and I wanted to stay on in Goa, which was a lie. We were both looking for an excuse to be rid of each other. I'm here, in India, for a special purpose of which he doesn't approve. And don't ask me what that mission is. I'm tired of defending myself. People think I'm naïve or crazy.'

'I won't. Try me.'

'I don't know. Incidentally, I've an Indian Airlines return ticket to Bombay. I could fly there, then catch a Bombay-Poona train. But if I do Jonathan will be at the airport. He knows the flight number. I did tell him not to meet me. He said awful things and I know he will again about my going to Poona.'

'Why?'

'Mother and he are against my going to live and work in an *ashram*. But I've made up my mind. That's what I want to do.'

'Is this Swami Govinda's ashram?'

'Yes. How did you guess?'

'I know he has quite a following from Canada and America?'

'A few Australians too. I stay clear of the Westerners, which is not difficult as the majority in the ashram are middle-class Indians. His preaches in English. Don't say anything if you've got nothing positive to say about him. It will spoil our friendship.'

'How did you get you know of him?'

'Through an Indian friend. We were at school together. She took me to a meeting, when he came to Birmingham. The Maharishi . . . Guruji, was wonderful. Spoke about the importance of neighbourly love and care. Love in general.'

'All religions preach love. Christianity certainly does.'

'Do you know much about Christianity?'

'I suppose as much as you know about Hinduism. Sorry, I didn't mean to put it like that. My old guru, Pundit Bhabha, believed in the goodness of all religions.'

'As a Hindu, do you think I'm doing anything I shouldn't do?'

'No. There's nothing wrong in choosing to have a religious experience. I should be proud of your interest in Hinduism. But keep your wits about you. In case the man's a fraud, as some are. If I sound sceptical, it's because these, in quotes, "holy men", end up either embezzling money or in some sex scandal.'

'He's different. I know. I've not rushed into this without giving it a lot of thought. I have always loved the *Gita*, and he preaches on it with such beauty and . . . His full title is Shri Govinda Devadasa.'

'That means a server or disciple of Lord Krishna. Tell me, does he preach about free love?' She nodded. 'Somehow I guessed he would. Krishna is said to have had 16,000 wives. That's probably a gross exaggeration, but clearly he was a great one for women. I accept I'm in no position to malign or praise your guru. I don't know him. Anyway, we have to solve the immediate problem of getting you to Poona. I could drive you to Poona, in my car. It will take seven to eight hours.'

'I couldn't do that! I'm sure you're a gentleman, but we've only just met.'

'I thought you trusted me. Well, as it happens, we won't be alone. I'll drive you to Poona in my own car. Ajit Singh will be driving. He has to drive the car back, because I've sold the car to Fernandez.' He smiled encouragingly. 'Please say yes. It's the best and most comfortable way to get to Poona.'

She nodded. 'Thank you.'

'We'll lunch at the Braganza and I'll remind you to ring . . .'

'Jonathan? No need. I said I'd ring if I wanted him to meet me.' She smiled. 'It'll be pointless my saying we'll go Dutch?'

Later at the Braganza she ordered a vegetarian meal, much to the disappointment of the waiter and to keep her company Dinesh did the same. The meal was excellent and rounded off with the finest coconut ice-cream they had eaten.

'Alice, I suppose, once we get to Poona, I'll never see you again.'

She reached across the table and touched his hand. 'You've been such a darling, but it is quite useless. You're married and while we may live in an age of promiscuity, it's not something I want . . . Please understand, I've committed myself, though, now I fear, I may not turn out to be a good disciple of my Guru, but I'd like to try.'

'My marriage is meaningless. I'm never going back to my wife.'

'How greedy and selfish of me! You were going to tell me. I've been eating almost without a pause. Made quite a pig of myself. Why are you smiling?'

'Whenever anyone said they were making pigs of themselves, Sandy would always say: "You may as well go the whole hog".' They laughed.

'You must have been very fond of Sandy. You remember so much about him.'

'Quite the opposite. He was an Anglophile. I was so anti-Brit then, I picked every opportunity to attack him. As a result, I missed out on his many endearing qualities. I regret my abominable conduct towards him. My mother deserted me, left me in his care. I probably made him the target of my anger against my real parents. But his love for all things English did, then, so annoy me.'

'And did he arranged your marriage?'

'Sandy? Oh, no. I fell into that pit myself. Sandy was an Englishman in all but birth. He was also a Christian. In opposition I was determined to emphasise my Hindu roots. I was a spiteful rebel. He raised no objection to the marriage. He said he'd never tell me what to do after I reached the age of twenty-one, and he kept his word.'

'Don't be hard on yourself. I'm not sure I would have liked Sandy if, as you say he was an Anglophile. I'm no fan of the British Empire. I think people should mind their own . . . though I suppose there were worse imperialists than the Brits.'

"Well, if you had met him, you would have changed your mind. He was one of the most charming people on earth. That's what made it so frustrating. He had friends and defenders who were Muslims, Hindus, and Sikhs. You had to be bloody-minded to be immune to his charm or, like me, obdurately critical.'

'So, what went wrong with the marriage?'

'Shanti, my wife, is spoilt and immature, as an only child of a rich doting father can be. And quite soon into the marriage we both realised we weren't as madly in love with each other as we thought. She preferred to stay with her father and in time I got used to her absences till it did not matter.'

'In arranged marriages these things are quite normal. Are they not? They succeed because the couple have low expectations and know they have to work hard to keep the commitment going?'

'There was also a long accepted cultural and religious depth to the whole thing, but increasingly that has weakened. I met Shanti before we married and the unseemly haste to marry, as I say, was entirely my irresponsibility. And soon I learned that she had for long and often been unfaithful. But I never thought for a moment it would turn ugly.'

'How did you find out?'

'Servants in India are the first to know about everything. Anthony warned me about her dance master. I gathered that he had an evil and hypnotic effect on her.'

'I can understand that. My Indian friend Veena would do anything our Guru asked her to do and that sort of implicit obedience is catching. This is a very Indian cultural thing, between teacher and pupil.'

'But isn't there such a thing as physical repulsion? Are women blinded by their sense of the devout . . . of devotion. I knew of a Swami Ananda, who was small and physically revolting. Yet women fawned on him.'

'Looks have nothing to do with the sheer beauty of a great soul.'

'But Shanti's music and dance master's ugliness is without relief—I don't even know his name. And he's no great soul. I suppose he's well endowed in . . . in that, that area. That could be one explanation.'

Alice giggled. 'And a typically masculine one. Men think women fall for men who are, as you put it, well endowed. How could you know about his . . . his equipment?'

'Don't make me laugh. But I saw it for myself. This chap had a studio off Bombay's Marine Drive. I caught them at it. Telling you now makes it almost a farce, but I assure you, I was devastated and angry.'

'I'm sure you were. You poor man.'

'When I confronted her she was defiant. I wanted nothing more to do with her. In that case, she said, she would go back to her father, and that I'd never see her again; and added, she would ask her dance master to accompany her back to Pathankot.'

'That would hurt your pride if you still love her.'

'I don't love her. In fact, I may never have. I realise, till now, if any woman really fascinated me it was Emma. My foster mother was much younger than Sandy. It was innocent and short-lived.'

'Did she know you had a crush on her? Emma I mean.'

'No. Besides she didn't like me and for good reasons. She tried hard not to show it. She was devoted to Sandy and although she seemed to live in a world of her own, they were seldom apart. It was a totally absurd secret love . . . I don't know why I mentioned it . . . unless its because I'm in love again . . . now.'

'What was she like, to look at?' Alice said with a detectable haste in her voice.

'A stunner. But she didn't seem to know it, or want to exploit it. Everyone loved her and treated her like a saint, which she was.'

'Well, if you don't want Shanti back, just be patient. Keep apart, and you can sue for divorce after two years separation.'

'Unfortunately, it's not that simple. Her father's issued a *fatwa*, a death threat, if I go ahead with the divorce. He's assured me he'll have me killed.'

'That's barbaric!' She took a deep breath. 'You didn't prepare me for that!'

'Sorry. You're looking at a jobless man on the run. I was working for him. He's a very rich businessman and my job in Bombay was a sinecure . . . a gift to the son-in-law. Losing the job poses no problem. I'm well off financially. As Sandy's heir, I've ample funds and investments . . . I don't need to work.'

'But can he really carry out his threat?'

'He's not just a powerful businessman, he's what people in Bombay call a *Dada*. A godfather, in a mafia sense of the word. He has people in his pay, who execute his threats. The hotels he owns, (I was a manager of one), make him respectable. But his trade is illicit and includes drugs . . . unfortunately I knew nothing of that side of his business till now. So I have no hold over him, and he knows it.'

'Pathankot is near Dharamsala. I know Dharamsala. It's a Tibetan Asylum. India is huge. Can anyone have influence from there to Bombay?'

'Most of his trade is in the Bombay area. Dharamsala is a hideout. If any honest civil servant should investigate the Seth—a title businessmen and landlords get in India—he will get wind of it in Dharamsala and disappear before the police can get him.'

'And you had no idea about the kind of man he was before you married . . .'

'None whatsoever. I was immature and, what Americans so concisely describe, "a mixed up kid". I wanted independence and he promised me riches beyond my dreams. Truly. Shanti and I were given a bank account from which we could draw unlimited funds. In practice it meant little because we lived in his house.'

'Where is your real mother?'

'In Fiji. With a step-father I've never seen. There are a lot of Indians in Fiji.'

'And you've never thought of making contact?'

'Fiji is what Sandy told me. But she broke off all correspondence with him when she left Delhi. It wasn't impossible to find out for myself, but Sandy discouraged me. You see, her husband knows nothing of my existence. She means nothing to me. It would be cruel to ruin whatever happiness . . .' He shrugged and gave a tired smile.

'You poor man! You've been so open and frank to a stranger and all I've done is to listen. There's nothing I can do to help.'

'Alice, that itself is a great help. If you can do nothing but listen, you can't betray me. I couldn't speak to anyone I know and be sure of their loyalty. I needed someone to talk to—to get it off my chest, as they say.'

'Well, then, at least let me say this. I am happy we'll be travelling together in your car, and even if this driver chap was not coming, I'll still be prepared to come.'

'Thank you. Alas, I can't shake off Ajit Singh even if I wanted to.'

'Then let him drive, we'll sit together in the back.'

Ajit Singh proved to be more than a good driver. He was a good mechanic as well, and a broken fan belt, fifty miles away from Poona, posed no obstacle to him, but they did lose forty minutes and arrived at the Miramar Hotel well after ten at night. Late as it was, Ajit insisted on setting out on his return journey to Goa, but assured Dinesh that he would be staying the night with his friend Gurbir Singh, in Nasik. Dinesh held out his hand and Ajit shook it warmly. A close friendship was established between the men, after Dinesh surprised Ajit with his fluent Punjabi. Staring at the neon sign of the hotel, Ajit said: 'I'll surely forget the name of this hotel, so I won't be able to remember where Dinesh sahib is staying in Punè, but,' he added with a sly wink, 'I will say that I overheard sahib planning an immediate trip to Satara.'

They embraced as Punjabis do, gripping each others shoulders. Dinesh waved as the car's square tail lights disappeared round the corner. He turned to Alice, who looked tired and wan in the pale neon light of the hotel porch. 'You must be starving?'

'That's not my immediate worry. It's too late to get to the *Ashram.*'

'I'll take you there in the morning.'

'Are you suggesting I spend the night here, with you?'

He looked apologetic. 'They've assumed we are together. But I'll get you a room.'

'It may be better not to disillusion them.'

'I know this hotel. The rooms are large. There will be a spare bed, or sofa.'

She took his hand. 'It's all right. I'll share your bed if I have to. Promise to behave and let me sleep. I'm exhausted. How long has it been since you've had . . . you know?'

'You don't expect me to answer that! Six . . . seven months.'

'You must be desperate, if you have been celibate?' She giggled. 'No lies please, I'm British.'

'Well, to parody Harold Wilson, a week of sexual abstinence is a long time.'

'You poor boy. You bring out the mother in me. But it would be all wrong. Dinesh, be good. I'm not prepared, physically or mentally. Neither of us want an accident!'

'I'll marry you, I promise, when this divorce comes through. If you'll have me.'

'In that case we can afford to wait. I'm not being virtuous about this. I'm sure the hotel staff already have a poor opinion of me.'

'After tomorrow, you won't just go out of my life? Promise you'll keep in touch?'

'Of course. I'd like that. I like writing letters.'

'When I said I'll marry you, you said "we can afford to wait", does that mean your answer is "yes"?'

She smiled. 'I'll give my answer when you ask me again, after your divorce.'

'I'll write to you, but you can't write back. I have to keep my whereabouts secret. I haven't had any post for months. It's awful. I've a friend in England, Emma's mother Edith. She must be wondering why she hasn't heard from me. I don't want to explain to her why she must not write back to me, and I don't know if she's still alive. I know Emma's brother too, Ted. His daughter Kitty, incidentally a spitting image of her aunt, arrived in India, not long ago, to live and work in Dharamsala. I was fond of her, but she was rather cold towards me. My reputation of being a prig reached her long before she even contemplated coming over. I would've liked to be friends. Now I can't even write to her.'

'I can write on your behalf, whenever you need to write to your friends. The more people know about your present situation the safer you will be.'

Dinesh collected his room key from Reception. 'Good point, I didn't look at it that way.' Dinner was available through Room service, but they settled for hot chocolate and biscuits. 'It's a beautiful room,' she said, 'with a comfortable double . . . Ah, look, there's a spare single bed.'

'Yes, what bad luck.'

She seemed not to have heard his remark. 'I'll take the small bed. I'm smaller.' She grinned. 'You're tall for an Indian. In my *ashram*, I can't think of any Indian taller than you, except the chowkidars, watchmen. They're Pathans. Now, I've a problem. Either I sleep in my petticoat or in the hotel dressing gown. In the ashram we sleep on the floor. Guriji encourages men and women to sleep in a simple wrap around cloth.'

'I'm sure he does, the man is no fool.'

'Now, you promised not to make snide remarks about him. He says, it's how people slept in the times of the ancient scriptures. It's healthy. I could use this top sheet, but with the air-conditioning on, I'll be cold.'

'Borrow one of the shirts I bought this afternoon.' He opened his suit case. 'I have enough. I bought four from the "Braganza Boutique" before we set out.'

'I think I'm growing to love you.'

'I've loved you since the moment I first saw you.'

'Then you deserve a kiss. May I?' She came up to him and rising on her toes kissed him softly on the mouth. His hands touched her breasts. She backed away.

'Sorry. Do forgive me. I've frightened you. Are you a virgin?'

She stared, wide-eyed, then burst out laughing. 'That's bold. Virgin? Verging on the ridiculous. I'm twenty-nine!'

'I did wonder, with all your good religious inclinations, you might be a . . . as I said.'

'Well, it was sometime ago. Two casual encounters. Of no insignificant now.' She chuckled. 'But I shouldn't say that. Everything in our lives, my Guru says, is.'

'I'll let you get ready first,' he said.

She threw his shirt on the single bed and rummaged in her back-pack. 'You could in the meanwhile read about my *ashram*.' She gave him a booklet.' When she came out from the bathroom his shirt barely covered her knees, but her look of anxiety struck him. 'Alice, what's the matter?'

'I've been selfish. I'd forgotten the danger you're in. I said, I couldn't help, but, silly me, I can. And we could be together in a place which is the safest of all asylums. Stay in the *ashram* with me.'

'I can't come on false pretences. I'm no disciple of your Guru. He'll know that.'

'You join as an observer. Guriji talks about his inner fold and his outer fold. you know what that means—the inner circle are disciples, the outer circle are those willing to listen. I hope, one day, I'll be accepted into the inner circle. Please Dinesh, do. Now that we have a solution, I could never forgive myself if anything happened to you.'

'What do I have to do?'

'Nothing. Stop being sceptical. You'll have to pay for your board and lodging'

'I'm a very private man. I can't rough it out, rub shoulders with all and sundry and use public baths and latrines. I suppose I'll have to sweep and clean?.'

'It's not that kind of *ashram*. It's more like an academy or college. Swami Govinda is very much a businessman. He believes, money must be made to serve.'

'I bet he has a string of Rolls-Royces.'

'He has two. But he is an honest man and does not hide the fact he is rich. He has always been rich. His father joined the Congress party and knew Nehru and Gandhi. The money we pay—I pay by cheque in sterling—goes to the administration. Let me explain.' She picked up the booklet and pointed to a diagram which showed what she described as the plan of the campus. 'This large square has the outer wall that marks the perimeter of the compound. That's the main gate. These two squares mark the living quarters. Men and women separate. They have three barrack-like buildings containing narrow, monastic cell-like rooms. No furniture, only a thin mattress. You sleep on the floor but you have your own small lavatory and a wash basin. It's simple and clean. In the centre of each square is a shower-room.'

'And what's that octagonal building behind the two squares?'

'That's the Prayer Hall and where Guruji lives when he's on the campus. He enters from behind the curtains and sits on a *gaddi*, on a raised dais, on a theatre-like stage. He only comes in when the audience before him are seated and waiting.'

'So the money for board and lodging goes in maintaining the buildings?'

'And pays for the small community of dhobis, cooks, servers and sweepers. They have quarters outside the compound and get free board and a small salary. At present, for the short term they live in tents but there are plans to house them in buildings. The *ashram* is only two years old.'

'I suppose they go into the fields beyond, each morning, with their *lotas* of water.'

'Yes. I've never given it much thought. Don't make a face. Behind the Prayer Hall, these two oblong buildings are the *langars* or the kitchens and dining halls. Again, men and women are separated. There's one new small brick building, not shown on here. Its the shop, where you can buy, bath rubber slippers, towels, soap, toiletries, oh yes, and bottled water. Guruji aims to attract Europeans. Men and women dress uniformly. This is given. Two pairs. One you wear and one you wash. For men it is a long saffron robe. You've seen the women's sari and blouse.'

'No books?'

'No. You're there to listen to Guruji. There is also a rota of duties, involving the supervision of the cooking and the cleaning.'

'I couldn't do that!'

'Stop being difficult. You've got to. It's a matter of life and death, Dinesh. Anyway, men have it easier than the women. Your father-in-law, even in the unlikely chance of learning where you are, wouldn't dare enter an *ashram*. Surely. Guruji will have no truck with drug-dealers.'

'There is no one in India who can't be bought.'

'Will you stop being difficult! If you will come with me to the *ashram*, I'll sleep in your bed and let you make love to me. Promise me you won't talk about it.'

It was nine in the morning when Alice, sitting up in bed shook him gently. Dinesh groaned. 'Let me rest.' He stretched himself across the bed. 'I'm tired.'

'I'm not surprised you're tired,' she said. 'I thought you were never going to let me rest.' He reached out to her. 'Now no more of that. That's your lot. Dinesh, I mean it. I had resolved to remain celibate, at least for the two years I planned to be in India. I'm going to have to pretend this night never happened. I shall feel such a hypocrite.'

'It was at your suggestion,' he grinned.

'I know. You're a very attractive man.'

'You made a sacrifice to save a life. Look at it as a religious rite.'

'Hindus are such optimists. They are so very good at explaining everything away, and there is always some god or goddess to turn to.'

'I suppose you're right. 'One god is a dictatorship. Many gods is a democracy.'

'Remember, you can't break your side of the bargain.'

'I won't. It's a brilliant suggestion. The *ashram* is indeed a safe place. Thank you.'

She sprang out of bed. 'Back to square one. From now on nothing doing.'

'Forgive me, but did you take precautions? I didn't, rather I couldn't.'

'I know. In the heat of the moment I didn't care. It's not the end of the world. The *ashram* doesn't exclude pregnant women, though when the time comes you'll have to own up to being the child's father. There's plenty of time for that.'

'Or nothing to worry about. One of us, that's Shanti and me, is not fertile, if you get my meaning. Eight months ago, I received a set of diamond studs, shirt buttons, with a message congratulating me on being a father. I'm not the father. I can't be.'

'How can you be certain?'

'Well, in any case, that is academic. I'm not going back on my decision to end the marriage. I have money and I have you.'

'And the diamond buttons.' She compressed her lips to arrest a giggle, then took a deep breath. 'We won't talk about us. You must give me time. I assume Sandy didn't have children?'

'That's not why he fostered me. He couldn't say no to his sister, my mother. And he did adopt, because of Emma's impetuosity, a Tibetan refugee. She was little more than a girl when they did. Sandy literally bought her freedom. I believe they loved her more than they did me. Sona, that's her name, and I, did not get on. But, I was difficult; an ungrateful child and, as I said, a foolish, angry young man.'

***

The Govinda Devadas Ashram impressed Dinesh. Compared to what he knew about *ashrams* or expected to see, this one was a genuine attempt to meet twentieth century standards. Much building work was still in progress. 'We asked for raised bricked paths to link the various buildings, Prayer Hall and shower rooms, because it's muddy during the monsoons,' Alice said. 'Now, wait here, while I have a word with our Secretary and Treasurer. Unusually a she. A pretty, efficient woman and an authority on the *Gita*. We call her Munshiji because she's in charge of the administration. She'll fix a meeting with my Guruji for his formal approval of your enrolment.'

'What if the place is fully booked?'

'I'm going to beg for asylum. He wont refuse that. Stay here and don't move.'

They were invited to meet Guru Govinda in the Prayer Hall that same afternoon, and if the *ashram* surprised Dinesh another surprise awaited him in the person of Guruji. He appeared majestically from behind bright green velvet curtains and stood in front of a crimson cushioned, gilt throne. Dinesh had expected to see a long-haired, full bearded holy man, but Shree Govinda Devadasa was not much older than him. With his clean shaven face and wearing a heavy Rajput turban—tied in bright orange ropes of silk material, sprinkled with gold, silver and green glitter—he looked more like a Maharaja than a holy man. Nothing, apart from the neat smear of the ostentatious Brahmin caste mark of a Vishnavite on his forehead, suggested any connection with the religious. The usual large bead necklace and garland of marigold were absent. He wore a below knee length saffron robe over an immaculately tied white dhoti. Alice touched his feet, and with a formal gesture and a 'no, no, that is not necessary' he raised her by her elbows. 'I see,' he continued in an even toned voice, which combined an acquired Oxford accent with an Indian lilt, 'I seem to have taken your friend by surprise. You see, Shriman Dinesh Thakur, I do not believe in the ascetic life, nor do other Swamijees I know, although they take great pains to make it appear so. I am here to enjoy, like the rest of you, the good things of life, the material joys that the Lords of the Universe have set before us. The goddess of wealth, Lakshmi, the Indian Venus, and Krishna, that great avatar of Vishnu and god of love are worshipped together. So I, who am dedicated to Him, whose name I've adopted, am here to preach the joys of free love.' Then pursing his lips and shaking his head knowingly, he added: 'I can see in the glow of your faces that the two of you have already communicated sexually, which I thoroughly approve. But, this *ashram*, is a place of abstinence and learning. For life is lived all the better by the adherence to rules and insights, which I shall give you, including those of the *Kama Sutra*, so that my disciples will later find joys in abundance. Shortly, should they desire sexual congress, my disciples will have my permission to use my House of Love, which is presently being built behind this Prayer Hall and my living quarters.' Then with an elaborate but unmistakable gesture of his hands he indicated that the audience was at an end. Dinesh folded his hands and bowed. But they had barely turned to go when Guru Govinda called out. 'And Thakurji, should you feel that the board and lodging fee is inadequate, please feel free to make an added donation.' He gave a light chuckle and disappeared behind the heavy curtains.

Outside the Hall Alice and Dinesh stood together staring out across the campus. The builders had downed tools for the day and the silence now gave the hot sultry day a rare apprehension. Alice sighed. 'This is one of the hottest days I can remember.'

'I long for a shower,' Dinesh mumbled.

'Why don't you take one? You know where it is. Now don't fuss. Just get on with it. I have learnt how to use a bucket and a *lota*, you too can manage.'

'The tap in the loo is very low down.'

"That's there to wash your bottom after using the loo—the use of loo paper is not allowed, because it can block the drains. Bathing is outdoors. Keep your pants on. I've pointed to the taps for common use.'

'About the *langar*, the kitchen hall, that was a good lunch, but the thought of eating only vegetarian meals makes my heart sink.'

'Do you like your room?'

'If I didn't, there's nothing I can do about it, can I? And they've taken my suitcase and left me with this . . .' he looked down miserably at the cassock-like saffron robe.'

'Stop moaning. Look at your stay here as a kind of penance for all the luxuries and indulgences of your wicked past.' She smiled. 'You look different in that robe. Saintly. Well, this is where we part. You to the men's quarters and I . . .'

A little man came out of the Prayer Hall with a hammer and struck the hours on a suspended piece of steel rail.

'What do you think of GD, that's short for Govinda Devadasa.'

'I really can't say. He looks very impressive. But when he started talking and went into all that rigmarole about love, I felt a cold shiver go down my spine.'

'I must be going. In less than an hour there's a women's committee meeting, and I'm part of it. Any favourite vegetables that I can suggest to the Mess Secretary?'

'Brinjals and bhindi. That's aubergines and okra? Did you know that brinjal is a corruption of the Anglo-Indian, brown jolly?'

'No.'

'Brinjal curry reminds me of Bill Clayton. A big man in every sense of the word, and a truly good man. He liked being called a Christian sadhu. I didn't like that. Seemed to me like an attempt to fuse opposites and make of them a Trojan Horse. After all he was a missionary. I argued with him. I know better now. I should've sat at his feet, listened. If you knew him Alice, you wouldn't run after new ideas or bogus teachers who preach free love with such lecherous delight. What he said was calmer than the *Kama Sutra*.'

'You're not to talk like that about GD. Stop grinning. I haven't missed the pun, but what I seem to miss is what you stand for. Apart from being Hindu. What are you?'

'I don't know what I am. Yet I'm reluctant to change. India and Hinduism are my birthright. I'll stick to them, even when at times I hate both. I'll never understand why Sandy's father turned to Christianity. He was a schoolmaster and like Sandy a lover of English Literature. Sandy once said that you can never get to grips with English unless you knew the Bible. And the Bible is a dangerous book.'

'I like GD's teachings and I'm interested in Hinduism. I want to learn about it, and why it makes Indians the sort of people they are. But I'll probably die a Christian.'

'You mean why it makes Hindus the kind of people they are. You could learn about Hinduism from me, and people like Dr Radhakrishnan; or from books.'

'I like it here. Don't discourage me. Let me find out things for myself.'

'I don't like it here, but I suppose I'll survive.' A forced smile failed to hide her annoyance. 'Sorry,' he said hurriedly. 'I know I'm being a pain. Don't go off me?'

'I'll never go off you,' she said with a frown. 'Whatever that means.'

As she walked away with determined strides he had to agree with Fernandez, the sari did not suit her. But he knew better. He knew what lay beneath those clumsily tied folds of cotton fabric and it was enough to trouble him like a fever. He shook his head sadly. They would have little time together, here. Not only were women housed separately, they ate separately. He looked forward to the evening prayer meetings, when they sat together. But that was little consolation. The four meetings each week, some lasting three hours, were dull, and apart from listening and joining in the *bhajans*, hymns of prayer and praise, there was little communication. Alice's concentration and devotion were remarkable and it astonished him to see her next to him, listening to GD with rapt attention, while he found him tedious. Then after the first week she started to sit with her friend Veena, leaving him desolate and feeling utterly neglected. He feared this was the beginning of the end of their relationship. She did introduce him to Veena, to whom he took an instant dislike. Her black mascaraed eyes bulged prominently and when she spoke her lips pouted irritatingly. Through her neat, discreetly wrapped sari he sensed a pair of shapely breasts but their otherwise attractive effect was marred, for him, by her high hips and long legs. The raven black hair, which framed her pale face, was pulled into a top knot, emulating the traditional Hindu art illustrations of pious women.

In spite of the rebellions spirit, he had acquired, without realising it—from his life with Sandy and Emma—a westernised outlook which protected him from much of India's ugliness. Now, in isolation, with time to think, the scales fell from his eyes, revealing the fraudulent life he had led. Now, as India's ugliness stared him in the face, he felt unable to deal with it and the frustration, turned inwardly, upset him. All the nationalistic ideals he had borrowed and fostered in his youth were disappearing, and gradually it was beginning to dawn on him that he disliked Indians; their deceptions, intolerance, and their anti-social habits. Every public clearing of the nose and throat, the spitting, and the belching, made him shudder. Now, here in the *ashram*, his sensitivity was assaulted by the lack of privacy. He could not bear strangers approaching him to ask his age, his past life; his income, his marital state, and how many children he had and, if not, why not. He marvelled at Alice's equanimity and realised how close he was to Sandy, and what a happy bond of friendship they could have shared. But in those student days, moving with friends, equally ignorant, shallow and supercilious as he had been about realities, he attacked Sandy's love of England and, for what he claimed to be, in some measure, disloyalty. Now he found himself open to censure by the very criteria he had judged and condemned Sandy; and here, without a servant to shield him, he had to rub shoulders with people who made him feel uncomfortable.

Convinced that Alice had grown cold towards him, he decided to stop attending meetings, where he had to listen to bogus theology and witness a poorly disguised exploitation of tourists, and other gullible searchers for consolation. He pretended to be sick, but feared the *ashram* executives would ask him to leave. Then, he concluded that as long as he was making a good financial contribution, they would keep him.

In the middle of the third week he heard a gentle knock on the door. It was Alice. She slipped quickly into his cell and shut the door behind her. 'Where have you been all this time? I thought you had left.'

'I wouldn't do that without telling you, and I would have had to face GD in order to retrieve my suitcase. I suppose I'll have to buy my freedom.'

'Why? Is this place so awful that you'd rather face mortal danger outside?'

'I don't know what to say. Incidentally, I need to get to my suitcase. My cheque-book's almost run out . . . Alice, I hate this place, it's an open prison!'

'No, it isn't.' They sat together on his narrow bed. 'We're free to do what we like.'

'Are we? I hardly saw you. That's why . . . Good Lord! Are we breaking the rules? You're not supposed to be here. You'll get into trouble.'

'No, as I said we're free to do what we want—except that, of course. This is a free community.'

'You mean I could have come over to see you?'

'Yes. Separating men and women is for administration purposes only. I should have told you, but I wanted time away from you and thoughts of you, for the short-term.'

'I thought GD wants to establish a community of free lovers?'

'Yes. I suppose, in the end, only those who want to indulge in free love will stay on and move to his new house and gardens in Mathura, which he's named Brindaban.'

'Don't tell me. There'll be a lake and fountains and open air bathing. Men will steal the women's clothes and play games of "catch me if you can", all to mimic or recreate the sexual frolics of Lord Krishna.'

'Can you be serious for a moment. GD says, whatever people may think about those who indulge in free sex, at least they are not criminals. But to answer your question, in theory, even now. GD's serious about his free community, even if it's a small group of volunteers. He personally told me that. Veena has agreed to . . .'

'Gosh! Alice, you're not going to join . . .'

'No, Dinesh, I've no such intention. That is when I leave. It is going to take at least two years before the move to Muthura.'

'What will happen to this place?'

'It will be a community for widows and orphans. A primary school too. Anyway, he's going to talk about both projects. He's also showing films of the temples at Puri, Konarak, and Khajuraho.'

Dinesh laughed ironically. 'The man's no fool. Those temple sculptures are highly erotic. I don't suppose you have seen them.'

'No, but I know about them. GD says they prove that in eleventh century India, there was an idyllic, free and enlightened society.'

'Now that can't be true. There are a few theories about what those erotic sculptures are about. The widely accepted one is that they depict the women of the temple. Sort of vestal virgins, exploited by the priests, who suggested that sexual orgies were a way of having communion with the gods. I bet, rich men paid liberally and filled the temple coffers for those favours. There's enough lies and legend in Indian History to mislead the simple. Next GD'll give a talk about the *yoni* and the *lingam*, how they symbolise the unity of Shiva and Parvati and procreation. If you're not careful you'll be feeling his *lingam* up your *yoni*. Alice, for heaven's sake, what's a sensible girl . . . sorry woman . . . Sorry, I've no right . . . I get so easily worked up.' He leaned forward and covering his face began to cry bitterly. Alice froze. Then she put her arm round him. 'I know how you feel,' and cupping his face in her hands, wiped his tears with the end of her sari.

'You can't know how I feel,' he whimpered. 'I'm afraid for my life. I'm a coward, in spite of not wanting to be one. I feel like dirt. It's not as if I'm a nobody.'

'Yes, you're proud and don't want to be intimidated. But you have to be sensible.'

'And now I'm in love. Madly, deeply, and I'm left here alone. I hate every moment I'm away from you.'

'Hush, I can't stay. I'm going to open the door. Veena's here too, with three other women to divert attention. There they are. Now, I'm going to slip out. We'll join them and talk outside. I want my visit to look innocent.'

'I don't like Veena.'

'Dinesh, from all you have told me about yourself, it s clear you are a bad judge of character. She's a sweet person. It was her idea, my coming here. You don't know her yet you dislike her. You don't know me, you can't know me, yet you like me.'

'But I haven't got you wrong? You do care for me, don't you?'

'Of course, I care. But that's all you know about me. Come on, let's join them, and do thank her for planning this. I came with a group, a group of women.'

'Do I know the others?'

'No, and you don't need to. One of them is rather dishy.'

'Stop! Keep looking at me. Don't turn round. You believe I'm safe here?'

'Yes.'

'Well, all this past week, I can swear I'm being followed.'

'What makes you think that?'

'There's a horrid little man. He keeps grinning at me. Turn slowly and look towards where I am looking. He's moving away now.'

'Oh, him. I've seen him too. He's new. He's to be seen a lot with GD, these days. I assumed he's a Brahmin priest. By the way he's dressed.'

'Any Brahmin can wear a loin cloth and the sacred thread across the chest.'

'He looks perfectly harmless, my sweet.'

Veena had left the group of women and came down to join them. She smiled shyly and folding her hands greeted Dinesh. '*Hare Krishna*! Babuji. Now start attending the prayer meetings again.'

'Yes, I will. And thank for getting Alice to visit me. I'm very grateful.'

'Alice will sit with you from now on. And did she tell you, you can go out to town together? Saturday afternoons? No! *Arrey*, why not Alice?'

'I was about to, then we got distracted.'

The Lotus And The Rose

'You mean by that thin man. Such a miserable specimen he is, no. Kept grinning at us so shamelessly. If he wasn't a priest, I'd have told him to keep his eyes to himself. Well, it'll soon be time for the meeting. Come, Alice, they're serving *chai,* tea.'

'You go ahead, Veena. There's something else I forgot to tell Dinesh.'

'*Chale, chalo,*' Veena said. 'Follow close behind us, then. Oh, look that little man has popped up again. He's watching very suspiciously.'

'I've had to confide in Veena,' Alice whispered, as they followed Veena.

'What, everything?'

'About us. Not about why you're here. Something else. You asked me to write to Ted. I did. I told him the whole situation you're in, why you had not written. I've got a reply from him. He had wondered why you had not answered his letter. One he wrote some months ago. You see, Edith . . .'

'Edith! What about Edith. She has . . . don't tell me she has . . .'

'Died. Yes.'

'Great God, am I to be left with nothing!'

'Darling she was an old woman. She died peacefully. Ted also says, your simplest and best way out is to live in England. I didn't know you had a British passport? You didn't tell me. I would have said the same thing, had I known.'

'I had planned not to renew it. But I still have two years left on the current one. I'm a mess. I wanted above all to be an Indian, living in India. Now, I can't do even that.'

'Be patient then, time heals all wounds . . . what are you laughing about?'

'A black and while old American movie, I recently saw but I forget the name. The down and out hero says, rather sadly, "time wounds all heels". That applies to me. I've been a heel in every sense of that American word.'

'Dinesh time is on your side and time will change things for you. This threat will be forgotten. Your wife's father, can't have long to live. We'll talk later, let's have tea. I've started liking this hot, sweet, milky strong tea, but I haven't got use drinking it from a glass beaker . . . thank you, Veena.'

Veena brought the tea and they sat together on a bench facing the Prayer Hall. 'So,' Veena said, conspiratorially, 'you two planned trip to town? Tomorrow's Saturday.'

'Not really, but we will.'

'I can't be seen in town,' Dinesh blurted out and then bit his lip. Veena's ears pricked up almost visibly. 'Why not?'

'Well,' Dinesh said, 'it's a long story. Alice, if you go, get me some money from my Bank—State Bank of India—and I'll authorise you to collect a new cheque book. I had asked them not to mail . . . God! there's that man again, watching.'

※

Then as suddenly as he appeared the Brahmin disappeared. For the next three days there was no sign of him. Dinesh kept his eyes peeled and at times retraced his steps to make sure the little man was not hiding round corners. Then on the fifth day, returning from lunch, he saw the Brahmin waiting for him outside his cell. The supercilious grin had gone but the steady gaze from feverishly yellow eyes was evil, making his greeting with folded hands distinctly false. 'I yam here to be of service to you.' The shaved head wobbled as he spoke and the smile returned with an obsequious leer.

'I don't need any service from any one. Who are you? What do you want?' Dinesh spoke in Hindustani.

'You may speak in English. I yam educated.' He pointed to the sandalwood paste that marked his forehead. 'Hear me out, Mr Dinesh Thakur.'

'How d'you know my name?'

'Never mind dat. All will be clear in good time.' He spoke with great deliberation, stressing each syllable in an attempt to disguise his strong Tamil accent. 'There is no thing to fear. Yev'rything to gain. I can be of service to you, service that I know will give much pleasure. You rich man, but I yam not seeking single paisa in recompense. You may reward, for services rendered, in which case it's entirely up to you.'

Dinesh waved his hand and was about to shut the door when the little man spoke again. This time the voice was slyly menacing. 'I know your predicament. The terrible quandary you're in, Mr

The Lotus And The Rose

Thakur. I yam good man but bad enemy. I help, I also hinder. So can I speak frankly. I see how much you desire that white woman and I can see she is not unwilling. If I may say so, her body promises all the pleasures a man may want.'

Dinesh slammed the door angrily but waited behind the door, listening for the man's departure. He could hear heavy breathing. 'Thakurji, yev not heard me out.' Dinesh's curiosity weakened his resolve. He opened the door slightly. The wild look of the little man and his yellow eyes and teeth, sickened him. 'You, dat woman want . . .' He made a vulgar gesture with his hands, 'but you have no place, where to satisfy your desires . . .' The head wobbled knowingly. 'Is that not so? This is where I can help you. There is a special room next to GD's quarters behind the Prayer Hall. You may have the use of it for one hour yev'ry Monday and Thursday night. There is a mattress on the floor and mirrors and pictures from the *Kama Sutra*. You can practice all the positions you want undisturbed. Door bolt from the inside. Talk with woman. Feel free to approach me . . .'

'Stop! Enough!' Dinesh sounded hoarse and breathless. 'You must think I was born yesterday,' he said, trying not to shout. 'I know all about such rooms. A friend took me to one of them in Bombay, all lit up and equipped with video camera and recorder . . .'

The Brahmin laughed. From a man of his size, the laugh was surprisingly loud and raucous. 'Do I look like man who can use such modern technology?'

'There had to be some catch,' Dinesh thought, and the image of a hired cameraman came to mind. He spoke firmly: 'I'll report you to GD.'

'Dat will be most unwise. The room has been hired for me and GD has received a big donation for that purpose. Besides, your word against a Brahmin priest will not be believed. You can prove nothing. Also, I warn you against such action. You will put yourself in greater danger. I know why eyow have confined yowself to this *ashram*.'

Dinesh slammed the door and sat down on his stringed cot heavily

'I yam leaving,' the Brahmin could be heard chuckling. 'There she is, waiting, alone, on the edge of indiscretion.' He laughed wickedly. Dinesh sprang to his feet and opened the door. The man's bow-legged walk took on a sinister aspect. Then he saw Alice. He ran past the man to Alice and led her away. 'You mustn't come here again. In fact we must keep away from each other for some time. Sit with the women. I'll find a moment to explain. I'm so afraid that because of me you're in grave danger too.'

'But what has that horrid little man got to do with . . . ?'

'I've a hunch. He's a plant. It explains his sudden appearance, and why he knows my name and about me. And I don't believe he's a Brahmin, I mean he's disguised as one. It's why I didn't recognise him. Something about the way he walked rings a bell. I've seen him, I can't think where.'

A week later Dinesh's hunch was to be proved right. It was late afternoon and as he walked up the slope towards the Prayer Hall, he saw the Brahmin grinning down at him. Suddenly the true identity of the man struck him. 'Why, its you, Kuryan . . .' he stopped. The woman next to Kuryan, in gold-rimmed spectacles and a bright red sari, was none other than his wife. He stared aghast. 'Good Lord!' he cried, 'Shanti!'

Shanti made a wild gesture with her hands. 'Yes, your wife. Have you no shame! So you're hiding here with a new sweetheart! A bitch of a whitey woman!'

Dinesh took a deep breath to regained his composure.

'*Arrey!* You shameless husband,' she screamed, 'what have you to say!'

'Nothing, I have nothing to say to you.' A crowd of men and women began to gather behind Kuryan and Shanti.

'Nothing to say! Huh!' Shanti stared hard at him, arms akimbo, and swaying like a cobra, ready to strike. He knew any reply would be unhelpful.

'Keeping *chup*. Nothing to say. *Harami*! After all my father did for you!'

'I didn't need your father's help.'

With a piercing scream she rushed at him. Kuryan attempted to restrain her. It was a mistake. 'Take your hands off me!' she howled and pushed the little man, who fell flat in front of her, causing her to trip and fall across him. Dinesh laughed. He knew he was making matters worse. Shanti stood up, slinging her sari *pulloo* over her shoulder, she removed one of her sandals and raised it to throw at Dinesh. But Veena, who seemed to come from nowhere, caught her hand by the wrist. She was a strong woman, and the struggling Shanti was soon subdued. 'Please don't make a scene here. This is *ashram*. If you have got anything to settle take it to Panditji.' Veena always referred to GD as Panditji. She had barely finished speaking when GD himself appeared with his *munshi* and a train of acolytes. He was looking particularly regal in his silk saffron robes, and white satin turban. He did not need to speak. A ripple of awe silenced the crowd before him. He raised a hand, the palm of which had been freshly hennaed, and with the other he gestured to his *Munshi*. '*Shrimati*, bring the offending parties before me. I will be in the Prayer Hall and see that we are not disturbed,' he said, in Marathi.

When Dinesh, Shanti and Kuryan entered the Hall, GD was seated, crossed-legged on his crimson plinth, with an attendant ceremoniously swaying an elaborate peacock feathered fan behind him; and standing close to him, was his serene *Munshi*. Dinesh was seeing her for the first time and noted that she was very pale skinned and handsome to look at. Her tranquil presence intrigued him. 'What's all this *Tamasha*?' GD stared at Shanti. 'You have mocked and disgrace this *ashram*. Have you no sense of right and wrong? No sense of propriety or place. Have you no feminine dignity? No, no, I don't want to know. Non-spiritual matters do not concern me. Leave these premises and take your fellow conspirator with you. I gave him room, hospitality and let him stay, even when I knew he was a fraud.' He addressed the man. 'Yes, yes, I let you stay because for your six weeks sojourn you brought a large donation from an anonymous party. Bhola Nath, you are a wicked man. I found out that you are neither priest nor Brahmin.'

'But, but, how can this be?' Kuryan stammered.

'Shrimatee Munshiji pointed to the fact you wore the sacred thread over the wrong shoulder.' The woman gave Kuryan a cold stare and nodded. 'For your most deceitful behaviour, consider the donation forfeit. The *ashram* will put bad money to good use.' Both of you will be seen off the premises.' Another nod from the Munshi brought four men from behind the curtains. They led Shanti and Kuryan out of the Hall.

GD waited till they were gone, then he turned to Dinesh. His voice gentler in tone. 'Fortunately for your case, Sister Alice confided in me yesterday. So, you are a Hindu, and a married Hindu; and you want to live with a white woman. That is not orthodox Hindu conduct. But no matter. Love has neither colour, creed nor limits. But, a shared life without a *bandan*, that is a tie or commitment, is exploitation.'

'I mean to marry Alice and start a new life.'

'So be it. But these private matters, as I always say, are no concern of mine. I hear your life is in danger.' He turned to the statuesque woman next to him. 'Shrimati, has she been sent for?'

'Yes, Guruji, she will be here soon.' The voice was deep and her accentless English, smooth and unaffected. Dinesh had never heard her speak before. He studied GD and the woman and wondered if they shared more than just religious or administrative ties.

'Let her come in as soon as she arrives. So, Mr Dinesh Thakur, have you learned anything during your time here. Please be frank.'

Dinesh thought for a moment: 'Only this, that when we arrive at the truth, it turns out to be a collection of platitudes.'

'Not a very original statement, Thakurji, but if it expresses your feelings, I'll accept it. Truth is also a path. A path is of no use until you travel on it; and to the traveller it is of no use unless it leads somewhere. Destination is the point where meaning or absence of meaning disappears. For destiny means peace and an end of questing.'

Dinesh folded his hands and bowed.

'Ah, your partner is here.'

Alice ran up to GD and touched his feet. 'Please Guruji, don't send me away.'

'Child,' he said, 'whatever your mission was, now it has changed. I'm afraid the two of you must leave the *ashram*. The ashram must be free of scandal.'

'I am sorry, Alice,' Dinesh said almost inaudibly, but she heard him, and rising took his hand and led him up to the step below the throne.

'Guruji,' she said, 'if it has to be this way, give us your *arshidvar*, your blessing.'

'I'll do more than that. I may not be able to protect your man from danger or death, but I'll give you both a good start. Go, collect your things now. In the morning, you'll be driven in my personal car to wherever you plan to go in Punè.' He made a sign. The *Munshi* handed Dinesh a white scarf. 'Wear this, and may it protect you.'

'I will always make an annual donation, Guruji.'

'But not to me. When I have left this place, there will be an orphanage and a home for widows. Support that.' He turned to Alice and from a brass tray picked up a small silver fial, dipped his finger in it and placed a red *tikka on* her forehead. Then he laid his hands on their heads, and blessed them.

CHAPTER SEVENTEEN

'So back where we started,' Alice said as the saffron yellow Rolls-Royce stopped outside the closed gates of the Ambassador Hotel.

Dinesh nodded. 'Almost. Don't forget Goa. We'll always have Goa!' He grinned. 'Remember *Casablanca*? The film. At the end, Bogart, Humphrey Bogart, says to Ingrid Bergmann, "We'll always have Paris!"'

The driver sounded his horn.

'I wish I could mimic Bogart,' Dinesh went on. 'Sandy could. But I see my little joke has fallen flat on its face.'

'I'm in no mood for jokes.'

'What more can I say. I'm sorry you couldn't say goodbye to Veena. And I know how you must feel about all that's happened. Forgive?'

She gave his hand a squeeze. 'No point fretting. One has to move on.'

The gates opened automatically with a plangent grind.

She sighed. 'No more talk about the *ashram*. That the past. I'll return to the peace of non-demanding Christianity.' The Rolls glided regally up the long tree-lined drive.

'But Christianity is very demanding, although there are questions it does not answer, or rather the answers are unsatisfactory.'

'And Hinduism has the answers?'

'Yes, summarised in one word: reincarnation. I believe in it. With one reservation. Humans return to human, not to animal life. When I die, I'll be born to new parents in a new place. That's why the past is forgotten.'

'Because humans are superior to animals. I'm not sure Hinduism supports that.'

'In any cycle there has to be a hierarchy.'

'Surely, cycles are circular. By definition.'

'The Hindu cycle aims for the tangents. A "stop the world I want to get off" sort of thing. To have been human is already to have reached a higher, though not the highest level of attainment. To be one with God, is the highest level. God is not in the cycle.'

'We'll return to this another time. Back to now. What *are* we going to do? I'll go back to England. Dinesh, are you coming with me?'

The car stopped under the Hotel porch and was immediately surrounded by what seemed like the entire Hotel staff. Dinesh smiled. 'All this attention is for to the Rolls.'

He acknowledge the askew salute of the doorman and asked if "Chopra Sahib" was in. The man nodded. A porter took their suitcases and clearly showed his surprise at their lightness. He left them at the Reception Desk and left to find "Chopra Sahib." Dinesh asked Alice if she would like separate rooms.

'That would be a charade.' She smiled and blew him a kiss. 'Sorry I was so grumpy a moment ago.' She looked around her. 'This is another five star hotel. I can't imagine how much you paid at the last hotel.'

'Not a penny. Here too. Anil Chopra won't hear of it. You'll see.'

'Goodness! Why?'

'When I was a director of Agarwal Hotels, I got Anil this job. When I said I've no friends I can trust, actually I have two. Both school chums. Anil is one . . . Ah!'

A door opened into the foyer and a tall well dressed man in blazer and grey flannels came out with open arms. 'Hello, there! Dinesh old chap.' He bowed to Alice.

'Alice, this is my dear friend, Anil Chopra.' They shook hands. 'Now Chops, you must let me pay. I insist.'

'*Arrey, yaar*, what bloody nonsense! *Bhai* sahib, please don't insult me.'

'Well, it's not for long. An hour or so, just a room to freshen up and make plans.'

'Then I'll tell Biba. You know my wife Biba? We'll have lunch together.'

'That's very kind but that will delay us. You've been a good friend; and I know you will keep everything I say to yourself. There one last big favour I ask of you.'

'Ask? *Arrey*, no need to ask. Tell me!' Anil grinned and turned to Alice. 'We're old friends you know, can't think why this fellow has to stand on formalities?'

Alice smiled. 'I don't know what he's going to ask,' she said. Since Anil entered the hotel lobby, she had had time to study this bluff mannered man. As Dinesh's classmate she was surprised to see a much older looking man and she put it down to his greying hair and heavy moustache. She also noted that Dinesh's good looks shrank before Anil Chopra's handsome and very masculine face. He spoke with a deep voice, punctuating every other word with a brush and twirl of his neat moustache.

'All right. But Anil, this has to be treated as a straightforward business deal. Does the hotel still provide its car hire service?'

'Still all silver-grey Hindustan-Ambassadors. But I have contracted out that side of the business.'

'Good. Then we don't have to argue over payment. Now, could you arrange it? I'll pay you by cheque. I need to go to Belapore and from there on to Bombay.'

'No problem. "Dandekars Car Hire" is big company. This is branch. Main office is in Bombay. You can leave the car there. I'll give you their Bombay address and fix it all.'

'Many thanks, Anil,' Dinesh said. 'And keep this.'

'What's this, Dinesh Bhai?'

'I know you, Anil, That's why I've taken this precaution. It's a signed blank cheque. Just put in the amount.'

'You trusting me with a blank cheque? Brother you've made my day. You're on the run? Thought as much. Bastard!' Anil glanced at Alice. 'Sorry, but there is no polite way to refer to that swine, Agarwal. At least have a drink with me before you set off. Bar is on the first floor lounge.'

'Not for me. Alice? Thanks, we just want to freshen up.'

'Then, I'll get the chappie to show you the ground floor suite.'

The Lotus And The Rose

Twenty minutes later they were in the car. 'Happy?' Dinesh asked.'

She said nothing. He could see she had been crying. He took her hands in his. 'Please!'

'You've talked so much about yourself and your family, you've never asked about mine. All you know is my name?'

'Because I took you as you. You were all I needed to know. It's different now. You asked me if I'm coming to England. Yes. I'm setting aside my cocky nationalist ideas. The short stay in the *ashram* was enough to make me think how wonderful it would be to live in a civilised country, where one can have a decent shower and loos. But all that wouldn't have been enough. Knowing you'll be there, helped me make up my mind. If Sandy's watching, he'd be amused at the irony of it all. Anyway, we'll be together, and I'm full of questions. About where you live in England? All about your family. Will they accept me, an Indian? A married man . . . a divorced one?'

'I don't know. Mother's an enigma. You'll have to charm her. I think you will. As for Jonathan, you don't have to worry about him. One or two of the family might be, how shall I put it, prejudiced. We're not a posh family, but mercifully a small one. An aunt and uncle, their families, and all in Yorkshire. Apart from exchanging cards at Christmas, mum avoids contact. I'm the only one who's been to University, Warwick, and we live, mother and I, in Ludlow.'

Anil Chopra tapped on the window. 'Everything okay?'

'Yes, Chops, thanks. Darling wave to . . .' Dinesh started the car and they moved off. 'So, you're a Shropshire lass.'

She smiled. 'The house is lovely. Quite impressive. It's been in the family for a long time. We couldn't afford to buy it now. House prices have gone mad. We're lucky.'

'But you'll be with me in London?'

'Oh my love, I've so misjudged you. You have friends in England. I bet they'll be grand and genteel.'

'Genteel? I never quite know what that means. It's only Ted Franks I can claim to know well. His mother liked me. I didn't impress him. His beautiful daughter even less. I want to make a new life with you. Now I must concentrate on the driving. Chops has given me a map to the new motorway. I don't want to miss the turning to get to it.'

'This place we're going to . . .'

'Belapore. Yes?'

'Why?'

'You must wonder, all this roaming around with little more than a toothbrush . . . But I do have stuff, furniture, books, clothes, most important of all, my passport. The other friend, besides Anil, I said I can trust, he's been mopping up my stuff from Bombay and giving it storage space . . . Apart from what goes on the plane, I'll have to ditch the rest.'

'I could carry some of it on my baggage allowance.'

'Yes. And there are some fine books. Why don't you look at them? Take what you want. Talking about ditching stuff, get rid of that sari. I'm dying to see you in a dress. Show off those lovely legs. I'll buy you one in Bombay. There's a boutique at Kemp's Corner.'

'You'll do nothing of the sort. No more risks. We're going straight to the airport with your passport. Promise me!'

'I promise. Oh, one piece of good news I forgot to tell you. Anil found out that I could hand over the car at Santa Cruz Airport. I don't have to go to their City depot.'

'It must break your heart to leave so much stuff behind?'

'Incidentally, much of the furniture and books I had stored in Dharamsala has been eaten, demolished by white ants—termites which go for wood and paper. Nothing lasts. I may as well be philosophical. And accept my losses. Look what I've gained!'

'I suppose your friend in Belapore will have much to gain . . . why do you laugh?'

'Dhanraj, that's his name, is a prince, a Raja. He probably has my stuff stacked in one of his many godowns, store rooms. His father left him a large rambling old palace he doesn't know what to do with. I'd drew plans to turn it into a luxury hotel, with a large investment from Shanti's father. That's gone. Mind you, Danny, that's Dhanraj, said he hopes to find other investors to fund the project.'

'If he does, you can still see your project through.'

'True. Danny's in no hurry. He spends a lot of time abroad. In fact, he may be away when we get there. Not a problem. The servants know me.'

'I remember now, he's the one you bought the car from.'

'Yes. Tell me about your father. You've said nothing about him?'

The Lotus And The Rose

'Nothing to tell. One day he went out of the house and out of our lives. I've been alone with my mother since I was sixteen.'

'The packet of cigarettes syn . . . sorry, I'm being silly.'

'I don't know if he's alive or dead. Jonathan tried to find out. He's been on the trail ever since. I don't think about it. Mum took it well, too. Seemed not to care. Went on with life as if nothing happened. She won't talk about it.'

※

The massive cast iron gates were chained and padlocked. Through the bars Alice saw the pale sandstone palace gleaming in the evening light. 'Mother wouldn't believe it. We could be in France. It's like a French Chateau!'

'Yes, though I gather the architect was an Italian. Stay in the car, I'll find someone to open the gates. Danny must be abroad.'

'I can guess that from the locked gates.'

'The gates are always kept locked. When he's in he hoists his flag, a black elephant on a red background, copying the idea of flying Royal Standard when the Queen's in residence. Another Anglophile. We argued. He didn't care what I thought.'

'Is he married?'

'He'll never marry.'

'Not interested in women?'

'Not what I think you mean. He's more interested in horses. I know little about his private life, but at one party I went to, he turned up with his German mistress . . . ah, here comes . . . I'll give a beep to catch his attention.'

'Are you sure? That is one big Pathan charging down the drive with a *lathi*.'

'It's Motta Khan.' Dinesh got out of the car. The Pathan saluted him. They shook hands through the bars. A moment later the man ran back. Dinesh returned to the car. 'Gone for the keys.'

After a short wait, two figures approached the gates. Motta Khan's companion was a slight, bent figure, wearing a brown pillbox cap. He greeted Dinesh with folded hands and a toothy smile. 'Raja sahib gone Vilayat. Coming back another three weeks.'

'I'm good friend of Raja Dhanraj,' Dinesh said, recognising Mr Banerji.

'Dat I knowing. Also your *bibi* Shanti.' The man bent down and peered at Alice. After a moment's blank stare he recovered himself. 'What service I do for Dinesh sahib? I am also discreet gentleman.'

'This, Alice, is Dhanraj's long serving Secretary, the venerable Aurobindo Banerji, a fine Bengali gentleman; he began service with Danny's father when he was in Calcutta in the early nineteen sixties. Mr Banerji, this is Miss Alice Turnbull.'

'I used to know a Mr John Turnbull of the Hong Kong and Shanghai Bank in Delhi. Could he be related?'

'Not that I know of. Turnbull is not an uncommon name,' Alice smiled.

'Mr Banerji,' Dinesh broke in. 'I need to collect some of my things. I don't expect to be here for more than two nights.'

'I see no problem, gentleman, except for tonight the cook has gone home early. In any case there's no goods for him to prepare a meal. So if you give Motta Khan some money, he will get some *Rogan Gosh* and *roti*; some soda water maybe for a whisky drink or other hard stuff. I open bar room for you. From tomorrow, every hospitality at your disposal. Miss Turnbull, the Rajasahib insists his guests be treated well.'

'Will sixty rupees do?' Dinesh asked, counting the notes in his wallet.

'That is more than sufficient for the purpose.'

'Then tell Motta Khan to get *sabzi, dhal* and rice. Miss Turnbull is vegetarian.'

'A white woman! Vegetarian like me! Most wonderful!' Mr Banerji rolled his head, while, behind dark, heavy-rimmed spectacles, the rheumy but kindly eyes, gleamed his astonishment. 'Then my wife will be glad to provide the evening meal, she is excellent vegetarian cook. So if I can sit in the back seat of car, I shall guide you to my abode.'

Mrs Banerji appeared to be several years younger than her husband. She took the news about having to extend the evening meal with a calm roll of her head. 'Please to sit down, be homely. I'll make hot, hot, onion bhajias. To have with drinks.'

The Lotus And The Rose

Mr Banerji smiled sheepishly at Alice. 'You see, I indulge in a little hard stuff.'

After the meal, Mr Banerji led Dinesh aside. 'I will accommodate you in the main bedroom. It is one always kept in readiness for such contingencies. The bed is a little noisy, but there is no one to disturb, so enjoy the solitude.'

'Mr Banerji, let me explain . . .' Dinesh gaped as the old man gave a knowing wink.'

'No need for explanations. I have been long in the Raja's service to know that the watchword is, how d'you say it, "Mummies the word?"

'Mum's the word. Well, thank you. As I said, no more than a couple nights.'

'I shall tell the *khansamah* to see that you are provided with tea and breakfast, then I shall come with godown keys . . . ten o'clock. Your keys are in the writing desk.'

Banerji and Khan came to collect Dinesh and Alice punctually at ten. Mr Banerji said: 'The storerooms are back of the palace, therefore, I suggest you bring car round.'

'I'll do that,' said Dinesh, 'and thank you for all the trouble you have taken.'

'Mr Banerji bowed graciously to Alice. 'I trust you've slept well.'

Alice ignored the wicked twinkle in the old man's eye. 'Yes, thank you, and once again please thank Mrs Banerji for the lovely dinner.'

'That I will do with pleasure. And please note, before you leave tomorrow, to call on her. It is her intention to prepare some comestibles for your journey to Bombay.'

'That is so kind. Tell her not to take too much trouble.'

'Most considerate. One o'clock bearer come with tiffin lunch. Thakurji has pleaded for a non-vegetarian meal, so there shall be one dish of lamb curry, with puris and rice.'

Alice watched the retreating figure of Mr Banerji and noted his highly polished black brogues, neatly folded down blue cotton socks and white calico dhoti. The collar of his ill-fitting brown *achkan* jacket was unfastened, but what made her smile was the sight of a large amber handled, unrolled umbrella tucked under his right arm. 'That,' Dinesh remarked, 'is a sight which would have been familiar to Rudyard Kipling.'

'Why the umbrella, under a hot cloudless sky?'

'Just that. He'll have it up in the afternoon, against the noonday sun. It also makes an indispensable part of the typical Bengali Babu's uniform. His is a dying race.'

'Have you ever worn a *dhoti*?'

'On one ceremonial occasion.'

'I know. On your wedding day.'

'I hate them. Given a gust of wind, they reveal more than they hide. It is mostly worn in Bengal and South India. Gujarat too. Not much in the Punjab. Gandhi's was little more than a loin cloth. In Britain, he was asked about it. Gandhi, never slow to answer, promptly said: "You English have your plus fours, I have my minus fours."'

'Good. That was clever. But do the young middle-classes of India, wear *dhotis*?.'

'It's more important for India to be a modern industrialised nation, moving with the times. It's one thing to wear handwoven *dhotis* as a demonstration against British rule and to boycott Bristish goods. But all that is behind us, now.'

'Gandhi was a great man.'

'India's youth were fans of Nehru rather than Gandhi. You said Gandhi was clever. Sandy said so too. This was one of the areas in which we saw eye to eye. Gandhi was shrewd, but he is not above criticism.'

'Who isn't?'

'We should get on. You see those steel trunks . . . I'll open them and you can then pick the books you want. Put them to one side. Remember books are heavy. I won't bother to take any . . . maybe the set of Gibbons, some shirts and the two suits I'm rather fond of. I'll find and empty two suitcases.'

'First find your passport.'

'It's in that desk . . . I can't open the drawer . . . give me a hand to get this sofa out of the way . . . careful, don't hurt yourself.'

'Don't fuss, I'm stronger than you think.'

'Yes.' Dinesh pressed his hands against the small of his back. 'How can I forget.'

'I refuse to be embarrassed and I won't talk about it. I've said this before, that sex, according to Henry James, is highly overrated.'

'I'm afraid I haven't read James . . .'

'A gap in your education. When we get to England . . .'

'I was put off reading him . . . put the box on that table, then we won't have to bend. Yes, by Somerset Maugham. He said that James is like a mountaineer who collects all the equipment necessary for the ascent of Everest, in order to climb Primrose Hill. Or words to that effect.'

'You'll change your mind. At least I hope . . . you might want to see this. It's a box file, with letters and some photographs.'

'I'll take them for Ted. He's writing a book about Sandy and Emma . . . I thought he had all the relevant . . . No, these are addressed to me. I gave Kitty some of Emma's stuff three years ago, before leaving Dharamsala.'

'Kitty? Oh, yes, Ted's daughter, and Ted is Emma's brother. Here's something else. A brown paper parcel. Too light and soft to be a book.'

'Open it.'

Alice did. 'It's a dress. A beautiful maroon dress. It's old, but it's back in fashion.'

'Gosh! Emma's! I missed that. Edith, her mother, made it and sent it to her. She, Emma looked smashing in it. Wore it once, then took to wearing Punjabi clothes.

Alice held the dress against her. 'It's the right length but it will be a little tight above the waist.'

'Put it on. Please. I want to see you in a dress. It's just past eleven, no one will be here till one. You heard Banerji say that.'

'All right. Look away. I mean it!' Alice undressed and slipped the dress on. 'Now you can turn around. A little tight round the bust, as I thought. It could do with another inch in length. Why are you looking . . . Don't. Stop it.'

'You look different. Younger and absolutely wonderful. I could make love to you.'

'Love among the boxes! You'll do nothing of the kind. And not tonight either.'

'Last night did you take precautions?'

'I did. It was the right time.'

'But I didn't see . . . good Lord, are you Roman Catholic?'

'Guruji also opposes the use of contraceptives, because it's against nature.'

'But it's not a fool-proof method.'

'If you're worried, you may use . . . in England, there are contraceptives all over the place. By the way, if Shanti's child is less than a year old, he could be yours.'

'I've told you what I believe. Anyway there's no turning back.'

'I don't want you to.' She stroked the front of the dress. 'It's a beautiful dress. I like the material. Non-iron linen. Maybe synthetic. Is Kitty the same size as Emma?

'Yes, as I said, Emma's double in every way, except the eyes. Emma's were blue.'

'Then post it to her. To Kitty. You should, when you can. There's no need for you to keep it. What's Kitty doing in Dharamsala?'

'Near Dharamsala, Nurpur, a mile or two higher up the Himalayan foot hills. She came to be a teacher and social worker at the Christian Missionary School . . . but she left. Resigned. Found the rapid changes in the area too much to cope with. It is now more Tibetan than Indian. She's staying on in Mcleodganj, in Fern Cottage, which was Sandy's old cottage . . . and Emma's.'

'Doesn't that belong to you?'

'Yes. I'll sell it the first chance I get. It's a beautiful cottage, but I can't live there. Painful memories. Someday I'll take you there. You'll think you're in Scotland.' He laughed. 'Without the rain and the midges.'

'I've heard about Mcleodganj becoming Tibetan. Little Lhasa they now call it.'

'Actually it's more than a cottage, its a house, with orchards and farm lands. All on a separate spur of hillside, north of and apart from Mcleodganj. The land is out on hire to farmers. I get a third of the revenue. It does well, and my friend Mohan Singh, a Sikh magnate and tea planter, keeps an eye on the property, for me. He knows I'll sell it to him. To anyone but the bloody Seth.'

'I wondered how you prevented your father-in-law getting hold of your property. If all was well with you and Shanti, would you have let him?'

'Yes. Actually, though I said Mohan Singh keeps an eye on the land, Ted Franks is a trustee. Sandy thought I was too young. Thank God he did.'

'But you're Sandy's heir.'

'There's another reason why I can't just sell it. I have to share a small part of the cottage with Sona—Sona my long standing rival. Sandy wanted to protect her. I'll need the consent not just of Ted Franks, but Bill Clayton as well. He's the missionary I told you about. He was a trustee too. But Bill was killed in an accident. I learnt about that in Bombay, long after the event. The cottage, more for the sake of the servants than anything else, has to be kept going, so, I begged Ted to persuade Kitty to live there. Fortunately it coincided with her decision to give up her job at the Mission.'

'Is she alone?'

'She's unmarried if that's what you mean.'

'What about Sona?'

Sona disappeared after Sandy died. She was eventually traced by Bill. Ransingh, the chowkidar, turned out to be her husband. They had kept their liaison a secret. Ransingh is happy to live in the little more than a hut Bill Clayton provided for them. By the way, Bill Clayton was from an aristocratic family with property in England. He sold all that to build a school for the Mission to run. It's all very involved . . . enough to say that Sona visits the cottage frequently; Ransingh her partner is our chowkidar. Now he serves as school chowkidar. Then there's the mali, cook and servants, so, Kitty's well cared for.'

Alice sighed. 'What complicated lives we lead! So, it's dead property? Such a waste. I mean, it's of no benefit to you.'

'It is. But I do get a regular income from the estate.'

'And you can trust that man, the Sikh . . .'

'Mohan Singh's a big businessman. Not just in Tea, but also in turpentine. I trust him not only because he wants to buy the cottage and estate, but also because he's not the sort of chap to let Seth Agarwal intimidate him.'

'Now no more talk. We really must get on. You're a very open person. I like that.'

'Only with you. I want you to know all about me.'

'That's sweet. We've achieved little. Soon it will be lunch time.'

'Tiffin time. It won't take long to fill two suitcases. We don't really need to spend a second night here.'

'Yes we do. We need airline tickets, both of us! We can't just turn up at the airport on spec, can we? I'd rather spend a night here, than one at the airport.' She walked up to the open door. 'It is so beautiful. The palace looks magnificent. This is quite a rare experience for me in India. I mean this opulence. My image of India is of teeming life, jostling crowds, poverty and beggars. Where are all the people of this town?'

'They're there all right. In the bazaars and streets. Here you'll only see those who have a job of work to do in this palace. The gate and high walls shut the town off. Do you know the story of Prince Siddhartha, the Buddha? All the misery of the world was similarly hidden from him till he set out beyond the gates of his palace.'

'Here comes Mr Banerji. I better change quickly.'

'Keep it on, you look good in it. Old Banerji's quite taken to you. I'll rely on that charm of yours to get him to book our airline tickets.

CHAPTER EIGHTEEN

'I wanted to talk . . . Dinesh, keep the bar pressed or the trolley won't move.'

'Alice, I had spotted a porter, you should've let me . . .'

'No. You're not in India. In England live as the English do. Listen, during the flight, I wanted to talk about our future plans. But you were sleepy tired.'

'Sorry. I couldn't sleep the night before. I was so afraid something might go wrong. Once the plane took off, you told me to relax and I did.'

'I know. I hadn't the heart to disturb you. It's all happened so fast, and we've talked about everything but the future. How well do you know Britain?'

'Apart from London, not much. Two holidays. One in Scotland, one in Wales.'

'We need to find you a place to stay in London. A one bedroom flat to start with.'

'I thought I was going with you to . . .'

'I'm sorry, my love, I can't. I haven't told mother about you. It wouldn't be fair to spring you on her without warning. You have to give us time. It's going to be a quite a shock for her. She's sweet and friendly but old fashioned about things like sex and marriage. For my sake she'll eventually accept you, but then she'll want to be told why we can't get married. Don't look at me like that. I know, till now, I've made us being together look so simple. It isn't. We have to consider other people.'

'Dear Alice, it might be better to tell her the whole story in one instalment.'

'Maybe. She'll be moved by your situation and I'll say how much I love you. Let me do it my way. It won't be long. I'll be in touch. Here we can communicate openly. You brought me back to her. That's in your favour. She expected not to see me for years.'

'Tell her I've filed for divorce. That, according to my solicitor, the case will be heard and settled in my absence. I don't have to be there. But it will take time, because the wheels of Indian bureaucracy move slowly. One advantage of being here, there can be no doubt about judicial separation. England's my alibi.'

'One can divorce only on grounds of adultery or proof of two years separation?'

'Yes. But my solicitor is a clever man. If there's a loophole, he'll find it.'

'And how are you going to manage for pounds sterling?'

'I've a bank account from my time as a student. I can keep that topped up through Ted Franks.'

'I gave you his letter. He's no longer at Chalfont St Giles. He's back in Winchester.'

'He was a doctor. You told me Ted was a doctor. A GP in London?'

'Yes. He lived in Chalfont after he retired. He must have sold that place, if he's back in Winchester. That's the family home. I don't really know him all that well. He's very English. Reserved and all that.'

'Which reminds me. Don't expect stereotypes in Britain today. Don't fall for that "rolled umbrella, bowler hatted, stiff upper-lip" image. Nine times out of ten, reserve is an act simply to avoid involvement. Meet Ted without pre-conceived ideas. If he's a trustee to much of your funds and property, you'd better become friends. You have more money than sense. Sorry, but you do give me the impression of being rather slap-dash about keeping track of all your wealth.'

'That's because its in bits and pieces. You are looking at a businessman. A shrewd one. Six months before I decided to divorce my Shanti, I gave myself a fat salary rise and tucked away a full year's bonus. I was in a position to do that. Believe me, I give a lot of thought before making any move. I will contact Ted, and keep close touch with my solicitors, Mohan Singh and Fernandez. I've a pocket book with addresses.'

'Then you won't forget to thank Anil Chopra and the Raja of Belapore?'

'Yes, bossy boots. Not Chopra. We don't know who's checking his mail.'

Paddington Station looked cleaner and brighter than Dinesh remembered it. 'Are you sure this is the right platform, Alice?'

'It is,' Alice said a little impatiently. 'Put the suitcase down and don't sulk. You must accept I need to sort things out in my own way. If I can accept you staying in a hotel, which I didn't want you to do, and if I can make allowances, you must do the same! There are things that I need to do!'

'I didn't want to run out for meals or prepare them myself, which I can't. In a hotel I'll have more freedom than if I rented a studio flat.'

'All right, I've apologised. You're fortunate to be rich enough to do that, just don't let it spoil you. It makes me feel redundant, and I'm not used to that. I'm very grateful for all you've done. I really have had a wonderful time, but now, if I'm to think clearly, and pick up where I left off. I need to go to Oxford first? Be sweet and stay here while I buy my ticket, yes?' She kissed him lightly on his cheek. 'There, I won't be long.'

'I still don't see why you need to go to Oxford?'

'Sweetheart, you're going to make me miss the train!'

'You didn't tell me about Andrew.'

'Sorry, but you mustn't imagine I've lied to you. Had you asked I would've told you. At my age, surely you would expect me to have a boy friend? All right, let's have a heart to heart. I owe you that. I'll take the next train. Forty minutes won't matter. Take the case to that café. I'll join you there, after I've got my ticket. I'll feel relaxed once I've bought my ticket. Just coffee, nothing else.'

When Alice joined him Dinesh was sipping his coffee thoughtfully. He pushed a cup towards her. She put it to one side and reached out to hold his hands. 'Don't make a big thing out of this. We'll be seeing a lot of each other. Andrew means nothing to me.'

'Then why see him? You could write to him.'

'Don't be jealous of someone who's no threat to you. Nothing will happen. He, more or less gave up on me, when I told him I would spend two years in an *ashram* in India, while he did a post-graduate teaching course.'

'Do you still love him?'

'No. But I like him.'

'Is he handsomer than me?'

'Possibly. But I love you.'

'Does my being an Indian . . .'

'Don't be absurd. I've been with you all this time, haven't I? Anyway most people here must take you for an Italian or a Spaniard. Look around you. The place is full of all kinds of people. I should get cross with you for bringing this up.'

'Didn't you like the dresses and the jewellery I got you?'

'You're determined to be miserable. I'm wearing this blue dress just for you.'

'Alice, you looked fantastic in it.'

'Well, then, be happy? I shall see Andrew wearing jeans and shirt.'

Dinesh smiled. 'I'm being silly. But I can't help being jealous about other men.'

'Dinesh, because I love you it doesn't mean you own me. I'm not going to be a shy and meek little Indian girl walking two paces behind you. This is England. Adjust to that. Understand and trust me. I'm lucky to be loved by someone like you, rich and generous to boot, but I'm no gold-digger. I'd be equally loving and happy if we were an average couple. Drink up and see me off on the train, which I'm happy to learn I haven't missed, and give me a good hug and a kiss. Write. Don't forget to see Ted.'

'So, this is where Sandy met Emma,' Dinesh said, looking about him.

'Did Sandy say that?' Ted Franks studied Dinesh and thought he had changed since he last saw him. 'Actually he first met Emma in the local cemetery. He'd gone to visit my father's grave.'

Dinesh found Ted's steady grey-eyed stare disconcerting. 'You're looking well,' he said, defensively. They walked through the French windows and on to the terrace.

The Lotus And The Rose

'You're looking well, too.' Ted smiled.

'I meant to say, Ted, you look the same as when I last saw you in . . .'

'It wasn't many years ago, Dinesh.'

'I would like to visit Edith's grave,' Dinesh said after a moment's silence.

'My mother was cremated. It was her wish. Her ashes are interred in my father's grave. We could go there this evening before you leave for London.' The grey eyes softened. 'I'm sorry to hear about your troubles and I wish I could be of more help. But now that you're here, you can safely let time bring about a change.'

'Yes, that's what Alice said too.'

'Alice? oh, yes. I'd like to know Alice.'

'A friend. Someone I met. She's been a great support. I met her in Goa. It's a long story.'

Ted waved a deprecating hand.

After a pause Dinesh said: 'I've brought you some letters. Hope they'll be of use.'

'Thank you. I thought I had all their letters.'

'These were addressed to me.'

'You won't mind if I use them.'

'No. Ted, I'm not the chap you knew . . . I was a pompous ass. I've changed.'

'You were very young. One must always make allowances for the young. As you'll no doubt find out, in time, when you have youngsters to bring up.'

'I still think my conduct inexcusable. How is the book getting on?'

'As well as can be. At times I wish I hadn't taken it on. I'm not a natural writer.'

'And how is Kitty?'

'She's well. You could've seen for yourself, but she had to go to London on some unavoidable business. She wanted very much to see you. But there'll be other times.'.

'She's not in India? I thought she was staying in Sandy's cottage.'

'She was. I was there too, on a short holiday, four months ago. I went to bring her back. It was mother's wish. This house is hers,

Kitty's. But I'm settling down here. It is the family home. Has been for five generations.'

'And has she got India out of her system?'

'Not quite, but she now wants to work in the South. In Kerala. It may not happen. There has been a new development which has to do with her trip to London today. If it resolves the way I hope it will, then this house has a future.'

For a moment the two men looked at each other, and Dinesh recognised the glint in Ted's grey translucent eyes. 'Do I hear wedding bells?'

'My arthritic fingers have remained so crossed that I can't uncross them. Yes. It's not to late for her to have children. She'll make a good mother.'

There was a light tap on the window pane behind them. 'Ted, someone is trying to get your attention.'

'That'll be Sarah and a signal that lunch will be served in half an hour. Shall we go in. She doesn't like lunch to be kept waiting. Sarah's a good cook. A small repertoire but good wholesome stuff. She comes in the mornings.'

'What about dinners?'

'I'm quite a dab hand at opening cans of soup and making cold meat sandwiches. And Kitty's learned a lot. Makes a good authentic curry. By the way, you must come again. Spend a few days here. There's plenty of room. Bring Alice too.'

'Thank you, I will. But it'll be some time. Next week I'm meeting her mother for the first time and I hope to stay there for a fortnight.'

'So, Alice lives outside London?'

'Yes, Ludlow in Shropshire. Ted, a silly question, but I noticed your neighbour's thatched roof is an unusual colour. I thought thatched roofs were almost black.'

'That's because it's new. The neighbours are new too, fairly. We don't really know them as well as we did the Williamses. Close friends of my mother, particularly Mary Williams. She had a young son, a little older than Emma. If it wasn't for Sandy, Emma would've been another Mrs Williams. They sold the house and settled in South Africa.'

'Talking about selling. We need to get down to the real purpose of my visit. You know I've been keen to sell Fern Cottage, and you also know that the best person to sell it to is Mohan Singh.'

'I remember now, Alice, she wrote to me on your behalf. Mohan Singh had agreed to buy it at the best price we hoped to get. He also agreed to take on the servants. As for Sona's bit of the house, he would like to negotiate with her directly. But whatever sum of money he'll pay her, we will have to reimburse that amount.'

'A good arrangement,' Dinesh said, 'I'll readily sign on the dotted line.'

'I suppose fifty thousand pounds is a good price. A pity though,' Ted sighed. 'A fine house on a beautiful site. And all that land as well. It's less than a tenth of the price it would fetch here.'

'Ted, it's quite isolated.'

'That can be seen as a plus.'

'And expensive to run.'

'You're thinking about the generator. Emma quite liked using oil lamps. Mohan Singh's a resourceful chap. He'll put in electricity. The plumbing's good and the pipes are in good condition. I've always wondered why, if the builders troubled to lay down pipes, why they missed out on electricity.'

'At that time much of the area was without electricity.' Dinesh raised his brows as Ted shifted uneasily in his chair. 'There something else you want to say? Bad news?'

Ted nodded. 'I've been trying to pick the right time to say it. There never is a right time for bad news. I would have preferred to write. But it coincided with Alice's cable telling me you'd soon be in London and would be contacting me. So I waited.'

'Mohan Singh has backed out?'

'No. That remains the only good part of the terrible news. He phoned me a week ago, and followed it by a letter I received yesterday. There was a fire. More than half the cottage has been gutted.'

'My God! Was it an accident?'

'The locals have been told to say that. And the story going the rounds is that the generator exploded, setting fire to the oil tank. Mohan thinks it was arson and firemen and the police agree with him. Mohan and I have a hunch. You can guess what that is.'

'Shanti's father? Seth Agarwal's henchmen? So he's discovered I've left India.'

'Yes. Vendetta. There's worse to come.'

'Casualties? The servants?'

'The servants are fine. Their quarters are right at the back. Only the front half of the house has been destroyed and one death. Sona!'

'*Hai Raam*! My God! Sona.'

'Mohan Singh wondered why she was there.'

'Good God, it just occurred to me, you and Kitty have had a narrow escape.'

'When we were there, you were in India and his quarrel's with you. While there, you may not like this, but Kitty and Shanti became quite good friends. Kitty's been to the Seth's house several times and he's grown rather fond of her.

'I'm not surprised, the Seth had a theory about faces. Women's in particular. He believed a woman is beautiful because a goddess chooses to dwell in her body.'

'How would Shanti fit into that theory of his . . . I'm not suggesting she's ugly, but . . .'

'I suppose he makes exceptions.'

'Incidentally, Alice wrote about your situation—rather what you told her in detail.'

Dinesh sighed. 'You were going to say something more about Sona . . .'

'Oh, yes. I think Sona and Ransingh got wind of the news . . . that the house was to be torched. There can be no other explanation for what happened subsequently.'

'Was Ransingh also, I mean how is Ransingh?'

'He's been arrested. I expect he's languishing in jail. You do know he was Sona's husband? Arrested on a charge of murder. Mohan and I believe his story, and it is also the reason why we think it was arson. Ransingh found a man lurking in the stable. This is after the fire had started; and learning of Sona's death, this normally sober man, in a wild frenzy, beat the intruder to death. With his *lathi*.'

'But if he was there, why was he not with Sona?'

'I don't know. Mohan has worked it out. His letter tells the full story as if he was a witness to the whole incident, which, of course, he wasn't, and why he can't take the witness stand to defend Ransingh. He could've got the story from Ransingh, which is that Sona rushed into the burning house before Ransingh could stop her, and she was killed by a falling beam. Poor man, he'll be hanged.'

'But it's a case of self-defence or mitigating circumstances, at least!'

'There is no one to corroborate Ransingh's story. He killed his only alibi. And he proudly admitted killing the man.'

'We must stop that. I mean Ransingh being hanged. Sona's death has to be a plea for mitigating circumstance. Don't you agree?'

'Yes. Mohan's made a deposition and produced a petition signed by over a hundred local people. But murder is murder and Ransingh's confessed to it. If he escapes the gallows,which is unlikely, he'll get life imprisonment. I've asked Mohan to engage a good lawyer.'

'Yes, Ted. At my expense.'

'We'll split the costs. The Seth is not leaving it at that. He claims the murdered man was an employee, and that the man had seen the fire and ran into the premises to help.'

'I really should go back, back to Pathankot.'

'That's madness! You'll achieve nothing. Let's see what can be done about the sale of the house. Mohan has not changed his mind, but in the circumstances he now offers £40,000. I'm sorry, but I can only think in pounds sterling. Keep an eye on it, inflation in India is on the rise. Repairs will, by Mohan's calculations, exceed £10,000, but he'll bear the excess, because he feels, in fairness, he had originally intended to spend about £5,000 to refurbish the place. Don't rush to a decision. Think about it.'

'Ted, I don't want to think about it at all. Accept Mohan's offer. I suppose Sona's share will make it another £5,000 less.'

'Six, actually.'

'That's fine. Ransingh can look forward to that, if . . . Didn't he have a son?'

'Yes. His son enlisted. Second Gharwal Rifles. He got a fortnight's compassionate leave. There's nothing he could do, apart from giving support and comfort. Now he's back with his regiment, in Ranikhet. It's awful business, the whole shocking affair. I've always liked Sona. I thought she was a lovely woman and Ransingh a lucky man.' Ted got up and looked through the French windows. 'It's stopped raining,' he said. 'Let me give you a lift to the cemetery.'

'Cemetery? Oh, yes! Where Edith's ashes are buried. My car or yours?'

'Mine. I see you have got yourself a brand new car. They're good, Japanese cars.'

'I did think of buying British but I liked the look of this one.'

'When I was a boy, the name Japanese was synonymous with rubbish. Not now.'

'I see yours is a Ford.'

Ted smiled. 'Sandy would have said, "you can af-ford better".'

Dinesh got out of his car and consulted his map. He could see the castle and soon located it on the map. Then he read Alice's instructions for the umpteenth time and failed to understand where he went wrong. A young man walked past him. 'Excuse me!' he called. 'I'm looking for Church Crescent.'

'Fuck off!'

Dinesh was taken aback and just about managed to mumble: 'I beg you pardon!'

The youth took a step nearer. 'I said "fuck off", get it, now eff off.'

'I will, when I get there,' Dinesh said, and immediately regretted it.

'You trying to be funny, mother-fucker.' The young man moved up to Dinesh, his eyes wild, threatening. 'I say!' A voice rang out accompanied by a loud tapping of a walking stick on the pavement. They looked in the direction of the sounds. An elderly man was drawing attention to himself. He was smartly dressed in a sports jacket, grey flannel trousers, a tweed cap, and a handsome Red Irish Setter on a lead. 'I say, are you lost. Can I be of help?'

The youth grunted and loped away. Dinesh walked up to the man, and held out the open map. 'Yes, thank you. I'm looking for Church Street.'

'You must mean Church Crescent. Would've been easier if you'd approached the town from the Ludforth Bridge. Never mind, I can point to it from here. You see the church? St Laurence. Its the road behind it. You can't see the turn in, the great tower's in the way.

You've come much too high up. It's no good showing me a map. Go back and start again.'

'Thank you.'

'Don't mention it. Where do you come from?'

'India.'

'Ah! Then you must see Clive's House. Clive? Robert Clive. Clive of Plassey.'

'Sorry, I was taken by surprise. Yes, I certainly will, thank you again.'

'I served in India, and my father before me. I was with a tank regiment. Saw action in Burma. Knew a chap called Jarvis. Can't forget him, saved my life.'

'An uncle of mine served in Burma. I only know of him. But he was there. That's all any one knows about him. He never came back.'

'You don't think he went over to join the Indian National Army, eh, what?' The old man laughed and coughed at the same time. 'Just joking, you know. But quite a few did. Believe you me, that chap, I forget his name, a nasty piece of work.'

'You may be right. I assume you're referring to Nataji Chandra Bose?'

'That's the man. We called him the "Natter Toad". Nasty piece of work. No offence meant. It's all in the past now. They thought the Japs would welcome them with open arms. Never happened. Japs despised any form of disloyalty.'

'I really must be going. Thank you.'

'Goodbye! I loved India, you know. Has it changed much?'

'I'm sure it has since your time. Have you never been back?'

'No. This country's changed too. Much for the worst. Well, it's a lovely day. Warm for the season. An Indian Summer, what!' The man laughed. 'Goodbye!'

'Goodbye!' Dinesh looked back as he walked to his car. The man's laughter made him cough and splutter, and his excited dog pranced up and down.

Alice and her mother, Kay, waited for Dinesh in what Kay called the parlour. They sat on the chintz covered sofa facing the bay window. The opened curtains gave them a clear view of the paved path that led from the little cast-iron gate to the ivy-covered stone porch outside their blue front door. Behind them, a small, oval dining table was laid out for tea with Alice's freshly baked sponge cake and Kay's banana, walnut and date sandwiches. On a third plate were squares of chocolate fudge brownies—another of Kay's specialities, and of such acclaim among the parishioners of St John's Church, that it helped to make its December Christmas Bazaar an annual success. She was tall, lean, pleasant looking with curly white hair; and it was easy to see what Alice would look like twenty years on. But in one prominent feature they differed. Kay's eyes were strikingly blue.

'I wasn't sure about the roast ham, Alice,' Kay said. 'I remembered something about Indians not eating pork. You should've thought of that, love.'

'No, Mum, you should've trusted me. It's Muslims who don't eat pork and Hindus who don't eat beef. Dinesh is Hindu. In any case he eats everything. Yes, even beef. He loves a steak. We'll plan for that. Then you can make your delicious mushroom sauce.'

'I'm all at sixes and sevens. But one lives and learns. I'm sure to make mistakes and cause offence. Still it's some consolation to know he's not fussy about food. Have you warned him how cold it can get?'

'Yes. Relax. You're far too lovely to offend by anything you say or do. Everyone says I look like you. Not true. At your age I won't be half as attractive.'

'I don't know what you're on about. I'm what did you say, charming? I'm not. I do offend people you know. I'd best keep my mouth shut. "Count up to ten before you speak", as my father would say to me. I also find it hard to talk to Indians. Even harder to understand them.'

'Mother, the only Indians you know are the waiters in the Shalimar Restaurant.'

'There's one that comes to church.'

'He's West Indian. From Trinadad. Dinesh is very different. You'll see. And you'll only rarely detect an accent. He was educated in England.'

'He's still a foreigner. A young man in a house with two women. People will talk.'

'People will talk even if Andrew came to stay. Or Jonathan.'

'What did happen? With Andrew, I mean. You said you'd tell me about it. It's not really over between you two, is it?'

'Don't mention Andrew when Dinesh is here. Please ma, he's jealous. He was very unhappy about my seeing Andrew, at all. Quite cross.'

'Does he know Andrew?'

'Of course not. Nor do you. The meeting was a disaster. He really upset me, In a cold sophisticated way he told me all that could go wrong with my "Indian attachment" as he called it. He can be downright offensive.'

'And you can be stubborn. Alice, I also have my doubts and fears about this whole affair. When it comes to the crunch, we're all racist. Those who are not are the ones who can afford to be.'

'What *do* you mean?

'It's easy to be broadminded, when it's someone else's problem. When it personally enters your life and you've got to face . . . I'll say no more. You're never going to agree or change your mind. It's all too late for that, anyhow. I can see. I know.'

'Mother stop talking in riddles.'

'I've let you have your way in everything, and I know when your mind's made up. We have to learn the hard way. My mother said, marry in haste repent at leisure.'

'We're not marrying in haste! We couldn't even if we wanted to.'

'So, you'll be living in sin; for who knows how long? I can't see you pressing him to do the right thing. It's worse than marrying in haste. You could be left stranded, with a little one to boot. Sorry, I can't help wanting to know. I worry. I don't know why you stopped going to Mass. Why you turned to these mad newfangled religious cults . . . say what you like, they're heathen. Dangerous too. That friend of yours, Veena, she's been a bad influence. Don't turn away, I am your mother. I care. You're all I have.'

'Please! You mustn't cry. He'll be here soon.' Alice put an arm round her mother. 'We've been through all this before. I'm sorry I hurt you. I'm here and I'm not going back. About Dinesh, it happened. I didn't plan it. But please understand, I've told you how much I love him. Andrew doesn't need me. Dinesh does.'

'Those marriages seldom last... where the man needs the woman, and you're quite bossy, you know. I don't want to frighten you, but no man likes to be bossed over. Just remember that. You're a good girl. Always one for caring, getting mixed up in all sorts of things, like a cat, wandering off, and returning with strange creatures, strange ideas, strange people, strange fads . . . all this business of Guruji . . . and becoming a vegetarian.'

'Right. Give me a big smile and I'll stop being a vegetarian. Truly! I mean it.'

'Now you're going to make me feel bad.'

'No. It's no sacrifice. I've been thinking about it, recently, and weakening. Dinesh has taken me to so many grand restaurants. I've been sorely tempted. What he ate was so much more delicious than the insipid stuff served up on to my plate.'

'Then it'll please him too. Alice, what should I . . . I'll have so little to say to him.'

'Don't worry, He's talkative and he likes elderly women. He really will be the right person for us. He wants you to live with us. He said that, the moment he realised you'll be alone. "Oh, you can't leave your mother on her own", he said. That's the Hindu side to him, extended family and all it means in his culture. He might be westernised but his roots are still Indian. I've watched him. Odd, at times, to be reminded how very Indian he . . . I shouldn't say odd because it's also fascinating.'

'That won't help, love. You know me. I like to be independent. Have a place of my own. I'm all right. I've managed so far. Maybe, it made you think I didn't care. Didn't need you. But I do, have always done. And this is different. Not because he's Indian. No couple wants another, and surely not a mother . . . I'd be in the way.'

'I just want you to know he'll be an easier son-in-law to like than any Englishman would be. And, of course, I've always known you care. All the more because you make living with you easy. Other girls leave home in their teens! We've been together longer than most. Now I'll just go up to put fresh towels in his bedroom.'

Her mother nodded. 'And thank you, love, for not . . . you know what. I couldn't bear it. Not under my roof.'

'Yes, mother, we'll abstain. Its only for three nights. Dinesh will understand.'

'I suppose that will mean you'll be joining him in London, soon?'

'Yes, but not simply for the sake of a life of sin. I need to earn a living, mum, and my Training College is in London. Besides, he couldn't stay here for a long time?'

'I'm wedded to the Church. Father McCowan knows that.'

'And friends know about Jonathan. Don't make a face. You're beautiful. He should consider himself lucky.'

'Which reminds me, Jonathan is furious with you.'

'I don't care, as long as he's not furious with you. I had lied about him to Dinesh. It didn't seem right to tell him I had travelled with my mother's intended. And I wasn't to know then that Dinesh was going to be part of our . . . I hate lying. I saw no need why he had to know. Besides it concerned you. I felt I had no right too . . .'

'Well, Jonathan isn't going to turn up to prove you lied. If things had worked out as you expected, Jonathan would be sort of related or connected. But that's not to be. As I said, I'm wedded to the Church. My mind's firmly made up.'

'Poor Jonathan. But he did find out about dad and got the death certificate. There's nothing to stop you now . . . You won't be breaking Catholic rules.'

'I couldn't go through with it. I loved your father very much. He was so handsome and gentle. Why he did what he did I'll never know.'

'He was neurotic and prone to bouts of depression. Davidson said that.'

'Davidson?'

'You remember, Davidson? Dr Hugh Davidson at the clinic?'

'Oh, yes. I remember Dr Davidson. Did Graham go to see him?'

'Yes. And when Davidson left to practice in Manchester, dad wouldn't see anyone else. I thought you knew?'

Kay sighed. 'I did. And Graham took to drinking. Let's not talk about it . . . . As for Jonathan, well, I hate to be unfair to anyone, but I do believe he was more interested in the house than he was in me. When he was last here, he'd looked around the place as if he was making a mental inventory.'

'Maybe if . . . if you'd given the poor man a chance to demonstrate his love.'

'I was being a good Catholic. He's a bachelor. There was nothing to stop him doing the right thing. Oh, we did hug and kiss . . . you're making me say things I don't . . . you've always been good at getting people to talk . . . to bare . . .'

'I'm like you. Chip of the old bitch!'

'Hush, Alice. Watch your tongue girl. You mustn't use foul language. Anyway, you didn't like Jonathan. I thought about that, too.'

'It was none of my business, whatever I felt. I didn't mean to stand in your way.'

'You should've seen Jonathan's face when I made it clear that the house is in your name.' She chuckled, looking and sounding like Alice. 'Its now water under the bridge. I do hope, when, what's his name . . .'

'Dinesh?'

'When Dinesh sees us living in a fine detached house, knowing it will be yours . . .

'Mum, I didn't want to tell you, because you know how you get all respectful and over attentive when rich people are about . . . you know what I mean. But Dinesh, oh, he'll like the house, who wouldn't, but he's not going to eye it. He's a very rich man. Can't say how rich, because I don't know, but money's not something he's short of. Look at this.' Alice thrust her left hand under her mother's eyes.

'Oh, that's beautiful. You haven't worn it before. I wouldn't have missed that.'

'Dinesh gave it to me. I wearing it now for him. It's a real ruby.'

Her mother dropped Alice's hand. 'Love, he's here.' They watched Dinesh open the gate and shut it behind him. 'He is posh. He's got a bunch of flowers. Mind you, its like carrying coals to Newcastle. No, look! They're orchids.'

'They're for you mother.'

'Are they! You forgot the towels. Let me lay them out. When I'm down you can introduce me. Darling, I'm happy for you. I can only hope it all works for the best.'

'Mum, hurry up now.'

Alice went out into the porch to meet Dinesh. She took his extended hand limply and as she looked past him beyond the gate, across the road, the curtains of number 6 Church Crescent moved. She smiled smugly, pleased at the thought Dinesh wouldn't do anything to embarrass her. It was not like him to show affection in public. In fact, as she now turned to him, Dinesh was clearly abashed and nervous. 'Come in. Keep the flowers, mother will be down in a moment, give it to her then.'

'Gosh, what'll I say to her?'

'Just be yourself. We'll have tea in a moment. You must be famished. Would you like to freshen up? Use the loo? There's one here at the end of this hall. And one up the stairs, but then you may bump into mother without being introduced.' She chuckled.

'I've been. At a service station, about an hour ago.' He followed her into the sitting-room. 'Gosh!' he said looking around. 'Is that your mother coming down the stairs?'

'Yes,' Alice said as Kay entered the room.'

'What a lovely face!' Dinesh said involuntarily.

Kay blushed and looked appealingly at Alice. 'Mother, this is Dinesh Thakur.'

'Dinesh. May I call you Dinesh? I've heard a lot about you.'

Dinesh bowed and looked down at the flowers in his hand. 'For you, Mrs Turnbull.'

Kay hesitated, then she looked up at him and smiled graciously. 'Alice, put these in a vase and I'll see to the tea. Do sit down, Denis. Anywhere at the table. Sorry did I say Denis. Dinesh. Did you have trouble finding us?'

'Actually I did. My fault entirely. Alice's instructions were clear. I took a wrong turn somewhere. But a kind old gentleman put me right.'

'What was he like, this gentleman?'

'Very ex-military. He had a dog with him. A big dog. Brown, long-haired.'

'An Irish red-setter?'

'I wouldn't know.'

'That almost surely would be Colonel Mortimer,' Kay said.

'I'm sure you're right, mum.' Alice said, as she placed the vase on a corner table.

'Then you've met one of our prominent citizens. I'll be back in a moment.'

'Your mum's beautiful,' he whispered to Alice across the table. 'Is she formal? Do I ask for your hand in marriage? If so when?'

'No, you don't. You wouldn't be here if she didn't know. But you'll have to behave yourself. No hanky-panky.'

'You say it with such delight. You're a masochist.'

'You mean sadist.'

'Yes.'

Kay returned carrying a brown teapot. 'You've been very quiet, you two. Cat got your tongues?'

'No, mother, he's been whispering. Dinesh thinks you're very beautiful.'

Kay laughed. 'Not again! He's being very kind, I'm sure.'

'Oh, no, Mrs Turnbull . . .

'Do call me Kay.'

'Kay, You remind me of an actress. I forget the name, ah, Kim Novak.'

'Oh, don't. I can't. Well, fortunately I don't know what she looks like. Alice?'

'Like you. I should know but I don't. Anyway all this is making me a trifle jealous.'

'Hush, child. You mustn't say that, I'm your mother.'

'But you're tickled pink, I bet.'

'He's just . . . buttering me up, I'd say.

'Kim Novak,' Dinesh said, 'she was in a Hitchcock film with James Stewart. An old film. Just shows how old Hollywood films still do their rounds in small-town India.'

'Old films do their rounds here too,' Kay said. 'Our Church has a film club. But it's late in the evening for me. We could go now that you and Alice are here.'

'Mother's a telly addict. No, don't worry, mum. Dinesh is mad about the telly too.'

Dinesh grinned. 'You get excellent programmes here.'

'The tea's getting cold.' Kay said. 'Now, Dinesh, help yourself to sandwiches while I'll pour the tea. If you like it strong, I'll let it mash? There's sugar if you want it. Is the milk all right? I should have asked. I always put the milk first.'

'If there is a right or wrong, I can't see what difference it will make.'

'You're such a comfort, Dinesh. Alice, cut the cake. Oh, Alice did you . . .'

'Yes, mum, it's the first thing I asked.'

Dinesh smiled. 'That's new to me, "mash", though I can guess what it means.'

Kay passed the cake to him. 'Alice's sponge cakes are very good.'

'You could be sisters.' Dinesh said, helping himself.'

Kay blushed. 'I was very young when I married. Nineteen when Alice was born. I never went to college. Alice did. She's very bright, you know. Got a first in History. Did you know that?'

'Indeed no! But I'm not surprised. Much to clever for me, at times.' He noted the quick glance mother and daughter shared. 'History's not my subject. I've dabbled in the sciences and engineering. Not for long.'

'Here in England?'

'Yes. About twelve years ago.'

'And do you find England has changed since your time here?'

'Yes. This used to be such a polite country. Now people can be so rude.'

'In the big cities, but not in the country and small towns. You look doubtful.'

'Well, Kay, before the kind old gentleman, I did ask a young man for directions. He told me where to go.'

Alice laughed. 'Did he tell you to fuck off?'

'Alice, darling, how could you! Did he really say that, Dinesh?'

'He told me to go forth and multiply, not in the Biblical sense. I borrowed it from some film. Like all Indians, Kay, I love the cinema.'

'Is that so. I haven't been to the cinema for ages. Indians also love cricket too. And what about an interest in flowers and gardening.'

Dinesh hesitated. 'I'll be lying if I say we have more than a passing interest.'

'Mother's an avid gardener,' said Alice.

'Of course,' Dinesh quickly piped in, 'I'd love to see the garden. I know quite a bit about gardens and growing, even a little about farming. I was forced to, being brought up in one of the finest cottage gardens. Emma, my aunt, was a brilliant gardener.'

'I told you about Emma, mum.'

'Actually as a boy, I was more interested in drawing flowers—but I gave up before I got to the painting stage.'

'And why?' Kay asked.

'Emma was too good an artist. I was no match. It seemed such a waste of time.'

'Did she discourage you?'

'No Mrs . . . Kay, she didn't. I was being over sensitive and distinctly unfriendly.'

'You must take it up again. Drawing. You've got such soft and sensitive hands.'

'Those hands have never seen a day's hard work,' Alice teased.

'But now that he's here. Life's different. I'm sure he wouldn't want to do nothing, even if he can afford to while away his time. Is that not so, Dinesh?'

'Yes. Alice would like me to. But, I'm not qualified or trained or experienced in any job-like sphere.'

'Mum, I've told Dinesh, he could take up teaching.'

Dinesh nodded. 'Alice says its a rewarding job. Do you agree, Kay?'

'Yes, and you'll easily enter a teacher training college. At no expense. All you'll have to do is apply. More or less.'

'Well, then, I'll think about it, seriously. Sandy was a teacher, you know, before he married Emma and before he inherited money and property from his uncle Jaggers.'

'That will be Dinesh's great uncle, mother,' Alice interjected.

Dinesh nodded. 'Yes. I never saw him. Jagdish Thakur. That was his name. He was a Nawab and very rich. And what Sandy inherited from him is now mine.'

'Teaching is a tough and thankless job too.' Kay said.

'But they train you to be a teacher,' Alice insisted. 'And you get an education as well. There's even an allowance or grant . . . no, not in your case, you won't, I forget.'

'He doesn't have to work, Alice. I was thinking of hobbies and . . .'

'Alice is a puritan, Kay. She hates the idea of whiling away time, though I've said I intend to get on with my own reading list. I have one, you know. Sandy made one for me years ago.'

For a while no one spoke. Then Kay said: 'We mustn't be hard on the boy. Let him enjoy himself. There are a lot of good things to see and do in London.' She rose from her chair and stood next to him. 'For one so young, you've had quite a life.' Then she bent down and kissed his forehead. 'You'll look after Alice, won't you?'

'Oh, mother, please!' Alice cried.

'Sorry darling, but I don't want either of you to be hurt. Now, why don't you two stroll in the garden. I'll clear up. Off you go.' Kay patted Dinesh affectionately.

'In England, gardens are at the back of houses. In India, in the front, after the style of Raj bungalows, with their wide gates and long gravel drives.' Dinesh stood up and looked at Kay. He wrestled with a new found emotion. Not having known maternal affection, she had, by her show of it, stirred a latent hunger within him. It prompted a spontaneous, filial response and a yearning that was almost physically painful. He was caught unprepared. Kissing was not, except in the height of making love, a gesture he was comfortable with. His hand involuntarily reached out and cupped her chin tenderly. 'I promise, I'll never harm or hurt Alice, or let you down. Trust me. Kay, I . . . whatever the future holds, I'll always do the right thing, the right thing by both of you.'

'Thank you. I know you will. There now, let me give you a hug. It's good to have someone taller then me.'

He embraced Kay. 'You must be five eight, because I'm barely an inch taller.'

'Will you both stop being soppy, tell mother about the Fern Cottage garden.'

Dinesh nodded, released Kay and took a deep breath. He opened his mouth as if to speak. No sound came. The whole frame of his body shivered, visibly.

Alice's eyes widened. 'What is it. Darling, what is the matter. Something, something has happened? For goodness sake tell me!' The weight of a presentiment made her sink back into her chair.

'The-the cottage,' he stammered, 'was set fire to. More than half of it, gutted.'

'Oh my God! Dinesh! Why? Was it . . . arson . . . It was arson!'

'Yes, without doubt.'

'Does that mean,' Kay asked, 'you have suffered a loss, a financial loss?'

'Oh, mother, how can you.'

'No, Alice.' Dinesh wagged a finger. 'It's a right and sensible to ask. Yes and no, Kay. It doesn't immediately affect me. I own the cottage, but I get no income from it. I do from the land, which is not affected. The cottage was being cared for and lived in by some of uncle Sandy's friends. They're back in England and the cottage was put up for sale. Actually we didn't have to wait for a buyer, but we had to wait for an agreement to be drawn out. The fire is a set back.'

'You mean, the sale has fallen through?'

'Not really, Kay. I'll get less for it. Less all the expense of repairs etc . . . but that's not the only bad news. There's been, Alice has rightly guessed, no accident, but a criminal act leading to a tragic death. What can I say? I hope you understand. I've had a hard upbringing. For much of my own personal unhappiness, I am to blame. What I taught myself to hate in childhood, and longed to break away from, is back to haunt me. I can't handle it. It's destroying me.'

Kay put an arm round him and drew him to the sofa. 'There, sit by me. We may run away from things and people that were part of our past, our childhood,' she said softly, 'but we can't escape them. I understand your feelings, but you must learn not to blame yourself. Youthful irresponsibility, is part and parcel of life, a growing to maturity . . . All of us, have memories that leave us with a sense of guilt.'

'There's more than just the fire, mum. Dinesh, tell us about the accident?'

'The Tibetan woman, who was like a sister, a harsh sister, but a sister nonetheless, has died in the fire. Sona, that's her name, was killed, and her husband, Ransingh, the family chowkidar—Kay that means watchman, caught the man he believed had set fire to the cottage, and in a frenzy beat the man to death.'

For a moment no one spoke. They stared hard at each other. Then Alice went up to Dinesh and Kay moved away. 'You poor boy,' Kay said. 'All this time you've had this terrible news on his mind?'

'There's nothing any of us can do, mum,' Alice murmured almost inaudibly.

'Ransingh's been arrested and because he has confessed to the crime of murder, he'll surely hang. The poor man is in prison. I should go back.'

'But Dinesh,' Alice pleaded, 'there's nothing you can do. They want you dead, you know that. Why you had to flee India and why you're here. They couldn't get you, so, this is how they've retaliated. Nothing you do now will make things right.'

'If I compromised, made a plea for Ransingh's life, Seth Agarwal will ensure that his life is spared. He won't care what justice his henchmen get. They're in his pay. He will just compensate the family of the man Ransingh killed.'

'Compromise? You mean, go back to your wife? What are you saying?'

'Oh, Alice! Kay! Forgive me. Heavens, how can I put this? I won't do anything . . . without my lawyer's advice. He's brilliant. A Parsee friend of Sandy. Only if he fails, and only if I have too, and only if I can achieve something by doing so . . .'

'How are you going to protect yourself from being murdered,' Alice cried, 'except by being agreeing to go back to your wife?'

'I'll pretend I'm going back and then, at the first opportunity, I'll escape, back to England, back to you. Kay, this man, who's in prison on a murder charge, I was close to him. From the age of six, I grew up with him. Ransingh is someone special. If you saw him you would see that immediately. A man of few words; an upright ex-soldier, cool, brave, strong. I used to call him the iron man, because he seemed to have muscles of steel . . . I want to help him if I can. But, I won't do anything foolish. I also want to live and start a new life with Alice.'

'Are you're trying to say,' Kay said evenly, 'that you need to be in London and be ready to fly back to India at a moment's notice.'

'Yes, Kay. But I'll stay the night here, if I may.'

Kay moved silently to the window and looked out. 'Alice, it's getting dark and it's started to rain.' Alice joined her.

'My stuff is in the car,' Dinesh said. 'I won't be a moment.'

'Take the large umbrella in the hall.' Kay said.

The women watched him leave the house from the very window they had seen him enter. Alice touched her mother's arm. 'You wish he hadn't come?'

'No, love. I'm glad he came. I'm glad I saw him. But I fear he won't settle here, in England, I mean. Not for long. India has a tight grip on him.' She sighed. 'You must go with him, back to London, tomorrow. And India, when that becomes necessary.'

'He hasn't asked me to.'

'You'll have to suggest it. He needs you. He won't say no if you suggest it. He'll be grateful.' There were tears in Kay's eyes. 'Make the most of your time together, as if you were husband and wife. After all, you are carrying his child.'

'You can't know! How can you know? I'm not sure myself. I've only missed one . . . and I haven't been sick?'

'Some women don't. At least, not so early.'

'Then how could you know?'

'A mother knows. The way you've been looking at him, Saying so little all evening.'

'I would have told you but I wanted to give it more time, and to be sure. Mum, now that you know . . . Oh please don't cry! Now that you know, what shall I do?'

'Do? I've told you what you must do. There, he's back.'

'All right, I'll go back with him, but I won't say anything about . . . not yet, I don't want to add to his . . . Please don't tell him!'

'Just stick with him. As for that, he'll find out soon enough. I'll be in the patio.'

Alice went into the hall as Dinesh shut the door behind him. 'You're are wet.'

'It's wind and rain, I'm afraid. Luckily I've got a spare suit. Where's Kay?'

'You'll see her when we come down. Follow me now. Leave the brolly in the stand. It's the room on the first landing.'

Dinesh entered the room as Alice held the door open. He put his suitcase on the straight back chair next to the wardrobe. 'Is it all right to put it here?' he asked. She nodded, shut the door behind her, and looked at him.

'Don't I get a kiss, Alice?' She rushed at him, put her arms round his waist and clung tightly. 'Hey! I'm wet!'

'I don't care,' she said. 'I'm going back with you to London, tomorrow.'

'But what about Kay?'

'She suggested it!' Alice burst into tears. 'You don't know, you can't know how hard this past fortnight's been without you. Kiss me, Dinesh. Make love to me, now. Dinesh, now!'

It was eight when they came down to find Kay watching television. 'Ah, there you are,' she said. 'I see you have both changed. Good. What shall we have for supper?'

'No supper,' Dinesh said, 'we, the three of us, are going out for dinner. Choose a restaurant Kay. The best in town. I won't take no for an answer.'

'Why don't you two go. Enjoy yourselves. I'm happy for both of you.'

'No, Kay, please! I so much want you to come. Thanks to you, Alice is coming back with me to London. You've made me . . . so very happy.'

'All right, I'll come. You'll have to give me time to change.' She switched the telly off and as she passed him, touched his arm. 'Promise me, when you to go back to India, you'll take Alice with you.'

'I will. And Kay, don't worry. I've decided to name Alice my sole . . . you know, in the event of . . . well . . . should anything happen to me.'

'Thank you. Because, you know . . .

'No mother, please!' Alice pleaded.

'What's all this about?' Dinesh looked from one to the other.'

'Nothing,' said Alice. 'I'll tell you. But, it can wait.'

Kay raised her brows.

'Oh, my God,' Dinesh struck his forehead, 'you don't mean . . .'

'Yes,' said Kay. 'Alice is carrying your child.'

'In that case . . .' he gave a little skip and in an attempt to contain himself, bit hard on the knuckle of his forefinger. 'Gosh, Kay, you must think I'm an awful, terrible, cad. Forgive me, but I love Alice.'

'No point crying over . . . over the past. Prove your love. Do the right thing by her.'

'I'll open a special bank account for Alice, and—and come what may, into it will go all the money I'll get from the sale of Fern Cottage. And lots more. You'll see.'

'Oh, mum! My teacher training course!' cried Alice. 'I'll have to . . .

'Yes, darling, you'll have had to . . . in any case. Under the circumstances.'

Alice nodded.

Later that night Alice knocked on the door of her mother's bedroom. 'It's only me, Alice.' She looked at the double bed. 'Can I?' She crept under the blankets.

Kay watched her quizzically. 'What's all this about, love?'

'Nothing. I'm leaving for London tomorrow. I wanted to be with you tonight.'

'It's been years since you've done this. The last time was the night after your father left and you realised he wasn't coming back.'

'The sheets are cold. Let me cuddle up to you.'

'Yes, but we're not going to talk long into the night. Now, what is it?'

'Mum, have you been dabbling again? You know what I mean. You must tell me. Have you been seeing Margaret again? It's dangerous. Unhealthy. You'll be unhappy. I'm not saying she's a fraud. Just strange. A little mad. And you know you shouldn't. Not as a good Catholic. Hindus, at least the ones I've met, don't go for spiritualism.'

'I haven't, what you call dabbled. Not, as you know, for years. Only since the news Jonathan brought of Graham. I so wanted to know. Why he left and what happened?'

'And did you? Get to know, I mean.'

'No. But you know, I'm psychic. Always have been.'

'Like knowing I'm preggers. It gives me the shivers, this clairvoyant business . . .'

'What's that, in simple words?'

'Your telepathy. And what you said about Dinesh. How could you know . . .'

'About him not being happy to settle here because of his deep attachment to India? I didn't. I was being clever. It worked. I wanted both of you to think seriously about the future. You can be irresponsible, Alice. Now is no time for that. And before you ask, I needed to test him. See what he would do when faced with being a father. That worked too. I had to protect you.'

'He thinks you're wise and wonderful.'

'It's not hard. If you watch people carefully, you get to guess a lot about them.'

Alice thought for a moment. 'I suppose, when you love, are close to someone, you can . . . I can't think how I felt something tragic, other than the cottage fire, had . . .'

'Wouldn't you call that telepathy? Now off you go. Don't leave before breakfast?'

'No. Oh, I know what he loves. Scrambled eggs on fried toast.'

'Turn off the light and shut the door.'

CHAPTER NINETEEN

'Ted's a doctor, you know.'

'Yes,' said Alice, 'that's the second time you've told me. Dinesh, he's not going to know just by looking at me. But it wouldn't matter even if he did. Did know, that is.'

He nodded. 'You don't look any different.'

'It's far to early for that. Stop being self-conscious about it; and stop fussing.'

He gazed at her with pride. She was going to be the mother of his child and he must come to terms with this new strange feeling of being on the threshold of a new beginning; a promise that would banish the sadness of past loneliness. The thought of bringing into main stream humanity, a new life, was exciting, a mental leap to get used to it. And he found her assured serenity comforting. Women, immensely practical, repair the broken timber of men's lives and stir a new desire to live. That thought took him by surprise. Where did it came from? Not Sandy again! Must all his thinking come second-hand? Sandy must have acquired his thoughts too. Was that not the nature of the human condition, to browse in libraries of past thinking, and borrow to rationalise the impact of life's challenges? Is much of our imagination simply memory? Answers did not matter. We must live the questions. He would dismiss needless speculation. A good healthy, sensible policy, lay in taking part and moving on. He was proud to be a Hindu and pleased that Alice had sought consolation in Hinduism. For more than any other philosophy, Hinduism elevated the women, to take their place alongside the gods in the cycles of life, co-creators, through their role of child-bearers. A pregnant woman was, indeed, a sacred vessel.

Alice turned. 'What is it? You're not going to be soppy?'

'I won't. I'm resolved. I'm thinking about you and about how lucky I am.'

But she sensed his real thoughts and loved him for it. 'It must be time now.'

Dinesh glanced at his watch then at the pub sign of The King's Arms. The board outside the entrance read: "Lunch now being served". He turned on the engine. 'Ted did say twelve thirty for one. We could drive slowly up to the house. I'll park outside the gate and we could then walk up the drive. So that we're not too early.'

'It's quite grand,' she said, taking his arm. 'The house must be listed.'

'Alice, before I forget. I've been meaning to ask . . . are you really going to return to Christianity, become a Catholic again?'

'Why, will you go off me if I did?'

'No. Hindus are a tolerant lot. Only Hinduism could produce a Mahatma Gandhi.'

'Don't be so sure. You're very facile in your judgements. Christianity has its saints, too. Saint Francis of Assisi, to name one? Anyway, I don't know about where I'll end up, darling. But Hinduism will always be a part of me. Though I still find some of its practices at odds with it's philosophy.' She mused. 'I like what I understand.'

'I see what you mean. My beliefs have little to do with temples and I've no time for priests. Most of them are rascals. Fortunately they are not necessary for salvation. The Hindu needs only to do good works, *karma*, good *karma*, to be on the right path. The rest is lip service and going through the motions.'

'Can I, as the Americans say, take a rain check, on this discussion. Right now I'm a little concerned. There's no one around. Have you got the day right?'

'Yes. Kitty said to go round the back into the garden.'

ॐ

'They're getting on, as my father would say, like a house on fire. It's good for Kitty. I'm glad Alice came.' Ted Franks turned to faced Dinesh. 'You'll make a good couple.' 'But, for her sake, you've got to see your divorce through; and that quickly.'

Dinesh nodded and wondered at the emphasis on "for her sake" but decided to let it pass. 'Kitty's looking well', he said, 'and beautiful as ever.'

'As Emma was.'

The remark caught Dinesh unprepared. He gave a gentle cough. 'When I was last here I asked about Kitty, did I hear wedding bells?'

'I'm afraid they've been silenced. Kitty's called off the engagement.'

'I see,' Dinesh paused. 'You don't seem too disappointed.'

'*I am* disappointed. I was looking forward to grandchildren. Still, it's her life to live the way she wants to. I suppose he was awed by Kitty. Kitty does that to men. He's another weakling, another Trevor Williams. I told you about our old neighbours and how close Emma got to being Mrs Williams. Kitty needs a man like Sandy, who'd risk all and sweep her up . . .' Ted's voice trailed off into a thoughtful silence. Dinesh waited. 'It was Kitty who broke off the engagement. I never ask for explanations. That may be a parental failing. Can you blame me? Her love sustained me through dark times . . . from the time she was six . . . Ah! here they come. There's something about Kitty as there was about Emma, which is completely disarming,'

Kitty gestured as she and Alice walked up to the terrace. 'Daddy, don't go into the dining-room just yet. I'll call you. Alice can keep both of you company There's nothing to do. Just a little organising. You'll love Sarah's cooking. She's a wizard. Oh, dad I forgot, you do the wine.'

Alice waited till father and daughter went inside. Then she squeezed Dinesh's arm. 'You said she was beautiful, but I wasn't quite prepared . . . what a loss to the cinema. I must look so drab next to her! Is she really older than me?'

'No, you don't and yes by at least three to four years.'

'Stop. You don't have to flatter me, like you did mother. You really overdid that. I'll accept I'm not ugly, but I would be lost in a crowd.'

'Nonsense. You were picked out in a crowd. We, Fernandez and I, did in Goa.'

'Well, that's reassuring. Right now, next to Kitty, I feel . . . well, homely.'

The Lotus And The Rose

'Kitty and Emma are like beautiful porcelain, which one keeps in a show case. You are like soft furnishing. One can be uncomfortable in the presence of too much beauty. I remember Sandy saying, he thanked his lucky stars Emma seemed blissfully unaware about her looks. You're a cushion . . . the best pin cushion if you get my lewd meaning.'

Alice boxed his arm.

He put his arm round Alice. 'You're matchless, in that area.' He pressed her against his side.

'Come in you two.' Kitty called from the terrace. 'You'll have all the time in the world for that, Dinesh.'

Dinesh grinned. 'There is not world enough and time,' he said, and then whispered to Alice: 'I wonder where that sentence came from?'

'You know,' Alice said as went into the dining room, 'your past stays close to you. You're constantly being reminded of the past and always quoting someone.' She tried to picture the sullen, watchful boy, who by his own account, he would have been. 'You should take up writing.'

'Did you say he should write,' Ted asked. 'Good, do encourage him, he can then take over the book I've started. I'm on the verge of giving up.'

Alice blushed at having been overheard. 'He'll be good,' Dr Franks, 'Dinesh is very observant and has an excellent memory.'

'Add to that . . . Dinesh won't mind my saying,' Ted raised brows, as if waiting for a cue, 'a passionate and angry young man.'

'No longer Ted. I was. I'm a penitent now.'

'Then, my boy, you have all the ingredients for the making of a writer.' He held a chair for Alice. 'You're next to me, and do call me Ted.'

There was much idle chatter during luncheon, from most of which Dinesh felt left out. He tried hard to think of things to say, but found it difficult to join in. He gave up and almost instantly stopped worrying about it. Sitting opposite Ted, he was ideally placed to observe. The doting affection Ted and Kitty had for each other was obvious and expected. But Sarah intrigued him. For the first time he got a chance to study her closely. It struck him that her attitude towards Ted had a kind of relaxed familiarity, which one does not associate with a paid housekeeper. She was short and stout with a clearly defined round face; while her movements and manner were that of a prim but not unfriendly matron. Could she be living in? There was no sign of a car by which she could have arrived, or a bicycle, nor had he seen buses or coaches in the area. But, short of asking, he saw no way of finding out. He turned back to study Kitty, and then glanced at Alice, who sat opposite her. What he saw pleased him. He was right. Kitty didn't overshadow her. He marvelled at their clear skins and fair complexions and was reminded of his Sikh friend, Mohan Singh. '*Arrey*, you know why English women have such smooth skins? It's climate. The British weather. Yes, that awful weather! That's why they have best complexions in the world.' Dinesh chuckled audibly at the memory. He caught Ted's attention, and a sudden silence descended in the room.

'A penny for your thoughts, young man?' Ted said.

Dinesh spread his hands. 'Nothing worth the telling.'

'Come on, Dinesh,' chimed Kitty. 'You've been very quiet.'

'Something amused you?' Ted put down his napkin next to his plate. 'That was a lovely lunch, Sarah.'

'You're welcome,' Sarah said, in a soothing voice one might expect her to have, and as she picked up his plate, Dinesh saw her hand lightly touch Ted's arm.

'You should have joined us, Sarah.' Ted said, looking up at her.

'I'm on a strict diet, Ted. Don't tempt me,' she said and left the room.

'Go on, Dinesh,' Alice coaxed. 'Share the joke?'

'I was thinking about our friend Mohan Singh, Ted, who can be quite amusing.'

'A good man Mohan Singh. I have a lot of time for him.'

'Me too,' Kitty trilled. 'And for his wife, Bunty. But Dinesh, I feared you were quiet because you were thinking about your immediate plans to return to Dharamsala. Daddy and I haven't forgotten and we've got some suggestions to make. But let's move on to the terrace and talk about them over coffee. Yes?'

'This time, Kitty, I insist on helping.' Alice said.

'Good. Then we can give Sarah a rest.'

The Lotus And The Rose

Later on the terrace Kitty chaired the discussion in a business like way. 'Dinesh, I want you to seriously consider what I'm going to say. It concerns all of us. Yes, you too Alice . . . sorry, there's sugar and milk. Help yourselves. Of course, none of this would be necessary if Dinesh gave up his mad idea of going back to India. Yes, I'm sorry Dinesh, no one will think any the less of you if you just stayed put and let the lawyers to deal with it. You know Ransingh better than I do, but I know he won't expect you to be in court. I can't see what you are going to achieve by being there. You're not a witness and any good conduct testimony can be put in writing.'

'I accept all that, Kitty. It's moral support I want to give Ransingh. To see a friend in Court will boost his morale. I gather from what Ted tells me, he won't even stand up for himself. He never should have admitted anything. He ought to defend . . .'

'What about Alice? Have you considered the risk you're putting her in. You owe it to her not to put yourself in danger.'

'He has, Kitty. he has thought about me. But he feels he has a moral obligation.'

'He could end up being killed and so could you. Anyway, I can see there's no point labouring over this. Let's assume the trip is on. Dinesh, at least give up the pretence of a reconciliation with Shanti.'

'Yes,' Ted said. 'You could jeopardise or compromise your divorce proceedings. Worse, you might end up under house arrest and be unable to get out when you want to. Your movements would be closely watched. The Seth is unlikely to trust you, after all that has happened since you left his employ. I suggest you listen carefully to what Kitty says. The Seth's rather fond of her and has shown a great deal of respect for her advice and opinions. If anyone can charm . . .'

'So Dinesh,' Kitty interposed, 'in order to protect yourself from being bumped off or risk house arrest, we have to find another way. The Seth's highly suspicious nature is a weakness we could use. It is vital for Alice to realise she can't be seen with Dinesh, or be seen on the same plane with him. Agarwal has a net work of spies. We know that for a fact. And don't ever call him a drug dealer, even though he is one. Yes, Alice?'

'Shanti's seen me. At the Ashram. I know Bombay. I could find a place there.'

'Alice', Dinesh said, 'I'll put you in a comfortable flat in Bombay, with a woman to care for you. Sorry Kitty, I know you and Ted have a plan to outline.'

'My plan is simply for me to get the Seth to give you and Shanti a chance to meet and discuss matters privately, unhindered by threats or third parties. That he has to be patient if he really wants a reconciliation. That, had he not scared you away, you might already have been in Pathankot. I'll improve on it and make it more convincing. Then assuming he agrees, you press your case for Ransingh. Say you're unhappy about the whole affair, which could be settled amicably. Dad, have I forgotten anything else?'

'Only this. Dinesh make sure all charges are dropped, and before you leave ensure Ransingh is not just free but back home in Rohtak. I don't for one moment believe the Seth is interested in justice for his henchmen. If he can avoid public scandal, he'll pay them off . . . after all those thugs are mercenaries. That said, Dinesh, I can't see how you are going to make good your escape. You must seek the help of influential people. Get Mohan Singh and your lawyers to draw a protection order, soon after the Ransingh business is over. You could suggest, once Ransingh is freed, that that proves what took place at Fern Cottage was a case of arson, but that in the light of the Seth's reasonable conduct towards you, you'll drop charges.'

'And Dinesh,' Kitty said, 'I just remembered, when you do get out of Dharamsala, I would avoid public transport. I know someone in the army who'll arrange to get you out in a military truck . . .' She paused. She and Ted exchanged glances. 'I'll give you his name and address—fortunately he's just been posted to Pathankot. No civilian will dare stop a military truck.'

'But Kitty, is the Seth a reasonable man?' You make it sound so simple.'

'Yes, Alice, he can be reasonable, but he's not a fool. Dinesh will have to be very convincing. He truly was fond of you Dinesh. He told me so many times. But as I said, he's superstitious. Work on that. Find something that will shake him. Oh, and when you get to Delhi—because that's as far as Dusty will take you—make for Calcutta. For some unknown reason the Seth has few if any contacts there. In fact, if I were you I'd take Alice there. It will be the safest place for her.'

'But Kitty, I have no one I know in Calcutta.'

'Well, then put her up in a hotel. You can afford it.'

'Yes, of course. Is Dusty someone I know?'

'No, Dinesh, I met him after you left. He's someone you can trust . . .'

'And will do anything for Kitty,' Ted said. Glancing at her, his eyes twinkled.

'Ah, the power we women have over men.' Alice said knowingly.

But Kitty seemed not to have heard. She was looking at her father. 'So, now you know, dad,' she said just above a whisper.

'First Emma, then Kitty, and now you, Alice,' Ted said. 'India reigns supreme.'

'Hush,' said Kitty, and as she said it, Dinesh was reminded of Emma. She looked at him and smiled sweetly; and the resemblance became even more marked. 'We must rehearse our plans, make notes, so that there's no mistaking our cues.'

Dinesh gave a thoughtful nod. 'Kitty, I hope this does not involve you further than meeting the Seth. As it is, I'm not happy about you taking risks for my sake. If the Seth finds out you've deceived him, you could be in serious trouble.'

'It will be some time before he does. By then I will be away with no reason ever to return. My part is simply to lie for you to him and Shanti . . . and, having got you there I can't be held responsible for your subsequent behaviour. Now you and Alice are not to hang about either. Once you join her in Calcutta, fly back to London, immediately.'

Dinesh nodded. 'Will you be keeping Kitty company?' he asked Ted.

'I'm afraid not. Not after the last trip. One dose of hepatitis is enough for anyone. Of course I'd be worried sick thinking about Kitty.' Ted rose to go indoors. 'You will have tea before you go? Then I'll see you later.'

'Excuse me,' Kitty said and caught up with her father in the dining room. 'Dad, it's not as bad as you think, I wouldn't take a risk if I thought I couldn't handle Agarwal. And I'll take Dusty with me, in his uniform. He's a Major now. Indians respect army officers. With him around the Seth wouldn't dare harm me.'

'That's some comfort to know, because Agarwal could hold you hostage.'

'I won't be there when Dinesh arrives. Once the Seth agrees to see Dinesh, I'll say I'm going to Delhi (I shan't mention Calcutta) to tell Dinesh in person. And dad, you know I'm doing this as much for poor old Ransingh as for Dinesh; and now for Alice. I like Alice, don't you? She's like the sister I've never had.'

Ted looked at his daughter sadly. 'I thought this Dusty business was over?'

'I tried, dad. But I can't . . . I really do love him. I've never stopped. It's just that I felt he deserved better. Someone better than me, that is. So I wanted to free him.'

'You silly girl! No one in the world is too good for you! But that's neither here nor there. I presume you've heard from him?'

'Yes, we're going to marry soon after he gets permission from his CO. It's a mere formality, once an officer is past twenty-five. Dusty is well over forty.'

'Is he! Indians don't look their age.'

'Why are you shaking your head like that?'

'When I was a young man, India was a foreign land. Now, I'm surrounded by an English-Indian epidemic. Emma, Alice, now you. I'm being a bore repeating it.'

'I suppose Sandy started it all. You know, as a little girl I had a crush on him.'

'A good looking Indian can be irresistible.'

'Dusty's not good looking. Well not in the Sandy league.'

Striking eyes, though. And the most graceful man I know.'

I like his face. Dad, there's something uniquely attractive and comfortable about it. Large nose and all.'

'He's a Dustoor. All Parsees have big noses.'

'Dusty's not Parsee. Dustoor is not his real surname. He took it for the sake of his foster father. I thought I'd told you. It's a long story. You'll come to the wedding?'

'Not even hepatitis will stop me. Just for the ceremony. I'll survive the few days.'

'Good. I must get back to Alice. I've seen enough handsome men . . . but should I ever miss them, there's always you, my dishy dad.' She put her arms round his neck and kissed him. 'Sarah said the other day, you're her image of Richard Hannay.'

'She's been reading Buchan. Sarah is an incorrigible romantic. But it doesn't mean anything. When she returned my copy of *King Solomon's Mines*, she told me she saw Jack Barlow as an Allan Quartermain look-alike. Jack's her husband, remember?'

Kitty laughed. 'Still, it's a compliment. You mustn't think of yourself as old. What are you, now? I forget. Sixty-one? Two? Never mind, you could marry again. Wasn't Granny in her nineties? You've got her strong constitution, unlike poor aunt Emmy.'

'Granny was eighty-seven. But I get your point. I've never been a good judge of women. I don't want to make the same mistake a second time round. Once bitten, as they say. I'm all right. Sarah takes good care of me and Jack's good company.'

After tea Kitty went into the kitchen to help Sarah and Ted invited Dinesh and Alice to join him in the library. Sandy would not have recognised the library where, seated at the writing desk, he had looked though a portfolio of Emma's paintings, as she stood over him, inches away from actual physical contact. Now the desk was no longer there. In its place a long mahogany showcase displayed Emma's sketch books and smaller ink and wash drawings. Another change was the blocking up of one of the two windows, that looked onto the drive, to provide more hanging space for larger paintings. These were the first to catch Alice's eye and she studied them for some time before speaking. She turned to Dinesh. He joined her and pointed to the largest painting. 'That,' he said, 'that's Fern Cottage, as seen from the paddock outside the garden gate.'

'Alice, have you at any time in London been to Kew Gardens?' Ted asked.

Alice nodded. 'Oh, yes. Once.'

'And did you see the botanical paintings of Marianne North?'

Alice shook her head. Ted turned to Dinesh. He shook his head too. 'But,' Dinesh said, 'I know about her. Sandy once told me that Emma's work was very like hers?'

'Indeed,' Ted said. 'Very perceptive of Sandy. We went there together to see them. That's when I was practising in London. Marianne North's paintings are all under one roof, covering every square inch of wall-hanging space. I was astounded. Astounded at their likeness to Emma's work.'

'Dr Franks . . . I mean Ted, I'd love to see them. You must take me there, Dinesh.'

'Yes. Make a day of it. It's a lovely part of London. But now you must see some of Emma's paintings. I've framed quite a few. Many of the early ones, were painted here, the oils in particular, will be new to you, Dinesh. I plan to give many to an institution. They really deserve to be a national treasure. This library was father's, and as he and Emma were close, I decided it is the best place to display some of her work.'

'That one of the cottage is beautiful,' Alice said. 'Why is it called Fern Cottage?'

Dinesh shrugged and looked at Ted.'

'No one knows.' Ted said. 'I assume it was called that when Sandy's uncle bought it from the Englishman who owned it. I forget the man's name. Sandy told me, Philip something. One of those "staying on" civil servants, who only return to England to die, and to mark a corner in some Home County graveyard.'

'I see a porch, so I guess that's the front of the cottage . . . I love the bougainvillaea. Just a few dots of colour and it looks like the real thing!' Alice sighed. 'Don't tell me all that's gone with the fire.'

'No,' said Ted. 'I'm now told the fire was at the back. Where Sona was killed.'

'I still believe she had a hand in Sandy's death.'

'Steady on, Dinesh,' Ted said sharply. 'I thought you had got over that.'

'Sandy may have begged her to . . . but euthanasia's still a crime, still murder.'

'We've been through all this and there's absolutely no proof to your accusation. I wished you had, and now, under the circumstances, forgotten all about it.'

'Yes. I'm sorry I said it. I certainly remember her now with a deep respect. Her love for both Sandy and Emma was dog-like devotion.'

The Lotus And The Rose

'And Sandy would have been desolate without Emma.'

'Yes, I apologise. Ted, as I said, I'm not the same Dinesh you knew.'

'Really, Dinesh, believe me, Sandy was a dying man . . . and with a death wish.'

'God, I'm sorry.' Dinesh shook his head and Alice put a hand on his shoulder.

'There now,' Ted said quickly. 'All's well and forgotten. We were talking about the fire at the cottage . . . Emma certainly did one of the kitchen garden at the back. Quite a blueprint for anyone who wanted to restore the cottage to its former glory. I'll give it to Mohan Singh if he needs it. He may have other ideas.'

Alice gave a long sigh. 'Mum would love to have seen those paintings. We, neither of us are artists but, she's a good gardener. When she buys cards they are invariably of flowers and gardens.'

'Come again and bring her with you.'

'I'm sorry, I didn't mean . . .'

'No need to apologise, Alice. I'd be happy to meet her. Dinesh, can make another trip before he leaves for India.' Ted moved up to the window as a car drew up the drive. He waved. 'That will be John Barlow, Sarah's husband, come to collect her.'

Dinesh started. He was wrong, but still wondered about Sarah's intimate gesture during lunch. He got his answer immediately.

'John's an old friend.' Ted went on. 'We went to the same prep school here, then he went on to Wellington and the army, while I stayed here. Good. Kitty and Sarah have gone out to him. That gives me a chance, before you leave for London, to have a word with you two.' He led them back to the sitting-room. 'Why don't you two, sit together, on the sofa, while I talk to you as a doctor should. I'm going to be intimate, but you can shut me up and tell me to mind my own business. And you don't have to answer if you don't want to. What do you say. May I?'

'Yes, Ted.' Dinesh leaned forward. 'By all means.'

'Good. Then, speaking as a doctor, I'll get straight to it. Alice, are you pregnant?'

'There, Alice, I told you Ted would know!'

'Oh, Dinesh!' Alice said. 'You're such an innocent. Ted is only asking. Yes, I am.'

'In that case, Dinesh and Alice, I want you to think carefully. Be sensible about this Dinesh. I think you ought to go alone to India. Leave Alice with her mother. She and your child need to be medically cared for, here in England.'

'But, Ted, there are excellent private hospitals in India.'

'I know, and excellent doctors too. But remember court proceedings in India are slow. It will be quite sometime before you need to go to India or even before Kitty has had time to soften up the Seth. Alice's pregnancy will be fairly advanced by then. Well, if it's within the first four months you could risk it, but when it's five and over, long distance travel is not advisable.'

'But Ted,' said Alice, 'there is nothing to stop us going to India almost at once? We could be waiting, as Kitty suggested, in Calcutta?'

'You can't till the Seth has assured Kitty that it will be safe for Dinesh to see him?'

'The more I think about it,' Dinesh said, 'Calcutta does offer a safe place to hide.'

'But the worry will put a great strain on Alice. That won't be good for the baby.'

'It will be a worse strain,' Alice said, 'sitting here, thousands of miles away, waiting for news of Dinesh. The nearness will be far less of a strain.'

'I agree. I just wanted to make sure the two of you know what you're doing. I felt I had to say this. I spoke confidentially. Kitty plans to fly next week.'

'Thank you, Ted. It's sweet of you,' said Alice. 'And it won't matter if Kitty knows.'

CHAPTER TWENTY

Ram Nivas, Seth Agarwal's residence, was a square, two-storied mansion, with brick walls faced with pink stucco to match the red sandstone *chattris* that crowned the corners of its flat, roof-top terrace. Here, on hot sultry summer nights, residents slept on rope sprung *charpoys*, family and servants on either side of a curtained divide. From the main entrance a paved path runs through a front garden, to a grand Mughal barbican of red sandstone and marble. This path went out of use after an invasion by stray cattle caused the gates to be locked. Behind the barbican is a courtyard enclosed by two arcades of pillared and scalloped arches. One leads to the offices of Agarwal Industries, which overlooks Pathankot's busy bus station, the other, to the living quarters and a large unkempt formal garden with a disused fountain. In the centre of the courtyard, a large mulberry tree shelters a well and a small silver and gold shrine to the goddess of cash registers, Lakshmi.

Old Gopal, the ill-tempered *mali*, found the task of maintaining the garden, single-handed beyond his efforts. Being a father figure to the Seth, he was allowed to do as much or as little as he liked, and no one dared to criticise the old retainer. He potters around his domain like a hoary and eccentric botanist muttering to himself and cursing the fountain whenever he passes by it; and spends much of the day talking to a tall pipal tree, which stands against the boundary wall, where he had built a hut for himself. Next to it he keeps a store of firewood, chopped from fallen trees. This he said was for his funeral pyre.

Visitors enter Ram Nivas by the large iron-spiked, oak side-door, where on a hard wooden stool sits the watchman, a sleepy Gurkha, armed with a rusty Enfield rifle. Above him, the office veranda, hangs over the Booking Office of the noisy bus station, for services to Delhi and towns en route. A team of sweepers attempt to keep the Bus Station clean, fighting a losing battle against the constant litter from hawkers and food vendors; while nothing can be done to protect the stout concrete pillars of the loggia from the splattered spittle of betel nut pan. Adjacent to the Booking Office is Munshi Popatlal's personal office, with stairs that go up to the veranda above. He is the Seth's secretary and head of the clerical staff; and for the job has one of the two telephones in the building. The other had been recently installed, on Shanti's insistence, in the living quarters. The Seth dislikes telephones and never uses either. As to why a rich tycoon should choose to live next to a bus station, surprises only those who do not know that his mock-Mughal stone house had preceded the bus station by sixty years; and that the *uddah*, or bus station, was there precisely because the Seth asked for it to be there. It is secretly rumoured that he is the proprietor of the Haryana Bus Company, and that he makes several trips during the day to the first floor veranda, screened from view by a pea-green painted bamboo screen. From there he surveys the bustling scene below, like a modern Roman Emperor.

On the morning on which Dinesh was escorted to this first floor veranda, he found the Seth squatting cross-legged on the carpeted floor. A wet hand-towel lay round his fat neck and in front of him, frog-like on his heels, is his barber busily stropping a cut-throat razor on a leather belt, held between his teeth and stretched along his left hand.

With a wave the Seth dismissed the man, who vanished, silently and as suddenly like a frog off a rock into the depths of a pool. Dinesh started. He glanced in the direction the man went. The Seth was on his feet, dabbing his face with the wet towel, looking fatter than Dinesh remembered. The pale flabby body, bare to the waist, presented the comic vision of an over-grown, twenty-stoned baby in a white nappy, and required all the gravity Dinesh could muster. A minion ran up to the Seth with a freshly laundered, white, muslin *kurta* and disappeared into the shadows, leaving behind him, like a vague memory, the echoes of bare feet on flagstone. The Seth donned the voluminous *kurta*, letting it slide down his raised hands.

The Lotus And The Rose

He then waddled up to Dinesh, as only a big man, almost as broad as he was long, could do. He puffed and wheezed and his protruding eyes regarded Dinesh with an angry stare. Something Teutonic about his stance gave him the appearance of Field Marshal Goring in *kurta* and pyjammas.

'So,' he roared. 'Got your fill of England? Chi, Chi, what happened to your Hindu principles? Wanting to stay in that filthy country with your prostitute friend? Huh! And now coming with tail between your legs?'

'Sethji . . .'

'What Sethji? You called me, papaji. Yes, father. *Yad hai?* Remember.' He hesitated once more. His English was limited. 'Lost all respect for your elders?'

'Sorry, papaji, but if you hadn't threatened . . .'

'*Bus, bus*! Enough of this *Angrezi* talk. Speak Punjabi or Hindi or forgotten both?'

Dinesh shook his head. In fluent Punjabi he said: 'If you hadn't threaten to kill me I wouldn't have gone to England.'

'So I drove you to cross the black waters. What about that woman?'

'She's a better Hindu than you and me,' Dinesh said, plucking up courage. 'I met her in the *ashram*.' He lied and regretted it.

'Liar! You met her in Goa. I know all your movements. How you managed to slip from me so far, I don't know. But don't lie to me. I'm no fool.'

'Goa is just a few hours. Enough time for her to tell me about the *ashram*.' Dinesh persisted, relying entirely on his friend Anil's discretion. It paid.

'And why? She's no great beauty. My Shanti is a princess compared to her.'

'Why do you keep talking about her? She doesn't mean anything to me. I am here, am I not? Would I be here if she was anything more than someone I met?'

'You've made a fool of me and disgraced my daughter over one small mistake. You forsake honour, tradition. I should call my *gundas* and give you good thrashing.'

Dinesh raised his voice. 'Your daughter forsook all honour and wifely duty! You say small error?'

The Seth clenched his teeth. 'What's done is done. Forgive, forget.' He took a succession of deep breaths. Then, almost paternally, 'you should have come to me.'

The Seth's conciliatory tone embolden Dinesh. 'What would you have done? You would have done nothing. Your daughter can do no wrong. And the music master . . .'

'Shut up! Don't talk. He will never be heard off again. I've taken care of that.'

'How can I forgive or forget? In my place, what would you have done? Forgiven? As a man and a good Hindu, you should have sympathy with my position.'

'I did. But for that you would be dead by now. Much pity I've shown.'

'Well, I'm here. And I am prepared to keep up appearances.'

The Seth put his arms round Dinesh and gave him a bear hug. 'I've always looked upon you like a son. My *beta*. The son I never had. The son I lost with his mother at childbirth. You know all about that story. *Chaloo*, come, meet my *beti*, Shanti. Come, come. She made one mistake. Have you not made mistakes? You have been *chutia* too, and not once but two three times.'

'What do you mean?'

'You also . . .' He paused, then with added emphasis: 'You fuck, yes you fucker too. *Arrey*, do not deny. My chaps watching you. We have proof. That Anglo-Indian nurse you took to Bombay flat?' He started to laugh.

Dinesh stared. 'That was for the Court. Pretence. I was pretending.'

'What you mean. It not changing facts.'

'I took the blame to protect your daughter's and your *izzat*. Even if I did. It is less serious than what she did. You know what the Chinese say?'

'What?'

'When a man is unfaithful it is like someone spitting from the house into the street. When a woman is unfaithful it is like someone spitting from the street into the house.'

The Seth shook his head ruefully. 'This is no way to talk to your elder?' He looked away as they walked through the pillared arcade. The brown neglected lawns made him grit his teeth. 'Bloody man!

That mali does no work.' He pulled the collar of his *kurta* and blew down the front of his chest. 'So hot . . . now, why not . . . You, me, Shanti, why not we go to Varanasi. Bathe in Ganges. Washing away all sins. New start? Hey boy! Her young body will be new. Make you forget . . . You still filing for divorce?'

'Papaji, that is done. I have got my *decree nisi*. Three weeks ago.'

'What! What you saying? What for *nisi*. You intend to marry again? So then, what are you here for? You joking with me? Want me to kill you?'

Dinesh felt he owed it to Alice and their child to see the divorce through, even at the risk of failing in his present mission. 'Papaji, it was too late to stop.'

'What, too late!' The Seth barked. 'Nonsense you talking?'

'But, I'm here, now.'

'But *nisi* not absolute. Don't make absolute. Say never happened. I told you what we do. We be like family again. What say you?'

'Papaji, You know I'm here, prepared to sacrifice my pride. For Ransingh.'

'Yes, yes, I know. Kitty told me. But what do I get? And Shanti, what she get?'

'When you drop all charges and Ransingh is free, I will agree to stay here, with you. Nobody will know about the divorce. I won't talk about it. But don't press me to do anything more. You owe me that.' Dinesh had to say it all over again in Hindi.

The Seth stared at Dinesh sullenly. '*Challo*, we'll talk later. After you seeing wife and son. Then maybe your heart will speak to you. He's just over one years old. Your *beta*, idiot, your son.'

'Why do you call him my son? He's not my son. You know he can't be my son.'

'*Arrey*, what nonsense, boy. He's the image of Shanti.'

'Because she's his mother. That doesn't mean he's my son.'

The Seth put his arm round Dinesh and squeezed, more with anger than affection.

Dinesh freed himself. 'You must know, papaji, that a lot of people know that I am here. They will not keep quiet, if any harm comes to me.'

The Seth lashed out with his right hand. Dinesh ducked, causing the Seth to lose his balance and snatch at a pillar for support.

'Speaking me like this!' He wheezed between each word. 'What you become. Changed from the *beta*, the son, I knew.'

Dinesh opened his hands in a gesture of placation. 'I'll keep my side of the bargain. You keep yours regarding Ransingh.'

'I have given Kitty my word. I am a man of *izzat*.'

'Yes, papaji. I have always known you to be a man of honour.'

'The lawyers, both parties meet three days from now. Settlement making. Man of honour, yes, but don't think me to be fool. No enemy of mine can escape my revenge. Remember, nothing tracing back to me. So not afraid of threats. Go now. No urgent to see Shanti, after all you telling me. Also, time for my *bhojan*. I take light repast, about this time. Six light meals, Dr Chaudhuri say, for my gastric acid problem. Later we join family for the evening meal, seven p.m. What time now?'

'It's just past four o'clock.'

'*Angrezi* tea time. You can order *chai* . . . cup of tea. Any my servants will . . .'

'It's all right. I'll go to the station café.'

The Seth laughed. 'You not leaving here. My men told, instructions, not to let you leave the building. And you going nowhere alone.'

'Papaji, as you say, "no problem". Eat your *bhojan*. I'll take a walk in the garden and have a chat with Gopal.'

'That old man not die. *Arrey* make him see sense about garden. He was good mali, once. I wanting to employ young mali to help him make garden looking decent. I am one of the richest man, and look, what garden . . . I should be living in house like palace.'

'I'll try. But Gopal listens to no one. Shanti tried, remember. He should listen to you. Be firm with him. And, papaji, eat some of those special sweets I brought you.'

'I eat nothing which my Munshi not first tasting.'

'They're too good. Indian sweets made in Britain are better than anything you'll get in India. Because the ingredients are pure.'

'What have you bought?'

'*Peda, burfi,* and *gulabjamin.*'

'Then let Munshi eat them. *Hakim* Dawood say to give up all milk sweetmeats and no more *ghee* in my food. So, you want *gup shup* with Gopal, and not seeing Shanti?'

'You must give me time. It will be good if our first meeting is by chance.'

The Seth gave a sardonic laugh. 'And little Manjit? You say not your son? Do you realise what you saying. You're useless. All years married to Shanti, nothing happened. Are you not man. So this why, all this problem! She wanted man.'

The insult caused Dinesh to react without thought. 'I'm not impotent, I know.'

'Oh, so you have produced a child.'

'No but,' Dinesh lied, 'doctors have tested me.'

'You marry three years. Taking all that time.'

'Papaji, we were young. You treated us like children. We felt like brother and sister. We had no privacy. I married when I wasn't ready for it. To spite my uncle Sandy. But now, I think, possibly, I never loved Shanti. See, I am confiding in you like a son . . .'

'Stop this *buckvas*. Nonsense talk. Bloody *chukram*. Get out! You want privacy? I give you privacy. I'll tell Munshi, make sure you three seen like family. Shanti, Manjit and you. The world must know that. You want favours from me? Treat Manjit as son. Make an old man happy. And have bloody haircut. You look like . . . Beatles.'

'Papaji, before you go, remember Dusty is coming tomorrow to meet me.'

'I know. Munshi tell me when getting phone call.' Then speaking in fluent Punjabi, he said: 'We'll all meet in my room. Shanti and Manjit will be there, so he will see the family. Major Dustoor came with Kitty. I do not know what she sees in him but I like the smart fellow. After my repast I'll rest. Come over at seven for dinner with Shanti. You know where and you'll find your suitcase, there.'

'I see, so you have already decided to treat me like a prisoner.'

'Up to you . . . This big house. Ayub Khan, he will keeping watch on you. You know, that Pathan chowkidar. He never liked you.'

'So you don't trust me?'

'After five years, I trust. Not now.' He grinned wickedly. 'And don't worry, I won't be dead soon. My horoscope, it say, I'll be seventy, maybe more.'

Dinesh watched Seth Agarwal enter his Munshi's office. As he did so Popatlal came out. Dinesh turned away and sat down on the low skirting wall of the arcade, deeply distressed. Kitty had achieved her hopes for Ransingh's early release, but any hope of making good his own early escape had receded. Here he was a friendless prisoner in a fortress teaming with loyal servants of the Seth. True, Dusty would be here tomorrow but the chances of keeping in touch with him were slim.

He heard a light shuffle behind him. It was the Munshi. The man bowed, and a wide skull-like grin split his thin face. 'May I?' he said and sat down next to Dinesh. 'Had you listened to me, on that earlier occasion, in Bombay, matters would not come to this pass. So much evil and sadness would not have taken place. Now, respected sir, now is the time to let bygones be bygones. You have great expectations. Accept as inevitable your place here. Whatsoever your qualms, Shantiji, if I may say, is not made of rubber. Her body will retain its voluptuous qualities, whatever use it was put to. It is only our images of what is right, wrong or proper, that drive us to despair.'

'Munshiji, what on earth are you talking about?'

'I'm thinking you understand, my import, despite your protest.'

Dinesh did not answer. He kept his gaze away from the Munshi, whose eyes he could feel fixed on him. He knew the man was prying, as he had done when last they met in Bombay and he was determined not to fall into a trap. 'Permit me to say this,' continued the Munshi, 'this one thing, and I ask to crave your indulgence. You see, I trust you to treat what I say with uttermost confidentiality. I am assured, because you have English education, and so have those admirable virtues and upright qualities that Englishmen of the Raj imbued into the educated Indian.'

Dinesh chuckled. 'How would you know about English virtues.'

'I have it from most impeccable source, my father. He worked for them, as a head clerk. As a boy returning from school, I would spend time with him, sitting by his desk. Often his white bosses would address my father, sometimes sternly, sometimes kindly. At times, I thought, insultingly, addressing him as "babu", but my father always said it was basically done in good humour and without malice. They were most even handed in the way they treated him and punctilious about office timings and holidays.'

'Munshiji, if you don't mind, I want to be left alone for a while.'

'You see, Dinesh sahib, I know I can trust you to keep what I say, confidential. You see, it will not be long before, assuming you will now make the correct decision, before all this will be yours, along with the vast complex of Agarwal Industries. That you will, with your England background, right many things that are wrong practices, even in the treatment of your employees. I am not thinking of myself. I will be sixty next month . . .' he paused to let Dinesh study his face and misread Dinesh's astonishment. 'Yes, as old as that, but I know that under your fair regime my reward will be just, and I shall spend my last days in my beloved Gujarat in come-fort-table retirement.'

Dinesh smelled a rat. 'Thank you for your compliments. So the Popatlals hail from Gujarat and Maharastra?

'They come from all over the place. Why do you laugh? Is it because of the name?'

'No, Munshiji, I would never do that.'

'You may joke. No matter. Like my revered father, I take all in good humour. And you, young master, as I was saying, will make a great tycoon. You will grow confident and wise.'

Dinesh desperately wanted to scream at the man. Tell him to shut up. That nothing he could say would change his mind. He had no need for more riches. He longed to be back with his beloved Alice. God, how he ached for her. He said: 'Munshiji, right now, I would like a tray with a pot of tea.'

'Most certainly. And, if I may suggest, a slice of fruit cake. Tea should not be taken without a little something to eat. I shall order it from the Madras Hotel.'

'You'll need money. Let me . . .'

'Never, young master, that will be an insult. Where will you want it?'

'There, by the fountain.'

'*Chee, chee!* The fountain is filthy, with no where clean to sit down at ease. I will send for a light chair and table. I suggest you sit in the shadow of the *neem* tree,'

'Why not the gulmohur tree?' Dinesh teased.

'No flies or unwanted insects under the *neem*. It is tree of great medicinal properties and sundry cures. Ramoo! *Arrey* Ramoo!' A thin man sprang out from the Munshi's office. Bending forward from the waist, and moving with rapid steps, he resembled an ostrich on the run. '*Mez aur kursi lao*, sahib *ke liyeh. Ek dum jaldi!*'

Dinesh walked towards the *neem* tree, but before he reached it, the minion shot past him with a metal folding chair and table. Ramoo stood with downcast eyes waiting to be dismissed. The single word "Jao!" would have sufficed, but Dinesh hesitated as he had never done before. What a change being in England had wrought! Now the idea of thanking subordinates and treating them with due politeness appealed to him, and he recalled with disgust the way he had behaved towards them in the past.

'Thank you.' he said. The man looked confused. '*Dhanyavad*, Ramoo.' Ramoo looked up and grinned. He folded his hands against his forehead, bowed obsequiously and left.

Dinesh sighed. He took out his handkerchief and dabbed his eyes. Tears? He clicked his tongue. He must steel himself. Tears for the second time! Earlier that day he broke down as he stood in front of Fern Cottage, for the memories it evoked. Mohan Singh and Dusty Dustoor saw those tears. The shame of it! He had to convince himself that the past was not all bad. That with Sandy, Emma, and even Sona, there had been good times together. He turned and caught a glimpse of his jailer, the big Pathan, Ayub Khan. The man was armed. A rifle slung over his left shoulder. Dinesh looked away.

Ramoo was back with the tray of tea and sliced cake. He seemed more cheerful and upright. The West had made its impact. What, Dinesh once asked Sandy, had stirred his love for England? History? "Yes," Sandy replied, "but more its Literature, particularly Poetry." It was not answer enough for him. Sandy saw that. "If I had to name a single poet," Sandy went on, "it would have to be Blake." "Not Kipling?" Dinesh had queried pointedly. They were together in the garden, working on a jig-saw puzzle that was a picture of the Bridge at Henley, when Sandy looked up. "Suddenly I see a link! Blake's "Tiger", India, and Blake's "Jerusalem", England." And Dinesh remembered his mood turn ugly and resentful. Now, he shook his head, sighed and said aloud. 'I suppose from such anger and regret the young gain maturity.' It startled Ramoo, who pretended to understand by pointing to the tray. 'Sahib, *chai*, cake, *aur biskoot.*' Dinesh made a face at the cake which looked sticky and sweet. 'There,' he said in Hindi. 'Ramoo, you have the cake. Go

The Lotus And The Rose

on!' Ramoo, after an incredulous hesitation, took the cake, moved behind the *neem* tree, and ate it hungrily.

The tea, in a fluted glass tumbler, was sugary, milky and strong. Dinesh sipped it gingerly and continued sipping ignoring the taste. A sudden movement from behind a frangipani tree caught his attention. He waved to Gopal, who was carrying a sickle and adjusting a dhoti no larger than a loin cloth. Gopal waved back, then ambled on to the bramble covered gates and there began hacking away with the sickle, aimlessly.

Dinesh leaned back, his hands behind his head. Apart from the orange flowers on the gulmohur, no other colour relieved the dun brown of the garden. Kay would have been delighted with a garden this size . . . and Alice, sweet, fresh faced, generous Alice . . .

'She your wife?' asked the bold, inquisitive Bengali gentleman, who sat next to him in the waiting-room of the Tagore Natal Clinic. 'That lady, who just went in?' Dinesh feigned not to hear. 'My wife, also, four to five months. This place,' the man rambled on, 'bloody expensive. But money, what's money? My wife must have best attention.' He paused briefly and, not deterred by the lack of response, went on. 'So you not find good Indian woman? Pardon my saying so, but nothing like an Indian wife. Faithful, dutiful, in best Hindu tradition. Always I say to bachelor friends, making business trips to America and the West, beware white women. All flirtatious by nature and hoodwink husbands.' Dinesh smiled as he remembered the delight with which he disabused his obnoxious interlocutor. 'That's what every Indian says, I was married to one of your virtuous Indian women and was hoodwinked, under my very nose. Now, let me read my book?' The irrepressible Bengali asked the title. 'Gibbon, and it's not about monkeys?' The effect was magical. The Bengali crossed the room to sulk in the opposite corner. Dinesh chuckled, recalling the fit of giggles Alice went into, when, back at their hotel, he recounted the incident. That memory was vivid because that very day she decided to fly back to England. They agreed they had been silly, unthinking about being together. That Ted was right. Alice should be with her mother. Also, since the good news of his divorce had reached them while they were on holiday in the Nilgiri Hills, it was time to be sensible. 'I can wait patiently till you come back,' Alice said, 'darling, take care.' He waved goodbye to her at Calcutta's airport and then left for Delhi the next day, where Kitty was waiting with news that the Seth had agreed to see him; and that Dusty, who was posted as a liaison officer with an Infantry regiment stationed five miles west of Pathankot, would meet him at the Pathankot Railway station . . . That was this morning, but before dropping him here at Ram Nivas, Dusty suggested they first went on to Fern Cottage where Mohan Singh was waiting to see him, and that he would then come over to see Dinesh and the Seth tomorrow . . . Dusty also stressed that Dinesh must play his part with patience, and give the impression that he was genuinely here to be reconciled and to settle down with Shanti, because it was vital to remove every suspicion the Seth may have. Then after the Seth drops the case against Ransingh and Ransingh is freed, Dinesh was to look for any loophole that would help make his escape from Ram Nivas a certainty. Dusty would then need two days notice to arrange a secret rendezvous, where Dinesh would be collected and driven to Delhi. In Delhi he was to take the first flight out to London. Dusty's personality and supreme panache made it look that simple.

But now, faced with the realities of his situation, Dinesh despaired. He put the glass of tea down and sighed. As a prisoner, unable to telephone or post a letter, it would be impossible to communicate with Dusty. They had not taken this into account. He stood up and walked sadly towards the gates. A confused Ramoo followed discreetly. Dinesh swung round. 'What!' he raised his voice. 'Sorry, yes, you may take away the table and chair.' Just then the Ayub Khan stepped into the open, his Semite face, hard, unsmiling. He was a major obstacle. And Dusty would have problems too. As a serving officer, he would have to pick on a day, time and place, which fitted with his timetable. This tight situation called for regular contact and communication.

Dinesh walked on casually to study the perimeter walls which enclosed the garden. They were seven feet high. The locked gates offered no respite either. The vertical iron bars had sharp spear heads. Of course, there was a way out, and into the open, through the Munshi's office on the ground floor. Could he as a last resort make a dash for it? It was so temptingly easy, that there had to be a trap. And to make good his escape, he would need a clear two hours before his absence was discovered. That was also Dusty's estimate, who had been to Ram Nivas with Kitty and managed to note the geography of the garden and house while Kitty and the Seth were busy negotiating.

Dinesh returned to the gulmohur tree and looked up at its feathery branches, then at the trunk where he had carved his initials three years ago. They were there. Someone left a small wooden stool. He flicked the top of it with a handkerchief and sat down. As he did he remembered the pipal tree. It was there, next to Gopal's hut, right against the garden wall! But any sense of elation soon turned to dismay. He could not see himself climbing it and jumping down seven feet to the other side. He was no athlete. Attempts by rope or ladder would be discovered, even at midnight. Shanti was a light sleeper and knowing the Seth and a little about Ayub Khan, a sentry will surely be posted at nights. The Pathan may have orders to shoot and, claiming to mistake Dinesh for an intruder, get away with murder. He looked back to study Ayub Khan, all six-feet four of him, in the usual dress of a grey *kurta* and *salwar pyjamas*, that Pathans wore. Over the *kurta* he had a black, gold-thread embroidered waistcoat and slung over his left shoulder was no rifle but a *jazail*, which looked as if it had seen service. Dinesh was no hero. He had to rely on men like Dusty.

He tried hard to cheer himself by thinking about Dusty's brimming confidence. Their first meeting earlier this morning, when Dusty met him at Pathankot Railway station as Kitty said he would. How without the slightest hesitation he came straight up to him. 'You must be Dinesh, come with me, I've a staff car outside.' He smiled. 'Don't look surprised. People expecting to be met invariably betray their anxiety. *Coolie*!' They waited for the man to collect Dinesh's luggage, while he moved briskly down to the far end of the platform. Dinesh and the *coolie* tried hard to keep up with him. 'Pay the man whatever he asks, we don't want to draw attention to ourselves.' He spoke like an army officer, clipped, clear, affected.

There was a chill in the air. The mists had not yet lifted. 'We'll go through Town, past Seth Agarwal's house, on our way to Mcleodganj. I've a flask of hot coffee and biscuits to keep us going. Do get in at the back. My man Lal Singh will drive us. I see you've cut yourself? There was no need to shave. You're not trying to impress Shanti.'

Dusty laughed. He immediately saw why any woman would find a face, so ostensibly plain, attractive. Dusty eyes were strikingly beautiful, dark, long-lashed, magnetic. It was charm, not looks, that made Kitty fall in love with this graceful, athletic man.

Dinesh said he hoped he was not going to be an inconvenience. 'Not a bit,' Dusty said. 'A cavalry officer, attached to a regiment in an advisory role, has more freedom. Now, I'll tell Lal Singh to expect us back at three.' Lal Singh was in uniform. He gave a smart salute. Dusty, who was immaculately dressed in flannels, a blue shirt, red cravat and Blazer, acknowledged it with a click of heels and a stiffening of his arms . . .

The prospect of seeing Dusty tomorrow lifted Dinesh's spirits and he told himself it was good to have someone like Dusty around. But the tension got to him. He rose to retrace his steps to the Munshi's office, when a discreet cough drew his attention. Gopal was standing by the pipal tree beckoning to him. He hesitated; then with astonishing alacrity he saw Gopal dart into his lean-to and come out out waving his sickle. 'Keep out!' he growled and drew a line with his sickle on the brown grass. He stood, arms akimbo. Dinesh stepped back astonished, then realised Gopal's confrontation was directed at Ayub Khan, who was behind him. Gopal waved his sickle menacingly. The Pathan gazed down at Gopal, a shrivelled dry shrub before a tree of a man. 'Stop there! No mussalman here! No musssalman!' bellowed Gopal.

The Pathan twirled his moustache and adjusted his *pugaree*. 'Seth Agarwal Sahib *ka hukum*,' he said and then made the mistake of adding: '*soowar ka bachcha*,' child of a pig. Gopal saw red. The Pathan sprang back as Gopal made a sudden swipe. The sickle caught the sling of the Ayub's *jazail* and sliced through the strap, causing it to fall to the ground. The Pathan cursed fulsomely as he picked up his weapon.

'The Seth knows,' said Gopal as he extended the line he drew to include the lean-to and the pipal tree. 'This Hindu holy ground. *Khabardar!*'

The Pathan waved a hand and said: 'You may call down all the curses and spells of your gods and demons. A mussalman has no fear!' But having said that, he stepped back and stood still, his *jazail* resting horizontally across his shoulders. Gopal grunted and glared

The Lotus And The Rose

at the Ayub. Then he invited Dinesh into his hut. Dinesh bowed low to enter and on entering realised that the thatched roof covered not only an open outer space but also a reasonably large inner room with neatly appointed bricks and a central doorway. The roof sloped down from the seven foot high boundary wall and was supported, at the front, on a cross beam, held by the forks of two dried tree trunks. Gopal flung his sickle in a far corner and entered the room, only to return with a light charpoy. He gestured Dinesh to sit down on it, while he sat on the cow dung plastered floor, frog-like on his heels, in front of him. Having calmed down, the venerable, grey-stubbled face regarded Dinish quizzically. Dinesh waited a moment then asked what Gopal was thinking. For an answer, the old man laid a thin gnarled hand on Dinesh's knee. Dinesh stared at the dry, heavily veined hand. Then he took it in his hands and leant forward. 'And how is my old friend?' he asked. Gopal looked at Dinesh searchingly. In the short time Dinesh had lived in Ram Niwas, he learnt something about this grumpy octogenarian. How the man increasingly had less time for humanity, and preferred instead to commune with nature, his gods, and himself.

Gopal was twenty when the Seth's father employed him, first as a mason and later as gardener. As a gardener, he struck a close friendship with the present Seth, who was then ten years old. Gopal told the boy stories from the Hindu scriptures, and soon it was discovered that he had been a *chela*, a disciple, to a holy man from Hardwar, and with whom he travelled from Banares to the Cow's Mouth, which is the source of Mother Ganges. It was also noted that since his employment, Agarwal Industries prospered greatly and the superstitious Agarwals, father and son, entreated the young Brahmin to make Ram Niwas his home. Gopal, who trekked every day to and from Jor, his village, agreed on condition he could follow in the footsteps of his old guru, by leading a pure, contemplative, unworldly life. He wanted no money but asked to be allowed to build himself a shed near the pipal tree and to have a male Brahmin to cook his midday meal. This meal almost invariably consisted of slow cooked unleavened corn bread, which he ate after crumbling it in buttermilk. "Best diet for maintaining a healthy body" Gopal once told Dinesh, who remembered how every morning at six, Gopal rose to pray, then ground the dried maize corn by hand on the millstones that were on the floor behind him. 'Are you still able to turn the millstone?' he asked. For an answer, Gopal freed his hand and gripped Dinesh by the wrist. Dinesh winced. His grip was like a vice.

'You are unhappy,' Gopal said, taking Dinesh by surprise. Gopal spoke in Marwari, a dialect he knew Dinesh understood, for Dinesh's forbears came from Rajasthan. 'Tell me. You can trust me. I can help.'

Dinesh hesitated. After all Gopal was the Seth's man.

Gopal rose to his feet and beckoned Dinesh to come with him into the inner room. It was dim but light enough to see. Against the wall was a shelf, on which was an array of three gleaming brass cooking utensils. In a corner, on the floor, was a brass bucket and a *lota*. On the wall above the shelf, two framed pictures were garlanded with a string of dead marigold and jasmine. Below them, from a single lit joss-stick rose a fragrant curl of blue smoke. A glance at the larger of the two pictures revealed a print of the blue god Krishna, but it was the other picture that held Dinesh's attention. A photograph of a woman. A woman with a familiar face. Emma. Yes, his beautiful aunt, Emma Thakur, Sandy's wife. Gopal was watching him. 'Devata', he said, and folding hands against his forehead, bowed.

'Where did you get that picture?'

'Sona,' Gopal said simply.'

'How did you know Sona?'

Gopal pointed to a side of the hut where on a ledge below a small barred window, were a row of glass jars containing a variety of dried berries, twigs, leaves and flowers. 'Sona and . . .' he pointed to himself, 'we know a lot about herbal medicine.' He stared at Dinesh, and kept nodding his head. He lifted a black glazed pottery jar, put it down, and mimed "fast asleep". 'Yes,' he pointed to the jar again. '*Aram se*, peaceful sleep.'

Then it dawned on Dinesh. 'You mean, you gave Sona . . . for Sandy?'

Gopal gestured fiercely. He didn't want to talk about it. 'I can help you?'

'I don't want to die! I want to live.'

Gopal waved his hands impatiently. 'I was very good *mistri*, building mason.' He took Dinesh's hand and drew him to the perimeter wall

The Lotus And The Rose

and thumped on it. 'You know, this garden wall. Behind it is road. I can breach the wall, let you through to the outside world, and seal it again so no one would be any the wiser.'

Dinesh felt his heart beat. He smiled, but checked himself. It was a matter of life and death. Death if Gopal betrayed him.

'Tell me when you're ready,' Gopal whispered. 'When you want my help.'

'But Gopal,' Dinesh risked the plunge, 'you're a friend of the Seth. You're like . . .'

Gopal shook his head. '*Kharab admi*! Seth is bad man. He was like my son, long ago. But he has turned evil. A sinner.'

'Gopal!' Dinesh could contain himself no longer. 'I am afraid and alone. Can I trust you. I don't mean to insult you, but . . .'

Gopal stopped him. 'I am speaking before my Lord, after whom I am named.'

'Gopal, you are a good Hindu. I try to be a good Hindu, too.'

'I know, but your wife has defiled the marriage bed.'

'How do you know?'

'The Seth cannot hide things from me. When the boy was born, I knew he was not your son. The Seth wanted life to be as if nothing had happened. I then knew he would even kill to preserve his good name.'

'God bless you Gopal. Thank you. I'll never forget you.'

'When you are gone, I will never see you again. But you must be free to take the road of life. Life's *yatra*. Life's journey.'

There were tears in Dinesh's eyes. But he did not mind them. He stared at the little man and wanted to embrace him. Give me your *arshidwar*, your blessings.'

'I will, when I send you on your way.'

'Master Dinesh! Master Dinesh!' There was no mistaking the Munshi's voice.

Dinesh brushed his face and came out from the hut. 'What is it Munshi?' he asked.

'The *malik*, Sethji, he has asked me to accompany you to the family quarters. Soon it will be supper time.'

'I'll say goodbye to Gopal.' But before Dinesh could turn, Gopal had joined him.

'*Namaskar*, Panditji,' the Munshi addressed Gopal with a slight sarcasm in his voice. 'Gopal, our gardener is a very righteous man, therefore, I call him, Panditji.'

The irony was wasted. Gopal gave a dismissive wave of the hand and went inside. Dinesh joined the Munshi. 'I note, an emotional meeting with Gopal has taken place?'

Dinesh wanted to strangle the man. 'No more than the one I had with you.'

'That was never my intention, dear sir. For I do believe emotional encounters ought to be avoided. It is harmful to one's health.'

'Then you should not take me to meet Shanti, should you, Munshiji?'

'Indeed, young master, but my hands are tied in this matter.'

They walked down the arcade in silence. The Munshi, lean and bent. Dinesh with a spring in his step. 'Munshiji, will you never seek to be free of your yoke? Strike out for independence, free yourself from unquestioning obedience?'

Munshi Popatlal cast a sideways glance at Dinesh. 'You look like one who has had good news, master Dinesh, if I may say so. As for concern for my own future, may I assure you, a time in the near future will come when I shall shed cares of this world, make my peace with the gods by immersing myself in *Gunga Mata*. She washes all sin. Thereafter, I shall seek peace in the hills. As good Hindus should.'

Dinesh intensely disliked the Munshi's ability to end with stings to his tales. They had now reached the family wing. 'I shall leave you here, young sir, and wish you well in all your enterprises. Whatever opinion you may have of me, I assure you my slavery is limited to obedience. I am not an informer.'

A baffled Dinesh watched the bent figure merge into the evening gloom. Entering the front room he found himself facing Shanti; and was shocked to see she had grown fat and her eyes, always large, were now bulging like her father's. She reached for her spectacles and stared at him. Her face crumpled and she bellowed, throwing herself on the floor in a fit of hysteria. 'O God!' she screamed, 'what have I done to deserve this. Hi, Ram! Cursed be the day I set eyes on you!'

The Lotus And The Rose

There were sounds of heavy feet rushing towards the door. Instinctively he dashed to the far end of the room and waited behind a chair, rigid with fear. He wanted her to be quiet but stared helplessly. The first to enter was Ayub Khan with his gun against his hip. He was immediately followed by another Pathan carrying an ugly looking knobbed *lathi*. They took positions on either side of the door and glared at him. Their sudden appearance had the effect of silencing Shanti, who now ogled them with astonishment. A few minutes later the Seth arrived, puffing and panting. Then before he could regain his breath he shouted at Dinesh. 'What did you say to her? Heh!' He then turned to the men. 'What are you waiting for? Take him out and give him a thrashing.'

Dinesh picked up the chair and backed against the wall. '*Thairo! Khabadar!*' The men hesitated. 'Papaji, I've said and done nothing. Ask her. Ask Munshiji.'

'Indeed, Seth Sahib,' said the Munshi, standing in the middle of the doorway, and looking over a pair of thin spectacles. 'I barely got even halfway to my office when the screaming began. I left Master Dinesh only a minute ago.'

'He must have said something to make her scream. *Beti* what did he say to you?'

'Hai! The gods have cursed our marriage. I am bereft. My son is fatherless!'

'But, what did he say to you?'

She stared, wildly. 'Nothing. Shameless man! Heartless monster.'

'*Beti*, Shanti, this no way to behave. Screaming. Shouting. Call Manjit. Let the boy see his father.' The Seth looked at his audience triumphantly. 'You and Dinesh need to sit and talk quietly.' He turned to the three standing at the doorway. 'Go, now. Leave us, I say. Munshiji, tell the cook, servants, arrange the table, bring the food nice, hot.'

The Munshi left with the two Pathans, but not without casting a sly look at Dinesh, and a gentle shake of his head.

Shanti returned to the front room with a little boy whose shaven head looked much too large for his body. The Seth picked him up. 'Look! Look! Manjit. That is papa.' The boy yawned and rubbed his eyes. 'There, that man. No, no! wake up, look.' The sleepy child had buried his head into the Seth's ample neck and shoulders. The Seth put the child down. 'Go to daddy. You asking where's daddy? There.'

'Papaji!' Dinesh said, irritated by this charade. 'Don't do this to the child. I am just a stranger to him.' And as if in confirmation the child burst out crying. 'Put him down.'

The Seth did so. The boy ran to Shanti, who took him to an inner room, as a line of servants came in with *thalis*, a basket of fried *puris*, silver bowls of steaming hot lentils, vegetable curry, curds and a flat dish of *pilau* rice.

Shanti returned. '*Chale, chalo*,' she said. 'Let's eat. I'm starving.'

'Is the boy all right?' The Seth asked

'Of course, daddyji. The ayah is sitting, keeping watch.'

'*Achcha*, then we can eat in peace, *aram se* and after, talking future plans. What say you, *beta* Dinesh?'

'Yes, but don't insult me in front of servants. Like you did. Think before you lose your temper. Have you no respect for me. Telling minions to beat me?'

'See, how he talks to me. No respect. But *beti* you did wrong. Shouting, screaming, for no reason. That made me *ghusa*, angry.'

'Daddy, this filthy man's been hobnobbing with white woman.'

'Then don't have anything to do with me,' Dinesh muttered.

'Enough! Shanti. Listen to me!' It was the first time Dinesh heard the Seth speak to her with any harshness. 'I know what you have been through,' the Seth continued in a more conciliatory tone. 'You too seriously misbehaved. Forget past. Enough. Dinesh has come, ready to talk things over, live here, become a member of the family. Give him time. And when we four become family again, he must be rewarded greatly. Hear that Dinesh, my son. You have a lot to gain. Okay, now we eat.'

After dinner the Seth asked Dinesh if he would like a glass of cold beer. 'I don't drink wine or spirits, but sometimes glass of beer taking. Today I keep you company. Good. Is that Ramoo there? *Arrey*, Ramoo!'

Ramoo came up to the Seth and bowed low. He avoided looking at Dinesh, and his whole demeanour was one of mortification. The Seth told him to bring a bottle of beer and two glasses. 'Ask Munshiji. He's got the keys.'

When he left, the Seth said to Dinesh: 'I have had to give boy good thrashing. You must not spoil servants. They take kindness for weakness. Remember that. I had report of what you did. Cake eating. No, no. Wrong,'

Dinesh shut his eyes. He had got Ramoo into trouble and because of his carelessness the man had been punished and humiliated. He would find some way of compensating the man. 'Papaji, this must be clearly understood. Manjit is not my son.'

'Why not? If Manjit is the result of what happened in Bombay with dance master fellow, he would be less than a year old.'

'Please daddy, I can't follow all this Punjabi talk, will you both speak Hindi.'

'Okay, Shanti. I saying Manjit is over one year old, so his son.'

'That would mean,' Dinesh said, 'he was conceived two years ago. Two years ago I was alone in Bombay, or travelling all over Maharashtra State on official business. She, remember refused to join me because she said it interfered with her Kathakali dancing.'

'But did you not come home on two weeks leave . . .'

'I did, after we acquired that flat on Malabar Hill. I came to collect her. But she was not there. She was in Allahabad, for some dancing competition. When she came, she travelled to Bombay with the music master.'

'*Arrey*, you mean, cunning man. Are you telling daddy you've never slept with me? So many times you fuck. Not my fault if . . .' She checked herself. 'Useless man.'

'See papaji, she's calling me impotent.'

'*Arrey*, in anger women say anything.' The Seth waved his hand.

'If he's my child's, papaji, he'll either have to be nearly three years or less than ten months old. So, don't insist Manjit is my son, otherwise you are making her shameful behaviour public, as it means she's been unfaithful long before I found out. People and servants can work that out. Some already know that Manjit is not my son.'

'But if you say he's your son, people will shut up!'

'Then papaji, as the English say, least said soonest mended. It's not necessary to lie or pretend. Give me time to forgive, forget, and carry on as if nothing happened.'

'I don't understand this fast, fast, English speaking,' mumbled the Seth.

'Oh, God,' Shanti began to rant in Hindi. 'So the whole world will know I'm a slut and Manjit is a bastard.' Then in English, she repeated: 'So, my son is a bastard?'

'Shanti,' Dinesh couldn't repress a smile, 'that's the truth. I'm saying, keep quiet about it. Or, if you care about Manjit's status, start a new life with his real father.'

'*Bus, bus.* Enough.' Seth Agarwal stood up. 'So, Dinesh, give me word of honour. You not talking about of this to anyone?'

'Yes, but you must respect the fact that I am the injured party.'

'So, are you ever going to fuck me ever again?'

'*Beti*, Shanti. How can you talk like this in front of your father?'

'Daddy, I thought you didn't understand English.'

'Stupid girl! Even simple Ramoo knowing "fuck"; whole world knows.'

CHAPTER TWENTY-ONE

'Mr Dinesh, my good sir, I have just received a message from Major Dustoor. He will be arriving here at eleven thirty sharp.'

'On the telephone? Did he ask for me?'

Popatlal bowed.

'Then why didn't you send for me?'

'I had to say you were occupied elsewhere. But that I would convey his message.'

'Next time you must send for me. I insist on receiving my calls.'

'I have strict instruction from boss. For you, no telephone, till he say. I dare not go against the Seth's wishes. No intention to displease. If it be a matter of most expressed urgency, I shall secretly send for you, my good sir. I wish very much to be in your good books. But as things stand, the Seth has upper hand. You realise we are being watched. This, I say, at some risk to myself.'

'All right, all right. I'm not here to get you into trouble or betray you, Munshiji.'

Dusty's punctuality came as no surprise, and the brisk tramp of his footsteps in the arcade alerted the Seth, Shanti and Dinesh, who were waiting for him. The Seth, lazing on the sofa, sat up to buttoned his black waistcoat. He adjusted his dhoti, as he crossed the room to sit on a velvet cushioned, winged-back chair. Shanti went to the window and looked down the arcade. 'Look at that smart fellow.' she drooled, as Dinesh went past her to meet Dusty. 'That's the sort of husband I should have had.'

'*Chup, beti.* Shut up, I telling you.' the Seth growled. 'No more nonsense like that before guest. Act like good Indian wife. Show full respect.' He waved Dinesh on. 'And tell the fellow with him . . . Is it our Premchand? Tell him, to order coffee and cakes.'

Dinesh nodded. In front of guests the Seth made a point of speaking in English and where he failed to follow the conversation, he relied on his Munshi to fill in the blanks. 'What is this fellow going to talk about? And call Munshi, too?'

'Yes, papaji,' Dinesh shook Dusty's hand warmly. 'God, I'm glad to see you.'

Dusty stood in the centre of the room and with supreme aplomb surveyed all the occupants. He struck the side of his olive green trousers with his swagger stick and smiled at the Seth. 'I haven't come to talk about anything in particular. Just a friendly call to see how Dinesh is getting on.'

'He is as you see.' The Seth rolled his head from side to side. 'Please to take seat.'

Dusty was immaculately turned out in his uniform. The highly polished leather Sam Browne belt contrasted well with his olive green gabardine tunic and the shining brass Ashoka Lions on his epaulets, indicated his rank of major.

'Now tell me,' said the Seth, 'how is wife, Kitty?'

'She's well, thank you.' Dusty frowned.

'But funny kind of newly married couple?' Shanti said, making a face.

'What d'you mean by that, Mrs Thakur?' Dusty smiled as he saw Munshi Popatlal slink into a dark corner of the room.

'I mean, you here, she Goa, all alone. She's too pretty to leave alone.'

'She's not alone. She's with a lot of nuns and teachers at the Convent. And we'll soon be together again, when my new posting comes through. I get joining leave, so we'll have a second honeymoon before we settle down to regimental life.'

'Second honeymoon? Great. Vee never had first honeymoon, even.'

The Seth shot an irate look at his daughter. '*Bus*, my Shanti. Major sahib, women loving gossip talk. So, Kitty's got job. What teaching?'

'Teaching? English, what else.' Dusty said. 'Goans are quite keen to learn.'

The Seth rolled his head. 'Especially white or half white Goanese.'

'Goans. They don't like being called Goanese, because of the way it sounds. Go and ease.' The Seth stared at Dusty blankly. 'Never mind, Sethji, never mind.'

'Okay, what language you speak when not English. Do you not speaking Punjabi?'

'No. Army Hindustani, Gujarati, and now some Gurkhali.'

'*Arrey*, this England returned Indian vant to speak English only.' Shanti chimed in, waving an accusing hand at Dinesh, while the wrist of the other hand rested on her hip. 'And useless Indians, whose families licked the boots of Englishmen, talk like limeys.' She stuck her chin out and gave a look which Dinesh ignored.

'For many years I was a radical nationalist. If any member of my family worked for the Raj, it was ages ago. I certainly did not lick any Englishman's boots.'

'It's no sin to have worked for the Brits, Shanti,' Dusty said. "It made good sense to be involved in the government of one's country. Not to do so was a dereliction of one's duty. Well, not quite duty, since there was no compulsion, but to be criticised, for participating, is unfair. Gandhi and Nehru were what you call "England returned". As were many Indians in government. Nobody insults them. Seth sahib, many Indian boxwallahs minted money, working for the Brits. You must know that?'

'What is this "boxwallahs" you say?'

'Businessmen. The *banya* caste. The true freedom fighters were those who stood up against the Brits and were sent to prison. That's the acid test. Were any of your family sent to prison in the time of the Raj?'

The Seth stared at Dusty open mouthed. 'What is he saying Munshiji?'

'It is a fair question, Seth sahib. But, but, you see, Major Dustoor, Sethji's family believed in minding their own business.'

'I'm sure they did, Mr Popatlal.' Dusty raised his brows and the Munshi bowed.

Dinesh laughed.

'Why you laugh, you silly man,' Shanti turned on him. 'You hated uncle Sandy, for being so like Englishman. You were ashamed of him.'

'True, Shanti. I've learned my lesson. Sandy, and great uncle Jagdish, and his father, were great men. Don't remind me of my foolishness. I have come to my senses, now.'

Shanti stood up, but before she could say anything her father interjected. "Shanti! Beti! Just see what that Premchand is doing about the coffee.'

'Thank you,' Dusty said, 'but please don't bother about coffee.'

'No, no, Major. Guests in this house are always . . . *arrey, hah*! Here it comes! But if you're preferring strong stuff, that too arranged can be. Gin, bitters, rum, whisky, you say. I know army types drink good spirits.'

'Thank you, Seth Agarwal, coffee will be just fine.'

Coffee was served to all except the Munshi, who declined because soon he would be having his "tiffin" 'Then, Munshiji,' the Seth said, 'pass the sweets round.' He gave his heavily sugared coffee a vigorous stir. 'So, Major Dustoor, *ye nam kahanse* . . . sorry, where does this name, Dustoor, come from?'

'A long story, Sethji. But I assure you it is as worthy a name as Agarwal. My father may not have been a business man but he was a damn good lecturer.'

'Damn good!' Agarwal chuckled. His body quivering like blancmange. 'Now you sound like Army Officer. "Damn Good! Bloody good show!" That's how army fellows talking. Listen, Major, I could have gone to England for school and all education. Also speaking English like Dinesh boy. Money was in plenty. But I said to father "no, no! India is where I stay". You sound English, too, but I have respect for you. Kitty says, you do not want go live in England. Is that not so?'

Dusty smiled and did not answer. The Seth waited for a moment, then he sipped his coffee noisily and called out to Premchand to take his cup away. Premchand, smartly attired in his white *Chaparasi's* uniform, adjusted his red turban nervously and came forward. He took the cup and saucer with great deference. The Seth stifled a yawn. 'So, Major, you have come with your driver in army jeep. If you like I send Ayub Khan with tea and snacks for driver?'

'That will be appreciated,'

'Consider it done.' The Seth nodded to the Munshi. 'And then you may go back to office and eat your tiffin. Dustoor sahib is not here for any business matter.' The gaunt and bent Munshi left noiselessly. 'He is my most loyal and trustworthy servant.'

'Indeed, Sethji, you are well served. I won't take up any more of your time. But I'd like to have a chat with my friend Dinesh before I go.'

Seth Agarwal's face clouded. 'Friend? What friend? You see him second time only. Is that not so?'

Dusty regarded the Seth steadily. 'Any friend of Kitty is my friend.'

'Say what you like here. No secret talk. You not planning to take him away from his wife and son?'

'His private life is no business of mine. A happy man has no reason to leave. Keep him happy, not a prisoner. Treat him like a free man. Son and heir. That's what he is.'

'If he's unhappy, then he must tell me. Hah Dinesh?'

'You are a great and noble man.' Dusty went on. 'Many people look upon you as their godfather. You have money, power and total hold of this place. You have nothing to worry about giving me a private moment with Dinesh. We will simply walk and talk in the garden. He has come here of his own accord. Why would he wish to leave?'

The Seth purse his lips. 'Okay, okay. Go, go, in garden. Bloody garden? What damn garden? What *bageecha*? We had grand *bageecha*. Look at now. But go. You, Dinesh, be happy. This is home.'

'One more thing Sethji. Make him happy. Me happy. Kitty happy. See that Ransingh is set free. That was why Kitty came to you. Be *malik*. Act now, with honour.'

'I keep to promise. See me before you go. I'll be at my usual place upstairs after my bathing before meal time. *Arrey*, Shanti, I can hear Manjit crying. Look to him.'

'Okay,' Shanti gave a petulant nod. Gazed at her departing father, glared at Dinesh, and smiled at Dusty. 'You two, you may gossip like women but Dusty, I hope you'll also tell him to . . . you know, to be proper man and husband.'

'Patience, Mrs Thakur, he will.' Dusty watched her leave with a provocative swing of her hips. 'Good grief, the woman's a nymphomaniac. Didn't you spot that the first time you set eyes on her? Steel yourself. Sleep with the bitch. It can only help. Don't tell me you can't? It will help things along.'

'It's not impossible. But Alice?'

'Oh, come on. What she doesn't know won't hurt. Look at it as a sacrifice for her sake. Don't worry, my lips are sealed. It will please the Seth and relax the atmosphere. Besides I'm for anything that makes my task easier. Thanks to Kitty' charm, the CO is bending backwards to help. I don't do anything without his permission and I don't like taking advantage of his kindness. Too many visits will raise suspicion. So next we meet it must be for the real thing. Ransingh will be freed in a matter of days now. I believe the Seth is keeping his word.'

Dinesh sighed. 'I can't forget the sight of that panting music master on top of her.'

'From what you said, you must have left your mark on his offending bottom. Ugly brute, was he? The mind boggles. Women are a mystery. As I said, steel yourself. It's not for long. And it doesn't have to be every night. Just show you care. Look, its vital you get their defences down. Shut your eyes. Don't look. As we say in the army. You don't look at the mantelpiece when stoking the fire.' He laughed. 'By the end of next month you could be back with Alice. Why are you looking at me like that?'

'Sorry Dusty. Sheer admiration. I wish I was like you.'

'It's against regs to have a civilian in a military vehicle. But you'll be under cover . . . Is that your guardian angel? There, under the gulmohur tree, the tall Pathan?'

'Yes, that's Ayub Khan.'

They were now out in the open. Dusty looked about him. 'It doesn't look hopeful. This place is an open prison.'

'I may have good news, but I'm not sure. You see the end wall of the garden. On the right. You see that high stack of firewood and the pipal tree in the corner? Next to it, the hut, that's where the mali lives? Well . . .'

'Keep walking and don't fix your gaze at any one place.'

The Lotus And The Rose

'The mali, Gopal, is prepared to help. His hut is built against the wall. Behind that wall is the road . . . well, he'll breach the wall, let me out, and then seal it up again.'

'I see. So, if I'm waiting on the other side of the wall . . . I get it. That's brilliant! It's simplicity itself. But you have to be absolutely sure. It could be a trap.' He prodded Dinesh in the midriff with his cane. 'Keep fit. Exercise. If you increase your naval base, you may not be able to call your ships back.'

'Naval? Ah. I see. I get it. The belly navel. But what's the bit about ships?'

Dusty laughed. 'It's a joke. At the Military Academy we had a fat lecturer, who said one's sex life was inversely proportional to one's waistline, because "when the stomach advances other things recede." Doesn't quite fit. Tell me about Gopal.'

'I've known him to be very close to the Seth. But he's convinced me that's not the case any longer. I'm strongly tempted to trust him. Should I?'

'There, old boy, I can't help. You know the man, I don't . . . you must make up your mind whether it's a risk worth taking. It is a risk. But only you can decide.'

'He wants two days notice. My problem is how to inform you.'

'No. My problem. I'm afraid I must name the day. It has to be a Wednesday, three in the afternoon. It's most important you remember that. When I telephone, I know I'll get the Munshi. The message I'll leave with him for you is that I will be calling for you on Thursday. But now you know I really mean the day before, that is Wednesday.'

'Yes, and as I'll need to give Gopal two days notice, confirm by telephoning Munshi on a Monday. I've got the picture. The Munshi, expects you to turn up on a Thursday but we'll be off the day before, Wednesday.'

'Good. But I won't be there. It'll be the driver of the Regimental water carrier. He drives to town every Wednesday and Sunday. I'll do a "dry run" with him, that means I'll time it. After he fills the water tank, from the Railway Station—from the main hose that's used for the steam engines—he'll drive to the road behind that wall. You have to be punctual. He won't wait longer than ten minutes. He'll bring you to me. Then after a drink in the Mess, I'll smuggle you in a lorry. Won't bore you with the details now, but as I retire in six months, I'm gradually transporting some of my stuff to a warehouse in Delhi.' He grinned. 'Any questions, as they say in the Army?'

'What does the water truck look like?'

'Chev fifteen hundred weight, fitted with a water tank, olive green, I pointed one out to you at the railway station. Military policeman may be about. If stopped, insist on them escorting you to see me. I'll take the rap if I have to.'

'Dusty, it's decent of you to help me. I'll never be able to thank you enough.'

'Then don't try.'

'I was afraid you may not take my plight seriously. The Seth can look avuncular. I mean, he does not look the nasty man he is.'

'Why should he? It's only in the cinema that villains are typecast. In real life they plan to deceive. But he almost betrayed himself. Now, make life easier for all of us by making love to Shanti. I meant that seriously. She'll relax. The Seth will get to know. Then both will treat you with less suspicion.'

'I'll try. God, how I miss Alice!'

'Stop thinking about her, unless it helps to get it up. Don't look at me like that, I don't believe in mincing words.'

'It is frustrating not being able to phone you. What if something goes wrong and I can't make it?'

'We'll have to make other plans.'

They went past Gopal's hut. Dinesh peered in. 'It's a pity, he's not in.'

'I don't need to meet him. In fact, it's better I didn't. That wall looks rather solid.'

'Gopal showed me. He can do it. He started off as a mason. He can do it.'

'Fine. But Dinesh, if things go wrong on that Wednesday and it gets serious, don't hesitate. Make a desperate dash out of the Munshi's office, as if it's the end of the world. Get to the bus station. Shout at the top of your voice. Draw attention.'

Dinesh shook his head. 'That's not possible. I was wrong to think it was. I managed to check. The door from the office is kept locked. The Munshi has the keys.'

The Lotus And The Rose

'Find out where he keeps them. Smash the window with a chair.'

'You think Gopal might let me down?'

Dusty grimaced: 'I'd hate to be in your shoes. I must go now.'

A fortnight later it was all arranged. Ransingh had been freed from prison four days earlier and was safe and back in his village miles away. The Monday call from Dusty was relayed by the Munshi and Dinesh paid Gopal a visit that very afternoon. Gopal nodded conspiratorially.

'Ready by Wednesday, are you sure?' Dinesh stared at Gopal gratefully.

Gopal nodded impassively. 'Baba, no problem.' He looked feverish and frail. Dinesh reached out and held him firmly by the shoulders. 'Can you really do it without help?'

Gopal rolled his head slowly. 'Come tomorrow, at night. I will show you the hole. Then,' he said, with a gesture of his hands, 'you push and *jao*!' He dusted his hands.

But on Tuesday morning Gopal died.

The Munshi brought the news after breakfast. Shanti was also in the room, lying on the sofa with little Manjit climbing all over her. During the night Dinesh steeled himself and managed to make love to her. For the past few days the three, with scarcely a hard word from Shanti, had lived like a family.

'Good,' Shanti greeted the news of Gopal's death heartlessly. 'He vas real jinx. Now we can have a proper mali and a decent garden. Good riddance.'

The Munshi shook his head. 'No, dear madam, that is most unfortunate way to look upon this tragedy. Your father is most distressed.' He said, studying Dinesh's look of undisguised horror. 'Your husband is unhappy too. Harken to the mourners. They are arriving in increasing numbers.' He was wearing a grey *pashmina* shawl over his brown Nehru jacket and carrying a small brief case.

'I can hear a lot of chopping and hammering. What is that?' Dinesh asked.

The Munshi jiggled is head. 'Now I can hear chanting.'

They paused to listen. Shanti put her child down, stood up, went to the window and opened it. 'Vate till the vimen from his village turn up. This place will become one big howling. *Toba!. Toba!* And daddiji vill have to pay them and feed them. They are not coming for Gopal. All the howling and rocking, banging of chests and slapping heads, all done for money and food.'

'It's custom to have professional mourners, Mrs Thakur. Master Dinesh, you need to come with me to Gopal's hut. The Seth has not yet arrived.'

Still in a daze, Dinesh nodded. 'Where is the Seth?'

'At the Kailash Temple, making an offering to the gods. He is ordering garlands of marigold to be sent on to the funeral party.'

'Kailash? Then he has gone by car.'

'Indeed, chauffeured by Jarnail Singh. In the red Mercedes. The Seth will bring the priest or panditji, who will have a basket of things necessary for doing the funeral rites and mantras.'

As they drew near to the gulmohur tree, the Munshi said: 'Please, master Dinesh, there is no actual hurry. If we sit here,' he pointed to the table and two chairs that had been placed under the shade of the tree, 'I will disclose a matter of utmost importance to your person.'

'Some other time Munshiji. Where will the cremation take place?'

'At the burning ghats, as it the custom, by the river side.'

'I know that, I just wondered if the body was being taken in procession back to his own village. There are burning ghats there as well.'

'This has been Gopal's home for many years! Please master Dinesh, I beg you stay a moment! It is vitally urgent that you hear me out.'

Dinesh stopped. 'Had Gopal left any specific instructions?'

'Not that I know of. Even if the Seth was privy to any of his specific wish, he would have confided in me. As for final last minute wishes, the sudden onset of death would have made it impossible. All I have been asked to do, is hire a bullock cart, for loading the firewood that Gopal collected for this occasion. No cause for anxiety.'

'And who will be performing the rites?'

'Premchand. His eldest and only son. Did you not know, about Premchand?'

Dinesh shook his head. 'Only that he lives in town.'

'There is much you do not know. So, it is important that you hear me. Your life, if I may say so, depends on it.' They sat down. 'Dinesh baba, I know much of your present feelings. Please do not distress yourself over the death of Gopal. Believe me, he indeed was your enemy. A loyal slave to the Seth. You have been living here under the sword of Damocles. That sword was Gopal. The one person convinced your intent, to return to the family fold of Ram Niwas, was false. With the Seth's assent, he was testing you. The gods have smiled on you, my good sir.'

'What on earth are you talking about, Munshi?'

'Well done! Good sir. Keep this up. Deny everything. It's the best policy. But, kind sir, concerning ourselves, we may be open and frank with each other. I may not know the exact details of your plans, but I know you would have found Ayub Khan waiting for you on the other side of the wall. Thus, caught red handed, your life would have been forfeit. It is why I say, the gods have smiled upon you, Master Dinesh.'

Dinesh stared at him in troubled silence.

'You have never trusted me, Master Dinesh. Never mind. I am the Seth's official right hand man, so I can understand your suspicions. I also know that you do not like me. That I do not understand, for in truth I look upon you as I would my son. Truly I had rested my hopes on you, as my future, nay, imminent boss. I wanted very much an end to opium trading. That being very much against my cherished principles. Together we would have put an end to much evil practices. But now, I accept this is not to be and, therefore, logically, your future should be of no interest to me. But, believe it or not, I am a man of non-violence. Gandhi was my hero. To my lasting shame, I have stood aside, plunged my head in sand, like an ostrich, and shut all my scruples against cold-blooded murders. I cannot in your case.' He paused as his eyes took on a rheumy tenderness Dinesh had never seen before. 'Will you trust me?' He gave a low chuckle. Something of his old wily expression returned. 'If I may say so, you have no option.'

Dinesh leaned forward and stretched out a hand. The Munshi raised his hands. 'No, no, my good sir. There must be no fraternisation. It must not be seen.' He bowed his head and allowed himself a smile.

It gave his face an air of comic irony. 'But if you place your hand next to me, I will make bold to hold it.'

There were tears in Dinesh's eyes. 'Dear kind Munshiji. Can you forgive me? I have never been a good judge of character. Take comfort in the fact that I would have been an incompetent boss. A disappointment.' He took a deep breath. 'I wonder who'll take over when the Seth dies.'

'Premchand. Yes, your successor. Gopal knew. Your elimination meant his son's elevation. Yes, Premchand is Gopal's son. And Premchand will take your place on that other front as well, if you get my meaning. There has already been some jiggery-pokery in that area.'

Dinesh gaped. 'You mean Shanti and . . . He was dressed like a *chapprasi*!'

The Munshi giggled. 'He is a poor student of history. The young man thinks he is dressing like a prince. Actually, the difference is slight. It amused those mischievous Britishers to dress their office peons like Indian princes.'

'I have never seen you laugh before Munshiji. You should do that more often.'

For a while neither spoke. Dinesh looked up. The sky was blotted out by a cloud of fierce orange flowers. It took him by surprise. 'What a change a week makes!'

'My good sir. It is April, when gulmohur trees blossom in all their summer glory.'

'Are we waiting for the Seth to get back?' A sudden sound of voices and axe on wood drowned the Munshi's answer, but a nod of his head sufficed. Dinesh turned to look in the direction of the sounds. Three men armed with axe and sickle were working hard at clearing bush and bramble from the main gates.

'It won't be long now,' the Munshi raised his voice. 'You can see the mourners crowding behind the gates. Soon they will be let in. Then the whole garden will be a seething mass of cacophonous humanity. It was thus when the old Seth died. Why do you smile, master Dinesh?'

'Because, Munshiji, you have such a rare and extensive English vocabulary, and I see great charm in its precision.'

'I say what I mean and mean what I say.'

'Indeed. But tell me, who are the people in Gopal's hut?'

'That is the funeral party. I let them enter through my office. It would have been a disaster to let the vast crowd that way, so I ordered the main gates to be cleared.'

'When did Gopal die?'

'That I cannot say, exactly. Maybe small hours, early morning. could be night time even. He was found on the main path between the fountains. The sweeper, Manju, he saw the body and brought news to me. I had him carried, Gopal I mean, back to his hut. It was then about seven a.m. or so.'

'And does Premchand know?'

'By now he must. The Seth has taken him to the temple.'

Dinesh looked at his watch. It was five minutes to eleven. 'So you have had a busy morning making all the other arrangements. Tell me, since I have never seen a funeral, what are those men doing in the hut?'

'They haven't been there long. After I let them in, I came to see you. They will wrap the body in saffron cloths and bind it to a stretcher. Then it is be covered with flowers, pink roses, but mostly *gaindas*, that is, marigolds.'

Dinesh squeezed the Munshi's hand. 'What is to become of me?' He shivered.

'When the Seth gets back, with him will be the panditji and Premchand. I then let in the crowd. So, in the midst of all commotion, mourning and funeral chants, you must seize the opportunity to escape from my office out into bus station. There is a steel filing cabinet next to the door. You will have concealed yourself behind it. I open the door, let the Seth and his party in, keep them talking, occupied and looking away. That is your opportunity to make a dash for freedom.' He smiled. 'You look doubtful. You must have courage. Good sir, you have no option. Do not hesitate, for after a moment I shall make great show of locking the door, as per standing orders of the Seth.' He stared hard at Dinesh. 'I do not know what part your army friend can play in all this, but do not think about it, you have not a moment to lose. Be single-minded.'

'The bus station and café are full of the Seth's people, Munshiji.'

Popatlal winked and smiled cunningly. 'I know you to be an excellent driver. Here, keep a good hold of this, my son. They are duplicate car keys of the Mercedes, always kept in my desk drawer. Now son, the car will be outside the door. Take it. Dash off! Go as far as you can, then abandon it.'

'But Jarnail the driver will be in the car!'

'Not so. I feel sure he will be carrying panditji's paraphernalia from the temple. If not, I will call to him to fetch and carry to Gopal's hut a basket of flowers that is on my desk. The flowers, I will say, is for Mr Premchand.'

'Mr Popatlal, my dear Munshi, you've thought of everything. Won't they suspect you? I'd hate to feel you have put yourself at risk for my sake.'

'On Monday when I learned of the trap set for you I had the keys copied. That extra pair is now in the drawer where the duplicate is always kept. So, nothing is missing. No charge of carelessness on my part may be levied against me. You have the original set of duplicate keys, to ensure there is no hitch, and in case the copy made is imperfect . Nothing about your disappearance can be traced to me. They will have seen me locking the door. The stable door, if I may think of you as the horse that has bolted. How you got out will remain a mystery. So, play your part well, good sir, for if you are caught, I cannot then help you.' He pushed the small black leather brief case with his foot. 'Take it. There is fifteen thousand rupees, in ten rupee notes. You need cash to speed your journey hence.'

'But Munshiji, the money? Where did . . .'

'Revenge is sweet. It's the Seth's money. All accounted for. You will remember me now as an embezzler. No matter. I have no sense of guilt. Because my boss is a wicked man, a crooked fellow, I consider myself absolved. During the last twelve years I set aside for myself . . . what people call a nest egg for my old age. This is a small bit from it. But I trust it will suffice. It in no way represents a measure of my regard for you.'

'But one day you could be caught. If you continue to embezzle.'

'The Seth's profits are in the lakhs. A drop from the ocean is not missed. Also when it comes to accounting, if I may boast, no man can match me. I have now another three to four years, before I retire. I will stop before then. I am not a greedy man.'

'What about Mr Pramod Jha, the Auditor?'

'All covered. Mr Jha is my cousin brother. As I said there are many things about the business of which you are unaware. Today, you are the only other person who knows. And you will not give me away.' The comic grin returned with a vengeance.

'Never Munshiji, even if I'm caught. And if I am, I hope you'll take all you can.'

'Go now. To my office. Ayub Khan is outside with mourners. Drive on the road to Delhi, far as the car can take you, then dump it.'

'But Munshiji, Shanti's seen you come to fetch me?'

'I shall say I last saw you going towards Gopal's hut. Go now. Don't fail, my son.'

'When I'm gone, will you inform Dusty, I mean Major Dustoor?'

Popatlal rolled his head. 'Indeed. Maybe I should accompany you to my office, and I better carry the case, since you may have been seen empty-handed.'

'How will you know when they have arrived?'

'Jarnail blows horn thrice, when turning into bus station. What he always does. An arrangement of long standing. Also I have sent the Gurkha watchman on an errand.'

They stood up. 'I'll write to you, my dear Munshi.'

'That', said the Munshi, 'will be most foolish. You must never do that. Think well, young master. From now on, think most careful, every move you make.'

They walked in silence till they entered the office. 'How can I show my gratitude!'

'Show nothing,' the Munshi's voice cracked. 'For our mutual benefit. I am very much used to people not liking me. Believe it or not, that keeps me calm. You see it is best for me to feel I mean nothing to you. Affection or caring is upsetting. I rather not be upset. Here, take this. This money has the blessing of goddess Lakshmi. May Hari Krishna and her Lord Vishnu, preserve you.'

Dinesh took the brief case, then he bent down and touched the Munshi's feet.

Munshi Popatlal drew back. 'Please, that is not necessary.' He pointed to the steel filing cabinet by the door. 'Stand between the door and cabinet. Stay calm. I will take party to the other end of the room and engage them in conversation with their backs towards you, so that you can quietly slip out. I will then say in Hindi: "Now Sethji, let me lock-up and join you all to pay my respects to Gopal." I will then turn round, with a prayer in heart and a hope that you have gone.'

'And . . .' Dinesh began to tremble, 'if I don't get that opportunity . . .'

'I will make excuse to return and let you out. That is the most I can do.' Popatlat gripped Dinesh's arm firmly. 'I see you are not yoga student. A yogi can control his heart beat and keep his nerves calm. We are not heroes. But try to keep heart calm by taking deep breaths. Be assured, I will make certain that attention is kept away from the door. When you get to car, lie low. Don't drive off till I have locked the door.'

CHAPTER TWENTY-TWO

Kay picked up the telephone. Dinesh apologised for the lateness of the hour. 'Kay, I've had days in hell and I'm dying to come home.'

'It's wonderful to hear your voice. No need to apologise. Alice is asleep, but I've been up, keeping an eye on the baby.'

'Baby?'

'Yes. A week now. Ted cabled Kitty. Dusty was to tell you after he got you out. We wanted you to choose a name. I've been calling him Denis. Sounds like Dinesh.'

'He's a boy then? Of course, sorry, you know what I mean. I couldn't see Dusty. It's a long story. I'll tell you later. I don't know what to say! How's Alice?'

'Recovering. She had a hard time. Denis was two weeks late and big. Ten pounds. Where are you?'

'Heathrow. I'll come at once. By taxi, all the way. No point going to London first. My car battery'll be dead. I suppose it'll take four hours from now. To get to Ludlow, I mean. I look terrible. You've been warned.'

'You'll be a sight for sore eyes. Alice has been weepy these past few days. Your home coming couldn't have come at a better time. This is just wonderful news.'

'What's he like, the baby? I hope he looks like Alice?'

'Something of you both. One can never be sure at this stage. He's got beautiful light brown eyes. How did you manage to escape . . . Never mind. Tell us when you get here.'

'You were not here when I needed you.'

'I'll make up for it, Alice. At last I'm free. From now on, nothing's going to stop us being together and having a great time. Tell yourself, I would have been in the way. Of no help at all. Hospitals scare me. But now, we'll do lots of things together. Holidays in Venice, Florence, Spain, anywhere you'd like. We'll go as soon as you're . . .'

'We can't. Not for sometime. Not till he's a toddler.'

'Oh, you don't have to wait that long,' Kay said, 'Once he's weaned, I'll be able to let you have a holiday. You both deserve it. Oh, that reminds me, day after tomorrow, Saturday, we're spending the weekend with Ted. It was planned last week.'

'Then I'll wait to tell him I'm back.'

'He knows, Dinesh. I rang him early this morning, while you were asleep.'

'We've got wonderful news to share, Dinesh,' Alice said.

'Hush, Alice, not now, love.'

Dinesh looked from one to the other. The happy twinkle in Alice's eyes was now doubly familiar. He lifted his son above his head, 'I'm glad he's got your eyes, Alice.'

Kay took the child and lay him in his cot. 'Tell me the wonderful news,' he said.

'The news can wait,' Kay said.

'Mother and Ted are . . . they're getting married. It's a June wedding.'

'July, Alice dear. There, I told you the news could wait a better moment.'

'No, Kay, just a delayed reaction.' Dinesh shut his eyes and shook his head. 'You both will have to get used to my clumsy ways. I'm happy for you, my beautiful Kay, you deserve every happiness. And Ted's a great guy. So this is what's been going on behind my back.' He gave Kay a big hug.

She kissed him. 'And I want you to look well. You have lost a lot of weight.'

'I'll do my best. Saville Row . . . I suppose it will have to be a morning suit affair?'

'No. Just a quiet affair at the Registry Office. But check with Ted'

'It's going to be a family affair.' Alice said.

Kay laughed. 'Not our family.'

'Not even Jonathan?' Dinesh teased.

'No, especially not Jonathan,' Kay looked at her daughter and smiled. 'Alice, its time for his feed. Kitty and Dusty will be there. George and Sarah, too.'

There were tears in Alice's eyes and her lips started to tremble.

'Dinesh, haven't you got something to say?'

'Gosh, Kay! I'm such an idiot. Stupid and tactless. Alice, will you, marry me?'

Alice kept her eyes on the floor and sniffed thoughtfully.

'And, if you, Kay, and Ted won't mind, we can combine our weddings?'

'And can you? Marry Alice, I mean?'

'Yes, Kay. The decree absolute will come through in a week or two. It's all smooth going from now on. Will you, sweet Alice, marry me!'

'I will.' Alice started to laugh and cry at the same time. Then covering her face, she sobbed bitterly. Amazed, Dinesh looked on helplessly.

'Go on,' Kay nudged. 'Put your arms round her. And sit with her while she feeds . . . It's time, Alice. I know it is.' She offered Alice a box of tissues. 'Sorry, I made a scene, mum.' She wiped her eyes, watched Kay coaching Dinesh, and laughed. 'Leave it mother, Indian men don't do that sort of thing.'

'This one will.' Dinesh sat next Alice.

'There,' Kay said. 'Now I'll leave you two. I'll be in the garden. Well done Dinesh!'

Dinesh had kissed Alice as she bent down to pick their son from his little cot. 'Isn't he a darling,' she said, 'a good sleeper and so little trouble.'

'Don't say good things about the boy.' Dinesh hissed. 'The evil eye!'

'Hush now! Mother hoped you'd suggest a double wedding.' Alice unbuttoned her blouse and held the little head as the baby sought and found the nipple.

'You're not wearing a bra.'

Alice smiled. She lifted the child higher and rocked gently. 'Mum showed me how.'

'Did he hurt you? I mean at . . . when . . . you know . . . the birth?'

She shook her head. 'I don't want to think about it. It affects the flow of the milk. Ouch . . . he's a bit rough today. I wanted to ask you about the cottage. Is it sold?'

'No. And I don't know what to say. I've had so much on my mind . . . my lawyers would have informed me if . . . but I've heard nothing. Ted might have letters for me.'

'Darling, you may think it's no business of mine . . .'

'Good grief, Alice, you have every right to know . . . but I haven't got the foggiest. I've heard nothing from Mohan Singh other than he's definitely buying the place . . . Ted may have news. We'll find out tomorrow.'

'I know nothing about your finances. You behave as if . . . are you a millionaire?'

'Oh, no. But we could live well on interest and not have to touch capital. And when the sale of the cottage . . . I mean, when that money comes through, we'll use it to buy a place for ourselves.'

'You don't have to worry about that. Mum's giving us this house. It's her wedding present to . . . That's if you don't mind living in Ludlow.' She gave a tired smile and changed the baby's position to suckle the other breast. He watched fascinated. 'Don't look, it makes me feel . . . I can't think of the word . . . uncomfortable. What is it? I can see you want to say something.'

'Nothing. I wanted to ask . . . but I know the answer. Are you out of bounds.'

'Out of bounds? Where did you pick that up . . . from Dusty, I suppose. Yes, you'll have to be patient. Not for long. But you'll sleep with me. I want that.'

He nodded. 'Of course. I think I'll go out and chat with Kay.'

'Not yet. You poor, poor thing! You've had such a hard time. I try to get close but you seem always to raise a barrier. Come, sit with me, and put your arm around me.'

'If I was Sandy you wouldn't have had to ask. He understood Emma so well.'

'Did she mind? I mean, a woman can get too much attention.'

'True. But she didn't complain. I know, because I heard her tell Bunty, Mohan's wife . . . I was twelve or thirteen . . . they thought I

The Lotus And The Rose

wasn't listening. She said she let Sandy do what he liked with her and that was the measure of her love for him . . . no, not love, she used the word "gratitude".'

'I bet she enjoyed every minute of it. Women don't always say what they truly feel. Even when they complain, it's not to discourage the man. You'd better digest that . . .'

'We are very alike, you know, you and I.'

'Oh, look, he's gone to sleep. I'll put him in his cot. I should have stroked his back to let him burp, but he'll wake up if he needs it. There. Now hold me and kiss me, and tell me you love me.'

'I do Alice, I do! If only I could make you understand how much I missed you!'

'I thought about you a lot. Especially when I was having the baby. And I was cross with you for not being around.'

'You had your mother to comfort you.'

'I wanted the father of my child to be there.'

'I had no one . . . no not quite. There was Dusty and then a father figure . . . the Munshi. Surprised? I'll tell you all about that later.'

'You did, and to mother, but I want to hear it again, in more detail.' She sighed. 'I was prepared for the worst . . . while you were away. I used all I learned at the *ashram*, to face the likelihood of-of being alone.' She led him back to her bed. 'Yes. Guruji once said, if it wasn't for death and loss there would be no love in the world; and that it's because of death we hold life precious . . . loss and pain make us cling to each other. Wasn't that profound?'

He made a face. 'I don't know. But it confirms what an English friend of mine, chap called Webb, said of Hinduism. It's a religion without hope in the present. Every good thing is deferred to a future time; and that present circumstances were meant to be.'

'You mustn't judge Guruji by that old Hindu outlook. Gurus of today are as modern and often as humanistic or sophisticated as any in the West.'

'Indian Gurus may not feel bound by Hinduism, but their philosophy is of the East, and largely Hinduism. Your Guru linked love and death, I knew one, well, he wasn't a Guru, he was a pundit . . . He linked death with time, but like . . . what's that chap who did those geometry theorems . . . proofs?'

'Pythagoras? ... Euclid?'

'Yes, Euclid. Then in a Euclidean, if that's the right word, way, he reduced the whole thing to nothing. I didn't quite understand, though at the time I was terribly impressed. And that's what makes all this kind of thinking dangerous.'

'What do you mean?'

'His reduction went something like this. Because there's death we can record time. But there is no time, so what is memory ... memory passes, so no death, no loss.'

'I think you just made that up. Anyway, forget it. Dinesh, now we need to come to a decision about the boy's name. Mum's been calling him Denis. I want him to have your name. Whatever we decide, we need to have a formal, a proper naming ceremony.'

'What does your mother say?'

'She's a romantic. We don't have to do what she wants.'

'Baptism makes him a Christian.' Dinesh shrugged. 'I don't mind if that simplifies matters. We'll bring him up to feel free to choose ... if that's possible?'

'There's one way out. Baptism in the Church of England. Less pressure. He'll feel less bound. I oughtn't say that, but you know the West enough to know what I mean. Ted is C of E. He could fix that, if you agree.'

'Yes. That's fine. Though I have to say, when we think about Christianity, Hindus have a greater affinity with Roman Catholics. Their style of worship. Worshiping and prayers to images, in particular to Mary. Many Hindus pray to her, as a mother goddess. But, he's your son, do as you please. My opinion matters little. I'm a defeated man. Just thankful to be alive. Without you and Kay ... Ted, Kitty ... I'd be dead.'

'You mustn't think like that. You are your own man now. Good-looking, rich, and you've got a family; a new life here, England ... And another thing. Forget Sandy. Stop comparing yourself with ... you're different ... sometimes, I think, you want to be him.'

'Impossible. I couldn't; and I tried to destroy him.'

'Dinesh, don't go on. Forget him!'

'Yes, sorry. I'd prefer a Hindu name. It doesn't matter which Church. You decide.' The baby started to fuss and whimper and

The Lotus And The Rose

Alice rushed to the cot. 'Right on cue. He must know we're talking about him.' Dinesh grinned.

'It's wind. I should have done this before,' she said holding the child against her and stroking his back. 'It's all right. Go to mum. I'll join you both later. Oh, before you go, what would you say is the difference between a pundit and a guru?'

'A pundit's a scholar and a priest, and he's part of society. We pay for his services, marriages, funerals etc. Gurus are cult makers and while a pundit may be cunning and placating, gurus are frauds . . . You did ask! Gosh! I've never seen you look so angry.'

'I am. But I'll let it go now. In consideration for all you've been through. But I've told you before, you can't tar my guru with the same brush you tar others. In the end you were very impressed by him.'

'Yes. True. Sorry. Oh, that reminds me. I'll go to London tomorrow. To collect the car. Get it going. Then I could drive us all to Winchester.'

Dinesh found Kay sitting on her hands on a wooden bench, pensively studying the gold fish in the pond. The sound of trickling water enhanced the stillness and peace of the evening. She did not hear him coming and started when he came up to her.

'You gave me such a fright,' she said breathlessly. 'We're not used to having a man about the place. Come walk with me to the far end of the garden . . . to that bench. It's my favourite part of the garden.'

'A green thought in a green shade . . . who said that?'

'What? Oh, don't ask. I'm the last person you should ask about things like that.'

'I used to know, sorry I wasn't trying to be clever. I got it from Sandy . . . sorry, I've been given strict instructions to set Sandy aside . . . by Alice.'

'Quite right too. Now, I want to have a chat with you, if I may?'

'I'm listening.'

They walked in silence till they sat down. 'It is nice here.' she said. 'This is where I have my crocuses and daffodils. They were out early this year. I'll miss this spot. Will you make big changes when you take over this place?'

'Changes? I don't know. I'm no gardener.'

'You haven't said much since you've been back, Dinesh?'

'I'm sorry. I'm tired. Exhausted mentally and physically.' He turned to meet her steady gaze. Something in her piercing look made him feel uneasy. He looked away.

'You have had to compromise. If you get my meaning?' She paused then added: 'Don't punish yourself for it. You had no choice. No one can hold that against you.'

'But, Kay! How could you know? Ah, you trapped me. Or is this clairvoyance.'

'The important thing is, you must never tell Alice. The thought would've occurred to her. She'll dismiss it, but wouldn't want it confirmed. That's the sort of girl she is.'

'Alice is sweet and understanding.'

'It's a big risk. Don't chance it. Anyway, to be understood is to be complacent, and it will be good for you to have a sense of guilt. Good for you to start again. You need to stir yourself and reach out to where you left off. All I'm asking you to do is to woo her again. Begin at the beginning, like you did in Goa. I know all about that. Start all over again. It's terribly important. When she began to think you were not coming back, she steeled herself to be quite resigned, and once again be her old independent self. She even talked about returning to the *ashram*. You mustn't let her. I'll be unhappy if that happens because, in time, she'll probably drag the boy with her. She's not tempted by drugs, but a young boy may not be able to resist. I want you two to plan an extended holiday. You mentioned Venice. That's just the romantic place to be in.'

'Thank you Kay.'

She reached out and took his hand. 'Did there have to be a lot of intimacy? More than you could handle?'

'No Kay, just enough to allay suspicion.'

'As long as it didn't reawaken old passions.'

'Whatever passion I had for Shanti has long been dead.'

'Alice has come out to join us. Is Denis asleep, dear?'

'Yes. But I'm staying by the pond, in case he wakes. I want to call him Ganesh.'

'Darling. Stay there, we're coming. Why not let Dinesh choose a name.'

The Lotus And The Rose

'I've got it!' Dinesh said triumphantly. 'We'll call him Davy. Short for Davinder and David and English enough, not to be picked out when he starts school.'

'That's it, then,' Alice said in a matter-of-fact way. It made Dinesh smile. 'Mum, Dinesh is going to London in the morning. To fetch the car. For Saturday.'

'Oh, that'll be good. And don't forget to get something to secure the baby. One of those safety things. But, it'll be a wasted trip if you can't get the car going.'

'I'd left it in a garage. I've checked with them. I'll just have to pay for the new battery. I'll ask them about the baby seat, or whatever it's called. I'm sure they will arrange that too.'

'Money talks,' Alice said with a wry face. 'Life's easy when you have money.'

'You poor boy,' Ted said, pushing his coffee cup to one side. He was sitting opposite Kay at the dining table. 'You've had a hard time.'

Dinesh gave Kay a quick side glance and looked across the table at Alice. 'Ted, I don't suppose you've met Shanti?'

'No, nor the Seth. But when I was in Mcleodganj there was talk about her. Not very complimentary. Sandy was concerned. Rightly as it happens. You were too hot-headed to listen to any criticism that involved either you or Shanti. I wonder if things might've been different if she had a mother. I gather she was five when her mother died.'

Dinesh traced a pattern on the table. 'Sandy said . . .' He began, saw Alice's raised brows and checked himself.

'Go on.' encouraged Kay.

'Sandy said to attain maturity, one has to grow away from a mother's love. Mohan felt that that can never happen. Love for one's mother never dies.'

'Typically Mohan,' Ted chuckled. 'I wonder why Sandy said that. He adored his mother. But he may have a point, because although one can't be whole without having known a mother's love . . . a mother's love both supports as well as smothers.'

'I hardly knew my mother,' Dinesh frowned. 'Would you say that affected . . .'

'No, please don't misunderstand me. I hardly knew my mother. She wasn't always around. When she was, she raised all sorts of barriers. Sandy's was a psychological observation. A mother's love is necessary for childhood, but one must shed it in order to become mature.'

'But,' Kay intervened, 'the power and quality of that love depends on the mother, and a child needs time and separation to grow out of it. On the other hand, some good character building qualities come from the fact of having to face the world alone.'

Ted smiled. 'What is the abiding character defect from not having known a mother?'

'Resentment,' Dinesh almost growled. 'And pessimism.'

Ted took a sharp intake of breath. 'Good God, I wish I hadn't started . . .'

'There.' said Kay. 'Now why don't you two go out into the garden and leave us, Alice and me, to clear up.'

Ted stood up. 'Just stack the stuff around the sink. Sarah will soon be here. She'll deal with it. She likes to put things away where she can find them.' He went out on to the terrace. 'That's no good. It's raining. We'll go into my study. You won't recognise it. It's brighter and more spacious. Kay's handiwork.'

Dinesh hesitated. He looked at Alice. He wondered why she had been silent. Alice understood and going up to him, gave his hand a reassuring squeeze. He smiled weakly and followed Ted, who pointed to a chair in the study and sat at the desk. He unlocked a drawer and took out a file. 'Now, about Sandy's cottage. There's nothing to worry about. It's all settled to your advantage. I know you've been hurt about Mohan Singh not making contact. He terribly ashamed about that. He's making up for it by being prepared to pay you the original full price—full, as if the fire never happened. It's a fine and generous gesture. And if you agree to the terms in this document—my advice is you should—you stand to gain. Try to understand his position. He's a businessman after all. The Seth, to borrow a phrase, made him an offer he couldn't refuse. I don't mean threats. Mohan can look after himself. In fact I feel protected by his friendship. His silence, as far as you are concerned, protects you, remember that. He's convinced the Seth that your whereabouts are of no interest to him or the new business plans.'

'What are their, his and the Seth's, plans for the cottage?'
'To turn it into a Hotel.'
'And the land? There's quite a bit of land.'
'It's going to be a grand hotel. One of these five-star affairs. The "Punjab Hotel", or "Hotel Punjab"; with annexes and stables—pony riding for tourists.'

Dinesh laughed. 'But Ted, the area is full of Tibetans.'
'They must know what they're doing. The Punjabis are a large community there. It could encourage more Punjabis to settle and take over more land and businesses, they could curb further Tibetan expansion. Or force them to go elsewhere. They believe the hotel's name will suggest an exclusivity. A carrot to the Punjabis. And Mohan certainly believes an expensive hotel will automatically exclude the average Tibetan. But it's of no interest to us, whether they succeed or fail.'

'What about your own interest? Have you approved? Are you in on the deal?'

'That's three questions. First, you must know, I did consider your feelings.'

'I'm sure you did . . . you're my friend, but if you can make money . .

'Dear boy, I didn't for a moment imagine you'd misunderstand me if I did, but making money is not a matter I spend time thinking about. The immediate problem is to work out how he's going to remit the moneys to you?'

For a while the two men studied each other, then Ted continued. 'I have not told Mohan where you are and I don't intend to—though he's a decent chap and I can trust him to keep a secret. I know, he's using the Seth as much as the Seth thinks he's using him, but it's wiser and safer not to disclose your address, even to friends, unless one has to. The Seth's your enemy and will remain so as long as he's around. You have Alice and the child to consider.'

'Yes, thanks. Ted, you take the money. Let him give it to you, in trust. In any case, I'd like you to arrange for all of it to go to Alice; for our son.'

'Good. Then I'll get on with it. These things take time. I've planned to make a trip to India as soon as I can. There's another matter I want to attend to, and I hope you'll have no objection. I intend to bring Sandy and Emma home. They belong here. You know, my father loved Sandy. I've known that for a fact. He thought a lot of him. And here, in this very house Sandy met Emma—actually, first in the cemetery nearby, where they'll finally rest, next to my father's grave.'

'But Ted, can you? Even if permitted. Its been some years now.'

'It's their ashes. Once exhumed, they'll be cremated with all due respect. I've made inquiries. This is where Mohan will help. He has a lot of influence, and in government circles too. Also it's private land and the local community is not raising objections. Bill Clayton's school and orchard are, as you know, adjacent to the Chapel graveyard.'

'Yes, but Ted you still haven't answered . . .'

'Ransingh says, he and Sona made the burial arrangements, the coffins should be in good preservation. Good quality wood. And the masons built a mini vault of flagstones and brick, well cemented over. I'll be present at the exhumation—being a doctor helps. The cremation will be by the graveside on a traditional Hindu pyre. Emma and Sandy will like that. It also means that some of their ashes will remain in India.

'And the gravestone?'

'No. That's much to heavy. It will be left in the chapel. A Memorial.'

CHAPTER TWENTY-THREE

It took Ted Franks nearly two years to bring the ashes back from India, which came in a beautifully carved casket of polished walnut wood. Inside, the casket was lined with copper and the outer floral design, of delicate brass inlay, was tooled by artisans from Benares, at one of Mohan Singh's workshops, and personally supervised by him. In a private and simple ceremony, the casket was laid in the Franks family plot, next to the grave of Ted's father, Colonel Ian Franks. Ted, Kay, Alice and her three-year-old son, Davy, were present. Dinesh was away. Four days earlier, he had left for London after suddenly announcing he must be there on a matter of great urgency. 'There is,' he said, searching their anxious faces, 'no cause for alarm. I'm not in a position to tell you why I have to go, and frankly, I don't quite know myself what it is about. But in a few days all will be clear. I'll be back, soon.' Alone with Ted, on the day before he left for London, he had more to say. 'Ted, it is really a matter of life and death, and not just for me; for Alice, the boy; even you and Kay. Can you ever forgive me for putting all of you into this predicament.'

'Predicament? Now you sound like the Dinesh I knew. But seriously, as a family, we're in this together. Alice took her chances with you, and now we must face up to whatever comes our way. Take appropriate precautions, even get police protection if necessary. This is England. But, I can see you know more than you are letting on.'

'It is why I must go. Promise me, Ted,' his voice was hoarse, and a violent tremor shook his body. 'promise me you won't tell Alice. Not even Kay, till I return.'

Ted nodded, 'You will return? And you have to go?'

Dinesh cleared his throat. 'Yes. I can't protect them if I don't. Believe me, I have to do what this letter asks. Read it, Ted. Read it. You'll see what I mean. We have time. They won't be back till after six.'

'Remind me. Where have they gone?'

'Salisbury Cathedral. Davy's into towers and spires. Your calendar of England's Cathedrals has stirred him.'

'Davy's terribly bright for his age.' Ted glanced down at the letter.

'You can disclose the contents of the letter to anyone after I get back. I would like to explain matters to Alice in my own way. If I'm not back in a week, hold on another four or five days, then get in touch with the police. After that, Ted, will you take care of Alice and bring the boy up as if he were your own son?' Another fit of the shivers gripped him. He crumpled up and wept bitterly. Ted held him firmly.

'There now, my boy. You mustn't. Or you'll make it impossible for me to keep any of this secret. Kay or Alice have only to look at you . . . There's a brave lad. Now, can I keep this letter?'

'No, Ted! I must have it back. It was for my eyes only. But read it now so that you know . . . in case I can't make it back.'

Ted nodded and moved away. He glanced at it for a minute or two. 'I can't read it! It makes no sense. Half of it is in Hindi . . . or is that Punjabi?'

'Punjabi. Yes. The Punjabi bits are meaningless. Just pointless abuse. Start here.'

'There's no signature. Who's written the letter? There's no signature.'

'It's been typed, except the Punjabi bits. That's written by Shanti, I know her hand. Dictated by the Seth, I'm certain of that. There's no mistaking his style and tone. The abusive language is all his.'

Ted, began to read in a low but audible whisper. "If you thought you could escape, then you are bloody fool. See how I found address in London . . ." he skipped the few lines in foreign script. "Tell me, you ungrateful *soovar*, what happened to your love for India?" 'What's *soovar*?'

'Pig.'

The Lotus And The Rose

Ted read on. "Have you no shame! Don't you want to see your son? Bring him up like a father should? He's your son. No doubt. What is in London for you? You seem to be alone in London but never there. Living with some cheap English prostitute, are you? I'll find out. She too will be . . ." What's K-H-A-T-A-M? No, I know. *Khatam*. Finished, that is, eliminated.' Ted returned to the letter. "No escape from me. Munshi tried, but now he's *Khatam*." God, that means the poor man's been bumped off?'

'Yes. The Seth's no fool. I'm sorry for Popatlal. The old man saved my life.'

'Hm.' Ted shook his head. 'But surely . . . What happens in India? When a body is discovered, don't the police investigate?'

'It would've been made to look like a natural death. An injection. By a doctor in his pay. That would have been my fate, had they got me.'

After a moment Ted handed back the letter. 'I can't read this. Tell me what is being asked of you and, of course, I agree you must protect Alice and Davy at all costs.'

'I'm to be in London for the whole of next week. Sometime in that week, Shanti and the boy . . .'

'Is he your son? Tell me, frankly.'

'I can't say. He an image of Shanti. It's possible. I really don't know. If it's the case, it's so unfair. The cruel irony of it all, that I, and not that awful music master, made her pregnant. All my life I've had bad luck.'

'They probably took precautions.'

'Not from what I saw, with my own eyes.'

'Anyway, go on.'

'No actual date or time has been given, but I'll be contacted.'

'Contacted for what?'

'For a meeting with Shanti and the boy. They are in London, with that awful creep Premchand. He is the new heir to the Seth's estate and Shanti's future husband. So I have to make a signed statement that breaks any claim on them or be eliminated.'

'I don't see why all this elaboration is necessary. Why this meeting? You're legally divorced and so the woman is free to do what she likes.'

'It says here, it is my last chance to return with them to India . . . sorry I forgot that bit, or sign away all claims to the Seth's financial empire. I think the Seth has used my name, separately and jointly with Shanti's to launder black market money. There is also our joint account he would like me to surrender. Premchand will have papers for me to sign on the dotted line, which I'll gladly do, if that will ensure my safe return.'

'This is all rather complicated, dubious and fraudulent.'

'But not, I'm afraid uncommon in India. There was some talk, some years ago, of a secret fund, when the Indian Government, in one of it sporadic, anti-corruption moves, threatened action against the Seth. Somehow he managed to get round that. Bribery, I assume. Clearly he didn't always confide in me . . . the Munshi would have known . . . may well be the account from which he has been siphoning sums for his retirement.'

'But you haven't put your signature to anything that is illegal?'

'No, I was in Bombay, and these dealings may have taken place during my absence from Pathankot. Yes I'm certain I haven't . . . probably why he wants me to sign now.'

'He may have named you and Shanti next of kin . . . no, that shouldn't be a problem. I don't know. It's all very underhand. Well, he might leave it at that . . . especially if he has found a new loyal young man to replace you. I don't like this one bit. You should go to the police. This is Britain. Ignore the whole thing and you stay put here. Exercise care from now on. You don't have to work. And you don't have to keep your studio flat in London. Someone has been keeping tabs on you. And by now all our addresses are known. I think the sooner you report all this to the police, the safer all of us will feel.'

'Ted, to go back what you said earlier, he says at the end of the letter that if I *do* what he asks he'll just, the nearest equivalent to the Punjabi is, "wipe the slate clean", and as if I never existed.'

'Can you trust him?'

'No, but going to the police is not going to improve friendly relations.'

'Yes. I take your point. And if you don't do what you are asked to . . .'

'He will take revenge. The letter makes that very clear, and why I can't have that sort of threat over all your heads. I have to settle matters between the Seth and me, once and for all. I owe it to you and Kay, as much as I owe it to Alice and Davy.'

'I'm still uneasy. You could be playing into their hands. This can be a very risky and dangerous trip you're making.'

'Ted, I want to end the uncertainty. I must protect the family. I can't keep running away from it. I'm not interested, and I can assure them, absolutely, I'm not interested in any claim, financial or otherwise. I'll appeal to Shanti's self-respect. She must know by now that I had deceived her, that she means nothing to me, and that she's better off starting a new life with Premchand.'

'I'd gladly dog your tracks, shadow you, but I'm too old . . .'

'No! Don't even think of it. Or even get the police to . . . You have no idea what the Seth is capable . . . The slightest suspicion . . . This may be the only chance to negotiate.'

'But, you must tell Alice and gently assure her. Give something she and Davy can cling to. They must not be left to think you're making some foolhardy or unnecessarily futile gesture. And don't leave her behind without a hint of the danger and risk you are taking . . . You owe her that. They can't know what you've told her?'

'If Alice knows, she won't let me go.'

'No Dinesh. Alice is immensely practical. She'll understand.' Ted paused. 'Dinesh, I've been meaning to say this. Recently I've noted you two have been distant towards each other this past winter, particularly over Christmas. Is something the matter? You *do* still love her? Frankly, I've been a little puzzled why you, a staunch Hindu, could contemplate marrying an English woman?'

'Ted, Alice came into my life when I was most vulnerable . . . and she made it easy for me. She was wearing a sari, looking demurely Indian, when first I saw her. Remember she was going to live in an *ashram*. She's Hindu. Possibly a stauncher one than me.'

'But Alice tells me you have been avoiding the boy. You know he's fond of you.' He waited. Dinesh remained bowed in thought. 'He'll be four next month, and doing extremely well in nursery school.'

Dinesh nodded and gave a little laugh. 'Yes, growing up to be the perfect English gentleman. His accent is quite posh.'

'Quite like his father.'

Dinesh shook his head. 'I suppose I'm a good mimic. But I would say "daddy". He says "deddy". He'll be another Sandy. How ironical. I attacked Sandy, only, in the end, to produce another Sandy . . .' he clicked his tongue.

'Take it on the chin. Say good-bye to the lad. Make up some story about your trip?'

'He is breaking my heart . . . and I'm trying . . . I want him to forget me. I want you to be a father to him. Go on outings together.' Dinesh waved a hand. 'I've long accepted he'll grow away from me.' He laughed involuntary. 'He certainly won't be a Hindu.'

'What's so funny?' Ted asked, rather sternly. 'Do share the joke. I could do . . .'

'No please, I'm not being frivolous or do I mean callous. Did Alice tell you what Davy said the other day . . . it was the day I received this letter . . . as we got into the car he heard me whisper "Hari Om". "Why, deddy," he said, "why must we hurry home?" I laughed . . . oh, God, Ted! Promise me. Promise you'll see that he'll never know about Shanti, the Seth and all that . . . that awful episode. Please will you?'

'I can't, my boy. I'll tell Alice how you feel, but you have to trust her judgement . . . and Davy, to her. And I'm sure Alice will see that he knows his father's religion and philosophy . . . as you said she's quite a Hindu herself. England is changing too. It is so very different from the England I knew. Soon there'll be a few Temples in London . . . and other cities. Like all Hindus you are being very fatalistic.'

Dinesh gave a tired smile. 'A common mistake. Hindus are not fatalistic. They are resigned. Which is not the same thing. As you sow, so shall you reap: is not fatalistic. There's no judgement, hell or damnation, in Hinduism.'

'Sorry, it was a thoughtless remark. I know so little about Hinduism. And I suppose, people who believe in transmigration of souls, cannot be charged with pessimism.'

'Hold on to that, Ted. It's a timely thought. Transmigration offers hope. It explains inequality and why some are born with genius. As for why there is pain and evil in the world, Hindus explain that as the result of men's actions.'

The Lotus And The Rose

'I'm sure you're right. Religion is not my forte. All I'll say is that we can't control the future. None of us can, but children are observant, resilient; and, because of both, you and Alice, India is very much part of Davy's life. Hinduism will have a place in his life . . . and in his heart. Also, as I said, you must trust Alice. But, do explain the joke, I didn't quite get it. You know, the "hurry home" bit?'

'Ah, that. "Om", said with a deep, resonating stress on the m sound, is the Great Universal Hindu prayer to God. The music and echoing sound of creation. One of the chief names of God is Hari. Hari Om.'

'I see. I'll remember that. Did you explain to the boy?'

'Alice did, when she stopped laughing.' He walked towards the French windows and stared into the garden. 'Right now, I'd wish I could say, I will always be around in spirit; and that one day we'll meet again. As a Christian would.'

'Now my boy, you mustn't get morbid. You're coming back, though why you have to go in the first place . . . I know, I know, but I wish I could convince you to ride this out, so that we could present a united front. It's almost as if you have a death wish.'

'You know Ted, there are three stages in the life of a Hindu: The Student, the Householder, and the religious Pilgrim. I've covered the first two.'

'You're far too young for the third stage. You've hardly been a householder.'

'The stages have little to do with length of time. They are phases. I've lived life fast, and I have served my purpose.'

'Nonsense, my boy. I won't hear such talk. Come sit down and take our minds off all this. You never talk about your father. Your real father. You were far too young . . .'

'He meant nothing to me.'

'Is that why you took on Sandy's surname, not his?'

'It is what mother wanted.'

There followed an awkward pause. Ted looked at his watch. 'I hope they'll be back soon. Sarah has to prepare dinner.'

'Has she gone with them too?'

'Yes. She loves taking care of Davy, and it gives Alice and Kay time to themselves. Now that you've given Alice her own car, there'll be a season of picnics this summer.'

'Join them, Ted, as much as you can. Davy is lucky to have you as a father and grandfather figure. I wish I'd had someone like you. Sandy was far to young.'

'When do you leave, I mean how soon?'

'Day after tomorrow. I have to be in London on Monday.'

'Oh, before I forget, Dinesh. I've been meaning to mention this before. You know when I was there, for the cremation and to collect the ashes, on the grave I noticed a big bouquet of dying flowers, and as we moved it there was a card. I couldn't read the first sentence. It was faded and smudged. But below it, in clear writing were the words, "We came. With love Nigel and Sally Carr", do any of those names ring a bell?'

Dinesh thought a moment, then he shook his head.

'I remember a Sally Watson, Sandy once told me about. She was a colleague. If it's her, she must have gone to India, with her husband Nigel Carr, possibly on a holiday, and decided to visit Sandy; and got there not long before I did. Never mind. I hope that's how it was. When I've time I'll make inquiries. We put the flowers on the pyre.'

'I don't see why you must go. It's been three years. I thought we had seen the end of it? Is there never to be an end? I can't take anymore of this, Dinesh. I really would rather be alone. Alone and happy as I was at the ashram till you . . .'

'Alice!'

'No, mother, I mean it. I'm not going through all that again. I'd rather tell myself I'm not going to see him again and learn to live with that.'

'Dinesh dear, I'm sorry. Don't be hurt by what she says. I don't know what's come over her. Alice darling, you must apologise. Dinesh has done so much for us, for you, the boy, and . . .'

'Would you say all that if he was poor?'

'Alice! How can you! What's the matter, child! That's downright wicked. Rude!"

'Sorry, Mum, Dinesh, Ted . . . all of you. I'm sorry. But you can't know how I feel. Why must he go back into—into—into the jaws of death, when not so long ago he escaped from it. In Heaven's name, why go back? Oh, all right, he'll be in England, but I mean, you know what I mean! He's meeting the same people!'

'Alice,' pleaded Dinesh, as he opened the car door, 'trust me. I have to go. If I told you everything, you'd be unhappy and you'd worry.' He looked at Ted. 'I'm thinking about Davy. He must never know the whole truth. Give him a story to live by. Not the full . . . not this awful story!'

Ted walked up to Alice and took her hands in his. 'Dear Alice, believe me, he has good reason, very good reason to go, even a most noble one. You have to be patient, and strong, and when he's back, you'll be the happier for it.'

Alice nodded and walked back to Kay.

'Now Dinesh,' Ted said, 'drive carefully. You don't have to break any records and, dear boy, protect yourself as much as you can. Take care.'

Kay kissed Alice and nudged her. 'Go on, darling, run to him. Give him a hug.'

Dinesh started the engine. Alice hesitated and the car moved. 'Go on,' Kay urged. 'He has to open the gate, you can catch up with him.'

Alice rushed forward, and as Dinesh got out off the car, she flung herself at him. Kay moved towards Ted. They held hands. 'He's a strange lad,' she said. 'I know he loves her, but he doesn't show his love. Not even to the boy, he doesn't.'

'Alice, emotional and impulsive as she can be, is not demonstrative either,' Ted said quietly. 'But look now. It couldn't be more . . .'

'Oh, thank God,' Kay said, a catch in her voice, 'because I don't think we'll ever see him again.'

'Gosh! Kay, you've make the hairs to stand . . . I know you are clairvoyant, but for the sake of Alice, I hope you're wrong?'

She shook her head sadly and turning into his arms buried her face against his chest. 'Poor Alice,' she whispered and sobbed quietly.

There was a sound of running footsteps. They looked behind them. Sarah had come out with the boy. Kay stared at her, astonished. Alice had asked Sarah to keep the boy away, because that was what Dinesh wanted. But Sarah's expression was one of grim determination. 'Go on Davy,' she said firmly, 'run to daddy, give him a great big kiss.'

With a squeak of delight the boy ran up to his mother and father.

※

Dinesh regained consciousness. Like a drowning man coming up for air, he gasped with a noisy splutter. He felt icy-cold and wet, and couldn't understand why. He tried to cover himself, but was unable to move till, with horror, it dawned on him. His hands and legs were tied; that he was cold because he was naked, lying stretched out on a drenched rough carpet, on a hard floor. He wriggled, turning his aching head to one side, to sniff and sense what lay beneath him. But he gave up as a stab of pain, like an electric current, ran the length of his body. The room was dark, the moist air, heavy. Where was he and why? 'Shanti!' he called out 'What is the meaning of this. I came. I came.' He was hoarse and barely heard himself. A beam of torch-light pierced the darkness. He froze. An intuitive foreboding urged him to stay very still. He shut his eyes tightly and turned away as much as he could, determined not to wince. The beam crept searchingly over his head and then went out as suddenly as it came. Left in his darkness he sensed a movement of darker shadows, and tried hard to remember. A fog of weird images drifted in and out of the void, coming unbidden, piecemeal, erratically, while all his awareness seemed to concentrate on pain. There was a lot of pain, at times too overwhelming even to feel. There had been a car journey? Oh, yes, a juddering car journey. Heavy feet on his chest and that sensation of choking and pain; coughing and pain; such pain, pain . . . he wanted an end of it, to forget it, to die. But no, he must keep awake. Why? He couldn't think why. Why keep awake or alive, when each conscious moment brought pain, excruciating pain? He would rather drift into nothingness. Then like an answered prayer, the pain went. He tried to open his eyes with a great effort. He couldn't and it hurt terribly. He cried out as he drifted once again into deeper darkness. Now, he was a boy of four and someone was holding his hands. He looked up. It was his mother. There was no doubt about that, though her face kept changing from mother to Sandy, Sandy to Alice. They were all in a room. It was the kitchen in Delhi . . . and peering at him, an old, woman, a tiny shrivelled, dried walnut of an old woman, sitting, frog-like on her haunches, with a wide toothless grin and tender soft eyes . . . 'This is my son,' his mother said. The old woman reached out her bony hands towards his face and pressed her knuckles against her temples. '*Jiteh raho*', she said. Her cheeks puffed as she spoke. 'May you live forever . . . Live forever?' The woman had gone . . . his mother too. Instead, under a banyan tree was his dear friend, Pandit Bhaba: 'Can one live for ever, panditji?' The pandit wobbled his head. 'Life is energy. One can convert life, not destroy life. All good Hindus believe that. Do you not believe in re-incarnation.' 'I do,' he heard himself say, 'but once human, always a human!' Pandit Bhaba smiled. His face elongated and merged into the overhanging branches of the tree. The pain returned and faded away in a fog . . . he woke and with great effort rolled on to his side. His face felt a draught of fresh air, as his cheek touched a grassy softness that was damp and yielding. My God! He wasn't in a room after all, but open ground. A dull jab, a pressure against his back . . . he was being pushed . . . the ground disappeared and a sudden rush of cold wind buoyed him up a split second. He fell freely and the whistling wind numbed his bruising body. Then a hard thud broke his fall . . . the pain, pain beyond coping. A slide, another roll, another free fall, then oblivion . . . In the far distance, a far far distance . . . a child cried, waking to life, and a mother, forgetting her birth pangs held him against her chest and looked down. He stared at the smiling face. That face is mother? Remember that face! All else will be forgotten. Nothing else mattered. Here was a new beginning.

There was a knock on Kay's bedroom door. She turned on the bedside lamp. 'That you, Alice? Come in.' Alice entered dazed and looking very frail. 'What's the matter love. Come,' Kay moved to one side. 'Get in and cover yourself.'

'I can't. I used to love doing that. When we were together. Now you're with Ted.'

'Silly, it not that kind of marriage. Just keeping each other company and liking it.'

'But love. Lots of love. I see it all the time.' Alice started to cry.

'What's all this about? You have lots of love. You, Dinesh, the boy. I've seen it.'

'He's dead, mother, he's dead.'

'Nonsense. You mustn't talk like that. What makes you say that? There, don't be silly. He'll be back in a day or two. Say a prayer for him. We'll say one together.'

'I know he's dead. And you know it too.'

Kay sighed. 'I'm tired darling. We'll talk in the morning. Yes, do push the covers back. It's hot for April. Hush now. We'll talk after a breakfast, in the garden, among the Indian marigolds he loved . . . don't go . . . stay with me . . . sleep. Is Davy asleep?'

'He's with Jack and Sarah, as you well know. It was your . . .' Alice put her arm round her mother's waist, bit the corner of her pillow and cried herself to sleep . . .

The report of the tragic news by the Press, caught the public's attention because the circumstances were strange—a crushed, naked body, found among rocks at the foot of Beachy Head, carrying no identification. But a week later, during the autopsy, a piece of paper, not much bigger than a postage stamp, was prised out of the clenched fist of the broken body. An enlargement of it was printed in newspapers along with an appeal to the public for identification. Ted recognised the bit of paper from the script on it—the script in which Punjabi is written. Now, he could tell Kay the whole story.

'We won't talk about my "canny intuition" as you put it, Ted,' she said, when he told her. 'Alice may not have seen the news. We'll wait till you return from Brighton after you've formally identified the body. She's already prepared for the worst. Still I dread to think how we are going to tell her.

'You needn't worry about me,' Alice was standing against the light in the doorway.

Kay leaned forward. She couldn't see Alice's face. 'Since the day he left, I've been expecting it every passing day.' She spoke without the slightest tinge of emotion. 'He told me he was doing it for Davy and me. He wanted to settle matters once and for all. There was no need for him to have gone.' She walked past Kay and sat on the edge of a chair, very calm. 'He could have let the courts handle it. But he feared they would take revenge on us. He was a fool. How could dying make a difference. Or does it?'

The Lotus And The Rose

'Oh, it does.' Ted said as he went up to her and took her hands in his. 'Dinesh has wiped the slate clean. The Seth has got his pound of flesh. But I won't leave it at that. I'll tell everything I know to the police. And I'll pursue it as far as I possibly can, even internationally. The poor boy. He deserves all we can do . . . more. We mustn't let go.'

'His assassins will still be in the country.'

'Assassins? What makes you say that, Alice?'

'I don't know. I feel it in me. They tricked him. All that nonsense about Shanti and the boy being here. They enticed him to a meeting, then assaulted him, tied him up and threw him over the cliff. That is how I'll remember it.' There was a long pause. Then Alice said with great determination. 'I'm coming with you. I'm coming to Brighton. I want to see him. I don't care how he looks. I want to hold him in my arms. I'll bring his suit. The one he wore at the wedding.'

Kay studied her daughter for a moment. Then she nodded. 'We'll all go. All of us. But we must be sensible. Spare Davy the shock of seeing what he doesn't have to.'

Alice sighed. 'After that mother, I'm going back to Poona.'

'You have a lot of money to do what you like.' Kay said simply.

'And money for Davy's education,' Ted added. 'I'll see he gets to a good school and Winchester. Sandy would like that. After all he *is* Sandy's heir. In a real sense.'

'And Alice,' Kay said. 'the ashram's no place for a child. My grandchild.'

'Then you bring him up as your son. You and Ted.'

'Alice, darling you don't know what you're saying. Think, be sensible. He needs his mother.' Kay got up and faced Alice with outstretched arms.

Alice shook her head and turned away. 'I've said all I want to say.'

'And Alice,' Ted said. 'In time you'll see that Dinesh's sacrifice was not useless. I will see that his death is avenged. The Seth will pay for it. Besides Mohan Singh, Dusty, Kitty, I have other contacts in India. They will help. Mohan looked upon Dinesh as a son. He's pressing the Indian Internal Affairs Ministry to investigate. In fact they already are on to the Seth for fraud and drug dealing.'

'Ted, it could be ages before . . .'

'Alice, I gather the man's not long for this world. I'm told he's a sick man, and the prospect of a probe into his affairs will hasten the end. And remember, that in the end Seth Agarwal lost. Dinesh escaped from his clutches.'

'There,' Kay opened her arms. 'Darling Alice, come. Don't reject your mother.'

Alice moved towards her in a daze, stopped and took a step back.

Kay put her arms down. 'Darling, Davy's your link with Dinesh. By loving him you are loving Dinesh . . . keeping alive his memory. One day the boy will . . .'

'Oh, mum!' Alice cried. 'Oh, mother! I'm angry! So very angry.'

The next day, Alice received Dinesh's letter. It was hand-written.

Dear Alice

I write while waiting here to be contacted, by those who have taken me away from you and I've asked my friend in the garage to post this letter exactly a week from now. If I should get home before it reaches you, we'll read it together and laugh. If I don't, then it makes good sense to have written it, because if this letter gets to you before I do, it means I cannot get back to you. In which case, please do not grieve. No good Hindu believes life ends. I'll be somewhere on earth growing up again into manhood, but alas with no memory of you and Davy, Kay, Ted and all the past I hold dear. I know this idea of mine is not true to the Hindu theology of reincarnation, but there's no certainty on earth. Even the gods, if they are part of our lives, cannot know all the right answers. You said the creator of the universe would. But creation involves the three great gods, Brahma, Vishnu and Shiva, who are not in single agreement. I suppose a Creator has to be outside and apart from his creation—like the Judeo-Christian Jehovah. Maybe, an answer lies there. But not consolation.

For much as I've grown to respect Christianity, comfort can only to be found in Hinduism, because we fool ourselves. There's nothing right or wrong about that. Farewell, with a love that's more than I can say. Dinesh

༺ൟൟൟൟ༻

Lightning Source UK Ltd.
Milton Keynes UK
UKOW050227221211

184235UK00001B/6/P